The Hallowed Isle

THE HALLOWED ISLE

The Book of the Sword
The Book of the Spear
The Book of the Cauldron
The Book of the Stone

DIANA L. PAXSON

FANTASY

THE BOOK OF THE SWORD Copyright © 1999 by Diana L. Paxson
    Avon trade paperback: February 1999
THE BOOK OF THE SPEAR Copyright © 1999 by Diana L. Paxson
    Avon trade paperback: April 1999
THE BOOK OF THE CAULDRON Copyright © 1999 by Diana L. Paxson
    Avon trade paperback: November 1999
THE BOOK OF THE STONE Copyright © 2000 by Diana L. Paxson
    Avon trade paperback: January 2000

First SFBC Fantasy Printing: January 2000

Visit The SFBC online at *http://www.sfbc.com*

ISBN 0-7394-0776-7

CONTENTS

In Memoriam
Paul Edwin Zimmer

ACKNOWLEDGMENTS

My special thanks to Heather Rose Jones, who took time off from her doctoral studies in Welsh philology to advise me on the mysteries of fifth-century British spelling. I would also like to thank Alexei Kondratiev for his suggestions regarding the origins of the Wild Man legend.

I direct the reader to the work of C. Scott Littleton and Ann C. Thomas for more information on the Sarmatian origins of Excalibur. For those who would like an excellent historical overview of the Arthurian period, I recommend *The Age of Arthur* by John Morris, recently reprinted by Barnes & Noble.

Through the fields of European literature, the Matter of Britain flows as a broad and noble stream. I offer this tributary with thanks and recognition to all those who have gone before.

THE BOOK OF THE SWORD

Contents

Prologue

The first living thing was fire.

Erupting from the silent womb of infinite space, it devoured all matter within its reach, grew, raging, and expelled bright showers of sparks to beget new flames. Fire lives still in the glowing heart of the world and in the sun that shines above. All green and growing things feed on that light; it burns in the red blood that pulses through each vein, and in death, all become food and fuel for other things.

Fire is magic.

Above the waving grasses of the steppe, light slashes through the heavens and a solitary tree explodes into flame. Chanting, men carry away the burning branches and fire the coals in their forge. Cunning ironsmiths, their magic is composed equally of skill and spells.

Soon the hearth is ablaze, and in the trough, a lump of rock that fell from heaven begins to glow. It bubbles and cracks, flows out in a river of liquid fire to fill the mold. Once more it grows solid. Sparks fly as hammers beat out the hot iron bar into a shining wire. Again the metal is heated; glowing bundles of wire twining together, fire sparking furiously as the hammer strikes once more.

Twined and twisted, cooled and heated, each particle in each rod is realigned until the mass is no longer iron but something more. As the earth was born out of a spinning star, the steel is born from the forgefire. From the whispering of the flames grow whispered spells; each hammer stroke beats out a complex rhythm; and the steel sings in triumph as its apotheosis nears.

The mage-smiths' chanting compels the steel to hold its shape, slim and deadly and beautiful. Their spells impress upon that shape its nature and its name. They cry out to their god, drawing down his power, precise and anxious lest their work be too weak to contain what comes.

Again the bellows heave and the forge fire furiously glows. Again the blade is heated; the chant marks out the time, wise eyes watch the colors change, and now, with a cry, the steel is lifted. Its shining length seems to ripple as heat-shimmer blurs the air. The mage-smith wraps its tang in leather, and quenches the blade in the heartblood of a captive warrior, chosen for his courage on the field. Sheathed in that throbbing flesh, the sword drinks life. The blade is jerked free, and blood gushes onto the ground. The mage-smith raises it, and lightning sears the sky.

Seven smiths alone know all the spells and secrets to make these blades, the seven mages of the Chalybes. Seven swords they have crafted, forged from star-steel, bearing in their hearts the war-god's name. To seven sacred kings they are given, to deal death in the service of life.

Fire is power.

Ceremony of the Sword

Britannia was burning.

Artoria Argantel pulled her veil half across her face and took a careful breath, staring at the flames. She told herself that this one burning villa was not the world, but even the sun seemed afire in a molten sky, and blue smoke hazed the hills. Her cousin Maderun coughed painfully, then pulled the mantle that covered her bronze-brown hair down as if to shut out the sight of what had once been a prosperous estate. It was a smoldering ruin now, and another column of smoke beyond the hazel wood bore witness to the fate of the next farm along the road.

"Lady, you must come away—" Junius Lupercus reached for her bridle rein. The mare danced nervously as Argantel pulled her back.

"Not yet." He was only doing his duty as captain of her escort, but he did not understand why she had to see.

She stared at the bodies that lay sprawled on the trampled ground. The nearest had been an old man. Blood from a great gash in his crown stained his white hair, but he still clutched a legionary spatha and shield. *A veteran*, she thought, *who had settled near the fort he once defended.*

She nudged the mare forward. Junius reached out once more to stop her, but she was already looking at the thing he had not wanted her to see.

Behind the man a little girl, perhaps his granddaughter, stared sightlessly at the sky. The corpse of a red-haired barbarian lay across her bloodied thighs. At least the old soldier had avenged her before he himself was struck down.

"Who did this?" Maderun asked in a shaking voice, putting back her veil.

"Dalriadan raiders, come over from Hibernia," Junius said grimly, pointing at the bloodstained length of checkered cloth. "They will have landed at Bremetennacum and raided northward."

"That's where we met your ship—" said Argantel, her gaze moving from her cousin to the body of the little girl and back again. Maderun nodded, her eyes widening in comprehension.

The captain grimaced. "You were lucky, my lady. Their ships have no comforts, but they are agile and swift. The boat that brought you here would have had no chance if they had caught her at sea." He had evidently given up trying to spare them knowledge of danger.

Maderun grew, if possible, more pale, and Argantel swallowed. At that moment, her cousin's white face and gray eyes must be a mirror of her own. Barbarian raiders, whether from the Scottii or the tribes of Alba who had never come under the yoke of Rome, had been a fact of their lives for as long as they could remember. But for Argantel, learning her lessons among the priestesses of the Isle of Maidens, and for Maderun, safe in her father's court at Maridunum, the attacks had been only a tale of terror.

Until now.

"They must be punished!" she exclaimed. "They cannot be more than a half day ahead of us! Go after them, Junius!"

"And leave you undefended? I will not betray my oath to protect the Lady of the Lake, even at her command. Come, my lady, let me take you home—" He gestured northward. "There is nothing we can do here."

Home. . . . She peered through the smoke as if she could see through its filthy veils to the green mountains that rose beyond. No enemy had ever penetrated those forests and fells. Even the Romans had built no more than a guardpost there, and soon abandoned it. She closed her eyes, remembering the silver lake within its circle of sheltering heights and the tree-clad island it protected. No raider would ever breach the Isle of Maidens' sanctity. Then she looked at Junius once more and shook her head.

"These people trusted us to defend them and we failed. I will not leave them for the wild beasts to devour." Argantel straightened in the saddle, drawing about her the aura of the high priestess as she held his gaze. "Lay them in the ashes of their home and pile more wood over them. If it can no longer shelter them, let it be their pyre."

She could feel his resistance, but her will compelled him. Even Maderun, watching at her side, eyed her uneasily, as if she could see that invisible mantling of power. It would not be surprising, thought Argantel. Maderun was untrained, but their mothers had been twins, the elder bound to become Lady of the Lake and carry on the family tradition on the druid isle, the younger married off to Carmelidus, the lord of Maridunum. Argantel's hair was more red, and she was seven years older, but they looked enough alike to be sisters. She turned her awareness from the residue of fury and fear that hung like smoke in the air and fixed it on the girl.

"*Don't fear,*" she sent the thought on a wave of reassurance, "*the ones who did this are nowhere near. I would know.*" From Maderun she sensed astonishment, and then relief.

"How could this happen?" her cousin said aloud. "How could God allow it?"

Of course, thought Argantel, Maderun had been raised a Christian. But her question went beyond theology.

"God, or the gods?" she said bitterly. "Your clerics say that these disasters are a punishment for our sins. But whatever evils the old man might have done, I cannot believe that little girl deserved such agony. The god of the Christians does not protect his worshippers, and the gods of Rome fled with the legions."

"Then who will you pray to?" exclaimed Maderun. "Who will give us justice now?"

"I am sworn to serve the Lady who is the soul of this land," said Argantel slowly. "But I think the time has come to wake a different power. By oath I am a priestess of the Goddess, but by blood I have the right to call on the God in the Sword. It is dangerous, but I will dare it. You have the right as well as I, Maderun. Will you stand with me?"

Maderun gazed at the flames of the villa where the bodies of the folk who had lived there were burning. The firelight lent color to her cheeks, and glittered in the tears that filled her eyes. After a few moments she shivered and turned to Argantel again.

"I have no training in such arts as you have learned, but I hope my courage is the equal of yours. In God's name I swear that I will stand behind you, cousin, and do whatever I can to help defend our land."

Maderun reached out and Argantel took her hand. Where their flesh touched she felt a tingling, and then that odd shift in awareness that came when she directed her attention to the gods.

"May the Holy Mother bless us," she whispered, feeling Maderun's wordless assent like an echo, "and bless Britannia!"

The Sword stood upright in the altar stone. Sometimes, as a shift in the air fanned the flames of the tall torches set to either side, it would catch their light and refract a fiery flicker across the stone floor, as if something that lived within had momentarily awakened. Then it would become plain steel, a third of its length sunk into the stone, once more.

With the patience of long practice, Argantel stood before it, as motionless as the Sword. Behind her, footsteps whispered on granite as the others filed in, the black-robed priestesses with their hair unbound, the girls they were training with heads wrapped tightly to protect them from the power. At her back she could feel the cold weight of Ebrdila's glare, as if the older priestess would continue their argument by sheer weight of will.

"You must not do this! Your mother was a greater priestess than you will ever be, and even she did not dare to awaken the Power that sleeps in this Sword! If I were High Priestess, I would never allow you to risk yourself, and the rest of us, this way!"

"But you are not," Argantel had replied. Not for want of trying—but when their Lady died, the priestesses had chosen her daughter to lead them. *"And even if you were, by birth I am the Keeper of this blade."*

"At least leave your cousin out of this. If he knew about this, her father's wrath would strike us all!" It was capitulation, even if Ebrdila did not want to admit it.

"Maderun has the right to be here. The Sword will recognize her and do her no harm. . . ."

Looking across the stone at the younger woman, Argantel hoped that was true. Maderun had been garbed, like herself, in red. Beneath the fall of shining hair her features were pinched with strain, and her eyes flicked uneasily as each newcomer entered the House of the Sword. It was barely large enough for all of them, round, in the ancient fashion, but built of native granite instead of daub and wattle. The walls were low, but the roof timbers met almost thirty feet above her head.

Argantel sent the other girl a pulse of wordless reassurance. Maderun's gray gaze shifted from the Sword to her cousin, and she tried to smile.

The priestess felt a pang of misgiving. She did not doubt her cousin's courage, but she was increasingly aware of the girl's vulnerability. Yet

Maderun would have been shamed if Argantel had tried to exclude her now. And it had seemed to her that the God in the Sword might hear the voices of two who came of the blood of its keepers more clearly than one.

As the women entered they moved deosil around the room, and that constant sunwise circling was altering the sense of watchful expectance which Argantel usually felt in this place to an active anticipation. This chamber needed no warding. Five centuries before, it had been hallowed by priestesses more powerful than any that she would ever know, when Roman legions destroyed the sanctuary on the isle of Mona and the last of the druid priesthood fled northward.

In her grandmother's time it had become something more than a ritual chamber. Her grandmother had brought them the Sword. And what, the priestess wondered, would the Sword bring to them? For fifty years the druids of the Isle of Maidens had preserved it. Each year they had dutifully honored the god who dwelt within. But this ritual was different. This was the first time Argantel had taken it upon herself to ask His aid.

The torches flickered wildly as the great doors were closed. When they had stilled, the priestess nodded to Maderun, who began to sprinkle herbs from her basket across the coals in the brazier before her. In moments their pungent scent filled the room. Smoke spiraled lazily toward the thatching. Argantel took a deep breath, feeling the familiar lift and swing of awareness, as if her ordinary self were being pushed aside to let the persona of the priestess take control.

Maderun's eyes were already unfocused. The priestess smiled a little and reached out with her own awareness until she sensed the younger woman like a blaze of light before her. A little further, and she felt her cousin's spirit awaken within her own. It was not the steady support of a trained priestess, but it was familiar, as though a forgotten piece of herself had just been found.

She let her breath out slowly, releasing her own tension, listening as the other women began to sing. There were no words to it, only tones that built a bridge of ascending harmonies. Slowly she lifted her arms, compelling their attention.

"Behold the Sword of War!" she cried. "God-steel, star-steel, cast flaming down from heaven to bury itself in earth's womb. Spell-steel, forged by Kurdalagon, master of Chalybes's magic. Neither breaking nor bending, neither rusting nor tarnished, this immortal blade we honor!"

"By what right?" called Ebrdila from across the circle, her voice ringing with a sincerity that was more than ritual.

"By right of birth and blood," together, Argantel and Maderun replied.

"We are the granddaughters of Rigantona daughter of Gutuator, who came to be high priestess on this holy isle, and of Artorius Hamicus Sarmatius, who was the last priest of the Sword. From the land of the Royal Scyths his fathers brought it, to guard as a holy trust until the time comes when it shall be wielded by a king once more."

"And when shall that king come?" asked one of the other priestesses.

"The God of the Sword shall raise up a king to serve him when his people are in their greatest need," Argantel answered. "And who can doubt our need now? The Eagles have flown, and Britannia's enemies beset her from every side." For a moment she smelled the reek of the burning villa in the smoke from the brazier and her breath caught in her throat.

"It is so—" came the murmured answer. "Call upon the God of the Sword, and we will abide His will."

Maderun, who had been warned, shut her eyes. Argantel swallowed. The next part she did not like, but she had learned to do it. The high gods needed no sacrifice, but the power that lived in the Sword came from an older time. In a wicker cage at the base of the stone a red cock was waiting, victor of many a battle with other champions bred by the men whose fathers had defended Hadrian's Wall. The priestess bent, murmuring, and slid open the door to the cage.

The bird stared about fiercely, but it did not struggle as she drew it forth and held it high. A good sign, for its tattered comb bore witness to the cock's fighting spirit, and the men who handled these birds were accustomed to wear gloves to protect them from sharp beaks and spurs.

"So, my warrior, be still," she murmured, stroking its feathers and feeling the rapid heartbeat gallop beneath her hand. "Here is a more noble death than the cock pit. You shall go undefeated to the god."

The cock's beady eyes fixed on her own, and then, slowly, closed. Her own eyes stung with mingled exultation and pity, and for a moment she could not move. It would be sacrilege to bungle this, but the cook had made her kill chickens for the pot until she could do it with a merciful efficiency, saying no one should be allowed to eat meat who was not willing to take responsibility for the act that transformed it from living flesh to food. Then she took a quick breath, and twisted, holding tight to the twitching body as the hot blood sprayed across the gray stone.

As the blood flowed she could feel the life leaving, first awareness, and then the energies of the body, and finally an indefinable change that left the cock lighter by more than the weight of its blood. But as the bird became a dead husk in her hands, the stone before her began to pulse with energy.

She laid the body of the cock at the base of the stone, straightened, and lifted her hands; and Maderun, feeling the pulse of power, opened her eyes and raised hers as well.

"Sword-God, War-God, God of Justice, we call you. Cocidius, Red Lord, and Shining Belutacadros we call, as the folk in this land hailed you before the Romans came. Mars of the Soldiers, hear us, and forgive us that we have no knowledge of your other names." She stretched out her hands and set them about the hilt, and Maderun covered them with her own.

Argantel had been taught the secret twist by which the Sword might be withdrawn, but though a woman could guard the blade, it was not for her to wield it. And indeed, as she felt the power focused in the Sword growing, she would not have dared. It was hard enough simply to hold onto it, and she was glad of the strength of Maderun's hands enclosing hers.

"Hear us!" she cried, "as you heard your servants in years of old. Grant us a vision! Show us the Defender who will restore peace to this land!"

She felt Maderun's clasp loosen, freed one hand and gripped her cousin's hard over her own. The younger woman's eyes had closed; she swayed, tremors shaking her body. Argantel suppressed a surge of panic. This wasn't supposed to be happening! Maderun's role was to support, to add her energy, her need, to that of the priestess to whom the God would send His words.

Fool that she was, to think that because her cousin was untrained she had no ability. They shared the same blood and the same potential—and without the disciplines of a priestess, Maderun had no defenses against the force that lived in the Sword.

She moved again, this time trying to detach Maderun's fingers from the hilt. But now it was the other girl who clung with a grip she could not break. Argantel straightened, fighting to control her own breathing as Maderun twitched and moaned.

"Belutacadros!" she cried, choosing the most beneficent of the aspects she knew. "We have called you, and given you honor. Go gently with this woman, daughter of your priests of old. Speak through her, that we may hear, and leave her without harm!"

Very carefully she let go of the Sword and edged backward, lifting her hands in salutation. For a moment longer Maderun jerked, gasping, like a horse that fights the rein. Then she stilled, and the tension went out of her in a long sigh. When the girl drew breath once more, Argantel could *see* how, with the air, something else was flowing into her. Or rather

Someone Else, for the figure that held the Sword now stood like a warrior, tall and grim.

"Long . . . it has been long since I wore flesh. . . ." The first words were a whisper, then the voice strengthened. It was deep, with a faintly gutteral accent.

Argantel blinked, for laid like a veil above the form of her cousin she saw a man's shape, clad in a hauberk of overlapping scales, features half-hidden by a helm. For a moment he gazed around the chamber, and the priestesses flinched and bowed their heads, afraid to meet his gaze. Trembling, Argantel held her own head high, praying she would have the courage to face the power she had invoked.

The dark gaze turned to her at last. "Why have you called Me here?"

"My people perish, beset on every side. The Romans forbade us to bear arms, and now they have abandoned us. Send us a Duke of War." He looked at her and suddenly he laughed. It was not a comforting sound.

"You have asked for War and War you shall have. The enemies of whom you now complain are children compared to those who shall come after them."

"What do you mean? Is there nothing we can do?"

"I am a god of Justice. What you ask for you shall receive. If your leaders act in honor, they may yet be saved, but if they are ruled by greed they will lose all. I do not ordain this fate; I only read men's hearts and tell you what I see."

"Then I ask you to give us a King who will rule with honor, a King who will be worthy to wield this Sword!"

For a long moment he looked at her, and the pressure of his gaze forced her to her knees. "He will come," he said softly at last, "not from your womb, but from your blood. You will ally yourself with a husband who is skilled in war and true in heart, and sworn to shed his blood for this land. He will defend the North by force of arms, and you will defend it by the force of the spirit. Tigernissa, High Queen, you shall never be, but *Branuen* I name you, the White Raven of Britannia who rules the hidden realm. You have the will. It remains to be seen whether you have the wisdom. Use your power well."

Argantel felt the color leave her cheeks and then flood back again.

"And what of my cousin, whose body now serves you. What will her fate be?"

"She is an empty vessel, that any power that passes can fill. A wilder power than my own will possess her, nor can you protect her. But from wildness shall come wisdom, and the child she bears must live, for by his magic you shall gain your king."

Once more he glanced around him, and as she heard his voice ringing across the room Argantel realized that his previous words had been for her alone to hear.

"Endure, resist, meet honor with honor, and your Duke of War shall become a Peace-King whose name will live as long as this land lasts."

He looked back at the Sword, fingering the hilt regretfully. Then, with a little sigh, his eyes closed. For a moment Argantel was not sure who she was seeing. Then it was only Maderun who stood there, dazed and pale, and as Argantel realized that the god had left her, the girl swayed and crumpled to the floor.

"You will ally yourself with a husband who is skilled in war, and true in heart, and sworn to shed his blood for this land."

Beneath her lashes Argantel considered the husband the Sword-God had given her. At least she supposed it must be the work of some god, from the rapidity with which the marriage negotiations had been concluded. Amlodius Licinius, Protector of Brigantia, had the height of his barbarian ancestors, tribesmen from the north coast of Germania who had crossed the Rhenus to enter the service of Rome. His fair skin was reddened by exposure to wind and weather, his pale hair thinning, as if the pressure of a helmet had worn it away. His blunt features bore the marks of a decided character, but she did not yet know if he was kind.

To those who had argued out the marriage contract, that had not been important. What mattered to them was that he represented the last legitimate government established by Rome. As for Amlodius, he recognized that the times were changing, and wished to found a dynasty that would endure in the North by allying himself to the oldest blood in the land. He would respect her birth, and if he did not, she was Lady of the Lake, with her own defenses.

She mopped up some of the meat sauce with a bit of bread and chewed it slowly. She had thoroughly considered all the aspects of this alliance. Amlodius needed her link to the land, and the Old Faith needed a protector. The marriage had the blessing of the gods. The table was strewn with the remains of the wedding feast, and soon it would be time for the bedding. Only now, confronted with the physical reality of her new husband, did she wonder if among all the reasons of state that bound them there might be room for love.

The great hall which had once been the basilica of the Roman magistrates of Luguvalium was garlanded with greenery and crowded with all those who had come to honor the occasion. She supposed she should be flattered, although they had come as much to win favor with Amlodius as to honor her.

Coroticus, newly come to his grandfather's high seat at Dun Breatann in Altacluta, had been given a place at the high table. Flushed with wine, he was debating policy with Vitalinus of Glevum. Vitalinus was as wily, it was said, as the fox from whose pelt he might have taken the color of his hair. Antonius Donatus, Protector of the Novantae country, watched them sourly. He was an old man now, appointed to his post by Theodosius, the last ruler of a united Empire. He had fought the Picts and the Scotii most of his long life, and seen the power of Rome drain away from Britannia like blood from a wound.

At one of the lower tables her cousin Maderun sat with some of the princes' wives. As if she had felt the thought, Maderun looked up and smiled. Smiling back at her, Argantel realized that most of those here were friends to her husband, not to her. Abruptly she found herself wishing she could go down to sit with the other women, and wondering whether anyone at the high table would miss her if she did.

But then she would have had to talk to Ebrdila, who could not quite hide her satisfaction. Argantel remained High Priestess and Lady of the Lake, but at least until Amlodius had got her with child, she must remain in Luguvalium, and the older woman would rule the priestesses in fact, if not in name.

"They say that Ambrosius is dying—"

A sudden tension in the man beside her recalled Argantel's attention. It was Coroticus who had spoken, but everyone was looking at Vitalinus.

"Who will wear the purple after him?" Argantel said then, since no one else seemed willing to ask.

"Does it matter?" asked Coroticus. "The time of the emperors is ended. It was ever the way of our people for each tribe to choose a king, as we do in Alba. Even in Britannia the authority of Ambrosius and the House of Constantine was not everywhere accepted, is that not so?" He looked at Vitalinus again, and Argantel remembered hearing that the Lord of Glevum had opposed Ambrosius to the point of civil war.

"Emperor or overking, the name does not matter," said Vitalinus, pushing away his platter. "But someone must exercise supreme authority. If our people had stood together, Rome would never have conquered us at all." He lifted his goblet, found it empty, and set it down again. Argantel gestured to one of the serving lads to go around the table refilling them.

"I agree," rumbled Amlodius. "Today, Britannia is more than just the British tribes, and the Picts and the Scotii threaten us all. What use is it for me to fight them off here if they then turn their keels northward to attack you, Coroticus, in Dun Breatann? When wolves attack a herd, they separate the weakest animal from the rest and bring it down, but if the others make a ring of defense around it, the attackers can do nothing. We must stand together or they will gobble us up piecemeal."

It was the longest speech she had yet heard from him, thought Argantel. Clearly he was articulate enough in court or camp. She would have to teach him that women were capable of sensible discourse as well.

"My thought exactly!" Vitalinus looked at him gratefully.

"Perhaps such measures are required in the south," objected Coroticus, "where for generations the men of the tribes have been forbidden to bear arms. But the men of the north still know how to use their swords, and we need no emperor who will take more in taxes than the enemy takes in spoils!"

Amlodius shook his head. "There are strong arms in the south— twenty-year men of the Legions who have retired near the old fortresses. They are not British, but this is their home, and they can teach their skills to the sons they have bred up in this land."

"Will you seek to be emperor if Ambrosius dies?" asked old Antonius Donatus.

"I will!" Vitalinus answered, his gaze continuing on to the other men. "Will you support me?"

Amlodius nodded. "I will uphold you, so that you confirm me in my lordship here—" His glance went to Argantel, as if that had reminded him of the other source of his authority.

"I will swear alliance," Coroticus said then, "but my people were never ruled by the South, and will not accept an overlord."

Antonius Donatus nodded his agreement. "But it is not the men of the North that you must convince to help you defend them, Vitalinus. We love our independence, but the Pictish wolf is always at our door. Your task will be to persuade the great folk of southern Britain, who have lived in peace for so long they cannot believe anyone would dare to do them harm."

"I will persuade them," Vitalinus said soberly. "And I will rule."

Amlodius lifted his goblet in salutation. A silence fell as the others drained their own. Then Antonius Donatus looked at Argantel and laughed.

"Well, this is fine talk for a wedding feast! I wonder that your bride has not fallen asleep waiting for you to pay her some attention."

"I am not sleepy, I assure you," said Argantel tartly. "I saw the ruin the Scotii leave behind them only a few months ago. We women may not take up a sword, but we can die on one. Should we not be as concerned with what plans are being made for our defense as you?"

"Ho, you have married a fire-eater!" Coroticus laughed. "Take care lest you set the bed aflame!"

Argantel was interested to see a flush of embarrassment redden Amlodius's neck and ears.

Some of the other guests, overhearing, were beginning to shout that it was time for the bedding of the bride. Argantel felt her own cheeks grow warm, and wondered if her face were as crimson as her veil. Ebrdila was advancing towards her with Maderun and the other women close behind.

"We will escort the Lady to the bridal chamber," she said grandly, "and inform you when she is ready."

It was like a ritual, thought Argantel as she rose to her feet. All the decisions had been made, and it only remained to go through the ceremonial motions. Wordless, she allowed the other women to lead her out of the hall.

Argantel sat wrapped in a nightrobe in front of the hearth, her waistlength hair spread out across her shoulders like a veil. The other women were busy turning back the bed and arranging the greenery with which they had adorned the room. Maderun drew the brush through the last strand of hair and stepped back, head tipped to admire her handiwork.

"Look how it gleams!" Maderun lifted it so that her cousin could see. Argantel nodded. As Maderun laid the lock back again it shimmered with little fiery glints from the flame on the hearth, reminding her abruptly of the Sword.

"Lord, I consented to this marriage because of your words," she prayed silently, *"grant it your blessing . . ."*

Maderun, misinterpreting her stillness, laid a hand on her shoulder.

"Argantel, are you afraid?"

She shook her head. "I have served the Goddess in the holy rites, and I am not a virgin. It is only that this life will be such a change from all I have known."

Maderun sighed. "That is true for all of us. I used to dream of entering a holy sisterhood, but if what spoke to you in the Sword-rite was a divine being and no demon, we must bear the children Britannia needs. No doubt my father will be arranging a match for me when I get home."

"I suppose so—" Argantel looked up at her cousin, and saw something vulnerable, almost fey, in her expression. The other women were already moving toward the door. Filled with sudden tenderness, she took the other girl's hand and kissed it. "Thank you, Maderun, for staying to support me on this day. May your god bless and protect you on your journey home."

Maderun caught Argantel's hand to her cheek and smiled. "And may your goddess fill your new husband with love for you." She smiled tremulously and, turning, followed the others from the room.

Argantel was not left long alone.

Barely a moment had passed, it seemed, when the door was flung open again and the men, laughing, thrust Amlodius into the room.

"Be off with you, now! You have seen us put together in the bridal chamber. Go get drunk or something, and leave us alone!"

Propelled by a volley of bawdy commentary, the door slammed shut. Amlodius drew a deep breath, some of the high color leaving his face. Clutching her robe closed, Argantel rose. She was a tall woman, but he towered over her.

He cleared his throat. "We have not had much time to become acquainted, but I will try to be a good husband to you. You must tell me if there is something you need."

She nodded. "Most of all I will need you to talk to me. I have been used to ruling the priestesses on the Isle of Maidens, as you rule your warriors here. Do not treat me like a woman who knows no more than her distaff and her cookfire, Amlodius. Like you, I serve this land. Do we have an agreement?" She paused. "You are looking at me as if you were surveying a battlefield."

Amusement sparked in his blue eyes, and as he shrugged off his robe, she saw that if this was a combat, his forces were ready. Argantel felt a slow fire kindling beneath her skin.

"That bed is our field, lady, and you shall be my fellow-warrior. . . ."

With a swift step he bore down upon her, and letting her own garment fall, she readied herself for the fray.

The Wild Man

A.D. 425–29

The road from Luguvalium to Deva ran south through the hills and then straight across the levels beside the sea. In these times no route could be said to be completely secure, but after what she had seen the preceding autumn, Maderun feared to return to Maridunum by sea.

The weather grew warmer as Beltain neared. Creamy primroses clustered beneath the hedges and the first starry blooms of the hawthorne appeared. As each day came to a peaceful close, the fear that had made Maderun tense against each jolt of the horse-litter faded and she began to enjoy the journey. She had never, she thought, known the land to be so beautiful. She laughed at the antics of the new lambs on the hillsides, and plaited the flowers that the men of her escort picked for her into wreaths for their hair. Maderun listened to their singing and laughed, for it was the tune that the lads and lasses sang when they went out to gather greenery for Beltain.

Two weeks of journeying brought them in sight of the northern coast of the old Deceangli lands that curved west into the sea. Here the road ran between the water and the forest. Another long day's journey would bring them to Deva, and a bath, thought Maderun longingly, and a soft bed.

Looking around their campsite, no one would guess that a major center of Roman civilization lay so near. Tonight she would lack even the poor comforts of a shepherd's shelter. Since noon they had passed only one ruined farmstead. The men were already busy cutting branches to build her a leafy bower. However, they had water and firewood, and the evening was calm and beautiful. She watched the sun go down across the Hibernian Sea and knew herself at peace with the world.

Peace there might be in field and forest, but it was otherwise in the world of men. Just before dawn, Maderun found herself sitting up in her blankets, wondering what had awakened her. She looked around for the warrior on watch and could not see him. Alarm burned the last of the sleep from her brain and she drew breath to call out a warning, and in that instant the darkness exploded.

Sword blades flared red as someone kicked the coals and the banked fire burst into new flame. Maderun heard a grunt and one of the struggling bodies fell; warm blood splattered her hand. She gasped and struggled to her feet. *Scottii raiders . . .* the thought came through the gibbering in her brain. *But the sea had been empty. Where had they come from?*

Clutching the blanket around her, she tried to distinguish friend from foe. In the growing light she saw that several of her escort were down. The others were too few to hold all of the raiders, some of whom were already beginning to paw through the piles of gear.

One of them caught sight of her and grinned, and Maderun remembered with appalling clarity the burned villa and the body of the little girl. As the Scot started towards her the horror that had frozen her limbs became a hot tide of terror and she ran.

She fled like a frightened doe, blundering into branches and stumbling over roots and stones. When she came to a halt at last, breathless and bleeding from a dozen scratches, she heard crashing in the undergrowth behind her, and compelled her trembling legs to carry her onward.

When fear-begotten strength finally failed, Maderun forced her slim body through a hole some creature had made in the tangled lower branches of a hazel copse and lay still. Whether she fainted then or only slept she did not know. But when she became aware once more it was full daylight, and in the forest there were no sounds but the musical gurgle of a nearby stream and the cheerful morning song of the birds.

She had lost the blanket, and the undergown in which she had slept was dirty and torn. But at least no one was pursuing her. Slowly, for overstressed muscles had stiffened and she ached in every limb, she crawled out of the hazels and down to the stream. The cool water eased her thirst, and bathed some of the hurt from her face and arms. She sat up then, looking around her, and realized that she had no idea where she might be.

Argantel would know how to find her way out of the forest, she told herself, looking around her. *What would she do now?* Water ran toward the ocean, she thought, and the road ran beside it. She had only to follow the stream.

But perhaps in her panic she had run south instead of east, or perhaps it was only that the forest brook meandered where it chose, in no hurry to reach the sea. Maderun was still lost when darkness fell on the forest—and hungry, for aside from a few greens whose leaves she recognized, she had found nothing to eat all day. Weeping a little from fatigue and hunger, she curled up between the gnarled roots of a great oak tree.

Maderun woke once in the night, whimpering from a dream of terror; finding herself safe and warm, she dropped swiftly into sleep once more. When she woke again she sensed light through her closed eyelids. She started to move and winced. What had she been doing yesterday to get so sore? She remembered men fighting, and a terrified flight through the forest, but surely that had been in her nightmare, because now she lay in a warm bed. . . .

Her eyes opened. Above her light filtered through green leaves. But the air was quite still. She listened, and realized that what she had taken for the wind was the sound of someone breathing. Her groping fingers closed on fur. She jerked upright, turning, and found herself staring down into a flat, wide-nostriled face. Brown hair thick as a bear's pelt grew low above a pair of dark eyes.

Maderun gasped and started to scramble away. A long-fingered hand, attached to a sinewy arm which was also covered with hair, reached out and grasped her ankle. The grip was not tight enough to hurt, but quite secure. She could not get away.

Swallowing her fear, Maderun looked at her captor. If the beast had meant to eat her she would be dead already. She saw long legs, and feet very like those of a man, a thick barrel, and—she looked quickly away. He—not it—was unmistakably male, but not quite a beast. Seeing him whole, she recognized the original of the distorted masks and tunics of tufted wool in which men cavorted at festivals. It was a Wild Man.

She had been told they were all dead, or at least withdrawn to the far northern lands. What was one doing here? Around his face white hairs sprinkled the dark fur. Was he the last in Britannia?

She searched her memory for the old tales. The Wildfolk were shy creatures, but could fight fiercely if captured. At times they had rescued lost children and cared for them until they were found. That gave her hope. She licked dry lips and pointed to the stream.

The Wild Man chuffed deep in his throat and released her ankle. Carefully she made her way to the brookside and cupped water in her hands to drink. Then she made her way behind a clump of sallow to relieve herself, still uncomfortably aware of his watchful gaze. But when she tried to go further he half rose, growling deep in his throat until she turned back.

Later that morning the Wild Man left her and she tried to escape once more, but he found her when she was scarcely out of sight of the oak tree and carried her back under his arm. Some tender roots and new greens lay on the ground beside the tree root, and a piece of honeycomb. Still weeping, Maderun ate greedily.

The infant moon began to wax with little change in Maderun's captivity. By day she followed the Wild Man, learning which plants could be eaten. By night she slept warm in his arms. She grew thin on a diet of tubers and raw greens, and wept again when the grubs and raw birds' eggs the Wild Man brought began to look good to her. She tried to pray for deliverance, but prayers to the Christian god seemed irrelevant here in the wildwood, and she had never learned how to address the old gods of her tribe. Argantel would have known. "Cousin, help me!" she cried, but her only answer was the wind in the trees.

To think about her situation brought pain, and so as the days passed she avoided thought and banished memory, taking refuge in the forest's eternal *now*. To live was to feel the warmth of the sun or the cool wind, the satisfaction of food in the belly and the sweetness of water on the tongue. Wordless, she seemed to sense the life that flowed through all the green world around her in a way she had only glimpsed when she was part of the world of men.

Bright eyes gleamed through the sparkle of a waterfall; willowy maidens emerged from the trunks of their trees to dance in the moonlight, and once, just at sunset, she glimpsed the turf of a forgotten mound opening like a door, and saw a radiant figure that beckoned to her to come in. She might have gone, but her captor, growling deep in his throat, had grasped her arm and dragged her away.

The Wild Man had a territory through which he ranged, gathering the sweet onion in one place, mustard in another, fish from a forest pool, grubs from beneath a fallen log. It took most of his time and energy just to find enough food to support his giant frame. Maderun tore off the ragged hem of her skirt, and clad now in what was no more than a short tunic, followed him. They slept sometimes in a hollow tree and at others in a kind of nest lined with soft grasses, but always they returned to the oak tree by the stream.

The moon grew full and round, blessing the woodlands with her silver light. In the world of men, if Maderun had had any way to calculate the calendar, it was the moon when men and women danced together around the Beltain fires. In the forest, Maderun lay curled beneath her captor's hand as once she had curled around her pet kitten. The Wild Man stroked her as she had touched her cat, drawing his long, lightly furred fingers through her hair and humming tunelessly as he often did at such times. She held still when he sniffed along her body, nostrils flaring. Sometimes he licked her skin and she shivered, simultaneously repulsed and pleasured. In this state of mindless endurance, it seemed inevitable that one day his touch should grow more intimate, and when he thrust her down and dog-fashion, entered her, she did not try to pull away.

While the moon remained full this usage continued. In that corner of her mind that still could think Maderun knew that reason was her enemy. If she allowed herself to understand what was happening, she would be reduced to gibbering hysteria. And if she recognized that she had come to welcome it her mind would snap entirely.

When the silver round began to thin, the Wild Man seemed to lose interest, though he fed and protected her as before. One night, when the moon was only a thin sickle in the sky, Maderun dreamed. She was looking in a mirror, and then she realized it was not a mirror but Argantel who was facing her, calling her name. And when she replied, the other woman cried, *"Remember the hope of Britannia! Remember the Sword!"*

When she woke, Maderun knew herself as human for the first time in many days. But she scarcely recognized the gaunt features that stared back at her from the forest pool. *If I stay here, I will die*, she thought, and then, *Better to die than to live as an animal. . . .*

The Wild Man was watching her, his dark eyes sorrowful as if he sensed her unhappiness, but Maderun refused to pity him. She no longer feared him, nor did their strange life together disgust her, but from that time she began to actively try to recover her humanity.

It was three days later that she heard in the distance the melancholy belling of a hunter's horn. The Wild Man was off somewhere, seeking food. Heart pounding, Maderun set off toward the sound of the horn. For a time she waded in the stream, hoping to throw him off the scent if he should follow her. Then she took to the bank once more, moving as swiftly as she dared.

The horns grew louder, and she heard the yapping of hounds. But closer still she heard a familiar deep chuffing and knew that the Wild Man was coming after her. Her first cry was a squawk, and for one panicked moment she wondered if she had forgotten how to form human words. Then she filled her lungs and tried again.

"Help—help me!"

For a moment there was silence, then she heard a change in the calling of the hounds. Rapidly they drew closer, but the Wild Man was gaining too. Panting, Maderun leaped for the lower branches of a gnarled apple tree, survivor of some forgotten orchard, and began to climb, seeking the topmost branches that would bear her slender weight but not that of her pursuer. Clinging to the bough she cried out again and again.

The Wild Man splashed through the stream and paused at the foot of Maderun's tree. For a long, wordless moment she stared into his eyes. Then the yammering of the dogs grew deafening and he crouched to meet them, the rough hair over neck and shoulders rising to a crest as he bared his teeth.

"Run!" cried Maderun, gesturing towards the undergrowth. "Run, or they will kill you!"

Once more the Wild Man looked up, jaws opening in a very human moan. Then, as the first of the dogs leaped through the undergrowth, he whirled away into the forest and was gone.

Let the hunters think that the dogs had treed her, thought Maderun as they milled around the base of the beech, whining. Let them think that her tears were from fear of them, and not because now, when she was sure of rescue, she could at last afford to pity the creature that was more than a beast, if less than a man, and who in his way had loved her.

To her rescuers, Maderun would say only that she had wandered in the wildwood, living on roots and greens, meeting no man. Her father received her with astonished joy, for her marriage had figured in his plans. But she continued to weep, and so he sent her for healing to the quiet confines of the convent next to the church of Saint Peter in the town.

The nuns were kind to her, and if their garden was not quite so peaceful as the forest, it was far better than the smoky clamor of her father's hall. Maderun sank gratefully into the routine of song and prayer, and her memories of the wildwood became as faint and disjointed as images in a dream.

When her bleeding did not come at the change of the moon, the

Infirmary sister patted her hand kindly and assured her that when a woman had suffered a shock or was as thin as Maderun had become, it was often so. With good food and rest, surely she would grow healthy once more. And indeed, as the summer passed, she began to fill out a little, though her face was still gaunt and pale. But her moon blood did not return.

She dreamed, sometimes, that she was back in the forest. Sometimes she relived the terror of that first flight from the raiders, and would wake in a cold sweat, babbling of blood and monsters among the trees. But sometimes her dreams returned her to the oak tree, and she smiled, thinking she still slept cradled in the Wild Man's arms. Those were the times when she reached out to him, and writhing on her narrow bed, touched herself as *he* had touched her, until she passed into peaceful sleep once more. The other girls in the novices' dormitory would ask her what she had been dreaming, but Maderun could not answer them.

On a warm autumn day just after the Feast of St. Michael, Maderun went out with a few of the older nuns and the three novices to gather apples.

"Have you heard?" said little Felicia as they searched for windfalls among the tall grass, "Ambrosius the Emperor is dead and Vitalinus of Glevum has proclaimed himself Vor-Tigernus—High King!"

"And how would you know that?" asked Thea, the brown-skinned daughter of a legionary from Numidia who had married a British woman and settled in Demetia when his term of service was done. "Did an angel announce it to you in a dream?" The folklore of the convent was rich in tales of supernatural visitors.

"I heard it in Maridunum, of course," retorted Felicia, "when I accompanied Sister Ildeg to market last Saturday."

"God prosper him," put in the third girl. "For well He knows how much we need a strong lord. But I do not think that the chieftains of the West Country will accept Vitalinus's rule."

The others nodded. They were all, if not the daughters of princes, girls of good family. And in the West, even the poorest hill farmer felt free to criticize the doings of those who claimed authority over him.

Thea laughed. "Of course not—it is Ambrosius Aurelianus who has the right to claim his father's honors."

"But he is still in Armorica with his brother. My father says we need a king who will care for Britannia first and foremost," Felicia replied. "Vitalinus doesn't want to be emperor. He titles himself in our own language, *'over king.'* "

Maderun nodded. "I met him at the wedding of my cousin in Luguvalium. He seemed a very determined man."

The others looked at her in surprise, unaccustomed to hearing her speak and remembering now that she outranked them all.

"He will need to be," Felicia said finally. "He is trying to raise an army, and our men will not want to fight for people at the other end of the country when the Dalriadan warriors are at our door."

Maderun shuddered, remembering the raiders, and the others fell abruptly silent.

"They say that is why Vitalinus claimed the power—" Felicia added softly. "Because of what happened to you. He has said it is a disgrace that a princess of a royal house cannot travel safely through the land, and Britannia needs a defender."

"A Defender . . ." Maderun spoke softly in the cadence of prophecy, recalling fragments of the knowledge that had passed through her awareness, it seemed a lifetime ago, "but it will not be the Vor-Tigernus, but another, who shall come after him."

"What?" asked Thea, but Maderun shook her head, losing the memory. This had happened to her often since her ordeal. She lived in the present; all her memories were like fragments of dream, and as easily whirled away.

"We have gathered all the windfalls," Felicia said brightly into the silence. "And for all our shaking, no more apples will fall out of this tree. But there are still some clinging to the upper branches. They are almost ripe, and it seems a shame to leave them there."

Maderun looked up, dimly remembering that trees meant safety. "I will go after them. I am the lightest of you all." Kirtling up her skirts, she began to clamber upward.

From the top of the tree she could see over the convent walls. She could see the roofs of Maridunum, and beyond them a patchwork of field and forest. But inevitably her gaze turned northward, where the land disappeared into a blue haze, and the wind dried the tears that sprang beneath her eyelids before she could wipe them away.

"Can you reach the apples?" the call came from below.

Recalled to the present, Maderun stretched to grasp the fruit, and the wind flattened her gown against her body and blew back her hair.

There was a stifled exclamation from below. Maderun plucked an apple and settled back, turning to look down. Felicia was staring up at her wide-eyed.

"What is wrong?"

"Daughter of Carmelidus, I think you go with child!"

The apple slipped from Maderun's grasp, missed the basket, and rolled across the grass. Only a convulsive tightening of her arms saved her from falling as well. She shook her head and reached for another apple, then picked a third and two more.

By the time she climbed back down the tree, Maderun could almost believe she had not heard it. But the flushed faces and avid eyes of the other girls forced her to remember Felicia's words.

"It is not so—" she said quietly. "I have never lain with a man."

"But your breasts are so round, and your belly—"

"Hush!" said Thea, taking pity on her. "If she is a maiden, then time will proclaim her innocence, and time will accuse her more harshly than any man if it is not so. It is not for us to judge."

It is not true. . . . Maderun repeated to herself as they carried their baskets back to the convent. *I have never loved a man.*

But as Thea had said, time did indeed accuse her—time, and the wagging tongues of two dozen cloistered women, who began to watch Maderun's belly as a farmer scans his newly sown field. And by Samhain it was apparent to everyone that the princess was expecting a child.

Then the questioning began.

"It is a great sorrow, but no shame to you, child, if one of the Scottii raiders who attacked your camp caught and raped you before you fled," said Mother Paterna.

"They were still busy fighting. I got away."

And indeed, the evidence of Maderun's maidservant, who had rolled under a pile of luggage and watched till the fight was over, did seem to confirm that when Maderun ran, the men who followed returned quickly, complaining that she had gotten away.

"Escaped slaves and outlawed men take refuge in the wilderness. If it was one of these who abused you, tell me, and we will hunt him down!" said her father.

"I ate at no hearth and met no human soul from the time I fled to the day that I was found," answered Maderun, and it was true, said some, that even outlaws would not have allowed the girl to live in such a condition as she had been found.

"Why will you not believe me?" she cried. "Put me to the ordeal, let me swear on holy relics that I have not lied to you!"

And she swore, and was not blasted, and so her accusers were no closer to the truth than before. In the convent they whispered that if she had lain with no man in the wilderness perhaps something worse had come to her then, or even—and here the voices of the novices grew faint with excitement—within the convent walls.

"We will wait until the child is born," they said then. "Whether its father be man or devil, the babe itself will proclaim its paternity."

And so Maderun's pregnancy continued through the winter. Her belly grew ever larger, and the older women counted the months, nodding wisely. But the ninth month since Maderun's rescue passed, and there was no child. The whispers changed then, to talk of the incubus who lies with women in their sleep, or the Devil himself, seeking to beget an Anti-Christ into the world.

"Perhaps it is so," said Maderun wearily above the great round of her belly, "for indeed I sometimes have strange dreams. . . ." But the next day she was talking of a prince of the faerie folk whom she had met in the forest, who had fed her on cakes made from sunbeams and moonlight wine. And that might be so as well, the gossip ran, for the girl had been starving when they found her and surely faerie food, like faerie gold, would vanish in the ordinary light of day.

The bishop heard of the case and sent one of his priests, a Father Blaise, to question her, but if Maderun told the truth to him, the seal of the confessional protected it.

Maderun's child was born at Beltain, when the folk of faerie come forth from their mounds and move from winter quarters to their summer homes. But it was no faerie child she gave birth to, for when he arrived, after a nightlong labor in which the midwives almost despaired of saving either mother or child, he was large, lusty, and covered with a fine pelt of dark down.

"The Devil's child," said one of the midwives, listening to him squall.

"*My* child—" whispered Maderun. "Give him to me!"

They exchanged worried glances, for they had meant to carry the babe away to the forest and leave it there. Exposure of unwanted children was forbidden to Christians, but this, surely, was no Christian babe.

But Maderun was a king's daughter, and though she had babbled strangely during the labor, she spoke with authority now, and so they shrugged and gave her the child. But the rumors did not cease from flying, and when storms ruined the harvest that summer, and gave way to a freezing winter, and the next two years were seasons of little rain, folk began to murmur that it was because the King of Demetia was harboring a witch-daughter and her demon child.

Maderun sat in the convent garden watching her boy playing in the sun. From the little church came the sound of chanting; Maderun leaned back against the cool stone and let the sound carry her spirit upward. After

Ambros's birth she had asked to be admitted as a novice, but although she was still welcome to dwell among the nuns, the bishop had forbidden formal vows to the mother of such a dubious child. Perhaps it was for the best, she thought dreamily. She had recovered her health, but she found it hard to concentrate, and could never seem to remember the prayers.

Ambros was squatting on the path, making patterns with the pebbles he found there, his dark hair, coarse as a horse's mane, hanging over his eyes. After his birth most of the fuzz that covered his body had fallen out, except for a line of black down that followed his spine. Carefully he made a circle, and then a square, and other figures, over and over again.

Sometimes he raged, and raced in circles until he was exhausted, but on other days he could play such games for hours. Though he was nearly three, he had never yet spoken a word, but as he worked he hummed softly. The sound made her feel soft and sleepy, and she found it familiar, but could never think where she had heard such humming before.

A winged shadow flickered across the path. The child looked up at the wren that had made it and laughed. Maderun watched in astonishment as the bird fluttered down to alight on his outstretched hand. The wren chirped, and Ambros chirped back at it. Then it took fright suddenly and flew away.

Ambros sat up, dark eyes fixed on the path. Only then did Maderun hear the footsteps and see Father Blaise approaching them. His hair, as always, stood half on end, so that he reminded one of a startled bird, and his step hesitated as he peered nearsightedly around him. But his face was uncharacteristically grim.

"What has happened?" She rose to meet him.

"Three landowners whose hayfields were washed out last summer have brought suit to try you for a witch and sorceress because of the child!"

Maderun made a hushing motion. Because Ambros did not speak, people often did not realize how much he could understand. Then the sense of what the priest had said sank in and she sat down.

"Why?" she whispered. "What harm have I done to them? Surely I am as good a Christian as any woman in this land."

"You will not name the father of your child."

"I cannot—" Sometimes Maderun remembered him as a shining youth and sometimes as a comforting presence in the dark, but she knew that he had no human name.

"God send they will believe it. They have brought the case before their kindred court and the *caput gentis* has chosen Uethen son of Maclovius to judge it, so your father has no power to gainsay them. You must think of something to tell them, Maderun. They have the power to drown you, do you understand?"

She looked at Ambros, and for a moment saw in her mind's eye moonlight sparkling on a forest stream. Then the picture darkened. "I don't remember. . . ."

Ambros, who was having one of his quiet days, sat on his mother's lap, surveying the scene with eyes as bright and dark as a young bird's. Even though the sky was cloudy, the court had been convened in the meadow beyond the king's hall, the only place large enough to hold so many. The people made a circle, chattering. On the isle of Mona, they whispered, a cow had dropped a two-headed calf. In Londinium, Vitalinus, despairing of building a fighting force from the men of the South and East of Britannia, had followed the ancient tradition of Rome and hired Saxon mercenaries from across the sea.

A damp wind fluttered veils and mantles. Maderun shivered. Once, she thought, there had been someone who would have protected her—a mighty presence who had kept her safe and warm.

Uethen son of Maclovius settled himself on a bench on the hill. His robes were white, but his cloak was woven in many colors, his right as a man who knew the law. He draped the folds more majestically and cleared his throat.

"I call Maderun daughter of Carmelidus into this court—" His voice, trained and resonant, carried clearly, and Maderun felt a changing tension in Ambros's body as he stilled, listening.

She tried to speak, and could not. She knew this feeling of being helpless—the other time, it had been no use to struggle. She shook her head, feeling awareness begin to slip away like an unmoored boat that the current will carry downstream.

Father Blaise, beside her, responded, "She is here."

Uethen nodded. "Who brings suit against her?"

One of the farmers stepped forward. "I bring suit against the daughter of Carmelidus on the charge of *maleficium*, in that she willingly gave herself to the Devil in order to bring his child into the world, who has tampered with the order of nature and brought us nothing but disaster since that day!"

A murmur of interest swept the crowd and all eyes turned toward Maderun.

"That is two accusations!" exclaimed Father Blaise. "I can bring witnesses to testify that the child was born in a normal manner, and duly baptised when he was three days old. The good nuns of Saint Peter's have watched him grow, and seen him do no magic. If the weather has been bad, it is not his doing. Have you known no other seasons of disaster, when there was no babe to blame? It is for your sins that God has brought this upon you, not his!"

The babble this time was louder, and once or twice she heard laughter.

"It may be so," said the second farmer. "But it does not absolve Maderun of *her* crime. Whether the father be demon or mortal, she has brought dishonor on her kindred by having a nameless child."

"He has the name with which he was baptised," said Father Blaise, "which is Ambrosius, after the emperor."

"And where is the rest of it? Of whom is he the son?"

"He is the child of the nun. And that would be enough among the northern folk from whom this girl's mother came."

"But this is Demetia, and we hold by our own law," said the judge. "If the whoredom of a girl of the kindred dishonors her people, then that of the daughter of a king brings shame upon the whole kingdom, and she must pay the penalty."

"Will you kill *your* mother?"

The question was voiced in a clear and piping tone that carried to the edge of the crowd. Only slowly did men realize that its source was the child who sat in his mother's arms.

"What did you say?" Uethen was staring as if he thought Maderun had played some trick, but in truth she was as surprised as anyone. Could Ambros know what he was saying? Certainly the case had been discussed in his hearing, but how could he understand?

"Your mother doesn't say who *your* father was," Ambros repeated with patient clarity. "Do you drown her too?"

"My father was my mother's husband!" the judge exclaimed.

"How do you know? Do you ask her?"

The first shocked astonishment was giving way to laughter. Somehow, Ambros's question had turned the temper of the crowd toward sympathy.

"That's so, Uethen—it's not fair to condemn the boy's mother until you know about your own! Send for her, man, and let us all hear."

Uethen was flushing angrily, but he could interpret the murmurs around him. People respected his learning, but he was not a popular man. Someone had already gone to fetch his mother. Glowering, he agreed to wait until she should come.

When the woman arrived, escorted by a grinning warrior, Ambros straightened.

"I do not know my father. I know my mother, and they want to kill her. Does your son know his father?" The tone was clear, wistful. The old woman looked at the child and all saw her eyes fill with tears.

"Ah, little one, there's no man born that can be certain of more." She sighed, and looked up at her son. "It is glad I am that my husband is not here this day, for I came to love him. But he was not the father of my child."

The face of the judge set like stone, and the people whispered, divided between shock and glee. His mother looked at him once, and then away.

"It is our law that a stranger who lies with a girl of the kindred must stay and marry her. But my lover was thirsty for learning, and when he had learned all there was to know of Maridunum, he went away. When I knew that he had left me with child I gave myself to Maclovius, who had long courted me, and so I got a husband." She sighed. "If I may speak in your Assembly I counsel mercy, for Maderun at least has practiced no deception."

There was a long silence, while all eyes turned back to the judge, who had drawn his mantle over his head in mourning.

"I cannot judge this case," he said harshly. "The king is your father, woman. Let him deal with your shame!"

King Carmelidus pushed through the crowd, followed by his house-guard, the high color returning to his face as the tension left it.

"My daughter shall have a husband, and her child a father, as good as yours! Matauc Morobrin has consented to wed her." One of the warriors came forward to stand beside him.

Maderun looked at him, ordinary as bread and solid as stone, and felt the last of her bright dreams mist away. But her child had been saved, for whatever future God, or the old gods, had in mind. Ambros tugged at her gown. With a sigh, she put him to the breast. Upon her head, like a blessing, she felt the first drops of rain.

III

The Red Dragon
and The White

The ball, made from a calf stomach stuffed with hay, hurtled through the air. Ambros, who was faster than the others though he was only seven, darted beneath Dinabu's arm and whacked it with his hurley stick as it fell. He straightened to watch as it arced over the other boy's head toward the goal.

"Curse you, that was *my* ball!" cried Dinabu.

"But it is a point for *our* team—" answered Ambros, watching the other boy warily. He had attempted to play with the boys before. It usually ended in a quarrel, but he knew how much it mattered to his mother that he be accepted, and so he continued to try.

The others began to yell as the ball smacked into the bush that was serving as goal, and the horsemen who had paused to watch them play set up a cheer.

Ambros hung back as the ball was put in play once more, aware with all his senses of the pattern that was emerging, the energy of the other players, even the life in the grass. He had learned, painfully, that other people did not sense these things, and so he tried to hide his knowledge.

Sometimes he thought his mother felt things also, but she did not seem to be aware of what she knew.

The ball spun toward him. He could see Dinabu running, and knew in the same moment that the older boy would not get there in time. The others were shrieking encouragement. Dinabu would be angry if Ambros hit the ball, but *they* would be pleased. Before he had completed the thought he was moving, placing himself in the correct relationship to ball and goal. Muscles flexed as the stick swung; he felt the vibration all the way up his arm as it struck the ball, the sweet "rightness" as he continued to turn, and the ball soared straight for the goal.

Dinabu turned on him, features contorting. Ambros saw the hurley stick whip toward his head and ducked. Fury reddened his own vision; like a thing foreordained, he could sense how his own blow would strike the other boy's head. With a final effort at control he let go of the stick and saw it whirl away. Dinabu struck again; Ambros plucked the wooden shaft from his grasp and sent it after his own. Dinabu grabbed for his arm, and Ambros danced away, knowing that if they came to grips his own anger would overwhelm him.

"Bastard . . ." panted the older boy, stumbling after him. "No-fathered, demon begotten—"

Ambros avoided his attacks and shut out his words. He had heard it all before. But the other boys, with the pack-mentality of their kind, were taking up the chant, even those on his own team.

"Go away," they cried. "We'll have no devil-child on our side!" Someone picked up a clod of earth and threw.

Ambros knew it would hit him, but held his ground. The tears that smarted in his eyes were of rage.

"You'll ask me—you'll beg me for my help one day!" he growled.

Then, ignoring the insults and the clods that followed him, Ambros stalked away. At the edge of the field a stand of hazels marked the beginning of the woodlands. There was no one in Maridunum who could follow him once he was among the trees.

His rage carried him farther than he had intended. He came to rest at last where water from an unfailing spring trickled down over rock to form a small pool. He bent over it to drink and remained, watching his image take shape as the ripples stilled. Eyes as dark and watchful as a beast's gazed back at him beneath the fall of coarse hair. His brows were heavy, his forehead low. He tried to smile, and large teeth snarled back at him from a heavy jaw. Only in his high arched nose did he resemble his mother's kin.

But I am no child of the Devil, for the priests say that when he comes to tempt humankind his face is fair, and I am as ugly as a hobgoblin. But the hobgoblin was a little fellow, and it was clear already that Ambros was going to be a very big man. *Whatever I am, it is nothing human,* he thought unhappily. *Perhaps I should run away and live in the forest. I am happy here.*

He had considered this before, many times, and always it was the thought of his mother's pain that prevented him from running away. Morobrin was not unkind, but there was no love between them. Maderun and little Ganeda, the girl-child she had borne her new husband, were the only human creatures Ambros loved.

He gazed around him, looking for the other being that cared for him. He used to think she was the spirit of the waterfall, for he had first seen her here. But he had found that if he unfocused his eyes in a certain way he could see her elsewhere, just as he saw the beings that lived in rock and bush and tree. And sometimes, just lately, he would hear her talking to him even when he could not see.

"Girl . . ." he whispered, "will I ever find friends?"

And in the silence of his spirit he heard, faint but clear, *"I am your friend, and I am always here. . . ."*

He lay back upon the bracken and then for a little while he must have slept, lulled by the sweet singing of the waterfall, for when he sat up again, the sky was growing gold.

When he set out for home it was already dark beneath the trees. But Ambros seemed to have eyes in his feet, so swiftly did he go. He was never clumsy in the forest, only in the hall.

Ambros came over the hill to Lys Morobrin as the first stars were kindling in a purple sky. His nostrils flared at the scents of woodsmoke and roasting meat. He began to run, slowing only when he noticed the three strange horses in the pen. They were fine beasts; he frowned, memory supplying an image of them saddled and mounted. They belonged to the men who had been watching the hurley game. What were they doing here?

He doused his head in the horse-trough, combing back his hair with his fingers in an attempt to bring it to some kind of order, but as he thrust aside the spotted cowhide that curtained the doorway he had an unhappy feeling that he had only succeeded in making it stand up in spikes like a bogle's. And his tunic was torn; he had not noticed that before.

Something stirred in the shadows of the entry. Ambros whirled, then relaxed, sensing, even as his eyes adjusted, that it was little Ganeda who was hiding there. He bent and took her into his arms.

"Guests, with pretty clothes!" She pointed into the hall.

"Who are they, sweetling?" Her soft hair, pale as duckling's down, tickled his nose and he set her down again.

"They asked for you," she said, "to bring you honor! Come and see!" She took his hand and pulled him into the center of the hall.

His stepfather and the strangers lay at their ease on dining-couches on the other side of the fire. His mother looked up from her embroidery as he entered, as if that breath of air had alerted her. Maderun was vague about many things, but surprisingly alert where her son was concerned. With one glance she took in his appearance and shook her head with a sigh. In another moment she would try to hustle him out to put on his good tunic, but before she could rise, Morobrin spied him and pointed.

Ambros, still standing in the doorway, found himself the target of all eyes. Flushing, he stood his ground.

"That is the boy?" asked one of the strangers, a tall man with a grizzled beard.

"Ambros," said Morobrin, "child of the nun."

"She will have to come with him," said the other man, "to tell her story."

"Where?" Ambros found his voice at last. "Where are we going?"

"To Vitalinus, to the Over-King."

"The king has promised gold and a bull from his own herds if you can help him," said Maderun as they rode northward. "Your father is very pleased. . . ."

He is not my father, thought Ambros, *and he is pleased to be rid of me. You are chattering, mother—what is the knowledge you are trying to hide?*

He knew already that the Over-King's messengers had not told the whole truth to him. They said that a fatherless child was required to bless the king's new fortress, but what if he failed? Ambros did not believe that his mother would knowingly lead him into danger, but she was very good at seeing only those parts of a picture that fitted her vision of reality.

She even thought *he* was handsome, and Ambros knew full well he was as ugly as Imacdub who was the ugliest boy ever born. The goddess Cerituend had brewed up a cauldron of magic to make her son wise if he could not be beautiful, but the serving-lad Viaun had drunk it all instead.

Perhaps my mother's cousin Argantel could teach me wisdom—I have heard she is a mistress of magic, but I think I will have to be Imacdub and Viaun both if I am to survive.

But whatever happened to him in the Over-King's hall, it would be a change from listening to the taunts of the lads at Maridunum, and the little girl who talked to him in his head had told him he should go. He turned to look at the road behind him. The town was already hidden behind a wooded ridge, and they were passing through the last of the farmsteads.

"I met Vitalinus once, you know," his mother chattered on.

"Who?" Lost in his own thoughts Ambros tried to pick up the thread again.

"That is his name. Vor-Tigernus is only the title he has taken, though I suppose it might be courteous to use it when you address him." She frowned. "He did not seem overweeningly proud, as I remember, but he did have a great many opinions. . . . Great lords do not like to be contradicted—" She turned to Ambros again. "Be careful how you speak to him, but remember that your blood is as good as his."

On one side, thought Ambros unhappily, but he nodded.

"And perhaps," she went on, "it would be better not to tell him about the Sword."

He turned to her. "That will be easy. You have never more than mentioned it to me!"

His mother's face brightened. She liked to tell stories about the past— it was safely over and done. Sometimes, though, the past was like an adder that seems dead until it rolls over and bites you.

"Two hundred years ago there was an emperor in the lands of the Romans who was called Marcus Aurelius." Maderun glanced up and down the road and decided that the riders in their escort were out of earshot. "In his time there was war between the Sarmatian peoples beyond the borders of Dacia, and one of the losing tribes, the Iazyges, came to the Danuvius and asked for asylum in the Empire. The emperor replied that he could not take all of them together, but if they were willing to be divided, he would let them in.

"Five hundred warriors were sent here to Britannia and stationed at Bremetennacum, to guard the western shore. When their twenty years of service were up, they settled here in the North and their sons entered the *Auxilla* after them. When the veterans were given citizenship, as the custom was, they took the family name of their commander, Artorius."

Ambros nodded. "Wasn't your grandmother named Artoria?"

"Just so. My cousin Argantel bears the name also, and keeps the Sword. It came to us through our great-grandmother, a druid's daughter who married the last of the Sarmatian soldier-priests who guarded it," Maderun went on. "It is an ancient blade, forged from star-steel by a magic that no smith in our day understands. In the hands of a great king, born of the ancient blood, it will bring victory."

"You are telling me that Vitalinus wants to be a great king, and would take the Sword?"

"He would," she said softly, "but he is not destined to wield it." She moved her mare up beside Ambros's hill pony. "A god lives in that Sword, who has promised that the Defender of Britannia will come of my cousin's blood. But the druid who must help him will come of mine."

Ambros's pony started to trot at the involuntary touch of his heels. He hauled back on the reins, abruptly making sense of a number of comments his mother had made in the past.

"And you think that *I* will be that Man of Wisdom?"

"I know that you are—" she said serenely. "And you must remember it when you go before this king."

Ambros felt his heart beat as if he had been running. "But what if I say the wrong thing?"

"Say what your heart tells you, and trust in God."

Which one? he wondered grimly. *The god of the Christians, or the one in the Sword, or whatever power my unknown father served?* He had been christened as a babe, but he thought sometimes that his alien blood had somehow repelled the Christian blessing. He attended mass with his mother, but he felt the mystery of the Spirit more strongly in the depths of the forest than he ever had within the chapel's walls.

Ambros grew very silent as the journey continued, for he had much to think about. Two days' travel brought them to the western coast. From there they rode northward, into the old Ordovici lands. Presently the way became more traveled. Boats were drawn up on the shore, and sacks and bales lay stacked under rude shelters.

They camped overnight by the water, and Ambros ran about talking to the sailors and workmen. If he was to grow up into a man of wisdom he would need to know about everything. And so he asked the sailors how they knew when a storm was coming, and the builders how they laid a foundation, and noted not only what they said but the pitying looks they thought he did not see.

Three more days of travel brought them to the Over-King.

Ambros sensed the hill almost before he saw it. A round summit, separate from the surrounding hills, it commanded the vale. The eastern face rose steeply, but their escort led them around to the southwest, where a path meandered slantwise across the slope. From here, one could see to the peak, where the trees had been felled to make way for the building. But there were no walls, only a great deal of tumbled stone.

The royal encampment sprawled over the meadows by the lake. A roundhouse had been erected to shelter the king; a gaggle of rudely thatched lesser buildings clustered around it, leaning a little drunkenly as if they had been built for a temporary use that had extended well beyond its term. The men were as motley as the dwellings.

Many were native British of types he recognized—horse-faced and redheaded Celts from the south or midlands, or the smaller, darker folk of the west. He saw men with the brown skins of legionary forebears from every corner of the Empire who spoke the British tongue with as pure an accent as any tribesman. But there were others, big, heavily muscled warriors with brown or ash-blond hair who exclaimed in deep-voiced gutturals. He knew these must be Saxons, hired mercenaries from across the sea.

A new language, Ambros thought with interest. He was quick at such things, and could read Latin from the church books almost as well as the priest already. He wondered how hard the Saxon tongue would be to learn.

Their escort brought them through the camp and drew up before the big roundhouse. Ambros felt his heart thumping heavily as he slid stiff-legged off his pony.

"The Vor-Tigernus is down by the lakeside," said the warrior who guarded the door. He was a big man called Hengest, the leader of the Saxon mercenaries. "He said you should take the boy to him when you came in."

Ambros was glad for the chance to walk some feeling back into his legs. He did not want them to think they were trembling because he was afraid. Still, as they made their way through the camp and down to the waterside he could not help holding very tightly to his mother's hand.

A group of older men stood on the lakeshore, watching another, who stood thigh deep in the water, holding a slender pole.

"He is fishing," said one of the men as Ambros looked up inquiringly, "we must keep still."

At home people generally used nets, which were more efficient both in time and results, but Ambros had sometimes caught fish in his hands, and knew how silent and attuned to the flow of the water one must be. The man who stood in the water did not move, but his mind was unquiet. And if Ambros could feel that, surely the fish would too. But maybe he did not care if he caught anything, so long as he could get away from other people for awhile.

Maderun was speaking in low tones to a tall man, richly dressed, with silver in his fair hair.

"This is Amlodius, your cousin by marriage. It seems a long time ago that we met—" She turned to the big man again. "Is Argantel well?"

"She is well in body. We had hopes of a child earlier this year, but it was not to be."

"That is always hard for a woman," Maderun sighed. "Take my love to her, when you return."

Amlodius started to reply, then stilled. The fisherman was coming in. The skin on his head was sunburnt beneath the thinning ginger hair, and the skirts of his tunic flapped wetly around his legs, but no one laughed. Instead of the kind of majesty Ambros had expected, he moved with a driving purpose that was in its own way just as compelling. A slave brought up a stool for him to sit on and took his fishing pole. Ambros stiffened as the Over-King's gaze swept the little group and fixed upon him.

"This is the boy, sir," said one of the messengers. Vitalinus beckoned him forward.

"Do you know why you were brought here?" His voice was an even tenor, neither warm nor cold.

"You are building a fortress and it keeps falling down. Your wise men said I could help you, and you will reward my family if I do—" Ambros shrugged and glanced at the two men in the multi-checkered mantles of druids who stood nearby.

"Perhaps, if you are the right boy," said Vitalinus. "Lady Maderun, I understand this is your son. You must tell me truthfully how he was begotten."

Maderun came forward to stand beside Ambros and he took her hand.

"I can say this, my lord, and may God be my witness. Until I was married, after this boy's birth, I never lay with a man. They will have told you that on my journey home from my cousin's wedding I was lost for a time in the forest. What happened to me there I do not remember, but my son was born a full twelve-month afterward, so I do not think he was gotten then. When I lay recovering in the convent I dreamed often of a man as fair as the dawn who came to me. Be he angel or demon I do not know, but that he was my child's father I believe, and no earthly man."

Ambros looked up at his mother with interest. *Does she have an invisible friend too?*

"Maugantius, is this possible?" The king turned to his house-priest, who was looking thoughtful.

"As you know, I have studied the writings of the Romans as well as the Church fathers," he said at last. "And it may be so. In *De Deo Socratis*, Apuleus tells us of beings that live between the earth and the moon which have partly the nature of men and partly that of angels. The ancients called them *daimons*, but we know that they are *incubi*, or *succubi* if they come in female form. It is said that they delight in tempting mortals to impurity. Perhaps one of these appeared to this woman and begot the lad."

"He does not look like the son of an angel," said Vitalinus thoughtfully. "But he does seem to fulfill the terms of the prophecy. My druids have told me that the blood of a fatherless boy is needed to bless the foundations of my fortress. What have you to say to that, Ambros who is no man's son?" he said suddenly.

Maderun gasped and gripped his shoulders protectively.

They did not tell my mother why they wanted me, but I think they told Morobrin! Ambros felt terror shock through him and then drain away, leaving him very still. Neither of the two druids would meet his gaze.

"They are fools," said a still, sweet voice in his head. *"Go to the hilltop and the spirits in the earth will tell you what is wrong."*

"I think that they are stupid," he said in a voice he did not recognize. "You need me with my blood in my veins, not on the ground. The earth speaks to me. Take me to the top of your hill, and I will tell you what she says." Saying the words opened his awareness to the voices in the wind and water. He could feel the flow of energy beneath his feet as he did sometimes in the forest at home.

"It is true that death is very final," said the Vor-Tigernus. "But you must understand that this fortress is an essential link in the chain of strongholds I am building to defend this land. I will do whatever is needful to establish it."

Ambros met the Over-King's eyes and saw something, perhaps a spark of recognition, kindle in that amber gaze. "You act from need . . ." he said, "but I, from necessity. . . ."

Ambros felt as if he was two people, the one who was climbing the hill, answering questions as if he were a spirit himself, and the other, who was only a little boy, and afraid. But there was a third within him, and it was she who comforted the one who feared and counseled the one who climbed. Perhaps, he thought, she was a *daimon* like the one who had come to his mother. It was a long climb, but Ambros noted with some satisfaction that the adults tired before he did.

Except for the Over-King. Agile as a fox, Vitalinus mounted the path ahead of him, and when they arrived at the summit he was not even winded.

"Behold Britannia spread out before you," said the Vor-Tigernus. "Is it not a fair prospect?" Below them the lake shone bright as blue enamelwork in the sun, surrounded by folded green hills.

"Is that why you want to build a fortress here?"

"I will be remembered. I will defend this land!"

Ambros looked at him, and echoing the voice within, replied, "It is true. You will be remembered."

Vitalinus, sensing something sardonic in the boy's tone, turned to him with narrowed eyes. "And what do you say now that you are here? Your life hangs on it, boy, so speak to me."

At the center of the summit was a hollow, where coarse marsh grasses grew. Ambros made his way to the center, squatted down, and laid his two palms against the ground. With his eyes closed his hearing sharpened, and it seemed to him he could hear running water. His awareness expanded, and he felt two streams of energy, one coming all the way from the farthest point on the holy isle of Mona to the northwest and the other from the Isle of the Dead to the southwest, winding through the earth like serpents to cross beneath the peak.

"The Dragon Path . . ." he whispered, looking up at the king. "You are building on the Dragon Path. Why have your druids not told you?" Once more he sent his awareness downward where the forces churned uneasily, disturbed by the digging.

"Tell the Vor-Tigernus he must dig down until he reaches the water—" came his inner voice. Ambros did not realize he had repeated the words aloud until Vitalinus began to shout for his builders.

"Your head is not safe yet, boy," he said as men ran off to do his bidding, "but if you are right about this I will begin to believe."

For the rest of that day and the next every man who could hold a shovel was set to digging, stopping only when darkness fell. Ambros and his mother were treated well, but they were carefully guarded. The boy slept fitfully, dreaming of warring dragons.

On the third day the mud the workmen had been digging gave way to a bubbling spring, which rapidly washed away the remaining earth around it until they were looking down at a clear pool.

"Your druids could not even tell you what was underneath the ground," said Ambros. "They were wrong about me as well."

"Perhaps. But I still must make the foundations for my fortress."

Ambros eyed him uncertainly, but the Over-King was smiling. A little wind ruffled the surface of the water; or was it something from below? The boy looked upward and saw clouds moving in from the northwest, but the disturbance he felt came from somewhere deep in the hill.

The two druids watched him, muttering, and he turned to them.

"If you are so wise, tell the king what is underneath the pool!"

"Earth and stone are underneath the water," said one, but the other kept silent.

"And what do you say is underneath the pool, oh fatherless child?" asked the Vor-Tigernus.

"Dragons . . ." whispered Ambros. "I would tell you to leave this place, but you will not do it. Command your men to drain this pool, and you will see."

Once more the laborers were summoned. Working with pick and drill, they made a channel through the side of the hill. As the work proceeded the wind grew stronger, blowing now from one direction and now from the other. Overhead, clouds were gathering. Light from the westering sun slanted golden beneath them, gilding the metal of the shovels and turning the grass a vivid green.

Ambros sat on the ground, frowning beneath his heavy brows. He could hear men marveling at how swiftly the wind was driving the storm, but he knew it was not the wind, but an echo of the disturbance in the hill. As the level of the channel neared that of the pool, he got up and edged backward. When he approached the oak trees that grew at the rim of the hill, two warriors barred his way.

"Very well, I will stay—" He sat down again. "But take my mother a little ways down the hill. Tell her it is because of the storm."

The man's grim expression softened a little and he turned to do as Ambros had asked. Vitalinus had been eyeing them suspiciously, but when the boy sat down he resumed his watch on the pool. The last cut was made, well below the level of the pool, and the water began to sink rapidly, swirling in a widdershins vortex toward the hidden hole. So swiftly did it spin that a fine spray flew up from it, continuing to whirl in the wind. In another moment it seemed as if the clouds themselves had caught the motion. Wind whipped at men's mantles and blew anything lightweight away.

Ambros hunkered down where he was, fingers digging into the grass. Leaning against the wind, Vitalinus stumbled toward him.

"What is it?" he cried, staring up at the storm. "What is happening?"

Ambros looked up at the clouds shot with lightnings, partly a dirty white, and partly tinged red by the setting sun. Then his focus changed and he allowed himself to see the energies that other senses had shown him.

"The Dragons are fighting!" Ambros shouted back, waving upward. "The Red Dragon, and the White!" Storm-white and crimson, the sinuous forms roiled; now the white one taking the ascendant and then the other claiming victory. "Don't you see them? Can't you *see*?" He gripped the Vor-Tigernus's shoulder and felt the man stiffen and knew that at least for that moment he *did* see.

The White Dragon had risen from the path that came up from the southeast toward Mona; the Crimson from the line of power that crossed it. The earth trembled with the force of their conflict. But gradually, as he watched he could see that the White Dragon was forcing its opponent downward. Lightning flared, and in the next instant they were deafened by a clap of thunder. Blinking, Ambros saw the Crimson Dragon sink into the earth and disappear. But the White circled upward on the storm, spiraled three times widdershins around the hill, then sped away in the direction it had come.

The great wind died away as suddenly as it had appeared, and the hilltop stood silent. The last light of the sun picked out the wreckage strewn across the grass and the empty hole in the ground. Men picked themselves up, staring about them. One by one, they gathered around the Vor-Tigernus and the boy.

"What does it mean? Why did they come?" Vitalinus picked Ambros up and stood him on his feet. The boy rubbed his eyes. He felt dizzy, and his vision was still seared by that last lightning flash, so that he saw in shadows speckled with little sparks of light.

He started to say that he did not know, but in his head his invisible friend was speaking. As he listened he began to weep, because he was very tired, and what she was saying filled him with fear. He shook his head, but the terrible knowledge would not go away, and in the end, it was easier to close his eyes and let her use his voice to say the words.

"The Red Dragon belongs to the tribes. It is part of this land."

"And the White?" The question seemed to come from a long ways away.

"The White comes from over the sea. It follows the path of the conquerors, the way the first Romans came. The White Dragon belongs to the Saxon folk that you have called into this land. In blood and fire they will rise against you, and only in these mountains will the Red Dragon find refuge from the foe. . . ."

With the words came images: burning cities, dead children lying sprawled like abandoned dolls, fleeing families pursued by fair-haired men with bloody swords. It was too much for him—consciousness fled inward, while from his lips the dreadful prophecies rolled on and on.

*   *   *

When Ambros awakened he knew it had been a long time because it was dark. Beside the empty pool a bonfire was blazing. He lay with his head in his mother's lap, wrapped warmly. He felt empty, as if only his mother's touch anchored him to earth. He stirred a little, and one of the people who had been watching over him ran off. Presently a shadow came between him and the fire, and he looked up and saw the Over-King.

"So, Ambros, you have confounded my men of wisdom," said Vitalinus.

"They were fools. . . . Will you give my mother the gold?" Ambros swallowed. His voice was hoarse, as if he had been shouting. Maderun offered him some warmed milk in a panniken and he drank it gratefully.

"I will keep my word," said the king. "But if my druids are fools I must send them away. Stay with me, Ambros, and be my prophet."

"But he is only a boy!" exclaimed Maderun.

"Is he?" Their gazes locked above Ambros's head.

If I go home, thought Ambros, *Dinabu will tease me and my stepfather will glower and wish me gone. Here, where so many men come and go, maybe I can find out who I am. . . .*

"I will stay," the boy said into the tense silence, and Vitalinus turned back to look at him. Ambros gazed up into those yellow eyes, and in the end, it was the Vor-Tigernus of Britannia who looked away.

IV

The Forge

The Wise Men of Britannia were debating in the Over-King's hall. In the portico of what had once been the palace of the Roman governor of Britannia, the philosopher and priest Maugantius, who studied the stars; a druid from the lands of the Votadini called Maglicun and another from Guenet named Melerius; and Godwulf, the Saxon thyle, argued beneath the dispassionate gaze of painted gods. With them sat Father Felix, who had been a student of Pelagius, and Martinus, come over from Gaul to preach the new theology by which Augustinus of Hippo explained the disasters that had overtaken the empire. And just beyond the circle of light cast by the brazier, the king's prophet, Ambros son of Maderun, sat listening, with his back against a marble pillar and his arms around his knees.

Some of the Vor-Tigernus's wise men viewed Ambros as a mindless vehicle for prophecy. Such creatures were born from time to time—unable to speak properly or care for themselves, but capable of great feats of calculation, or of repeating back lists of names and lore. But Ambros was something else, a wild child with an endless thirst for knowledge. Remembering his mother's teaching, he kept quiet and made himself useful, and they condescended to let him listen to their discussions, though they did not suspect how much he had learned.

At eleven, he had the growth of a boy of fourteen, all long legs and clumsy feet with a head that seemed too large for his body and teeth too big for his jaws. It had been some time since Vitalinus had called on him for prophecy. *Maybe*, thought Ambros as he listened to the men's voices, *when I grow up the gift will leave me, and I will be an ordinary man.*

"It does not matter how hard you strive," said the new priest, Martinus. "You will still fall so short of God's perfection that only His grace can save you, as He has predestined."

Ambros did not yet know what Martinus might have to teach him, for the Gaulish priest still crossed himself and muttered charms against the devil when the boy came too near. Now, he saw Ambros watching him and his fiery gaze flinched away.

"And I call that a heresy!" exclaimed Felix. "I believe in a God of justice, who will reward good works done in His name. Will you tell our lord that all his labor to protect this land meant nothing? For twelve years the wolves have been kept from our borders, and Britannia has prospered as never before."

Felix was a priest in the civilized tradition of the later empire, able to argue philosophy as well as theology, viewing other faiths with an easy tolerance so long as they prayed for Britannia. He had taught Ambros to work hard and to value the wonderful variety of humankind. The boy smiled as Felix continued, for he had heard all this before.

"The Vor-Tigernus has pacified the men of Eriu by marrying his daughter to their king, and the Irish who remained in Guenet are being cast out by the Votadini. Those who tried to take Dumnonia were defeated by the Cornovii whom he has settled there. Coelius and the Army defend the lands around Eburacum, and Amlodius those of Luguvalium, and our allies in Dun Breatann and Dun Eidyn are a further bulwark against the painted people of the North. In the South and East we are protected from the Saxon wolves who formerly savaged these shores by Hengest and his men! All these forces are commanded by the Vor-Tigernus!"

"Praise ice when you have crossed over it, and a king when he is on the funeral pyre . . ." rumbled Godwulf. "Hengest guards you now, but he cannot do so if Vitalinus does not pay his men."

"Let the men of the South and East who have grown rich in these times of peace pay them!" exclaimed Maglicun. "The north must support its own defenders."

It had taken some time for the druids' suspicions of Ambros to ease, but in the end they had remembered his mother's connection to the Isle of Maidens and accepted the boy. Perhaps the alacrity with which he learned from the other sages had something to do with it also, for as Maglicun said, it was not fitting that a child of the ancient priestly line of Britannia should grow up knowing nothing of his true heritage.

"I do not think they will," Father Felix said unhappily. "They complain about the Vor-Tigernus's taxes and talk of calling the sons of Ambrosius Augustus back from Armorica to rule them."

"It is not Justice that Vitalinus needs, but Mercy," put in Martinus. "If all his labors are in vain, will not that prove the truth of Bishop Augustinus's teaching?"

"The stars show that a time of changes is coming, but whether for good or ill I do not know." Maugantius pulled at his beard thoughtfully.

Ambros had found Maugantius more approachable than most of the others, and through many long nights had kept him company as the philosopher watched the constellations wheel across the sky. Maugantius was a follower of Plato and his later disciples, Iamblichus and Porphyry, an initiate of Greek mysteries and Egyptian magic dedicated to the Great Work by which a man might re-forge himself into a god.

Maglicun snorted. "Of course there will be changes. Night gives birth to day and winter to spring. It is the way of the world to turn in a circle, not in a straight line as you Christians say. The end of one thing is the beginning of another. The wise man learns to interpret these cycles, and moves with them rather than fighting the flow."

Ambros nodded. This was the wisdom of his mother's people, and it nourished something in his soul. But all this talk of change was making him uneasy. Would Vitalinus ask him to prophesy? Could he still do it? At the thought, he felt the familiar wave of dizziness and the presence of his invisible friend, awakening suddenly in his mind like an old tune.

He shook his head and pinched himself to reconnect with his body. *No! I don't want to see what is coming! I don't want to know.*

"That is so," Godwulf was saying, "but the little priest says truly that those threads the Norns have spun may not be broken. In the end, it is not the outcome that matters, but the way a man meets his wyrd. Still, one may face what is to be all the better for some warning. I will cast the runes and see what they say."

From the thyle, Ambros had learned some of the runelore of the Eruli, and found it powerful but strange. Godwulf turned, as if he had felt Ambros staring at him, and the boy felt that premonitory dizziness brush his mind once more.

"We must speak to the men on the Council, and to the Over-King," Melerius said then. "We must make them understand."

These were wise men, thought Ambros, and they would speak with wisdom. But in the end he knew that the Vor-Tigernus would call on the wild power that spoke through the boy without a father, and Ambros could not predict what that power might say.

The river Ictis meandered gently through reedbed and meadow, its quiet belying the proximity of Venta Belgarum, whose tiled roofs could just be glimpsed beyond the trees. The spring had been wet, and the water ran high and strong, but its surface was calm, veiling its power. With the warmer days of summer, vegetation had grown lushly green, at times almost blocking the path beside the stream. But Ambros pushed determinedly onward, looking over his shoulder from time to time at the roof of the basilica where the Vor-Tigernus sat in Council with the lords of Britannia. He was well out of earshot, but it seemed to him that the sound of angry voices still echoed inside his skull.

The day had the sultry stillness that heralded a storm, though there was no cloud in the sky. He paused, looking down into the brown waters, his sharp eyes catching the sinuous movement of the speckled bass and silver-scaled bream, but although he might for a moment touch the slow, quiet thoughts of the fish that hid in those depths he could not forget the passions of humankind. Maugantius had tried to teach him the skill by which a man can barrier his soul from the emotions of others, but Ambros had not yet mastered it. He wondered if even Maugantius had the power to shut out awareness of what was happening today.

For three days they had been arguing, Vitalinus insisting that the rich landowners of the Midlands and the West should contribute to the defense of their eastern neighbors. And for three days the magnates of Britannia had countered that the danger from which the mercenaries had been hired to protect them was past, and it was foolishness to maintain an army when there was no enemy. And throughout it all Hengest, Vitalinus's *magister militum*, stood at his master's right hand and said nothing at all.

Ambros turned his back on the city and kept walking. From above, the musical "ke-ar" of a hawk came drifting down on the wind. He peered upward, shading his eyes with one hand, and glimpsed a tiny speck against the blue. From such a height the doings of men must seem without significance, he told himself. And yet the hawk's sharp eyes caught the tiniest movements of the small scurrying creatures that moved through the grass. *Is that how the gods see us?* he wondered. It was an uncomfortable thought, and he moved on.

Presently, over the gentle murmur of the stream he heard a musical "tink, tink." In another moment a shift in the wind brought him the scent of charcoal and scorched metal, and he knew he was nearing a forge.

The noise grew louder. Ambros saw a path leading away from the river and followed it. Beneath an ancient oak tree stood an unhitched wagon. Nearby, the cart-horse was cropping the grass, while the smith, barrel-chested and bandy-legged, with arms like gnarled trees, hammered at a horseshoe for a dappled mare. He was a freedman, Ambros saw from the Phrygian cap he wore; probably one of those who traveled from farm to villa, plying his trade. Two more horses awaited his attention, tied to trees.

As Ambros neared, the smith finished hammering, took the shoe from the anvil and lifted the horse's hoof to try it, then swore softly and laid it back on the coals of the forge. As he did so, he saw Ambros watching.

"You, boy—come give me a hand with the bellows. You look strong, and my own lad's run off to gawk at the great ones in the town."

Amused, for even the Vor-Tigernus did not order him about in quite so peremptory a tone, Ambros set his hand to the work and quickly got the knack of it.

"Fire's like a man, you see," said the smith, "that will die if you don't give him air."

"And the iron?" asked Ambros.

"Ah, that's like a man too, a strong man who's hardened and shaped by the blows life deals him. But sometimes you'll find a piece of metal, or a man, with a hidden flaw. You strike him wrong and he'll shatter." The horseshoe glowed a dull red when he plucked it from the fire, but the color faded quickly as he began to hammer it once more.

"Are the best pieces the purest?" asked Ambros as the smith got the horse's leg between his knees and set the shoe against the hoof once more. The metal was still hot enough to singe, and the boy wrinkled his nose at the scent of hot horn. This time the shoe fit, and the smith changed hammers and began to nail it down with swift, precise taps.

"Not always." He let go and the horse stamped, unused to the weight of the shoe. "For some things, like swords, you want to melt a little of something else, nickel, for instance, into the iron. If you forge rods whose metal is different together, the sword has the strength of all of them, not just one. Do you understand?"

Ambros nodded, and the smith took up another shoe blank and laid it on the fire. The boy had sometimes watched the smiths who traveled with the Vor-Tigernus, but his ambiguous position in the court constrained communication. To this man, he was only a boy. Ambros applied himself to the bellows once more, watching with satisfaction as the coals began to pulse and glow.

"You work well," said the smith. "Have your people set you to a trade?"

"I'm only eleven."

"That's not too soon to begin, if you're strong. What do your folk mean you to be?"

A Man of Wisdom, thought Ambros, but that was his mother's saying, not his own. And there were many kinds of wisdom.

"I don't know what metal I'm made of . . ." he answered, "or who's to have the forging of me." A flock of rooks flew overhead, calling raucously; he looked up to follow their flight and saw the sun disappearing behind the trees. He let go of the bellows and straightened. The work had freed him from his worries for most of the afternoon.

"I have to go. I'm sorry—" he added, "I liked helping you."

"Did you?" The smith's laughter echoed from the trees and the horses tossed their heads nervously. "Do not grieve then, for we will meet again, and when we do, perhaps you will know what you are."

Ambros's steps dragged as he headed homeward, watching the white swans sail the quiet stream. But as he neared the bridge the echo of the smith's laughter was drowned out by a great clamor from the town. He stopped, staring, as riders clattered over the bridge and set their mounts at a gallop down the road—they belonged to Gerontius of Dumnonia, by the emblem. A few moments later they were followed by a horse-litter surrounded by guards. That was Sulpicius from Deva. What was going on?

He crossed the bridge between cavalcades and tugged at a shopkeeper's sleeve.

"Vitalinus has dismissed the Council!" came the answer. "Or they've dismissed him, it's hard to say. But the great ones are off to their own lands, and talk goes that they've sworn to bring Ambrosius Aurelianus and his brother back from Armorica to be our emperors!"

Vitalinus moved swiftly, marshalling the forces that were left to him. But with the warriors of Dumnonia and Guenet turned against him, and Coelius protesting that the Painted Peoples would attack if he weakened the Army of the North, they were few. Even Amlodius, protesting that after so many years of marriage his wife was about to give birth to a living child at last, refused to come, though he sent a subcommander with some of his men.

From his own lands around Glevum the Vor-Tigernus had the men he had trained, and some from the south coast, but for the most part his strength lay in the barbarian troops who for the past ten seasons had guarded the land. And where they had come from there were many more.

While the sons of Ambrosius gathered forces in the west country, Hengest sent swift ships across the channel to bring more warriors from the German lands. While he waited for them to arrive the Over-King evaded Aurelianus's attempts to bring him to battle, knowing that if he could delay long enough, many of the rebels would go home to help get the harvest in.

The two forces came together at last just before the festival of Lugos at a place called Uollopum, north of Venta Belgarum. Not all of the Vor-Tigernus's reinforcements had arrived, but Aurelianus forced the issue, for he was beginning to lose men. Through all one bloody day they struggled, while Ambros and the other noncombatants watched from a hill nearby. And because their numbers were almost even, when darkness fell neither side could claim the victory. The Ambrosian forces withdrew to Dumnonia to lick their wounds, and Vitalinus and his men fell back toward Glevum.

The sword flares down, slicing through leather armor, cleaving flesh and bone. A man screams as his arm is torn from his body; then blood sprays crimson and the voice is stilled. Others fill the silence, crying out in pain or rage. The clangor of weapons assaults the senses. The smell of blood and sweat and shit fouls the air.

He whimpers, trying to find a way out of the carnage, but everywhere he turns he finds faces contorted in rage, and the swift flare of bloodied swords. . . . He curls in a ball, trying to get away, away. . . .

"Ambros!"

He flinched as a hand gripped his shoulder and jerked upright on the bench, flailing. The fingers let go and someone laughed. Ambros blinked, saw Hengest looming over him and behind the Saxon, Vitalinus.

"Wake up, boy. Your master needs music to sweeten his mood!" The Saxon laughed again and turned away.

Ambros rubbed his eyes. The only fighting he could see was the battle between the Greeks and the centaurs painted on the wall of the villa where they had stopped for the night, and the angry voice he heard belonged to the Vor-Tigernus.

A slave scurried in with a pitcher of spiced wine. Vitalinus took it before the slave could set it down and refilled his cup, drank deeply, coughed, and drank again.

"Emperor! He dares to take the purple on the strength of one battle which he did not win!" Vitalinus glared around the room.

As his senses returned, Ambros remembered the messenger who had ridden in just before suppertime. That was what had sent the great ones to council. From the sound of it, nothing had been resolved.

"Neither did you," Hengest said drily. "Nor will you, unless you get more men." Despite the guttural accent, he spoke Latin fluently and could make himself understood in the British tongue. He stood with his back to the fire, his face hidden, but his shadow stretched dark across the room.

The Vor-Tigernus poured more wine and began to pace up and down. As he passed Ambros he paused.

"You heard him, child. Take up your harp and see if music will soothe the savage heart of your king!"

Eyeing his master warily, Ambros reached for the harp, a simple crescent of oakwood joined to a soundbox, with five horsehair strings.

"Go on—or do you think yourself a David to my Saul? I will not throw a lance at you!" He jerked into motion once more, slopping wine upon the floor.

No, Ambros thought, *I am not David, for I will never be a king. . . .*

He settled the harp against his shoulder. He had learned to play simple chords and accompany the bards when they chanted the old songs, but he did not think that singing was wanted just now. Softly he began to pluck the thirds and fifths of harmony.

Perhaps the sound did have a soothing effect, for he saw Vitalinus's high color recede and presently the king sat down. He looked at his *magister militum* and sighed.

"You are right. I need more men. Can you conjure them out of the air?"

"Out of the air?" Hengest's deep laughter rumbled in his chest. "That I cannot do. But I can bring them out of the water—over the sea—"

There was a long silence. Ambros clutched the harp, scarcely daring to touch the strings.

"I know. In your country there are many warriors. But they will not fight for love of me," Vitalinus said at last. "If I had the gold to pay them—to pay *you*—I would not be sitting here now."

Hengest sat down before the hearth, clasping his knees. Sitting so, his head was still as high as the king's shoulder, but he no longer loomed over him.

"When I give the gold you pay me to my men, they send it home so that their kindred can buy food that their sea-soaked land will no longer bear. If you have no gold, you possess what my people hold dearer— black earth from which grows the golden corn."

The Vor-Tigernus started, staring down at the other man, but he made no sound. After a moment the soft rumble of Hengest's voice resumed.

"Hirelings must be paid, but there is no question of payment between allies. Give us land, Lord of Britannia, as the emperors of Rome gave Germania Prima to the Burgunds, and Aquitanica to the Visigoths. As guest with host we shall dwell, and take our living from the produce of the land."

"As *feoderati*—" said Vitalinus.

"As allies," repeated Hengest. "And to seal the bargain I will give you a hostage from my own family. You have seen my daughter—"

She had come over from Germania just this year, Ambros remembered, a tall woman, with red-gold hair, and beautiful.

"Reginwynna . . ." breathed Vitalinus.

"You have no woman. Take Reginwynna as your wife, and give us Cantium."

"It cannot work!" Vitalinus jerked out of his chair and began to pace about the room. "The lords of Britannia will never stand for it."

"It has worked for the Romans," Hengest objected. "Are you not the emperor?"

Vitalinus shrugged. "My fathers were magistrates under Rome, but I do not come of the old princely lines. Aurelianus is kin to the old kings of Demetia and Guenet. If I had something—some symbol of sovereignty that might command men's allegiance, I could rule as I willed." For a long moment he stared into the fire. Then he turned.

Ambros felt the hairs rise on the back of his neck as he realized that the Vor-Tigernus was looking at *him*.

"Your mother comes of the old blood of the North, is it not so? I have heard tales of a Sword. . . ."

Ambros was shaking his head, but he could feel the pressure of Vitalinus's will like a fire.

"Put down your harp, son of Maderun, and speak to me words of truth and prophecy—" the Vor-Tigernus's words sparked through his awareness.

I cannot. . . . I will not. . . . I swore not to speak of the Sword! thought Ambros, but already his vision was blurring. His will was a fraying tether, and his consciousness a wild thing eager to break free.

"In the name of God and his holy angels I command you, and in the name of the Old Powers of this land. Four winters I have fed and clothed you, and I am your lord."

He was a king, and accustomed to be obeyed. Against the authority in that tone Ambros had no defenses. Desperate, he sought his inner *dai-*

mon, and as the inrush of her presence released him from himself, faintly
he heard a voice that was not quite his own begin to answer the king.

"Woe to the lord who summons powers he cannot command!" An
eerie, tinkling laughter made Vitalinus step back. "You have asked, oh
King, but can you understand the answer? I see the White Dragon growing
strong; his children flourish in the land. The Red Dragon rises to fight
against them, and blood covers the ground. The children of the Red
Dragon are slain."

"And what of the Sword?" As from a great distance, he heard the
Vor-Tigernus ask.

"The Boar of Dumnonia rages and the White Dragon is brought to
bay; but he in turn shall be brought low and his brother shall rule. But
the Sword of the God of War is not for him, for he shall be slain. After
him shall come the young bear, begotten by a man who is dead upon a
secret queen. No man but he may draw the Sword from the Stone."

"And what of me? How shall I save this land?"

"You have sown the teeth of the dragon and you must reap the harvest. . . ."

The voice came to Ambros like a whisper on the wind. His body was
falling, but his spirit fell further, descending forever down a tunnel of
night until he knew no more.

Ambros opened his eyes to darkness. He lay on the bench, and someone had covered him with a cloak, but he was alone in the room. He sat
up, rubbing his forehead to relieve the dull ache behind his eyes, and
pulled the wool around him. A dim glow from the hearth enabled him to
make out his surroundings; from somewhere nearby came a faint snoring.

What had the daimon that lived within him said to the king? Nothing
good, for he could remember someone shouting. If he was still alive and
free it must be because the king thought him too weakened by his trance
to be worth guarding. But tomorrow the Vor-Tigernus would certainly
punish him.

At the thought, volition came back to his limbs. Ambros wrapped the
cloak around him, took a partly eaten loaf of bread from the Vor-
Tigernus's plate and stuffed it down the front of his tunic, and poked his
head out the door.

He heard snores and harsh breathing, but nothing stirred.

The gods of his people must be protecting him, thought Ambros as
he passed through the gate of the villa, for the one guard he had seen had
been sleeping. A waning moon showed him his way, and soon he was on

the Londinium road. No one would expect him to flee that way, but from there he could double around to the north and then head west to Demetia.

Though the road was not so well maintained as it had been under the Romans, Ambros made good time, and by dawn he was approaching the White Horse Vale. He paused, gazing southward in wonder, as the first light revealed first the noble curve of the downs against the eastern sky, and then, as the sun rose, the attenuated curves of white that revealed the Horse shape carved into the chalk of the hills.

Ambros's breath caught. He remembered suddenly the sculptured curves of bone in the skull of the White Mare that led the procession at Samhain. Swathed in a white horsehide, the Mare was at once the face of Death and the promise of life to come, for she brought the spirits of the ancestors in her train to take flesh once more in the wombs of the women of the tribe. The blood of his mother's people beat in his temples as he gazed upon that mighty form, bound into the very bones of the land.

"White Mare, protect me—" he whispered, then glanced behind him. There was nothing there now, but soon, folk would be stirring, and might remember a strange lad hurrying down the road. But if he struck out across country here, he should strike the Ridgeway, that ancient trail that followed the top of the downs east and north. From there he could spot any pursuers long before he could be seen.

The Vale was bigger than it had looked in the deceptive light of dawn. All that day, the boy struggled to cross it, detouring around meadows whose green hid marshland still soggy from the spring rains. Farm roads petered out in woodlots or pastures, and sometimes he had to hide from men working in the fields. Thus, by the time he began the long climb up to the Ridgeway, dusk was drawing a veil of shadow across the land.

Ambros found the ancient track more by touch than by eyesight, stumbling even when he reached the summit and the smoother ground. He flinched from a flicker of motion, then saw it was a hunting owl, gliding by on noiseless wings. With nightfall, the downs became a different country. He was acutely aware of the mighty swell of the chalk, as if the bones of the earth were pushing through the soil. And the longer he followed the Ridgeway, the more conscious he became of the many feet that had trod that path before.

This was an ancient land, where any stone might be an elf-bolt lost before the fathers of the British tribes ever came over the sea. Some said that the little dark hunters, or their spirits, wandered here still. Ambros glanced over his shoulder, wondering if they hunted by night or by day. The open expanse that had attracted him in the morning seemed now to impose a terrible vulnerability. Uplifted on the shoulders of the downs, he cowered beneath the huge expanse of sky, seeking, like some small scurrying animal benighted far from its burrow, a place to hide.

And so, when he saw a stand of beech trees in dark silhouette against the southern sky, he turned off the path.

Almost at once an odd scent stopped him. Ambros sniffed cautiously, and his nostrils flared at the harsh reek of a charcoal fire. He took a step forward, fancying he saw the glow of flames behind the trees, and then, unmistakably, came the chink of metal on metal, and he recognized the music of the forge.

"Come warm yourself—" a deep voice called him forth from among the beeches. "I have stew to fill your belly as well."

Amazement warred with caution, for this was the same man Ambros had met beside the river at Venta Belgarum. But more powerful still was hunger, for beside the bread he had eaten nothing that day. Licking his lips, he stepped into the light of the blacksmith's fire.

The flickering flames showed him the horse and wagon, and behind them a tumble of stone like a fallen wall. But four mighty uprights still stood among them, flanking a dark passage that led into the mound.

"What are you doing here?" He heard his own voice, stupid with fatigue.

"Shoeing horses—what else?" The smith grinned. "In this country there are many fine ones. The people will bring them to me when they gather in the old fortress for the fair."

There is a fine white mare on the hillside, thought Ambros. *Will you set shoes on Her as well?*

But more important than fear or fancy was hunger, and he dug into the bowl of stewed pork which the smith handed him. There was ale as well, stronger than he was used to, with an aftertaste of honey. The smith continued to tap away with his hammer, talking of the the fair with its horse races and peddlers from many lands, when the people scoured away the grass that encroached around the edges of the Horse's limbs. Ambros could not quite see what he was making, and after a time his eyes grew heavy and he forgot to look.

The chink of the hammer came regular as a pulsebeat, but as Ambros began to drowse, it seemed to him that what the smith was beating out was not metal but memories, a sequence of bright images that passed before him until he walked among them. The dark hunters of the hills chipped skillfully at the flint to make their arrowheads and axes. They were followed by a bigger, brown-haired folk who tilled the land and dragged great stones from the mountains to entomb their dead, using hand axes to peck cups and spirals into the rock. Ambros saw the first mound made beneath the beech trees, and then the building of the barrow of stones.

He was sitting in a place of ghosts, he thought dimly, but he sensed a circle of safety in the light of the blacksmith's fire. In dream he saw the leaves of countless seasons drift down across the stones. A new tribe came who drank their ale from beakers of fired clay banded with patterns made by cord or comb, and after them people whose smiths crafted fine weapons of polished bronze, who brought more stones to set in careful alignments where the dragon power flowed through the land. Circles of shaped stone marked the movements of sun and moon with more precision than any of Maugantius's formulae. The makers of the old tombs were forgotten, and bronze-smiths plied their craft before the mound.

And yet these tribes also passed into memory. The weather grew colder, with more rain, and the upland farms were abandoned. Men used new and better weapons of bronze to fight for what arable land remained, and built earth-walled fortresses to defend their territory. Ambros did not understand all that he saw, but he could see a pattern, in which one people succeeded another in lordship of the land.

And presently there came tall, bright-haired folk from across the sea who carried swords of iron, and worked their ornaments in sinuous spirals varied with palmettes and scrolls. He knew them for British, his mother's people, but in his dream they seemed no more than another layering of leaves on the mound. The click of stone axe on stone became the ring of bronze, and then the heavy clangor of iron as, generation after generation, the smiths worked their magic, compelling the inert elements of earth to the service of man.

His head throbbed to the ring of those hammers until he could no longer see, and then it seemed to Ambros that he himself was lifted and laid upon the anvil. The hammer swung, shattering his old form and shaping him anew. He understood at last what the atoms of which the old Greek magi had written must be, for he could feel each atom in his body realigning beneath the blows. And as he looked up, he saw that somehow the gnarled blacksmith had become a radiant goddess, with hair of flame.

"You were a raw lump, but I have made of you a mighty weapon for the hand of the destined king. But let the lord who makes use of you remember that truth is a two-edged sword. . . ."

Then he was taken from the anvil and sheathed in something soft and warm, and sank into a sleep of darkness too deep for dreams.

Ambros woke slowly. He ached as if he had been beaten all over, but at least he was warm. One eye opened, and then the other. He lay wrapped in the cloak on a bed of sweet-smelling grasses, but above and to either side of him he saw stone. With a shiver he realized that he was lying inside the mound. Still, the light had to be coming from somewhere. Wincing, he turned over, and saw at the end of the passageway a pale square of sky. He caught a whiff of woodsmoke and then the scent of meat, and his stomach rumbled.

After a struggle, he freed himself from the cloak and crawled toward the daylight.

There was the fire, as he remembered. But there was no wagon, only a muddy horse cropping the grass. Blinking, he peered at the man who sat toasting strips of venison over the flames. The broad shoulders were familiar, but they did not belong to the smith. It was Hengest who was sitting there.

The Saxon lifted a strip of meat and handed the end of the skewer to Ambros. It was hot, but perhaps his encounter with the smith had been a dream, for he was furiously hungry.

"How did you find me?" he asked when he had finished the first piece and was working on a second one.

"I followed the White Horse," came the reply. "For my people, the white stallion is holy. The way he runs tells the priests what is to be. Sometimes when a tribe must move, they loose the stallion, and where he goes they follow. You also see the future—I knew he would lead me to you."

"Did the Vor-Tigernus send you after me?"

"My lord is not happy—" Beneath the grizzled mustache Hengest's lips twitched. "But in this he does not command me." His blue gaze fixed the boy. "Our wise men teach that Woden, who gives the ecstasy that carries men to victory in battle, gives also staves of verse to the shope, and the spirit speech of the *witega*, the wise-man. I think that you belong to the god."

He frowned, and gripped a hank of grass. Earth crumbled dark between his fingers as he lifted the clod. "This is a good land, and my people are hungry for a home. You said that the White Dragon would conquer."

"I do not remember—" Ambros whispered.

"Then the god gave you the words. This land will belong to us, and we to this land."

Ambros shook his head, denying it, but the stones of the barrow, that had seen so many peoples pass, told him that it was true.

Ambros did not protest when Hengest took him back to Vitalinus, nor did he repeat what the Saxon leader had told him. The Vor-Tigernus had heard the prophecy; if he did not heed Ambros when he was inspired, he was unlikely to believe what the boy said in his ordinary senses. But from that day, Ambros avoided the Saxons.

For a time, Ambros dared to hope he had been mistaken. He was growing fast now, as if the hammering he had received from the blacksmith—from Govannon himself, and Brigantia, if he had not been dreaming—had unbound his limbs, which seemed to lengthen day by day. Hengest's son Octha and a chieftain called Ebissa, who was his nephew, were sent to garrison the lands below the wall, and the Picts kept close to their own hearthfires. Ambrosius did not dare to challenge the Vor-Tigernus again.

But while Ambros gained in height, Hengest gained men. Keel after keel rowed past Tanatus to beach their boats where Caesar had landed. Others ran ashore below the white cliffs at Dubris, and their crews marched overland to Durovernum. Prince Gorangonus lived a prisoner in his own city, but the Over-King would not hear his complaints.

In the year that Ambros turned sixteen, the distant storm whose lightnings had played upon the horizon for so long broke upon the British in all its terrible power.

Cantium had been more than sufficient for Hengest's original warband, but it could not support the horde that had followed them. Hengest no longer came to Londinium; it was Godwulf who presented his demands for more gold. But the Vor-Tigernus had already given the Saxons all the gold he had.

And so the Saxon wolves turned at last upon the poor sheep they had guarded, and all the south and east of Britannia were engulfed in blood and fire. Venta Icenorum vanished, Camulodunum was overrun; the gate of Lindum was burnt down. And if walled towns fell, how much more vulnerable were the isolated villas and farms. Where the Saxons did not strike, fear of them wielded a keen-edged sword. Everywhere folk fled, and even when the first fury of the revolt ebbed, they did not return.

But in Londinium, the Vor-Tigernus clung grimly to his imperium. The barbarians were not invincible. Even the terrible Attila had been defeated by Aetius at the Catalaunian fields. Vitalinus had sons, Vortimer and Categirnus, who were now come to manhood, and together they set out to reconquer Brittannia.

V

The Night of
the Long Knives

"**A**mbros son of Maderun, you are welcome to Luguvalium—" Amlodius led the guest toward the hearth. "We have not seen you here in the north for far too long."

Igierne resisted the temptation to whirl around to look at him. At twenty, a married woman with a child of her own, she was surely too mature to leap up because the Vor-Tigernus's prophet had come. Then her father and his guest moved into her line of sight and her eyes widened; kinsman though he might be, she had never seen anyone like Ambros before.

His height was not so surprising—her own father was tall. But she had never encountered so hairy a man. The hair of his head had been trimmed, but his eyebrows bristled, and the short beard merged with the dark hair that grew thickly on neck and his arms below the embroidered borders of his sleeves. No doubt his legs, covered by loose breeches of fine wool, were furry as well. Then his swift, evaluating glance, moving over the assembly, crossed hers. For a moment black eyes stared into blue.

He is proud, she thought, marshalling her own self-respect to withstand that scrutiny. *He has reason to be.* All men had heard how even as a child Ambros had confounded the wise. During the Saxon wars he had become the Vor-Tigernus's most valued counselor. He wore the garments of a prince, and around his neck hung a pendant of a running stag on a chain of gold. Then his gaze passed on, and she let out her breath in a long sigh.

"Sit—" said Argantel, gesturing to a servant to bring food. "You have had a long ride."

"I have, but my lord wished to honor you by sending his message through one who is kin."

Ambros's voice was deep, with a curiously husky timbre. They said his father had not been human, and Igierne could believe it, for the red glints in his hair were the only feature he shared with his mother's kin.

"The proclamation states that we have defeated the Saxons. Horsa was killed at Rithergabail, but Hengest holds Cantium, and his son, Octha, the old Iceni lands. Is that a victory?" Amlodius asked as they sat down.

"It is all the victory we will have in this generation." Ambros threw back the folds of his mantle, a druid's cloak, checkered in many colors and held by a silver pin, and took his own seat. "He has given both his sons to defend Britannia. If the princes of the West and North would fight under his banner, the Saxons might be swept from our shores, but they will not do so, and he will not submit himself to Aurelianus. Therefore this treaty that Hengest has offered is the best outcome we are likely to achieve."

"But a partition!" exclaimed one of the other men. "It is a recognition that they will never go away."

"This Wall that you guard so carefully is a partition, but the religion and culture of Rome are found in Dun Breatann as well as in Luguvalium. Men from every part of the world have become good sons of Britannia. We will trade back and forth across that border, and in time they will learn our ways."

Amlodius laughed. "I suppose you are right. My own grandfather came from the same lands as Hengest, but I am a Roman."

"And you are one of the masters of the North. Vitalinus summons all the great lords who are sworn to him to come to Sorviodunum by the first day of May. His sons may be gone, but it will be well for the Saxons to know what strength is united against them when the treaty is made."

Amlodius frowned. Igierne had been surprised, when she arrived for this visit, to realize that his fair hair was now all turned to silver and the massive shoulders a little bowed. In contrast, her mother, despite a sprinkling of silver at the temples, seemed young. It would be a long trip for an old man, but he was nodding in agreement.

"It has been many years since I visited the South. I would like to see what the Saxons have done to the land."

"They have destroyed it," said one of the men who had come with Ambros's escort, "as the wolf who gains entry to the sheepfold in his bloodlust rends and slays far more than he can devour."

"We drove them back, but we cannot force those who fled before them to return," said another. "Good farms lie abandoned, and the towns that remain are dying, for there is no way to get the goods made in one place to market in another. And the weather has been so bad these past years it seems that even God has turned against us, and is giving the coastlands back to the sea."

The servant brought round a tray of silver cups and Argantel poured wine from a pitcher made of Roman glass. Igierne sipped appreciatively. In Dumnonia, they had wine often, brought over by the ships that traded with Gaul, but this was an old vintage, hoarded in the cellars of the Roman fort.

One of Ambros's men asked where the wine had come from, and Amlodius began to talk about the vintages he had known as a young man. With a start, she realized that Ambros was watching her. Argantel followed the direction of his gaze and smiled.

"I forget that you will not have met my daughter, Igierne."

"You are the wife of the Prince of the Dumnonii—" he stated, as if, she thought with a spurt of irritation, he were labeling her. But she smiled sweetly in return.

Igierne had grown accustomed to being viewed as an appendage of Gorlosius when she was in Dumnonia, but returning to the North, she had begun to think of herself in the singular once more. What was he seeing, she wondered, beyond a tall woman with her father's fair hair?

"I was married three years past, and have a little daughter who is just a year old."

Morgause was auburn-haired and strong-willed like her grandmother, and Igierne loved her dearly, but it had been a relief to get away from her for a little while.

"It is well that you are both here at the same time," Argantel said softly. "You two are the only heirs in the next generation of the line of Artorius Hamicus, and it is in my mind to take this opportunity to teach you the rites of the Sword."

Ambros's eyes widened. "My mother told me its history, but I thought the priestesses—"

"On the Isle of Maidens it is guarded, but it can be touched only by those of our line. Will you come, son of Maderun, and take up the priesthood that is your heritage?"

For a moment something unfathomable stirred in his dark eyes; then they became opaque once more. He nodded, and Igierne felt her heart bound in her breast and did not know if it beat with anticipation or fear.

It was inevitable, as they rode south from Luguvalium, that Igierne should find herself often in the company of her cousin. Argantel rode in a horse-litter, but Igierne was mounted on a sturdy hill-pony, and Ambros on a bigger mount of the old cavalry breed. He was interested in her impressions of Ambrosius Aurelianus, who had guested with them several times at Bannhedos, and she, of course, was curious about Vitalinus and the Saxon woman he had married.

"She went back to her father when Hengest broke faith with the king. Among her people it is a woman's right to leave a marriage, and though they were wed in a Christian ceremony, I think in her heart she was a heathen still. But it is true that she was very beautiful."

He frowned, and Igierne wondered if that beauty had stirred him. She had observed that he did not look at women with lust, as some men did, but rather as if they were a puzzle to be solved.

"To be pagan is not so great a sin in the North," said Igierne. "I was raised to be a priestess and my mother's heir, though it proved necessary for us to make an alliance with Dumnonia. Perhaps when I have given Gorlosius a son I will take my daughter and return here."

He looked at her curiously. "Do you not love your husband?"

The undertone of bitterness in her answer surprised her. "Love has little to do with the matings of princes. From me he expects fertility and faithfulness, and he gives me support and protection. Like most of the Dumnonian lords he has interests in Armorica. He may have a concubine there—I have never asked."

She kept her eyes on the road ahead, where the great crouching shapes of the hills guarded what lay within. The country around Luguvalium was rolling, and in Dumnonia one always felt exposed to the immensity of sky. But the Lake country was a land set apart; those whom it called to itself might find a path through the wooded dales, but the way could not be forced by an enemy.

"Among our people it was not always so," he said softly at last. "The druids teach that the king serves the land and if need be, dies for it. But it is through the queen that he touches its power. But not since the days of Brannos, I think, have we had a High King of all Britannia, and even he had no Tigernissa, no High Queen."

"My mother is Branuen, the hidden queen who performs the rites for the sake of the land, and I suppose that I will bear that mantle after her."

"But what if Branuen and Tigernissa were the same woman, a priestess-queen? Might not the king then become Brannos as well as Vor-Tigernus, a sacred king who would rule over a golden age?" His voice trembled, and turning, she saw that he too was staring at the holy hills.

"Have you seen this in a vision?" she asked softly.

"A vision?" He shook his head. "I have learned more certain ways to foretell what the future holds, and the magic, if need be, to change it."

As their journey continued, Igierne continued to consider his words. He sounded very confident, but Ambros was by his very nature a creature half of myth and magic. If he seemed arrogant perhaps he had reason. As for herself, the latest, and it seemed to her the least, in a long line of priestesses, what power could she have in a world where priestesses were becoming as legendary as the gods they had served? If men honored her it was only because she was the daughter of one great lord and the wife of another.

And yet, as they wound their way into the hills, Igierne felt herself slipping backward in time. Her mother, also, seemed to become younger as the Lake grew near. But Ambros grew strange, as if the veneer of sophistication which he had acquired in the Vor-Tigernus's court was peeling away to reveal some other being, more ancient and elemental, that lived within. He spoke less and looked around him more, and when they paused to rest the horses he would dismount and move to the edge of the forest with a grace so alien and still that she half-expected him to disappear into a tree.

On the fourth day of travel they reached the top of the pass. From here they could look down into the vale whose center was the blue lake with its tree-crowned islands.

"There lies the Holy Isle—" Igierne pointed to the largest, which lay close to the eastern shore. Here and there the gold of thatched roofs gleamed from among the trees; the long feasting hall, the roundhouses where the priestesses lived, and a little apart from the others, the House of the Sword. "We will be there by the time night falls."

"I will be glad of it," he answered harshly. "This wilderness makes me afraid."

Igierne looked at him in surprise.

"—Not of the mountains," he added then, "but of myself. When I gaze at these hills the great prophet and learned counselor of Vitalinus seems a crawling insect that one shiver of the ground could knock away. And if I am not the Vor-Tigernus's mage, what am I?"

She nodded. "I have sensed that strangeness in you. It is different for me. Here, I come into my own power."

He considered her curiously. "Is it because you are a woman, I wonder, or because—" He did not finish the thought, but turned to gaze down at the Isle of Maidens as if it could give him his answer.

As soon as he stepped through the door Ambros could scent the power. He stared around the House of the Sword, hair lifting along his spine at the growing sense that something that had been patiently waiting was now awakening. Light flickered madly across the floor as Igierne fixed torches in the sockets, and the draperies that shrouded the altar flared suddenly crimson. He found himself watching her as he had ever since he came to the North: a swift glance, swiftly turned away, lest she should see. Was it because she was a woman of his own blood that he felt drawn to her, or was there some other reason, that he was not yet ready to understand?

He heard Argantel draw a careful breath, then she pulled the cloth away from the Sword, murmuring words of praise and salutation to the spirit that lived within.

The blade stood upright in a block of stone. Perhaps half its length was free; its surface, of some polished metal that had neither tarnished nor rusted during all these years, gleamed red in the light of the fires. Ambros did not use weapons, but he had learned to judge them. The crossguard was plain, but the hilt had been wound with gold wire. It was a sword sturdy enough to serve a warrior, with a stark elegance worthy of a king.

"I will teach you the prayers later," said the priestess. "Tonight I will do no more than introduce you. . . ." She lifted the cage which held the cockerel. "But it is for you to make the offering. Daughter, you must assist him."

Biting her lip with concentration, Igierne extracted the fowl from the cage. Ambros looked from her to her mother in confusion.

"What, have you never killed a chicken for the pot?" Argantel laughed. "Well it is time you learned!"

He blinked back vertigo. Eating at the king's table, he had never killed anything before, but he could not admit that while the women were watching him so expectantly. He took a firm grip, feeling the fowl's frantic heartbeat. Then he twisted its neck, and gasped as he *felt* the life departing. Hot blood gushed over his hands.

In the next moment his revulsion gave way to an appalling surge of hunger. Then the priestess guided his arm so that the fowl's blood dripped onto the altar stone. His own sensations paled before the approach of the god as the light of a candle dims in the sun.

Argantel was saying something, but he could not understand the words. He saw Igierne reach out, saw her face change as she grasped the hilt of the Sword. Argantel set her own hand over that of her daughter, and together they pulled the blade a handsbreadth further from the stone. Another twist, and the Sword was thrust back. Then the priestess grasped his wrist and pressed his own hand, still red with the blood of the rooster, around the hilt of the Sword.

"You must twist as you withdraw the blade . . ." her words seemed to come from a great distance, "or it will not move." Her grip tightened on his hand, but he did not need the instruction, for the blood of his great-great-grandfather was awake within him. Smoothly he turned the blade and felt it slide freely through the stone.

"Not too far—" said Argantel. "The time to draw it has not yet come."

He stared at her through eyes that he knew were rimmed white with the effort of keeping control. A voice that was louder than the drumming in his blood began to speak in his soul.

"Not yet, man of the ancient blood. You are not the King who shall wield this blade, but the time will come when you shall enable him to claim it. Lift up your eyes, for she in whose womb he shall be cradled stands before you. . . ."

Ambros looked up, blinking as if he had been staring into the light, and saw Igierne. Her face was shining, and her pale hair flared out around her head like rays of gold, and in that moment she was beautiful beyond mortal imagining. He stared at her, and understood at last that for him she was the Goddess, and that what he felt for her was love. What she heard he did not know, but she stretched out her hand and set it upon the pommel of the Sword, and together, they thrust it home.

Radiance flared around them. Dazzled, Ambros tried to look back at Igierne, but it was the face of a boy he saw, brown-haired and intent, with Igierne's blue eyes.

The treaty talks took place at a shrine north of Sorviodunum, on the edge of the broad central plain. Ambros supposed it must qualify as neutral ground, having belonged to both British and Saxons in turn during the past few years. The Saxons had built a shelter for the meetings—no more than a framework with a thatched roof to keep off the rain. Between the posts one could look out past the last sheltering swales of grass to the broad sweep of the plain. It was an empty land, haunted by memories of peoples so ancient no one even remembered their names. Perhaps that accounted for the unease that had troubled him since the meetings began.

They had feasted on beef and pork, a raider's menu. The rich scent of roast meat still hung in the air. But now, at last, the eating was over. When the drinking horns had gone round a few times for men to toast the new treaty, it would be done.

They sat at long trestle tables covered with an assortment of cloths. Hengest, to emphasize the peaceful nature of this festival, had forbidden the usual barbarian custom in which men came armed to a feast and hung sword and shield behind them on the wallposts. But the Saxons still looked like savages. Ambros sighed, remembering the last time he had come to Sorviodunum with the Vor-Tigernus, when he was still a child. They had dined in one of the great houses of the town, and eaten off the elegant table service that had once belonged to the Roman magistrates. Its pieces were probably scattered through half the Saxon army by now.

Not, strictly speaking, that it was all Saxon any more. The chieftain sitting next to Amlodius was Aelle, whose Saxons had settled into the coastal lands to the east of Noviomagus. But Hengest himself had peopled Cantium with Jutes and Frisians. There were Franks as well, and others whose names he did not know. The ravens who feasted on the carcass of Britannia were drawn from half a dozen northern tribes, paired one by one with the British councilors.

Ambros pushed the meat on his platter distastefully aside. *Ah Vortimer*, he thought, *we should have honored your dying wish and buried you on the eastern shore. Then, perhaps, your spirit would have saved us from this day . . .*

His own dinner partner was Godwulf, who had once taught him the Eruli lore. The Saxon thyle had always been hard to read, but tonight he seemed as impenetrable as Hadrian's wall. In the days when he had cast runes for Vitalinus, Ambros had thought him old. But by now Godwulf must be in his eighties, a truly remarkable age.

"You are in health, I see. Your gods have been good to you," Ambros said politely.

Godwulf smiled. He was missing some of his teeth, and could only eat his food chopped fine. It gave him a more sinister appearance than Ambros remembered.

"It is so," the old man answered. "Woden gives victory in the battles of the mind as well as those of the body, and he likes this land. You should make him an offering."

Ambros lifted one eyebrow. Powerful the god might be, but all his help had no more than won his people a toehold in Britannia.

"You may offer to your demon, and I will honor mine," he said wryly, for the Christian priests would characterize the heathen god and the spirit that spoke to him in his soul alike as devils.

Or that used to speak to him. These days, he commanded spirits rather than praying to them. He tried to remember how long it had been since his inner voice had counseled him.

"If different peoples are to live in peace, their gods must make peace as well," unfazed, Godwulf was answering. "So it was when Woden and the Ase-gods fought with the Wanes. Neither side could conquer, and so they became allies."

"Do you mean to put an eyepatch on Lugos and call him Woden-Lugos, as the Romans used to honor Mars-Belutacadros and many another, proclaiming that all the deities of the peoples they conquered were only faces of their own? They are not the same!"

"Your Lugos is not Woden, not as we encounter him, though they both carry a sacred spear," agreed the thyle, "but there is a place where they meet. Those who can come there will understand how disparate peoples can become one."

"Is Hengest such a man?" asked Ambros, looking at the high table. The Saxon leader sat next to Vitalinus, like an old stallion, scarred and gaunt, looming over a grizzled fox. He sat at his ease, but his eyes were watchful, like a man awaiting the beginning of battle, not one who sighs relief at its ending. Once more, Ambros felt that little prickle of unease.

"Hengest loves this land . . ." Godwulf said ambiguously.

"Will he honor the treaty, now that we have given him what he asked?"

"He will keep the oaths he swears on the sacred ring." The thyle touched the silver arm-ring, graven over with runes, that he wore.

Ambros nodded. It was the oath-taking, not the writing of words on parchment, that would bind the Saxon.

A serving lad bore the mead pitcher past the benches and refilled his beaker. Ordinarily Ambros did not drink deeply, but he had felt the strain of this long war more deeply than he realized, and drinking brought release. He looked at the other British lords and saw that for them it was the same. Faces grew flushed and voices louder; laughter filled the air. The Saxons, eyes bright with excitement, were laughing too, but they were accustomed to deep drinking. Indeed, they were being remarkably temperate this evening, as if they feared to shame themselves.

The platters of roasted meat were taken away, and the ill-assorted collection of plates. Did the fact that nothing matched matter to the Saxons? Ambros thought of a Saxon warrior he had seen emerging from a burning village, wearing a Roman helmet and a woman's gown. Perhaps they liked the variety. Perhaps they were naturally perverse. . . . He realized that the mead was affecting him and set down his beaker.

"It is good mead," said Godwulf.

"It is indeed, but do not your own shopes warn against allowing the heron of heedlessness to steal a man's wits away?"

"You are, as always, wise," said Godwulf with a peculiar smile. He swung himself around and eased off the bench. At the high table, Vitalinus had risen to face the man who had been first his greatest servant and then his greatest foe. A priest stood behind him, holiding a reliquary. Gradually a hush spread through the crowd.

The Vor-Tigernus set one hand upon the casket. He looked sour, but determined, as befitted a man who was about to swear part of his native land away.

"We have labored as hard to frame this treaty as ever we fought on the battlefield," he said. "And all the harder, because our goal was not victory, but a settlement that would be fair to both sides. The details are written, but to this I will now take oath: that the lands which were formerly those of the Iceni and the Cantiaci shall belong to the Saxons and Angles who now dwell therein, and such other smaller enclaves as are specified in the treaty. I pledge that my people will honor their tenure and recognize their borders. In the name of the Father, Son, and Holy Spirit." He crossed himself, a gesture which was echoed by most of the British lords.

Godwulf drew the oath-ring from his arm and held it out to Hengest.

"On the ring of Thunor I swear, and in the name of Woden—this land that we have taken, we shall hold—and as much more as the gods shall give into our hand!"

He released the arm-ring, and turning, held out his arms to Vitalinus as if to embrace him. *"Nimet oure seaxes!"* he cried.

Vitalinus recoiled, but with another step the Saxon swept him into a bear hug that carried him away from the high table and toward the end of the hall.

Staring in amazement, Ambros caught the first flicker of movement only from the corner of his eye. Then someone screamed. Steel flashed in the light of the torches—a dagger, when by agreement all men had come unweaponed to this feast. Coelius of Eburacum and three others lay sprawled in their blood already. But the Saxons were not having it all their own way. Those who had not been felled in the first moments still struggled with the men who by chance or design had been placed to partner them, who had shared the same meat and mead, making missiles of their drinking horns or laying about them with benches. Eldaul of Glevum had pulled up a tent stake and was using it like a club.

Following his example, Ambros wrenched a post from the ground and started toward the nearest Saxons, but Godwulf was before him. As Ambros started to swing, the thyle pulled a short wand from his belt and swiftly drew several symbols in the air.

"Eees—" The thyle drew out the syllables of the bind-rune in a pulsing drone. *"Nyd—"*

Ambros felt the air congeal around him; he could still move, but slowly, far too slowly, like a man struggling through a storm.

Why not kill me? Ambros's mind raced. Did the old man hesitate to murder one who had been his pupil; or did he lack the power? With that thought, Ambros summoned his own energies, drawing on earth and air as Maugantius had taught him, and where they met in his solar plexus, kindling a fire that shocked through every limb.

In another moment he could move again, but in those few minutes the British princes had passed beyond his aid. Men lay sprawled all about him, silent in death or groaning while their murderers stood panting above them, still clutching the dripping daggers they had brought hidden beneath their leggings when they came to the hall.

Ambros forced stiff limbs to carry him across the ground to Amlodius. His cousin's husband still breathed, but life was ebbing out of him from many wounds, and blood frothed at his lips with every gasp. An animal moan of dismay passed Ambros's own lips as he bent over him, pressing a corner of the older man's mantle over the worst of the wounds.

"No use . . ." The whisper was almost too faint to hear. "Tell Argantel . . . choose Caidiau to rule in . . . Lugu—"

If Amlodius completed the word, it was too softly for Ambros to hear. His gaze became fixed, and then the soul-light faded like a dying flame and was gone.

Slowly, Ambros lifted the old man's body in his arms and got to his feet. The air vibrated with the passage of spirits reft untimely from the flesh that had housed them; they made a roaring in his ears that drowned out all other sound. Where his gaze fell men flinched, but he had no interest in lesser murderers, even Aelle. It was Hengest whom his eyes sought, standing like a deity of carnage in the midst of the slain. Vitalinus, his arms pinioned by a grinning warrior, stood beside him, weeping and shouting words that Ambros could not hear.

He drew breath, and Godwulf, eyes widening, lifted his staff and began to draw runes of protection. But the spells of the thyle could no longer hold him. Ambros opened his mouth and released the words that all those wailing spirits no longer had breath to say—

"In the name of Britannia's gods I curse you, and by the power of all the spirits of this land!" Power shuddered through him and he recognized the oncoming Presence he had sensed when Argantel showed him the Sword. This was not the gentle wisdom of his daimon, but a force that expanded his aura beyond even his own great height.

"Hear Me, men of the forests and fens and hear Me, you who lead them." The voice of the god boomed through the hall. "As you have been false to your trust, so shall you be betrayed by those you trusted. As you have usurped the lordship of this land, the leadership of those peoples you have brought here shall be given to another! You have slain the flower of Britannia, but from their bones a host shall rise up to confront you. I will raise up a Defender, and he will strike you with a Sword of Fire!"

Ambros could not hear the sound of his own words, but Hengest heard them. Yet if some of the triumph left his face, it was replaced by a stubborn pride that would neither defend nor deny what he had done.

The warrior who was holding Vitalinus let him go, and the old man sank weeping to the floor, a dead man who still moved and breathed. Ambros wondered if the god would curse him too, but there was no point to it; the man who had been the Vor-Tigernus had destroyed himself, the White Dragon savaging the Red as Ambros himself had foretold so long ago. His very name would be a curse so long as Britannia endured.

He swayed as the power of the god began to leave him, but enough strength remained for him to bear the body of his kinsman through the door, and no man sought to bar his way.

"Ambros, what has happened? They told me you had come to the Lake, but not your errand. Is my lord—"

Argantel's brisk greeting faltered. Something in Ambros's face must be conveying the message for which he could not yet find words.

"You have had no news?" he asked hoarsely.

"Neither enemies nor news of them can find their way to this holy place without my will." Her words were proud, but he could see the beginnings of a stricken look in her eyes. His mother had said once that Argantel's marriage had been a political arrangement. But the priestess had come to care for her Roman commander.

"I have brought your husband home."

Once more his throat closed. His memories of that journey were confused. In Sorviodunum he had found a man who would build him a coffin, and a wagon to bear it, and up the Great North Road he had driven, pausing only to rest and feed the horse, neither knowing nor caring what tales might follow him. It occurred to him now that the goal of bringing Amlodius back to his people was the only thing that had kept him sane.

But Argantel was a priestess, accustomed to reading men's souls.

"He is dead?" Her voice cracked on the words. She must be guessing already that no simple illness or stopping of the heart would have made Ambros bring him here himself, and in such a state as this.

"They are all dead—" Ambros whispered. "The Saxons killed—" he gasped, and then, like water breaking through a dam, all the dreadful tale poured out of him at last.

He was weeping by the time he finished. Argantel remained calm, but her stillness seemed the quiet of an autumn forest silvered by a sudden frost. She gave orders for the coffin to be brought into the sanctuary and the horse to be cared for. Hot spiced ale was offered and Ambros drank it gratefully, but when she showed him a bed he shook his head.

"I cannot rest, not yet. I have pushed too hard and long. Perhaps if I walk along the shore I will find peace. . . ."

Argantel nodded. "If there is peace anywhere it is here. Thank you for bringing Amlodius back to me."

Ambros stared at her. Didn't she understand? If not for him, her husband would never have gone into danger. She lifted her hand in blessing and left him, and he saw that in those few moments she had become old.

He took up his cloak and went out, turning down the path that led to the shore. The Isle of Maidens was no more than a few boat-lengths from the mainland. The flat-bottomed barge that had brought over his wagon lay drawn up on shore. He turned away from it and began to pick his way among the rocks that edged the water.

Hills rose sheer to the south and west and north, dark shapes humped like sleeping beasts against the starlit sky. By habit his gaze found the pole star and he marked the constellations around it. He could name the fixed stars and those that wandered, foretell their conjunctions and oppositions, but he had failed to read Hengest's heart. He was a fraud and a failure, all his vaunted wisdom worth nothing. He had been a better prophet when he was seven years old!

Ambros looked back at the clustered buildings. By morning they would all have heard the news and know how he had failed. Indeed, by now all Britannia must know how the Vor-Tigernus's prophet had walked into the trap and stood gaping while the princes of Britannia were slain.

How could he face them? How could he face *anyone* now?

Before him the dark waters lapped quietly at the shore. Let them swallow him, he thought numbly, and drown his shame. . . .

Ambros let his cloak fall to the ground and moved forward. The water was very cold, but it did not stop him. Steadily he continued as the water rose to his knees, his waist, his chest. In another moment it would close over his head and he would be at peace.

But instead it receded to his waist again. The lake bottom was rising. For a moment he stood undecided, but if he returned to the island now he would appear not only a failure but a fool. Perhaps the shadows of the forest would be deep enough to engulf him. Shivering, he pushed forward, and when he reached the shore he kept going, blundering blindly on.

Several times during that night he fell, and lay for a time in mindless exhaustion. But always a moment would come when self-awareness returned, and the voices in his head would begin to accuse him once more. Then he would stagger to his feet and push onward. By the time dawn banished the darkness he had covered many miles. He burrowed into a tangle of vines then and sleep delivered him from his accusers at last.

When he awoke, he was aware only of hunger. A heedless squirrel came within his reach, and he, who in all his life had killed only the cockerel he had offered to the god in the Sword, pounced on it and tore it to pieces, ripping off the pelt, crunching up flesh and bone. Wild onion grew nearby and he ate that too, and lapped water, wolf-fashion, from the stream. Then he began to move once more, south and westward, ever deeper into the hills.

As day followed day, the voices grew fainter, and after a time he ceased to think in words at all. His body hardened and he no longer noticed the cold. The strange flapping things that covered his limbs became encumbrances, and he tore them off and threw them away. He became more clever at foraging for food, though he never found quite enough to satisfy his large frame.

He saw deer, and once a thrown rock even brought one down. He smelled bear and avoided them, and became acquainted with beaver and badger and the wild pig and wolf that roamed these hills. One day he came upon a new creature, furred like a beast but standing upright in the rapids to snatch fish from the stream. As he approached it took fright and ran off, still on two legs, and he came down to the waterside to drink.

The backwater was still. As he bent, something moved in its depths and he jumped back. Then, more cautious, he leaned over the water, and saw a creature covered with bristling hair. It strongly resembled the one that had run away.

Wild Man. . . . A distant memory stirred of men dressed in garments tufted with colored yarn who ran shouting through the streets at festivals. And in that moment of clarity he understood of what blood he himself was come.

Were there more than the one he had seen, and would they accept him among them? He sat back on his haunches, the realization that he was himself a beast making it possible, for the first time in weeks, to think like a man.

Sunlight glanced blindingly from the water; he blinked and stilled, for someone was standing there. Not a Wild Man; it was a human woman's form, veiled in shining hair. She turned and he saw a face he remembered from dreams. When she spoke it was the voice he had so often heard in his soul. Among human women, only Igierne had ever stirred his heart. But this being touched a place that lay deeper still.

"It is so—you stand between the worlds of beast and man, and you can choose what you will be. You are a mule, and will have no offspring of your body, but if you return to humankind you will have a child of the spirit, and he will be the greatest of Britannia's kings."

His throat worked as he struggled to form human words.

"If I go, will you be with me?"

"If you will open your heart," she answered, "for I am the Bride of your Soul, and in truth I have never been far away."

The angle of the sun changed and the vision vanished. But he could still feel her presence. He waded into the river and began to scrub the dirt away. Then, when he was as clean as he could manage, he started out again, not back to the Isle of Maidens, but south, to Ambrosius Aurelianus and his brother Uthir, who were now the undisputed leaders of Britannia.

VI

The Dragon Star

"**Y**ou have sinned against the Lord of Hosts, and the Devil has sent his legions to chastise you!" The tattered sleeves of a robe that had once been white fluttered as the priest shook his fists against the sunset sky. "For your greed you are punished; for your faithlessness you are cast down. You have followed the heretic Pelagius, and thought that your own deeds could save you, and this is the result—rivers running with blood and a land in flames!" Spittle flew from parched lips as the priest brought down his arms.

"It is true!" wailed the people. "We have sinned! We must flee this accursed land!"

The tall figure at the edge of the crowd moved forward, leaning on his rowan staff. These days he called himself Merlin, the name that "son of Maderun," misheard, had become. He did not trouble to correct it. Ambros had been a human name, and that man had died in the forest. It seemed fitting that he, who was not really a man, should bear what was not a real name.

Merlin had come into the wayfarers' encampment hoping for food and fire—this close to midsummer a day's journey was long. Instead, he had found this haranguing cleric, whose whine made him want to turn back to the quiet of the hills.

"You sought to cast out the devil Hengest, and as happened to the man from whom they cast out the devil, seven demons worse than the first one have invaded our land!" the priest was continuing.

And that was true enough, for the German tribesmen who had hung back when Vortimer was battling Hengest to a standstill had come howling like wolves to tear at the poor bleeding carcass of Britannia once the way was opened by treachery. Aelle and his sons held the lands east of Sorviodunum, and the Jutes and Frisians had taken back all their old lands in Cantium and more. The walled cities of Londinium, Verulamium, Regnum and many others still held, but throughout the eastern half of the country the enemy ranged freely.

"Should we have welcomed the Saxon?" asked someone, and a few people grimaced with what might have been laughter if they had not forgotten how.

In truth, they were a sorry lot; even those who had fled with some of their wealth were worn and dirty. The skin on the priest's face hung in folds, as if he had once been a much heavier man. Those whom Merlin passed edged aside, crossing themselves. He had become accustomed to that, for if they were tattered caricatures of their former prosperity, he had abandoned all its trappings, and now went barefoot, in a garment of deerskin, mantled with a wolf's hide that he pinned with the curving tusk of a wild boar. But he knew how to veil his presence so that even those men who had been startled by his appearance in another moment forgot what they had seen.

"Leave the land to the sea wolves, and may they have joy of it," answered another. "We'll make a new home in Armorica."

Many of his countrymen had done so already, following the men whom the Emperor Maximian had led away two generations before. War and plague had left Armorica nearly empty, and Riothamus, who ruled there now, welcomed the men of Britannia.

"Will you leave the land to the wolves, or to those who still have the balls to fight for it?" A new voice cut through the babble of agreement.

Merlin turned. Several horsemen had pulled up at the edge of the firelight. The speaker urged his mount a few steps forward, and they saw a big man with mouse-brown hair cut short in the Roman manner, a weatherstained crimson cavalry cloak wrapped over his mail.

"Where are your sentries?" snapped the officer, or rather, the prince, for as he moved Merlin glimpsed at his throat a torc of gold. Three of the men at the outskirts of the crowd hung their heads. "We'd have caught you with your breeches down had we been Saxons!"

"My lord, you have no right to talk to us this way!" the priest exclaimed.

"Do I not?" The prince urged his horse through the crowd until he was almost on top of the cleric. "My brother and I were already safe *in* Armorica! You called us back to Britannia, promised to stand behind us if we would lead you. And now we are here, and when *we* start to plough a furrow, we don't leave the job half done!" He made an obscene gesture that left no doubt of his meaning.

Some of the men looked shamefaced, but others faced the prince with a mutinous glare.

"God Himself has cursed this land. Who are we to fight against the will of God?"

The prince glared in frustration. Clearly, if calling men cowards did not move them, he was at a loss for persuasions. Merlin smiled. He had met neither Aurelianus nor Uthir, but this must be the younger brother, for the emperor was said to be a man of some subtlety. One virtue they both had was energy. They had hunted Vitalinus down already and burned him in his tower.

Then Uthir turned, and Merlin's breath caught as memory overlaid that face with another, seen once in vision, with Igierne's blue eyes.

This was the man who would beget the Defender.

Merlin surveyed him with new interest, searching for lines of character in the pleasant face, for a strength of will to match the powerful body. He saw endurance and determination there; it was the face of a good commander. But was there greatness? He could not tell, but then he had not seen the treachery in Hengest's soul. His own judgment had proved lacking, and he could only trust the gods.

"Blame God for the storm that drowns your crops, but not for the fear that makes you flee." He allowed the power of his personality to blaze forth so that to the people, noticing him for the first time, it was as if he had appeared among them by magic. Even Uthir's horse tossed its head in surprise and had to be reined down.

"Rome protected you as a parent protects a growing child. But now Mother Rome is gone. Will you cling to her skirts when she can no longer even guard herself, or will you defend yourselves like men? Fleeing to Armorica will not save you—the barbarians are everywhere. If you do not stand together to fight them here you will have to do it later, in a foreign land."

"Who are you to condemn us?" someone cried.

"I am no man's son and no man's father . . ." Merlin's voice rang out through the darkness. "I have been a wolf on the hills and a stag in the meadow. . . . I soar with the eagle and root with the wild boar beneath the ground. I am the Wild Man of the woods and the prophet of Britannia, and my spirits tell me what is to come. . . ."

"Prophesy the future, then!"

"Why should I prophesy what logic can reveal?" Merlin asked contemptuously. "The mysteries of heaven cannot be revealed except where there is the most pressing need for them. If I were to utter them as an entertainment or where there is no necessity, the spirit which controls me would forsake me in the moment of need."

But as he drew breath to continue, he felt the dizzying shift in awareness that told him his daimon was awakening. His face must have changed then, for the man stood openmouthed as Merlin put the knowledge that was coming to him into words.

"You would do better to search your own heart than to question me. Confess yourself to this whining priest while you can, for this much is given to me to say—neither here nor in Armorica can you evade your doom. This very night you shall stand before your God!"

"You dare to curse—" the priest began, but Merlin's gesture silenced him.

"I neither curse nor bless. I only say what I see." He turned back toward the prince.

Sputtering, the heckler started toward him, fist raised. No man could say precisely what happened after, whether the fellow tripped and hit his head, or if he was felled by some invisible foe. But it was certain that when they lifted him up again he was dead and staring.

"Sorcery!" came the whisper, but it was not a loud one, and no one raised a hand to stop Merlin as he continued to Uthir's side.

The prince had gone pale beneath his tan, but he was not one to waste an opportunity.

"Death can strike you anywhere—" he said in a strong voice. "March with me, and if you die, at least it will be *for* something, not running away. Any man who can stiffen his rod to beget a child should be able to stiffen his spine enough to defend it. March with me, and your sons and your daughters will grow up free in their own land!"

Uthir's gaze met Merlin's as the whispers became a babble of discussion. "I know you now. You were Vitalinus's prophet. You will come with me to the emperor."

"I offer you my service."

"I hope you serve us better than you did him," said Uthir, but mingled with the trouble in his eyes was a hope that had not been there before.

North of Sorviodunum, the land rose to a broad plain. Even in more peaceful times it had been sparsely populated, and now it was nearly empty. But ghosts whispered on the wind. There were more ghosts now, thought Merlin, looking at the covered carts that the emperor's men were driving up the track from the shrine. He could sense the spirits of the British princes hovering over those mingled fragments of ash and bone.

Did Aurelianus understand what fulfilling this task, the first the emperor had asked, would cost Merlin? To other men, Sorviodunum, battle-scarred but bravely flaunting a few remnants of past glory, might be no different than any other place recaptured from the enemy; but for him, its population of dead was more numerous than the living, and more vivid, and the ghost of the man he himself had been was the most terrible of all.

To come before the emperor in Sorviodunum was hard. To ride with him to the shrine on the edge of the plain where Hengest had slain the princes was harder still. About the round huts where the monks lived, a military camp was growing. They called it Ambrosiacum now, or Ambrosius's hill.

The Saxons had burned the thatched shelter above the bodies, and though the monks had chanted prayers over them, they had no cemetery. And so Aurelianus had decreed that the princes must have a monument. To create it was Merlin's penance, and the first test of his wisdom.

One of the riders in the lead lifted his lance, pointing. Uthir kicked his horse alongside Merlin's.

"Where is the place?"

The shallow valley that the Abona had carved through the plain was falling away behind them. Ahead of them, grass and heath stretched away toward a line of hills, broken with occasional clumps of trees. Merlin pointed.

"Do you see that lump, perhaps a mile from here? That is the first mound, though indeed, such ancient burials are scattered throughout the plain. But these form a line that points back to Sorviodunum, and extends northward up the backbone of Britannia. East to West, another line passes through the Giant's Dance, and links it to the Isle of Glass, which is also a place of ancient power."

He had first come here with Maugantius during one of the Vor-Tigernus's visits to Sorviodunum, when he was a child. The wide plain had frightened and exalted him then; it continued to do so now.

"What did you tell my brother to get him to come here?" asked Uthir.

Both of them glanced back at the horse-litter in which Ambrosius Aurelianus was following. The emperor was considerably older than his brother, and at times his joints pained him too greatly for riding to be easy. But there was nothing wrong with his mind.

"I told him that this is the most important focus of power in this part of the island," said Merlin. "The spirits whose bones are laid to rest in this place will join with those who were buried here in ancient days."

"Now, this is the border of Britannia," said Uthir with a sigh. "We don't even call ourselves Britons any longer, but *Combrogi*, the countrymen." He was an interesting contrast to his brother. Both had been educated by Greek tutors, but Uthir, perhaps to distinguish himself from the emperor, had adopted the rough language of the soldiers he commanded.

They rode on a little further, and Uthir stiffened in the saddle, pointing. "What is that?"

Out of the grass dark shapes were rising. A few more steps and they became a circle of standing stones, linked uprights surrounding grouped trilithons. The Romans had built works of greater height and complexity, but never with such massive blocks of stone. Stark against the empty plain, the henge waited with a brooding power.

"That is the Giant's Dance."

As the days shortened toward Samhain the men labored, and when they were finished, the line of barrows was longer by one. Beneath it lay the remains of the leaders of Britannia. On the eve of the Festival, Merlin commanded the workmen to build a circle of fires around the barrow and then to withdraw to the river, leaving the fires to burn through the night.

"I will go to the stone circle and make the magic that will bind these spirits to the land."

"Do you have to go alone?" asked Uthir, and Merlin raised one eyebrow, for on such a night any other man would have covered himself with protective charms and huddled by the fire. "If not, I'll go with you."

"As will I," the emperor echoed him.

Merlin bowed. He had not yet had much chance to know Aurelianus, but though the emperor's body was not strong, it was from him that Uthir had gotten his strength of will. He could see already that if Vitalinus had possessed such a purity of purpose, and such ability to make men follow him, the Saxons would never have gained a foothold in Britannia.

"For lesser men it would not be safe. But it is fitting that the kings who rule now should stand where the chieftains of ancient times held sway."

"Was this a druid temple?" Uthir had asked as they passed beneath the portal of stone.

"A temple of sorts, but not made by the druids, though they learned some of its secrets. It was built before ever our people came to this land."

"Was it the Trojans, as some have said, or wise men from Egypt who taught the people how to raise these stones?" asked Aurelianus. Well-wrapped in cloaks against the chill, he sat throned on one of the fallen stones.

"The traditions I was taught say it was neither," answered Merlin. "The mages who built the stone circles came from the west, from a land of magic far across the sea. To Eriu they came and then to Britannia. It is from these isles that the knowledge was carried southward, all the way to the lands around the Middle Sea."

It was almost midnight. They looked across the grass to the fires that circled the mound, and then up at the starry radiance of the sky.

"The stars are like the watchfires of a great host encamped in the heavens," said Uthir. "Will those spirit warriors come to help us in our need?"

"They will come if I call them. You must keep silence now, no matter what you see or hear." Merlin drew from his pouch a handful of herbs and sprinkled them in a protective circle around the princes. Then, chanting softly, he paced sunwise around the henge. As he reached each stone, he saluted it, and within the lichened rock he seemed to see the beginnings of an answering glow. The henge was awakening.

He stripped off his own clothing, laid his wolfskin on the ground halfway between the two pairs of trilithons, and sat cross-legged on the hide. He gazed upward, watching as the great round of the sky wheeled towards the sacred hour, and in the moment when the stars stood still in mid-heaven, the spirit awakened within him and he began to sing.

Bright-shining stars, brilliant above,
As fires of foemen burn below,
Silent, you shall tell your story;
Stones shall sing histories. . . .

He remembered that night he had spent in the barrow with the smith when he was a child. Then the visions had come uncontrolled and unexpected. Now he was a man in the fullness of his power, and he called them. He sang, and slowly the shining shapes began to come forth from the mounds.

He heard the rhythmic chanting of many voices as men strained to pull the massive blocks over the ground. Stone by stone, the circle was completed. He saw the blood of bulls poured out to bless them; he saw kings with gold upon their shoulders, and queens with gold twined in their curling hair. Season by season he saw the ceremonies; the inaugurations and burials and the foot races and chariot races around the mounds.

All these things he saw; these things he sang, and as the stars began to pale with the approach of dawn, he summoned the spirits.

"You who have loved this land, defend it from those who would destroy. You whose bones have become this earth, defend it from the death-bringers. You who have dwelt here in a time before time, welcome the spirits who are newly come to your realm!"

The glow from the stones grew brighter, raying out across the plain. Where it fell, transparent figures rose from the earth, more and more of them with every moment. As the wind lifts the leaves, his song moved them toward the new mound. In the east the sky grew bright with the approach of dawn. The fires were veiled by an opalescent cloud, swirling ever more swiftly until the earth of the barrow opened and the spirits of the newly dead burst free.

In that instant the burning edge of the sun rimmed the horizon. Merlin heard a gasp of awe from behind him; then he blinked at the explosion of radiance above the mound. The sun lifted free of earth's shadow and light flamed in a burning path from the mound across the grass to flare from the stones of the henge.

The living and the dead and the earth itself joined in a great shout of praise. Merlin felt his spirit reft away in a timeless moment of unity. Then he fell back into his body, and sat up, blinking at the morning light of Samhain Day.

"Their sacrifice has been accepted," said a voice behind him. "They are one with the land."

It was Aurelianus, his face still radiant with awe. He looked younger than Merlin had yet seen him, but fragile, as if the spirit within him burned too fiercely for his flesh to bear. He knew then that the emperor would not live long. Uthir stood beside him, steadying his elbow.

This was the king that he would serve, thought Merlin, until the time for the Defender should come.

"They would ask no greater honor," said Uthir, "nor would I."

From that day, Merlin rode with Uthir's band. While Aurelianus traveled back to Venta to direct the defense of Britannia along the new frontier, his brother marched toward Demetia. While the combrogi had been focused on defending their eastern territories, the Picts and Scotii—the ancient enemy—took advantage of the situation to renew their raiding. Their numbers were reinforced by a band of Saxons led by Pascentius, who had been beaten off by Amlodius the year before, and had taken refuge in Eriu.

For a time, the heavens themselves seemed to be fighting on the side of their foes, for clouds rolled in from the west, washing out tracks and slowing the combrogi army. Uthir rallied them with cheerful obscenities and said that the storms had been sent by God to pin the enemy down until they could catch up with him. He was, observed Merlin, a good commander, willing to listen to advice when there was time and decisive when there was not. He asked his men to endure no hardship that he himself did not share.

As the campaign continued, Merlin grew to know the other commanders as well, Caius Turpilius, whose family had a prosperous estate near Venta Silurum and still held to the old Roman ways; Eldaul of Glevum the younger, a distant cousin of Vitalinus who always sought the most dangerous fighting in an attempt to avenge his father, and Gorlosius of the Cornovii, eldest son and heir of Gerontius, who ruled Dumnonia.

Igierne's husband.

Merlin studied him more closely than the others, and found little to like, though there was much to admire. He too fought fiercely, though it seemed sometimes that his ruthlessness came from outrage that anyone would dare to oppose him. If ever Merlin had thought of offering Igierne more than a kinsman's love, recognition of his own origins would have prevented it, but it galled him to think of her bound to this arrogant princeling, when she was herself the equal of a queen.

They had marched all the way through Demetia and were pushing up the coast toward Guenet before the clouds began to break up and they saw the naked heavens once more.

When they made camp that evening, the only remains of the storm were a few tattered banners of flame across the sky. Merlin—whose usual reaction to rain was to bundle his leather clothing into a chest and go clad only in the twist of linen about his loins—was salving a sore where the wet saddle blanket had galled his pony, when he heard a shout. It was not the standard alarm for an approaching enemy. He turned and saw men pointing at the heavens.

Half these men had been shepherds before the wars. Even the farmers among them were accustomed to tell the seasons by searching the skies. Merlin had been making regular observations since Maugantius began to teach him when he was ten years old. It took no more than a moment for him to see what they were looking at—a brilliant point of light in the southeast where there had been no star before. For an hour it was visible in the heavens, then it sank behind the trees.

The next night it was brighter still, and they could see a blur of light behind it. It was a comet, Merlin told them, such as often foretold events of great import. But it was still rising. They must wait until it reached full magnitude before he could attempt to discover what it might mean.

The three nights that followed were overcast. The combrogi pushed northward, eager to come to grips with the foe. Smoke still rose from the burned timbers of the looted farmsteads they were passing now. The enemy army could not be far away.

The next day a wind came up that tossed the treetops and scoured the clouds from the sky. They made camp early that evening, choosing a rise with a clear view to the south. Merlin put on a good tunic of white wool that Aurelianus had given him; it made no difference to the magic, but to look like a druid would inspire confidence. By now, he himself was as anxious to know the comet's meaning as any of the men. But mingled with his anticipation was fear.

As daylight faded the tension grew. Merlin felt their apprehension as a pressure against his awareness and braced his mind against it. His discomfort lessened, but so did his ability to perceive the subtle currents of the universe. Frowning, he chose a good vantage point on the hill and drew the circle of herbs around him. Not even Uthir would dare to cross it, and as he closed it he felt the strain ease.

He took his place upon the wolfhide, breathing deeply and regularly and rooting his soul in the earth below. He sensed the delicate branchings of power that nourished the land; but they were only tributaries, not a mighty river such as he had tapped at the Giant's Dance. Yet even these tiny channels were troubled. Some change was coming, and soon.

The blue of the sky deepened to a luminous cobalt. The first stars gleamed suddenly, but where had the comet gone? A murmur from the men brought his attention upward and he realized that it was traveling more quickly than he had expected, for it was already high. Merlin lay back, gazing upward and, anchored by his link to the earth, allowed his spirit to soar.

The head of the comet blazed more brightly than Venus when she is the morning star, and its tail seemed to stretch halfway across the sky. Transfixed by its beauty, it took Merlin a little while to realize that someone was calling him.

"Prophet, tell me—" Uthir's voice was thin with strain, "what is this wild star?"

Already half-tranced, Merlin responded to the note of command as a horse obeys the rein. Awareness of the outer world faded; he stared up at the comet until it filled his vision. Its head had seemed a ball of light, but now it was pulsing wildly, and suddenly it was the head of a dragon. Distantly he heard his own voice reporting what he saw.

There was a mutter of awe from the men around him. Then the prince spoke again.

"Such marvels don't come by chance. What does this one mean?"

At the question, knowledge cascaded into conscious awareness with an intensity that brought Merlin upright, tears welling in his eyes.

"Woe and sorrow," he whispered, "woe and weeping for you, my lord, and for all Britannia. Your brother is dead. The noble prince is gone, and the people left without their leader." Blindly he turned toward Uthir and stretched out his hand. "Arise, son of Ambrosius, and hasten to strike your foe. Go now, while the head of the Dragon rules the sky and promises you victory. Destroy your enemy and take Britannia into your keeping."

He gazed upward once more and saw the mouth of the Dragon opening, and from its jaws blazed a tongue of fire. "You will have victory!" he shouted suddenly, "and a son greater even than his father who will save his people and win fame unending!"

Now others were clamoring, asking how Aurelianus had died, where the enemy was, what they should do. Merlin shook his head, striving to hear the voice that spoke within.

"You shall find your foes camped on the shore where the Isle of the Dead guards the bay—" he whispered. "March now, and take them as they are sleeping. You must move swiftly, for they mean to sail on the morning tide!"

They marched through the night, and the Dragon blazed above them, showing the way. And just as it was growing ghostly with the approach of dawn, the combrogi army wound down from the hills above Madoc's Bay and saw the enemy encampment sprawled across the sands below. They had sent out scouts, and every man knew what to expect and what he must do.

Except for Merlin. Uthir had made it quite clear that he must not risk himself. In any case he had never learned how men fought with weapons of iron, and he had been taught that to use his other gifts to take life would destroy both those gifts, and him. He waited on the brow of the hill, in the shelter of a thornbush. To an enemy passing by he would have been invisible, but his prophecy had brought these men to battle; he owed it to them to watch them fight.

The raiders had thought themselves safe. But they were not stupid.

As Uthir's force came sweeping down the hill, guards gave the alarm, and men burst from their rude shelters or struggled free from the cloaks in which they had wrapped themselves to sleep, weapons in hand. Uthir had divided his men into three wings; one to strike from each side and the third to circle round to the shore. In such confusion the horses gave little advantage. After the first wild ride through the encampment, stabbing with lance and spear, most of the riders slid off their mounts and began to lay about them with their swords.

Surprise had evened the odds, but the enemy fought well, and all the more so when the men Uthir had delegated to the task waded out with torches and fired the vessels waiting to carry them away. Most of the plunder had already been loaded into them. Deprived of both escape and reward, the enemy had little to lose, but Uthir was determined that this lot of raiders would not return another day.

The prince had kept his mount. From the hill, Merlin marked him, reining the bay mare in tight circles, stabbing with his lance as if each man he faced was responsible for Aurelianus's loss. It was one way to deal with grief, or at least to put off facing it. The true pain would come later on.

Gorlosius was still mounted as well, on a wiry stallion with a coat as black as his own hair. What he might lack in brute strength he made up in quickness. No sooner had an enemy focused on him than he was gone. Eldaul, on the other hand, was too big a man for most horses. He waded into battle with a sword in each hand, and when one blade shattered, replaced it with an axe he had won from a foe. As he fought his way through the camp the bodies piled up behind him like earth thrown up by the plough.

Then the men who had attacked the ships regrouped at the water's edge and drove those who were trying to escape that way back onto the attackers' swords. The incoming tide ran red above the bloodstained sands.

After that it was soon over. Merlin made his way down the hill. The Frisian, Pascentius, had been killed, and the Irish chieftain, Gillomanus, was captured. But in the battle his leg had been half severed. Even if he were ransomed, he would fight no more against Britannia. Most of the other prisoners were put to the sword.

Merlin moved among their own wounded, cleaning and binding the dreadful gashes, stitching when there was need. Most of these men were scarred already, and they were as healthy as their own ponies. There was good reason to hope they would heal, though he had known a tiny scratch to bring death to a man in his prime. He wondered how Aurelianus had died—for after finding the enemy where he had predicted, he no longer doubted that the first part of his vision was also true. Had some disease stricken the emperor, or had his heart given out at last?

Angry voices roused him from his absorption. He finished securing a bandage and got to his feet. One voice was that of Uthir, clipped and low. The other, louder, belonged to Gorlosius.

"All that those wretches had stolen was on those ships, and you burned them!" exclaimed the Cornovian.

"Would you rather they escaped with it?" Uthir was hanging onto his temper surprisingly well.

"We would have prevented that—" Gorlosius gestured toward the bodies being dragged towards the pyre.

"Perhaps. I had to be sure."

"We should have returned that wealth to its owners, or used it to feed our forces if the owners could not be found. We all bled for this—we deserve a share in the reward!"

"Do you?" Uthir's voice sharpened. "Dumnonia has suffered least of all. If the rest of us can do without, you can afford it as well!"

"Don't use that tone with me!" exclaimed Gorlosius. "You have only the word of this sorcerer that the emperor is dead and yet you are claiming his mantle. Do you think because you're his brother it will automatically go to you? The new High King must be elected from among all the princes when that time comes."

"And so he will be." Uthir's voice shook with the effort he was making to retain control. "But until we return to Venta, the command of this army is mine, and you will obey!"

They took the road south as soon as their wounded could travel. By the time they reached Demetia the messengers had found them. Aurelianus was dead indeed—of illness, said some, while others whispered of poison, though no culprit could be found. The comet had been seen all over the land, and its meaning widely disputed. But by that time, one of Uthir's men had made a banner bearing a red dragon, its head haloed in light. *Pendragon*, "Dragonhead," they hailed him, and the word ran ahead of them so that by the time they reached Venta Belgarum, the whole countryside was calling him by that name.

And it was as Uthir Pendragon that the princes of Britannia hailed him as their High King.

A Heritage of Power

The house of the High Priestess smelled of sickness. After the fresh breeze off the lake, it was almost overpowering. Igierne stopped short in the entry, summoning her self-control, and little Morgause bumped into her. The message had said that Argantel was ill and wanted her, but the figure in the bed seemed shrunken, and even the lamplight could not lend a healthy color to her skin. The old woman who sat by her stood up and motioned to them to enter; Igierne recognized Ebrdila, who had served as Argantel's deputy when the High Priestess was away.

Igierne grasped the child's shoulder, holding her tightly, and Morgause, who could never bear to be restrained, struggled to get free.

"Your grandmother is resting, little one—" With an effort she kept her voice steady. "Why don't you run down to the shore to play?"

She felt the girl shake her head. "I want to kiss her."

Igierne looked down at Morgause's ruddy curls with the exasperation her daughter so often aroused in her. This was not how she wished the child to remember her grandmother, but Morgause was almost six, old enough to face the reality of death. With a sigh she released her grip, and followed her inside.

"Mother—"

Argantel's eyelids quivered. For a moment she gazed unseeing, then the blue eyes focused and she smiled. Her hair had just begun to gray before Amlodius died; it was white now. Igierne swallowed. Her parents had always been so matter-of-fact about their marriage. Who would have thought that losing her husband would blight Argantel's autumnal splendor?

"You came . . . and the little one too. . . . It is well that you had a daughter first . . . to inherit . . . the trust."

"I'm not ready," said Igierne.

"Neither was I. . . . Your path lies still in the world . . ." Argantel reached out and grasped her daughter's hand. "You must go back, and be Tigernissa. But a time will come when you will return to be the Lady of the Lake on this Isle. And this one . . . shall rule after you. . . ." She reached out to the child.

Was that a curse, wondered Igierne, or a promise? Morgause's dark eyes grew round, then she bent and kissed the old woman's papery cheek.

"Grandmother, are you a queen?"

Argantel smiled. "In a way I am. . . . Remember, whatever happens in the outer world, so long as the Lady of the Lake . . . rules here . . ." she paused, fighting for breath, "the Goddess still lives . . . in Britannia."

"Not in the South," Igierne said bitterly. "The bishops preach against the old festivals, or change their meaning, and call woman the root of evil. The Saxons are pagans, therefore no loyal Briton can honor our ancient gods!"

"That's enough," said Ebrdila. "You are tiring her." Igierne remembered her mother telling her that the older woman had wanted to be High Priestess once. But she seemed honestly grief-stricken now.

Argantel's features twisted in a grimace that was trying to be a smile. "Let me talk. . . . I will be quiet soon."

"Cannot you do something?" Igierne asked Ebrdila. "You know all the secrets of healing here! Cannot the power of the Cauldron make her whole?" She did not speak of the Sword. Its power was of another kind.

Ebrdila drew herself up. "Do you understand so little? The Hallows can set aright only that which counters the way of nature. But even the Cauldron cannot mend a heart which is outworn!"

Argantel shook her head. "Truly, daughter, if you had not been here,

I do not think I would have lived so long. . . . Do not waste the time I have left in mourning. You may weep when I am gone."

Igierne bit her lip and looked down. Morgause had slipped away from the bedside and was wandering about the chamber, fingering the hangings and carved beams, the vessels of silver and bronze, all the odd bits of paraphernalia that had accumulated there.

"You have borne your daughter for the Lake. Now you must bear a son for Britannia."

"How? It has been months since Gorlosius sought my bed. But I was married by Christian rites. I cannot divorce him."

"Gorlosius will not . . . father your child."

"Who, then?"

"You will know. . . ." Argantel's smile faded. "But you must not fail . . . in your trust. Guard the Sword until your son is a man!"

Igierne stared into her mother's blue eyes that were so like her own. Argantel's fingers twitched anxiously, and Ebrdila lifted her hand and set it on her daughter's head.

"Witness!" whispered the High Priestess. "To Igierne I pass the power! May the gods of our people bear witness to what I say!"

She fell back and lay gasping, but Igierne swayed and nearly fell, dizzied by the pulse of energy, as if her mother's life had passed into her through her hand.

"Go. She will sleep now. I will call you if there is need."

There was command in Ebrdila's voice, and Igierne rose, looking down at her mother's closed face. She wanted to throw her arms around her, weeping, but Argantel was already leaving her. She bowed her head and turned, and as she did so, Ebrdila also stood, and made her the obeisance due a High Priestess, or a queen.

That night, after Morgause had been put to bed, Igierne walked upon the shore. A little after Igierne had left her, Argantel had slipped into sleep as well, a slumber from which she could not be wakened. From the house of the High Priestess Igierne could hear singing as the women of the Isle of Maidens chanted the verses that guide a departing spirit home.

The past few days had been cloudy, but tonight the sky was clear, and the quiet waters of the lake glittered with reflected stars. As she gazed, light seemed to blossom beneath the waters. She looked up and saw the comet, hanging like a firedrake in the sky.

For a long time she watched it, her heart wrenched between anguish and exaltation. When at last she sought her bed, she dreamed of a battle on the sands. In the chill hour just before sunrise, Ebrdila woke her to say that her mother was gone.

*   *   *

Londinium was hot and crowded and full of bad smells. The only thing it did not have in overabundance, thought Igierne, was Saxons. Riding through the empty lands along the Tamesis, she had longed for the safety of the Lake. Now she longed for its peace. Her horse snorted and tried to rear as a peddler waved a tray of glass bangles almost under its nose. She reined the beast down, glancing at her husband in irritation.

"If you were going to ask me again to allow you to return to the Isle of Maidens," said Gorlosius, "the answer is still no. I gave you leave to attend your mother's deathbed, not to become the High Priestess of a pagan cult. You will not speak of that while we are in Londinium, do you understand? The princes will not choose a man who would bring them a pagan queen!"

Since the death of his father, she thought angrily, he had become even more autocratic.

"Do you think my silence will make any difference?" asked Igierne. "They all know who I am. I thought it was for an alliance with the powers of the North that you married me."

"The *secular* power of the North," he snapped in reply. "And you should not have left my daughter on the Isle."

"Your message commanded my presence at your side," she answered sweetly. "It said nothing of Morgause."

"Well, that is past praying for now, and perhaps it will do no harm. Until she reaches an age for marriage no one will care too much where a girl-child is bestowed."

"I wonder that you men have not found some other method of begetting offspring if you consider females of such little worth."

Gorlosius refused to dignify that sally with an answer. The old governor's palace was before them; the warriors guarding the gate straightened to attention as the Cornovian prince rode in, and returned Igierne's smile. It was not their fault that her husband had ordered her to join him, she thought as they continued across the inner courtyard. And she might need friends one day.

The basilica of Londinium was the largest building Igierne had ever seen, and drafty. It was a place for court and council, and so it remained. The altar which had once received incense for the emperor had been taken down, but the flaking portraits of dead Caesars still watched from the walls. In Byzantium, she had heard, the emperor was still treated as if he were a god. She sighed as she watched the gesticulating figures below from her place with the other wives. Things were different in Britannia.

"There was a time," Eleutherius of Eburacum was saying as he addressed the other princes, "when our numbers would have been too many even for this hall! Too many of our men of good family have gone to Armorica. It is those of us who have remained, standing fast against the enemy, who should rule, not a man whose family fled."

"Nonsense!" Uthir answered him. "Half the lords of Dumnonia and Demetia rule more lands in lesser Britannia than they do here. My father never ran from the Saxons; my brother and I went only to avoid weakening this island by civil war. And when Britannia called we came back again. *You* summoned the 'sons of Ambrosius' to come and lead you—not Aurelianus alone. You've already chosen me!"

He had not raised his voice, but it carried clearly. He was too far away for Igierne to make out his features, but she wondered if the relaxed lines of his body represented unconcern or an exquisite control.

The woman sitting beside her leaned closer. "He only says the truth. And they say his soldiers love him. If he went outside and appealed to the men, they would raise him on their shields as emperors were made in the old days."

Why was it only the men who were deciding? wondered Igierne. The Saxons killed women as well as warriors. It was said, of course, that a woman influenced the outcome by influencing her husband, but to Gorlosius, she was only a symbol of his status, like the golden torque he wore. Her father, she remembered, had valued her mother's wisdom. In that moment she missed them both acutely. How foolish she had been to expect that her own marriage would be the same.

"Your husband is not a candidate, then?" asked Igierne.

"Oh no. He is Caius Turpilius, a gentleman of good family, but no prince. I am Flavia. But Uthir will have his vote. My husband has served with the prince through several campaigns."

"So has mine," answered Igierne dryly. "But I think I would rather have Uthir as High King."

Flavia, once she had started talking, seemed eager to be friendly. Igierne learned in short order that she had a young son at home and would like more children, but feared it was not to be, for the child was large, and the birth had been a hard one.

"A fine strapping boy is my Cai, but it's hard to bear sons, knowing that as soon as they can hold a blade they'll be off to war. I could almost wish he had been a girl."

"Girls can be a trial too," said Igierne, remembering how Morgause had wept when she rode away. But she was more certain than ever that she had been wise to leave the girl safe in the North.

Eldaul of Glevum was speaking now. His connection with Vitalinus gave him a claim, but was also his greatest liability. Fortunately he seemed to be without ambition, and was supporting his commander.

"Do you think the Protector of Eburacum a serious contender?" asked Flavia.

"He would like to be, but he is young and untried," answered Igierne dispassionately. "The same goes for Agricola of Demetia, and Honorius. Many of the men who might have been contenders died at Sorviodunum. Northerners from beyond the Wall, like Ridarchus, are too far away to be considered, though they make useful allies. I hope that they will choose Uthir."

"You know a great deal about it—" said Flavia.

"Really? You would never think it, to hear my husband. . . ."

Flavia followed the direction of her gaze and understanding dawned suddenly. "You don't want to be queen?"

"I don't particularly want Gorlosius to be High King," Igierne replied.

Flavia raised one eyebrow, then her eyes widened. "And who in the name of Christ and His holy mother is *that*?"

She pointed, and Igierne saw a tall figure that appeared to have formed itself from the shadows behind Uthir. A singularly inappropriate invocation, thought Igierne, recognizing, even at this distance, the slightly stooping posture and the dark hair. But he had changed; his finery had been replaced by a plain white robe and his beard swept his chest. As if he had felt her gaze upon him, he looked up, eyes fierce as a hawk's beneath heavy brows.

"That is my cousin," she said softly, "Merlin. . . ."

She did not encounter Merlin again until the Council was over and the princes and their wives gathered at the church to see Uthir anointed and crowned. Despite the arguments, the choice had been, she thought, inevitable. The Pendragon's name was on every tongue. If the princes had chosen another ruler, no one would have followed him.

During the Council, Igierne had come to value Flavia's simple friendliness. They stood together now outside the little church, mantles wrapped tightly, for a damp wind had come up, promising rain. With the other women and less important chieftains they waited for the princes to emerge, for the little church could not hold them all. Merlin stood apart, appearing rather monkish himself in his white robe. But from what she had heard, he was no longer any kind of Christian at all. From time to time she would find him watching her, but when their eyes met he looked away.

Before we leave here I will find time to talk to him, she thought, *even if Gorlosius disapproves.*

If the bishop sealed the rite by offering communion she wondered if her husband would receive it. It was a sin, she had been told, to take the sacrament when one's heart was full of anger or envy, and Gorlosius had been festering with fury since the decision was made. She listened with half an ear to Flavia chatter about her eagerness to get back to her child and her home, reflecting that this was what a marriage should be.

I will go home to Dun Tagell with Gorlosius, she told herself, *but when he goes off to fight again, I will leave as well. The Lady of the Lake should not be at any man's beck and call.*

The church doors swung open. From inside came a wave of incense and the sound of voices joined in song. Men began to come out of the sanctuary, blinking in the light. A murmur of anticipation spread through the crowd.

"The Pendragon! The High King comes!"

Igierne felt a wave of dizziness and took a deep breath. Interesting, she thought—his brother had been addressed as emperor, but Uthir obviously favored a British title, accepting that the Roman days were done. More men emerged, a guard of honor, who stood away to either side, drawing their swords. She moved back a little and felt a hand grasp her elbow. It was Merlin.

"You must stay here until they come. . . ."

Before she could ask why, color blazed at the church door. The bishop was coming through, clad in his embroidered cope, and beside him, his brow bound with gold and his shoulders draped in a purple mantle that flowed over a white garment like a priest's gown, came the king.

He looked dazed, thought Igierne, and not because the sun was coming out at last. His gaze was the rapt stare of one who has looked on a holy thing. Two priests guided him between the lines of warriors; he blinked and lifted a hand to acknowledge the cheers.

The crowd surged toward him, shouting, but somehow Merlin was in front of them, still holding Igierne by the arm.

"All hail to the Pendragon of Britannia—" said Merlin. Igierne knew that the people were still shouting, but the noise was muted, as if the three of them stood within a bubble that shut out sound. "I bring you the blessing of the ancient powers, and I bring you the White Raven, the hidden queen!"

Slowly, Uthir's gaze moved from Merlin to Igierne. What was he seeing? She had cast back her hood when the sun came out and with it her veil; she could feel the sun warm on her hair. She felt herself flushing as the dazed wonder in his face became a very focused awe.

Abruptly she understood that he was seeing not an ordinary woman, the wife of one of his chieftains, but the Goddess in mortal form. And understanding, her own awareness became that of the priestess, and looking upon him, she saw not Uthir the man, but the King.

It was Gorlosius who broke the spell.

"Come away, woman!" He took her arm and pulled her after him. "And put on your veil. Our great king has better things to do than stare at you!"

They turned a corner and he let her go, glaring. "What did Uthir say to you?"

Igierne straightened her mantle and drew her veil back over her hair. "He said nothing. Nothing at all," she said coldly.

He had not needed to, she thought as she turned and began to walk toward their lodgings. As king and queen their spirits had touched, and she could not predict what was going to happen now.

Igierne had been taught that the six weeks before the equinox were a time of change, in both the inner worlds and the lands of men. True it was that no sooner had she and Gorlosius arrived at Dun Tagell than the weather grew stormy. From then until the autumnal equinox, the outer coasts of Dumnonia were lashed by violent weather, but the conflicts in the skies were only a mild reflection of the tumults in the affairs of men.

For Gorlosius, overriding by sheer force of will his father's old councilors, had declared Dumnonia a kingdom separate from Britannia, and renounced his oaths to the High King. The rock of Dun Tagell, which had known peace since Vitalinus brought the Cornovii down from the north to drive the men of Eriu away, became a garrison.

The Latin name for the place was Durocornovium, the stronghold of the Cornovii. Its defenses were limited to a wall that enclosed a hall and a barracks built of the native stone, but it needed no more, for it was set on an outcrop at the edge of the sea, with only a narrow bridge of rock to link it to the land. It was not clear to Igierne whether her husband had settled her there to hold it for him, or whether the dozen men assigned to it were there to keep watch on her. Gorlosius himself paid her only an occasional visit. Isca Dumnoniorum and Durnovaria were the first lines of his defense, and to her relief he had little time for his western holdings.

From time to time word came to them of the progress of the war. The new High King, desperate to settle the situation before the Saxons could organize themselves to take advantage of British disunity, had struck

swiftly and hard. Gorlosius had fallen back from Durnovaria and made a
new frontier at Isca, but Uthir, seeking to besiege him in the city, left a
back way open, and instead of driving his enemy down toward Belerion
in the toe of the peninsula, had allowed him to escape toward the western
coast where Gorlosius had hopes of joining with allies from Eriu.

By the time Uthir caught up with him his enemy had gone to ground
once more in an ancient hill-fort called Dimilioc, a few miles south of
Dun Tagell. And there they held, as the cold winds blew and the nights
lengthened toward winter, until the feast of Samhain, when the dead come
home.

Torchflames flickered wildly in the draft, chasing shadows like fleeing
bogles into the corners of the hall. Try though they might, thought Igierne,
they could never make the building completely proof against the wind.
Always before, she had spent the winter in the villa above the sheltered
waters of the Fawwyth, on the protected southern coast of Cornovia. In
the summer Dun Tagell could be delightful, with the gulls calling as they
wheeled above and the sunlight sparkling on the waves. But it was a cold
and damp and dismal place to spend the wintertime!

With a silent curse for the husband who had left her here, Igierne set
the basket of apples, last of the summer's store, up on the table. It was a
poor feast—if they had any sense, those spirits to whom it was offered
would return to some table that was better supplied. If there were enough,
she reflected, frowning, to go around. In these past years so many had
died, and so many of the families who did survive had fled the land. Any
ancestors who sought them would have a long way to go.

And so she set out the fruit and the barley bread, and the dishes of
boiled meat and cheese. And despite the draft, she fixed the great doorway
just a little ajar so that any spirit that might wish to share the hospitality
of Dun Tagell could come in.

Certainly the men of her garrison appreciated the break in the mo-
notony of their duty. There was no mead, but when she brought round
the ale pitcher they grinned and held out their cups. The drinking went
on until late, for there were many toasts to be made, to comrades lost in
the recent fighting, to her mother, and to Aurelianus, who lay now in the
barrow beside the Giant's Dance with the lords whom Hengest had slain.

By the evening's ending, sorrow had been translated to melancholy
on a golden tide of ale. The men went singing to their barracks, and even
Igierne's two women were nodding. She herself had drunk enough to feel
an unaccustomed detachment, but she was not yet sleepy. When she had

helped her women to their beds, she eased out the door and climbed carefully to the lookout post on the wall.

A three-quarter moon glimmered between tattered clouds, touching an occasional glint of silver from the restless waves. And from time to time the water would catch a flicker of light from the torches that burned on the walls, as if the people of the sea were celebrating their own festival. Lights had been kindled over the gates, and at the other end of the arching causeway, to aid any spirit that might be uncertain of the road in finding its way.

Though surely, she thought as she gazed at the shadowed masses of the cliffs beyond it, any spirit that could find a path between the worlds could manage to travel this last little way. She blinked—for a moment she had thought she saw something moving—but when she looked again the land was as dark and featureless as before.

It is the ale, she thought, shaking her head. *I had best seek my bed before I try to walk the moonpath across the sea.*

She made her way down from the wall, choosing her footing with conscious care. The hall seemed warm after the brisk wind outside, and she cast aside her shawl. The pitcher still stood upon the table, half full of ale. It would be flat by morning, and it seemed a pity to waste it when there were so many dead whom she had not yet honored. She filled her cup and raised it high.

"To Amlodius, shield of the North!"

She had barely begun the tally of her father's dead companions when the lamplight flickered wildly and a gust of wind stirred her hair. She looked up. The door to the hall had swung open; three figures were standing there.

"Be you living or dead, I give you greeting—" She held out the beaker. "In the name of the old gods and the new, be welcome to this hall."

They came forward, and the third man closed the door behind them. Igierne blinked, thinking she must have drunk more than she thought, for she found it hard to focus on their features. Then the leader stopped before her and held out his hand to take the cup. He was wearing a checkered mantle she knew only too well, with a golden griffin pin.

"Gorlosius!" she exclaimed, almost dropping the cup. "What are you doing here?"

For a moment he hesitated. "Where else should I be on this holy festival?" His voice seemed strained and hoarse, as if he were very tired. "I gave my army the slip and came here. I couldn't go any longer without seeing you again."

Igierne took a step back and snatched up the lamp, but his features were still in shadow.

"You come here on Samhain Eve, like a spirit from the Otherworld, and you expect me to welcome you?"

"Is it so strange to expect a wife to welcome her husband?"

"It is when I am the wife," she said with a bitter humor, "and the husband is you."

One of his men—she thought his name was Jordanus—hovered anxiously behind him. The third man kept to the shadows by the door. Perhaps they were spirits, she thought, her skin prickling, for surely this was not the Gorlosius she had known.

"Nonetheless," he said harshly, "this night I'll claim a husband's place in your bed!" Before she could react he was beside her, gripping her shoulders with a warrior's callused hands.

But not the hands of Gorlosius. He was a living man—so close, she could feel the warmth of his body; her nostrils flared to the scents of sweat and horse—but her flesh knew that this man had never touched her before.

"I am the Lady of the Lake," she said in a still voice, "and not to be deceived by lesser magics. In the name of the gods my people swear by I conjure your true form back again."

Whether the change was in him or in herself she could not say, but the air seemed to ripple around him, and when it cleared she was looking up into the face of the High King.

"Why?" she said softly. "Why have you sought to dishonor me?"

Uthir shook his head. "The disguise was to protect you. The man at the gate thought I was Gorlosius, and let me in."

"I asked the wrong question," Igierne said then. "Why have you tried to deceive me? It is not the way of a lover to court in the guise of another man, nor is it the way of a king."

"It is the way of a desperate man . . ." he whispered then, glancing toward the man by the door in appeal.

"What is that to me?" exclaimed Igierne. She was slow to wrath, but she was growing angry now. "If this is love, it can learn to wait; if it is lust, then burn!"

"This is the hour in which the Pendragon is destined to beget his son," said the third man, coming at last into the light. "The child which you conceive in this hour, and no other, shall be the Defender of Britannia."

"Merlin . . ." she breathed, remembering how she had faced him across the altar of the Sword. "Is this truly so?"

He bowed his head. "I have seen it in the heavens."

"I will not be coerced . . . even by the stars. . . ."

Uthir stared at her, his desperation gradually giving way to the awe with which he had looked upon her as he came from his crowning.

"Lady—I won't force you." Taking a deep breath, he got down upon one knee. "You are the White Raven of Britannia; you decide." He took her hand and gently kissed the palm.

At the touch of his lips a little shock traveled up her arm. She bit her lip, feeling a warmth spreading through her despite the chill air. She held out her other hand, and trembled as he kissed it.

"You are so beautiful, Igierne," he said softly. "You haunt my sleep, and I dream you are my queen."

"Truly?" She laughed suddenly, her anger giving way to a fierce exhilaration. "Then as a queen I will claim you! You shall come to my bed, and we will see what ancient soul is hovering in these shadows, waiting to take flesh in my womb!"

One end of the hall had been partitioned off with curtains and woven screens to give the master of the fortress some privacy. A few swift steps brought her to the entrance. Uthir surged to his feet and followed her.

In the dim light that came through the curtain she saw him in silhouette, stripping off his mantle and heavy outer tunic, struggling with the buckles of his commander's belt, and finally letting it drop with a clatter to the floor. She unhooked belt and brooches, pulling first the short-sleeved outer garment and then the long-sleeved undertunic over her head so that she stood shivering in her shift before him.

He had got as far as his braes. Her eyes had adjusted to the dim light, and her breath caught as she took in his breadth of shoulder and the fine modeling of muscle in belly and arm. She knelt to unknot his leg wrappings and he bent, plucking the pins from her coiled hair so that it fell in silken masses about her shoulders.

"Lie down," he whispered. "If you touch me now I will waste the good seed."

She pulled away, looking up at him, and saw that it was true. She wanted to laugh, but her pulse was leaping erratically, and she realized that she had come already to a state of readiness that Gorlosius, with all his efforts, had rarely been able to bring her. She tugged at the neck ties of her shift and as she rose it slid off her shoulders and pooled around her feet. She padded to the bed and lay down upon it, clad only in her hair.

For one moment longer Uthir hesitated, then he surrendered himself to her embrace, and as the embers flare when new fuel is thrust into the hearth, their bodies caught fire. With arms and legs she held fast as the flames rose higher. Then they exploded in a shower of light, brilliant behind her closed eyelids, and he cried out and arched hard against her and then fell like a slain man back into her arms.

For a few moments they lay gasping. Then Igierne ran her hands down the rippling muscles of his back and felt him come to life again between her thighs. This time their joining had a sweet deliberation that left her panting and helpless in his arms. They made love a third time before they slept, but long afterward, when she thought about that night, it seemed to her that it must have been in the first encounter that she got her son, when all the High King's hoarded passion was released in that great cry.

She felt Uthir's contentment change to the relaxation of sleep, and had time only to draw the blankets over them before oblivion claimed her as well. It was some hours later that she awakened, wondering what had disturbed her, for Uthir lay still beside her and there had been no sound. She opened her eyes, abruptly certain they were not alone.

Beside the curtains a pale shape moved.

She blinked, remembering how a trick of the light on the bedcurtains had been able to frighten her when she was a child. But this image grew ever more distinct until she could make out the tense, wiry shape beneath the mantle, the shock of dark hair and staring eyes. Spectral lips shaped her name.

"Gorlosius . . ." she whispered, answering.

The shape reached towards her. Then from the pen beside the garden came a cock's crow, and its features contorted and began to fade.

Was it Gorlosius's spirit body or his shade? Igierne lay trembling until in the gray hour just after dawn, when the mist lies heavy on the sea, the stillness was broken by someone shouting. She heard the door to the hall slam open and sat up, pulling the blanket around her, as Uthir began to stir by her side.

"My lady, my lady! The High King's men have stormed the fort and struck down Gorlosius. Come quickly, and we will help you to flee!"

The curtains were flung back. She saw two of her husband's men, their armor bloodied, their frantic faces stiffening to astonishment as the torchlight showed them who was sitting there. For a moment Igierne's mind went blank with terror. Then the warrior went down on one knee.

"Lord Gorlosius, I saw you fall!"

"I escaped," said Uthir. As a commander, Igierne thought numbly, he must have developed the ability to sound sensible moments after being awakened by an alarm.

"Then you must flee again, for the Pendragon will surely come here to secure this stronghold!"

"If he's taken Dimilioc then my cause is lost, and I must make peace with him. Go back—tell the men to lay down their arms. The High King won't condemn them for following their prince!"

"Aye, my lord—" said the warrior, sorrow replacing the terror in his eyes. He regained his feet and pushed back out through the curtains.

Igierne let out her pent breath in a long sigh.

Uthir was already pulling on his clothing. "What a tangle—" he muttered. "But with all the rumors that will fly, I suppose no one will know what's true!" He belted his tunic and reached for the checkered mantle.

Igierne still sat with the blanket around her shoulders, watching him. "Does anyone know that?" she said softly.

He stilled, and the warmth came back into his eyes. A swift step brought him to her side and he kissed her.

"I know that you're my queen! Bar the gates after me; and don't let anyone in until I come for you!"

It seemed very quiet when he had gone.

I am a widow . . . thought Igierne, remembering Gorlosius's anguished ghost. Then, deliberately, she thrust the memory away. *I am a queen*, she told herself, and set her hands above her belly, where even now the future Defender of Britannia, planted in her womb like a seed of light, was beginning to glow.

VIII

The Sign of the Bear

"Morgause, your hair is like my mother's, the way it was when I was a child," said Igierne, drawing the comb through the long strands. "It shines like a dark fire."

Through the narrow window of the tower a thin spring sunlight glowed on rich fabric, sparkled from the jewelry waiting in its casket, and struck fiery glints from the girl's long hair. Once, this had been part of the Roman fortress of Eburacum, but Coelius had made it a royal residence. Now his son Eleutherius ruled, and seemed happy to host the wedding of his overlord's daughter to Leudonus of Dun Eidyn.

Morgause shrugged as if she were not convinced, but she stood still as her mother took up the next strand and began to tease the snarls free. Poor child, thought Igierne, at fifteen her hair was almost her only beauty. She herself had been the same at her first marriage, a pudgy adolescent with no graces to charm her new husband. She wished they could have delayed this wedding until Morgause grew into her own looks, but Uthir needed the northern alliance now. She could only hope that Leudonus would have the sensitivity to cherish this flower until it bloomed. Now in his thirties, he had buried one wife already, and was newly come to his grandfather's throne.

She finished the last lock and smoothed it into place. "There now. Put on the jewels and you will look splendid!" She picked up the necklet of Alban gold.

"I look terrible," said Morgause. "I hate this color—"

"Crimson is traditional," Igierne began, although she had to agree that this particular shade did not flatter her daughter's complexion.

"—and I hate this city. You should have left me on the Isle of Maidens to finish my training. The Isle needs a High Priestess, and if you do not want the position, I do not see why it should not go to me."

Igierne stared at her. *I do want it*, she thought, and each time she had visited Morgause she had wanted to stay with her. But Uthir needed her, and when she was with him, her memories of the Lake became a fair dream.

"Perhaps one day it will," she said aloud. "But the Lady of the Lake needs to know the ways of the world as well. And we need you here—"

"Then why are you sending me to Dun Eidyn?" retorted Morgause, sliding the bracelets onto her wrists.

"Would you rather we had wedded you to some southern magnate who thinks the old ways are a sin?" exclaimed Igierne. "At least the Votadini still honor the gods. Leudonus's mother was a Pictish princess. He will know how to value you not only as Uthir's daughter, but as my heir."

Morgause looked thoughtful as she hung the discs of gold filigree in her ears, and Igierne was unhappily reminded that the girl was her only heir, so far as the world knew. In ten years of marriage, she had given Uthir no other child than the one tiny son, born six weeks before his time at Dun Tagell, the Midsummer after his conception, and handed over to Merlin to foster as soon as it became clear that he would live. She had given him her mother's family name, Artorius, but she would not even know him if she saw him now.

"Well, at least Leudonus is not a bad-looking man," Morgause said finally, finishing with the second earring. "And, as you keep reminding me, he is a king." As she held up the bronze mirror Igierne saw them both for a moment reflected—Morgause ruddy with her father's dark eyes, and herself still pale and fair. But the bronze canceled out such differences, revealing the elegant modeling of cheek and brow, the firm line of the jaw, and beyond such surface similarities, their pride.

There was a stir at the doorway. Igierne turned, expecting the women whom she had banished from her chambers, wanting a little time alone with this daughter whom she was about to lose once more. But it was the High King—with Merlin, as usual, behind him.

"Go out now," she said briskly. "The other ladies are waiting with your wreath and veil. In a few moments I will follow you."

Morgause looked from her mother to Uthir with thinly veiled hostility, but she went without arguing.

"I hope this marriage will work," said the king, looking after her.

"That is the chance you take, is it not, when you marry girls off so young, and without consulting their inclination," Igierne replied, a bit more sharply than she had intended. "What's to say they won't find someone that suits them better when they are grown?"

Uthir had the grace to flush, and her frown softened. Since their marriage he had put on flesh, and from time to time he experienced episodes of dizziness and joint pain that worried her, but he still looked at her with the ardent gaze that had won her ten years ago. With Uthir she had the kind of partnership she had dreamed of, and their physical harmony had only increased with the years.

"It will be enough if Leudonus is as brisk in bed as he is in battle, since her children may be my heirs . . ." he said thoughtfully.

"But what about our son? Isn't it time you brought him to court and acknowledged him? How can he be a king if he is not trained up to rule?"

"How can he be a king if he's dead?" Uthir responded. "People tried to poison my brother and me three times before we were fifteen. Aurelianus never did get over it, really. And we were Ambrosius's legitimate sons!"

"Are you saying that Artorius is not?" Her voice shook.

"Not by Church law—we weren't married 'til Midwinter. A pity the child came early. Curse it, I myself proved how Gorlosius could have visited you six weeks before. The boy's too young to face the whispers that will follow once I claim him. People know you bore me a child, but many think he died, and they don't know where he is now. He is safe, Igierne; let him be!"

"Is he?" Igierne whispered. She turned to Merlin. "He was such a tiny mite when you took him away from me. Have you told me the truth, cousin? Did he live and thrive, or is he only a few tiny bones in an unmarked grave?" It was a nightmare that haunted her—that Gorlosius's ghost had somehow blighted Uthir's seed.

"On your mother's soul I swear, I have seen him every year since he was born," Merlin said quietly.

"Have you seen him this year?" she exclaimed. "You made me Tigernissa, and as High Queen I command you. Go to him, Merlin, and report to me every detail of how he looks and what he does! Then, perhaps, I will believe."

Over her head the two men exchanged a look. Then Merlin nodded. Igierne knew they were humoring her. Perhaps it was seeing Morgause again that made her so desperate to know about her son.

"I will go to him," said the druid, "as soon as the marriage festivities are done."

She drew a trembling breath. "The wedding procession will be forming. You must take your places. Give me a moment to compose myself, and I will come."

On the table there was a flagon with wine. She poured some into a goblet and drank, waiting for her breathing to slow. There was a sound from the entry and she turned. Morgause was standing there, with two spots of color blazing in her cheeks. How long had she been there? wondered her mother. What had she heard?

"It's *him*—it's my brother that you really want, isn't it?" the girl said in a low voice. "But he doesn't even know who you are, and Ebrdila was more of a mother to me than you. You might as well never have had any children at all! If I have babies I swear I will keep them by me! They, at least, will know they had their mother's love!"

She turned in a swirl of draperies and swept out.

After a moment Igierne's fury turned to a laughter that edged hysteria. She gulped down the rest of the wine and strove to control her breathing. It seemed a long time before she was calm once more. But when she emerged at last, the wedding procession was just getting underway. She took her husband's arm, and the High King and High Queen of Britannia escorted Morgause to meet her destiny.

Always, when Merlin came into the pleasant lands above the Sabrina estuary, he felt he was moving back in time. The Silure tribesmen to whom they had once belonged had long ago embraced the manners and culture of Rome, and though the old tribal capital of Venta Silurum now went by the name of Ker-Venta, on Saturday evenings the gentlemen of the countryside heated their baths, and they rode to visit, in the old fashion, in a carriage and pair.

Merlin traveled on a sturdy gray mule, and he preferred to lie upon a patch of woodland rather than seek shelter with folk he did not know, and to bathe in the cold stream. The silence of the forest eased his spirit, and he blessed Igierne for sending him on this errand. Caius and Flavia would be surprised to see him, but their son Cai and Artor their fosterling knew him only as a wandering druid, and accepted his comings and goings without questioning.

He came to the villa a week before the old festival of the goddess of the harvest and Lugos her defender at the time when the grain begins to ripen in the fields, which the Christians now called the Feast of Mary. To the people it made little difference; as always, they prepared to offer their first fruits to the Lady, and pray to the Lord to protect the harvest. It was not only the wheat that was growing stiff and golden and the barley heads that were beginning to hang low. In the orchards, the topmost apples were blushing red and golden with promise of sweetness to come.

As Merlin turned down the lane from the High Road the branches of one of the trees began to shiver as if agitated by an extremely localized storm. From within the tree came high-pitched shouting. The druid reined in, and after a moment's reflection, spun around himself the sphere of shadow that kept him from being seen.

The branches thrashed again and a small, copper-haired figure dropped to the ground. Merlin recognized him as one of the villa's Irish slaves.

"I can't get them, Cai, no matter how hard I shake. Those apples may look ripe, but they aren't!"

"I have sworn to offer them to Our Lady tomorrow!" said the boy who was standing by the trunk of the tree. Big-boned and black-haired, he had the look of Caius Turpilius senior already. "Climb back up and pick them if they will not fall."

"The top branches are too little—they will break, and *I* will fall!" objected the slave.

"Well, *I* am certainly too big to climb up there!" said Cai rather smugly. "Try again! I order you!"

"No," put in the third boy, younger and smaller than the other two. His hair was the color of the tree trunk and he seemed nondescript, until you looked at his eyes. "That is an unjust order, and he doesn't have to obey."

"Be quiet, Artor! I am the master's son, and you are only a nameless fosterling! Treni, get up that tree!"

Merlin bit his lip with remembered pain at the old insult. No doubt Caius Turpilius had kept his promise to raise the child as his own, but boys were acutely sensitive to questions of status; they should have anticipated that the other children would mock Artor.

The boy himself did not change expression. Perhaps he was used to it or perhaps, like Merlin, he had become an expert at hiding his wounds.

Cai gripped the slave's arm and dragged him forward, but before they reached the tree, Artor scrambled up the trunk and gained the lowest branch.

"I'll do it—I'm the lightest of us three. Lie down, Cai, so I can land on something soft if I fall!" A sudden grin transformed his rather stiff expression into a look that caught at the heart. The branches shook as he clambered upward.

Merlin nudged his mule forward, rehearsing spells to knit broken limbs. He could see the topmost branches, and as the Irish boy had stated, they were indeed very thin and small. For a few moments the motion ceased. Had Artor decided not to try it after all? A little way down from the crown of the tree he could see a thickening that might be the boy.

Then something poked up through the leaves. It was a branch, with a twig pointing down like a shepherd's crook. In another moment the branch on which the apple hung was hooked and pulled down into the leaves. *He thinks!* thought Merlin. *He thinks as well as feels.*

"Throw it down, Artor!" came Cai's voice from below. "I'll catch it!"

"You couldn't catch the sun if it fell from the sky," Artor called mockingly. "The apples shall come safe in my tunic, one each for the Virgin, the Mother, and the One who sorrows." Another branch was captured and its fruit disappeared. A third apple went the way of the first two, then the hooked branch dropped and the tree began to shake as the boy started down.

Merlin, who had brought the mule up behind the other two, let out his breath in a long sigh, dropping his concealment, as Artor appeared beneath the leaves and slid to the ground. The boy's gaze traveled past Cai to Merlin and his eyes widened.

"Lord Ambros! Cai—look, the druid has come! Treni, run back to the house and tell Lady Flavia! My lord, we did not expect you until autumn—you've never been here in the summertime!"

He took one of the mule's reins, and Cai took the other, and so escorted, Merlin passed through the orchard and up to the villa where Flavia was waiting.

"You've not come to take him away?" Caius Turpilius asked as they waited for the evening meal. The long porch of the villa faced westward, so they could watch the sun set above the hills.

"Not yet," answered Merlin. "He looks healthy. He is doing well at his studies?"

"Well enough," Caius smiled, "though it is hard to keep the boys to their books on these summer days. His tutor says he asks too many questions."

"And physical exercise?" Merlin already knew that Artor was nimble, but the boys had sworn him to secrecy.

"Cai is better at swordplay—of course he has the advantage of size. Artor is very quick, though, and no quitter. When he has his growth I think he will do well."

A gong announced the imminence of dinner, and they went in. The Turpilius household dined in the old Roman manner, reclining on couches around a central table. The food was simple, but well prepared: the usual hard-boiled eggs; a dish of lentils with cow-parsnips, seasoned with mint and coriander; fried trout from the river with a sauce of herbs and peas from the garden; and a boiled chicken with honey sauce. Merlin had often eaten worse at the table of the High King.

It was more than enough for five adults, for Caius had invited their nearest neighbors as well. Caius and Flavia, of course, knew who and what Merlin was. To their household and neighbors he was merely Ambros, a wandering druid always welcome for his news and his wisdom.

Tonight, they wanted to hear about the wedding. It was surprising, they thought, that the betrothal had not been longer. But perhaps, commented Caius, the High King wanted to secure his northern borders in case Hengest's son Octha returned from Germania.

"What were they about to let him escape?" asked Flavia. "Because the old wolf had lost his teeth, did they think the young one had no fangs?"

Hengest still lived and held his lands in Cantium, but he had not stirred outside his borders in many a year. No one knew whether he was still the leader of the invasion, or barely holding his own. When they were not attacking the British, a new generation of heathens squabbled with each other, and Octha, who had nearly overrun Eburacum some years before, had been among the most successful.

But after several defeats, Uthir had taken him captive, and instead of killing him outright, as many advised, had held him as a hostage.

"Did they think that Brannos's ravens would guard him? They say that the heathen devil, Woden, is the lord of ravens. Perhaps his birds proved stronger than those of our ancient king!"

They all laughed, but in truth, Merlin had wondered. As long as men could remember, there had been ravens on the hill by the Tamesis that was called the White Mount. According to the ancient lore, it was there that the head of the divine king, Brannos, had been buried, with the promise that so long as it stayed there Londinium should never fall.

After the other guests had departed, Merlin took Caius aside.

"It is in my mind to take Artor with me into the mountains after the festival. There are things that I can teach him there."

"Very well. I will instruct Phylox to pack his things."

Merlin shook his head. "No baggage. To live off the land is part of the teaching."

They left the villa before dawn, for the hills were farther off than they seemed. To Artor, Merlin said that he needed help to gather the herbs that grew wild there. At first Artor skipped ahead, exclaiming at the first birdsongs, the swift dart of the awakening swallows, the flicker of motion as a fox disappeared into the hedge. But as the sun climbed higher, he settled to an observant silence, imitating the druid's ground-eating stride as well as his shorter legs could manage.

Merlin had hoped that they could talk during the journey. When he had visited before, they had always been surrounded by the folk of the villa, and in planning for this journey he had realized that although he had been acquainted with Artor since his birth, he knew only the bright surface that the boy presented to the world. Was this reticence a natural characteristic, he wondered, or a response to the boy's ambivalent status in Caius's family?

Merlin had spent his life gathering knowledge. Since the Night of the Long Knives, when he had failed so disastrously to see through Hengest's cordial mask, he had devoted himself to the study of men's souls, seeking to understand what lay behind their surfaces as once he had studied the secrets of the sky. Uthir depended on him to reveal the hidden motives of the men around him; it should not take long for him to learn the secrets of one child.

By midafternoon they reached a band of open pasture, studded with limestone outcroppings, and began to search for herbs. In the deeper soil they found self-heal, paired leaves marching up the stem to the long purple flower head. In an ointment with goldenrod it was good for infected wounds. Among the rocks twined the strands of mountain pea with their paired leaves and tiny blue flowers.

"Say a prayer of thanks to the spirit of the plant," said Merlin, "and then dig it up and strip off the tubers that cling to the roots."

"What are they good for?" asked the boy.

"Clean one off and chew on it, and you will see. The druids call this *corma*; it will stave off the pangs of hunger and give you energy."

Artor looked dubious, but he did as Merlin asked. In a moment his face changed, and the druid smiled.

"It tastes good . . . sweet. . . ."

"Save the others—you will need them for our journey."

Artor frowned and gazed back across the banding of grass and woodland that fell away toward the valley of the Wae, veiled by blue summer haze.

"It is midafternoon," he said thoughtfully. "Shouldn't we be turning back soon?"

"Not yet. Just beyond this ridge there is an oak wood that has other plants I need."

At the edge of the forest they found bilberries and brambles whose fruit was just ripening. Artor began to pluck and eat with a boy's enthusiasm, moving deeper and deeper into the wood. Even Merlin was not immune to their attraction, though the taste brought back memories of his wanderings.

What am I doing? he asked himself. *I carry the blood of the Wild Men, who live on such things, but this boy is all human. Can he survive? What will he learn by starving here?*

"He will learn what you learned," his daimon replied. *"He will learn what he is made of . . . and so will you—"*

It seemed to Merlin that the answer was somewhat ambiguous, but he could get nothing more. Still, in this smiling weather, the boy could come to no harm wandering in the woods for a day or even two, and so he watched the sun dip towards the hilltop and kept silence.

The sudden chill as the sun disappeared brought Artor back to awareness of the passage of time. He straightened, looking at Merlin accusingly. "It will be dark long before we get home!"

"That is true," said the druid. "Perhaps we should make camp here and start back in the morning. It will be an adventure—" He added, as Artor looked dubious, "It is something Cai has never done."

As he had expected, that argument had power, and the boy began to look about him with a new interest.

"But what if we get lost?"

"So long as the sky does not fall and the earth stands solid you cannot be truly lost," said the druid, leading the way down the hill. "Have I not taught you how to observe the sun and judge the lie of the land, and what herbs will serve as food?"

"Where will we sleep?" asked Artor.

"Farther down the hill we'll find water, and the trees will shelter us from the wind. Wrap yourself in your cloak and burrow into the leaves and you will sleep warm."

Artor nodded. "Soldiers camp out like this when they're on campaign."

"Do you want to be a soldier?"

"I have to know how to fight. We all do. My foster-father says that if we British had not forgotten how to be warriors, the Saxons would never have come."

"That's so," said Merlin. "That is why Vitalinus hired Hengest in the first place. He begged the magistrates and the chieftains to raise armies, but they were too accustomed to being defended by Rome."

"That was years and years ago—" Artor looked at him skeptically.

"Ah well," said the druid evasively, "that is what I have heard."

Beneath the trees it was growing dark already. They followed the sound of water until they found a grass-grown mudflat above a little stream.

"Are the Saxons truly devils, as Father Paternus says?" asked Artor as they heaped up bracken for bedding and gathered sticks that the spring floods had lodged against the tree-trunks to build a fire.

"There are Saxon slaves in Caius Turpilius's household," answered Merlin. "Are they demons?"

"No . . . but they have been baptized."

"The priests make great claims for that holy water of theirs, but I have never noticed that it stopped any man from doing evil if he saw some great advantage in it, or that its lack prevented men from doing good if that was their will. No doubt those same Saxon devils are loving husbands and fathers when they are at home."

"But this isn't their home!" exclaimed Artor.

"The Wild Men might say the same to you. . . ."

Merlin shut his mouth, wondering why he had said that. Even his mother, before she died, had managed to persuade herself that her child was the offspring of an angelic visitor. He rubbed his arms, with their telltale covering of hair. He had never spoken to anyone of his time in the forest and what he had learned there.

"Wild Men are a legend . . . aren't they?" Artor gave him an odd look, and Merlin wondered what the boy was seeing in the flickering light of their little fire.

"This whole wide earth is a matter of legend. The water is holy, and the stones, and the fire. The wind whispers tales of times that are gone. Maybe you and I will be legends one day."

Artor laughed, and somewhere within, the druid felt a pang. He had plotted and planned for this boy's birth since he first set his hands upon the Sword of Kings. Only by raising up the Defender could he expiate his failure to avert the massacre at Sorviodunum. Only now, gazing into those clear eyes, did it occur to him to question his right to cast Artor in that role.

His mother had cast *him* in the role of Prophet of Britannia. Did it matter that his childhood would have been even more unhappy if he had grown up in Maridunum? Her words, and the Vor-Tigernus's need, had set his feet upon the path, and now he could not choose but follow.

But Artor still had a choice. Igierne wanted to bring him up as a prince, but the dangers that had forced his guardians to raise him in ignorance of his destiny had also protected him from its stresses. Unlike Merlin, Artor had been allowed to be a child before he was forced to become a man.

I will teach him all I can, thought the druid, *but in the end, it is the spirit within him that must seek this fate. He must be allowed to choose.*

But that spirit must be tested. A young raven spent many days clinging to the edge of the nest, stretching and beating his wings against the air. Only if he did so would his wings be strong enough to bear him when his spirit finally compelled him to fly.

"You are a good climber," he said aloud. "Perhaps tomorrow we will find some mistletoe. In the lore of the druids it is called all-heal, and the powdered berries have great power against fever and diseases of the heart. But it must be used sparingly, for like many herbs, in the wrong dose it can be a poison."

As the fire burned down he continued to speak of the herbs of the forest and their lore, and which plants were good for food and where they could be found. Artor's eyelids began to droop, for it had been a strenuous day, and presently he sank down upon his leafy bed.

Merlin rubbed out the remains of the fire, but he did not sleep. The stars pricked through the velvet of the sky and the moon rose, and still he watched over the child.

It was nearing midnight when his senses told him that Artor had passed through the borders of sleep and lay now in the deepest slumber, and he arose. First he stripped off his own clothing and rolled it into a tight bundle to carry, for it would only slow him, and in truth, his own body heat made clothing a formality. Then, murmuring spells to keep the boy dreaming, he lifted him in his arms. Artor was no great burden, for he was small for his age, and Merlin's strength was beyond that of humankind. Moving quietly, the druid bore him away.

His long strides carried him through the forest and into the next valley, over a second ridge and down into woodlands that grew beside another stream that like the first flowed into the Wae, but several miles away. There he found a drift of leaves beneath an oak tree and carefully laid the boy down. Chanting softly, he paced a circle around him and sealed it with a sigil of power.

Then he climbed into the tree and curled his long limbs into a fork where the foliage would prevent him from being easily seen from the ground. His situation did not permit deep slumber, but as the night turned from midnight toward dawn he passed into a state halfway between wakefulness and sleeping, suspended between the earth and the stars.

In that dream his spirit hovered above the clearing. With spirit sight he saw the life-force flow through every tree; each leaf outlined in light. And as he watched, the light grew stronger, resolved itself into forms which his mind interpreted as human as they stepped forth from the trees. Merlin's circle had been meant to repel all evil, but these beings were beyond such considerations, like the land itself. The hazels, the green herbs, even the blades of grass had spirits, and all of them gathered around the sleeping boy.

Were they simply curious, or were they drawn by something within him? As Merlin hovered, wondering, he saw Artor's lifelight pulse, and the spirit of the boy, detaching itself as often happens during dreaming, rose up from his body, connected only by a silver cord. He laughed with delight, seeing those bright beings around him, and they bent—in homage, or in welcome?

The rippling stream made a soft background for the chirring of the crickets as the tree-spirits began to dance. At first Artor simply watched in wonder, but presently they drew him into their round. They continued to dance until the moon disappeared behind the hill. Then, one by one, the bright spirits drifted back to shrub or tree, until only the spirit of the oak remained. She it was who escorted the boy's spirit back to his slumbering body, and then herself merged into the solid trunk of the tree once more.

When Merlin woke, it was a little past dawn, and the pile of leaves that covered Artor was beginning to stir. The druid peered through the branches, watching as the boy sat up, rubbing his eyes. It took him some time to realize that not only was the druid not sleeping on the other side of the fire, but that this clearing and this stream were not the ones beside which he had fallen asleep the night before. Merlin could see the moment when his eyes went still and watchful, count the minutes it took for Artor to decide that though he might be lost, he was in no immediate danger.

He got to his feet, brushing off the leaves, and with an instinctive courtesy whose source his waking mind did not remember, relieved himself against a rock instead of a tree. Then he went to the stream to drink, and stayed there for a time, gazing at the light on the trees.

Good, thought the druid, *he is getting his directions from the angle of the sun.*

Artor had already passed the first test, having neither wept nor run screaming in circles, though his face was rather pale. Now he proceeded to pass another, cutting reeds whose tender inner stems were edible and catching several of the big frogs that hid among them. He gathered tinder and managed to get a spark from his flints to light it, and soon the frogs' legs were sizzling on twigs above the fire. Some rather squishy bilberries from his pouch completed his meal—a better breakfast than the druid was having, still perched in his tree.

Then, when the sun was high enough to cast a good shadow, the boy put out his fire and buried the remains of his meal, rolled up his cloak and tied it across his back. But before he set out he paused, looking around him.

"Green lord of the forest," he whispered, "it is not by my own will that I must pass through your realm. Guard my ways until I come to the lands of men."

From what he remembered of the night, Merlin thought the prayer would be heard. But whether it was or not, he himself, unseen, would keep watch until the boy reached safety. With considerable relief he slipped down from the oak tree as Artor moved off down the stream.

The boy went slowly, and Merlin had time to take care of his own necessities before he followed. Woodland streams could be deceptive, but eventually they all flowed downhill. Artor had correctly judged that this tributary would in time reach the Wae, where he could find the road that would take him southward again and home. It was only a matter of keeping his nerve and keeping on.

Will he thank me for the adventure? wondered the druid, *or will he be angry with me for abandoning him?*

Perhaps it was a little of both, for as the journey continued, Artor's set features relaxed, and he paused more often to watch the glittering dance of the dragonflies over the water, or the swift dart of a swallow above the trees. Once he surprised a lordly stag who had come down to drink, and they stared at each other in mutual astonishment that turned on the boy's part to awe before the deer, deciding this two-legged creature posed no threat to him, stalked away.

This is my gift to you, thought Merlin, watching. *Whatever you may inherit from your father, this is your inheritance from me.*

And so they continued on as the sun rose past her nooning and began to arch westward. The trees were still too thick to see the end of the forest, but Merlin knew that the road was near. He lagged behind to put on his crumpled garments, intending to double around to meet the boy on the road. And so, Artor was out of sight when the wind shifted and Merlin smelled the rank scent of a bear.

For an instant, shock held him immobile. He had encountered bears in the northern hills and avoided them, for their tempers were uncertain, and nothing less than a band of armed men could make them afraid. He had not thought any still roamed in these hills.

Then, skirts flapping, he began to run. Self-castigation could come later, when he had saved the boy, or failed. Even in the tunic he went swiftly, but before the boy was in sight he heard the bear's cough of warning. Moving silently, lest his presence set off the attack he feared, he covered the last few feet to the stream.

The bilberries were thick here, growing nearly to the water, and Artor had stopped to pick them, apparently surprising a bear who had come this way with the same thing in mind. It was still standing half-reared in the midst of the bushes, trying to decide whether this two-legged being was a threat.

It was a young bear, perhaps a season separated from its mother, big enough to be dangerous, but perhaps not old enough to have learned to hate humankind. Artor stood absolutely still, the bilberries he had already picked still cupped in his hand. All the color had left his face, but his eyes were very bright. He looked, thought Merlin, *present*, as if by danger the essence of his being had been focused and revealed. At that moment he saw in Artor a spirit that burned like a flame, and knew that men would follow him.

If he lived.

The bear's wet black nose wrinkled as it sniffed the unfamiliar scent mingled with that of the fruit. Branches crackled as it moved toward Artor. The druid drew breath to cry out, but the boy was stretching out his hand, fingers folded flat as if he were offering grain to a pony. The bear lowered its heavy head, and a rough pink tongue swept the berries from Artor's palm. Its sun-bleached brown fur was exactly the color of the boy's hair.

The bear nosed at his hand, then licked his berry-stained cheek, and Artor lifted his other hand and gently stroked the thick fur. For a few moments they stood, man-cub and bear-cub together, then the bear snorted, dropped to all fours, and moved off through the bushes.

The blood pounded in Merlin's head as he remembered to breathe. Artor blinked a few times, then he turned, eyes widening only a little as if after what had just happened the appearance of the druid was no surprise.

"Did you see?" he whispered.

"I saw—" Years of discipline gave Merlin his voice again. "You are Arktos, the Bear, and your totem has blessed you."

IX

The Birds of Battle

A.D. 473

"The command will have to go to Leudonus—" the king's words came out like a curse. "If he can stop ploughing your daughter's field long enough to get into his armor!"

The warm light of a summer's morning on the Tamesis reflected through the window of the old Roman tower and glimmered on the whitewashed ceiling; a clear, pitless light that illuminated his face and showed every line worn there by the past year's pain.

"Uthir!" Igierne shook her head, torn between anxiety and exasperation. He must be feeling particularly bad today, for in general when she was present he guarded his tongue. "Morgause is pregnant with their second child, and Gualchmai is just a year old."

"Two brats in three years is a good yield," growled the king. "Time we made sure there's something for them to inherit. Leudonus is the best of the lot—if I can't take the field he'll have to command."

"That is why you gave him Morgause in marriage," Igierne reminded him.

"Hoped it wouldn't come to this—Damn!" He swore again as he tried to shift position on the bed. It was as comfortable as his household could make it, but the old garrison fort had never been intended for long habitation. Londinium was a commercial city, not a fortress, and the old tower, with the river to the south and a rampart and ditch between it and the city, was the safest place they could find.

In the past three years the episodes of joint pain and muscular weakness had become ever more frequent. At times, when the weather was mild, Uthir would be free of it, but Octha and his warband would not wait on the king's convenience. Hengest's son had kept the oath he swore when he escaped from Londinium, and the army he had raised among the tribes of Germania had made a landfall in the country south of Eburacum.

"My lord, be easy," said Jordanus. "I will send the message by swift riders. If the enemy strikes north, he will be ready."

"And if they move south?" asked Igierne.

Uthir frowned. "Cataur of Dumnonia is energetic, and so are his brothers, but he doesn't have the experience. Catraut is a good fighter, but headstrong. Maybe Eldaul . . . but some still don't trust him. We've worn out our best men in these endless wars! If they come south . . . I'll have to get myself out of this damned bed . . . somehow." He tried to raise himself and fell back again, grunting with pain.

Igierne knelt by his side, wiping the sudden perspiration from his brow. She kept a smile on her lips, but she was weeping within. All his life Uthir had been a warrior—he could have faced death in battle gladly, but not this invisible enemy that was making him a prisoner in his own body. There must be something that would ease this lingering agony!

That night she dreamed of blood and battle, but just as the darkness was about to engulf both friend and foe, light flamed in the west, and she saw riding through the carnage a figure with Uthir's brown hair, grasping in his hand a blazing sword. Where its radiance fell, the Saxons hid their eyes and fled, but the British rose up like souls on the Day of Judgment, crying out in praise of the High King.

"The Sword of Kings. . . ."

She woke in the dawning, whispering its name. Her dream fled away, but the image of that burning blade remained before her. She sat up, drawing the covers around her against the morning chill.

Decision came to her. "I will bring the Sword from the Isle of Maidens. Its power will make the High King whole!"

The House of the Sword had that indefinable air of damp and emptiness that marks a place not often used. Or perhaps not quite empty— Igierne's gaze moved to the shrouded shape in the center of the chamber.

Even covered, she could sense the presence of the Hallow it concealed, but the energies of the Chalybe blade were muted, as if it dreamed. Brows bent in concentration, she returned to her sweeping. It had always been her task to clean this chamber when she lived on the Isle. But today would be different. Today, she would unsheath the Sword.

Ebrdila had sought to dissuade her, but she could not stand against the queen's resolve. Morgause might well have argued, for she had never had any great love for Uthir, but Morgause was Leudonus's broodmare now.

Igierne had made her preparations carefully. The old sheath had fallen to dust years ago, but she had prepared a box, bound in iron and lined with crimson silk, to carry the Sword. For a week she had taken no flesh-meat, and today, only water. She could not rival Merlin in knowledge of the stars, but she knew enough to calculate an auspicious configuration, and to perform this rite at the waxing of the moon.

When she had cleansed the chamber, she went back to the lake for her own purification, shivering as the chill water touched her skin. Only the lapping of the little wavelets against the shore disturbed the hush that lay upon the lake. It had often seemed to her that the great hills gave off silence as the sun gives off light. Here, it was very easy to listen to the voice of the soul. Perhaps that was why the priestesses had made it their sanctuary.

She sat back on her heels, letting the cool morning air dry her skin. *I may be a grandmother, but I am still young and strong. And the Sword will restore my beloved!* That was the voice of her will, she knew it. But if her soul had any different wisdom, even in this silence she could not hear.

As the sun was nearing the heights of noon, Igierne put on her crimson robe and entered the House of the Sword. Twelve dark-clad priestesses stood in a circle around her, chanting softly, drawing power from the earth as she drew strength from them.

"Cocidius, Belutacadros, Mars of the Soldiers—" she whispered.

"Hear and bless us . . ." chorused the priestesses.

"Star of Hope, Hand of Justice, Pillar of Power—" And indeed, Igierne could feel the power increasing; she scarcely heard the other women now.

"Sword of the Defender, Sword of Kings, Sword of God!"

She twisted the red cock's neck and the blood flowed over the stone, and then, as in the world outside the sun reached her zenith, grasped the swordhilt, twisted, and pulled the Sword out of the stone.

"For Britannia I draw this blade, and for her lawful king!" With trembling arms she held the weapon high, and the shining steel refracted the light of the torches in red lightnings around the room.

The priestesses recoiled, but Igierne stiffened, shuddering as she tried to control the uprush of power. Behind her closed eyelids cities burned; she saw a crimson sky, swinging swords and bloody spears. In another instant the bloodlust of the blade would overcome her—

—and in that moment of panic the spirit of the sword-priest who was her ancestor spoke within her and she remembered the words that she must say.

"Fortitude binds fury. . . . Strength binds savagery. . . . Right binds rapine. . . . Lord of the Sword I summon Thee; control Thy power!"

For a breath longer the blade's hunger blazed; then something immense and ancient and cold descended from on high to enclose it, and Igierne was left gasping, hanging onto the sword. With her last strength she dragged it into the box, for it had grown heavy with the power it contained. She closed the lid, and then her knees gave way and she sat down beside it on the cold floor.

Igierne had waited almost too long. While she was traveling to the Isle of Maidens and claiming the Sword, Leudonus and his army were halting Octha's northern campaign. Just after Beltain they fought a great battle near Eburacum, and though it ended in victory for the British, Leudonus's forces had been too well savaged to pursue their advantage, and the Saxons retreated unhindered toward Londinium.

Now, the great city's inadequate defenses turned to its advantage, for the enemy wanted a walled town where they could halt and lick their wounds in safety. Just north of Londinium lay Verulamium, and there Octha took refuge.

As Igierne came back down the Roman road, she encountered roving scouts who told her that the army of Southern Britannia was besieging Verulamium, where the martyr Albanus had his shrine, and that the Pendragon had had himself carried there in a litter so that he could command.

"You should have stayed on the Isle," said Uthir when he saw her. "You'd have been safe there."

"My mother may have been Lady of the Lake, but my father was a warrior who died on the Night of the Long Knives. I hope my courage is no less than his."

Uthir cleared his throat gruffly, but his eyes had kindled when he saw her, and she knew he was glad to have her at his side. Indeed, the excitement seemed to have distracted him from his troubles, and though he looked feverish, he did not seem to be in so much pain as before.

They had found quarters for the king in a partly ruined villa near the town. That evening, the British commanders gathered in what had been the dining chamber for a council of war.

"Another few days of siege and we'll have them!" exclaimed Cataur.

Still young enough to be enthusiastic, there were times when he reminded Igierne painfully of his uncle Gorlosius, but he seemed to bear the High King no enmity for a death which had, after all, put him in line to inherit Dumnonia. His wife had recently borne him a son whom they named Constantine, for they were descended from the grandfather of Uthir in the female line.

"But do we want them—" objected Eldaul, "if it means a house-to-house fight where we can make no use of our cavalry?"

"Do you propose to leave them there unmolested?" Cataur replied.

"Of course not," said Ulfinus. "Give them a good scare on the walls, and perhaps we can winkle them out of there!"

Matauc of Durnovaria, who had created a princedom from the old Durotrige lands, shook his head. "Beseige them long enough and they'll starve to death inside!" Leonorus of the Belgae, who was even more cautious by nature, nodded agreement.

"We don't have that long," exclaimed Ulfinus. "It is high summer now—if there is to be a harvest, our men must be getting away home!"

"There is a way." Merlin, who as usual had been effectively invisible until he wished to be heard, came forward. Several of the commanders jumped, and one of them crossed himself.

"The Saxons are concerned above all with their reputation as warriors. They will pursue glory even to their own disadvantage. You complain, my lord, that your weakness will not allow you to fight—" He turned to Uthir. "Let it work for you. Have them carry you in your litter before the walls, and let your men mock the enemy by saying they are too cowardly to fight even a man who cannot ride."

Uthir flushed angrily. "And what about my honor?"

"Is it dishonor to tell the truth?" Merlin spoke dispassionately, but Igierne could see the sorrow in his eyes.

"It's not, but you're the only man who would dare say it to me—" growled the king.

"And what if it works, and they come out to fight us?" Jordanus said into the silence that followed. "We can use our cavalry then, but they still have the greater numbers. We must not only win, but win so decisively that the Saxons will run away to lick their wounds and not come back again!"

"Merlin . . ." the king said slowly. "In all these years I've never required you to take a role in the fighting. But I'm asking now, for I see no other way. Can't you find a spell to cast madness on the enemy? To call spirits from the earth to fight them?"

Those parts of the druid's face not covered by beard went perfectly white. Igierne realized suddenly how much silver there was in her cousin's hair.

"You don't know . . . the cost of what you're suggesting—"

"Maybe not. But I think you know what it costs me to ask!"

For a long moment dark eyes met gray, and it was the druid who first looked away.

"I do . . ." whispered Merlin. "I will do what I may."

From there, the conversation turned to ways of disposing of their forces if the plan to draw the enemy out should succeed. Merlin went out almost immediately, and presently the others also took their leave and went away.

"They're so hot for the fight," Uthir said painfully. "I'd give my soul to stand with them, but I can hardly hold a sword!"

"There is a Sword that I think you could hold," Igierne said softly, "and it will not require your soul, but only your promise to serve this land."

"I gave that at my anointing—" he began, not understanding.

Igierne shook her head, pulling the long box from beneath the cloak she had laid over it and laying it on the bed beside him. "This belongs to an older mystery." Feeling her own heart beat faster, she opened the box and turned back the cloths that wrapped the Sword.

"Touch it—"

Uthir gripped the hilt and jerked, let go, then carefully grasped it once more. The color came and went in his face as power pulsed through him, then, with an effort of will, he released the hilt and covered it with the silk again.

"By Beli's blazing balls!" he breathed, which if not precisely the same god, at least belonged to the right religion. "That thing will either kill or cure me! Where—"

"It will cure you!" Igierne exclaimed. "It must!" She could not allow herself to contemplate any other possibility, for he had pulled the box closer to his body, and it was clear that he would never now give up the Sword.

And so, as the British prepared for battle around them, Igierne recounted to her king the history of the Chalybe blade.

*   *   *

Merlin watched, frowning, as Uthir's litter was carried onto the battlefield. Behind him, the British were moving into position before the western gate of Verulamium. Smaller forces had been delegated to watch the other gateways, but it was here, where broad pastures spread out to either side of the road, that the major fighting must be. Overhead the sky was clear, but to the west, gray clouds were building, and a restless wind bent the grass.

The men seemed grim, but determined; there had been little rest for anyone the night before, as warriors sharpened weapons and checked the straps of their armor or simply sat by their campfires, too tense to sleep.

Merlin's preparations had been more complex, if less tangible, as he searched his memory for the appropriate spells and contemplated the ways in which they must be focused and combined. He calculated their interaction as carefully as a master chef making choices from his spice jars. But a cook could only ruin a meal; if Merlin made a mistake, both armies might be destroyed. When he tried to rest, his sleep was troubled by images of destruction from whose midst rose a flaming sword.

Uthir had given them their instructions with a kind of febrile gaiety that Merlin found disturbing. Was he fey, or had the prospect of battle simply made him forget his pain? Either way, he should not be out there. Merlin had only meant to suggest that Uthir have himself carried before the walls to taunt the Saxons, not station himself in the midst of the battle line. Even if the British did not win this battle, their cause would not be lost while the High King lived. He had to survive long enough for Artor to grow up.

Thus the druid in him had reasoned, but as he watched the king go by, the tears on his cheeks were those of the man.

He turned his attention inward, seeking solace from that invisible companion who had been his inspiration and comfort for so long.

"I give life—I do not take it. I cannot help you here. What you do today will be done on your own. . . ."

"So be it—" whispered Merlin, but there was a knot of unease in his belly that would not go away.

"Hai, you Saxon dogs!" cried the British warriors, "why are you hiding behind those walls? Are you afraid to face us? Even our sick are a match for you! Come out and play!"

From beyond the wall they heard shouting, then above the gate a Saxon head appeared.

"We have no need for children's games," came the guttural answer. "We are men!"

Another helmed head appeared beside him. "What honor is there in killing a man who is half-dead already? Take your king home and let him die in peace!"

Merlin looked up and saw a buzzard circling hopefully. He climbed into one of the wagons where no one would trip over him, lay down, and sent his awareness arrowing upward to seize the mind of the bird, then directed it to fly toward the town.

"Skulk inside there and starve if you want to," called the British, "but we give you a chance to settle this now. The only peace between us will be in the grave. See, we will withdraw to give you room!"

The escort surrounding Uthir's litter began to retreat. The buzzard soared over the walls. Through the bird's eyes, Merlin could see Saxon warriors crowding toward the walls, knots of men tangling and separating as they argued.

"*Pee-oo,*" called the buzzard, "*Fight, kill, win—*" Carried by the force of his will, the message arrowed down. "*Charge, strike, destroy! Pee-oo, pee-oo, pee-oo. . . .*"

This time the noise from inside the town was louder. The fair-haired man who had first replied seemed to be arguing with the others. It was Octha, Hengest's son. Merlin guided the buzzard closer.

"*Pee-oo, pee-oo, blood will flow and I will feast! Go out and win glory!*" Three times widdershins he circled the Saxon leader, then winged out past the gateway, and Octha's disputation became a battle cry.

The gate trembled as men hurried to draw the bar, then swung open. The Saxon warriors began to form up into their battle array.

Soaring back towards the British, Merlin saw their spearmen ready, the cavalry wings waiting to either side. Uthir's litter was still in the center, but the High King was sitting up now, speaking to his men.

"The Saxons called me the half-dead king," Uthir burst out laughing, "because I lay flat in my litter, felled by illness. And it was true, but I'd rather fight them half-dead than live healthy as a horse and have them think me afraid! Better to die with honor than live disgraced!"

From the gateway came the thunder of spear-shafts beating on shields.

"Do you hear them, lads? They are coming out—will you show them how rough the men of Britannia can play?"

The British replied with an ululation of defiance whose echoes left a mist of brightness in the air. Merlin released the buzzard and sank back into his body. Even with his eyes closed, he could sense the High King's presence as a radiant sphere of power. Had the exultation of the moment released some potential the druid had never noticed before, as Artor had been transfigured by meeting the bear? Or was it something else—

There was no time to wonder. Octha and his warriors were coming out of Verulamium. More and more of them poured through the gate. The mournful call of a cowhorn sounded above the noise and the drumming of spear on shield gave way to the thunder of feet on sod as they began to run.

From the British side trumpets blared. The sound of thunder was abruptly amplified as from one side, Cataur of Dumnonia and his horsemen, and from the other, Eldaul and his cavalry, began their own charge. The wood of the wagon shivered to the vibration. Merlin got to his feet, holding to the side for balance, just as the charge hit, and the separate groups of combatants became a single struggling mass.

In moments, Uthir was surrounded, as in the game of *tabula* the enemy pieces attack the warriors guarding the king. The clangor of clashing weapons smote the ear, pierced by the cries of those who were struck down. Merlin had been present at other battles, but before, he had always waited with the physicians. Now he forced himself to really look at the carnage, striving to understand what was happening.

The Saxons were experienced fighters. Once the British had charged, they lost their main advantage. Horsemen skirmished around the edge of the battle, picking off foes with their lances, but they could not affect the fighting farther in. The British were going on the defensive. This, then, was why Uthir had insisted that the druid help them; without Merlin's magic to tip the balance, the British might well lose.

Once more he sat down. This time, he could not merely ride a passing raptor; he must *become* it. Focusing inward, he formed the image of the raven, Cathubodva's bird.

Goddess, it is your people who are suffering—come to us, blast our foes!

His breathing grew deeper; awareness of his body faded, to be replaced by an alien sense of taut strength, of lightness, of the air. Spirit borne by the raven, he opened his eyes, spread wings to catch the wind, and beat heavily into the sky.

To spirit sight, the forms of the men locked in that mortal struggle were no more than shadows. What he saw was their spirit bodies, flaring brightly as courage spurred them against the foe or fading as they were overcome. Those whose lives were severed floated free, gazing down in confusion at the battle in which they could no longer join.

The raven dove downward, beak opening in the terrible cry with which the Lady of Battles freezes the courage of her foes. Glossy feathers flared white in the light of the sun. And though fleshly ears might hear nothing, the souls of the Saxons heard, and quailed. That moment of hesitation put heart into the British warriors, who drove with renewed vigor at their enemies.

The raven, flapping skyward once more, saw a knot of combatants at whose center swayed Octha's fair head. They were perilously close to the High King; Octha could reach him in a moment if he broke free. The raven circled, gathering momentum, but before he could dive, two dark shapes sped between her and her goal—two other ravens, cawing defiance, which Merlin heard as words.

"This man is my kin through many sons . . . I remember!" called the first raven, and Merlin recalled that Hengest's family believed themselves to be descended from one of their gods.

"I protect him, for he plans wisely and well—" the other echoed.

"What is that to me?" Cathubodva's voice came through her bird. *"He has attacked my land and killed my people! He must die!"*

There were two of the enemy ravens, but the one who was Cathubodva was bigger. Wheeling and slashing, they joined in a battle as furious as the one below, the German god and the Celtic goddess confronting one another.

Even the overflow of power from that conflict of forces was enough to madden the human warriors. Shrieking and grunting, they dropped their weapons and went for each other with teeth and fingernails. The impact of that violence reverberated from one plane of existence to the next. Merlin felt his own mind disintegrating into a madness in which he had no thought but to rend and slay.

And then the fabric of the world was rent by a Sword of Light, and a great Voice that cried out—

"Stop! If they must fight, they shall do so within the bounds I establish—not as beasts, but as men!"

From the Sword came the shape of a Warrior. To some He seemed the helmed Mars of the old shrines, and to some, red Cocidius of the Wall. To the Saxons, He appeared grim and tall, with only one hand. He lifted the blazing sword and swept it above the battlefield, and everywhere combatants sprang apart, staring about them like men waking from a dream.

But the power of that stroke swept Merlin back to his own body, and for some little while he knew no more.

Merlin opened his eyes and groaned. His head hurt—indeed, every part of his body ached as badly as if he had been out on the battlefield. In a sense, he thought painfully, it was true. He should have anticipated that his astral activities would be reflected in his physical body. He sat up, wincing. Then he remembered.

Fear sent its own anodyne through his body as he jumped down from the wagon, but now there was nothing to distract him from the images that flooded his memory. And there before him was the reality of the battlefield. Where there had been green fields was now a trampled mass of mud and blood and the remains of men. Already the ravens—the real ones—were gathering. With all his senses still open, he felt the agony of the wounded, the confused spirits of the slain.

My fault . . . he thought. *It was I who made this a conflict of forces beyond the nature of humankind.*

In the distance he could see fleeing figures; a few horsemen were chasing them. The British were not running. From that, he supposed that they must have won. He certainly could not tell from looking at men's faces. They all looked as stunned as he. But they did not carry his guilt. Already he could feel the madness that had driven him to the mountains once before nibbling at his control. Rubbing his forehead, he looked around him. Where was the king?

In the center of the carnage, men were moving. They lifted the litter and bore it slowly toward the villa, stopping often to rest, for all had wounds of their own. Leaning on his staff, Merlin hurried to meet them.

Uthir opened his eyes as the druid bent over him. He was splashed with blood, but none of it seemed to be his own.

"Octha's dead—" he whispered. "We have the field."

Merlin nodded. "My lord, how is it with you?"

"As if I've been ploughed . . . by a red-hot poker." Uthir coughed painfully, and lifted his mantle so that Merlin could see what he had hidden there.

The druid stopped short, appalled recognition making everything suddenly very clear. He had never seen the full length of the Chalybe sword until now, when it gleamed with deadly beauty at the king's side. Now he understood where Igierne had gone, and why she had avoided him when she returned.

"I should have known!" Merlin exclaimed. "I sensed its presence—" It was one more thing in which he had failed.

"I didn't have the strength to wield it. The power . . . burned through me . . . killed everyone around."

"And no matter what Igierne may have said, you did not have the right," the druid replied.

Uthir grimaced. "Don't tell her . . . she'll blame herself. Must . . . keep it safe. . . ."

"I also am of the blood of its keepers. I will guard the Sword for your son, who is its destined lord." He pulled off his cloak, and kneeling beside the litter, wrapped it around the blade.

"I'm sorry I won't see him grown. . . . I always thought there would be time. Give him a father's blessing for me. . . ."

Merlin looked down at that white face and nodded.

The king smiled faintly. "But at least . . . Octha is dead."

Some of the servants who had stayed with Igierne at the villa came out, saw the litter, and began to run toward them. Merlin stepped back, still watching Uthir, as they took him up and carried him inside.

For a few moments Merlin stood unmoving, the shrouded Sword held close against his breast. Overhead, ravens were flying, calling harshly to their kin. Already he could smell a charnel scent from the battlefield. If he stayed here, with the Sword, he would indeed go mad. He took a deep breath, drawing up a cloak of shadow around him. Then he strode swiftly away.

Merlin had planned, insofar as thinking was possible, to carry the weapon northward, back to the Isle. But three days later, when the daze in which he had been wandering began to lift at last, he found himself many miles to the southwest. The Saxons had raided through this land several times, and many of the villas and farmsteads were in ruins, but there were buildings enough left to shelter him, and food in the gardens that had been left to run wild.

Only Calleva, on the old Roman road, still maintained itself as a center of civilization. Near an abandoned chapel just outside of the town Merlin came to rest.

"Stop here . . ." said his daimon.

"Make me a house," said the god in the Sword.

When Merlin began to rebuild the roof, folk from the town decided he must be a hermit, and some of them started to leave food as an offering. They were not so far wrong, though his devotions were not quite what they might have expected. As the days passed, he fell into a trance of labor in which the task of rebuilding kept his madness away.

He repaired the roof, and thatched it securely. He brought stones and mud with which to repair the shattered wall. While he was gathering them he had noted a boulder half his height, and almost as wide. When all else was done he went out during the night, and chanting to focus his strength, managed to roll it inside. Then, using a chisel and mallet that he had found in an outbuilding, he began to carve into the stone a new channel in which to sheathe the Sword.

It was precise and patient work. Long before he completed it he heard men in the road outside the chapel, talking of the death of the High King. Some whispered of poison, but others said it was only that he had exhausted his last strength in the battle. It was said that his queen was bringing the body to the Giant's Dance to lie with that of his brother and the British lords.

Merlin remembered a Samhain Eve beside the sacred stones and the wonder in Uthir's eyes, and wept, but he did not stop chiseling at the stone.

There were more rumors after that, as first one lord and then another sought support in order to claim the overlordship of Britannia. But there was no one on whom all the princes could agree.

The autumn was well advanced by the time Merlin finished his work at last, and slid the Sword into the channel with the secret twist that prevented anyone who did not know the secret from drawing it out again. And when it was sheathed, he carved into the front of the stone these words—

Quicunque me distringet rex iustus Britanniae est . . .

Then, at last, the compulsion released him. Over Sword and stone he draped his mantle, and walked out of the little chapel for the last time.

A ghost of the man he had been whispered that he should go to Igierne in Londinium, or to Artor in Demetia. But he no longer trusted his own wisdom. Let the men who lusted to rule Britannia and the gods they served do the fighting. He had had enough of humankind.

Merlin's feet carried him northward, traveling by night and speaking to no one. By the time he reached the Wall it was hard to remember human language, and so he passed into the shadows of the Forest of Caledonia and disappeared from the knowledge of men.

X

The Sword in the Stone

A.D. 475

In her dream, Igierne was sitting in an apple tree.

Cradled in its branches and rocked by the wind, she watched the slow-wheeling stars, yet even as she marveled at their majesty she knew that these visions were not hers but those of another, whose dream she shared.

Her tree was surrounded by oak and ash and stately pines, for the forest had grown over an old orchard and only the single apple tree remained. Hungry, she reached for an apple; the arm that moved was long, sinewy, and covered with coarse hair. Abruptly she realized whose mind she shared.

"Merlin," she called, *"where are you? We feared you dead—Britannia needs you, I need you!"*

"I am the Wild Man of Caledonia. . . . Merlin is a dream. Are you my little lass? I have seen you in a moonbeam, Lady, but you do not speak to me anymore. . . ." Through his eyes she saw leaves that glittered in the moonlight and the pale shapes of distant hills.

"It is Igierne who calls you. Return from your wanderings!"

He bit into the apple, and she felt the swift rush of sweetness on her own tongue.

"Merlin loved Igierne, when he was a man. . . . The Wild Man loves the little pig that roots beneath his tree. . . ."

For a moment surprise and pity held her silent, then need drove her on. *"If you ever loved me, find my son! The princes tear at this poor land like ravens at a carcass, and only he can make it whole—"*

A sudden wave of anguish blurred her vision; she smelled once more the deathly reek of the battlefield. Then the image faded, but the sorrow remained.

"Let the White Raven beware the Raven of Battle. To Calleva come the princes in search of sovereignty. . . . Where you find the Sword you shall find the King. . . ."

Branches tossed as he climbed downward. The ground blurred beneath her vision as he began to run, faster and faster until his awareness dissolved into pure motion and Igierne's consciousness fell away.

She opened her eyes, grasping for memories that were already fast fading, but on her lips the taste of apple remained.

How long had it been, she wondered, since she had awakened with happiness in her heart? Whatever her dream meant, it was better than nightmares in which Uthir died in her arms yet again. She had buried him in the barrow by the Giant's Ring, as he had asked, and then begun the long journey back to the north, staying for a time in one town and then in another, until she came to Isca in Demetia, where Bishop Dubricius had welcomed her.

Igierne was in no hurry to continue on, for what remained for her, even at the Lake, but to live out an empty existence mourning the death of Britannia's joy and her own?

But today she had hope once more, hope, and a fragment of prophecy. Bishop Dubricius was accounted a wise man. Together, perhaps they could make one last attempt to persuade the warring princes to seek unity.

In Calleva, one could almost believe that Rome had never departed from the Isle. Its walls were intact, its amphitheater only a little overgrown, its gracious houses, set amidst their gardens and orchards, still the homes of cultured men. It was also convenient in location, far enough to the west to be out of easy reach of Saxon raiders, and connected to the rest of the country by good roads. If summoning the lords of Britannia to this place had been no more than a night fancy, thought Igierne, then it had been a useful one.

For the warlords and chieftains and magistrates were coming in.

During the two years since Uthir's death there had been no central authority. Hengest, recovering from the shock of Octha's loss, had designated his grandson Oesc as heir, and though he no longer took the field, the chieftains he had summoned from Germania were swift to fall upon their British neighbors. In the North, Colgrin and Baldulf had made alliance with the old enemy, the Picts and Scots, and were extending their holdings. In the West the lords of Demetia and Guenet fought the men of Eriu and each other.

But now, when the first winter storms were putting an end to the fighting season, the British had braved bad roads and wild weather to converge on the old *civitas* of the Atrebates. The chieftains and their families were given hospitality in the better homes of the town, while the lesser lords and *gentiles* set up camp, with their men, in the fields outside. Even Leudonus had left the Votadini lands in charge of his clan chiefs and come south to the conclave, and with him came Morgause.

Igierne was sitting in the atrium of the chief magistrate, made pleasant by shrubs in pots and beds of late-blooming flowers, when a light step on the flagstones made her turn and she saw that her daughter had arrived.

Though the atrium was protected from the wind, Morgause's draperies fluttered with supressed motion. Clearly, marriage and motherhood agreed with her. What the girl's face had lost in childish roundness, her breasts had gained, and her complexion was blooming. Igierne frowned in sudden suspicion.

"Morgause, are you breeding again?"

Quick color came and went in the girl's face, then she set her hands over her belly and smiled.

"I shall have three children in four years of marriage. In all your years as a wife, you never managed but the two!"

Igierne's eyes widened a little at the taunt; she had not meant to sound disapproving—well, not very.

"I congratulate you on being one of those women who are built for bearing." She managed an answering smile. "Your husband must be pleased."

"I will give him enough sons to defend the North with the fruit of my own womb! Or perhaps they will rule a greater kingdom. Clearly, Uthir meant Leudonus to be his heir."

"Certainly he respected Leudonus's abilities as a commander," Igierne said evenly. "But the lords of southern Britannia may feel that his strength lies too far away."

Morgause shrugged and paced across the stones. Her mantle was dyed a deep crimson, not the color that had clashed so with her complexion at her wedding, but a shade like Gaulish wine. Heavy earrings of gold and garnet hung in her ears, and her golden pennanular brooch was set with garnets as well. Igierne remembered when she used to adorn herself in jewels. She had worn only black since Uthir died.

With a swirl of her skirts Morgause turned to face her once more.

"That argument might be used against any of them. At least Leudonus *has* strength. I will be Tigernissa, and it will be your turn, mother, to sit on the Isle of Maidens and watch the world go by!"

"Oh, the Lady of the Lake can do a little more than that—" said Igierne tightly. "Did you learn nothing when you were there?"

"I learned a great deal. And I am learning more in the North, where they revere their queens. Leudonus's mother was a princess of the Picts, who trace their descent through the female line. They choose their husbands to defend the land, but they are the source of power."

Igierne picked up her embroidery again and took a stitch or two. What Morgause had said agreed with the secret teaching of the Isle, but southern Britannia had been Roman too long, and the men who ruled it had forgotten many things.

"Neither queen nor king is the source of sovereignty," she said at last, "but the Goddess Herself who is Lady of this land. Do not forget that, daughter. Whatever I have done or you shall do, we are only Her deputies."

Morgause responded with a rather odd smile. "Oh, I have not forgotten. But the Lady sometimes wears a different face in the northern lands. . . ."

Igierne raised one eyebrow, but before she could inquire she heard voices in the entry and another woman, draped in a gown and palla of dusty blue, came into the atrium, followed by a lanky boy.

"*Domina*—" She made a reverence to Igierne, and then, after a moment's hesitation, to Morgause. "I do not know if you will remember me, for it has been many years—"

"Of course I do! You are Flavia, wife of Caius Turpilius." And indeed, though Flavia's figure had become more matronly, she had not really changed. "I am glad that you and your husband have come. They will need his good sense at the Council."

Flavia nodded. "He and young Cai are down at the meadow where the warriors will show off their strength in the games. God send that it does not become a battlefield!"

"Will not your younger son be fighting?"

For a moment Flavia looked troubled, then she smiled. "He is only fifteen, though he is taller than Cai. Time enough for him to be fighting when he has grown into his bones. . . ." She looked fondly at the boy, who flushed red as he realized he was the center of attention.

He reminded Igierne of a young colt, still all legs and neck, but with the promise of grace and speed. At least his skin was not disfigured by the spots that afflicted so many lads that age.

"If he has the time, perhaps you would lend him to me as an escort," she said to Flavia. "I no longer have a real household, and the town has become very crowded as the chieftains come in."

"Too crowded . . ." Morgause said softly, eyeing the newcomers.

Igierne frowned at her. Why should Morgause care if her mother showed some kindness to this gangling boy? But clearly it was so. *She still wants my approval*, thought the queen, *despite all her proud words*.

"I would be honored—" The boy spoke for the first time. If he resented being shuffled off among the ladies he was too well-bred to let it show.

"Come to me tomorrow," said Igierne. "You may be my escort to the warriors' games."

"My children in Christ, to this place I have called you to take counsel for the safety of your own children and the future of this land."

Bishop Dubricius stood on the dais at the end of the basilica, illuminated by light from the upper windows, which picked out the golden embroidery on his robes. He was a humble man, who on ordinary days dressed as simply as any of his monks. But he was not an unworldly one, reflected Igierne, watching from the gallery, and he knew the power of a judicious display of gold.

"The heathen encompass us on every side, and we have been abandoned by the eagles of Rome. Under the authority of our own emperors we have fought them; at times we nearly drove them from our shores. But only when we were united. When each lord cares only for his own lands, the devil's spawn can gobble us piecemeal, like a herd that has been scattered by the wolves!"

From his audience came a murmur of appreciation, if not for his text, at least for his rhetoric. The farther windows lit them as well, glinting on swordhilts and brooches and torques of gold.

The basilica of Calleva was second only to that of Londinium. The nave was seventy feet high, arches supported the upper walls and separated it from the aisle. In happier times, the decurions of the district had met there to conduct the business of government; now the benches were filled by nearly a hundred proud men from all over the Island.

"Indeed, your grace." Cataur of Dumnonia, representing his father and his grandfather, the prince Gerontius, rose from his bench to answer. His brother, Gerontius the younger, was at his side. "If we did not agree with you we would not have come here. But there is no man remaining of the direct line of Constantine to inherit, and how else shall we choose?"

His question seemed innocent enough, but every man there knew that through the female line Cataur was descended from the British emperor who had challenged Rome. It occurred to Igierne suddenly that Morgause, through her father, carried that blood as well. Had she thought of that? From the intent way in which she was watching, her mother felt it likely, and if so, Leudonus would be considering it as well.

Despite four centuries of Roman emperors, who were as likely to be raised to the purple for their popularity, or their power, their competence, or sometimes by pure chance, as for their heredity, an honored bloodline still carried weight with these descendents of Celtic kings.

If Uthir had allowed Merlin to bring back their son, thought Igierne, there would have been an heir in the male line. Where was he now, her little boy? Did he know of his heritage? Or was he dead, and had Uthir and Merlin resisted her pleas to bring him to her because they feared to tell her so?

It hardly mattered now. Cataur had just proclaimed himself a candidate. Igierne remembered him as energetic but headstrong, requiring a firm hand. Would he have the self-discipline to rule?

"Who is that?" asked Flavia as Eleutherius got to his feet.

"The prince of Eburacum. His father ruled the lands from the Wall to Lindum, but the Anglians are carving out a homeland there now."

Eleutherius cleared his throat. "Any lord we choose must care for the peoples of the North as well as the South; the remnants who hold out in the East, surrounded by Saxons, as well as the safe western lands. The sons of Ambrosius came back from Armorica to lead us. We do not want a High King who will flit oversea to Dumnonia if things go badly here."

That was close enough to a challenge to make all eyes turn to Cataur, for the northern coast of Armorica had been given its name by Britons who fled there from the lands his father had ruled. But before he could answer, Catraut, who had established himself in Verulamium after the battle, spoke in favor of choosing a man with experience on the Saxon frontier. He was followed by others, as each region proclaimed its importance, or its needs.

Throughout all this, Leudonus had sat in silence. He had put on weight since his marriage to Morgause, but he was still in his prime, broad rather than tall, with thinning reddish hair. His mantle was woven in wool

of many colors, in the traditional royal style. Igierne had seen him in
Roman dress, which he wore well, and knew that this appeal to Celtic
memory must be deliberate.

*He will let them talk themselves out before he makes his move, and
hope that in their desperation they will accept even a northerner, if he
has sufficient power.*

The light through the windows was deepening toward sunset when
Bishop Dubricius held up his crozier. Reluctantly, the men fell silent.

"We will not decide this issue today, but I think that those who have
spoken have set forth the qualities we must seek in our king—strength,
wisdom, a care for all parts of this land, a right to rule which can be
accepted by everyone here. . . ."

"A miracle . . ." whispered someone nearby.

"Christ Himself in His second coming could not win acceptance from
them all!" another voice answered.

One of the local men got to his feet. "We will never agree until God
Himself gives us a sign! But in the hermit's chapel just beyond the town
there is a sword thrust into a stone which no man can pull free. The writing
on the rock says it belongs to the king!"

Igierne sank back against the wall as if she had been struck to the
heart by that same blade.

Her dream of Merlin had been true! And this was what had happened
to the Sword, and why he had told her to seek Calleva! But why? Only
Merlin and she knew the trick of making a slot that would hold the Chalybe blade. Had he meant her to draw it herself and choose her king as a
priestess of the Lady of Sovereignty?

"My lady, are you unwell?" asked Flavia, and Igierne realized that
her skin had gone clammy and she was perspiring beneath her veil.

She shook her head, though she was trembling with a sudden awareness of great forces building around her. She dared not touch the Sword,
she realized then. She had given it to Uthir, and it had killed him. She
straightened, striving for calm. She could not interfere, but she would bear
witness to what must come.

The combats had already started when Igierne arrived at the amphitheater, accompanied by Flavia's boy. The horse races were scheduled for
later in the day. The amphitheater lay to the northeast of the town, where
it caught the morning light, but the day had dawned cloudy; now and
again a cool breath of mist touched her skin. She had wrapped up warmly,
and the people of Calleva had set up a shelter over part of the seating and

made it comfortable with rugs and cushions for the benefit of the noble ladies and the older men.

It was the Bishop's idea that a day of martial displays would relax the chieftains as well as enabling them to judge the temper of each other's men. And it was just as well, she thought, that they should have some time to get over last night's embarassment at having tried to draw the Chalybe Sword from the stone—and failed.

Once more she bit back her anger. *Curse you, Merlin, for preparing this test and then disappearing! If you know who is destined to draw the blade, why are you not here to make sure he does so?*

Originally the amphitheater must have seated nearly the entire population of the town. She guessed it was not now much used, for some of the timbers had decayed, but the stands that remained gave a good view of the arena, whose grass had been cropped by the sheep that ordinarily grazed here into a mat of green.

The boy leaned forward as two new combatants strode onto the green, armed as for war, except for the leather bands that wrapped their swords.

"Who are they?"

"One of Cataur's men and a man from Demetia, by the badges," she said. "I don't know their names. Do you want to be a fighter?"

He looked at her in surprise. "Peace is better than war, but nobody will have peace unless some are willing to spend their lives to guard the others. At least it is so in these times."

"Is that what Caius Turpilius told you?"

"It is what I believe."

His gaze returned to the field. The two men saluted the stands, then faced each other, feet braced and weapons raised.

"But don't you dream of winning honor, or hearing people praise your name?"

He colored, and she knew that she had guessed well.

"If I fought for the right things . . ." he said in a low voice, with a quick glance to see if she was laughing at him.

One of the swords slammed against the opposing shield and he looked back to the field to see the exchange of blows. The fighting settled into a pattern of tense pauses and flurried engagement. It was a shock when the Dumnonian's blade slipped past the enemy guard and stopped just touching the Demetian swordsman where the neck and shoulder joined. Igierne admired his control—if the blow had landed with full force it could have broken the man's neck even with a blunted edge. The Cornovians began to cheer and there was a patter of applause from the stands.

"I had a strange dream last night," the boy said as the next pair came out onto the green. "I was standing in a forge, watching a blacksmith at work, except that it was not a man, but a woman, like one of the old goddesses, with hair of flame. She took the fragments she was hammering from the anvil and cast them into a crucible. But they weren't metal, but the limbs of men. And then she turned and spoke to me—"

He fell silent, frowning. Igierne felt her skin pebble. Who was this boy to have a dream of such power?

"Can you remember her words?"

All that is made will in the end be broken. I gather the shards and try them in the flame. The dross I skim away, but the true metal runs together, all the stronger for its mixing.

"What happened then?" Igierne asked softly.

"The lumps melted and mingled until they were a single glowing mass. The goddess poured the molten metal into a mold, and when it was solid, she laid it on the anvil and began to hammer it. She hammered it into a sword . . . and when she was done," he swallowed, "she asked if I would serve her, and held it out to me. . . ."

Igierne's heart began to bound unevenly in her breast. "Boy, look at me—" She searched his face, striving to find something familiar in the curly brown hair or the blue eyes. But her own eyes blurred so that it was hard to see. "What is your name?"

"Arktos, because once I met a bear—well, really, it's Artor—"

Or Artorius? If this was her son, clearly he had not been told. She must speak with Flavia!

The boy was still staring at her in amazement when she saw a beefy young man with the Turpilius nose running toward them across the grass.

"Artor, Artor!" He pulled up in front of them, sketched a bow to Igierne, and grasped the rail in front of the boy. "I broke my sword practicing at the post! Run back to the camp and get my good blade— quickly!" He danced from one foot to the other. "I'm due to fight in the next round!"

Igierne looked from Cai to Artor, who was already on his feet, apparently accustomed to being ordered around in this way. "My Lady, do you mind? I will not be long—"

She gestured to him to draw nearer, and said softly, "You will return all the quicker if you stop in the old chapel just beyond the eastern gate and take the sword that is there—"

His face brightened, and he vaulted over the railing and darted away.

Well, Merlin, if that is interference then it is your fault for not being here to stop me, she thought defiantly. *If our blood runs true in him, he will draw the Sword!*

"It was kind of Artor to help you," she said to Cai, who was still standing there.

"Oh, well, he has some funny ideas, but he's a good lad all the same."

Not a bad recommendation from an older brother, she told herself, trying to gauge how long it should take the boy to get to the gate and find the chapel. Was he there already? Could he draw the blade, and if he succeeded, she wondered in sudden fear, what would happen then?

It seemed an eternity before she saw his tall figure across the grass, but Cai seemed surprised at how quickly he had made the journey. Artor was walking, not running, and a bundle, swathed in his cloak, was clasped in his arms. He seemed dazed, as one who has looked on too much light.

Igierne felt her heart begin that heavy beat once more.

"What's wrong? Did you run too fast?" Cai was hurrying toward him. "Here, I'll take it—"

For a moment Artor resisted, then he released the bundle, and Cai fumbled for the hilt.

"Ow! It *burned*!"

The blade slid from his hands and Artor bent to catch it before it could hit the ground. Igierne let out a breath she had not known she held, sudden tears blurring her eyes.

"That's not my sword!" Cai took his smarting fingers out of his mouth to cry. Artor looked at Igierne in appeal.

She got to her feet, pitching her voice to carry, though her vision came and went in waves, as if she looked through fire.

"It is not, nor ever shall be. It is the Sword of Kings that Artor holds, the Chalybe blade that the Defender of Britannia shall bear. By blood he is its rightful heir. Before his birth this destiny was written in the stars!"

Her knees gave way and she sat down again, but she had said enough. From every side, men were gathering. Caius Turpilius came hurrying forward. His face blanched as he saw Artor holding the Sword.

"Arktos, lad, where did you get that blade?"

"I found it in the chapel beside the gate. Father, did I do wrong? *She* said—" He broke off, for Caius, seeing the triumph in Igierne's eyes, had gone down on one knee before him.

"Boy, the druid told me that your birth was good, but I see now that you come of higher blood than ever I dreamed of!"

"Father, get up! I don't understand!"

"What he means is that you are my son, Artor, by Uthir the High King," Igierne said in a shaking voice, "the son that we entrusted to Merlin when you were a babe, that he might find you a safe fosterage."

"The druid came to us in the summer of the year Uthir made the lady Igierne his bride," Caius echoed, "with a boy-child a few weeks old."

The murmur of commentary from the men who had gathered around them became a clamor as word spread. Now the great lords were coming, Cataur and Leudonus and Eleutherius, with their champions behind them.

"What is this tale?" challenged Leudonus, fixing Igierne with his pale gaze.

"This boy is Uthir's son, and he has drawn the Sword!"

Leudonus wheeled round to glare at Artor, who still stood with the Sword clasped against his breast.

"Do you say so? We'll go back to the chapel and if he proves it, then, woman, you can explain!"

The word spread fast. By the time the procession reached the hermit's chapel, most of the chieftains and their men and half the town beside had joined it. Someone had even sent for Bishop Dubricius, who arrived, red-faced and puffing, just as they reached the door. With his usual imperturbable good sense he began to create order out of the confusion, calling on the chieftains to calm their men, and selecting, with an unerring grasp of the politics of the gathering, the witnesses, for it was clear that the chapel would hold barely a dozen men.

In the end, besides the Bishop himself, the group included Leudonus and Cataur, the chief magistrate of Calleva, Eleutherius, Catraut and Eldaul, Ulfinus, who had been Uthir's friend, Igierne, Turpilius, and his son Cai.

And Artor, who looked about him like a beast that scents the hunters closing in. But he was still hanging onto the Sword.

"Don't be afraid, lad," said the Bishop. "The truth will prevail, here on this holy ground."

Artor nodded, and Igierne knew it was not the men he feared, but his destiny.

"Will you swear before God and His holy angels that you drew the Sword you are holding from out this stone?"

All could see that the slot in which it had been fixed was empty. Artor nodded again.

"Then I will ask you to thrust the blade back into the rock, and draw it out once more."

Something grim in the set of the boy's jaw reminded Igierne painfully of Uthir as he moved forward. She heard Ulfinus's breath catch, and knew he saw it too. Artor dropped the swathing cloth, and with a swift turn of the wrist, brought the blade up, positioned it over the slot, and with the twisting movement that Igierne's own muscles remembered, thrust it home.

"There is blood on the stone—" said someone, pointing at the dark stain that had run down into the "r" of the *rex* in the rock surface.

"I cut my hand," said Artor, "when I pulled it out before."

"I have heard that such blades must be blooded when they are drawn," said Eldaul reflectively.

For a moment Artor studied the sheathed Sword, his brows bent in a frown, then he turned to the men. "There it is, as it was before. Try if you will. . . ."

"It has burnt me once already!" exclaimed Cai. "I have no desire to touch it again."

"Well I will try," said Catraut, grinning, "though I have no wish to be High King." He went forward, and though the sword did not burn him, neither could he budge it from the stone.

Cataur tried then, and some of the others, to no avail. And all the while Leudonus watched them, pulling at his beard, his gaze going from the Sword to Igierne and back again.

"I think my wife has told me something about this blade. There is a trick to its sheathing, is there not? Are you so tormented by your grief, my lady, that you have told this poor boy the secret and convinced yourself he is your son?"

"Indeed I know that Sword," Igierne said proudly, "for my family guarded it for many years. But I did not bring it here. And as for the boy—my heart began to whisper to me who he must be, and so I told him where to find the blade. But no more—before Our Lady's throne I swear it. I told him no more! It is not the drawing of the blade, but the wielding that is the test, Leudonus. Let Artor pull it out again for you and see if you can bear its power!"

"Do as she says, my son," Bishop Dubricius said softly. "As you did before . . ."

"I knelt down before the altar and asked God's leave," said Artor, "for I was not quite sure it was right to take something from a shrine." As he spoke, he knelt once more, head bowed in prayer. Then he signed himself and went to the stone. "But I did it all faster, because I was hurrying . . ."

He was not hurrying now. Igierne saw him swallow as he faced the Sword, this time knowing what pulling it out might mean.

He set his hand on the hilt, and she saw him stiffen at the first uprush of power. Then he set his feet more firmly and pulled, the muscles in his forearm rippling as he turned the blade, and with a faint hiss it came free. Artor took a step backward and swung it high, and no man could say after whether it was the last light of sunset coming through the open door that lit the Sword or some radiance from within.

Seen by that light, Artor's face was transfigured as well, the boy's unformed features overlaid with the stern majesty of a king. He brought the blade down and drew the keen edge across his forearm next to the other gash. Once more, blood dripped upon the stone.

"It is speaking to me . . ." he murmured. "It only whispered before—" He turned the flat of the blade against his wounds, and when he lifted it, there were two white scars. He straightened then, resting the weapon across his two palms.

"My son," said Igierne, "what does it say?"

"It tells me that the power to defend is the same as the power to destroy. One must balance the other. It says . . . it is a Sword of Justice, that will endure no lie." His blue gaze lifted to Leudonus's face, and the older man could not look away. "Stretch out your hand, my lord, and prove the truth or falsehood of your suspicions on this blade."

Leudonus did not lack courage, but as he neared Artor his steps slowed, as if he walked against a wind. Still, he managed to grip the golden hilt for a full minute before his features contorted in pain and he wrenched his hand away.

"Do not try to take the Sword again. From this hour to his life's ending it will bear no touch but that of the Defender," said a new voice.

They all turned. Merlin stood in the doorway, leaning on his staff. His hair and beard had grown longer, and he was clad only in a kilt of hide, but the Wild Man no longer looked out of his eyes.

"I took him from his mother's breast and gave him to Turpilius to foster. He is Igierne's son."

"But is he Uthir's?" asked Leudonus, recovering. "It was Gorlosius who visited her at Dun Tagell, as I have heard."

"It was Uthir, in Gorlosius's guise," said Merlin. "And Gorlosius himself lay dead already when the king came to her."

"Then it was not adultery," someone whispered. "Look at his face— who else could he be but Uthir's true son?"

"He is very young—" Eldaul began.

"Then you will advise him," snapped Igierne. "Does it matter whether he is my son or he dropped out of the sky? For many generations my family guarded this Sword. Now it has chosen its King."

She turned to Artor. "Will you accept the trust the Sword has laid upon you? Will you swear to defend, not one region, or one tribe, or one faith, but all this Hallowed Isle?"

Artor knelt before her, the Sword fixed upright before him. In his face shone exaltation, and terror, and joy.

"By this holy blade I do so swear . . ."

THE BOOK OF THE SPEAR

Contents

Prologue

In the beginning was the breath.

When the first Fire met primal Ice there came a wind, released by their meeting, feeding the flame. By virtue of that third element, the breath of life and the spirit that moves through all the worlds, matter and energy interacted.

It moves upon the face of the waters, and life begins to stir; the trees of the forest exhale it; the newborn babe breathes it in and becomes a child of time.

In the beginning was the Word.

Invisible, essential, it moves through all that lives, knowing everything, itself unknown. Aware, it wills the world to change and grow. Conscious, that will is borne on a breath of wind in the form of sound. . . .

In the morning of creation the god who gave men breath hangs on the Worldtree. Nine nights and days he hangs suspended, neither eating nor drinking, until out of his agony comes understanding, and he calls forth the primal energies of the world in sacred sounds. One by one he calls them into manifestation as Runes of might and power. And then he gives them to the world.

The Breath carries the Word.

In a northern forest, a rune-master chants, calling the wind. All through the night the wild storm rages. He stands to face it, hair streaming, garments blown to ribbons, shouting out the names of his god. When dawn breaks and the wind grows gentle, he sees before him the limb of an ash tree that the storm has speared into the ground.

Whispering a prayer of thanks, he pulls it free, finding it exact in weight and balance for his needs. From fallen wood he builds a shelter at the foot of a hill, and there, for nine nights and days he labors, eating nothing, drinking only from the sacred spring.

Carefully the wood is smoothed and polished, all irregularities planed away. As he works, he sings of the sun and rain that nourished the tree, the earth that bore it, the wind that ruffled its leaves. When he is finished, he holds a smooth shaft, almost as long as he is tall.

With his graving tool, he carves into the ashwood the angular shapes of the runes. One by one he carves them, chanting their names so that the wood vibrates with the sound. With the sounds come images, each rune name is a doorway to another realm. With blood and breath and spittle he colors and consecrates them, and as each one is added, the shaft gains power.

On the eighth night he is finished. To his eyes, the rune staff seems to glow. Now, it contains, but does not yet direct the power. In the dawning of the ninth day, he draws forth from its wrappings the one thing he himself has not made. A cleanly polished leaf-shaped blade of translucent, smoky stone, it came to him from his father. But it is far older.

When he holds it images come to him of hide-covered huts beneath a northern sky, and he feels the icy breath of eternal snows. The soul of the shaman who made that blade still guards it, whispering of ice and fire and monstrous enemies. Since the time when the fathers of the fathers of his people first spoke in human words, this blade has warded them; it comes from a time even before they knew the runes.

Handling it with reverence, he eases it into the slot that he has carved into the shaft, bedded in glue made from the hooves of stallions. With the sinew of wolves he wraps it, and ties two raven feathers so they will flutter in the breeze.

When he is finished, the wood feels different. It is not only that the balance has shifted. The power that was inherent now is focused. As the ninth night falls he climbs the hill. The wind that has sprung up with the coming of darkness is whispering in the trees.

He turns to face the breeze and it blows stronger. With both hands, he holds up the spear. Wind shrills down the shaft.

"Gungnir I name you, to Woden I offer you, to bear his word and his will throughout the world!"

The Wild Hunt

Wind gusted around the feasting hall, shrilling through the thatching and shaking the pillars. Oesc, leaning against the posts of his grandfather's high seat, could feel the wood trembling beneath his hand. *Maybe this will be the storm that destroys us,* he thought with a shiver in which excitement mingled with fear. *The wind will knock down the hall and then the sea will pour in over the fields and wash us away . . .*

Storms were common at this season, when the forces of winter fought a rearguard action against the advance of spring, but in all his nine years Oesc could not remember so mighty a wind. For generations the Myrgings had held this land, stubbornly clinging to their homes when other tribes passed away. Men spoke of gentle winters and good harvests when they sat around the fires, but since his birth, it seemed, the weather had been bad, and this was the worst year of all.

A cold blast whipped up the flames in the long hearth as the door opened. Several drenched figures pushed through and slammed it shut, stamping their feet and shaking themselves like wet dogs. Oesc listened with interest as they swore, testing the forbidden words with a silent tongue.

"The etins are pissing up a storm, curse them!" exclaimed Æthelhere, flinging his cloak at one of the thralls. "I swear the rain is coming in sideways, straight from the sea!"

"—And cold as the milk from Hella's tit, too!" echoed Byrhtwold, following him. Their boots squelched, and water ran down their necks from their wet hair.

"What of the tide?"

Oesc looked up at his grandfather, who had been sitting motionless since noon, listening to the wind.

"It will be high just past sunset, lord," said Æthelhere. "If the wind has not dropped by then—" He grimaced and shook his head.

He did not need to say more. At this season the wind, adding its power to that of the tide, could turn back the Fifeldor in its course. The storm tides and the flooding river between them would drown the newly planted fields.

"The Norns have cast for us an evil fate . . ." muttered Eadguth. "If foes attacked us I would go forth in arms, old as I am, but no man can hold back the sea."

Oesc looked up at his grandfather. Eadguth had always seemed eternal. Now the boy saw the sunken eyes and furrowed brow, the transparent skin on the thin hands, and knew that the Myrging-king was *old*, not as a standing stone is ancient, its rough surfaces weathered by the years, but like an old oak, decaying from within until it has no strength to withstand the storm. Already this wind had torn limbs from several of the trees that had rooted themselves in the wurt-mound on which stood the royal hall. What would it do to the old man? He crept closer and clasped his arms around Eadguth's leg as if his young strength could root him into the ground.

The old man's hooded glance turned downward and his lips twisted.

"Is it a curse on your line, boy, that has doomed you to find rest nowhere? I am glad that your mother did not live to see this day. . . ."

Oesc let go and sat staring. He did not remember his mother, a fair woman with eyes the rich brown of tree bark in the sun, so men said, who had run off with an Anglian adventurer called Octha and crept home again, heavy with child, when her man went over the sea to join his father in Britannia. Eadguth's sons had died in battle, and his daughter had been the apple of her father's eye.

"Or is it you who are the doom-bringer?" The king's gaze sharpened. "Doom to your mother in child-bed, and now the doom of my land?"

Oesc edged carefully away. He knew Eadguth's black moods too well. When he was smaller he had tried to say he was sorry, though he did not know what for, and only been beaten harder. He looked like his father, said the women. Perhaps that was why. But the old man, he could see, was too weary to strike him now.

Byrhtwold glanced from his king to the boy, pity in his eyes, and gestured toward the door. The old warrior would never criticize his lord, but he had showed Oesc what kindness he could. Nodding his thanks, the boy reached the shadows behind the row of pillars and slipped down the aisle between them and the bed boxes until he reached the door.

His grandfather, king of the Myrgings and lord of their land, was the supreme power in his small world, but Eadguth had ever been a chancy protector. Still, he was not the only power. Oesc slipped through the door, straining to hold it against the wind, seeking the one person by whom he had never been betrayed.

Before he had gone three steps he was soaked to the skin. The storm was driving down from the north, cold as the seas from which it came, lashing the land with rain. With each gust the big oak tree beyond the palisade thrashed wildly; the ground was littered with leaves and branches. Bent nearly double, Oesc splashed through the puddles, shielding his eyes with his arm. Even so, the wind slammed him against the weaving shed and sent him sprawling beside the storehouse before he came under the lee of the log palisade and crept along it to his goal.

Hæthwæge's hut was partially sheltered by the wall; the horse's skull on the post before the doorway rattled in the wind, and the raven feathers tied beneath it flapped wetly, but here Oesc could stand upright. He took a deep breath and wiped his eyes before knocking at her door. The moments seemed long before there was an answer. Surely, he thought, on such a day she would stay indoors, although the wise-folk were not like other men, and if her magic required it, even a woman who was a wicce might brave the storm.

The weight of the spindle drew out the thread, spiraling ever round and round like the turning of the seasons, the lives of humankind. Half-tranced by the motion, Hæthwæge did not at first distinguish the knocking from the sound of the storm. It was the flare of emotion that got her attention, rather than the sound. In another moment she sensed a pain more of the mind than the body, and recognized, as one identifies the pungence of bruised pine needles on the wind, that Oesc was waiting there. She twisted the thread through the notch in the shaft of the spindle, and before the knocking could come again, opened the door.

As the boy started to ease around it, the wind gave him a sudden push that propelled him the rest of the way inside. He fell to his knees, blinking at the darkness.

"Child, you are wet through! Take off your shoes—you are already making a puddle on the floor."

The words were harsh, but the tone was not. Hæthwæge had been Oesc's nurse when he was little, and knew that he was used to her scoldings.

The fire flared in the draft, showing her a boy whose hands and feet seemed too big for his thin frame, his fair hair plastered dark and flat by the rain. She took up a cloak and wrapped it around him. He sank down on the three-legged stool beside the fire, nose wrinkling at the smell of wet wool as its heat began to absorb the moisture from his clothes.

Hæthwæge took up her spindle again and began, humming softly and watching him from the corners of her long eyes, to spin. Oesc eyed her curiously, knowing that a wicce's spinning was sometimes more than yarn.

"It is black wool and white," Hæthwæge answered his unvoiced question, "carded together. Opposites entwined balance the magic."

"What do you use it for?"

"For healing, mostly. I can use this yarn to take a sick man's measure and seal it with a drop of his blood. Then I bring it home and sing over it, and the magic works as well to heal as if the man were here."

To heal, or, of course, to harm. . . . Those hanks of yarn measured trust as well. In the dozen years she had lived with the Myrgings, Hæthwæge had treated almost everyone in the king's household. She glanced at the boxes and sacks crammed into the space above the boxbed and around the room, trying to remember how many twists of grey yarn she had stored there.

"Can you use the measure to change my grandfather's mood?" Oesc said suddenly.

The twirling spindle stilled. "Has he beaten you again?"

Oesc shook his head. "I almost wish he had. He talks like one doom-fated, and blames it on me. Is it true, Hæthwæge? Is that why my father never came back for me?"

For a moment she considered him. She had known that one day he would ask her this question, and understood as well how careful she must be in her reply, so as not to alter the twinings of wyrd and will.

"Doom-fated you are, and so is Eadguth, and so is every man, all the more when they are god-descended, the children of kings. Eadguth traces his line to Ing the son of Mannus, but your father's family comes of Woden himself. When you were born, I cast the runes, and told your grandfather that he must lift you in his arms and give you a name." She fed out more yarn from the distaff and set the spindle to turning once again.

Oesc nodded. No doubt he had heard the maids gossiping when they thought he could not hear. Until the head of the family accepted the child, it had no legal existence. Her throat ached with pity for the boy whom she had taken as an infant from his dying mother's side, sensing his potential, and impelled by her god. She could not leave it there.

"I told him that you were the hope of his house, that if he gave you to the wolves, it was not Octha's, but his own line that would fail. And yet I do not see you sitting in Eadguth's high seat here. You will have a kingdom, but it lies elsewhere. The rune that goes before you is Sigel, the sun-road that leads to victory."

"Does my father know?" Oesc asked sullenly.

"A message was sent, but even I cannot tell if it ever found him. He has been fighting in Britannia. Perhaps he felt you would be safer here. And remember, the wandering shope who sang at last year's Yule feast told us that Uthir the British king had taken him prisoner."

"Perhaps he's dead . . ." muttered the boy.

Hæthwæge shook her head. "I have *seen* the two of you together. Your time will come."

Oesc sighed and let the blanket slip from his shoulders. His damp clothes were beginning to steam in the heat of the fire.

"Well, if it's not my fault, why does the king lay the blame on me?"

"Do not judge him too harshly. He is an old man. Since his own grandfather was slain by Offa of Angeln on the banks of the Fifeldor things have gone badly for the Myrgings. Now he sees his land being eaten away by flood and storm. When he goes to his fathers, the shopes will not sing that the harvests were good in his reign, and no one will lay offerings at his grave. Of all dooms, that one weighs hardest on a king."

As Hæthwæge played out more wool the thread broke suddenly, sending the spindle rolling across the floor toward the rune-carved spear that leaned against the wall, its head shrouded in a piece of cloth.

Hah, Old Man! she thought, *Has the time come for you to take a hand?* For a moment it seemed to her that a faint radiance played about the spear. A dozen years ago it had been entrusted to her, at the same time as her visions had instructed her to take service with the Myrging king.

Oesc bent to retrieve the spindle, his troubled gaze meeting her own, and carefully set it beside her stool.

"My grandfather hates me, and my father doesn't even know my name," he said bitterly. "Who will protect me?"

Hæthwæge twitched, feeling the first brush of power against her mind, subtle as the draught that stirred the fire.

"Look to the father of your fathers," she answered, her own voice sounding strange in her ears. Sight darkened as more words came to her. "Not the god of the land, but the one who hunts on the storm. He is coming—do you hear him?" She pointed northward, head cocked, listening.

The fire hissed, and above that came the sound of the rising wind, gusting through the branches of the trees beyond the palisade with a sound like surf on some distant shore. And beyond that . . . deep as her own heartbeat, the drumming of hooves.

Oesc's voice came to her as if from a great distance. "I don't understand—"

"Come—" The wicce rose from her stool. Without needing to think about it, she took the spear from its corner and started toward the door.

She could sense the boy's confusion, but to her spirit the hoofbeats were growing ever closer. If the boy's presence had been a scent on the breeze, what was coming now was the wind itself, a storm of terror and delight that could whirl consciousness itself away.

Hæthwæge pulled open the door. Wind swirled around her, insistent as a lover, plucking the pins from her hair. She felt the spearshaft vibrate in her hand and laughed.

I am coming, I am coming, my lord and my love. . . .

Laughing, she walked into the storm to meet the god, in that moment scarcely caring if the boy followed her.

Outside, dusk was falling fast. Oesc splashed through the puddles to catch up with Hæthwæge, raising his arm to shield his eyes from the driving rain. It came in flurries, as if the storm clouds were being broken up by the force of the wind. Head high, her hair streaming out behind her and with every moment growing darker in the rain, the wicce strode across the yard to the eastern gate. Oesc knew her as a woman just past middle life, her shoulders rounded and her body thickened by the years. But now she looked taller, and young, and by that he understood she was already in trance.

Below the mound that raised the village above the floods stretched a level land of wood and marsh and field, dotted and channeled by pond and stream. To the west, a little light shafted below the scudding clouds, touching the Law-Oak and the Field of Assembly where the tribal moots were held with a sickly yellow glow. In the distance he caught the pewter gleam of the sea. That last light gleamed on water that was closer as well, for from here he could see that the slow curve of the river had become a crescent grin of silver water that with every moment nibbled away more of the sodden fields. Monster-gate, they called it, but now it was not the etins who lived in the North Sea but the waters themselves that were devouring the land.

Beyond the palisade that sheltered the workshops and the king's hall, the long-houses of the villagers clustered closely along the slope. Oesc saw Hæthwæge disappearing between the last two and hurried to follow her. To the east stretched the home pasture, but on the west side, the marshes came nearly to the base of the mound. A narrow causeway, in this season half underwater, led through it. Picking his way carefully, Oesc followed the wisewoman. He could guess where she was heading now. In the heart of the boglands lay the dark pool where the Myrgings made their offerings under the staring eyes of the carven gods. Except at the time of sacrifice, most folk avoided it, but Oesc had gone there once or twice with Hæthwæge when she was gathering herbs.

Though the rain had diminished, by the time he caught up with the wicce, water from swinging branches had drenched him as thoroughly as the storm. Together they pushed through the screen of alder and willow that edged the pool, and at that moment the sun set and the clouds closed in once more, as if the mists of Nibhel had overwhelmed the world.

The wind stilled. Oesc shivered and drew closer to Hæthwæge. Reason told him that the horse whose hide and head were suspended on a framework of poles above the water was quite dead, but the water had risen, and it seemed now to be standing in the pool.

"What is happening?" Instinctively he dropped his voice to a whisper.

She turned, and this time she saw him, though her pupils were still dilated so that her eyes seemed to open on darkness.

"Wait." A tremor ran through her body. "Soon, he comes." With trembling fingers she unwound the cloth from about the head of the spear. The smoky stone glimmered in the shadows as if it shone with its own light.

Faint with distance, he heard a long horn-call. The raven feathers tied to the shaft fluttered in a sudden wind. Then came the hoofbeats. Men were riding on the wooden causeway that led through the marshes, he thought, but the sound grew rapidly louder. No horse could gallop safely on the rain-slick logs, nor could they cross other than in single file. What he heard now was the sound of many horses—or was it thunder? Was that the shrieking of the wind or the bitter answer of many horns?

He could not tell, but the sound sent a chill deep into his body. He crouched at Hæthwæge's feet, wishing he could burrow into the earth for protection. The animal heads spiked upon the offering stakes swayed frantically, and the horsehide heaved above the ruffled waters, straining toward the attenuated images of the gods.

In the next moment the tumult he had heard approaching was upon them. The last of the light had gone; he could make out only a confusion of shadows. Was it his imagination that shaped them into skeletal horses and wild riders who brandished spears or swords, or worse still, into wælcyriges, war-hags riding slavering wolves with serpents for reins. He bit back a cry as a gust of wind sent the horsehide flapping into the air to join them.

He cowered beneath their keening until Hæthwæge's hand on his shoulder made him look up again. The horrors had passed. The shapes that swept above him now, limned in their own light, were of a nobler kind.

"Behold, son of Octha, your fathers of old—Wihtgils, Witta, Wehta, and their sires before them. . . ."

Shaking, Oesc got to his feet and raised his arm in salute. The names rolled on, but he could not hear them. All his being was focused on those luminous shadows, grim or kindly, that looked on him with a considering gaze as if deciding whether he was worthy to continue their line.

And then, though all around them the trees still bowed to the storm, the air above the pool grew heavy with a sense of presence. Oesc remained standing, but he shut his eyes tightly. Whatever was coming now was something he was not yet ready to see. But he could not keep from hearing, though he never knew, then or thereafter, if the words had come to his mind or his ears.

"So this is the boy—" a deep voice seemed to say.

"Since his birth I have warded him," Hæthwæge answered. "When will the future I foretold for him come to be?"

"That is Verdandi's business. But when that time comes, he will have to choose . . ."

"What are his choices?"

"To stay here and live long in a dying land, or to risk all across the water. . . ."

"But the runes spoke of victory—" the wicce began. That other voice interrupted her.

"To endure the turning of the seasons is as much a victory as death

in battle. The one is the path of Ingvi, but the other is mine. If he chooses Me his name shall be remembered in a new land, and he shall sire kings."

"Is that your will, lord?" Now it was Hæthwæge's voice that trembled.

"I will what shall be, but it is not for me to choose how it shall come to pass—that lies with the boy, and with you."

Oesc had the abrupt sense of being the focus of attention, like a mouse trapped between a wolf's paws. He scrunched his eyes shut even more tightly. For a moment more he was held, then the pressure was released with a hint of laughter.

"I do not force you," came that whisper from within, *"but the Norns will force the choice upon you, my son, and soon."*

"I have chosen you, High One, since I was young—" Hæthwæge said then.

"It is so, nor have I ever been far away."

If there was more, it was not meant for Oesc's ears. He sank down at the woman's feet, and only afterward, when the god and those he led had passed, did he realize that his face was wet, not with rain, but with tears.

The wood seemed very silent. Oesc stood up, wiping his eyes. Then he stiffened, hearing once more the sounds of hoofbeats and horns.

But this was no spectral hunt—he could tell the difference now. Those were mortal horses whose hoofbeats he heard ringing on the wet logs, and mortal lungs behind those plaintive horns.

"There are riders, Hæthwæge! Riders on the causeway!" he exclaimed. "Hurry, we must get back to the hall."

She nodded, shrouding the spearhead once more, and he saw her face still luminous with memory. But as she turned her awareness back to the human world the lines deepened in her skin and she became merely mortal once more.

"So, it has begun. . . ."

Oesc peered through the door to the great hall, which only this morning had seemed so huge and empty. Now it was filled with men clad in well-worn war-gear and battered finery, with a liberal splashing of mud over all. The folk who served the hall were bustling around them, taking wet cloaks away and bringing beakers of heated ale.

"May Freo bring you blessings," said their leader, accepting a horn of mead from Æbbe, the king's widowed sister, who had ruled his household as long as Oesc could remember. He must have been handsome once, thought the boy, but now one eyelid drooped and the left side of his face was stiffened by a long scar.

"But where is your neice, Æbbe? Should it not be she who gives the welcome?"

"There is no other Lady in this hall," said the woman, taking a step backward. "And what unholy wight has taught you my name?"

The stranger frowned. "Did Hildeguth remarry, then? I suppose she thought I was dead—I've thought I was dead a few times myself, these past years!" His hand moved to touch his scar. "Have I changed so much, Æbbe, that even you don't know me?"

"It is my daughter who is dead," came a harsh voice from the far end of the hall, "killed by the seed you planted in her belly, and if you had not already claimed guest-right I would drive you from my door!" Leaning on his staff, Eadguth limped forward to his high seat and took his place there.

Oesc stared from one to the other, aware of every heartbeat that shook his chest, understanding without quite believing who the newcomer must be.

Octha, son of Hengest . . . his father.

Octha straightened, the muscles of his face stiffening into a battle-mask. "And the child?" he asked in a still voice. "Did it die too?"

"Shall I tell you it died in the womb?" Eadguth spat, "or that I set it out upon the heath for the wolves?"

"You shall tell him the truth, old man," said Hæthwæge, gripping Oesc by the shoulder and pushing him before her into the light of the fire. "Sore though it grieved you, you have reared up his son!"

For a moment longer the warrior's glance clashed with that of the king. Then Octha turned, his face changing as he looked at the boy.

"Come here—"

With feet that did not seem his own Oesc stepped forward. Octha knelt and gripped the boy's face between callused hands. After a moment he swallowed.

"You have your mother's eyes . . ."

Oesc nodded. Hæthwæge had told him so.

"But I see Hengest in your brow . . . What do they call you?"

"I am Oesc, son of Octha—" His voice wavered only a little.

"My son!"

Powerful arms closed around him; Oesc smelled horse, and wet wool, and the strong scent of the man. It was very strange. Not so long ago, Woden had also called him son—from being fatherless he seemed suddenly over-supplied with kin. He took a deep breath as Octha let him go.

"I am going back to Britannia, where the cows grow fat in green pastures and apples hang heavy on the bough. Will you come with me?"

Soon, Woden had told him, he would have to choose. Oesc looked into his father's storm-grey eyes, but when he spoke, he knew he was answering the god.

"Yes, father, I will come."

Since Octha's arrival three days had passed. The storm had moved on, but on the Field of Assembly scattered pools mirrored the blue sky. Only a few rags of cloud still clung to the southeastern heavens. As the people gathered, the green grass was being trampled to a muddy brown. But perhaps it would not matter, thought Oesc as he watched them from his place at his father's side. If the moot voted to follow Octha over the sea, the cattle would be slaughtered or sold and there would be no need for pastureland.

The thought awakened an anxious flutter in his belly. He knew there were other lands, for he had heard the shopes and gleemen sing of them, but Eadguth's hall was the center of his world. Most of the Myrgings had gathered, women and children forming a larger ring around the chieftains and heads of families. He looked around him for Hæthwæge, then remembered that the wicce had told him she had no need to watch. She had already seen this wyrd when she cast the runes.

Why did she not inform Eadguth, then, and save us all the trouble of deciding? he wondered, but as the wisewoman had often told him, you might predict the sun's rising, but you had to wait for it to happen just the same.

A bench had been placed for the king beneath the oak tree. His *witan,* the tribal elders, sat around him. Sunlight glowing through the young leaves dappled his white hair. Eadguth Gamol, they called him, Eadguth the Old, for of all the kings of the north, only Healfdene of Sillende had reigned longer.

His other grandfather, Hengest, was old too, thought Oesc. But he ruled a confederation of war-bands, like the sea-kings of Frisia. Eadguth was bred and bound through many fathers to his kingship and his land.

A murmur ran through the crowd as Geflaf, leader of the king's sword-thanes, stepped forward. He raised a great silver-mounted horn to his lips and blew, and as its echoes faded, the people also became still.

"Hear, ye chieftains and people of the Myrgings here assembled. A stranger, Octha son of Hengest, has come among us. The witan has called you to hear and consider his words."

"He is an Anglian of royal kin, and our enemy!" cried the chieftain of one of the older Myrging clans.

"He is not of the kin of Offa the king-slayer, but a lesser line, and has never borne arms against us," came the reply.

"Our kin serve in his father's war-band," said one of the Jutes who had settled among the Myrgings, taking up farmsteads left vacant after the Anglian wars. "Let us hear what he has to say."

For a little longer the clamor continued, but eventually it became clear that the mood of the moot was in Octha's favor.

Another murmur arose as he stepped forward, Oesc at his side. By now, of course, everyone had heard the rumors that the mysterious father of their Lady's son had reappeared. Oesc hung back as he realized that they were staring at him as well, but Octha's grip was firm.

He is using me to show them he is not an enemy, the boy realized suddenly, and allowed himself to be pulled along. For most of his short life he had been at best an embarrassment to his mother's kin; to stand forth before the people as one with a right to honor seemed very strange. For the first time, it came to him that he too might one day be a king.

"Men of the Myrgings!" cried Octha, "and all of you—be you Jute or Saxon or Frank, who by marriage or alliance have become part of this tribe. I come here as your ally, for it was a princess of your people who gave me my son!"

Someone started a cheer, and Oesc felt the hot color rise in his cheeks.

"Then why have you waited till now to claim him?" came another voice.

"There's many a man who goes off to war childless and returns to learn he has an heir. For ten winters I have battled in Britannia; I have slain many princes of their people, and cut down those who thought themselves the heirs of Rome. At first we fought for treasure, but now we fight for land. The British have little strength to resist us—their king is a sick man, and he has no son. The land lies undefended, ripe for the taking. To hold that earth men must till it, and so I come to you.

"Follow me to Britannia—bring your wives and your children. Bring your axes and your ploughs."

"Why should we abandon the hearths of our mothers and the howes where our fathers lie?" came the cry.

"Because this land is drowning!" responded Octha. "Look around you—the fields are blighted by bad weather and your cattle are dying. Each year more of your shores are eaten by the sea. In Britannia there are wide fields, fruitful and flourishing—good harvests of oat crops and broad barley-crops, white fields of wheat-crops and all that grows in Middle Earth."

"But they are not *our* fields. Will they bear for us if we do not know the names of the wights that dwell there?"

"Those fields have borne fruit for all the tribes the Romans settled in that land," said Octha. "Warriors from Iberia and Sarmatia and Gallia and other lands who took up farming after their time in the legions was done. Our cousins the Franks get good crops from the lands they have won in Gallia. Till the fields and make the offerings, and when your time comes, lay your bones in the soil. By blood and toil shall we claim Britannia and make it our own."

"We will go!" said one of the Jutish chieftains, a man called Hæsta. "There are men of my blood already in Hengest's war-band. They have said that Cantuware is a land of good soil and good grazing, where the cows give milk thrice a day at this time of year."

"And it breeds good fighters—" an older man spoke up, lifting an arm scarred and twisted by an old wound. "In my youth I too have been to Britannia, but all I got there was steel. It is well enough for warriors to take such chances, but I will not risk my family in a land whose native folk are awakening at last, determined to get back their own."

"Better to die by steel than starvation!" exclaimed another, and suddenly everyone was arguing.

"What says Eadguth?" someone cried at last. "What is the word of the Myrging king?"

Slowly, silence fell. When it was quite still, the thrall Cubba, who was even older than the king, assisted Eadguth to unfold his gaunt frame from the chair. The king came forward, leaning on his staff. For a few moments he looked around him, and those who had cried the loudest for emigration found it hard to meet his eyes.

"The gods have given me long life. For more than forty winters I have been your king. . . ." His voice did not seem loud, but it carried.

"In those years I have seen many things. I have seen five summers when the rains were so scant that the river sank down till its banks gaped like toothless jaws. That time ended. So will this. I have seen blizzards that heaped snow halfway up the walls and held us prisoner from one moon to the next. That time ended—this will too. And I have seen harvests so plentiful we had not the barns to store it all. And those times also came to an end. You cry out now like children who cannot go out to play because of the rain. And I say to you, neither will this time last."

He spoke slowly, a kindly grandfather chiding willful boys, and here and there a man would hang his head with a shamefaced grin.

"A man's mood changes, sometimes happy and sometimes sorrowful. Our holy mother earth has also her moods and changes. Will you desert her because now she is weeping? For men who have been uprooted from their homelands perhaps it is true that one land is as good as the next. But the Myrgings have been here since Mannus himself walked the earth. We are a free land and a free people, bound only to this soil."

Carefully, Eadguth bent and grasped a handful of muddy earth. He held it high, and the water squeezed out between his fingers and ran like brown blood down his hand.

My mother's bones lie in this earth, thought Oesc. *If I leave here, I will have lost her entirely.* But his father still stood beside him, and his bones were clad in warm and living flesh.

"Will you leave this holy earth, blessed by the blood of your fathers, for an alien land? Perhaps, as Octha says, in time it will accept you. But I say this—it will not be in your time, nor in that of your children. Stay, men of the Myrgings and those whom we have welcomed here. Stay, and defend the land that has nourished you."

Some of the men knelt in reverence and set their hands on the wet grass, but others were still standing, brows bent in thought.

Geflaf stepped forward once more. "The Myrging-king has spoken. Go now, carls and eorls, free men of our nation. Speak together, and when the sun is sinking toward the sea, return and say what your decision will be."

He turned away, and the men drew into knots and clusters as they began their debate.

"What now?" asked Octha, watching King Eadguth make his way slowly back toward the hall.

"Now we wait," answered Geflaf. He also was watching his king, and Oesc saw sorrow in his gaze.

That day seemed very long to Oesc, longer even than the day before the Midsummer festival. He tried to fill it by showing his father where Hildeguth was buried, and the best place to catch fish below the whirlpool, and even the god-images in the sacred bog, but he could tell that Octha's attention was elsewhere. And as the sun drove her wain across the fields of the sky his distraction grew, until the time came to turn their steps back toward the great oak tree.

Away to the west the sky was glowing in shades of amber and rose. Broad bands of light rayed out from the setting sun as if showing the way to Britannia. But a great peace lay on the Myrging lands. Even the sea lay still, its waters a lucent blue, and each leaf and blade of grass seemed to have caught the sunset's gold. Did it seem so fair, wondered Oesc, because he might soon be leaving it? Then he looked again and thought,

But perhaps we will not be going. It is too beautiful. On such an evening, no one could make the choice to go.

Once more King Eadguth came forth and sat in his carven chair, gazing at his people with hooded eyes. Once more the people gathered around the great tree.

"Men of the Myrgings," said Geflaf when they were quiet. "The sun has finished her course and it is time to choose our own. Are you ready to decide?"

"Aye," came the response from many voices.

"Then let the leaders of your clans and families stand forth and say your will."

Hæsta was first to step out from the crowd.

"I speak for the Jutes who dwell along the Fifeldor. For a generation we have guarded your northern border. We do not fear fighting. But the fields will not bear for us. We vote to seek the new lands across the sea."

There was a murmur at that, for the Jutes made up a sizable portion of their fighting men. A Myrging thane came forward next, and said that he would stay by his king. One by one others followed and spoke the will of their clans. And though there were some who swore to stay in the Myrging homeland, it became clear that those who had been convinced by Octha's words were in the majority.

"I would stay, but I see the choice being made for me," said one farmer, whose rich fields lay inland, away from the sea. "We cannot stop those who decide to leave us, and how can we defend ourselves against our enemies if only a tithe remain?"

A mutter of agreement swept through the people, and after that most of the men who stepped forward said that they would follow Octha. Now, only a few chieftains from the oldest families spoke for staying, and Eadguth's sworn sword-thanes, who said that while he lived, they would remain by their king.

Geflaf turned to his lord with troubled gaze.

"My king, the will of the moot is clear. Will you not change your mind and agree to lead us to the new land?"

Eadguth rose from his chair and set his hand against the rough bark of the great tree.

"Will you uproot this oak and carry it over the sea?" His voice grated painfully. "It is too old, too deeply rooted, and so am I. Go if you will—I cannot prevent you. I will remain with my land."

Oesc looked at his grandfather and felt a tremor beneath his heart as if someone had struck him there. *He looks like a dead man.* Suddenly he wanted to run to the old man as he had when he was little, before he understood why Eadguth hated him. But his father's hand was on his shoulder, and he did not move.

Once more Eadguth's dark gaze passed over his people, then he turned and started back toward his hall. His house-thanes fell in behind him, but their faces were grim.

But those who had voted to go with Octha pressed around him, clamoring with questions about the new land.

Oesc woke from a nightmare, fighting for breath. The bedclothes were strangling him—he fought free and lay gasping. In the hall, his own harsh breaths were the only sound, but outside he could hear birdsong. It must be dawn, he thought, blinking. Through the parted curtains of his bed-closet he glimpsed a faint glow from the long hearth and beyond it a colder light. He pulled back the curtains and looked out into the hall.

Along the hearth he could see the humped shapes of sleeping men. But beyond them, the little side door stood open. What clumsy thrall, he wondered, had left it so? Æbbe, who always rose early to supervise the thralls as they got breakfast, would have a thing or two to say about that when she knew.

But now he was curious. Who had gone out so early? He pulled his tunic over his head and tied on his shoes, and then, because the air was brisk, took his cloak from its peg as well. Silently he made his way between the sleeping men and sought the door.

Beyond the threshold the muddy ground showed many footprints, dusted by a light frost that was already melting in the growing light. But across that sparkling veil two sets of tracks showed clearly, and the larger prints were punctuated by the round mark of a staff. For a long moment Oesc stared, a cold feeling growing in his belly.

"Close the door, boy," came Æbbe's voice behind him. "You are letting in the cold."

"Æbbe—" he said, turning, "why has the king gone out so early?"

"What do you mean, child? Old men sleep late—he is in his bed still!"

"Look, are not those his footprints? Where did he go?"

For a moment she stared over his shoulder at the marked ground, and then, without a word, hurried back into the hall. Oesc sank down on a bench, shivering, but it was not from the cold. In a few moments the old woman returned with Byrhtwold and Æthelhere behind her. When they started out across the yard, Oesc followed.

The trail led toward Hæthwæge's hut, and when they picked it up again, there were three sets of footprints, one of them a woman's. Near the side gate they lost the trace, but the young warrior who guarded it, confronted with his king's senior thanes, confessed that his lord had passed through just as the first pallor that precedes the dawn was brightening the sky. The thrall Cubba was with him, and the wisewoman.

"I thought they were going out to make some offering to the gods. He told me to keep silence and stay at my post," said the warrior, "but my shift is almost over, and surely I do not break my oath to tell *you.* . . ."

"No doubt that is it," said Æbbe with a sigh. "I will go back to the kitchen—the king will be wanting his breakfast when he returns."

"I will go out to meet him," said Æthelhere. "It is not right for the lord of the Myrgings to go about without an escort."

Byrhtwold nodded, and when they passed through the gate, Oesc followed the two thanes down the hill.

Here and there a scar upon the frosted grass marked the trail. It led toward the Law Oak. As they came around the edge of the woods they stopped short, staring, for an untimely fruit was dangling from the oak tree's limbs.

It was King Eadguth's body that was hanging there. Blood from a rent beneath his breast had stained his tunic, and the thrall Cubba lay below him, a knife in his hand and blood from his slashed throat soaking the ground. *"An ætheling can look on anything, even his doom,"* Eadguth had once told him, but after Oesc had taken one look at his grandfather's purpled face and staring eyes, he fixed his gaze firmly upon the ground.

"Ah, my dear lord," said Æthelhere, shaking his head. "This is ill done, to go before me with only this thrall to escort you. Still I think your start is not so great I cannot overtake you."

"Why did he do this?" asked Byrhtwold. "We would have stood by him to his life's end."

"And so you have done—" came another voice. They turned, and saw that Hæthwæge was standing there, leaning on a staff whose top was swathed in a blue cloth. "Do you not understand? He had no son to follow him, and those who vowed to stay here are too few to defend the land. By his death Eadguth has freed them from their oaths and made offering to Woden for their protection. This was a noble sacrifice."

"By the knife of a thrall?" asked Byrhtwold.

Hæthwæge shook her head. "Cubba took his own life, but Eadguth's blood was shed by Woden's own spear." She lifted her staff, and Oesc's skin pebbled as he recognized the rune-carved shaft beneath the wrappings.

"This is the last and greatest act of a king," said Æthelhere, "to give his breath to the god and his blood to the land that his people may live."

Verulamium

A.D. 473

A dead horse lay stiff beside the road. The ravens, busy at their feasting, waited until the approaching riders were upon them before fluttering aside, cawing their mockery. Beyond them the Roman road ran straight southwards, where a thin haze of smoke stained the pale morning sky.

"We move from before your feet," they seemed to say, *"but one day you will be our meat!"*

Oesc suppressed a shiver; then his mare, scenting the carrion, tossed her head, and the boy reined her sharply in. His grandfather in the old country had not had the wealth to give him a pony, and in any case it was not the tradition of his people to fight mounted. But Britannia was a large island, and in the three years since Octha had brought him across the sea it seemed to Oesc they had ridden over most of the eastern half that the Angles and the Saxons and the Jutes and tag ends of other tribes were making their own. Through necessity, he had become an adequate horseman. He lifted his chin and straightened his shoulders in unconscious imitation of his father, sitting his big grey easily at the head of the column.

Most of the Myrgings had been settled in Cantuware, along with the

Jutes and Frisians and others who had answered Hengest's call. But the best of the warriors had left the rich fields of the south coast, settled for a generation already by men of the tribes, to ride north with Octha, where there were new and perhaps even richer lands to be won.

Hengest had wanted the boy to stay with him in Cantuware, but there had been no question, really, what Oesc would choose. He had spent most of his short life mewed up with one grandfather, and the other was past eighty, so ancient that many assumed he must be dead by now. No boy could resist the chance to ride with the men and share their glory. It was only sometimes in the night that he regretted the well-built hall and the peaceful fields of his homeland, and the gulls soaring over a sea that glittered with a golden treasure no Roman hoard could match in the light of the setting sun.

Oesc wondered now if he had made the right decision. Men of the German tongue held half the south and the fenlands on the eastern shore, and three years of campaigning had made the beginnings of an Anglian realm south of Eboracum. Only the valley of the Tamesis still separated the English lands. But Leudonus of Alba, having married the British king's daughter, had thrown all his strength into the reconquest of the north, and six days since, had brought the Saxons to battle on the banks of the Abus, and won.

Oesc kicked the mare's stout sides and drew up beside Colgrin, an Anglian who with the Jutish Baldulf was second only to his father in the band.

"Have the scouts come in? Is Leudonus following?" He glanced back, where the Saxon column, dissolving into its own dust, seemed to extend all the way back to Eboracum. Hæthwæge was back there somewhere, in the wagons with the wounded. Beyond them storm-clouds hung heavy in the sky.

Colgrin shook his head, the grey hair hacked short where they had bandaged a slash from a British sword. "Nay, lad, he will not catch us— we gave him too sound a savaging."

"But he is following . . ." Oesc repeated.

"Not yet . . ." the older man admitted. "There's no need to fret. By the time his men can march, we'll be safe behind Verulamium's stout walls."

"How long till we get there?"

Colgrin pointed to blue smudge that lay across the road on the horizon. "Verulamium lies just beyond those hills."

Oesc squinted ahead, and then, as a breath of cool air touched his cheek, looked back again. The curdled clouds were rolling after them, a visible expression of Leudonus' wrath. If the storm hit before they reached shelter the wounded would suffer. He looked at his father's straight back, frowning.

Colgrin, following his glance, sighed. "Not even the greatest of leaders can make the best decision always. And sometimes all choices are flawed. Octha thinks like a warrior, and takes a warrior's chances. Woden loves a brave man, and will give him victory."

"I know. . . ." Oesc nodded, but for the first time it occurred to him to wonder in what way the choices of a warleader might differ from those of a king. The wind blew once more, ruffling his pale hair, and with it came the first spatterings of rain.

The gates of Verulamium were open. Oesc, watching from the walkway atop the old Roman wall, gazed past the tower of the gatehouse to the British army encamped outside. But it was not Leudonus and his blood-stained veterans who were beseiging them. The forces outside the gate—dark-haired Romans in their grandfathers' breastplates or bright-haired British with checkered mantles over their mail, were men of the south and west, under the command of their dying king.

Octha's face had darkened when he heard that Uthir had come against him. He remembered his captivity in the Tower. And then he had told them to unbar and open the great gates that guarded the western route into the town.

"Why not just send Uthir an invitation to charge through?" Baldulf had exclaimed when Octha gave the order.

"That is what I am doing," answered Octha, grinning through his mustaches. "Or did you fancy spending the winter starving behind these walls? Inside the town they will not be able to use their horses, and we can overwhelm them."

"If they come—" said Colgrin.

"If they do not, it will not matter whether the gates are open or closed!"

And Oesc had heard the sharp silence, and then Colgrin's explosive laugh. But the British army, nestled in tent and brush shelter around the city, neither attacked nor lifted the seige.

As he had every day since the British came, Oesc watched them from the guard tower, curious, after all the stories he had heard, about this enemy. Sometimes the wind carried the swift, lilting gabble of the British speech, or the more sonorous cadences of Latin, but mostly he learned by watching. He had become accustomed to the diversity of the Saxon forces, composed of men from all the tribes of the north. But these Britons were more varied still, and in their faces he saw the mosaic, in miniature, that was the Empire.

To the Saxons, they were an accustomed and worthy enemy, but from time to time Oesc, seeing the British king being carried through the camp, would remember how his other grandfather had clung to his land, and feel ashamed. But when he saw his father again the feeling passed. Octha, his skin ripened to bronze by the weather and his body honed to muscle and sinew by the summer's campaigning, was now at the height of his powers, as great a hero as Sigfrid Fafnarsbane, of whom the shopes liked to sing.

Eadguth had been a landking, bound, blood and bone, to his native soil. Octha son of Hengest was a conqueror.

That night the Saxon chieftains met in the dining room, its walls painted in red ochre edged by a design of twining vines, of the house where once Catraut, the British prince who had been the city's chief magistrate, had entertained his peers. Its owner was fled long since—Oesc, bringing in more ale, wondered if he might be even now in Uthir's camp, gazing longingly toward the walls that hid his home. Most of the notable men of the town had escaped, or been killed when the Saxons marched in. But Octha had the authority to forbid looting, and if the common people had not accepted the warriors billeted among them with gladness, neither did they show active hostility.

"How long will we stay cooped up here?" asked one of the younger chieftains. "If we wait too long, Leudonus will come to his good-father's aid!"

"If he does so, I will close the gates—" The golden torque around Octha's neck glinted as he laughed. "But I do not think the British will maintain the seige so long."

"It is true. The British king is a sick man," said Baldulf thoughtfully. "And a military camp is no good place for healing."

"And unless you count Leudonus, he has no heir," said one of the others. "When Uthir dies, the British will be easy prey."

"Easy prey?" exclaimed Colgrin. "Is that the word of a warrior? The weaker Uthir becomes, the less honor there will be in defeating him. I say we should attack them now . . ."

But Octha was looking at the doorway, where Hæthwæge had appeared. "I called her—" He answered the question in the chieftains' eyes. "In the old days, the priestesses always went with the warriors. Hæthwæge is alone, but she was trained by the Walkyriun. Sit—" he gestured toward one of the benches, and then to his son, "bring her ale."

Hæthwæge accepted a sip from the cream-colored clay cup, but she did not sit down. Oesc's words of greeting stuck in his throat. He had grown too accustomed to her care for him, he thought, and forgotten what she was. Her eyes were wide and lightless, as if she had fared halfway down the road to the Otherworld already. As always when she worked magic, her face seemed simultaneously ancient and young.

"Wise One," Octha said softly, "our enemies surround us. Speak to the spirits and give us good counsel."

"I must have a high place . . ." she whispered.

Octha nodded soberly. "It shall be so—" He gestured to the others. Silent now, they rose, and as they moved down the empty street Oesc followed them.

Hæthwæge stared up at the dark bulk of the gatehouse of Verulamium, stark against the sky, its towers looming to either side of the arched gateway. The night was very still. It was only within that she sensed the slow stirring of power. Somewhere not too far away someone was working magic—perhaps it was the British witega they called Merlin.

They say you are strong to foretell the future, gealdor crafty. But I too am witege, and tomorrow you shall see that I too can sing battle spells. She moved into the darkness of the doorway, frowning. For a moment her questing spirit had touched something stronger and sharper, like the mind of a god.

The planks of the stairway rang hollow as they climbed, feeling their way along the curving wall, but when they emerged at the top they breathed freely beneath the starry vault of the heavens. To one side glimmered the lamps of the city and on the other the watchfires of their enemy glowed like red eyes in the darkness. A faint breeze stirred men's hair as if the night were breathing.

Hæthwæge sank down upon the bench beneath the parapet and pulled down her veil. One by one, the warriors sat on the cold stone walkway until only Octha remained standing, his speech becoming the chant of ritual.

"Wicce, hear me . . . to this high place I have brought thee. From here thou mayest soar between the worlds."

"This deed I will dare," her own voice came hoarse to her ears, "but the way is long and weary. It is your prayers I carry—let your power carry me. . . ."

Octha nodded, and began to strike the palms of his hands rhythmically against his thighs. The other men followed his example, swaying gently as the soft vibration pulsed in the air.

"Wicce, Woruld-Aesce ymbwend,
Wisdom innan thin hyde gewinn.
Wicce . . . Wicce . . ."

The word, repeated, became part of the soft susuration of flesh on cloth, a whisper of sound that lifted the hair and the spirit and whirled them away to journey around the Worldtree to the worlds it contained and gain access to the wisdom they held. *Wicce, to the Word-Ash win . . . Wisdom, shape-strong, find within. . . .*

Hæthwæge took a deep breath, and then another, letting her limbs relax against the parapet. Awareness extended into the stones, all the way down to the foundations of the tower and then back up again. As her consciousness changed she fancied she could feel it swaying, even though there was only a little wind. She focused on the singing, and with each repetition felt the links between body and spirit loosen, until like a boat that has slipped its mooring, she fell inward and away.

Images whirled past her—the tower and the army encamped around it, the undulating bands of field and forest, still under starshine, with the rivers, black and shining, veining the land. Then these too dimmed, and there was only the great plain of Middle Earth, and in its midst the huge column of the Worldtree, its radiant branches brushing the skies.

But the will that carried her drew her downward, diving into darkness beneath one of the three great roots of the Tree. Around and around her spirit spiraled, past mist and shadows, past the roots of great mountains where rushed the icy streams. Through the heat of Muspel's fires she journeyed, and sped by the cool grey mirror that was the Well of Wyrd. And still her way led downward, around, and deeper within, until she saw the great gorge of the worldriver and the last bridge, and beyond it the land where the Dark Lady rules and the apples of the blessed and the wild hemlock grow.

One final gate remained to pass. She dropped into darkness, and for a time beyond time, knew no more.

A long time later, it seemed, she became aware of a quiet voice calling her name. Unwillingly she forced her mind to focus. It was Octha, using the same calm voice with which he commanded his warriors.

"Wise One, say then, what dost thou see?"

At the words, images began to dislimn from the darkness. She struggled to make her lips form an answer.

"A dark plain, and a dark lake, and a black swan swimming . . ." she murmured, her voice sounding thready with distance. "My raven flies before me, and around me glimmer the pale faces of those who have gone before."

"Our enemies surround us. How shall we bring them to battle?"

In the pause that followed, her breathing came and went like the wind, fluttering the fabric of the veil. The scene before her blurred. There was still water, but in its midst now she could make out an island. From the woods that surrounded it she could hear the yammering of hounds, and in another moment she saw them, leaping up and down on the shore. What were they barking at? She strained to see, and presently became aware that she was speaking once more.

"I see a wolf brought to bay upon an island. The dogs wait on the shore. They will not swim across to meet the wolf's sharp fangs. He gazes around him and sees where the circle is weakest—where the old pack-leader watches—there he will make his fight." She drew a deep breath. "Wilt thou know more?"

"Will the British king die?"

"All men die!" the answer came to her immediately. "And this one is half-dead already."

"And will our sons inherit the land?" Octha added then.

Hæthwæge took a deep breath, releasing the vision, observing the ebb and flow of image until at last there came something she could put into words.

"I see the wolf and the dog running in one pack ..." more visions came to her "... I see the wheat crop and the barley crop growing in one field ... his seed shall rule men's hearts, but yours will rule the land...."

While they were still chewing on that answer, another voice, that she recognized as Baldulf's, spoke.

"And what about the battle?"

Hæthwæge shivered violently, her awareness battered and reeling beneath the onrush of vision. Ravens were fighting—not the friendly presence that was her own spirit guide, but feathered forms, huge and terrible, whose cries scored the soul.

"I see the Raven of Battle rising, men die when she screams. But Woden sends Hyge and Mynd against her; men battle as the god and the goddess strive...." Her spirit soared with the battling birds.

Then with a suddenness that seared her vision, the scene was split by a Sword of Light. Hæthwæge stiffened, features contorting. For a moment she glimpsed the figure that gripped it in all His glory. "Tir comes, Tir comes! Beware the Sword of War!"

Light and darkness crashed together around her and with it vision and consciousness were swept away.

When she could hear once more, she realized that she was lying on the cold stone of the walkway, her head resting on Octha's arm.

"Hæthwæge," he said softly, "do you hear me? Come forth from the dark plain and the dark lake. Return to Middle Earth—in Woden's name I summon you! Your raven will show you the way. Come to my calling until you can feel the night air on your skin and the bench beneath you. Come then . . . come. . . ."

With a murmur of soft speech, as if he were gentling a fractious mare, Octha continued to call her. Hæthwæge forced herself to breathe, to reconstruct the image of the dark lake and to send forth the inner call that would bring her raven to her side. She wanted only to float in the friendly darkness, but Octha's voice was insistent, and so, painfully, she moved to the gate, and image by image, summoned the landmarks of the spirit that would show her the way home.

By the time she had recovered control of her limbs and was able to sit up again, her memories were fading.

"What is it?" she asked, looking at the grim faces around her. "What did I say?"

"You called out to Tir, and told us," said Baldulf, "to beware the Sword of War."

For a moment she closed her eyes. "I remember," she said finally, "it blazed in the sun."

"What does it mean?" Octha asked then.

"I give you vision," answered the wisewoman tartly. "It is for you to find the meaning." Then a fragment of memory came to her. "But in the land of the Huns, I have heard, there were once great smiths who forged seven magic swords for the god of war."

"There are no Huns here," said Colgrin.

"Perhaps not. But there are swords. Make an offering to Tir before you fight, and perhaps he will spare you."

"Tir is a god of justice, not mercy," muttered one of the men, but Hæthwæge shook her head and would say no more.

The earth trembled beneath the tread of the warriors as the Saxon army marched out to meet its foe. Their footsteps rang hollow from the great arch of the gate and pigeons fluttered screaming from the cornices. Then five hundred spear butts smote as many shields, and thunder leaped from earth to heaven. Oesc, a helm drawn down to hide his features and a tattered cloak concealing his lack of armor, felt himself become one with the men who were crowding through the gate. The driving rhythm over-

whelmed thought and hearing, and with it, the fear that even now his
father might somehow discover he had disobeyed and send him back.

Then they were through the gate, and the crush eased as men began
to spread out into the wedge formation called the Boar's Head. Faint
through the thunder he could hear the blare of British trumpets, then the
irregular drumming of hoofbeats blurred the rhythm of spear and shield.
In the next moment the British horsemen struck the Saxon line, and the
thunder gave way to the clash of steel.

Oesc was lifted off his feet for a moment as the shock of the charge
drove the man on his left against him. Then the Saxons steadied, spears
bristling outwards, and began to drive forward against the foe. Oesc got
his breath back just as a horseman in a scarlet cloak crashed through. He
made a clumsy sweep out and heard the horse scream. Then another man
thrust upward and the rider fell, blood spraying red around him.

The boy stared, but there was no time to worry about his reaction.
Another enemy, dismounted, was slashing wildly with a long Roman cavalry spatha; a Saxon fell, then Oesc jabbed and caught the blade with his
spear. The impact jarred down the shaft, almost knocking him over, but
in the next moment two warriors speared the Briton through the body and
he went down.

A figure in Roman armor loomed up before him and he thrust, then
stared in horror as his point sank in and the man's face contorted in agony.
Oesc jerked the spear free, shuddering. Again and again his swordmaster
had told him that in battle there was no time for thinking. He had never
explained that no sane man would want to think about what his blade was
doing as it tore through flesh and bone.

Then another figure lurched towards him, and without his will he
turned, taking the attack on his shield and jabbing back until his foe fell
or the tide of battle tore him away, he never knew which, and the next
enemy came on.

Some endless time later, a scream from overhead recalled him to
himself. His spear had broken, and the short seax was in his hand. All
around him, Saxon warriors were staring upward, their arms faltering as
the raven wheeled above them, alternately black and white as the sunlight
flared from its wings. He saw the litter in which the British king had been
carried to the battlefield, and near it his father, staring upward with a face
as anguished as his own.

But the British returned to the attack with courage renewed. "Cathubodva, Cathubodva, Raven of Battle," they cried.

Oesc yelped at the sting as a spear tip sliced across his shoulder and
got his shield back up, striving to shut out that dreadful keening cry. The

enemy spear struck again and he felt the wood begin to crack, then two shadows flickered past and it seemed to him he heard a deep voice crying—

"Stand fast, son of Woden, and you shall have the victory!"

Wind swirled in the dust of the battlefield; suddenly the air had a bite that tingled through the veins. Now it was his enemy who paused. Oesc glanced up and saw two smaller, darker, ravens, engaging the first one in a deadly aerial dance. *Hyge and Mynd*—he thought. *Hæthwæge has called on the god!*

The British raven screamed her fury, and the two attackers replied, and as those cries clashed in the heavens, to Oesc's blurred vision his opponent was revealed as a monster, the foulest of etin-kin. The burning in his belly erupted in a scream of fury, and casting away both seax and shield, he leaped upon his foe.

It was a Sword of Light, searing through mind and vision, that separated man from monster and mind from madness. When Oesc came to himself he was on his hands and knees, with the iron taste of blood in his mouth and his chest and arms splattered with gore. Guts roiling, he struggled to his feet. All around him those who could still stand were doing likewise. Only near Uthir's litter were men still fighting, but as Oesc stumbled towards it, an arc of brightness seared his vision once more.

For a moment he saw, red against the radiance, a figure who rose from the ruins of the horse-litter, wielding in his single hand a Sword whose stroke scythed down all foes within a radius of ten yards. Then the light flared beyond his strength to bear it. Sobbing, he sank to his knees, arm raised to shield his eyes from that deadly flame.

And then it was gone.

The plain light of day seemed dim in contrast. But there was enough of it for Oesc's recovering vision to make out the body of his father, blood still pumping from the stump of his neck. The head had fallen a few feet away; its features still bore a look of appalled surprise.

Scarcely knowing what he did, Oesc crawled forward, pulled off the remnant of his cloak, and began, fumbling, to wrap the head. As he did so, one of the stricken figures stirred. It was Baldulf. Groaning, he gained his feet, then stopped short, features contorting with grief as he saw the boy, and the headless body of his lord.

He cast a quick glance around him, then limped forward.

"Tir's judgment fell against us—" he said hoarsely, "the field is lost, but our hope lives so long as you are alive."

Oesc looked up, dimly aware that most of the figures that were be-

ginning to move around them wore British gear. Beyond Octha's body he
could see the British king sprawled among his cushions, in his hand a
sword whose brightness still hurt the eye. Baldulf took a step towards it,
but the British warriors were too close. Swiftly Baldulf gathered up Octha's torque and his seax. Then he hauled Oesc to his feet and hurried
him away.

There was no wind.

Oesc was never able to recall much about the journey that followed.
His wound went bad, and at times he was fevered, but mostly he simply
did not want to remember. At some point Hæthwæge found them. He did
recall the foul taste of the herbal teas she brewed to bring down his fever,
as her compresses and charms fought the infection in his arm. For three
nights, he was told, they had hidden in the forest, waiting for the crisis
and muffling his delirious mumblings when British search parties went
past.

Of that, the boy had no recollection. All he retained were visions of
a dark land and a dark lake beside which he wandered, calling his father's
name, until the wisewoman came walking through the shadows, her raven
on her shoulder, and led him back to the light of day.

And through all his illness, and the travel that followed, the head of
Octha, hid now in a leather sack and packed with leeks to preserve it,
stayed by his side.

Travelling mostly by night, they fled to the East Saxon lands, where
they found a boat to carry them across the broad mouth of the Tamesis.
After that, they were in Hengest's country and could move openly, following the old Roman road between the sea and the North Downs. By
then, of course, word of their coming had gone before them, and Hengest
had sent an escort and a horse litter in which Oesc could travel like the
British king.

But Uthir was dead. Even in hiding, they had heard that news. The
High King of the Britons had died after the battle and left no heir. If the
Saxons had lost the battle, and with it the greatest of their own leaders,
at least that much had been achieved, and they, like the British, would
have time to heal before the warring began once more. Better still, the
rumor was that Merlin, the witega who had caused such devastation with
his magic, had disappeared.

For Oesc, life began once more when they drew up in front of the
meadhall Hengest had built in the ruins of Cantuware and he saw his
grandfather, tall and weathered as a storm-battered oak, waiting for him
there.

*   *   *

Oesc swung at the practice post set into the mud of the yard, wincing as the wooden blade hit the straw that had been bound around it and the impact jarred the weak muscles in his arm. In the three months since Verulamium his flesh had healed, but it still hurt at times. Since he left his bed, he had spent his days in ceaseless motion, hunting, running, even chopping wood for the fires. And whenever Byrhtwold was free, he had pestered the old warrior to give him more work with the sword.

His body was fined down to bone and sinew, and day by day he could feel his arm growing stronger. But no exercise he had tried could make his heart strong enough to deny the pain, and though each night he fell into bed, too tired to move, the hours of darkness brought dreams from which he would wake whimpering, his vision seared by a sword of fire and his cheeks wet with tears. But once awake, though his throat ached with grief, he could not cry.

Only when it grew too dark to see the post did Oesc give up. From inside the hall he could hear voices, but the yard was empty. Above the wall the first stars were glittering in the deepening blue of the sky. A bird flew towards the trees, crying, and then it was still once more. Now that he had stopped moving, fatigue dragged at back and shoulders. Sweat drying cold on his skin, he stumbled towards the hall.

After the brisk air outside, the warmth was welcome. His stomach rumbled at the scent of boiling beef and he realized that he was hungry.

His grandfather was already in the high seat, long legs stretched towards the fire, his gaunt frame as splendid in its ruin as a Roman tower. Once Hengest had fought to master all Britannia, but now he was content to cling to the corner that the Vor-Tigernus had given him. But his son would never inherit it now.

At his feet sat the shope Andulf, head bent as he tuned his harp. Firelight glistened on the silver strands threading his brown hair. As Oesc approached, the shope straightened, and the murmur of conversation began to still. Once, and then again, he struck the strings, then, in a voice with the honey of sweet mead and the bite of its fire, he began to sing.

Eormanaric, noblest of Amalings,
Great king of Goths, who got much glory,
Fought many folk and fed his people,
Lost land and life to Hunnish horse-lords.

Hengest beckoned, and Oesc joined him on the broad bench. In a few moments one of the thralls brought him a wooden bowl filled with savory stew, and he began to gobble it down. The first bowl took the edge off his hunger. He held it out to be refilled, able to listen now to the mingled honey and gall of the tale of the great king who a century earlier had led the Goths to create an empire, and when the Huns invaded, lost it. From the Pontus Euxinus to the Northern Sea he had ruled, and from the Wistla to the great steppes, conquering tribes whose names were lost in legend. He had defeated Alaric, king of the Heruli who had made a kingdom north of the Maiotis, and controlled the trade routes to the western lands.

Mightiest among his warriors, Eormanaric had been a man of evil temper, who had the young wife of a chieftain who had deserted him torn apart by tying her limbs to four wild stallions. Her brothers sought to avenge her, splitting the Gothic forces at the moment when they most needed unity. And so the Huns had rolled over them and the Goths who survived fled westward, some to cross the Danuvius and seek service with Rome, and some to push all the way to Iberia, where now they ruled.

Fierce to his foes and to the faithless,
Betrayed by trampled traitors' kin,
In old age he embraced his ending,
His blood in blessing fed the ground. . . .

In the end, ran the tale, Eormanaric had taken his own life, seeking by the offering of his own blood to placate the gods.

"It is said that one should not praise a day until it is ended," said Hengest, when the last note had faded to silence. "I suppose that the same is true of a king. He lost his empire, but perhaps his blood bought some protection for his people, since they have prospered in their new land. At least his death had meaning. . . ."

"That is what King Gundohar said—" answered the shope.

"You knew him?" exclaimed Oesc. He had been aware that the man was a Burgund, his accent worn smooth by years of wandering, but he had thought that everyone close to the royal clan died when the Huns attacked them a quarter-century before.

"He taught me how to play the harp," said Andulf, his voice tightening with old pain. "It is he who wrote this song."

"But you don't look old enough—" Oesc broke off, flushing, as the men began to laugh.

"I was a boy, younger than you," said Andulf smiling, "serving in his hall."

"And now the Niflungar themselves are becoming a legend," added Hengest, shaking his head. "And yet I myself saw Sigfrid when he was only a child and I scarcely older. Who, I wonder, will the heroes of this time be?"

"The deeds of your youth are meat for the bards already, lord," said Byrhtwold.

"Do you mean the fight at Finnesburgh?" growled Hengest. "To keep one oath I was forced to break another, but it is not something I remember with pride."

"You will be remembered as the leader who brought our people to this good land!" said one of the other men.

"If we can hold it . . ." someone said softly.

"Does that matter?" asked Byrhtwold. "Hunnish horses pasture now in the land where Eormanaric died, and the heirs of Gundohar have found refuge in Raetia. Sigfrid left only his name behind him. But in death they triumphed, and they are remembered."

"Do you mean that if we succeed in winning all this island it will be Uthir and Ambrosius about whom men make the stories?" Guthlaf, one of the younger warriors, laughed disbelievingly.

"It may be so," said Andulf, frowning, "for the winners will belong not to legend, but to history." He began to slide his harp into its sealskin case.

The conversation turned to other matters, and as the drinking horns were refilled, grew louder. Oesc leaned against the hard back of the high seat, exhaustion dragging like a sea-anchor at his limbs.

"Send the boy to bed, Hengest, before he falls asleep where he sits," Byrhtwold said presently.

"I'm not sleepy!" Oesc jerked upright, rubbing his eyes. "Grandfather, Octha was a hero, was he not?"

The old man nodded, his eyes dark with shared pain, and the boy knew that he too was thinking of the lonely mound just within the wall.

"Do we have to choose?" he said then. "Do we have to choose between a glorious death and living for our people?" He waited, realizing that his grandfather was taking him seriously.

"Many men fall and are not remembered . . ." Hengest said slowly. "It is because they died for a reason that we honor heroes, because they never gave up, but fought to the end. Death is not a failure, Oesc, if a man has truly lived."

"Then he didn't fail . . ." whispered the boy. "We lost the battle and they killed him, but Octha had his victory. . . ."

"Boy, is that what has troubled you?" Hengest set his gnarled hand on Oesc's shoulder. "Your father waits for us even now in Woden's hall. You must strive to live so that you will be worthy to see him again."

The ache in Oesc's throat made it hard to breathe. He sucked in air with a harsh gasp, and awkwardly, his grandfather began to pat his back, then seeing his face, gathered him against his bony breast. And there, breathing in the scents of leather and horses and the old man's flesh, Oesc found at last the release of tears.

III

Holy Ground

Every fall, when the raiding season had ended and the crops were gathered in, it was Hengest's custom to travel around the territory that the Vor-Tigernus had given him. At this time of year, when the quarrels of the summer were still fresh in memory, the king heard complaints and rendered judgment, lest resentment, festering through the dark days of winter, should erupt into bloodfeud and destroy the peace of the land. In the second year after Verulamium, Hengest took his grandson Oesc with him on the journey, that he might learn the land and its law.

That fall the first of the winter storms came early, soaking the stubbled fields. But it was succeeded by a season of smiling peace, and the king and his escort rode through a landscape as rich in autumn color as heaped amber, splashed with the vivid scarlet berries of rowan and holly and the varied crimsons of the vine.

Their way first led south to the coast, where the Roman fortress of Lemanis still guarded the Saxon shore. They travelled by short stages, for the king's age would not allow him to do more. In the mornings, when he stretched stiff joints, swearing, he would say that next year, surely, he would let Oesc do it all. But by evening he was smiling, and the cold knot of anxiety in Oesc's belly would disappear.

From Lemanis, they worked their way back north and east along the shoreline to Dubris, where the high chalk cliffs looked out across the sea. Their next stop was Rutupiae, where the Vor-Tigernus's son had once driven Hengest into the sea. The fortress was in ruins now, only the great triumphal arch still proclaiming the vanished glory of Rome. Here, the rich lands by the shore were thickly settled, and the cases being brought for judgment mostly quarrels over boundaries or complaints about strayed stock.

They passed through Durovernum once more and then made their way eastward along the straight line of the Roman road that led to Londinium. To their left the land rose in gentle slopes to the North Downs, scattered with ruined villas and new Saxon farmsteads. To their right the green fields stretched down to the estuary of the Tamesis, sparkling in the sun. Where the ribbon of the road passed, habitations, or their remains, were most thickly clustered, and as they neared Durobrivae, the Roman town that guarded the crossings of the Meduwege and the western half of Cantuware, the land became more populous still.

"The British have got themselves a high king!" Red-faced and perspiring, Hrofe Guthereson shouted out the words even before he greeted his king. He had come out with his houseguard to escort them into the city, but with his news the whole party had come to a halt in the road.

"Who?" barked Hengest. "Has Leudonus finally got the southern princes to accept him?"

"No—" Hrofe shook his head, eyes sparkling. "It's a fifteen-year-old boy! Uthir had a son!"

Fifteen! thought Oesc. *My age. . . .* How strange to think that the battle in which he had lost his own father had so deprived another boy as well.

"Legitimate?" asked Byrhtwold.

Hrofe shrugged. "That's not clear, but Queen Igierne has claimed him as her child by the king."

"I remember hearing talk of a babe," Hengest said, frowning, "but I thought it died. . . ." Slowly they had begun to move forward again.

"They say he was sent away to the west country for safety, so secretly that even the folk that fostered him did not know who he really was."

Hengest smiled sourly. "Well perhaps they had some reason. When you are trying to get rid of a family of bears, you should attack the den."

"Well this one is a bear cub, right enough," said Hrofe. "Arktos, they call him, or Artor."

Artor . . . To Oesc's ears, that name rang like the clash of steel.

"And they accepted him on the queen's say-so?" Hengest said dubiously. "I know the British princes, and they would be hard put to agree that the sun sets in the west without nine days of arguing."

The walls were quite close now.

"It was not the queen's word that convinced them," said Hrofe, with the air of one who has saved the best for last. "It was because the boy could handle the Sword!"

The sword that killed Octha. . . . Oesc's stricken gaze met that of his grandfather, and he saw Hengest's face grow grim.

"I had hoped that accursed weapon would go with Uthir to his grave."

"Oh no—" Hrofe babbled on with hateful cheer.

Unable to bear it any longer, Oesc dug his heels into his mare's flank and pushed past the king and through the shadowed arch of the eastern gate into Durobrivae.

Shaded by an awning of canvas, Hengest sat in judgment in the forum for five long days. Oesc fidgeted beside him, the arguments half-heard, dreaming of the hunting he was missing while the weather held fair. His other grandfather used to spend a lot of time listening to men complain against each other too. Why, he wondered resentfully, would anyone want to be a king? But even the master of a farmstead had to settle disputes among his people, he supposed. The men the king judged were more powerful, that was all.

"And how would you decide this matter, Oesc—" Hengest said suddenly.

Blinking, the boy tried to remember what the man before them had just said. He was a big, fair, fellow with the lines of habitual ill-temper graven deeply around his mouth and on his brow.

"He says," the king repeated, "that his neighbor deliberately burned down his woodlot, and nearly destroyed his house as well."

"It is not so!" exclaimed the accused, glaring. "I only meant to burn the stubble from my fields."

"But you burned my woods!"

"Is it my fault if Thunor turns the wind? Blame the gods, not me!"

Oesc gazed from one man to the other, frowning, as he tried to remember the law. "Was it a large wood?" he asked finally. Hengest began to smile, and the boy continued more boldly. "Were there many big trees?"

"A very fine wood," said the plaintiff, "with noble oak trees!"

"Untrue! Untrue! There was one tree of some size, and around it nought but hazels!" The accused pointed at an older man in the front row of the crowd. "Tell them! You know the place—tell them what was there!"

Oesc stood up, having remembered the relevant traditions now. He cast a quick glance at this grandfather, who nodded reassurance, then held up one hand and waited until silence fell.

"It is the law of our people that compensation shall be paid for deeds, not thoughts. It does not matter why you started the fire," he told the accused man. "If you were so foolish as to burn stubble on a day of wind, and it did damage to the property of another, you must pay for it. The fine for damage to a wood is thirty shillings, and five shillings for every great tree, and five pence for each of the smaller."

"It is his word against mine as to what was there . . ." the man said sullenly.

"Your word, and that of your witnesses," agreed the boy. "Let each of you call those who will take oath to support your assertion, and so the fine shall be set according to the decision of your peers."

"Unjust!" cried the plaintiff, but the men in the crowd were nodding and murmuring their approval of the plan. Clearly the fair-haired man's taste for contention had not endeared him to his neighbors, for only two men came to his support, while the accused could choose from a dozen or more.

"Did I do right?" asked Oesc when the oaths had been sworn and the fine paid over.

"You did very well," answered the king. "That man is a trouble-maker whom I have seen in court before. A more reasonable man might have settled the matter with his neighbor privately, and not burdened us with it, but he got his recompense, and will not, one hopes, feel compelled to get satisfaction by burning the other man's hall."

"I know it is law that the man who set the fire should be held responsible, but it does seem unfair when he intended no harm," said Oesc thoughtfully.

"Do you think our laws were made to do justice? No, child, if my decisions keep our hot-headed tribesmen from killing each other I will be satisfied. It is each man's wyrd, not I, that will give him the doom that he deserves."

Oesc was glad when they left Durobrivae behind them and took the road once more. Now they moved southward, climbing the tree-clad slopes where the valley of the Meduwege cut through the North Downs. From time to time the trees would part and he could glimpse the river below them, carrying the waters that drained from the Weald, the great forest that covered the central part of the Cantuware lands.

As the day drew to its ending, the road dropped downward into the valley, and he saw the red-tiled roofs of a cluster of Roman buildings set on an oval mound, and beyond them the thatching of a Saxon farmstead amid the water meadows by the stream. Closer still, he realized that the structures on the mound were temples, and that the farm had been built on the foundations of a Roman villa. Here the Meduwege broadened, running chuckling over the stones of a ford.

"Who holds this place?" he asked as they came to a halt in the yard.

"An Anglian called Ægele who sailed in one of the first three keels that came with me across the sea. He lost a leg in the fight at Rutupiae, and I settled him here," his grandfather answered him.

"And who lives up there?" Oesc pointed toward a small square building with a peaked roof, surrounded by a covered porch on all four sides. Some of the tiles were loose, and in places the white plaster was flaking from the stones of the wall, but someone had recently raked the path.

"Ah—that is the other reason we have stopped here. I am not the only one who will find in this place a friend."

But it was not until the following morning that Oesc found out what Hengest had meant, when together they climbed the temple hill.

She could hear them coming up the pathway, the old man's tread heavy and halting on the gravel and the boy's footsteps a quick brush against the stones, his rapid questions abruptly cut off as they paused in the shadow of the porch. A breath of air set the lamp flames to leaping, lending life to the carven eyes of the figures carved on the altar, and elongating her shadow across the wall. Oesc stopped in the doorway and she put back her shawl, smiling as his eyes adjusted to the dim light and he saw her sitting there.

"Hæthwæge!" The delight on his face was like another lamp in the room. "Where did you come from?"

"Where have I not been?" She patted the bench that ran around the wall and the boy sat down. Hengest eased down on the opposite bench and sat with his veined hands crossed on the head of his staff, watching them. "I have been going up and down, searching out the holy places of this land."

Brought back to awareness of where they were, his eyes flicked uneasily around the small room. He had grown, she thought, since she had last seen him. At fifteen he was leggy as a colt, with the promise of strength in his bony shoulders and character in the line of his jaw, where the first fuzz of manhood was beginning to appear.

"And who did the Romans worship here?"

"That is their image of them—" She gestured toward the altar.

Waist-high, the edges of its flat top were scrolled and fluted, forming a canopy for a bas-relief that showed a seated goddess in a wide sleeved, pleated garment, and three standing figures in cloaks with hoods. The goddess held something, possibly a spindle, in her hand. Below the figures there had been a Latin inscription, but the stone was too worn to make out the words.

"But who *are* they?" he asked again.

"They are not Roman, though they are figured in the Roman style," Hæthwæge said slowly. "This is an old place, where the track that runs along the downs crosses the river. It was here before Rome, maybe even before the British came. I have sat out all night upon a barrow beside that trackway and listened to those whose bones lie there."

She shivered a little, remembering voices in the windy darkness. She still limped where her knee had stiffened after that night's out-sitting, but she did not grudge it. The Romans, she gathered, had not bothered to listen, but had fastened their own names onto the native divinities and confined them in new temples, ignoring the old powers of the hills. The ancient ones had been pleased, she thought, that someone was paying attention to them at last.

"Why?"

"To learn about the spirits of this land so that we can honor them and gain their blessing. I left an offering at the barrow before I came away. You must leave a portion, also, when you go hunting in the Weald."

Oesc took one of the lamps from its niche and squatted, holding the flame so he could see.

"Do you think the Lady could be Frige, and the hooded gods Woden and Willa and Weoh?"

"Little by little our tongue is replacing that of the Romans on the land. I do not think its gods will mind if we call them by our names," Hæthwæge answered, and heard in her head a whisper of approving laughter.

Old Man, be still, she told the god within. *It seems to me you have too many names already! Are you greedy for more?*

"But is that who they really are?"

Hæthwæge shook her head. "Child, there is no name a human tongue could master that would tell you that. In many places, the Britons called their Lady Brigantia. But perhaps these are the names they will bear for us here."

"That is why I have brought the boy," Hengest said then. "So that we may make our offerings."

The wicce nodded and got to her feet. Taking up the second lamp, she moved around the altar and held it high. Light glimmered warm on the worn grey stones of the well coping, and glittered on the dark water within. Enclosed within stone walls, this place was very different from the pool in the marshes of the Myrging lands, and yet the power of its waters was much the same.

"The shrine was built around this spring. It rises from the same waters that feed the river, coming down from the Weald and the Downs. They carry the lifeblood of the Lady of this land."

Hengest had risen as well. Now he took from his belt purse three golden coins that bore the blurred image of some long-dead emperor. Carefully he bent over the well.

"Gyden . . . Frige . . ." he said in a low voice, "I took this land by the sword. But the folk I have brought to live here will tend and till it in love and law. All my days I have been a man of blood, but I have no strength now to force men to my will. Let this land feed my people. . . ." His voice trembled. "And let me leave it in frith to the son of my son."

As he spoke the air inside the temple grew heavy, as if something very ancient and powerful had directed its attention that way. Then the coins splashed into the pool and the tension broke.

It took a few moments for the king to straighten. Then he sat down again, his old eyes moving from Hæthwæge to the boy.

The wicce felt a pang of pity for this ancient warrior who had outlived his own strength and all his companions and now, at his life's ending, sought in a new land the justification for his deeds. For a moment her memory went back to Oesc's other grandfather, Eadguth the Myrging-king, who had been so bound to his land that like an ancient oak, he could not be transplanted from his native soil.

"Now it is for the heir to make his oath and his offering," she said aloud.

Oesc set the lamp he had been holding on the rim of the well and knelt beside it, staring down into the pool. The current, welling slowly from the depths, broke the reflection into a scattering of gold, as if more wealth were breeding already from Hengest's coins.

Rather reluctantly, he unpinned the silver brooch that held his cloak, the only thing of value that he had on. Once more the atmosphere changed, this time to a kind of singing tension that lifted the hair on Hæthwæge's arms and neck. Oesc felt it too. He cast an uneasy look in her direction before turning once more to the well.

"Lady of the spring, this is for you." His voice cracked on the last word and he flushed, swallowing, and swiftly tossed the brooch in. "Let me be worthy of my grandfather's trust. Body and spirit I offer, if you will give me this land as a home for my children and my people. And please, Lady, let me one day know your true name!"

The tension built to an audible hum, like crickets on a day of summer, though the leaves were turning and the air outside had the crisp clarity of fall. It intensified to the edge of pain, then, very slowly, ebbed away, leaving behind it a great peace and the conviction that all would be well.

From Ægele's ford the road cut southward through the Weald, dwindling to a rough track by the time it reached the southern coast. There, the Jute, Hæsta, had settled his clan near the old Roman iron workings where a low ridge ran down to the sea. Just down the coast, the sea-fort of Anderida provided safe harbor, and with a good wind and a pilot who knew the shoals of the coastline, they could return to Lemanis by boat in no more than a long day's sail. Hæsta's other guests had ridden eastward from the South Downs, where Aelle had been lord of his Saxons for almost as long as Hengest had held Cantuware, though he was thirty years younger. The farmstead, where the rich fields sloped down toward the sea, lay on the border between the lands the two leaders ruled.

Hæsta himself had come down to escort his guests from the landing. As they approached his hall, more men came out of it—a thickset, muscular man with grizzled hair and a king's torque who they said was Aelle, and behind him a tall young man with red hair. The child he carried on his shoulder stared at the newcomers with bright, considering eyes.

"He has brought Ceretic, I see," said Byrhtwold, "and that must be Ceretic's young son. That's a man to watch, lad. If he fights half as well as he talks, he'll be calling himself a king too one of these days."

Oesc nodded, understanding that this was one of the men with whom he would have to deal, in friendship or without it, when his own turn came to rule. Hengest's bid to claim lordship over all the men who had come over from Germania had failed, and Aelle seemed content with his coastal hills. Despite their numbers, the Saxon settlements were scattered, each under its own chieftain—men who had never gone under the yoke of Rome and saw no reason to bow down before one of their own.

Octha might have united them, Oesc thought grimly, until his battle-luck failed. But no—it had not been bad luck that felled him, but the sorcery in Uthir's sword. *I might do it . . .* he thought grimly, *and Artor will be my opponent if I do.* Then they were dismounting, and Hæsta led them into the friendly shelter, its air blue with woodsmoke and the welcome scents of cooking food, of his hall.

That night, new clouds rolled in from the sea. For three days, rain and sleet kept the Saxons inside the hall. They scarcely noticed. Hæsta had been brewing for weeks in preparation for the feasting, and so long as the ale-vats did not run dry, no one would complain.

In a break between the discussions, Oesc sat by the long hearth, carving scraps of wood into crude figures of horses and split twig-men to ride them. As each one was finished, he gave it to the child beside him. Cynric, he was called, with hair as red as his father's, the legacy of the British grandfather who had given Ceretic his name.

"That is a mighty army—" said Ceretic, looking down at his son. Cynric nodded, took the rider that Oesc had just finished and set it in order with the others.

"These with the bark on are Romans, because of their armor, and the peeled ones are Saxons," the child explained. Several of the figures fell over and he set them up again.

"I see you are placing your unmounted warriors in a wedge formation—" commented Ceretic.

"*He* told me—" said Cynric, pointing at Oesc.

"It was what my father used at Verulamium." Oesc swallowed, his stomach knotting as he remembered that day.

"Ah, yes." Ceretic transferred his attention from the child. "You were in that battle, I have heard."

Oesc flushed. "Against my father's orders," he said with a quelling look at Cynric. "But I brought away his head so that the British should not dishonor it. I have sworn that I will avenge him one day."

"Perhaps we will march to battle together. For now, I am in Aelle's following, but my father rules in Venta, and he refused to acknowledge Ambrosius as his master. It is certain he will not bow before this child the British are calling high king!"

"You are British?" Oesc stared at him. But of course, he thought as he looked at the milky Celtic skin and bright hair, it must be true.

"My father is—" Ceretic's lips twisted wryly. "Maglos took my mother as a second wife when he made alliance with Aelle. I grew up speaking both tongues equally. My father likes Saxons because they are good fighters, and if this new high king tries to recover the lands around Venta, Maglos will need more men to defend them. So he has sent me to Aelle."

"Does Aelle have them?"

"Not enough—hence, this meeting. Your grandfather's people have held Cantuware long enough for there to be a few younger sons who need new holdings. If they come to the Isle of Vecta, my father will make no objections. But I will need to bring more men from Germania to settle the land around Clausentum, along the estuary of the Icene. From there I can drive northward into the heart of Britannia. Maglos thinks he can defend the land with Saxon settlers and still call it British. But when I rule in Venta, I can strike northward to the British heartland!"

Listening to him talk, Oesc understood how it must have been for Hengest and Horsa when they were young. But in Durovernum the scars of warfare had been repaired, the burnt houses scavenged for building material or allowed to go back to the soil. The British who remained there were grateful for the protection of their new masters, and the Saxons were rooting themselves ever more deeply into the soil.

"And what about you?" asked Ceretic, as if Oesc had been thinking aloud. "Will you push westward as well? You are young, with your name yet to win. Have you no ambitions to take Londinium?"

"Londinium and the British lands around it divide us from the Anglians in the fen country, as Lindum divides them from the north. We would be stronger if we could take it," Oesc added thoughtfully, "but the city was more important when there was trade with the Empire. In itself, it is not so useful now."

"Go around it, then. If I push northward and you move west, our armies can join forces, and who will stop us then?" He threw his head back, laughing. In the flickering light his hair was as red as the fire.

"What armies? Are you Woden, to breathe life into these sticks your son is playing with, and make them men? Let us wait at least until the seed is planted before we sell the tree!" exclaimed Oesc. "When you have brought your warriors from Saxony and I command the men of Cantuware, we may talk of this again."

"It is so! It is so!" shaking his head, Ceretic hunkered down and began to help his son pick up his scattered men. "Always, my dreams have outstripped reality. But it will happen. Among the Saxons a second wife has equal standing, and my mother went willingly to Maglos's bed. But the Christian priests called her a Saxon whore and me a bastard. I had to fight for every scrap of food and nod of approval, but the sons of my father's Christian wife were killed in battle, while I survived and took a wife from my mother's people. Maglos has no choice now but to trust to me and my Saxon kin to defend him. I have come too far already not to believe it is my Wyrd to be a conqueror."

Oesc believed him. Ambition pulsed around Ceretic like heat from the flame. *And what is* my *Wyrd?* he wondered then. But even as he questioned, a memory came to him of lamplight on dark water, and a breath of wind.

My Wyrd is to be a king. . . .

Hæthwæge dipped up a spoonful of broth, tasted it, and decided that she could add a bit more of the infusion of galluc root and mallow without rendering it so bitter the king would refuse to drink it down. As she poured, she bent over the pot, whispering—

"Galluc, Galluc, great among herbs,
You have power against three and against thirty,
Against poison and all infection,
Against the loathsome foe that fares through the land. . . ."

In her mind's eye she saw the plant from which that root had come, its broad leaves frosted with prickles, the pale pink-purple flowers trembling like bells in the breeze. *Boneset*, they called it sometimes, but it had great power also to heal internally. The mallow would soothe and smooth it on its way.

Hengest would not admit that he was ill, though the cough he brought home from his visit to Hæsta's hall had hung on throughout the winter, and his frame grew as gaunt as the horsehide hung over the poles at the offering pool. Her more elaborate curing methods were useless if the patient would not admit he needed them. All she could do was to doctor his food and drink as unobtrusively as possible, and sing her charms over her pots as she prepared them.

Eadguth had been much the same in his old age. *Why,* she wondered, *have I spent so much of my life nursing old men?* But the god she served appeared most often in an old man's guise, so perhaps it was not so surprising.

And to balance the old man she had the young one, although these days Oesc spent most of his time outdoors, hunting, exploring the countryside, even helping the farmers with the work of each season as it came. She supposed it was inevitable, after his dedication at the sacred spring. The goddess of the land was speaking to him in each tree and hill, and as time passed, he would learn to understand her.

Oesc came to the wisewoman for liniment for sore muscles, and sometimes to dress a wound, but on the whole he was a healthy young animal, for which she thanked the gods.

She stirred the broth once more, then dipped it carefully into a carved hornbeam bowl, its wooden surface smoothed to a rich patina by the years, and carried it from the cookshed across the yard to the hall. In the years since Hengest had built it in the space adjoining two of the better preserved Roman dwellings, trees had grown up on the western side, screening the weed-covered waste where half-burned houses had been pulled down to serve as building material. Afternoon sunlight slanted through the branches, glowing in the new leaves. A pattern of shadow netted the path.

As she passed, a portion of that shadow solidified into a human shape: a tall man, wrapped in a cloak and leaning on a staff. Hæthwæge stopped, eyes narrowing. *High One,* she queried silently, *is it you?*

As if he had felt the touch of her mind, the stranger straightened, turning toward the light. The wisewoman noted the dark eyes beneath their heavy brows, the brown beard where only a few strands of silver yet showed, and let her breath out in a long sigh. It was not the god. But neither, she thought as other senses picked up the aura that surrounded him, was this entirely a man. And knowing that, she thought she could put a name to him.

"Merlin Witega, wæs hal! Be you welcome to this hall!"

His eyes widened at the greeting, and some indefinable tension in his posture ebbed away.

"A blessing on you also, woman of wisdom. I had heard there was a bean-drui in the house of the king, and I think you must be she."

Hæthwæge bowed her head, accepting the compliment. She should have expected that he would be able to see beyond the old shawl and apron to her own aura of power.

"Come with me, then. The king has been ill, but he is well enough to speak with you. Perhaps he will be ashamed to fuss about drinking this down if you are by."

His broad nostrils flared, though it seemed unlikely he could pick up the scent from there. Then he began to ask if the king's cough had lasted for long, and she realized that he had indeed recognized the herbs.

"We were not certain whether Hengest was still living." His deep voice rumbled up from somewhere near his belly. "I knew him when I was a boy in the Vor-Tigernus's hall."

"He is old, but he still has his wits." Hæthwæge answered the unspoken question.

A swift grin of understanding split the flowing beard. "Then he will remember me. But it might be better if to the rest I were known only as a messenger." He said, and Hæthwæge, remembering how Oesc still blamed Merlin for the magic that had caused his father's death, had to agree. Then he pushed open the door and together they entered the hall.

He is an old man, Merlin told himself as they made their way past the empty feasting benches toward the high seat. *He cannot hurt you now.* Somewhere inside him there still lived a child who remembered Hengest as a towering force that could break him without even breathing hard. But in the man before him there was nothing of the Vor-Tigernus's war leader but the eagle gaze. *Who would have thought that the terrible Hengest would live to be so old?*

"Am I well?" Hengest echoed his question. "At my age it is enough to be alive. No doubt you seem ancient to Artor." He chuckled grimly. "I have outlived all my enemies, and most of my friends. But I will last until my grandson is old enough to rule. Uthir's son has the name of king already, but is it he or his council who have sent you here?"

"His council—" admitted Merlin. "But the boy is no weakling. In time he will be a powerful leader in peace or in war."

"I don't suppose you have come to say that Artor wants me to give back Cantium. Even the hotheads on his council must recognize that we have sunk our roots too deeply into this soil."

"Nor have I come to ask whether you will try to take advantage of Artor's youth to attack Londinium," Merlin answered pleasantly. "What my king and his council offer is a treaty to confirm your possession of these lands, in return for your support against any of the Saxon kings who would try to expand their territories."

Hengest gave a bark of laughter, took a sip of broth, and grimacing, set it down again. "Why come to me? I am not high king of the Saxon kind. Do you think they will listen to me?"

They may not obey you, old wolf, but they listen, thought Merlin as the old man went on. *What is it that you are not telling me?*

"While I live, the warriors of Cantuware will not march against you. I can give no surety for the others, nor even for what my grandson will do when he has drunk my funeral ale."

He looked up, a warmer light coming into his old eyes, but Merlin had already felt the stir in the air as a youth who stood, like Artor, on the threshold between boy and man, came in. He was taller than Artor, and fair where the other boy was brown, and in his gaze Merlin perceived something watchful, as if he had already learned not to trust the world, where Artor's gaze was still open and unafraid.

"Not for a long time, I hope," he said, sitting down at the old man's feet.

"This is Oesc, Octha's son," said the king. But Merlin had already recognized the set of the shoulders and something of Hengest about the line of brow and jaw. "He is the one who will have to deal with Artor, not I."

"Yes . . ." Merlin shut his eyes, shaken by a sudden inrush of images—Artor and Oesc side by side on a hill where ravens flew, at feast and at hunt, and again, older, striving to meet amid the blood and terror of a battlefield. As foes or as allies? And if they fought, which one would have the victory? That knowledge was not given.

Then the moment of vision faded. When he looked up again, Oesc and his grandfather were still talking, but the witch-woman, Hæthwæge, was watching him with troubled eyes.

"If you wish to keep your anonymity," she told him when the interview was over, "you had better come with me. I will tell the thralls to bring food for us both."

Merlin nodded. He would lose the chance to pick up whatever revealing gossip the men might share in the hall, but it seemed to him that he knew the answer to his question already. Cantium would stay quiet, but the council had better keep a sharp eye on the South Saxons and the Anglians from now on. This wisewoman, on the other hand, clearly had considerable influence with both the old man and the boy. He could not afford to leave her a mystery.

He sensed a prickling beneath his skin as he entered Hæthwæge's house and smiled a little, recognizing in its pure form the feel of the wardings he had noted in the hall. Flame leaped as she built up the fire, and he looked around him with a fellow-professional's curiosity. Since his studies with the Vor-Tigernus's wise men when he was young he had had little to do with other workers of magic.

His nostrils flared at the mingled odors, spicy or musty or sour, that swirled around him, and with them the mingled currents of power. A witch he had called her, and the drying herbs that hung from the rafters, the sacks and baskets and packets ranked neatly on their shelves, confirmed it. What else she might be he could not yet tell.

Hæthwæge poured mead from a Roman flask into a silver-mounted drinking horn. "Do not fear," she said when for a moment he hesitated, "I know better than to set a spell upon it beyond a blessing on the yeast to make it brew, even if I thought such a thing would escape your notice."

"I did not doubt you," he said stiffly. He drank, savoring the fiery sweetness, and handed the horn back to her, then seated himself on the bench beside the fire.

The wisewoman drank in turn and took her place across from him.

She was a woman who would look much the same from her middle years to extreme old age, deep-breasted and broad-hipped, with a lacing of silver in her hair—ordinary, in fact, with no claim to beauty, until you met her eyes.

Those eyes held his now, with a silvery glow that hid the depths behind them like light on a pool.

"You ask Hengest what he will do with his warriors, as if those were the only powers at war over this land. Of another messenger I would have expected that, but not of you. Have you come to spy out our defenses, as you did when you rode the body of the bird at Verulamium?"

Merlin suppressed a shudder, remembering that day. Then the sense of what she had said reached him.

"That was you, with the ravens, opposing me?"

"For a little while—until it became a battle between your goddess and my god. You should know that Woden has long been a friend to the goddesses, and he will seek to learn her wisdom. Even then, it was not she who defeated him, but the god in the Sword. Will it kill its new master as it did your king?"

"Artor is its destined master, the Defender of Britannia. When he draws it in a just cause, it will bring him the victory." Remembering the particular pulsation of power the Sword carried, he became abruptly aware that he was sensing something similar here.

He turned, attention fixing on a long shape in the corner, swathed in leather wrappings and spells. Now that it had attracted his attention, its power overwhelmed all the other magics in the room. Behind him, Hæthwæge had gone very still.

"I should have realized that against you, the magics that hide it from other men would be useless . . ." She spoke slowly, as if listening to some voice within. "But perhaps . . . it was meant that you should see it." She moved slowly to the corner and began to unfasten the wrappings, and he saw that it was a spear.

For one moment only Merlin glimpsed the physical form—the wooden, rune-carved shaft and the blade of translucent stone. Then its power swirled through his senses in an explosion of meaning; its shaft a chain of incantations, its blade piercing the heart with pure song. Altered vision perceived it limned in light, as bright as the radiant being who was offering it to him.

"Take it by the shaft. . . ." Through his confusion he realized that Hæthwæge was speaking.

With an effort he managed to answer. "What will happen if I do?"

"You will know the god . . ."

"Woden? He is no god of mine!"

"You may say so, but still you bear a part of his wisdom in this world. You do not know him, but he knows you, and he claims this holy ground. . . ."

"Is it a weapon?" He mumbled, thinking it might be his duty to seize it. "Will your kings bear it against the Sword?"

"It is a weapon, but not for war . . ."

Sound came and went. He was not certain of her meaning, only of his own rejection of what she was telling him. And then the power was muted. Ordinary vision returned, and he saw that she had replaced the wrappings around the spear.

"I have walked this land through the seasons, and Woden went with me," said Hæthwæge. "He likes this country and will stay here. He says to me that you will serve him also, and it will be easier if it is with your will."

Merlin shook his head. "I serve the Lady of the Land."

"Of course," said the wicce, "but in time to come, their purposes may prove to be the same. . . ."

IV

The Ostara Offering

A.D. 477

In the second year after his acclamation, the High King of Britannia kept the feast of the Resurrection at Sorviodunum on the borders of the Dumnonian lands. The Roman town had been burned during the first Saxon rebellion and only partially rebuilt afterward. Merlin, riding in behind Artor's houseguard, had thought the intervening years would have faded his memories, but instead, the ghosts of Ambrosius and Uthir now haunted it along with the shades of those who had been murdered by Hengest's men.

The little church, only lightly scorched, remained. While Artor heard the Pascal mass inside with Docomaglos of Dumnonia and his sons, the rest of the princes and notables waited with more or less patience in the open area around it, nourishing their spirits on the incense that drifted from within, and the earthier scents that drifted from the cauldrons where the feast was being prepared.

Merlin sensed the strength of the mystery that was being celebrated within those whitewashed walls, but the power that he was feeling did not come from the church, but rather flowed through it, drawing him northward through the gate to stand staring across the plain. To the north lay the Giant's Dance. He could not see it, but he could sense its presence. As the Christian ritual built to its climax the power moving along the line between them increased until he could see a pathway of light. Did Uthir's spirit ride that road from his grave by the ring of stones to the church where his son knelt in prayer?

The druid lifted his hands in salutation as the light flared and then began to fade. With its passing, he was aware of the fragile balance of light and darkness as the world stood poised for the explosion of growth that the approaching summer would bring. Always, in the old days, men had propitiated those forces at this time with an offering. The Christian priests said the death of their god was a sufficient sacrifice for all times to come, and from the point of view of the divine powers, that might be so. But it seemed to him that sometimes it was men, like Abraham in the Christians' stories, who needed to make an offering.

Light filtered coldly through the interwoven branches to illuminate the features of the British princes. Brush had been bound over a framework of beams to shelter the council, since there was no building in Sorviodunum that would hold them all. The fire that burned in the center seemed to produce more smoke than heat, which might also be said, thought Merlin, of the arguments.

Artor had a place close to the fire, with Merlin behind him. From habit, the druid cloaked his aura. The British chieftains, at first inclined to be suspicious of his motives, had become accustomed to his silent presence. They did not accept his influence on the boy so much as ignore it.

"Last year they came by the hundreds, and the year before!" exclaimed Catraut, who had fought his way through two ambushes on his way down from Verulamium. "As a dead horse breeds maggots, Germania breeds men. Who knows how many more will arrive when the sailing season begins? There are so many Anglians now they have brought over their King Icel to rule them, with his lady and his sons, while *you*—" he swept an accusatory finger towards the Dumnonian lords, "flit back and forth across the sea to Armorica like migrating birds, preparing cozy nests to which you can flee when by sheer pressure of numbers the Saxons have crowded us into the sea!"

Docomaglos, who had inherited Dumnonia after his brother Gorlosius died, bristled indignantly, while his sons, Cataur and Gerontius, looked uncomfortable. "My home is in Isca of the Dumnonii, and I will defend it to my life's end!"

"That may be so," Catraut continued implacably, "but can you deny there's scarcely one of your lords who does not have a cousin or a brother waiting to welcome him across the narrow sea? You must forgive those of us who do not have such a refuge if we say that your risks and ours are not the same!"

"My lords, my lords—" Eldaul of Glevum extended a placating hand. "We have been hearing these arguments since the days when the Vor-Tigernus strove with Aurelianus. The men of the east protest their sufferings, and those of the west, their loyalty. If we had all been willing to aid each other then, we might not face this threat today. . . ."

There was an uncomfortable silence. Artor, whose eyes had begun to glaze, roused suddenly, looking around the circle. In the past year he had added several inches to his height, and he was beginning to learn how to manage his long limbs.

"It seems to me, my lords, that Eldaul speaks truly, and since it is so, surely we ought to be taking council on how we may meet the threat instead of wasting our energy accusing each other!"

For a moment they stared, as if one of the posts had grown a mouth to speak to them. Then Merlin saw their expressions change as they remembered that it had been their decision to make this boy their king. At this point, one might wonder if they had really meant it, or whether, to paraphrase that bishop Augustinus whose new ideas were upsetting everyone, they had prayed God to give them a king, "but not yet."

"My lord, it is clear that we must mount a campaign in the midlands," answered Catraut finally, "to destroy this Anglian kinglet before he is firmly seated in his power."

"From where you sit, that may be clear," said Matauc, who had ruled the Durotrige lands from Durnovernum on the coast for many years, "but when I look eastward, what I see is that Devil's cub Ceretic in Venta Belgarum!" His tone remained mild, and Catraut, who had begun to frown, sat back again.

"*He* has been bringing in more men from Germania as well," said Cataur, "with their families, so it is clear that these wolves are after more than plunder—they mean to plant themselves on the land."

"Leonorus Maglos has been a traitor since the time of Ambrosius," answered Eldaul, "but he is concerned only with the Belgic lands."

"He is an old man—" Docomaglos's second son, Gerontius, spoke then. "Ceretic speaks for him now in Venta, and Ceretic thinks like a Saxon, for all he bears a British name."

Artor nodded. For the past year Gerontius had captained the men who guarded the king, ate at his table and slept by his door, hunted and played at *tabula* and taught him the art of the sword. It was inevitable that the boy would end by either loving or hating him, and Gerontius was as good-hearted and fair-spoken as he was tall and dark and strong. No wonder, then, if his young king listened with admiration in his eyes.

Cataur, seizing the opening, leaned forward. "The word that we hear from Venta is that Ceretic means to expand northward. Do you want to fight the Anglians with his Jutes and Frisians snapping at your heels? Icel is not yet firmly seated in his power, and he must bring those chieftains who have grown accustomed to living without a lord into line before he can lead them against us."

One or two of those present looked embarrassed at that, for what he had said of the Anglians was surely true of the British as well. But Cataur was continuing—"Ceretic's men are sworn only to him. Your argument for fighting Icel applies to Ceretic as well—let us cut out this canker on our flank before it grows!"

There was a murmur of comment at that. Artor allowed it to continue for several minutes before lifting his hand for silence once more. In two years he had at least learned how to manage a council, even if he did not yet always have the confidence to impose his will. Silently, Merlin projected his aura towards the boy and allowed some of his own energy to flow into it. To the others, there seemed only an intensification of his presence, which focused their attention until everyone was still. At first, the fifteen-year-old king had needed such bolstering constantly, but along with his father's armor, he was growing into his power.

"I think we agree we're going to have to fight somebody—" Artor's grin was reflected in the faces of some of the younger men. "And the choice seems to be between Icel and Ceretic. They are both dangerous. Tell me what we have to fight them with, and maybe that will help us to decide."

If you want to know how the colt will run, look at his breeding, thought Merlin, hearing echoes of Uthir's easy style. It sounded ingenuous, but clearly Gerontius had been talking, for it was obvious, when you looked at the problem, where the men and resources would have to come from if the British intended a spring campaign.

"By the end of this month my people will be done with the spring planting," said Docomaglos. "I can have three thousand men on Ceretic's doorstep before he gets word we are moving. We can hit hard and fast and drive him into the sea by Pentecost."

"That reasoning seems good to me—" answered Artor. "Catraut is right—Icel is a problem, but I think we'll tackle him with more confidence without Ceretic's spears pricking between our shoulder blades."

Merlin suppressed a smile. Uthir would have said ". . . poking up our backsides." But without the crudities, the boy certainly seemed to have inherited his father's knack of putting men at ease. The northern princes not only dropped most of their objections, by the time the council ended, they had even promised to send men.

It was the sound of swordplay that led Merlin to the king. After dinner, most of the princes had gone back to sit and talk and drink by their campfires, watching the daylight fade from the sky. When the druid went to look for Artor, he found that most of the younger men had disappeared.

He hardly needed magic to find them. Just outside the town, where the river flowed quiet through grassy meadows, two figures strove, shadow against shadow, the last of the sunset flickering from their swinging swords. After the first shock Merlin realized that they were doing slow work, bodies moving with the graceful deliberation of dream. But it was still dangerous. He drew breath to stop them, then let it slowly out again. He could not keep the boy swaddled forever; Artor was almost a man.

But it was a boy's voice that protested, laughing—"But how can I touch you, Gerontius, when I can hardly see?" He danced back out of range and stood leaning on his sword, breathing hard.

"If the enemy makes a night attack you won't be able to see, or in the dust of the battlefield, or if you take a head wound and blood blinds you." Gerontius straightened, his voice cool and unstressed.

A third figure, by his voice, Cai, spoke up—"At least in battle you don't have to worry about hurting your enemy."

"If you can see which ones *are* the enemy," said Artor. "Once battle is joined, Gerontius, how do you *know?*"

"If his spear is pointed at your belly, he's an enemy!" said one of the others.

"If he shouts at you in Saxon—"

"If he's facing the opposite direction from your line—"

"Artor is right—" Gerontius cut into the discussion. "In the confusion of battle it can be hard to tell friend from foe, especially now, when our warriors and the Saxons copy each other's gear. What I am trying to do with this exercise is to teach you to perceive your opponent with senses other than sight or even sound."

"Ah . . . Merlin has showed me something of that . . ." said Artor. "He said you have to sense your enemy's energy, to become one with him. But I'm not good enough to risk it with the blade, so—" He stooped suddenly, scooped up something from the grass and flung it.

There was a blur of movement and then a thunk as Gerontius's sword struck the incoming missile and smote it to bits.

"Wretch!" he said, over his students' laughter. "If that was a cow patty, I will make you clean this blade."

"No," Artor caught his breath on a whoop, "only a piece of sod."

"Very well." Gerontius tried to sound stern. "And now it truly *is* dark, so I suppose we must bring this practice to an end. There should be time for some more work tomorrow morning, however, before the *consilium* begins again."

"Not more meetings!" exclaimed Cai over the murmur of talk as they began to gather up their gear.

"Do you think that several thousand men and all their gear are moved into place by magic, as they say Merlin sang up the stones to make your father's monument? There is still a great deal of planning yet to do . . ."

As the group started back toward the buildings, Merlin fell into step beside them. Artor had learned enough to sense *his* presence—Gerontius started and went for his sword when the dark shape appeared at the king's elbow, but Artor only sighed.

"Your teaching is done for the evening, but there is still time for some of mine," Merlin said to the warrior. "Take the others back to camp. I have something to show the king."

"He must be guarded—" objected Gerontius.

"Do you doubt my ability to protect him?" He drew in a breath of power, holding it until even the warrior must be able to see his glow.

"Do you doubt that I will track you down and break every sorcerous bone in your body if you fail?"

"Stop it!" exclaimed Artor. "I feel like the bone, with two dogs growling over it. Go on, Gerontius. I'm sure we will be back soon."

"Yes, my lord—" Gerontius's voice was harsh with reluctance, but he obeyed.

"We *will* be back soon, won't we?" asked Artor when he had gone. "I've worked hard this evening, and I'm tired."

"No. But we will take horses, so you can at least sit down."

Artor stopped short. "Horses? Where are we going at this hour?"

Don't you trust me? thought Merlin, but trust and reason made poor bedfellows. He remembered suddenly something that the Saxon witch had told him about her god, that he sometimes seemed treacherous, betraying men for their own good, or some purpose greater still. Maybe he himself was a little like Woden after all. *If you learn to trust me in small things, that I can explain, perhaps you will obey when the time comes to follow my lead without knowing why. . . .*

"We go to the Giant's Dance. It lies six miles hence. If we go now we can be there before the moon is high, and I do not know when we will be in this part of the country again."

There was a long silence. "My father is buried there . . ." Artor said at last. "Very well. I will come with you."

The standing stones cast long shadows, stark in the moonlight. In silence Artor and Merlin rode around the circle. The plain stretched away before them to a horizon dim with distance, its pale, moonwashed expanse broken only by the line of mounds.

"Who set up those stones? What are they for?" asked Artor, eyeing the henge circle uneasily.

His father had asked the same thing. Remembering, Merlin began to tell him of the ancient tribes and how they had watched the stars.

"The plain is so empty," Artor whispered when he had finished, "as if we were the only living beings in the world."

Merlin looked around him, seeing with spirit sight the need-fire that danced above the mounds.

"The only ones living, perhaps—but these spaces are thronging with the spirits of those who have gone before. That is what I have brought you here to learn. All things pass, but nothing is lost."

Artor swallowed. "Where is my father's grave?"

Merlin pointed toward the last of the mounds, the one they had raised next to the mound of the lords killed in the Night of the Long Knives.

"He lies there, with Ambrosius his brother."

"I never knew him . . . If I could meet him now, I wonder what wisdom he might have for me?"

"They say that if a man sits out the night on a sacred mound, by morning he will be mad, or dead, or a poet. We must be back at the camp before dawn, but if you wish, you might sit there for a little while."

"Is it dangerous?" Artor's voice, the druid was pleased to note, held not fear, but a healthy caution.

"The dangers are those you bring with you," he answered. "Anger for anger, fear for fear. Remember what I have taught you, and you will do well."

And if he does not, I may as well go back to my northern forest and stay there, Merlin thought wryly, *for my life will not be worth a denarius here!* But his fear was not for the boy's physical safety. If Artor failed this testing, then everything for which Merlin had worked and suffered would be lost as well. And for the druid, this place held its own dangers;

it would be fatally easy to come too close to the nexus of powers that met here, and be drawn through into some other world.

And so, as the young king took his place upon the mound that held his father's bones, Merlin his teacher sat down upon a boulder a little to one side of the line of power that ran from it to the henge of stones, to watch with him while the moon sailed serenely westward and the skies wheeled towards dawn.

When, in the grey hour before sunrise, the druid called his charge to come down from the mound so that they could begin the ride back to Sorviodunum, the boy's face was drawn, his eyes scarcely seeming to focus on the world. It was not until they were nearly back to the encampment and the first streaks of light were awakening the sky that Artor sighed and the bleak look began to leave his eyes.

"Did your father speak to you?"

"Don't you know?" The boy's voice held mixed wonder and bitterness.

"You are a child of prophecy, as am I, but our choices are our own. And this was *your* mystery," Merlin said gently. *I must learn . . .* he told himself, *to let him go.*

"Yes . . . I think he did . . ." Artor answered then. But he would not tell what the spirit of his father had said to him.

Oesc caught the blur of motion against the blue sky and dodged, thrusting up his wooden shield. The stave thwacked home with a force that nearly knocked him from his feet. He stumbled backward, shield-arm throbbing.

"You blocked well, but you were off-balance," said Byrhtwold, resting the oak stave on the ground and leaning on it.

"That hurt." Oesc let the shield slip off and rubbed his shoulder.

"No doubt. But without the shield a blow like that would have broken your arm."

"If I had a weapon I could hit you back," said Oesc. "You act as if I were still twelve winters old!"

"Maybe, but if you lose your blade in battle, only your shield will save you until you can grab another weapon," the old man replied. "Because you have been in a battle you think you are a warrior. I think you have habits which you must unlearn. So we go back to the beginning. When you can hold me off with shield alone you can practice with the blade. In the meantime, keep strengthening your sword arm."

"Chopping wood?" Oesc asked with a sigh. "That's thralls' work, I only did it before to strengthen my arm."

Byrhtwold grinned. "But good practice. And if you cannot master the skills of the folk who serve you, how will you keep them to their work?"

Oesc nodded, recognizing the futility of argument, and Byrhtwold handed him the stave.

"Tomorrow morning we will practice again." Byrhtwold turned away, then paused, relenting. "Be patient, lad—you will be chopping something more than wood soon enough. Ceretic has asked that you come with the men your grandfather is sending to Venta Belgarum. You are going to war."

Oesc stood watching as the warrior walked away, his mind in a whirl. The morning was sunny, though great puffy clouds like hanks of wool were moving in from the west, casting dappled shadows across the wall of the old theatre that dominated the remainder of the city like an old oak, after a storm has blasted all the lesser trees. No doubt there would be rain before evening. When his father first brought him to Cantuware, he had thought the buildings that still stood in Durovernum the work of etins. Then he had seen Eburacum and Verulamium, noble still despite their battle-scars.

But Venta had never been destroyed. Venta had welcomed the Saxons as the rightful heirs to the empire, as Gallia was welcoming the Franks even now, and the Visigoths had been received in Iberia. Even Durovernum was becoming Cantuwaraburh on men's tongues. *We are the future,* he thought, and if he marched with Ceretic, his own name might live in that future as well.

Ceretic assembled his allies in the fields outside of the old naval fortress of Portus Adurni that another German, the admiral Carausius, had built long ago, and there they held the feast of Ostara. It was a tribal celebration, in the old style of Germania, meant to remind men of their common heritage. The penned animals moved anxiously, as if aware of their role in the proceedings, but the rest of the camp hummed with anticipation.

Scouts had confirmed the rumors. The British princes were advancing, led by Docomaglos of Dumnonia with his sons and the boy whom they had made their king. Leonorus Maglos had fled Venta, and Ceretic had no desire to test the enthusiasm of his allies by exposing them to a seige. It would be better to meet the foe in open battle on the flood plain across from the Isle of Vecta, where the estuary of the Icene met the sea.

In the midst of the fields was a fine grove of oak trees. Here, some Roman had set up an offering tablet to Mercurius. It had been abandoned when the Christians came and grown over with vines until Ceretic had claimed the place and raised beside it an altar of heaped stones.

Oesc stood holding the tether of the white ox that Hengest had sent for the sacrifice. Across the field he could see the fyrd of Cantuware, farmers who had left their fields at their king's command, and the professional warriors of Hengest's household who had come to guard his heir. The ox stamped, and rubbed its head against his thigh, rocking him on his feet and leaving a smear of white hairs across the crimson wool of his tunic and knocking off some of the primrose blossoms from the wreath around its horns, then bent and lipped up more of the grain that had been poured out for it. A little of Oesc's anxiety eased. It was holy corn, mixed with sacred herbs and blessed by the priests, and for the ox to eat it signified acceptance of its role as offering.

He could see Hæthwæge standing with the other god-folk who had been assembled to bless the proceedings: the ancient Godwulf, who had once served at the court of Vitalinus, and two witegas who had been brought over from Germania with the most recent shipload of warriors. From the eagerness with which they surveyed the cattle, he guessed it had been some time since they had had sufficient beasts on which to practice their craft.

In the space between the animals and the men of the army three tumblers were performing, while another beat out a cheerful rhythm on a small hand drum. As the day drew towards its nooning, the clouds began to part, and the bits of metal sewn to the players clothes flashed and glittered in the sun. Then the light broke through completely, and from within the sacred grove came the call of a horn.

The chieftains who held the nine white horses began to lead them forward, followed by the oxen. As the beast next to him moved out, Oesc jerked on the halter of his animal and joined the line. From the sound, the pigs were being brought up behind them; he pitied the men who had to keep *them* under control.

In slow procession, men and beasts moved sunwise around the grove. Aelle's son Cymen was just ahead of him, with another ox, even bigger than his own. Men of the fyrd stepped out from the encircling crowd as they passed, draping the beasts with additional garlands, or simply patting the smooth hides as they murmured their prayers—"Let me fight bravely!" "May I kill many of the enemy!" and sometimes, "May the gods bring me safely home."

As they came around for the second time, each animal was led inside the grove. The beasts were becoming more restive as the blood-scent grew stronger, but when Oesc's turn came the ox followed docilely down the well-trodden path.

The heads and skins of the earlier victims already hung from the trees. Now the ox did plant his feet, nostrils flaring, and though the boy tugged on the rope, refused to stir. As Oesc struggled to make it move, Hæthwæge came forward, singing softly, a spray of ash leaves in her hand. He recognized "Ger" the rune of harvest, and "Sigel" for victory. At the sound, the ox calmed and stood quietly as the wicce moved around him, brushing the leaves across head and back and flanks.

Ceretic came after her, a knife in his hand. He cut a pinch of hair from the curling cowlick on the animal's forehead and stepped back, holding it high.

"Woden, to you this ox is offered, for you made holy. Accept it, Warfather, and give us the victory!"

The air around the altar tingled with the energy of the blood that had been spilled already. As the war-leader spoke, wind whispered in the leaves and lifted the hair from Oesc's brow, and as Ceretic opened his fingers, the white hairs whirled away.

Hæthwæge's fingers closed over Oesc's hand on the rope, and the ox followed them to the altar, where the butcher was waiting. He was a huge man, heavily muscled, with a hammer in his hand. As the ox reached the edge of the blood pit, he swung. There was a loud thunk as the hammer hit, and the ox went to its knees.

For a moment Oesc simply stared. Then he remembered to draw his seax, and Hæthwæge guided his hand to the pulsing vein in the throat of the ox and he struck and pulled the blade through.

The animal jerked, but within seconds the gush of blood dropped its internal pressure past the point of pain and the breath sighed out through the sliced windpipe in long gasps. Like everyone, Oesc had helped with the butchering each autumn, and when he was hunting, given the mercy stroke to hares or deer. Death was always serious, but he had never before understood that it was holy.

"Make your prayer now—" whispered the wisewoman, holding a brass bowl underneath the ox and letting it fill with blood.

"Woden, receive this spirit, and fill us with your soul. Father of Victory, bring my men back home to their fields, and me to my grandfather's hall!"

The eyes of the ox were dull already, and he could feel the life of the body ebbing from the flesh beneath his hands like grain from a torn bag. But the grain still existed even when the bag was empty, and he had the sense that the life of the ox had not been extinguished so much as drawn away.

Your flesh will give us power! he thought. *May my own blood, when the time comes, be as good an offering!*

The blood was draining now in spurts. Hæthwæge took Oesc's arm and pulled him to his feet, and as the last of the flow dribbled into the pit, men looped ropes around the ox's feet and hauled it away to be skinned and butchered for the feast that would follow. The wicce dipped the spray of leaves into the blood and sprinkled Oesc, then handed it to the boy and gave him the bowl.

Still dazed, Oesc made his way out of the grove to bless the men whom he hoped to lead to victory.

The armies came to battle three days later, under weeping skies. The Saxons formed their shieldwall on the shores of one of the streams that came down to the sound, feet planted in the muddy soil, watching the British cavalry sweep towards them across the plain. Rather than creating a solid line, Ceretic had ordered each contingent to form a wedge, so that more of the spears could come into play. It was a saw-edge that would cut the British to pieces, he had told them, riding up and down along the river bank.

Now the commander stood with his hearth-companions at the center, his white horse led off by a thrall to the rear. If he turned his head, Oesc could see the gleam of the gilded boar image that crowned the steel crest of Ceretic's helmet. On the other side, Aelle waited with his sons beside him. Oesc's helm was rounded, with a nasal and side flaps, and ringmail hanging around the back and sides. Beneath tunic and mail shirt he was sweating, but most of his men would fight with no more protection than a leather cap banded in iron, bodies defended only by their shields.

Beyond the reed beds, pewter-colored waters stretched away to a smudge of darker grey that was the island. Above the army, gulls rode the wind, crying like wælcyriges seeking out the slain. Soon they would be able to make their choices. The British were drawing steadily closer, trotting in close formation. Their shields were painted Roman-fashion, each contingent bearing its own device. He could see the glitter of their lance-heads as they came on. Perspiration made his hand slip on the shaft of his own throwing spear. Oesc leaned it against his shield, wiped his palm on the skirts of his tunic and grasped the javelin once more. Hæthwæge had a spear, he thought suddenly, as powerful as Artor's legendary sword. Why, he wondered, had Hengest not ordered her to bring it to war? When they got home he would ask her.

If he got home. . . . The British were cantering now, nearing with appalling speed. Surely the river would slow them, he thought, and then the hooves of the horses were churning the water into arcs of glittering spray. They surged up the bank like a rising wave, lancepoints dipping in deadly unison.

Oesc set his feet in the mud, lifted his left arm and felt his shield braced by those of Byrhtwold on one side and Eadric on the other, and raised his right arm, spear poised to throw. Wild-eyed horses expanded to fill his vision, the faces of the riders contorted above their shields. He felt a yell leave his throat, lost in the roar of the Saxon battle cry.

A ripple of motion swept the shield wall. Instinctively his arm swung forward, releasing the spear. Here and there the oncoming tide of horsemen faltered, but that first flight of spears was not enough to stop them. Oesc hunched behind his shield, straining to hold it in place between the others as an oncoming horseman struck the line.

The shieldwall rocked backward, and for a moment Oesc was lifted off his feet, but he did not fall. The enemy horse, pierced by spiked shieldbosses, reared, screaming. A lance thrust down at him, passing just above his shoulder. Oesc managed to get his sword free, and glimpsing a mailed body, stabbed upward. For a moment he felt as if he were supporting the entire weight of man and horse, then the foe recoiled and he caught his breath once more.

The British riders had broken the shield hedge in several places, and were in amongst the Saxons, stabbing with lance and sword. Others had swirled off to either side in an attempt to outflank them. Over the tumult Oesc glimpsed a dragon banner that he supposed must belong to Artor. It was being carried by a big man with dark hair. Then a horse loomed suddenly above him; a sword clanged against his shield boss and he gave ground, and for a long time after that was too busy to think about anything at all.

Consciousness returned gradually on a tide of lamentation.

Why are they weeping? Am I dead? Oesc wondered. But the dead didn't feel pain, and as awareness returned he realized he had a raging headache and was sore everywhere. For a few moments he lay still, trying to remember.

Then a flash of memory showed him Byrhtwold lying sprawled before him with a spear thrust through his chest. After that he had been seized by battle madness. That must be why he felt so awful now. *They must be wailing for Byrhtwold,* he thought then, and felt hot tears on his own cheeks. *He died saving me.*

Oesc opened his eyes. Blurred vision showed him a night sky and the shapes of men moving back and forth between him and the fires. Then he tried to sit up and discovered that his hands and feet were tied.

Alarm shocked through his body, sharpening his senses. The lamentations he heard were in the British tongue, and the faces and gear of the men around him were British as well. He had been taken by the enemy.

He knew enough of their language to make out the words—

Before Gerontius, scourge of the foe,
I saw white horses swiftly go,
After war cries, bitter the blow . . .

At least, he thought with grim satisfaction, the Saxons had accounted for one hero among their enemies. The British were not rejoicing, and yet he was a prisoner, his mail shirt enough to mark him as worth saving for ransom. Who had won the battle?

He took a deep breath and tried to break his bonds, and at the effort agony slashed through his head, dividing him from consciousness once more.

When Oesc opened his eyes again, it was morning. His other wounds had stiffened painfully, but the headache had subsided to a dull throb.

"Yes, that's him—" said a Saxon voice nearby. "Octha's whelp. I saw him in Venta."

Biting his lip to keep from groaning, Oesc rolled over. Squinting against the sunlight, he looked up at his captors. The Saxon was only a churl, of no importance. He blinked, trying to make out the features of the other two men.

"Let me kill him!" said one of them, a man of about thirty years with curling dark hair. "My brother's blood cries out for vengeance."

"Do you think I don't mourn him too?" said his companion. Oesc couldn't see him properly, but he sounded young, his voice hoarse with unshed tears. "He taught me to fight! He saved my life a dozen times yesterday . . . he was my friend. . . ."

"We all grieve for Gerontius, but this one is worth more to us as a hostage," said an older man.

"How so? He's no kin to Ceretic."

"True, but he is Hengest's grandson, and while we hold him, Cantium will stand surety for Ceretic's good behavior."

There was a long silence. Though his head was throbbing furiously, Oesc struggled to get up, refusing to remain bound like a thrall at his enemies' feet.

"Cut his bonds," said the young voice tiredly.

The older man sawed at the thongs with his knife and hauled Oesc to his feet, supporting him until the dizziness passed and he could stand alone.

Artor . . . thought Oesc, taking in the rich embroidery on the blood-stained tunic, and the golden torque beneath the thin fringing of brown beard on the jaw. He himself was a bit taller, otherwise there was little to choose between them for size.

"Can you understand me?" Artor asked, waiting for his prisoner's nod. "We didn't win the battle, but neither did you. You will come with us, bound by iron chains in a wagon, or bound not to try escape by oath before your gods, riding free. It's up to you."

Your father killed mine . . . thought Oesc. There was a dagger at the king's belt. If he could grab it and strike, Octha would be avenged. But at this moment it was taking all his strength just to stand. Once more he met Artor's eyes, and this time he could not look away.

He saw grief in that gaze, and a weariness almost as great as his own, and something else that he did not understand. Oddly, at that moment what he remembered was the trust in the eyes of the ox he had led to sacrifice. He had heard that the Christians of Eriu called it a white martyrdom, when they were exiled from their land. He swallowed, knowing himself self-doomed.

"I swear . . . in Woden's name. I am the offering."

V

The Raven's Head

A.D. 480

While Ceretic licked his wounds in the south and Icel gathered strength in the midlands, Britannia lay at peace. Even the Picts and the Scotti were keeping quiet, and Artor's advisors thought the time ripe for him to take possession of his father's city of Londinium. With him went his house-guard and his servants, and Eldaul of Glevum and Catraut of Verulamium, who had become his principal ministers. And with him also went Oesc, his Saxon hostage, riding sad and sullen in the rear.

Oesc's heart ached to think of his grandfather waiting for him in that shadowed hall. Hæthwæge would take care of the old man's health, but who now would play at tabula with him in the long evenings, or bring in venison when the salt beef of winter began to pall?

And more than he could have imagined, Oesc missed Cantuware. When he closed his eyes at night he could see how the waterfowl spiraled down into the marshes, or the wind brushed gentle fingers across the growing grain. He could see sunlight falling through the forest of the Weald in showers of green and gold, and blazing with pitiless clarity on the high shoulders of the Downs.

It was that day in the temple at Ægele's ford that had made the difference, he thought, looking backward. Sometimes he cursed Hæthwæge for having brought him there, and sometimes he took comfort in the memory. He was rooted now in Cantuware as deeply as if he had been born there, and away from it he would never be happy, even if he were free.

He was not badly treated. Rough repairs had made most of the old Governor's Palace habitable, and there was room enough for all of Artor's household there. Merlin had rooms in an old tower, but was rarely in them, being often away to other parts of Britannia, carrying messages, said some, while others whispered that he went off to consort with demons.

Oesc grew accustomed to carven pillars and marble facings and cold tiled floors. He had a whitewashed chamber to himself, with a shuttered window that opened out towards the river. Only sometimes, wandering through an empty passage or a courtyard where a dry fountain accused the sky, he remembered how he had felt once when he dressed up in his father's armor. It was as if he and all the others here were only children, playing at being kings, and soon the adults who had built these halls would reclaim their dwellings. Sometimes, watching Artor as he sat in splendor on the dais of the basilica, he wondered if the high king felt that way too.

But the legions were gone. Odoacer, a warlord among the Saxons whose father had been one of Attila's generals, ruled now in Italia, and unlike the barbarian generals who had gone before him, he refused to nominate a Roman as titular emperor. The Empire of the West was ended, and only in Britannia, and the parts of Gallia where Riothamus led British warriors whose families had fled the island after the Night of the Long Knives, did its memory live on.

On an afternoon in October, Oesc stood with the rest of the household in the basilica, watching as Artor welcomed a delegation from Gallia. He was placed near the front, with Cunorix, the son of an Irish chieftain who had been making trouble in Demetia. All the hostages were on display together, he thought bitterly, like the high king's sight-hounds, who lay panting on the mosaic floor, or the tiercel hawk on its perch by the throne.

With nothing much else on which to spend his energy, Oesc had found a certain interest in watching the young king grow into his power. Artor was now almost twenty, and a man's beard, clipped close, outlined the strong curve of his jaw. He had dressed for the occasion in a dalmatic of crimson silk, with twin bands of embroidery running over his shoulders and down to the hem on either side. Around his neck glinted the golden torque of a Celtic prince, but there was Byzantine enamel work on his diadem.

Oesc, who had become accustomed to seeing his captor lounging by the fire in his favorite tunic of faded green wool, suppressed a smile. But the dark-haired boy who followed the Gaullish envoy was gazing in awe at the marble facings on the walls and the gilding on the coffered beams of the distant ceiling, and most of all at the brilliant figure on the throne. To him, Artor *was* the emperor.

Eldaul stepped forward and read from a scroll, "Johannes Rutilius, Comes Lugdunensis, bears greetings from Riothamus, Dux of the Britons north of the river Liger, to Artorius, Vor-Tigernus of Greater Britannia."

"Let him approach—"

The dark-haired man with the boy bowed.

"My king, I bring the best wishes of my lord Riothamus for the continued good health of yourself and your realm." His British had an odd accent, but by this time Oesc understood the language well.

Someone in the crowd behind Oesc snorted. "About time—were they waiting to see if the lad could hold onto his crown?"

"My lord offers a treaty of trade and alliance. The Franks worry at our borders in Gallia as the Saxons trouble you here. Barbarians sit at their ease in the Holy City, and the Emperor in Constantinople is very far away. You and Riothamus, my lord, are the heirs of the Western Empire, and it is only good sense for you to work together."

"As you say," Eldaul interrupted him, "we are still fighting the Saxons. What help will Riothamus offer us?"

"Nay," growled one of the older men, "we need no help from men who fled Britannia when the Saxons first rose against us in blood and fire."

Artor frowned at both of them. "I think Gallia needs all her men for her own defense, and our own warriors can defend us here," he put in quickly.

"But the wharves of Londinium are often empty," Catraut added. "Trade has been poor while the Saxon wolves ranged the Narrow Seas. Once Britannia helped to feed the empire. Send us merchant ships, with war galleys to guard them, and we will send you corn from the rich midlands that we still hold."

The flush that had risen in Johannes's face subsided. "That is what I have come to propose, though I would add a provision that either ruler might call for aid to the other if times should change."

"That seems good to me," Artor said while his advisors were still drawing breath to answer.

"In earnest of our sincerity I have brought you my own son, the child of my wife who is sister to Riothamus, to serve you as part of your household." He set his hand on the boy's shoulder and pushed him towards the throne.

"What is your name?" asked Artor, learning forward with his elbows on his knees and the first genuine smile of the afternoon.

"I am Betiver, my lord." The boy spoke softly, but boldly enough—he must be accustomed to courts, thought Oesc.

"Then you shall be my cupbearer. Would you like that, Betiver?"

"I would like it very well—"

Betiver's eyes were shining. Oesc sighed. There was no denying that the British king had charm. All of the younger men were half in love with him. *Except for me . . .* he thought, glowering.

"Then you may stand over there, and tonight, when we feast in honor of your father, you shall serve me." Artor gestured towards the hostages.

As the business of the court continued, Betiver turned to his new companions.

"Who are you?"

"We're the king's hostages. This black-headed lad is Cunorix, an Irishman from Demetia, and I am Oesc from Cantium." Now, he thought, the boy would understand what his status truly was, despite the fine words.

"Do you dislike it?" Betiver asked with surprising perceptiveness. "They say that the great Aetius was a hostage with the Huns, and Attila himself hostage for a time in Rome. That's how we learn about other peoples and their lands."

For that to be any use, thought Oesc sourly, *you have to get home again.* But he said no more.

One evening just past Midsummer, when every window had been opened to let in whatever cooling breath of breeze might come from the river below, Artor came striding back from a meeting of the council with a face like thunder and Cai at his heels.

Oesc and Cunorix, who had been taking turns playing Round Mill with Betiver, stood up as the king appeared in the doorway. To try and get three counters in a row on the diagram was a children's game, but Oesc liked it because the pattern reminded him of a Germanic protective sigil called the "helm of awe." He made a grab for the counters as the board rocked, then straightened again.

"I've spent most of a stifling day listening to old men argue," said Artor. "They may have no blood in their veins, but mine needs cooling off. I'm going down to the river for a swim—would anyone else like to come?"

"I would!" cried Betiver, knocking the board askew as he pushed past. Cunorix rescued it this time and set it on his bed. He glanced at Oesc and then nodded.

"We'll come too."

As they trooped down the stairs towards the riverbank, it occurred to Oesc that Artor, surrounded by old men who all thought they knew what should be done better than he did, was in a sense a prisoner too. There was something sad in the thought that he had to turn to his own captives for company. It made Oesc uncomfortable to feel sorry for Artor, and he thrust the thought away, but as the evening continued, it kept coming back again.

The palace lay close to the river, but they had to follow the path along the banks for a little ways before they came to a landing where the bottom was shallow and firm enough to wade in. Some of the men from the town were already splashing happily, accompanied by shouting children. Someone looked up as they approached, saw they were strangers, and looked away.

Artor turned, his eyes alight, and held up one finger for silence. Oesc realized then that stripped down to thin tunics or breeches, with no mark of rank or royalty, they looked like any other group of young men out for a swim. He stepped out of his sandals, pulled off his tunic and laid it over a bush; in another moment his breechcloth had followed. Like all the children of the marshlands, he had learned to swim when he was small. He entered the water in a long, low dive that took him far out from shore. The current was stronger than he had expected, and cold. He had to swim hard to get back to the shallows once more.

Artor reached out and Oesc grasped his hand, a little surprised at the strength with which he pulled him in. Then he got his feet under him and stood, gasping.

"Don't go out too far—current will take you away," Oesc said in warning.

"I know . . . sometimes I wish it would. . . ."

There was a moment of strained silence. Then Artor saw Oesc staring at him, gave his head a little shake, and smiled. In the next moment he was splashing Betiver, and in the water-fight that followed the moment of understanding was gone.

But when the light of the long summer day faded at last and they reluctantly pulled on their clothing once more, Oesc still remembered that odd sense of equality.

The day might be ended, but they were young, and so was the night.
A century earlier, Londinium had been the metropolis of Britannia, and
for every one of the more utilitarian businesses there had been a wine
shop or taberna. Most of them had disappeared with the Legions, but now
that the high king was in residence, they seemed to be sprouting on every
street corner once more.

Betiver, who was the sort of child who never forgot his hat or broke
his shoe latchets, was the only one of them who had brought his belt-
pouch. It held enough coins for them all to drink at the first taberna they
stopped at, and the second. By the time they got to the third wine shop,
Cunorix had won more money dicing with an Armorican sailor. At the
fifth, Artor himself won them a round of drinks at ring-toss.

By this time, all of them were exceedingly merry. Oesc, a veteran of
serious Saxon drinking bouts with ale and mead, discovered that he had
no head for wine. But it didn't matter. Artor was a good fellow—Cai was
a good fellow—and so were Cunorix and the boy. The serving girls with
whom they flirted were all beautiful. The carters and tradesmen with
whom they were drinking were good fellows too, seen through a vinous,
rose-pink, haze.

"Got an idea—" He draped an arm across Artor's shoulder. "Take
your people, my people, get 'em to drink together. Make 'em be friends!"

"You're drunk, Oesc." Artor hiccoughed, then laughed. "Guess I am
too. Sounds good to me. Maybe that's how the Romans . . . got their empire!" They all laughed.

It was very late by the time they ran out of money again, and by then
the tabernas were beginning to close. Betiver had fallen asleep with his
head on the table, and Cai hoisted him over one shoulder as they staggered
out the door. The damp night air was bracing after the boozy warmth of
the wine shop, but their steps were still a little unsteady when they heard
the first light footfalls behind them.

Oesc shook his head in an attempt to clear it, and saw the stars spin.
If this was an ambush, he was going to have to fight drunk or not at all.

"My lord—" came Cai's voice from the darkness, the first time he
had used the title all evening.

"I heard. Take the boy on ahead."

How, Oesc wondered, could he sound so cool?

"Artor! My place is here—"

"Get Betiver to safety. That's a command! Cunorix, Oesc, stand back
to back with me!"

"I'll go for help!" Cai salved his conscience. He started to run, and
at the sound of his footsteps, their attackers came out from the alleyway.

At least, thought Oesc as he braced himself against the others' shoulders, *this way I won't fall down.*

"We've drunk up all our money," Artor said clearly. "You'll get nothing but blows for your trouble."

"Yon black-headed lad has a silver buckle, and you are wearing a ring. That's worth food and drink to starving men."

Oesc squinted at the approaching shadows. They didn't move like starving men.

"Go to the palace if you are hungry, and they will give you food. You are breaking the king's peace and will be punished if you harm us here."

As Artor was speaking, Cunorix whispered in Oesc's ear to watch out for the man on the right, who had a knife, while the others were armed with clubs or staves.

"Why should the king care what happens in the streets?"

"Believe me, he cares!" answered Artor. His laughter ceased as their assailants came on.

The robbers were five to three, and sober. Oesc drew a deep breath. "Woden!" he cried, as the first blow hit, and heard Artor calling out to Brigantia. The wine had blunted their reactions, but all three were warriors, trained to fight even when they could not see. With fists and feet they deflected the first rush and the second. When the third came they were gasping, but alarm and exertion had burned most of the alcohol away. What remained dulled the pain of the blows.

There were a few moments of furious action, followed by a pause while everyone stood gasping. One of their opponents lay on the ground, while another was holding his belly where Cunorix had kicked him. Oesc felt Artor straighten.

"Well, my friends, we have cleared the board a little. I think it is time for the king-piece to break out of the fortress!" Before they could object, Artor had sprung forward and scooped up a fallen club and was swinging it at the nearest foe.

Cunorix shrieked something in Irish, lowered his head and charged, and Oesc headed towards the third man. At last he was free to fight! The rage he had repressed during his captivity filled him with a new intoxication. He saw a stave whirr towards him, lifted his left arm to protect his head and heard a crack as it hit. The impact whirled him around, inside his opponent's guard, and his right fist drove towards the other man's throat. Something gave way with a sickening crunch and the man fell, gurgling.

Artor had felled his man, and Cunorix was grappling with the other one. Oesc drew breath to speak and gasped as the numbness in his arm began to give way to a throbbing agony. Artor held up one hand, listening.

More men were coming. But what they were hearing now was the ring of hob-nailed sandals and the jingle of military harness, not a foot-pad's stealthy tread. Cai had rousted out the city guard at last.

Oesc's broken arm healed slowly, though the tongue-lashing Artor received from his advisors when they returned to the palace no doubt left deeper wounds. Only Merlin, who had returned from one of his journeys shortly after, seemed to understand. Rumor had it that the reaction of Artor's mother, arriving for one of her periodic visitations, was more vig-orous.

To occupy Oesc's mind during his convalescence, a priest called Fas-tidius was sent to teach him the language of the Romans, and the others involved in their escapade were encouraged to study with him, whether as a punishment or to keep him company was not clear.

"*Arma virumque cano . . .* " The words were intoned with the sonority of a man who loved the language and a clarity of accent that Oesc was already learning to recognize as being of another order entirely than the camp Latin many of the soldiers used. "And what, my child, do those words say?"

"*Arma*—that means weapons," answered Oesc. This sounded much more interesting than the grammar the old man had been teaching them before. "Does *virumque* have anything to do with men?"

Through the open window he could hear the sounds of men and horses, and from farther off, a distant mutter of thunder. The heat wave had broken, and the air was cool and moist with the promise of rain.

"A man," Fastidius corrected. "The object of the verb. And the *que* at the end of it—what does that mean?" His watery gaze fixed on Cunorix, who stared as if an armed man had sprung from the ground before him. In fact, thought Oesc, he would probably have faced a warrior with less fear.

Artor took pity on him. "It means *and*, does it not? 'Of arms and the man I sing.' "

"Hmm," said the priest, "you have studied the language before."

"It was spoken in the home of Caius Turpilius, who fostered me," answered the king. "But I have not had much practice in reading."

"Ah . . . you will want to understand the messages you receive from foreign kings without depending on a scribe, and to make sure the mes-sages written for you express what you want to say."

It had never occurred to Oesc that a king could be his own interpreter, but he could see now that it would be useful. Certainly the priest seemed to understand. Fastidius was an old man, trained in the golden days before the Saxon Revolt when his namesake the bishop wrote letters of civilized amusement at the idea that sensible men could ever accept Augustinus's harsh doctrine. Their sufferings at the hands of the Saxons had made a belief in predestination more credible, but the old priest still behaved as if the purity of one's Latin were as important as the purity of one's soul.

Cunorix cleared his throat. "But what does it mean?"

Fastidius smiled, and without looking at the scroll, began to chant once more—"*Troiae ui primus ab oris Italiam fato profugus Lavinaque venit litora . . .* Who from Troy by fate caused to flee came first to the shores of Italia and Lavinium . . . It is the story of Aeneas, who escaped the fall of the great city of Troy and became the founder of Rome."

"I have heard of him," Artor said slowly. "They say that the ancestors of the Britons came from there with Brutus, his great-grandson."

But to Oesc it seemed that the story of this Aeneas must be very much like that of his own people, driven by need to seek a new home on a foreign shore. He pointed to the scroll.

"How did this Aeneas get to Italia, and what happened to him there?"

Fastidius smiled. "I thought that you might like the story. It is full of battles. Some of my brethren would say that you should study texts of the Holy Fathers. But it seems to me that you will learn better with something you find interesting, and also, Vergilius wrote much better Latin."

"Even Cai, here, might learn something if it is about battles—" Artor punched his foster-brother playfully. "He was a very poor pupil to our housepriest at home!"

It did seem that with the *Aenied* for their text they made better progress, following the adventures of the Trojan hero around the Mediterranean in his search for a home. And when the frustration of untangling Latin declensions became too much for their patience, Fastidius could be tempted into regaling them with tales of British heroes, for he came from the isle of Mona, where memories were long.

When autumn arrived, the whole court followed the Tamesis upriver to the hills for a few weeks of hunting, and came back brown from sun and wind and pleasantly fatigued by hard riding, with enough wild meat to vary the menu for some time. It had been good to get out, but in some ways the city seemed even more stifling afterward, especially when the weather changed and the early winter rains set in.

"Do you know any stories about Londinium?" asked Betiver one day when the leaden skies wept steadily and damp draughts crept in under every door.

Fastidius set down the tablet on which he had been checking Betiver's lists of Latin verbs and smiled. "I have told you already how Brutus founded the city and called it Troia Nova, which was in the British tongue, Trinovantum, because the Trinovante tribe came to dwell there. They say that his descendent, Lud, built walls and towers and renamed the city after himself. But that was just before the great Julius Ceasar brought the Romans to these shores. The Latin histories tell us that Londinium was only a small river town which the Romans rebuilt in stone, so I do not know what the truth may be."

"Buildings are not very exciting," said Cunorix. "Are there no other tales?"

Fastidius's brows, which were white like his hair, and rather bushy, bent. "There is another story, that ends here. If you will take up your tablets and write out all the forms of *placare,* 'to soothe or calm,' *conloquor,* 'to negotiate,' and *agere*, 'to make a treaty,' then I will tell you a story from Pagensis, where the Ordovici ruled, about a king who was so great in stature that no building could hold him."

"You think that we are so averse to using words of peace that we must be bribed to learn them?" asked Artor, laughing.

"I think that you are all young men, who believe that glory can only be won in war . . ."

Betiver had already picked up his stylus and tablet and was busily making marks in the wax. Grinning, the others began to work as well.

When they had finished and been corrected, Fastidius kept his promise.

"A long time ago there was a ruler of the Britons called Brannos, so great a king that men called him Blessed, and that became part of his name—in British, Bendeigid Brannos. He gave his sister Branuen in marriage to the king of Hibernia, but one of her half-brothers was angry because he had not been consulted, and he disfigured the horses of the Hibernian king, which was a great insult. Brannos paid compensation, and the girl went over the sea with her new husband, but the Hibernians still brooded on the insult, and presently they forced the king to punish his wife by making her a servant at his court. But Branuen had some magic of her own, and she trained a starling to carry the news of her torment to her brother in Britannia."

Nobody looked at Cunorix, who had gotten rather red in the face, but Artor motioned to Fastidius to go on.

"So the princes of Britannia went to war, the warriors in ships, and Bendeigid Brannos wading across the water, and there were great battles, and greater treacheries, and in the end, the Hibernians were defeated, but of the Britons only seven remained beside the king, who had been wounded by a poisoned lance in the heel. When Brannos saw that the poison would overcome him, he gave certain orders. And then, as he had commanded, they struck the head from his body, and took it back with them to Britannia."

"What were his orders?" asked Artor.

"What happened to Branven?" asked Betiver. Cunorix only glowered.

"The princess, remembering that because of her, two great peoples had been destroyed, died of sorrow. But the seven companions feasted for seven years in one habitation, forgetting their sorrows, and in another for seven again, listening to the birds from the Otherworld, and the head of Brannos was with them, uncorrupted. And when that time was done, they opened the door that looked towards the south, and then, as he had prophesied, they remembered everything."

It was a strange tale indeed, as Fastidius had promised them. To Oesc it seemed as if for him and Cunorix it had more meaning, for their people still lived as the Britons had lived before the Romans came. Cai was staring out the window, bored, as usual, by anything that was not about fighting, and Betiver listened with a child's wonder. But what did Artor make of this story of an ancient king?

He was already taller than Oesc, who overtopped most men. But in the past year Artor's body had thickened to match the promise of the strong bones. *This is no longer a boy to be led about by old men,* thought Oesc, *I wonder when his advisors will realize that their bear cub has become a bear?* The cold illumination from the window lit one side of the king's face and left the other in darkness, eyelids half closed to hide his thoughts, mouth grim. *His father killed mine . . .* Oesc told himself, but some other part of his being wished only that Artor would smile.

He cleared his throat. "What did they do then?"

"They followed Brannos's orders. They carried the head to the White Mount, the sacred hill by the river in Londinium, and there they buried it, face set towards Gallia. The word of Bendeigid Brannos was this, that while his head remained there, so also would his spirit and his power, to ward Britannia from plague and destruction."

"So, even in death a king may still watch over his people . . ." said Artor. His mouth was still grim, but there was a light in his eyes.

"It is so in the old Jutish lands," said Oesc. "There, when a king's reign has been peaceful, with good harvests, they build a great mound over his bones and set out offerings, so that his name is remembered and he becomes one with the gods."

"It is the bones of the saints and the blood of the martyrs that protect Christian lands!" said Betiver.

"Neither saints' relics nor a severed head seem to have protected the empire from the heathens," growled Cai. "I prefer to trust to stout hearts and strong arms."

"Perhaps Brannos's protection depended on a different kind of power," said Fastidius placatingly, and unrolled the scroll containing his grammatical notations once more.

The winter drew on, cold and wet. In the north and the midlands, it was a cruel season, with storms in which both men and cattle froze. But in Londinium, the sleet never quite seemed to turn into snow. The high king's household struggled with the old hypocaust system, but even when they got it working, the warmth that came up through the floors was never quite enough to offset the cold drafts that came in around the doors. There were many times when Oesc missed Saxon farmhouses. Dark and odorous though they might be, they were warm.

But presently the days began to lengthen, and occasionally they saw the sun. The skies echoed with the bitter music of the wild geese as they winged northward. Messengers went out to call the princes of Britannia to council. In the midlands, the snow that had fallen on hill and dale was melting, and the Tamesis began to rise.

"Am I or am I not the king?"

Oesc, who had been repairing his bow in hopes that they might soon get some hunting, opened his door and peered out. That had sounded like Artor's voice, but he had never heard it so angry.

Now he could hear a murmur of other voices, soothing or remonstrating.

"Be still—you prattle at me as if I were a fractious child!"

It *was* Artor. Oesc set down the bow and went out to see what was going on. He found Cai leaning against a pillar, watching the king stride back and forth across the cracked stones of the courtyard.

"He's always been like this, even when we were boys," said Cai. "He doesn't get mad often, but when he does, it's bad. He broke my nose and left me bruised for a week once when he thought I'd mistreated a horse, back when I was twelve and he was nine and I was a head taller than he."

Oesc didn't ask whether it was true. Cai was heavy handed with most things; he broke weapons and wore out his mounts faster than other men.

"He needs to crack someone's head or take a woman," Cai added, "but I don't suppose he will."

Oesc nodded. He knew that Cai sometimes went to the whores who served the soldiers, and Cunorix found comfort with the Irish serving girls. Oesc himself had always feared to be rejected because he was a Saxon. What Artor's reasons for continence might be he did not know.

"What's set him off now?" He asked.

"The old men on the council. They want someone to sit on the throne and look handsome, not a king. Artor got mad when they voted to exempt all Church lands from taxation."

"Does he want money?"

"Not for himself—for the troops up on the Wall. Your people have been quiet, but the Picts and the Scotti are always a threat, and all the regular army Britannia still has is up there. The landowners at least send men and supplies, but the Church expects to be protected for nothing."

Artor's long stride had slowed, and the high color was beginning to leave his cheeks. "Can't they understand? The time to build up your dikes is before it floods. We need to maintain a fighting force that can deter invasion, and that means money."

The placating murmur continued.

"I think God hears soldiers as well as priests. I have no quarrel with the Church, but its business is prayer, not politics, and not all in this land are Christian. Anyhow, that isn't the problem now. They wouldn't even listen to my reasoning! They as much as told me to run away and play, and I didn't—I couldn't—answer them!"

Oesc hid a smile. That's how it was for Saxon war-leaders most of the time. Except for the sword-thanes, vowed to stand by their chieftains till death, warriors served voluntarily, and felt free to argue. It amazed him sometimes that the Germans had been able to conquer as much as they had. But hunger was a powerful motivator. These Britons were too accustomed to safety. They had received a sharp lesson, but clearly it was easily forgotten. If they had been willing to pay the troops who protected them, Hengest would never have asked for land.

"If you could—if they would listen to you—how would you order Britannia?" he asked.

"With a strong government. Rome succeeded because there was strength at the center to make all the provinces help and defend each other. It failed because it got too big. Britannia is a good size for communications, with defined borders."

"You mean to rule all the island?" asked Betiver.

"What about the Picts? asked Cai.

"What about the Saxons?" Oesc echoed.

"It seems to me," Artor said slowly, "that when tribes or regions think too much about their own rights and practices and needs they fight their neighbors, and then they are easy prey for any better organized enemy who moves in. Julius Caesar conquered the British tribes because they could not work together. Your grandfather overran half the island because Vitalinus and Ambrosius would not make an alliance, and failed to keep it because your Saxon tribes would not accept a single high king. I know that rival emperors fought each other, but for most people, most of the time, within the empire there was peace."

"But at what price?" asked Cunorix. "Your Romans leveled peoples as they leveled the ground for their fortresses. Is peace worth losing everything that makes you who you are?"

"Did I say I thought it would be easy?" Artor said ruefully. "I would be king for the Romans and the British, the men of Eriu who have settled on these shores and the Picts and even the Saxons, if they would accept me, each with their own customs, living in peace with their neighbors."

"Foster-brother, you are crazy," Cai shook his head pityingly. "Even the Lord Jesus could not make them all agree."

"Jesus himself said his kingdom was not of this world, though some of our bishops seem to have trouble remembering it. What I am talking about requires an earthly king."

"You certainly seem to have spent some time thinking about it—" Betiver said admiringly.

Artor shrugged. "Sitting through all those meetings, what else do I have to do? I know that the king has to be strong enough to defend the borders and keep people within them from killing each other as well. He should encourage trade and sponsor public works. All this requires taxes, which people do not want to pay. He must keep local chieftains from oppressing their own people, but give them enough freedom so they will support him. Maybe it *is* impossible—but if they would stop treating me like a child, I would try!"

"You have a magic sword. Does not that give you the authority?" asked Oesc.

"That's an *old* miracle," Artor answered bitterly. "I need a new one to impress the princes—or maybe I am the one who needs a sign that this is what I am supposed to do. . . ."

Artor was still muttering when a workman appeared in the doorway, eyes bulging and muddy to the thighs.

"My lord, come quickly! They've found a head—some say it's a demon and some say it's a god. It was walled up, my lord, like a thing of power. They want to throw it into the river. I tried to tell them not to, but they wouldn't listen!"

"I know how you feel—" said the king. "Very well, I'll come. Perhaps the *people* will be willing to listen to me!"

"They call it the White Mount, my lord, but it's only just a little hill beside the water—"

Oesc saw Artor's step falter for a moment, and remembered suddenly where he had heard that name before. He hastened his own steps to catch up with them as the workman chattered on.

"The river's been rising, you see, and we was trying to drive in a few stakes to help hold the bank. And we hit something hard, though of course we didn't know that's what it was, and Marcellus says, 'That's funny—' and then the ground just sort of fell away and we could see the big slabs of stone with the water gurgling round."

Ahead a knot of people had gathered by the waterside. Someone saw the king coming, still dressed in the finery he had worn to the council, and shouted, and the crowd began to swirl towards them.

"I told them to leave it be, but Marcellus said that's good building stone, and he got a hook down the crack and pulled, and the whole slab came over, and then—"

But by then they were at the riverside, and Artor gestured for silence. As the workman had said, it was only a small hill, but it was crowned by three fine oak trees. Several ravens were sitting there, and as they approached, more came flying, calling as they circled the hill. Oesc felt a prickle of unease, and seeing Artor frown, knew that he too had felt the breath of the Otherworld. Cai stood with his arms folded, glaring back at the crowd.

People gave way before them. At the edge of the water the hill gaped open, the slab that had fallen revealing a small, square chamber, walled and roofed with stone. This was no Roman construction—the size of the stones reminded Oesc of etin-work he had seen. Water had seeped across the stone floor and around the stone block that stood in the midst of the chamber. On top of it was what appeared to be the head of a man of giant size, frozen in stone. Blank, almond, eyes stared out from either side of a long straight nose, the whole surrounded by masses of undulant hair.

Artor gazed at it for a moment, then bent to peer in. "Look, Cai—" he called. "It's pottery, not stone at all."

"Don't touch it—" Cai began, but Artor was already entering the chamber.

"Nonsense," he said over his shoulder. "If we leave it here it will be destroyed." There was a general gasp as the king grasped the pot in both arms and turned to carry it outside.

As he brought it into the sunlight, the shouting subsided. "Bendeigid Brannos . . ." said someone, and the whispers became a murmur of awe.

Seen full on, the features reminded Oesc a little of Merlin, and yet, though the druid's brown mane had the same wildness, Oesc had never seen on his face such a look of majesty. But he did not have long to compare them. As the light fell full on the surface of the pot, a fine network of cracks began to ray out across it.

Artor fell to his knees in the mud, cradling the pot against his chest, but in moments the clay was crumbling. As it fell away, they saw that it held neither ashes nor treasure, but a single human skull. For a moment only they looked upon the great empty eye-sockets and the mighty jaws, and then the skull also began to crumble. Clay and bone fell in fragments through Artor's fingers into the water, and the current whirled them away.

The ravens came skirling down from the trees after them, lamenting, but above their cacophony rose a woman's scream—

"The Raven of Britannia is gone! Brannos the Blessed has abandoned us and we are lost!" Now there was an edge of hysteria in the hubbub of the crowd.

Artor looked down at his hands, still white with clay and bone, then he stood up again, and there was something in his face that made Oesc go cold inside, for in that moment it held the same look he had seen in the statue's eyes. With a single easy movement Artor leaped up onto the grass.

"People of Britannia, do not despair . . ." The king's voice was not loud, but it carried. "The ancient king protected you for many years, but his task is done. His remains have been released to find rest with the sea, his father, but his spirit remains with me." He held out his arm, and the largest of the ravens, circling, alighted upon it.

"Do you see—the ravens recognize my right! Now it is I who shall be Brannos, and take upon me his duty. To the end of my life and beyond I will be your protector!"

"You are only a man, and one day your bones will be dust!" came a hoarse voice from the crowd.

Artor turned, and the people grew silent. "Keep this place holy, a sanctuary for the ravens, for I tell you now—so long as the ravens dwell on this hill, my spirit will ward Britannia!"

"Artor Brannos!" came the cry, "Artor the Blessed! Artor! Artor!" The echoes rang.

The people were all around Artor now, asking for his blessing, touching his hand. Oesc watched with wonder and pity in his heart. When he made his own dedication at the shrine it had only been for one lifetime.

He sensed in this spontaneous avowal a commitment far more binding than whatever oath Artor had given to the Christian god when he was made king.

Eventually the people dispersed and the king was able to return to the palace. The raven flew back to the oak tree, but it was a long time before the strangeness left Artor's eyes.

"It was only a skull," said Cai very softly as they passed through the gates. "And Brannos was only a legend."

Oesc nodded. That might be true, but the moment during which that skull, whoever it belonged to, had been visible had been long enough for him to see that it was larger than the head of any ordinary man.

VI

The Feast of Lugus

A.D. 486

Just after Beltain, in the eleventh year of Artor's kingship, Naitan Morbet, King of all the Provinces of the Picts, broke the peace that Leudonus had imposed upon him and came south in force. It was a year of barbarian victories. In Gallia, the new king, Chlodovechus, had led his Franks against Syagrius and defeated this last Roman at Augusta Suessionum. In Italia, the Ostrogoth, Theodoric, ruled as *magister militum* in the puppet emperor Zeno's name. And in Britannia, it seemed as if the time of the wild tribes had returned.

Before Leudonus could gather men to stop them, the Picts had swept around his eastern flank, across the tumbled stones where once the Romans had sought to establish a far northern frontier, and were swarming up the vale of the Cluta, burning everything in their path. King Ridarchus had warning enough to marshal his warband, but they were powerless against such a host and barely made it back to the safety of the Rock of Alta Cluta, where they took refuge, cursing. For this was no raid, but a carefully planned campaign. Leaving a swathe of destruction behind them, the Picts rolled up the old Roman road and through the passes, heading for the rich Selgovae lands and Luguvalium.

In Londinium, their first news came from a dust-covered courier whose horse fell dead beneath him as he pulled up before the palace. The scroll he bore was as clear a cry for help as anyone had ever heard from Leudonus. Indeed, commented Cai when he heard of it, ever since the British princes had chosen Artor over him as high king, the king of the Votadini had sent very few communications of any kind.

"Maybe so," Artor had replied, "but he has been sending his taxes, and even if he had not, this challenges the whole of Britannia."

Since the episode of Brannos's head, Artor had begun to assert himself. His counsellors protested, but they could not stop him from sending out messengers to speed past the fields of young grain, calling on the men of Eburacum and Deva and Bremetennacum and all the forts that were still manned along the Wall to gather to his banner at Luguvalium by Midsummer Day.

Oesc listened to the hubbub of preparation with mounting frustration. In the past, he had tried not to mind when Artor rode out against the Angles or the Saxons. But Artor and Cai and even young Betiver were already making names for themselves as fighters, while he, as young and strong as they were, practiced his Latin and his archery. Even if he were freed, why should his own people accept a man with no experience in war?

He was in the library of the palace, helping Fastidius to sort scrolls, when a sudden draft set the lamp flames to flickering and he turned and saw it was the king.

"It is your arms you should be sorting through, not these scrolls," said Artor, standing with arms folded in the doorway.

Oesc felt his cheeks grow red. He had never quite dared to think of the British king as his friend, but surely too much respect had grown between them for the other man to mock him.

"My lord, don't tease him—" said Betiver, appearing next to him. "Oesc, go get your gear—Artor wants you in his warband when we go against Naitan!"

From red, Oesc knew he was becoming pale. Artor came forward and grasped his arm. "I could not ask you to fight your own folk, but the Picts are no kin to you, and I will need every man. And indeed, I would be honored to have the grandson of Hengest at my side. . . ."

Oesc found his voice at last. "I have fought beside you once already, my lord." He rubbed the arm that had been broken in the fight, which still gave a twinge now and again when it was about to rain. "I will be glad to come."

Betiver looked up at the red sandstone walls of the great fortress called the Petriana with a grin of sheer pleasure. *This* was Rome, whose mighty works none of the new tribes would ever equal. The Petriana was still the headquarters for the senior officer of the Wall command, and it was better cared for than most of the forts the Legions had left behind them. When he surveyed the massive gatehouse and the strong walls that protected the city of Luguvalium, a few miles to the south, he was certain that the Empire of the West would be restored, with Artor as Imperator.

First, of course, they would have to do something about this troublesome Pictish king. But Betiver had grown from spindly youth to warrior in Artor's service, and it never really occurred to him that his king could fail.

Certainly, with the army that was gathering here to support him, Artor must have the victory. They had filled up all the empty barracks within the fortress, and more were camped along the banks of the river. And even as Betiver turned back towards the Principia, where Artor, following tradition, had made his headquarters, he heard a horn call from the eastern tower. Another band of warriors was coming in.

By the time Betiver reached the king, they all knew who it was. Leudonus of the Votadini, having come south by the eastern route and then along the Wall, was bringing all the men he could spare from the defense of his own lands to fight with them. Gualchmai, the eldest of his four sons and Artor's nephew, rode at his side.

That evening they feasted in the great hall of the Praetorium, where once Artor's grandfather had ruled with Caidiau, commander of the troops at the western end of the Wall. If there were a few more cracks in the tiled floor and a few more nicks in the pillars, still, it was a noble room, especially when the flower of Britannia filled it, glowing in their tunics of crimson and ochre and green, with gold at their necks and wrists and gleaming on the hilts of their swords. Artor himself had honored the occasion by putting on the Chalybe sword. It made some people uneasy, but there was no doubt it added to his majesty.

Artor had suggested that Betiver and Cunorix sit beside Leudonus's son, reasoning that he was the most likely to understand how a youngster new to the court might feel. Not that young Gualchmai had any problem with self-confidence—he was big for his age, with sandy hair and the promise of his father's burly build. One saw the resemblance to Artor only in the set of his eyes.

"My father is the greatest king in the north," he stated as the platters of boiled meat were being brought in. "Naitan Morbet is a sneak and a coward. If he had attacked Dun Eidyn instead of running around us, we would ourselves alone have been beating him already—"

"And saved the rest of us a very long ride," Cunorix responded pleasantly. "It was kind of you to let us share in the fun."

Gualchmai frowned, as if not quite sure how to take that. "I am hearing that my uncle Artor is a great warrior too," he said a little more politely. "It will be fine to see him fight."

"There are many fine warriors in your uncle's army," Betiver continued in the same tone. "There is Cai, who was his foster-brother, and Cyniarcus, son of the prince of Durnovaria. Beside them sits Cataur of Dumnonia, who is a very mighty man." He saw Oesc grimace at the name. Cataur had never ceased to hate the Saxons for killing his brother at Portus Adurni, and had made no secret of his opposition to Oesc's presence on the campaign.

"The men of the north are mighty too," Gualchmai said stoutly. "There is Peretur son of Eleutherius, come in from Eburacum, and Dumnoval of the southern Votadini over there by his side. But when myself and my brothers are grown we will be the greatest warriors in Britannia."

Betiver took a drink of ale to cover his smile. "How many brothers do you have?" he asked when he could control his face again.

"Gwyhir has thirteen winters, a year less than me, and wild he was that he could not come with us. But my mother would not allow it. If she could, I think she would keep all of us by her, but my father insisted, which he does not do often anymore. Aggarban is only ten, which is far too young for war, and Goriat is four and just a baby. But they are all big and strong for the years they have, and I have given my promise that the first of them who can knock me down shall have my dagger!" He patted the weapon that hung at his belt, a handsome piece of work with a cairngorm set in the hilt.

Later that evening, when Leudonus had taken his heir off to bed, Betiver found himself with Oesc by the fire.

"I am sure that Artor set me there so that the boy might have a friend among all these warriors, but believe me, that young man needs no reassurance." He proceeded to summarize their conversation, hoping to get a smile. Oesc was a good fellow, but too often one saw sadness in his eyes.

"Where does it come from?" asked the Saxon. "Leudonus does not seem so overbearing a man."

"Not now, I suppose, though I hear he was very ambitious when he was younger. And then there is their mother, who was trained on the Holy Isle. If we get to Dun Eidyn, maybe we'll meet her."

Oesc nodded. "If we get that far."

"You will get there—" rumbled a deep voice behind them.

There's no reason to be nervous, Betiver told himself as he turned to face Merlin. But he came from a land where druids, if indeed Merlin was not something worse, were only a memory, and he never knew quite how he ought to react to the man. Oesc had stiffened, his face showing no expression at all, but then where *he* came from, every chieftain had a witch or wise man at his left hand.

"My lord Merlin—" he said politely. "Have you seen this in the stars?"

"I have dreamed of Artor standing on the Rock as the sun sets behind him." The druid leaned on his staff, frowning. "You will fight Naitan Morbet, and pursue him." The great beard, streaked with silver now, twitched as he smiled. "But I do not think I will ride with you. My bones grow too old for long marches with armies. Perhaps I will walk in the forest of Caledonia for a time, and refresh my soul."

Merlin trying to be pleasant was even more unnerving than Merlin being grim, thought Betiver.

"Do you wish me to tell you if you will survive the battle? That is what all the other warriors wish to know."

Betiver shook his head, suppressing a shiver. For a moment Merlin's eyes were unfocused, looking through him. Then the old man blinked, and that dark gaze fixed Betiver once more.

"What you do not ask, the spirits have answered," he gave a bark of harsh laughter. "You will live long, and serve your lord to the end." For a moment he looked at Oesc, frowning, then without another word turned and moved away through the crowd.

"How very odd!" said Betiver, trying to laugh.

"He is a dangerous man," answered Oesc, but he would say no more.

With the Votadini, Artor's muster was complete. They moved out in good order past the fields of ripening grain, fording the rivers that emptied into the Salmaes firth until they came to the Stone of Mabon, a finger of rock set there by men of a time so ancient no one remembered their names, and honored ever since as the phallus of the god. In happier times it had marked the border between the Novantae and Selgovae lands, and the tribes had met on the flats beyond it for trade and festival.

Betiver took a deep breath of the brisk air, rich with the scents of grass and tidal mud and the salt tang of the sea. He had fought with Artor before, but this was different. They were beyond the Wall, now, in a land which had only intermittently accepted the yoke of Rome. He tried to pray, but the Christian god seemed irrelevant in this wilderness; he understood why someone had cast a garland of flowers around the Mabon stone.

He wondered how long it would take for the enemy to get there.

Any force moving down from the north with designs on Luguvalium must pass this way or take to the water, and the Picts had never been seamen. To the north, smoke hung like a dark smudge across the sky. The enemy was coming, and Artor's army took position to meet them—in the center nearly a thousand light infantry who had ridden to the battle and left their horses in the rear, and almost as many cavalry, armed with lance and sword, arranged in two wings to either side.

Betiver's mare stamped nervously and he patted her neck beneath the mane. His sword was loose in the sheath, his shield slung across his shoulder. He unfastened the straps of his round topped helmet to cool his head, then tightened them once more and changed his grip on the lance that lay along his thigh.

When were the Picts going to come?

Artor had taken command of the right wing, spreading his horsemen out in a curve across the rising heathland above the meadows. The warriors of his household were with him, except for Oesc and Cunorix, who had never learned to fight on horseback and were stationed among the foot fighters, mostly men of the hill country to the south of Luguvalium. Cador of Dumnonia and his seasoned troops held the left, on horses accustomed to the ocean, who would not panic if the battle pushed them into the shallows of the firth. And in the middle, Peretur of Eburacum commanded, backed by the band of Alamanni warriors who formed his personal guard.

Betiver had been in battle against Saxons, using the weight of the cavalry charge to break their line. He had never fought other cavalry before. Neither had Artor, he thought unhappily. They had all done practice fighting, but it was never the same.

Every time he waited for the fighting to start he hoped that this would be the time he learned how not to be afraid. The child Gualchmai, sitting his horse behind his father, was watching the road with barely concealed impatience. But he didn't know how it was going to be. Artor's face, as always, was a little pale, his eyes intent and grim. Betiver had never yet dared to ask him if he felt fear.

Would the Picts never come?

And then between one moment and the next, the skyline changed. Suddenly, not only the road, but the meadows and the farther hillsides were covered with moving dots. Metal flashed and flickered in the watery sunlight. They didn't seem surprised to see the British force awaiting them, but then they must have had scouts out, and he had heard that a Pictish scout could lie concealed in a clump of heather, and track a gull upon the breeze.

He felt hot and then cold. The dots were becoming tiny men on shaggy ponies. Most of the British had some kind of body armor—mail or scales of leather or metal or horn, as well as helms. The Pictish warriors rode with cinctured saddle cloths and only a few of them had helms. Many bore no more than a cloak or a sheepskin over their breeches; from a distance the tattooed beasts that spiraled all over their bodies made their skins look blue. But they carried stout shields, round or square and covered with bull hide, and long spears, and wicked looking swords. They seemed to be coming without order, but here and there a rider bore a wooden standard with a painted fish or bull or some other beast, so they must be riding in clan groups or bands.

Horns blared mockingly, answered by the bitter music of Artor's clarions. A shiver ran along the British line. Betiver picked up his reins and the mare bobbed her head, pulling at the bit. The clarions called again, and suddenly Artor's cavalry wing was moving, its line extending outward to hit the enemy on the flank and force them down upon the infantry's waiting spears. Ahead, he saw a larger standard with the elegantly executed image of a red stallion.

"Artor and Britannia!" cried the men. "Ar . . . tor . . ."

The shout tore through Betiver's throat. He dropped the rein on the mare's neck and shrugged his round shield down onto his arm; racing alongside the other horses, she needed little guidance. Without his will his arm lifted, lance poised.

And then the enemy horsemen were before him. A lance flew towards him and he knocked it aside with his shield, he stabbed, struck something and gripped the mare's barrel hard with his knees as he pulled it free.

"Ar . . . tor . . ."

Thought fled, and with it, fear, as Betiver was engulfed by the fray.

By afternoon, the battle was over. Oesc was glad to mount again, for what had been a fair meadow that morning was now a trampled wasteland, and blood ran in streams to redden the sea. He had come through the fight without much harm, though there was a slash on his thigh that made walking painful. The pony whuffed uneasily as he guided it back over the battlefield, calling the wagons to pick up British survivors and dispatching the more badly wounded of the enemy with a merciful thrust of his spear.

The fleeing survivors of Naitan Morbet's army were out of sight by now, closely pursued by Artor's cavalry. Perhaps he should learn to fight astride, Oesc thought grimly, so he could go with them. It was bad enough to fight a battle, but in the grisly work that came after there was neither excitement nor glory.

Where the land began to rise there was a heap of bodies, as if some desperate band of warriors had chosen it for their last stand. Most of them were Pictish, and all were quite dead. Among the corpses lay a wooden standard, carved and painted in the shape of a red stallion. Oesc frowned, remembering how it had threatened them in the morning light. He dismounted then, and began to pull aside the sprawled limbs of the warriors. Beneath them, as by now he was expecting, lay the body of a thick-bodied man with grizzled hair. Under the jutting beard a golden torque gleamed, and across the broad, naked chest was tattooed a horse and the double disc symbol of a king.

Oesc could see no mark upon him; perhaps the gods had struck him down in the midst of the battle. That happened sometimes with old men. But there was little doubt that this was Naitan Morbet, the lord of Pictland, who had set the lands from the Tava to the Salmaes ablaze. Oesc lifted his horn to his lips and blew, summoning the British captains to come and see.

Leaderless, the Picts fled northward like fallen leaves before the wind. Artor released his infantry and the men who lived farthest away to go home to their harvests while the British cavalry sped after the enemy, disposing of stragglers in a series of brief, bitter engagements that left the enemy dead, or less often, captive. The Picts were not destroyed entirely. Small groups of riders who knew the land could go where the larger, more heavily armed pursuers would never find them. Nonetheless, only a tithe of the great army that Naitan Morbet had led southward at Beltain ever returned to celebrate the feast of Lugus in the Caledonian hills and glens, and an unhappy line of prisoners followed when Artor's army at last reached Dun Eidyn.

From the high ridge of rock and the dun that crowned it to the flat meadow in the cleft below, the air pulsed with the sound of the drumming. From time to time a bitter skirling of pipes would gather the rhythm into their music, but when it ceased, the drums continued, the audible heartbeat of the land. The noise had continued since the beginning of the festival. By now, Betiver was aware of it only intermittently, when some shift in the wind amplified the volume, or when, for no reason that he understood, for a few moments it would stop. Sometimes, when the drums beat softly, he thought that pulsing might be the mead pounding in his brain, for during the past three days food and drink had flowed freely.

Those of Artor's men who had not gone home to help with the grain harvest camped in the meadow; it was a welcome opportunity to relax and recuperate from the long days on the trail. The hay had been cut, and the cattle brought down from the hills. The first fields of grain to ripen had been ceremonially harvested, and the clans of the Votadini, with the cattle they wanted to sell and the daughters they wanted to marry off, had come in. For the princes and lords of the king's household, it was a visit to a more ancient world that had never gone under the yoke of Rome.

"Is it so different?" asked Oesc, leaning back on the spread hides beside him. "My own people also make offerings at harvest time." Light from the bonfire reddened his fair hair.

Betiver shrugged. "At home in Gallia the priest offers prayers for the success of the harvest and the laborers feast when it is done. Maybe the country folk do other things, but I lived in towns and never saw them. There was never this great gathering." He sunk his teeth into the flesh that clung to the beef rib he was holding and worried it free.

"That is true. Among the Saxons, the next great feast will not be until autumn's ending, but that is for the family, like Yule. It is at Ostara and sometimes Midsummer that our tribes come together for the sacrifices."

"In Eriu, Lugos of the Long Arm is still honored," said Cunorix. "We hold a great festival for him at Taltiu, with a cattle fair."

Betiver nodded. For a moment it had seemed to him that the three of them, all born elsewhere and brought to Britannia, were equally foreigners. But he came from a land and a way of life long Christian, whereas Oesc and Cunorix were still as pagan as these Celts in their multicolored garments, dancing around the fires.

"Look there—" Oesc pointed. Gualchmai was moving among the feasters, his upper body swathed in a mantle of gold and brown and black checkered wool fastened with a silver penannular brooch. The skirts of a short saffron tunic showed beneath it, with black banding woven into the hem. In his hand he gripped a silver-mounted drinking horn.

He caught sight of the three Companions and made his way towards them, grinning widely.

"See—my father has given me this new horn! Tonight I have leave to stay and drink with the men."

"I am glad to see that you came through the battle unhurt," said Betiver. "Will you sit and drink with us, then, and tell us what is going on?"

"I will that—" Gualchmai said something in a dialect too thick for Betiver to follow to the wiry, red-headed tribesman who had been escorting him, and joined them on the cowhide. "Even my mother is agreeing that I am a warrior now I've seen battle. My brothers have to be staying up there with the women—" He pointed at the enclosure of loosely woven brush where the wives of the chieftains were holding their own festival. It was a flimsy barrier, but even a drunken man would not breach that sanctuary.

Not that the rest of them were without female companionship. The tribesmen had brought their families, and many of the girls had volunteered to help serve out the ale and mead. And when one of them, liking the looks of a southern warrior, settled down on the grass with him instead, no one seemed to think the worse of her. Betiver had noticed already that the women of the northern tribes had a freedom that would never have been permitted in a Christian land.

Gualchmai's red-headed servant returned with a pitcher full of mead and refilled their horns.

"Tell me, what is that platform with the fenced space in front of it?" asked Oesc.

"Oh, that is for the ceremony. Do you not have it in the south?" he asked as the men looked inquiring. "When Lugus kills the Black Bull who has carried off the Goddess and is holding back the harvest."

"Nay," Betiver said gravely, "I have never seen such a thing."

"Well, the sun has set," answered Gualchmai. "You will see something soon."

Westward, the sky blazed with banners of gold, as if to honor the vanished sun. The last light glowed soft on the rough rock of the cliff and the timbers of the palisade above them, and the thatched roof of Leudonus's high hall. Even as they watched, a spark appeared on the ridge below the eastern gate; in the next moment there were more, a line of torches winding like a fiery serpent down from the dun.

Closer, one saw the white robes of the men who led the procession, ghostly in the half-light.

"Druids!" exclaimed Betiver. "I did not know so many of them remained."

"in the north they do—" Gualchmai said smugly.

"And in Eriu," added Cunorix.

"They call Merlin a druid," observed Oesc.

"Merlin . . ." Betiver shook his head, thinking of the stories. "He has the druid knowledge, but he is something different. Some say the Devil fathered him and gave him his powers."

"If I believed in your Devil I could believe that was so," said Oesc somberly. "But my grandfather's wisewoman calls him witega, which means an oracle."

"My father's druids prophesy, and read omens," put in Gualchmai. "But they also conduct sacrifices and ceremonies."

Betiver twitched. He had been raised a Christian and held to that faith. But so had Artor. Whatever was going to happen, they could not insult their hosts by refusing to participate. If there was sin in it, he would simply have to ask Father Fastidius to give him a penance once they were home again.

The druids drew closer, men of middle-age or older, with flowing hair and beards. Upon the breast of their leader gleamed a golden crescent, and he leaned on a staff. Then Oesc drew his breath in sharply, and Betiver saw that behind the druids walked a group of dark-clad women.

"Those are the she-druids, the priestesses—" said Gualchmai. "And my mother . . ."

But Betiver had already noticed that one of the women had covered her dark robe with a mantle of crimson. As she moved towards them, her ornaments cast back the torchlight in running sparks and flickers of red gold. He did not need to be told that this was the queen.

Margause walked as a woman certain of her beauty and secure in her power, shoulders braced against the drag of her trailing mantle, head high. Her hair fell in waves of dark fire across back and shoulders, bound with a golden band. More gold swung from her ears and lay across her breast and weighted her wrists. Men fell silent at her coming; some bent, foreheads touching the earth in reverence.

It seemed irrelevant to call her beautiful. Deep-breasted and widehipped, her body was made for bearing. But from her face all the girlish softness had been fined away to reveal the faultless sculpting of bone at cheek and brow. At the entrance to the women's enclosure she paused, gazing across the assembly beneath painted eyelids. Then she disappeared into the shadows within.

Only then did Betiver realize that behind the women marched the warriors escorting Leudonus and the high king. Leudonus wore a plaid of the same hues as his son's; Artor a linen robe the color of the ripening fields. It was the first time since he had first set eyes on Artor as a child of thirteen that he had not been immediately aware when his lord drew near. He blinked, wondering if it was the mead that had dizzied him. Artor and his host were still talking. While the chieftains feasted, the kings had spent the afternoon hearing reports from the couriers sent to Caledonia to arrange for the ransom of prisoners. Men said that Drest Guithinmoch was the Picts' new king.

"And there is my father," said Gualchmai. "With the lord Artor. When you ride south again, I will be going with you. My mother was against it, but my father thinks it will be good for me to learn about the southern lands."

Betiver and Oesc exchanged glances, but managed not to smile. Until Artor married and begot a son, this boy had a good claim to be considered his heir.

The royal party ascended the platform and took their places on the benches there. The druids formed a line across the front and one of them lifted a bronze horn with a curious long shaft and blew. The sound did not seem loud, but it echoed from cliff to cliff and vibrated in the bones. When it finished, Betiver realized that every drum in the valley had stilled.

"The host of heaven, the summer stars,
Upon the sky fields they are gathered,
Upon the earth, fair Alba's children . . ."

The voice of the druid was thin and clear; Oesc felt the fine hairs on his neck and arms lifting at the sound. The northern intonation made it hard for him to understand some of the words, but it hardly mattered. The dark earth was sown with fire, and the cliffs framed a sky of luminous dark blue, blazing with a harvest of stars. The meaning of the words blossomed in his awareness without need for understanding as the ceremony went on. Woden had given the god-men of the Saxons this power, but until now he had not found its like in the British lands.

"Behold, Midsummer has passed,
the moon's sickle harvests summer stars;
The womb of the Mother swells:
Cattle grow fat, grain grows high.
Her children arise and flourish in the land.

The line of druids divided, revealing a throne set at the back of the stage, and upon it the shape of a woman, swathed in dark veils.

"The Mother has given birth, and her Son is grown;
Lord of the Spear of Light, the god of the clever hands,
Let the Son of the Mother arise and come forth to bless his
people—"

The hides nailed across the base of the platform shivered, and a new figure emerged, costumed in golden straw. Plaited and sewn, it formed a helm that covered head and face. Two tiers of straw flared out in a cape and a skirt below it. But his shield was of new wood with a gilded boss, and the head of his spear flashed gold.

For a moment he stood, staring around the circle, then, his voice slightly muffled through the mask, he began to sing.

"Well have you worked and long have you labored,
Now comes the time to receive your reward.
Rest and rejoice now, all uncertainty ended;
Laugh, make music, feast and frolic—
My love is the heat that warms you;
My light is the radiance that shows you the world."

"That is Lugus," said Gualchmai. "He is the bright god who can do everything. The ravens teach him wisdom."

"In my country they say that his spear is so powerful its head must be kept in a cauldron full of water or it would burn up the world," Cunorix said then.

Startled from his trance, Oesc stared at him.

"The god of my people, Woden, sends his ravens out to bring him knowledge, and claims the battle-doomed with his spear . . ." he whispered.

"My old tutor once told me that the mother of Apollo came from the land of the Hyperboreans in the far north, and that once he guided the people of Thera in the form of a raven," said Betiver. For a moment his eyes met Oesc's, then he crossed himself and looked away.

The god is here, thought Oesc. *Maybe this is the name he bears in the British lands.* After being for so long cut off from his own rites and his own people, he trembled, opened suddenly to awareness that the mummery before him was raising and focusing power. And even as this thought came to him he realized that the energy was shifting. The hides moved once more as a huge, dark figure shouldered between them, swathed in a cloak of some black stuff, helmed in leather that supported a pair of bull's horns.

"Lord of the Lightning, canst Thou deny me?" His voice was a deep rasp that raised the hackles. He lumbered back and forth, head lowered, while the bright god turned continually to face him. The druids moved back, and torchlight glittered from brooch and torque as the princes seated

on the benches leaned forward to see. Artor's eyes followed the mock-combat, bright with interest.

"I am the Shadow at Thy shoulder,
The darkness Thy light casts.
I come from the depths of earth
To devour the children of the day.
All that the Mother bears is meat for me—
The harvest and the cattle that eat it
And the men whose life the cattle are.
The Lady of Life I will hold prisoner—"

He made a rush towards the platform, feinting with his club, and the veiled woman who sat there flinched. He stopped then, club upraised, and the valley rumbled with his deep laughter.

"I am the Black Bull.
I am the plague that kills your young men,
the flood that drowns your fields,
the fire that burns your homes.
I am the Destroyer
Who shall trample your lives to dust!"

At the words, Lugus straightened, brandishing his spear.

"And I am the Defender!
I fight for all that the Mother has made!
I will stop the floods and free the Lady,
I will bring back the sunshine and win the harvest."

The veiled Goddess rose and came to watch from the front of the platform as weapon poised, he advanced upon his foe.

Once, twice, thrice, they circled, feinting back and forth in mimetic combat. But though their movements were stylized, the energy they were raising was real. With the third exchange, the Black God struck, and a sudden billowing of dust obscured the scene. When it thinned, in place of the human opponent stood a black bull.

It was, Oesc realized in astonishment, quite real. Like the men, it must have come from beneath the platform, but how they had kept it quiet there he could not imagine, for the beast was clearly in good health and full possession of its senses. Its dark gaze fixed on the glittering figure and it snorted, head lowering. A little shiver of tension ran through the crowd; there was hardly a man among them who had not at some point in his life been chased by a bull, and they recognized the warning signs.

The priest of Lugus shook his spear and began to sidestep around the bull, getting into position for a fatal blow. But the bull, shaking its head, turned with him. The priest extended his shield arm, shaking it a little to get the beast's attention. The massive head lowered, and suddenly the animal was in motion. If the priest had intended to strike as the bull went by, the beast was too fast for him. Even as his arm moved the bull was passing; the spearhead scored a long gouge in the animal's flank just as it hooked one horn into the shield and jerked it away.

The shield soared like a sunwheel, slapped against the fence and fell to the ground. The priest's gaze followed it, but the bull, with a better sense of priorities, was already wheeling towards the brightness of his cape and helm. The man was brave enough. He stood his ground as the bull surged forward, leaping aside at the last moment to stab.

But his courage was better than his timing. As he leaped, the bull swerved with a vicious sidewise swipe of the horns that hooked through straw and leather and grazed the priest's side. As the impact knocked him backward, the spear flew from his hand and slid rattling across the ground.

The torches flickered as a collective gasp of horror passed through the crowd. There was always this chance, that the Black Bull might win, and a murrain on the cattle and storms that spoiled the remainder of the harvest, would bring them a starving winter and death in the spring.

The bull, turned, pawing, as the priest struggled to his feet, eyeing the distance between himself, the bull, and his spear. At almost the same moment it became clear to both the man and the beast that he could not reach it in time. With preternatural intelligence, the bull moved, tail twitching, not towards the man, but towards the weapon that lay on the ground.

And then there was another movement, another figure that dropped, as if from the heavens, into the ring. For a moment Oesc thought it was one of the druids; then he recognized the barley-gold tunic and his blood chilled.

"Sacrilege!" cried someone. "He must not interfere!"

"Nay—he has the right," said another, "he is the king!"

A memory of his grandfather filled Oesc's vision, the body swinging from the old oak tree. *It is the right of the king to give his life for the people . . .* he told himself. Without willing it he leaped to his feet; his muscles locked with the effort it took to keep from rushing to Artor's aid. Betiver stood swaying beside him. Others had risen as well. But for each

British warrior there were two Votadini, ready to seize him if he should try to intervene.

The bull hesitated, for a moment uncertain as to what this new foe might be. It was long enough for Artor to pick up the spear. Muscles rippled along the dark flanks as the black bull charged. The king made no attempt to evade him. Still on one knee, he braced the spear and held it steady as the bull came on.

"Sweet Jesus," exclaimed Betiver, "does he think he's facing a boar?"

But a boar-spear had a cross piece to prevent the animal from running all the way up the shaft, and hunters could be killed trying that trick even so.

Then the bull was upon him. Dust swirled madly as the bull's own weight impaled him upon the spear. The wicked horns jerked savagely— was the man under them?

The thrashing figure changed shape suddenly; somehow Artor had evaded horns and hoofs and got astride the bull's massive shoulders. One hand gripped a horn; a dagger flashed in the other as Artor bent, reached, and ripped the sharp steel through the throat of the bull.

One last time the mighty body convulsed, nearly unseating him. Then the black bull collapsed, blood pumping onto the ground.

For a long moment nobody moved. Then Artor freed himself from the body and the druids, frantic lest the sacrifice be wasted, rushed forward with bronze basins in which to catch the blood.

Oesc remembered how the life of the bull he offered before the battle of Portus Adurni had ebbed away beneath his hands. But it seemed to him that the energy that flowed out of this bull was pouring into Artor, who stood wide-eyed in the torchlight, with a crimson stain across his golden robe.

Drums began to pound, a soft insistent rhythm that transformed shock and confusion into a mounting excitement. "Behold!" cried the chief of the druids, his voice steadying as he went on—

". . . the Goddess is freed and the monster is slain.
Now shall the sun return to those lands that need it.
To each power there is a proper season—
A time for the light to shine and a time for darkness,
A time for death and a time for life to flourish.
But now it is the time for harvest!
Therefore let there be no shadow on our celebration;
The Bull's blood buys your lives!"

The druids moved among the people with their blessing bowls, and Oesc pressed forward with the others, and felt, for a little while, as if he were no longer a stranger.

The priestess of the Goddess still stood on the platform, swaying to the drum beat. As she moved, her draperies swirled around her, and it became clear that, although she was masked, beneath the veils she wore nothing at all.

The druids finished cutting off the head of the bull and hoisted it onto a pole. On the platform before the Goddess they placed some of its flesh, along with bread baked from the first grain of the harvest. Some of the others pulled Artor back up onto the platform and set his hand in that of the priestess.

Lifting their linked hands, she cried out in a great voice—

"The grain feeds on the earth,
The folk feed on the grain,
Earth feeds on the folk;
So it is, so it was, so it will be—
Eater and eaten, feeder and fed,
All that dwell on earth must become.
Receive now the blessing of the harvest
the grain that is cut down,
the blood that is shed.
From these things, my children, your life shall spring."

Men moved through the crowd carrying platters of meat and bread. Girls followed them with skins of mead and ale. The drums grew louder and the pipes began to skirl above their beat in ecstatic melody. The rhythm pulsed through Oesc's veins like fire.

On the platform, the priestess had begun to dance—if it was the priestess, for to Oesc's altered vision she seemed suddenly taller. Beneath the half-revealing veils, her pale flesh glowed. Someone handed him a horn of mead and he swallowed. He heard laughter, saw a red-haired girl grab Betiver around the neck to kiss him. For a moment he resisted, then his arms went around her. After a moment she pulled back, laughing, took his hand and drew him after her. Vaguely he remembered Cunorix following another girl a little earlier; Gualchmai had disappeared as well.

Oesc looked back at the platform. Some of the priestess's veils had come off; he glimpsed bobbing breasts, a long, rounded thigh, and felt his flesh spring to agonized attention. *Frige . . .* he thought, *Desired One . . .* then he remembered that the Lady was called Brigantia here. But whoever

She was, she had the kind of beauty a man sees in dreams. Artor still stood before her, swaying in a tranced echo of her movements, his eyes wide and dazed.

A soft hand closed on his and Oesc looked down, glimpsed dark eyes and a merry grin and wildly springing black hair. But it hardly mattered what the girl looked like. He grabbed for her, groaning as soft breasts were crushed against him, a supple waist flexed beneath his hands. Over her head he saw the veiled Goddess take Artor's hand and lead him towards the back of the platform. In another moment they had disappeared into the darkness.

Then the girl's arms locked around his neck. Groaning, he let her draw him down to the hide, and after a brief struggle with their clothing sank between her welcoming thighs and came home.

VII

The High Seat of Hengest

The high king returned south by easy stages. By now only the core of his army remained with him, the others having gone home directly to help with the harvest. The feast of Lugus remained enshrined in their thoughts, but the men did not speak of it, neither to boast of their conquests, nor to wonder if some of the laughing girls with whom they had lain that night might come away from the festival with something more than a memory.

That winter they stayed with Peretur in Eburacum. The Saxons of the north remained quiet, for which Oesc was grateful. He was finding it hard enough to remember the brief time he had spent in this country with his father, without having to face in battle men who had given him his first lessons with the sword.

For he knew that if Artor asked, he would ride with him. The other men had accepted him as one of the high king's chosen Companions. At night he dreamed in the British tongue and by day found his memories of Cantuware growing dim. Even if he returned there, would the people accept him? He had become some curious hybrid, neither fully British nor truly Saxon anymore.

From Eburacum they moved south and west. For a time they stayed with Bishop Dubricius in Isca. There was some fighting as well, for Cunorix's kin in Demetia had been reinforced from Eriu, and were seeking to extend their territory. They proved more troublesome than expected, and the campaign lasted through the summer. And so it was not until early in the following year that the high king returned to Londinium.

Just after the feast of Candlemas, a rumor came to them that Hengest had died. Oesc knew of it first when men began to look at him oddly, whispering. An overheard remark revealed the cause, but he continued to behave as if he had not heard, grateful for time to try to understand his own feelings before he was forced to some public acknowledgment.

Oesc had at that time been among the Britons for nearly nine years. If this had come in the first years of his captivity, he thought, his grief would have been overwhelming. But for too long his memories of Cantuware had brought only pain, and so he had walled them away where even he could not reach them anymore. And that, he told himself, was probably for the best. No doubt Hengest's empty high seat would soon be filled by some ambitious Jute, or perhaps it would be seized by one of Aelle's sons.

By the time a month had passed, he had well-nigh persuaded himself that he believed this. And so when Artor summoned him it was, at least to his conscious mind, a surprise.

"Let us walk along the river—it is too fine a day to stay indoors." Artor reached for the crimson cloak that lay across the chair.

Oesc raised one eyebrow, for the wind had been brisk as he crossed the courtyard, and Artor flushed.

"Well, maybe it is a bit chilly, but I refuse to stay cooped up here. You can wear a cloak of mine—"

And so they fared out, wrapped alike in royal crimson and very much of a height. From a distance, the only difference between them would be his fair hair against Artor's brown. But Artor was lord of most of Britannia, and Oesc was, despite all the marks of consideration, his prisoner.

A brisk wind was blowing up the Tamesis, ruffling the ripples into little wavelets as it scoured the smoke of Londinium's hearthfires from the sky. They had both been right, thought Oesc, wrapping the crimson mantle more securely. It was cold, and it was a beautiful day. With the air so clear, he felt he ought to be able to see downriver all the way to the sea. A sudden memory came to him of sunlight on the water of the estuary below Durobrivae, and he turned swiftly away.

"Was there no one else to keep you company, or did you have something to say to me?" He realized too late how ungracious that had sounded and tried to soften it with a smile.

Artor, who had been gazing southward at the scattering of farms and fields and the distant blue line of the downs, turned back to him, frowning. Oesc felt himself being assessed and examined; it was a look he had learned to recognize when they were on campaign. Then the king released his gaze with a little smile. But there was still trouble in his eyes.

"What is it, my lord?"

"A messenger has come from Cantium. Your grandfather is dead."

Oesc felt a muscle jump in his cheek, but he kept his gaze steady. "He was very old. Many people think he died years ago." *When the Britons captured me. . . .*

Artor cleared his throat. "The message is from your witena-gemot, a formal request from the elders of your people to send you back to them to be their king."

Oesc felt all the blood leave his face and then flood back again. For a moment, staying on his feet took all his strength of will. Then he felt Artor's hand on his arm and his vision cleared.

"And what . . ." he swallowed and tried again, "what was your reply?"

"I have not yet given it. I have to ask you—do you want to go?"

Oesc stared at him. "I have a *choice?*"

"I cannot hold prisoner a man who has guarded my back and fought at my side," said Artor impatiently. "I blame myself now for keeping you by me. It was selfishness on my part. I should have given you this choice a year ago. I suppose it's time to let Cunorix go as well."

Thoughts and emotions suppressed so long Oesc had forgotten them battered against his awareness. Seeing his trouble, Artor went on—

"Oesc, you have earned a place among my Companions. You would be accepted. My own grandfather was a German in the service of Rome. As a man I would ask you to stay—there are many who fight for me because it is their duty, but few who do so because, if I dare assume so much, they are my friends."

There was a short silence. Oesc watched a gull soar towards the sun, then swoop earthward once more. He cleared his throat.

"And what do you ask . . . as a king?"

"If you stay with me, someone else will seize power in Cantium. I cannot afford to have an active enemy on my doorstep. As a king, I want a man in Durovernum who will at worst be neutral, and at best, perhaps, a friend." It was his turn, now to look away.

Gazing at that bent head, Oesc understood two things. The first was that what he felt for Artor was a love which he could never give to any other overlord, and the second was that he had to go home.

"Your grandfather was a Germanic Roman officer. Mine was the man who killed him, as your father killed mine," he said painfully. "If I were not who I am, I would serve you my life long. But if I were not Hengest's grandchild I would not be here at all. And there is another thing. Before ever I saw you I had made my dedication to the goddess who rules the land of Cantuware. I must go back to be her king."

"The Lady . . ." Artor turned back to him, his eyes clouded by memory. "I understand. I will miss you—" He reached out to grip Oesc's hand. "Because of you, even those Saxons whom I must fight will never be a faceless enemy, and to those who live in the lands I hold I will be a fair and honest lord."

Oesc nodded. Surely it was the wind that was making his eyes sting with tears.

"And one more thing, in thanks for the service you have done me. I will have a treaty drawn up between us, confirming you in the rights granted to Hengest by the Vor-Tigernus. It has been three generations since Cantium became Cantuware—even if we were to take it back tomorrow, the Britons who used to live there are scattered and gone. To you and your heirs I grant it, Oesc; it is Saxon soil."

The night of Oesc's farewell feast Artor got drunk for the first time since the rite to Lugus at Dun Eidyn. At least Betiver believed that the king had been drunk that night, certainly everyone else had been, and he did remember that Artor had been as red-eyed and dazed the next morning as the rest of them.

The feast was formal, the menu heavy on the Roman side, with spiced beets and wild spring greens dressed with oils, boiled grains with sauces, and chickens delicately seasoned as well as a suckling pig stewed in wine. For certain Oesc was not going to get a meal like this in his Saxon hut, thought Betiver, trying to decide whether he had room for just one more morsel of elderberry pie. But though his mouth still watered, his belly had another opinion, and he had let his belt out one notch already. With a sigh he pushed his plate away.

"Are you not wanting that?" Gualchmai reached across the table and scraped the remains from Betiver's plate to his own. Gualchmai had grown at least a foot since coming south with Artor, and was always hungry. He was going to be a big man.

Servants cleared the plates away and began to serve more wine. Oesc proposed a toast to the king; the king responded in kind, his cropped brown hair rumpled and his eyes very bright. Cai toasted the armies of Brittania; Artor drank to their commanders. It should have been Cataur, but the Dumnnonian, who had barely tolerated Oesc's presence with the army, had refused to attend. No one missed him. Indeed, by this time everyone was beginning to feel quite mellow, though Oesc looked depressed, except when he was forcing a smile.

The gifts that Artor was sending with his former hostage were brought in. Oesc went red and pale again as he accepted them. There was a lorica hamata of mail with punched and riveted rings and an officer's helmet with decorations in gold. But except for their quality, they would not make him stand out at home—half the Saxon fighting force was outfitted in looted Roman gear. Betiver did wonder, though, where Artor expected the Saxon to wear them. Perhaps he intended to raise auxiliaries from Cantium when the Picts made trouble again.

There were tunics of Byzantine silk, an officer's belt with gold fittings, a pair of arm rings, and a fine woolen cloak of deep blue that was the mate of Artor's crimson, with a great round brooch of gold. There was a table service of figured red ceramic ware and a silver ewer with goblets. Taken together with Oesc's share of the loot from the Pictish campaign, it was an impressive dowry to be taking home to Cantium.

Then the gifts were carried away again and the king called for more wine. Artor stood up and began to make a speech about how brave they had all been during the Pictish war. Betiver felt his eyes closing and surrendered to a dream in which he was dancing around the festival fire with a girl whose body he could still picture in arousing detail, though he had never learned her name.

He came abruptly awake again to find Gualchmai poking him.

"There's a man come from home to bring me messages, and he's asking for you as well. He has a young woman with him who says she's brought your child. . . ."

He had not spoken softly, and Betiver's progress towards the door was followed by a chorus of advice and comment that made him redden, though he pretended not to hear.

He went, determined to see the girl off in short order. There was a widow in the city whom he visited sometimes, but he knew that she was not with child. He was not like Gualchmai, who had progressed from kitchen maids to married ladies and was reputed to have one bastard already, though he was barely sixteen.

He was starting to question the messenger, a ginger-haired fellow wrapped in the yellowish checkered stuff Leudonus' people wore, when he heard a cry. A red-headed woman came forward into the light with a yearling child in her arms, and it was the girl he had just seen in his dream.

For a long moment Betiver stared at her. "What is your name?"

"Roud—" She took a deep breath. "Do you know me, then? I was fearing you might not remember after all."

"I remember."

"Well, that's a start—" Her words tumbled out as if she were afraid that she might not have the courage to say them all. "I know you are great among the princes of the south, and I don't ask you to marry me. But the boy deserves better than I can give him, out in the hills. There was no other man for a moon before or after the festival, my lord, so I am certain he's yours. If you will swear to do right by him, I'll trouble you no more."

Betiver lifted the blanket and saw a frowning, pug-nosed face topped by a tangle of dark hair that looked so much like his own father's that he blinked in surprise. *A boy child . . . I have a son. . . .*

"A child needs his mother," he said softly. "It would be better if you stayed."

Roud stared at him, then her eyes filled with tears. "We'll be no trouble to you, I promise—"

"Nay—you had the trouble of bearing him. If I had known of this, I would have provided for you before. Tonight you may sleep in my rooms here, and tomorrow we'll see about finding a house for you in the town."

By the time Betiver had settled Roud and the boy in his own bed and returned to the feasting hall, everyone had gone but Cai and young Gualchmai, who was pouring more wine for the king.

"You never knew you were planting a field, but it seems you got a fine crop all the same!" commented Gualchmai with rude good humor.

"I remember the girl," said Betiver, "and I'm satisfied that the boy is mine."

"You have a son?" asked Artor, his eyes dark with the wine.

"It would seem so. He wrinkles his forehead just the way my father does when he's annoyed. My memory of the festival in Dun Eidyn is somewhat confused, but I would guess mine was not the only seed to sprout from that sowing."

"Ah, indeed," said Gualchmai, "it was generous of you to replace the men we lost on that campaign."

"You are an unregenerate heathen!" exclaimed Cai.

"Maybe so, but in the north, festival babes are held to be a blessing from the gods."

"A man needs to know that his son is his own," Cai replied.

"Then get married and breed them!" exclaimed Gualchmai. "When will you be taking a wife, uncle? I'm heir to my father's lands already—I've no need for yours!"

His mother would be irritated to hear him say it, thought Betiver. By all accounts Morgause was ambitious for her sons. She had a fifth boy now to follow the others, he had heard.

Artor shook his head. "Kings don't make marriages, they make alliances. So long as I'm unmarried, any man of good blood can hope to make his daughter queen."

"I suppose that Oesc will settle down now and raise a troop of flaxen-haired brats," said Betiver.

"I suppose he will—" Artor sighed. Clearly the wine was wearing off. The sadness had returned to his eyes.

"Are you so sorry to lose him?" asked Cai gruffly. "Oesc is a good fellow, for all his moody ways, and I suppose we'll miss him. But *we're* still here!"

"That's true—" Artor reached out to grip their hands. "But I value each one of you in a different way. I'm afraid that when I see Oesc again he'll be a stranger, and then he might as well be dead to me—"

Betiver felt the king's hand strong and warm in his own, but in spirit Artor was far away. He tightened his grip, trying to draw him back again. *My dear lord, are we not enough for you?*

Oesc rode across the bridge into Durovernum on a fine spring evening just before Ostara, wearing a British tunic and riding a fine British horse that Artor had given him, and still thinking, despite a week of journeying with his Saxon escort, in the British tongue. The remains of the theatre still stood like a monument in the center of the walled town, but the walls themselves seemed lower, and several of the other Roman buildings he remembered had been scavenged for building stone. The long Saxon houses huddled under their weight of thatching like sheep in fleece, and everything he looked on seemed small, and poor, and old.

As they reined in before the hall, a figure appeared in the doorway, shading his eyes with his hand against the westering light. He shouted something, and in another moment Hæthwæge appeared, Hengest's silver-mounted meadhorn in her hands. There was more silver in her hair than he remembered, but otherwise she hadn't changed.

"Oesc son of Octha, waes hal—be welcome to your hall!" She came down the steps, and he took the horn. The mead was yeasty and dry, with an aftertaste of sweetness and fire. The taste of it brought a sudden flood of memories. He drank again, dizzied by the conflict of old knowledge and new, uncertain for a moment who he was or where.

"Thank you . . ." he mumbled, clinging to the formalities. A thrall came up to take the horse's head and he swung a leg across the high front of the saddle and slid to the ground. His escort were dismounting behind him. More thralls led their horses away. A horn blew and he heard people shouting.

For so long, he thought, he had dreamed of this moment, longed for it. And now, it seemed the capacity to respond was dead in him. *What am I doing here? How can I be a king to these people? Would Artor take me back again?*

Hæthwæge was saying something. He forced himself to attend.

"You are tired. Come into the hall."

He nodded gratefully and followed her.

Inside it was cool and dim. As his vision adjusted, light from the opened smoke vents beneath the eaves at either end of the hall showed him the carved and painted pillars that upheld the peaked roof and the curtained compartments to either side. But he had become accustomed to separate sleeping chambers and columns of stone. Then the scent, composite of woodsmoke and ale, dog and old leather and the sweat of men, caught at his throat, and for a moment he was thirteen years old once more. Someone opened a side door, and a rush of fresh air brought him back to the present.

"There are only half a dozen men now in the houseguard, and most of those are old," Hæthwæge was saying. "He gave the younger men land to farm. And there is only one cook and three kitchen thralls, but I have asked some of the women to come and help us."

Oesc nodded, thinking he would have to use much of the treasure Artor had given him just to set things in order here. Compared to the crowded, noisy place he remembered, this was like a hall of ghosts.

His footsteps echoed on the planking as he passed the boards and trestles for the tables that leaned in stacks against the walls, and he thought of colored mosaic floors. The raised stone hearth nearer the doorway was cold, but a little blue smoke rose from smoldering coals in the one before the high seat at the end of the hall. He remembered the clear light that fell through windows of nubbled glass, and Artor's marble throne.

The wisewoman paused as if she expected him to sit there. Oesc looked up at the serpentine carving on the posts, worn where Hengest had leaned against them, and at the cushion that still bore the impress of his body, and shook his head.

"Not yet. It has been a long time, and my soul is still stretched like a drying hide between here and Londinium. Build up the fire and let me sit on a bench beside it. I'll take the high seat when we drink Hengest's funeral ale."

She frowned at him thoughtfully and handed him the meadhorn once more. From outside came the sound of many voices. The light from the door flickered as if someone were hovering there.

"The people are gathering, wanting to see you. Two lambs are already roasting, and tonight you will feast. When you are ready, come to me and I will tell you how your grandfather died."

It was late before the shouting and the singing died away in the hall. But when the last of the revelers set off for his home or rolled up in his cloak beside the hearth, as Hæthwæge had known he would, Oesc came to her.

He had still been a boy when he left them, with the soft flesh of youth covering his bones. Now the strong structure of his face made the resemblance to his grandfather clear, all the more so because he looked so tired.

"Was it too bad?" He would have had more than enough ale in the hall. She dipped some of the mint tea that had been steeping on the hearth into a beaker and offered it.

Oesc sighed. "The skin of the boy who lived here nine years ago no longer fits, and the man he became is some sort of Saxon-British hybrid who doesn't fit anywhere. I told them I was tired from the journey, and they made allowances, but I am afraid my grandfather's thanes will think they have got a bad bargain in me."

"You have half a moon until the feast of Ostara when the æthelings and freemen will gather to drink Hengest's funeral ale. It will be better by then."

"I hope so! Otherwise I might as well lay myself in his mound . . ." He took a long drink of the tea and settled back on his stool. "This place is as I remember, and so are you. Talk to me, bind me back into this world again. . . ."

At least he knew what he needed, she thought, watching him. She would have to shape the man as she had shaped the boy, but it would be harder now because he was not so much scarred as armored by his time in the British lands.

"When one has a slow illness, or is very old, there comes a time when the spirit turns inward. Mostly our folk go quickly, in battle or sudden sickness, but I have seen this often enough so that when Hengest began to drift away from us I understood what it was. His health was no worse, nor was he in pain. He ate less and slept more, and delegated most of the household decisions to Guthlaf or to me. When he sat in his high seat he spoke of the battles of his youth sometimes, or of you, but as time went on, he mostly stayed in his bed."

Oesc frowned unhappily. "I should have been here for him. I knew how old he was—I should have begged Artor to let me visit him."

"It would have made no difference. It was that boy whose skin is too small for you that he remembered, not the man you are now."

"Whoever *he* is . . ." muttered Oesc, and refilled his cup. Then he straightened, obviously trying to lift himself out of the mood. "It is hard to picture Hengest, the conqueror of Britannia, dying in his bed like a woman or a thrall."

Hæthwæge shook her head. "He did not. There came a day when the hills echoed with the cries of new lambs, and the sky with the calls of returning waterfowl. There was a wind, and we opened all the doors to air out the hall." She shut her eyes for a moment, remembering the brilliance of the sky, and how life had tingled in that air. "The kitchen thrall who used to bring Hengest his porridge called me. The king was sitting up, asking for a basin to wash in and the Frankish lapped tunic with the gold borders to wear. The folk here rejoiced, thinking that he was getting well at last."

"Where did he want to go?"

"He asked me to take him to the god-grove, and to bring the Spear."

Oesc's eyes widened, and his gaze went to the shrouded shape by the door. Hæthwæge knew he was remembering how his other grandfather had died. In the same, measured tone, she went on.

They had brought a lamb, and the old king cut its throat and splashed its blood on the god-posts and the stones. She remembered how the air around them grew heavy, as if something had awakened and was watching as Hengest set his back against the ash tree and pulled open his tunic to bare his breast. The green shadows had given his old skin a sickly pallor, as if he were dead already.

And then, as he had commanded, she scratched Woden's knot into his belly just below the ribs, and tied the rags with which she stanched the bleeding onto the branches of the ash tree. And at that a great wind had shivered the new leaves.

"The god was there," she said softly. "The offering was accepted. But Hengest said that as the god had made him live so long already he would let him choose his own moment to claim him. And so he closed up his tunic and we went back to the hall.

"He sat down in his high seat and told them to build up the fire, but he would take neither food nor drink. Some of the men wanted me to force him to lie down, but the warriors of the houseguard backed me. They understood very well."

"How long did it take him to die?" asked Oesc in a still voice.

Hæthwæge drew a deep breath, remembering the old king sitting like a carven image in his bloodstained tunic, listening to Andulf sing of Sigfrid and Hagano, of Offa of Angeln and Scyld Sceafing, one of the few heroes who lived to be old. He had sung of Eormanaric. He sang until even his trained voice grew hoarse and Hengest told him to be still. That was the sixth night. Three days longer the king stayed, without eating or sleeping. By then he had stopped speaking as well, and only the occasional movement of his breast told them that he lived still.

"Nine days and nights altogether Hengest sat there, and when the tenth morning dawned, although he had not moved, we saw that his breath no longer stirred his beard. The god had come for him at last."

"And *that* is the high seat you want me to sit in?" Oesc said unsteadily.

"You will sit there, and Hengest's spirit will guide you," said Hæthwæge with the certainty of prophecy.

"I drink to Hengest, wisest of warriors, first to be king in the British lands—" Aelle lifted his drinking horn, and the others followed his example with a roar of approval.

Oesc, sitting on a bench before the high seat, gazed around him at the men crammed into the hall. They had begun to arrive just after the Ostara offerings, when by custom kings feasted with their chieftains, to celebrate Hengest's funeral ale.

He had expected Aelle to bring his son Cymen, and Ceretic to come over from Venta, and he knew that Hengest's thanes, Hrofe Guthereson and Hæsta and the others, would be there. But he was surprised by how many others made the journey—old men who had fought in Hengest's battles, and young men to whom they were legends. There was even a small party from Gallia, bearing the condolences of Chlodovechus, the Frankish king.

Each day more tents went up in the field beyond the hall as new groups settled in. It was just as well that Artor had gifted him with so much treasure, he thought ruefully, for this feast would exhaust their stores. He did not delude himself that all these folk had come for his sake. Hengest had been the father of the Saxon migration. With his death an era was ended.

Many times that night the meadhorn had gone round. Men laughed and said it was time the hall had a queen to honor the warriors. Hengest had been an old wolf, who had rather embrace his sword than a woman, but Oesc still had juice in his loins. He should take a wife—the talk grew ribald with speculation. Aelle had granddaughters, girls of good Saxon stock who would give him strong sons. Ceretic had a little daughter, but it would be a dozen winters before she was husband-high. The lords from the Anglian lands suggested that one of the Icelinga girls could bring him a useful alliance. Even Chlodovechus's representative joined the discussion, pointing out that his master also had marriageable daughters, and Cantuware possessed fine harbors that could benefit from Frankish trade.

Oesc shook his head, laughing. "Nay, I must see how my grandfather's high seat fits me before I seek someone to share it. Give me a year or three to settle into my kingship. I promise you I will consider an alliance then."

Hrofe began to talk of how Hengest had married his daughter Reginwynna to the Vor-Tigernus, and Oesc sat back with a sigh. For so long, even the idea of marriage had been out of the question; the thought of a connection more meaningful than his brief encounters with whores or serving-maids took some getting used to. More important still, any marriage he made would commit him to an alliance. If Artor had had another sister—his lips twitched as he remembered the overwhelming beauty of Leudonus's queen. Even if Morgause had been free, it would take a brave man to husband her. She was fertile, though. It was said that nine months after the feast of Lugus she too had been brought to bed of a fine boy that her husband accepted as his own.

Lost in his own thoughts, he did not realize that Andulf had begun to sing

". . . Where once he had held
most bliss in the world, war swept away
all Finn's thanes, save few alone
that he might not at that meeting place
with war against Hengest finish the fight
nor the survivors with warfare wrest free
from the king's thane. . . ."

It was the tale of the fight at Finnesburgh, the first of Hengest's great deeds, though Hengest himself had never boasted about it. That was a hard and bitter story, of the time when Hengest had led the warband of the Dane-king Hnaef on visit to his brother-in-law the Frisian Finn, and when enmity between Finn's men and Hnaef's had become warfare, first forced the Frisian king to divide the steading between the two sides and keep them through the winter, and when the Danes insisted on revenge, broken the peace-troth pledged with Finn in order to avenge his lord.

". . . But they bid him take terms,
that the king another hall should clear,
hall and high seat, that they half would hold
of all the Jutes' sons might possess,
and at wealth-giving, Folkwalda's son
every day the Danes would honor,
and Hengest's riders, with rings as was right
even as well with treasured wealth
and golden cups, the Frisian kin
in the beer-hall he bolstered in spirit."

Hengest had done the same thing again, he thought, when for the sake of his people he turned against the Vor-Tigernus and attacked the British princes. Oesc looked up at the empty high seat, contemplating once more the stature of the man who had occupied it. *What would I do, faced with such a decision?* he wondered then. *If I am ever forced to choose between my own folk and Artor, what will I do?*

Andulf ended the story of the slaying of the Frisians, and once more the meadhorn went round. The tales of Hengest's deeds had inspired his mourners to vows of emulation, most of them, as might have been expected, at the expense of their British neighbors.

"This is my oath, in Woden's name—" Ceretic lifted the horn. "To push the borders of the West Saxon lands outward until Dumnonia is ours, to found a line of kings who shall rule in this island for a hundred generations, to leave a name that shall be remembered as that of the father of this island's kings!"

That did not leave much scope for the other dynasties, and there were a few raised eyebrows, but neither was it much of a threat to the present balance of power. Oesc waited with growing apprehension for the horn to come round to him. Even when he took it in his hand he did not know what he was going to say.

For a long moment he stared at the empty high seat, then he turned to face his guests once more.

"I have fought in battles and killed enemies," he said slowly, "but all my great deeds are still in the future. I am too new in my lordship to make great boasts for my people. I was not here at Hengest's death to take his blessing. To sit in his seat without having performed some great exploit would be overweening pride. This therefore, is my boast. I will go from this place now, at night's high noon, and sit out upon my grand-father's grave mound. If I can sit in that high seat without scathe until dawn, I will claim his place as king."

As he finished, men began to nod and pound the tables in approval. Oesc's vow was unexpected, but not unworthy. It was true that Hengest had met his death in good heart as befitted a warrior and had no reason to hate the living, but the ghosts of the mighty dead could be unchancy, especially when disturbed in their howes.

At first the chill of the night air was welcome after the heat of the hall. But as Oesc approached the mound that had been raised for Hengest just inside the southeastern wall he began to feel the cold, and was glad of the heavy cloak he had brought along. Mist lay heavy on the fields, beyond the tumbled stones, luminous in the light of the waning moon. A dog howled in the town behind him and he suppressed a shiver, hoping that the two warriors who were escorting him had not seen. His shadow lengthened before him in the light of their torches, as if his fetch were hastening towards the mound.

The hill they had raised above the box containing his father's head was as he remembered, flattened a little by time and covered with green grass. Hengest's mound rose stark and black beside it, the colors of the white stallion carved on his grave-post still bright.

"Hengest son of Wihtgils, it is I, Oesc, blood of your blood, who come to your howe seeking counsel. Accept this food and drink, grand-father, and allow me to sit with you in safety until dawn." He unstoppered the flask of mead and poured its contents into the ditch that surrounded the grave mound, then crumbled the barley cake between his fingers and scattered it there.

He waited in silence, and presently it seemed to him that the night had grown a little warmer. "Woden, lord of the slain, be with me now . . ." he whispered, then he gathered up the folds of his cloak and leaped across the ditch onto the mound. He lifted one hand in salute to his men. Then they turned and left him alone.

Oesc's first awareness was of stillness without silence. From the woods beyond the fields he heard the bark of a fox and from the town a dog answering it. From time to time some unusually exuberant burst of shouting echoed faint from the hall.

He patted the earth beside him. "I am glad that you can hear the celebration, grandfather, and that you are not completely alone out here in your mound . . ."

The Christian priests would say that Hengest burned now in their

Gehenna, and that it was superstition to talk to him as if he were alive in the mound. But that did not stop them from praying at the graves of their saints, who were said to dwell with their god in bliss. Hæthwæge had always taught him that a man was a vastly more complex creation than the Christian duality of body and soul, and that while part of the being that had been Hengest feasted in Woden's hall, another part might still cling to the ashes buried in this mound, while the clan-soul which he had inherited from his forebears waited to take flesh again in some future child of his line.

He had seen how they buried Octha's head, and he supposed that after they burned Hengest's body, the bronze urn containing his ashes had been treated likewise, set within a wooden chamber with his shield and seax and spear, his helmet and arm rings, bronze-bound buckets and bowls with food and drink and all such other gear as he might need. Oesc tried to imagine what it was like down there in the heart of the mound.

"I have no wish to disturb your rest, grandfather, but I need your wisdom," Oesc said softly. "Give me your mind, teach me what you have learned from your deeds; and give me your luck, the might and main that carried you across the sea to claim this land, and that will help me to hold it. It is not your treasure that I need from you, Hengest, but this ghostly inheritance."

Once more the wind blew, ruffling the guard-hairs on the fur that lined his cloak. Oesc pulled it more tightly around him and settled himself to wait, breathing in and out in a steady rhythm as Hæthwæge had taught him. Time seemed to move slowly, but when a night bird's cry brought him briefly to awareness, he saw that the moon had moved a quarter of the way across the sky.

It was in the dead of the out-tide, when even the singing from the mead-hall had stilled, that Oesc became conscious in a way that was different from before. He saw the moon low in the west, but he saw also the grey shape that sat beside him on the mound. It was Hengest, the metal-woven braid on his Frankish tunic glinting in the moonlight, but though the wind bent the grass, it did not stir a hair of his flowing beard.

His lips did not move, and yet Oesc felt knowledge precipitating in his awareness like the dew on the grass. He knew the snarling faces of men now fifty years in their graves, the white cliffs of Dubris above the heaving grey waves of the sea, the clamor of a thousand fights, and the long slow years in Cantuware, growing into the land. Everything that had made Hengest a king was now his, if he had the might to use it.

"I see now what you have done . . ." he sent his own thought to that powerful presence, *"but not what I must do . . ."*

There was amusement in the answer that returned to him. *"That is your Wyrd, not mine. But this I will say—land-right belongs to those who give themselves to the land. Seek the Lady, and offer Her your seed and your soul. . . ."*

In the sky the stars were fading. Hengest's form dimmed—for a moment Oesc could see the shapes of field and tree through it, then it was gone.

He took a deep breath, returning sensation rushing tingling through hands and feet. Stiffened muscles did not want to move, but he got upright, and going carefully, for his balance was still unsure, descended the mound. On the other side of the ditch he fell to his knees and plunged his fingers through the new grass and into the soil.

"Earth, my mother, my life is yours. In return I take this kingdom into my hand."

As the first light of the new day scattered gold across the softly flowing waters of the Stur and glowed on the grass, Oesc son of Octha son of Hengest returned to his grandfather's mead-hall and ascended the high seat that was waiting for him there.

VIII

Battles in The Mist

A.D. 493

"Can there be any Angles left in Germania?" Artor slapped the table so hard that the map shivered and the inkwell skipped dangerously. "For fifteen years every spring has brought more of them flocking northward like wild geese across the sea. But these geese don't fly home again. The Iceni and Trinovante lands have long been lost to us, and now the Angles are spreading into the Coritani country. If they link up with their country-men above the Abus, King Icel will have a stranglehold on half the island!"

The flicker of a hanging lamp added an uncertain illumination to the grey light coming in through the thick panes of the window, further distorted by the rain that was streaming down them. It had been raining for some time.

"To answer your first question," answered Betiver, "in Gallia they say that the Anglian homeland has become a wilderness. There are no more reinforcements left to come. To answer your second question, the last messengers we had say that Lindum is surrounded. Even if he does not take it, eastern Britannia already lies in Icel's grasp. . . ."

"You are such a comforter," commented Gualchmai, lounging against the doorframe. He had grown taller even than Artor, and had to duck these days to go through. His brother Gwyhir, who had joined Artor's household two years after his brother, was almost as tall, and no doubt young Aggarban, the third of Artor's nephews to come to them, would be a big man too.

"Lindum was badly hit last time the Saxons attacked, and the walls were never repaired." Betiver traced the line of the Roman road northward. "By now it may have fallen. We should have reinforced it long ago."

"Gualchmai is right," muttered the king. "You *are* depressing."

"You would not thank me for lying to you . . ."

Artor looked up with that quick smile that took the sting from his words. "You are right, of course, but this is horrible weather for doing anything with cavalry. Do the Angles have webbed feet? I'm told that Anglia is all fenland—they must feel right at home."

Gualchmai guffawed. "I'll wager they do! I ought to have looked at old Oesc's feet when he was here. But he is a Jute of some kind, is he not?"

"His mother was Myrging, but Hengest was Anglian. Fortunately Oesc is rooted in Cantium, and content to keep to his own borders, thank God," added Betiver.

"But he is oathed to Artor—surely you could call—"

The king shook his head. "I raised a wild gosling once that followed me as if I were its mother. All through one summer it fed with the white farm geese and seemed content. But when the wild geese passed overhead in the autumn, my gosling opened her wings and flew away. I tried to call her back, and she circled thrice, but she could not deny her nature and so I lost her."

Gualchmai met his gaze blankly.

"I believe I have won Oesc's friendship, and I have his word," Artor said then, "but even though Hengest's line and Icel's were rivals, I know better than to overstrain Oesc's loyalty. There is more to kingship than giving orders—you must understand the nature of those you rule."

Gualchmai's ruddy skin grew redder. "Your orders are enough for me . . ."

"Because that is *your* nature," answered Artor softly.

"No doubt Cataur will send men, but it will take some time for them to get here," Betiver said into the silence that followed. "He loves killing Saxons, whoever they may be. There will be a troop from Glevum, and one from Deva—" He began to reckon the forces at their command.

"And we'll need some infantry. I wonder . . ." Suddenly Artor smiled.

"Perhaps Cunorix would like to bring me a band of his wild Irishmen. They should have no objection to fighting Icel if they get a good share of the spoils."

Outside, it continued to rain.

It was raining in Cantuware as well. Oesc made passing travelers welcome in his hall and listened to their news. Sitting snug by his fire, he told himself that he pitied men who had to march across the soggy soil of the Coritani lands, that there was no glory in that kind of fighting anyway.

The weather that had delayed the royal messengers also slowed the men who were responding to Artor's call. But the Angles, accustomed to muddy footing, pushed onward, and shortly after Beltain, word came that Lindum had fallen. Icel now possessed a base, if he could keep it, from which he might control everything between Eburacum and Durolipons.

Oesc tossed a coin to the pack-man who had brought the news and strode out of the hall. The fine drizzle beaded the blue wool of his cloak with tiny crystals, but he scarcely noticed the damp. He was seeing not the mud of the yard, but the bloody earth of a battlefield, and instead of Wulfhere and Guthlac and the other men of his household, Betiver and Gualchmai and Artor himself, riding against the foe. He should have been with them—but he understood why the king had not called him. Did Artor really fear that Oesc would have been tempted to fight on the other side?

He had faced Artor in battle once before, when he did not know him. His gut twisted unpleasantly at the thought of doing so again. But his body cried out for action, he wanted to fight. At that moment he scarcely cared who, and the folk of the steading scattered before him.

Presently he found himself in front of the barn.

He called for his horse. Someone asked a question about hunting, and he nodded, and a few minutes later he was trotting towards the south-eastern gate of the town. The road cut straight across the flats to the east of the river for several miles. To their right the river gleamed among marshy islets. Beyond it the skirts of the North Downs were clad in forest. But Oesc made no move to get to the other side—these woods, so close to the town, held no game capable of challenging him now.

It was nightfall before they crossed the river and came to the ancient trackway that climbed to the tops of the Downs. There they made camp, and before the sun was high they were taking the path into the hills. A night in the open had muted Oesc's sense of urgency. As riding warmed him, stiff muscles began to ease. He drew a deep breath of the morning air, heavy with the scents of leaf mold and new grass, and felt something that had been drawn tight within him grow easier as well. He actually *saw* the scenery he was looking at for the first time since leaving his hall. And when, just after noon, they crossed the track of a stag, awareness of all else fell away and he gave himself entirely to the joy of the chase.

By the depth of the prints, the stag was old enough to have learned all the tricks by which a hunted beast can elude its foes. But Oesc's tracker was a lad whose folk had lived on the Downs since before the Romans came, and he knew the beasts of his native woods as well as his own kin. A little past noon, they caught sight of the quarry and kicked their horses into all-out pursuit. Oesc's mount was the swiftest, and so he was out of sight of the others when, swinging wide to avoid a fallen tree, his horse put a foot into a hole. Oesc felt the beast lurch beneath him, but before he could get clear the horse went down. He was aware of trees blurring past, and then a resounding impact, and then, for quite some time, of nothing at all.

When Oesc came to himself again the clouds had wrapped the hillside in a damp embrace; everything beyond a few feet was dissolving into featureless grey. His horse stood a few feet away, one foreleg barely touching the ground. With a groan Oesc got upright, made his way over to the animal and gently felt the limb. It did not seem to be broken, thank the gods, though it was clearly a bad sprain. When he tugged on the rein, the horse followed, on three legs only, after him.

Their progress was painfully slow. It hardly mattered, thought Oesc grimly, since it was becoming increasingly apparent that he was lost. Even if he had known this countryside, the mists would have made everything seem strange. And yet to keep moving, even with no goal, was better than bleating like a lost sheep in hopes that someone would find him.

He could see nothing but the shadows of tree trunks in the mist, but downhill, he knew, the forest grew thicker still. His only hope was to struggle up to the bare open slopes that crowned the Downs, where he might strike the ancient track that crossed them. Local legend held that these hills had been well-peopled in ancient days, when the world was warmer and there were no iron ploughs to turn the heavier lowland soils. One still sometimes found the marks of ancient round houses in the soil. Even today, Oesc might hope to encounter a shepherd, or a pack-man trudging across the hills.

Once he found the track he could follow it back to the river, and have a good laugh at his escort, who must be quite frantic by now. But he had his bow, and had learned which of the spring greens could be eaten. He might be separated from his friends, but at least there were no foes hunting him. He was still better off than he would have been in Artor's army.

*   *   *

The same storms that pounded Cantuware had drenched the north as well, saturating the soil and exposing Artor's army to attack by the elements as well as the enemy. Rising waters lapped the raised Roman causeways, wagons bogged down in the sticky mud and animals went lame. Rain spoiled the rations they carried, and though water surrounded them, it was thick and foul. The fact that these hazards had been anticipated did not make them easier to bear. More than once men wished for Merlin to magic the clouds away, but the sorcerer was in the north on some errand of his own.

The Anglians, well aware of their danger, made good use of the country's natural defenses. And yet, though bowstrings stretched and leather rotted, still the Britons came on. In a battle near the ruins of Lactodorum they faced the Eslinga Saxons and had their first victory. Artor took oaths and hostages from their leaders and sent them eastward to Durolipons to garrison the fens against their former allies. Two more muddy skirmishes, hardly worth dignifying with the name of battle, could be counted as victories, since it was the Anglians who retreated when they were done.

Artor led his army along the old legionary road beside the Blackwater. By the feast of Pentecost the royal forces could see the smoke of Anglian cookfires in Lindum across the marshes to the northwest, where the Blackwater, curving into the lowlands, had breached its banks and made a lake of the land. Even in high summer the country of the Lindenses was largely water meadow and marsh. In a wet spring, it seemed an inland sea, in which the scattered bits of higher ground stood like islands. To beseige the city, surrounded by marsh in the midst of hostile territory, was not an attractive prospect, given the problems the Britons had already experienced with supply. But perhaps Icel, unfamiliar with both cities and seiges, would not be aware of Artor's difficulties.

Two days after Pentecost, the king sent one of his captured Saxon chieftains with a challenge. If the Anglians would wager all upon one battle, the Britons would abide by its outcome—to take back all the Lindenses lands if they won, and to abandon the campaign and cede the territory to Icel if their foes had the victory. When the delegation had gone, Artor ordered his army to make camp. The cooks began preparing the first hot meal they had had for a fortnight, and every warrior was set to repairing and preparing weapons and gear.

For three days they remained in camp, waiting for an answer. Then, leaving the baggage train on the high ground, they set out once more upon the road to Lindum.

*   *   *

"Be thankful, man—it could still be raining!" Gualchmai's beard and mustache glittered with fine droplets as he grinned. The clouds still hung low, but the weather had warmed, and the earth was giving back its excess moisture in the form of patchy mists that drifted among the trees.

"What's this, then? Liquid sunshine?" growled Betiver, shifting uncomfortably in the saddle. His thighs were chafed from riding in wet breeches and his nose was stuffy. But he was luckier than some, for the flux, plague of armies, was beginning to thin their line.

"Man, it would be counted a fine day in my own country!"

Betiver shook his head, wishing they had stayed in camp a day longer. But they might stay for a week and still be plagued by bad weather, while in the meantime the Anglians could be filling Lindum with supplies and men. Here, the Blackwater ran to their right, more or less paralleling the road. But soon, as he recalled, it would make a bend to the westward, where it flowed through the marshy valley. The Romans had made a ford there, so that the road could continue straight along the narrow neck of higher ground that led towards the town.

"Soon we'll be over the river, and then a straight march to Lindum it will be!" said Gwyhir, peering ahead. The mist had thickened. Only the ring of hooves on stone assured them they were still on the road.

"If the floods haven't washed the ford away," grumbled Betiver. Artor's companions headed the column, though the king himself had stayed near the middle to hearten the men. There were scouts out ahead somewhere. He hoped they hadn't gotten lost in this gloom. His stuffed nose was turning into a headache, and his back and shoulders hurt as well.

"Nay, they went out to look last night, remember, and reported that it was still whole," Gwyhir replied. He was, like his brother, exasperatingly cheerful in weather that made everyone else complain.

"If I were Icel, I would set stakes in it, or tear out the stones. He knows we must pass this way . . ."

"What's that?" Gualchmai checked his mount, peering ahead. Betiver strained to see, wishing he were taller. A touch of damp air on one cheek was echoed by a shift in the intensity of the greyness before them.

"The fog is lifting—" he began. A flicker of light rippled through the mist. He stiffened as the wind strengthened, rolling back the mist to unveil the road before them, where morning sunlight gleamed from the well-honed points of a host of spears. With each moment the size of the army that faced them grew clearer. A British horn bugled alarm.

Betiver let out his breath on a long sigh. "It would seem that Icel has given us his answer, after all."

Hooves clattered, and Artor pulled his big black horse to a halt beside them.

"Well. Now I know why our scouts did not return." He was scanning the foe, calculating numbers and dispositions. The Anglians had formed up on the other side of the ford, on the last broad piece of solid ground before the land narrowed. "They've chosen well. The ground's too soft for our heavy cavalry to flank them. Icel wants to force us into a slugging match. . . . we need some way to improve the odds."

The king's tone was detached, as if he were considering a board game. Could he really be that calm?

"Use your archers to soften them up, then," suggested Gualchmai. "They're mostly unarmored."

"Not yet—" Artor frowned. "First, let's try a parley."

"Do you think it will do any good?" Gwyhir asked.

"No, but I need a better estimate of their numbers, and a check on the state of the ford."

"I'll go—" offered Gwyhir.

"Nay, that you will not! You've not the experience—" retorted his brother. The king shook his head.

"The task is for neither. Your eloquence is all in your sword arm, Gualchmai—" Artor grinned. "This requires sweet talk and flattery, so Icel won't realize I'm playing for time." He looked at Betiver, who sighed.

"I understand. Let me wear that white cloak of yours with all the gold embroidery and I'll flatter him like an emperor."

It was amazing, thought Betiver as he splashed through the ford, how the imminent expectation of a spear in the gut put other pains in perspective. He could hardly feel the aches with which he had begun the day.

At least the ford had not been damaged. Perhaps, he thought as he looked around him, the Anglians had considered that precaution superfluous. There were certainly a lot of them, drawn up in groups surrounding their chieftains. Icel sat his white stallion in the middle of the line. He was a big man with a fair mustache, glittering in a shirt of ringmail and a spangenhelm inlaid with figures of gods and heroes in gold.

Meeting that cold grey gaze, Betiver found that respect came easily. Icel's homeland might be small compared to the empire, and poor, but he traced his descent, father to son, through a line of kings that went back to the god Woden, and that was an older lineage than either Artor or the emperor in Byzantium could claim.

"The king of the Britons has good warriors, but they are wet and weary. My men are fresh and strong," said the Anglian king when Betiver had stated Artor's terms. "It is not for him to demand surrender. This is our land now, and we will defend it. Eight hundred spears stand ready to prove my words—" He gestured. "We have heard much of Artor's battles and are eager to fight him. Go tell him so—"

As Betiver rode back towards the British lines it occurred to him that the Eslingas and Middle Saxons had been eager too, and Artor had beaten them, but Icel had spoken truly, and his own side, battered and muddy, seemed a rag-tag excuse for an army next to the barbaric splendor of the warriors surrounding the Anglian king.

But though Betiver's embassy had been fruitless, Artor had made good use of the delay. The British were armed and ready, their heavy cavalry in the middle, the archers positioned in the wings. The king was cantering along the lines, his red cloak bright against the black horse's flanks, his armor gleaming dully in the sun. He listened to Betiver's report with a smile that did not reach his eyes.

Then he wheeled the horse and came to a halt before the first line.

"Men of Britannia—" His voice was pitched to carry. "You have marched a weary way. But Lindum is in sight, and the Anglians have come out to make us welcome!" He waited for their answering laughter. "We have faced their kin three times already and beaten them. But Icel's own warriors have not encountered our like before. We are the heirs of Rome and the children of this island. Draw up strength from this sacred soil, and we will prevail. One more battle, lads, and we will break them. The way to Lindum lies before us—win this one, and tonight we'll lie in soft beds with roofs to keep out the rain!"

After the past few weeks, thought Betiver, dry beds sounded better than gold. He jerked the chin-strap of his helmet tight, wondering wistfully if the baths of Lindum were still usable. Artor was right. He would kill for the chance at a hot soak at the end of the day.

Artor lifted his hand and the air rang to the bitter calling of the horns. The enemy ran to meet them, intending to close the distance so there would be no room for a charge. A ripple of movement swept through the ranks of mounted men, and then the column was moving forward and Betiver's awareness narrowed to the area above his horse's ears through which he could see a glittering line of spearpoints that grew more distinct with every stride.

The air darkened as the archers let fly. The riders splashed through the ford. A horse went down on the right, where the bottom was treacherous, but the others kept their feet and labored up the far bank. An Anglian, outstripping his companions, cast a spear that sped past Artor's shoulder and gashed the flank of the horse behind him. The animal squealed and lurched, but its rider kept it going. Gualchmai plucked a javelin from its loop and cast, and the Anglian went down.

First blood to us— thought Betiver, but now all his vision was filled with grimacing enemy faces. He dug his heels into the horse's sides, striving for the momentum they would need to smash the Anglian line. More spears flew and he heard cries. One after another he reached for his own lances and threw. Then they were crashing into the first group of enemy warriors; for a moment the charge faltered, then they drove onward.

A spear jabbed up at him. Betiver swung his shield around to deflect it and pulled his sword from the sheath. It was all blade-work now, as their pace was slowed by crowding foes. But still they pushed onward, and then they were through. Artor called to them to form up again and hit the enemy from the rear. Light flared from his sword. In that moment of freedom Betiver heard shouting from the flanks. He blinked in confusion as figures rose up like ghosts from the misty waters. Then a familiar war cry shrilled above the clamor of battle and he laughed as Cunorix and his wild Irishmen emerged from the marshes and fell upon the foe.

Artor yelled again, and Betiver's mount, catching the excitement, lurched into motion after the others. His sword arm swung up, and screaming, he charged back into the fray.

The bay horse lifted its head, ears flicking nervously, and Oesc stilled, listening. In another moment his duller ears caught the bleating of sheep. He let out his breath in a long sigh, only then admitting his fear that he might have wandered somehow into Nebhelheim, and would never find his way back to Middle-Earth again. Through the thinning mists a ewe gazed at him with a flat, disapproving stare that could only belong to the sheep kept by humankind. Then the herd dog caught his scent and dashed forward, barking.

"There, boy, down—I mean no harm—"

The dog, a brisk black-and-white beast with a plume of a tail, did not seem convinced. It continued to advance, growling, and he looked around for the shepherd.

He was waving his hands to repel the dog when something moved on the hill. He looked up, saw a blur in the air, and threw up his arm. There was a crack. He reeled, then gasped as pain flared through his arm like white fire. Someone was running towards him, whirling a slingshot in one hand and brandishing a staff in the other; Oesc stepped back, caught his heel in a root and went down.

The stick whistled through the air where his head had been. He rolled as it thwacked downward, and made a grab for his assailant. His good hand closed on a slim ankle and he pulled. The staff went flying and they grappled, rolling over and over in the wet grass.

His foe was wiry as a wildcat, but Oesc was a trained fighting man, and despite his useless arm, in a few moments his size and strength began to tell. It was only when he had got his opponent's arm in a twist and the thrashing legs locked between his own long limbs that he realized his attacker was a girl.

For several moments neither could do more than gasp. He stared down into a heart-shaped face, flushed now with fury and surrounded by a Medusa-tangle of nut-brown hair. Her eyes were a gold-flecked brown, like amber, he thought, gazing into them, or honey-mead.

"A fine welcome you give to strangers here on the Downs," he said finally.

"I thought you were a robber." Her gaze fixed on the fine embroidery at the neck of his tunic, and the golden arm ring. "They've taken two sheep in the past week. I thought they'd come back again." She tensed, trying to free herself, and he was abruptly aware that it was a female body that lay crushed beneath his own.

"It's not mutton I would have from you—" He muttered, and kissed her, at first a light brush of the lips that held her still with surprise, and then hungrily, until she began to struggle once more beneath him and he came up for air, his heart beating hard in his breast.

"How *dare* you!" She got a hand free and tried to box his ear. He pinned her with his body, since he could not use his arm.

"You owe me some weregild—I think you've broken my arm—" he began, and felt her stiffen.

"You're a Saxon!"

He stared at her, and realized they had been speaking in the British tongue.

"A Myrging, to be more precise, and your master—" he said then.

"Then you *are* a robber, after all! My grandfather was lord of this land!"

"You're Prince Gorangonus's kin? We're well matched then, for *my* grandfather took Cantium away from him." He grinned down as her face flushed with angry color once more. His body was urging him to take her, but this was no thrall to be tumbled on a hillside, even if at the moment she looked more like a troll-maid than the daughter of a royal house.

"Hengest's brat—" On her lips it was a curse.

"Hengest's heir," he corrected softly, "and Cantium's king . . ."

"How can you be the king, when you were born across the sea?" She had stopped struggling, and sorrow was extinguishing the fire in her eyes.

"So were the Romans, when they came here—" He released her and sat up, wincing as the movement jarred his arm. "And it was they who put your father's fathers on that throne."

"Perhaps, but it was my mother's mothers who gave them the right to rule. That's why I came back—" She gestured towards the misty sweep of the Downs. "Folk of my blood have dwelt here since before the Romans, even before the Cantiaci came. This land belongs to me!"

For a moment Oesc felt the moist chill of the shrine on the Meduwege once more and remembered how its spirit had spoken to him there. There was a sense in which her claim was true. Men ruled by right of conquest, but sovereignty came from the Goddess and the queens who were her priestesses. Still, he knew better than to admit that, or to point out that without the power to defend it, she might as well have been the wild child she appeared.

"What is your name, granddaughter of Gorangonus?" He winced as an unwary movement jarred his arm, the same that had been broken in Londinium.

"I am called Rigana, for my mother said I should have the name of a queen even if I spent my days keeping sheep upon the hills."

"Very well, then," said Oesc. "I will treat with you as a king does with a queen. Give me shelter. Bind up my arm and tend my horse, which has gone lame, and when my men come to find me you shall have gold."

In a single supple movement she was on her feet, looking down at him.

"That is not the way you treat a queen, but an inn-wife. It is as a queen I will shelter you, for you are the suppliant. But the boy who helps us will go for your men as fast as he may, for I would not have the sight and smell of you in my house for one hour longer than hospitality compels."

Clean, warm, and dry at last, Betiver considered the captive Anglian lords. It made him shiver even now to remember what a near thing the battle had been. A score of times during that dreadful morning he had been sure they were beaten. But whenever he could stop to draw breath long enough to consider surrender he had seen that Artor was still fighting, and gritted his teeth, and kept on. He was not ashamed at his own grim satisfaction—now it was he who was dressed like a prince, and the Anglians who were gashed and grimy. However the reversal of fortune did not seem to have daunted their pride.

"Look at Icel!" exclaimed Gualchmai. "Lounging at his ease, as if he still held this hall! You would think he'd be showing a wee bit of apprehension. Did he never hear about the Night of the Long Knives?"

"He trusts to Artor's honor, and besides, that atrocity was the work of Hengest's Saxons. They may all look like the same kind of barbarian to us, but to Icel, his folk are as different from the other tribes as, say, your Votadini are from the Picts who are their neighbors."

"Hmph. Well, I won't deny the Picts have come to us at times for husbands for their princesses. But their sons are raised by their uncles, and mother's milk is stronger than father's blood."

Betiver lifted a hand to silence him. Artor stood in the doorway, drawing men's eyes and stilling their tongues. He too had taken advantage of Lindum's baths, and had dressed in a Roman tunic of saffron-dyed linen with bands of purple silk coming down over the shoulders to the hem and patches bearing eagles worked in gold. His mantle, also edged in goldwork, was of a red so deep it was almost purple, and he wore a Roman diadem upon his brow. Cai, behind him, was actually wearing a toga. Gualchmai whistled softly and grinned.

"Is it the emperor himself who's come to call on us? I hope Icel is impressed."

There had been a flicker of appreciation in Icel's grey eyes, but his face showed no emotion at all. That clothing had certainly never made the muddy journey from Londinium. Betiver, wondering which rich merchant had provided it, fought to keep his own face still. Icel had sought to impress them as a folk-king, lord of a mighty people, but Artor was meeting him as the heir of Rome.

Moving with conscious dignity, Artor seated himself on the carved chair on the dais, and Betiver and Gualchmai took their places with Cai behind him. Icel and two of his surviving chieftains, still in the grubby tunics they had worn beneath their mail, had been given low benches on the floor.

"You fought well, " said Artor, "but your gods have given you into my hand."

"Woden betrayed us," muttered one of the chieftains. "Nine stallions we gave him, and yet he did not give victory."

"But many of your warriors earned a place in his houseguard," said Artor, who had learned something of the German religion when Oesc was his captive. Icel responded with a rather wintry smile.

"Woden will take care of his own. My care is for the living. What is your will for those who are your prisoners?"

"Kill them," muttered Cataur, "as they slaughtered our men."

Most of those who had survived the battle, thought Betiver, belonged to Icel's houseguard, who had made a fortress of flesh around their king. If he had fallen, they would not have survived him, and only Icel's order could have made them lay down their arms. He leaned close to Gualchmai. "He doesn't ask about himself—"

Gualchmai snorted derisively. "He knows the high king cannot afford to let him go."

But Artor was leaning on the acanthus-carved arm of his chair, resting his chin on his hand, and frowning.

"What would you have me do?"

The question disturbed Icel's composure at last. "What do you mean?"

"You are their king—what did your people seek on these shores?"

"Land! Land that will not wash away in the winter rains!"

Artor raised one eyebrow, indicating with a turn of the head the flooded wastes outside the town, and someone laughed. But Icel was shaking his head.

"Oh yes, this land floods, but the water will go away again and leave it all the richer. We can ditch and dam and make good fields. The river is not so greedy as the sea."

"The Romans did not have that craft—"

Icel's lips twitched again. "The Romans built like etins, great works of pride and power that forced earth to their will. Our farmers are content to work with willow wands and mud and coax our Mother to be kind."

Artor's gaze moved slowly around the faded frescoes of the old basilica, and the worn mosaics on the floor, and he sighed.

"The Romans were mighty indeed, but they are gone, and the land remains," he said then. "And save for your folk, there are now none left to till that soil."

Something flickered in Icel's gaze at the words, but he kept his features still. Cataur's face began to darken dangerously.

"Many men of my blood have died," Artor went on, "but my duty is to the living also. To leave this place a wasteland and its shores desolate will serve no one. But I *am* high king, and any who would dwell here must go under my yoke." He frowned at Icel. "If I give you your lives, will you and your folk take oath to me, to hold these coasts and defend them in my name? As the Romans gave districts to the Franks and Burgunds and Visigoths, I will give the Lindenses lands to you, saving only Lindum itself, which I judge my own people better able to garrison."

As the Vor-Tigernus gave land to Hengest . . . thought Betiver grimly, *and look what that led to!* But Hengest's men had been a rag-tag of mercenaries and masterless men, not a nation. It was the same agreement

Artor had made with Oesc, in the end, and that seemed to be working well.

There was a short silence. "What guarantees . . . would you require?" the Anglian king said then.

"That you shall swear never again to take arms against me or my heirs, to defend these lands against all others, and to send a levy of warriors at my call. You shall pay a yearly tribute, its size contingent upon the size of your harvest, and in cases affecting men not of your people, be judged by my laws. I further require that you give up all looted goods and treasure, that one son from each of your noble families shall be sent as hostage to dwell among the youths of my household, and that all warriors who are not of your tribe shall remain my prisoners."

Cataur surged forward, and Gualchmai moved to stand between him and the dais. "My lord, you cannot do this! He's a *Saxon . . .*"

"An Anglian," Artor corrected coldly, "and I am your king—"

"Not if you betray us!" Cataur exclaimed, his hands twitching as if he reached for someone's throat. But Gwyhir and Aggarban had come to stand beside their brother, and Morgause's three sons made a formidable barrier. "You'll regret this day!" Still sputtering, Cataur whirled and strode from the room. Gualchmai started after him, but Artor waved him back.

It took a few minutes for the murmur of comment to die down. But despite the fact that there were those on both sides who like Cataur would obviously rather have kept on fighting, it was a fair offer. Indeed, it was more than generous, especially when the alternative was to be slaughtered like a sheep, without even a sword in one's hand. Icel must have hoped for something like this, even if he had not dared to expect it.

Icel got to his feet, his eyes still fixed on Artor. "I am the folk-lord, and I stand for my people before the gods. But for all things that belong to this land and the Britons I will give my oath to you."

Artor gestured to one of the guards. "Unloose his bonds." He looked back at Icel. "As you keep faith with me, so shall I with you, for the sake of Britannia."

A little past sunset three weeks after Oesc returned from his ill-fated hunting trip, the hounds who ran loose around his hall began barking furiously. Oesc, who had been drinking to ease the ache in his arm and trying not to think about Rigana, sat up, and Wulfhere rose to his feet, reaching for the spear that leaned against the door.

"Who comes to the hall of Oesc the king?"

"One who carried him on his saddlebow when he was a boy, came the gruff answer, "and I have not made my way across half Britannia,

beset by enemies, to be challenged in Hengest's hall!" Taking advantage
of Wulfhere's astonishment, the newcomer shouldered past him and into
the light of the fire. Two other men came after him, looking about them
nervously.

Oesc leaned forward, striving to see behind the dirt and the dried
blood and the wild grey-streaked hair.

"Is it Baldulf?" he asked, coming down from his high seat and opening his arms. "It must be! You stink too badly to be aught but a mortal
man! Old friend, what has happened to bring you to my door like—" He
shook his head, seeking words.

"Like a fugitive?" Baldulf sank down upon a bench, took the horn of
ale the thrall-woman offered and drank it down. "That's what I am, boy—
fleeing a lost battlefield and the wrath of your young high king."

"You were in the north—" Oesc said, "were you with Icel?"

Baldulf grunted. "I was safe enough in my dale, until that smooth-
talking Anglian sent messages around seeking allies in his campaign
against Lindum. All went well for a time, but Artor came at last, and
brought Icel to battle. Lad, I was lucky to survive that day, and luckier
still not to be captured. The Anglians have taken oath to Artor, but the
other prisoners were killed. If I never see another marsh I shall count
myself happy!" He shuddered reminiscently and held out his horn to be
refilled with ale.

"I won't give you up to him, if that's what you were wondering,"
said Oesc, "but I can't keep you here."

"Nor would I stay—help me to a ship and I'll be over the water to
the Frisian lands." He took another drink and reached out for a hunk of
the bread which had been set before him. "There may be no Anglians left
to replace those Icel lost, but there are still fighters on the coast who might
be willing to try their luck in Britannia. Two men only survived from my
warband—" He gestured towards his followers, who were being fed at a
table by the door. "But I'll soon raise another. The Britons have not heard
the last of me!"

Oesc nodded bemusedly. Listening to Baldulf was like stepping back
into another time, to the days when Hengest and his father tore at Britannia
like wolves. Things were different now. He understood why Icel had accepted Artor's peace. Now Britannia was his land, too. After a moment
he realized that Baldulf had asked him a question.

"Come with you? No—all that I want is here—" He shook his head,
smiling.

"All? What about a plump wife to warm your bed, and fair-haired children about your knee? Shall I look for the daughter of a Frisian chieftain, or maybe a Frankish princess, to be your queen?"

Oesc stared at him, all his frustration focusing suddenly into a single need. "I do need a wife," he said then, "but not a woman from across the sea. I must marry into this land if my heirs are to hold it. . . ."

Suddenly Rigana's face filled his vision. Tomorrow, he thought, he would ride to the hut on the Downs. After that first encounter he had not touched her, but one way or another, he knew that she would be his queen.

IX

Alliances

Torches had been set into the crumbling city wall and upon the green height of Hengest's mound. They flickered with pale fire in the last light of the soft summer day. The space before the mound had been cleared and spread with rushes to accommodate the tables for the wedding feast. The King's Hall had not room enough for so many, and in any case, this close to Midsummer it was far too warm to huddle indoors.

The sound of Andulf's chanting floated on the wind. He was old now, and his voice no longer as resonant as it once had been, but he still had the trick of pitching it to carry across the field.

"Hail the heir of high-born heroes—
Son of the Saxons who first to these shores;
West over whale-road, borne by the wind,
The old land left, new lives to fashion—"

Oesc, who had gone to consult with his steward about serving more mead, surveyed the scene and smiled. Two dozen tables rayed out in a semicircle from his own, where Rigana, draped in crimson silk and hung with gold, awaited him. Her features were half-hidden by the fall of her veil, but his pulse leaped at the sight of her all the same. In the month since he had brought her home to Cantuwaraburh, he had discovered that he could always sense her presence, and his pulse quickened at the mere brush of her hand.

But he had, in addition, a very different reason for feeling satisfaction. The Cantuware chieftains, nodding approvingly as Andulf began to recite Oesc's ancestry, had all turned out with their sworn men, but that, he had expected. It was their duty to witness the wedding of their lord to the woman who would give him his heir. But Ceretic had brought his West Saxons, and Aelle, his hair now entirely white but his frame still well-muscled, had journeyed up from the south coast to attend the celebration, and that was an honor on which Oesc had not dared to depend.

And beside Rigana, where her father, had he been living, would have had his place, sat Artor the High King, who had made time between campaigning against the Anglians and dealing with the new threat from Irish raiders in Demetia to come. He almost looked the part of a father, thought Oesc, watching them. In the past year or so Artor had broadened out—not with fat, but with the muscle that comes from wearing armor for long hours over an extended campaign. In Artor's eyes Oesc could still recognize the boy he had first faced across a battlefield sixteen years before, but the body was now emphatically that of a man, and a king.

It was with enthusiasm that Artor had accepted Oesc's invitation to stand for the family of the bride at the wedding. More eagerness, to tell the truth, than Rigana had shown when she heard about it. To be sure, it was Vitalinus the Vor-Tigernus who had given away her grandfather's princedom, not Uthir, but even though there was now no man of that line fit to hold Cantium, Rigana blamed the House of Ambrosius for not having won it back to British rule, and Artor for confirming Oesc as its lord.

It was no use to point out that if the Saxons had never come, she would most likely have been married off young to some lord living elsewhere in Britannia, whereas now she would be queen in her own country. Oesc was coming to understand the bride he had brought home from the hills. Courageous she was, as well as passionate, but logic was not one of her virtues.

"In wisdom he weds a noble woman," sang Andulf.
"Daughter of drightens, radiant as day.
Bold is her heart, as bright her beauty,
Lady who links the lord to the land."

Surely that must please her, thought Oesc. Artor had signed the marriage contract on her behalf, and now he was slicing meat from the joint that had been set before them, and as he transferred slices to her platter, she smiled. Should that make him uneasy, wondered Oesc?

Watching them, he saw in Rigana's face no coquetry, but it seemed to him that there was something wistful in Artor's eyes. The question of the high king's marriage had been often discussed, but although many maidens had been proposed for the honor, there had never been time, it seemed, for him to court one of them. But if Artor had found love of a more casual kind, no one had heard about it.

Oesc did not think the high king could have had a mistress in secret, but he was not a cold man. When he came to love, it would be deeply.

It is not my bride I should fear for, Oesc thought then, *but my king.*

He saw Ceretic's daughter Alfgifu approaching, bearing the great silver-mounted aurochs horn filled with mead. Andulf struck a last chord and finished his song.

Oesc strode quickly back to take his place at Rigana's side as Artor accepted the horn.

"It is my honor to be the first to offer a toast for the couple who sit before you. Any marriage is a harbinger of hope, for thus the race is renewed. But this wedding, more than most, gives me hope for the future, for the groom, who was once my enemy, has become a friend and ally, and the bride, a woman of my own people, is a living link between the old royal line and the new. It is always something of a miracle that two creatures so different as male and female can live in harmony—" He paused for the murmur of laughter. "But if Oesc and Rigana can do so, then there is hope that Britons and Saxons can live in peace as well.

"This, then, is my wish for the bridal couple—that as they join their lives, our peoples may be linked as well, and if they do not always manage to live in perfect accord—" again, he waited for the laughter "—then I wish that their differences may be quickly resolved, and that from their union new life shall spring!"

He turned the horn carefully so that its tip pointed down, and raised it to his lips, taking a long draught without spilling a drop. Then he handed it back to Alfgifu, who bore it to Aelle, and then to Ceretic and the other chieftains.

The other blessings were more conventional, with a heavy emphasis on the breeding of strong sons. Oesc scarcely heard them. His beating pulse reminded him that soon the feast would be finished, and it would be time to make Rigana his wife in fact as well as name.

When the toasts were completed, the women led Rigana off to the hall to be prepared for bed. As their singing faded, the sound of men's laughter grew louder as the male guests were released from such bonds of propriety as they had observed so far.

"Drink deep, my lord," said Wulfhere, refilling his horn.

Oesc took it and drank, fighting not to cough as he realized that this was not the mild ale mead they had been drinking, but a brew whose heavy sweetness did not quite hide its strength. He swallowed, feeling his head swim as the fire began to burn in his belly, and handed the horn back to the other man.

"That's fine stuff, but I'd best go easy or I'll be no use to my bride—"

"You'll be no use either if you cannot relax," said Ceretic with a grin, offering his own horn. "Drink up, man!"

"That's true," answered Oesc. He reached for the horn.

Ceretic moved closer, bending as if to continue his teasing. "At your wedding feast, the high king of Britannia himself sits down with his Saxon enemies. Are you not honored?" He was still smiling, but there was something unexpectedly sardonic in his tone.

Oesc raised an eyebrow. "Shouldn't I be?"

Ceretic shrugged. "Artor sings a sweet song about peace between Briton and Saxon, but it is like trying to build an alliance between dogs and wolves."

"You yourself are half Briton—" Oesc began.

Ceretic grunted. "But my heart is Saxon. The blood may mix, but the spirit must be singular. The Britons lick their wounds now, but they hate us still, especially Cataur, who has never forgiven us his brother's death at Portus Adurni. They say he protested making peace with Icel and left the army immediately afterward with all his men, nor will he take them to Artor's aid in Demetia. That man wants blood, and he'll not care where he gets it. I would put a guard upon your borders if I were you."

"Artor will keep him leashed—"

Ceretic shook his head. "Artor may desire peace, but one day his princes will force him to turn against us. When he summons you to war against your own people, which will you choose?"

For a long moment Oesc frowned back at him, the mead growing cold in his belly. "I will choose my own land," he said finally. "I will fight for Cantuware."

Ceretic opened his mouth as if he would say more, then closed it without speaking. The torches flared suddenly in a gust of wind, and Oesc turned. Hæthwæge had come into the circle of light. Silence spread as men saw her standing there, and one or two made a surreptitious gesture of warding where they thought no one could see. It occurred to Oesc that

Hæthwæge must be in her sixth decade by now, but as always when she put on the regalia of a priestess, she seemed beyond age.

The wisewoman looked around the circle, smiling slightly, then turned to Oesc. "This is a time of change, when the spindle twirls and new strands are woven into the web of Wyrd. Would you know, my king, what fates shall fall as a result of this marriage of yours?"

The men who stood nearest backed away uneasily. Oesc found himself abruptly sober once more.

"Are you afraid?" she asked then.

He shook his head. This was Hæthwæge, who had guided and guarded him since he was a child.

"I fear neither my fate nor you. Whether my Wyrd be good or bad, foreknowledge will enable me to face it well."

The guests drew back to leave a space around them. Hæthwæge spread a square of linen on the ground and drew the bundle of runestaves from her pouch.

"Say, then, what it is you wish to know—"

For a moment Oesc stood in thought, choosing his words. "Tell me if this marriage will prosper, and whether my queen will bear a son to follow me in this land."

Hæthwæge nodded. Her eyes closed, and she whispered a prayer he could not hear. Then she bent, and with a practiced flick of the wrist, scattered the runestaves across the cloth.

The yew wood sticks rattled faintly as they fell, bounced against one another, and then lay still. Oesc leaned forward, trying to make out the symbols incised and painted where the sides of the sticks had been planed smooth. It was quite dark now. In the flicker of torchlight the rune signs seemed to twist and bend.

Like any man of good blood he knew something of the runes, but their deeper meanings, especially in combination, were a mystery. The sticks the old woman had cast lay scattered across the cloth. Most of them had fallen near the edges; it was the ones that lay within the circle painted in the center that would provide the prophecy.

"*Ing,* the rune of the king who comes over the sea, the god in the royal mound—" Hæthwæge pointed to a rune of crossed angles that lay in the middle of the cloth. "Your seed will take root in the ground." There was a murmur of appreciation from the other men.

"And there, near to it, are *Ethel,* for heritage and homeland, and *Ger,* the rune of good harvests. It means that you will bring luck to your land. But *Hægl,* the hailstone, lies close by them. Some violent upset threatens as well."

"What is the rune that lies across the other, just to the right of the middle of the cloth?" asked Oesc.

For a moment Hæthwæge stared at them, swaying back and forth and muttering softly. Then she sighed.

"*Gyfu* is crossed by *Nyd*—the rune of gifts and exchange cut by Necessity. You see how similar they are—one equal-armed, the other showing the firedrill crossed by its bow. *Gyfu* is a rune that wins great gains, but it is also a sign of self-sacrifice. Some say that *Nyd* represents the slash of a sword, or the spindle of the Norns. Whichever is true, these two crossed runes intersect." The wisewoman looked up at Oesc, and his heart chilled at the sorrow he saw in her eyes.

The wisewoman sighed, then spoke again. "This is the Wyrd that these runes show to me. Your reign will be fruitful, my king, and your son will rule long in this land. But there is a price to pay. Always. Only if you are willing to give all will all you have wished for come to pass."

"All?" he echoed softly, remembering how his grandfather's body had swung from the tree. Since childhood he had understood what might be required of a king. "I made that offering before I ever ascended Hengest's high seat, when I sat out upon his mound."

"You have answered well." Leaning on her staff, the wicce straightened. "Your bride awaits you. Go now, and fulfill your destiny."

The light around them brightened. Oesc turned and saw that four of the women who had escorted Rigana to the hall had returned, bearing fresh torches whose flames were whipped out into ribbons of fire by the rising wind.

"To your destiny!" echoed Ceretic, grinning, "and a fair one it is!" He gave Oesc a push, and fell in with the other men behind him, cheering, as the women lit his way towards the bridal bower.

To satisfy his bride's Roman preference for privacy, Oesc had built a partition to wall off the end of the hall that held the king's boxbed from the rest. Four pillars still supported the framework, stuffed with straw and featherbeds. But instead of closing the space between them with wooden slats, it now was hung with lengths of heavy woolen woven in bands of crimson and gold. A wooden floor had been laid and a wolfskin rug cast over it. Terracotta lamps hung from brackets on the wall, and the women had garlanded the bed with greenery and early summer flowers.

More important still, the bower had a door. As he shut it firmly behind him, Oesc was suddenly extremely glad he had taken the trouble to build it. This moment would have been even more difficult if there had been no more than a single bedcurtain between him and the raucous encouragement he was being given by the men outside. He cleared his throat.

"Rigana?"

From the other side of the curtain came a noise that sounded suspiciously like laughter.

She answered, "The sooner you come to bed, the sooner those louts outside will shut up and go away."

Oesc fumbled with the clasp of his belt, dragged his tunic over his head and dropped it, and pulled off his breeches. As he pulled aside the curtain and climbed into the bed he could feel his heart beating as it did when he was going to war.

Light filtered through the rough weave of the curtains, glowing on the pale flesh of the woman who sat cross-legged on the coverlet. Oesc's breath caught as he looked at her small, uptilted breasts and rounded thighs, confirming with his eyes what his hands had learned about her body when they struggled on the grass. Since that day, she had scarcely let him touch her. But she did not seem to be afraid.

"Are you drunk?" she asked suddenly.

He blinked, then shook his head. "Did you think I would have to be drunk to lie with you?"

"I only wondered what was keeping you so long." She settled back among the pillows, looking at him with the same frank interest with which he had eyed her.

Hoping that the dim light would not show his blush, Oesc climbed the rest of the way into the bed.

"Hæthwæge read the runes. She says we will have a fine son to be king of this land."

"Does she? Then we had better get started on making him—"

Oesc could not decide whether her smile held eagerness or defiance.

He had meant to be tender, to take her slowly. He had dreamed of this moment in exquisite detail—how he would stroke first her cheek, and then work his way carefully down until her breast lay like a tender fruit in his hand. He had not anticipated the way that lust would flame in his blood in response to the challenge in her smile. *Frige be with me!* he thought desperately as he pulled Rigana into his arms.

The wiry, whipcord strength was as he remembered, but the feel of her smooth skin against his own as they wrestled together made his mind reel. His fingers tightened in her hair as he kissed her, his body straining against hers until she lay still. She cried out as he thrust through her maidenhead, and began to fight him again, but imperceptibly their struggles became harmony, their breath coming together in harsh gasps as they rode the storm. He felt her convulse in his arms, and her final frenzy swept his own awareness away.

An eternity later, they became aware of each other as separate beings again. Wind was whispering in the thatching, and from the feasting ground they could hear men's voices lifted in song. Oesc raised himself up on one elbow, looking down at his bride.

"Don't think it will be this easy every time . . ." she said shakily.

"Easy?" Oesc winced as bites and scratches began to sting. "I feel like a ship that has barely survived the storm. If this coupling has made a son, he will be a warrior!"

"A typical Saxon!"

"As fierce as his mother!" Oesc replied. He shook his head in exasperation. "If you hate us so, why did you marry me?"

"You carried me off—" she retorted, "what choice did I have?"

"You know very well I would not have forced you. And at the end there, your body seemed very eager for mine! Rigana—the same wind buffeted us both, and brought us in the end to safe harbor. Even now will you not give truth to me?"

"The truth is . . . that my body may have surrendered, but my mind still tells me that you are my enemy."

"And your heart?" he asked softly.

Rigana sighed. "My heart is a slow learner—you must give it time to understand."

In the weeks that followed, Oesc remembered those words. Marriage with Rigana was like sailing the sea at the mercy of conflicting winds. At times they blew as balmy as some fabled southern isle, and Oesc, half-drunk on his new wife's kisses, would swear that he had won her at last. But then some clash of culture or concept, or even the sight of the ruins over which her grandfather had ruled, would set the wind wheeling round to the north again, with a chill that could freeze his soul. But the body had its own imperatives. Their lovemaking, when Rigana would submit to it, was a force that shook them both to the core. And soon it became apparent that Oesc's seed had taken root in fertile ground.

Pregnancy, of course, gave the queen a whole new source of invective, especially during the early months, when she was often ill. Nonetheless, as the result of their lovemaking became increasingly apparent, Rigana began to turn to her husband more and more. It was a golden year, with a bountiful harvest and a mild winter, and Oesc tasted his new happiness with astonished joy.

Just after the spring equinox, when the rain storms followed each other in stately succession across the land, Rigana's pangs came upon her. The bed in the bower was spread with clean cloths and fresh straw for her lying in, and Oesc was banished from the room to wait beside the fire in the hall with the other men.

"Women!" exclaimed Wulfhere, "they act as if all men were monsters when one of them is in the straw!"

"Not all men—" said Oesc, wincing as he heard Rigana swearing from the other side of the wall. "Just me. . . ." He rubbed his left arm, where Rigana's slingstone had cracked the old break in the bone. He had still not gotten back full use of that hand.

"She has a good vocabulary," observed Wulfhere, running a hand through his thinning ash-brown hair.

Oesc managed to smile back at him. Wulfhere was a good friend, he thought, straightforward and steady, as good a man as one might find in the Saxon lands. But he had been born in Cantium, son to a man who had come over in Hengest's first warband. He understood Oesc's love for this land. More to the point, he was also the father of four children, and understood what his lord was going through.

Oesc looked up suddenly, realizing that he could hear nothing from the bower. He started to get to his feet, but Wulfhere shook his head.

"Someone will come out if there's news." He pushed the beer jug across the table.

"No. I don't want to be drunk when—if—she's been at it since morning and it is past midnight! I'd rather fight a battle than wait here. At least I could *do* something there!"

"This is a woman's battlefield. But life, not death, is the victory."

"I hope so—" Oesc sat down once more.

From the bower came a grunt, and then something very like a battle cry. The two men stared, scarcely daring to breathe, until they heard, like an echo, a thin, protesting wail.

Women's voices murmured busily as the door opened and Hæthwæge beckoned. Two steps brought Oesc to her side.

"Is Rigana—is the baby—" He could not find words. Beyond the wicce he saw his wife lying in the bed in which the child had been begotten. A pile of bloodstained cloths lay on the floor. She looked pale, but her eyes were very bright. Walking carefully, as if his footfalls might break something, he came to her side and took her hand.

"My dear, I'm so sorry—" he stammered, "I didn't know!"

"Sorry! When I've given you a fine son? Look at him!" She flipped back a piece of linen and he realized that what he had taken for tumbled bedclothes beside her were the cloths that swaddled a tiny being who mewed at the disturbance and rooted against his mother's breast.

"You're all right?" he asked.

"Of course. I've helped too many ewes bring their lambs into the world to make a fuss—though I must say the sheep seem to have an easier time! Pick him up—is he not beautiful?"

Oesc realized that the women were all watching him expectantly, and someone had summoned his sword-thanes, who were crowding into the room.

"Beautiful—" he muttered, although the crumpled red features looked more like those of a tiny troll than of a man. Carefully he got his hands under the small bundle and lifted it, and caught his breath as the slitted eyes opened and for a moment he saw his grandfather Eadguth's face overlaid on that of the child.

"Beautiful—" he said again, knowing what they were waiting for. "And I claim him as my son! Is there water?" He looked at Hæthwæge.

"Here—I brought it from the sacred spring . . ." She held out a bowl of dark brown earthenware incised with a zigzag design around the rim.

Oesc dipped his fingers into the water and sprinkled the cool droplets on the baby's brow. "Eormenric son of Oesc I name you, grandson of Octha and Gorangonus of Cantium, great grandson of Hengest of the royal Anglians, and Eadguth the Myrging king. I dedicate you to Woden, who has given you breath, and to the Lady of this land, who has given you flesh. Live long, my son, for Cantuware is your heritage!"

"I think I never knew what it was to simply feel happy before . . ." said Oesc. Wulfhere, who was riding beside him, laughed.

"Well, lord, you have reason."

Oesc found that he was grinning. The movement of the horse beneath him, the way the summer sunlight glowed through the whispering leaves above the track that led north through the Weald towards Aegelesford, even the sweetness of the air he drew in—today, everything gave him joy. But he had ridden through fine summer days before and never noticed their beauty. It was the happiness he had found in the great things of his life that allowed him to value the little ones as well.

"To the fortunate man, all things are golden—" he repeated the old saying. "It is true, I have been greatly blessed."

Still smiling, he silently enumerated the gifts that the gods had given him: Rigana had recovered well from the birthing, and Eormenric had outgrown the first fragility of babyhood and was now as fine and lusty a child as any man might wish for. The first, disturbing resemblance to his grandfathers had faded as he put on flesh. At three months, he was all plump cheeks and bright eyes, reaching out to grasp the world with chubby pink hands.

In his delight with the baby, Oesc did not forget the wife who had produced him. Rigana would never be an easy woman to live with, but after a year of marriage, she had lost the abrasive edge that had at first turned every conversation into a battle. Now they only fought once or twice a week, and since their battles more often than not ended in bed, Oesc could hardly regret them.

And Hengest's old hall had never been so bright. Rigana had the manner of a princess, but her life on the farm in the hills had given her a realistic understanding of the labor needed to maintain a hall. She asked nothing of her maids that she could not do better, and though at times they felt the lash of her tongue, they respected her.

His marriage had won him new respect among the men of Cantuware as well, especially the eorls and elders. *They no longer have to fear I will lead their sons off on wild adventures,* he thought. *I am becoming a land-king now.*

Certainly Hæsta seemed to think so. At this last law-giving, the southern eorl had praised his judgments. Even Hengest, he said, had not understood the land and its needs so well.

And Oesc was still young, and save for that lingering weakness in his left arm, in robust health. There was no reason he should not live as long as his grandfather and see his own grandchildren root themselves in this land. He had taken Rigana and the baby to Aegele's ford so that they could get the blessing of the goddess of the sacred spring.

Suddenly his joy demanded action. The ford was barely an hour away, and then he would see his wife and child, but he did not want to wait so long. The horse's ears twitched as he lifted the rein.

"Wulfhere, that nag of yours is plodding like a plowhorse. I have a mind to reach Aegele's ford by noon. Do you think you can match me?"

"I'll come there before you!" Wulfhere's eyes kindled.

"Do it and I'll give you the Frankish swordmount that Hæsta gifted me."

"And you shall have your pick of Prick-Ear's next litter if you win—" Wulfhere returned. The other men shook their heads indulgently, but they reined their mounts out of the way as with a shout their young king and his friend set their horses careering up the path.

Bent over the grey mare's neck, gulping in air strained through her flying mane, it was not until Oesc began to cough that he realized the air smelled of smoke—not the smoke of a hearthfire, or soapmaking or the burning of brush or any of the other uses of fire about a farm, but the acrid reek of a big fire, of burning timbers and smoldering straw. He had smelled it too often to mistake, when he was at war.

He straightened, shifting his weight back and hauling on the reins. For a moment the mare fought him, then she pulled up, plunging, just as Wulfhere thundered around the bend behind him.

"What is it? Is your horse—" he began. Then he too caught the scent the wind was bringing and his face changed.

"Go back and bring up the warriors," Oesc said softly. "Leave the baggage ponies to follow as best they can."

"But my lord—"

"I've done scouting. I'll go slowly and take care not to be seen."

Oesc waited until the clatter of Wulfhere's departure faded and the forest grew quiet around him. He could hear neither shouting nor hoof-beats, but the burning must be close for the reek to be so strong. Perhaps Aegele was only burning brush, he told himself, and the men would get a good laugh at his fear. Then a shift in the wind brought him a whiff of roasting flesh, and the mare lurched forward at the touch of his heel.

He slowed again as he started down the slope towards the ford, but now he could hear ravens calling to their kindred. They would not do so unless the fighting was done.

It was strange, some odd, detached part of his mind observed as he rode into the farmyard, how clearly he could still read the signs, though it was nearly ten years since last he had ridden to war.

The attackers had hit the farm without warning. The women had been dyeing cloth. Two squares of blue flapped damply from the rack, but the pot had been overthrown, its contents mixing with the blood on the ground. One of the thrall women lay beside it, her head crushed, her hand still gripping the wooden bat she had been using to stir the pot. But her skirts modestly covered her thighs.

Where is Rigana? Oesc forced the yammering voice within him to be still.

The raiders had not raped or even pillaged—cattle still lowed from the byre. But the hoofprints had already told him that these folk were riding good Roman-bred horses, not the shaggy hill ponies that outlaws would use. He found two more thralls by the byre, and then one of Aegele's men with a sword still in his hand. Outlaws would not have left the weapon, and the strokes that had killed the man had a military precision. This was not robbery, but a raid, conducted by trained warriors with a military objective in mind.

My wife and my son! Dead, or hostages? Once more he shut the voice away.

Methodically Oesc worked his way around the buildings. More men lay with their throats cut in addition to their wounds. The attackers had left no one living to tell the tale. Aegele himself lay just inside the ruins of his house, with his wife beside him. His body was partly burned, but the golden band that marked him as a thane was still on his arm.

Hæthwæge was with them. Could her magic have hidden Rigana and the child?

He left the mare standing and made his way up the path to the shrine. The devastation that had hit the farm had not touched it—more reason for that cold, evaluating part of his mind that kept his rage at bay to conclude British warriors had done this thing. He saw signs of a scuffle in the dirt before the shrine. Blood had been drawn—dark drops speckled the ground.

A breath of wind lifted his hair and chilled the sweat on his brow. He went inside.

The lamps were cold, but a bunch of summer asters, barely wilted, still lay on the stone, and beside it, a baby's teething bone.

"Lady—" he whispered, "they came to serve you. Could you not have protected them?"

Water murmured musically from below, the same song as it had sung for Celt and Roman, and for those who came before. *I am here as I have always been . . .* it whispered, *be still, and know . . .*

But Oesc could not listen. In his ears a furious wind was rising, sweeping both patience and reason away. A swift step took him back to the doorway and the devastated farm below. Wulfhere and his men were just riding in. But he scarcely saw them.

"Rigana . . ." he whispered. The roar of the wind grew louder, though no leaf stirred. "*Rigana. . . .*" Reason was reft away in a great shout that shattered the silence as her name became a berserker's wordless cry. Still shouting, Oesc ran down the hill.

For the next four days they followed the raiders. Messengers galloped off to raise the fyrd while Oesc and his best trackers kept on the trail. It was not difficult. The British had hit other steadings on their way into Cantuware, but in Rigana, they realized they had a prize beyond all booty and were losing no time in getting her away from the Saxon lands. North to Durobrivae led the trail, and then straight west along the old Roman road.

To those they passed, the attackers were no more than an echo of hoofbeats, a rumor in the night. But as word spread through the country-side, folk came from the places they had hit on their way in. By the time Oesc reached the borders of his own lands, his fyrd was over a hundred strong. But the British were a day ahead of them. They had left the road before it reached Londinium and headed cross-country, following minor paths that the Saxons did not know.

Clearly they meant to avoid Venta Belgarum as they had Londinium, but still their way led westward.

A week after Rigana had been taken, Oesc halted his warband at the edge of the British border. Their quarry had gone west and south into Dumnonia, where Oesc had not the force to follow them. But by then he knew whom he was chasing. The warriors who had captured his wife and child belonged to Cataur, prince of the Cornovii and enemy of the Saxon kind.

"What will you do?" asked Wulfhere, his face gaunted by a week of hard riding.

Oesc looked around him. "Beric—" he gestured to a red-headed lad on a roan pony. "Your mother was British, and you speak the tongue well. I will write a message in the Latin tongue, which you must take to Artor. I believe he is in Demetia—the Irish have been raiding again. It is time to hold him to his oath. Rigana and the baby are only valuable as hostages if they are alive. I have to believe that Cataur will take care of her. But he will have to give her up to his king."

"And if he does not?"

Oesc could feel his own features stiffening into a mask of rage. "If Artor does not get her back for me, then my own oaths to him are also void. I will go to my own kind, to Ceretic and Aelle, and together we shall make such a war of vengeance as will drive the British into the sea!"

X

Mons Badonicus

A brisk wind was blowing up from the Channel, bringing with it the scent of the sea. Oesc took a deep breath, and for a moment he was sixteen years old and on his way to the battle of Portus Adurni once more. *And at the end of it I was Artor's prisoner,* he fought down rage as that old sorrow amplified the new. Cataur still held Rigana and his son.

Struggling for calm, he told himself that this was the same war that his grandfather had begun, the war to make Britannia Angle-land. His alliance with Artor had been an interruption, that was all. The thought should have given him comfort, but the angry knot in his belly still throbbed.

"My lord, you must eat—" said Hæsta, pushing the wooden platter of swine-flesh toward him. Around the table of the kings were others for the eorls and the thanes and lesser warriors, and behind them the rush mats where their warriors were sitting, chunks of meat and bread before them and drinking horns in their hands.

Oesc ignored it. "Has there been any word from Beric?"

The thane shook his head. For a moon they had waited, while the news of Rigana's abduction spread as though carried by the wind. Had Beric found the high king? Had he even gotten through?

Artor—Artor— his heart called. *Why did you never answer me?*

Perhaps the king was unwilling to go against one of his greatest princes. Perhaps he had not the power to force Cataur to give up his prize.

I would have held to my oath to life's end! It is you who have broken faith with me. . . .

The wind shifted, and Oesc smelled the sweetness of curing grass. It was a moon past midsummer, and all over Britannia men were getting in the hay. The cornfields were ripening, the barley hanging down its head and the green emmer wheat turning gold. Who would harvest them, he wondered, once the Saxons had set the south aflame with war? The men they had sent directly to Cataur had returned with the message that Rigana was his guest, and would remain safe and comfortable so long as Oesc prevented his neighbors from attacking the Dumnonian lands. But if Cataur wanted peace, his own action had destroyed it. Wherever men spoke the Saxon tongue they were calling for revenge.

If Artor, who was acknowledged high king of the Britons, could not rule his princes, it was certain that Oesc could not control the Saxons, over whom he had no lordship at all. It was Ceretic, scenting the excuse that he had been seeking since Portus Adurni, who had summoned the tribes to gather here.

"Oesc, what are you doing?" Hæsta grasped his arm and Oesc realized that he had risen to his feet, his hand on his sword. He looked around him, blinking.

This army was already greater than the one that had challenged Artor eighteen years ago; each day more were coming in. A new generation of warriors had come to manhood, born in this land. They laughed as they ate, boasting of new conquests. His own men of Cantuware, with the West Saxons led by Ceretic and the South Saxons of Aelle, made a formidable alliance. In addition to the kingsmen, from the lands to the east of Londinium had come the Sunnings and the Mennings, the Geddings and Gillings, and more—warriors from a gaggle of clans who were oathsworn to no overlord.

Once more the wind changed. Now the scents were of horses and leather and roasted meat. Two thralls came past, pulling a cart with a vat of ale. Oesc held out his horn to be refilled and sat down. He took a long swallow, willing his racing heart to slow. For the others, avenging Oesc's loss was only the excuse for a campaign. Their beds were not empty, their children's first words would not be in the British tongue.

Gradually the muted roar of men's voices stilled and he realized that

Ceretic was standing. His voice rang across the field as he spoke to the kings and chieftains, chanting names and lineage, bidding them welcome. He knew them all, and their exploits as well. Even as Oesc twitched with impatience, he realized how long Ceretic had been preparing for this day.

"And so, we are come together—" he cried. "Against this army, the Britons will never be able to stand. All that remains is to say who will lead us against this foe!"

"Ceretic! Ceretic hail!" shouted his thanes.

But Hæsta had jumped to his feet as well. "Oesc son of Octha should be our leader! It is his wife who was taken, and he's the heir of Hengest, who brought us to this land!"

"He has not led men in battle—" came the rejoinder.

"But will Ceretic give up his lordship when the war is over? He wants to rule us all!"

"Oesc will be too rash against Cataur and too weak against Artor—"

The meadow erupted in disputation. The British had grown powerful because they all obeyed one high king. Who, Oesc wondered, could command the allegiance of the proud-stomached, hot-headed, independent-minded, warriors who were gathered here?

Oesc kept silent as the arguments went on. He wanted his wife back, but did he want to rule? *Artor won his kingship at the age of fifteen by pulling a God-Sword out of a stone. Shall I attempt the same trick with the Spear?*

He smiled grimly, remembering how even his own houseguard had grown pale when they realized just what the long, swaddled bundle he had taken from Hæthwæge's hut contained. At the time it had seemed right to bring it, but he knew that the Spear was not a token of sovereignty, even though it belonged to the god of kings. Whatever use he might make of it on this campaign, it would not make him Drighten of all the Saxon kind.

Oesc was not sure that anyone could claim that title here. The British were accustomed to overkings and emperors, but no Caesar had ever united the peoples of Germania. It seemed to him sometimes that to do so would be to pervert their very nature. German war-leaders who developed Imperial ambitions always seemed to come to a bad end.

Voices grew louder as tempers frayed. At this rate, the Saxon alliance would not last long enough to bring the Britons to battle. At the other end of the table Aelle was frowning, as if he had heard it all before.

Curse them all! thought Oesc. Rage roared in his ears. Suddenly he was on his feet; when no one seemed to notice, he leaped to the tabletop.

Platters danced and food flew, but he kept his footing. Pitching his voice as Andulf had taught him, he cried out—"*Hold!*

"You are squabbling like dogs while another hound takes the bitch away. I want my wife back, and I want Cataur's head—it doesn't matter to me who leads us so long as we win. We need someone with experience, with an authority that all can see. I will pledge myself and my warriors to Aelle of the South Saxons until this war is done!"

A murmur spread through the assembly like wind in the trees. Aelle's head came up and he frowned as if uncertain whether to be grateful. Oesc grimaced back at him. *If you don't want it, all the better! You will be less likely to cling to power.*

"He is right," said Hæsta. "It is the ancient way of our people to choose a war-leader. Aelle is an old wolf and will lead us well."

Everyone looked at Ceretic, whose face had gone dangerously red. But he was a wolf himself, and he could see that the temper of the gathering was against him. He shot Oesc a look of mingled amusement and fury and nodded.

"I agree." He lifted his horn. "In Woden's name I swear it—I and all who are sworn to me will follow Aelle for the duration of this war!"

"Aelle!" came the shout as more horns were raised. "Aelle!"

For a time Aelle listened, then he stood, and gradually the shouting ceased.

"As you have chosen me your leader, I accept the call." His deep voice rumbled through the air like distant thunder. "The Britons have given us fair words, but they cannot uphold them. There is no safety in oaths or treaties. Not until all of Britannia is Saxon will our wives and our homes be secure. Let us go forth in Woden's name, and fight until we have the victory!"

"Look, my lord—from here you can see the Isle of Glass. Beautiful, is it not?" Merlin pointed across the vale, where a scattering of hills rose from a sea of cloud. But only one of them compelled attention. The king reined in abruptly, and Merlin knew he had seen the Tor, its pointed cone dark against a sky flushed rose with morning light, its line pure as some Grecian vase.

"Very beautiful, had I seen it at any other time." Artor's lips tightened and he kicked his mount into motion down the hill. "Does Cataur think that because this is a holy place I will hold my hand? This war is his doing!" His horse broke into a trot.

Merlin held back a little, gazing across the vale. *You will not be stopped by coming to the holy Tor, but perhaps you will be changed.*

The druid had been in Isca when word of the Saxon outbreak arrived. For one terrible moment the events of the first Saxon Revolt had played themselves out in memory. Even before the messenger appeared his dreams had been filled with images of blood and fire. Was it because of them that he felt as if he were repeating actions performed long ago? Or was it only because this was the old enemy, the White Dragon, that had come forth to do battle with the Red once more?

Hengest was dead. This was his grandson, and his foe was not an old king worn out with wars, but Artor. Still, it seemed to Merlin that this campaign was only the culmination of the wars he had fought so long ago, and it was right that one more time he should ride to battle behind a king.

At this season the marshlands were mostly dry. As they reached the bottom of the hill and clattered across the logs of the causeway, cattle grazing in the water meadows looked up with incurious gaze. But mist still hung in the hollows and dimmed the copses, as if they were moving through a series of veils between the worlds.

Artor's face was grim. His control, thought the druid, was no doubt too rigid just now for him to sense any changes in the atmosphere. But the other men, less preoccupied, were looking around them with mingled distrust and wonder. As the Isle grew closer, its rounded slopes rising up to hide the Tor, Merlin felt its power growing steadily stronger, like the vibration of a great river, or the heat of a fire. It had been a long time since he had come here. He had forgotten how, to those with inner sight, the Tor could become in truth an isle of glass through which the light of the Otherworld shone clear.

Open your heart and your eyes, boy, he thought, fighting to control the intoxication of that radiance. The Christian wizard who had brought his followers to this place and built the first church at its base had known what he was doing. The Tor was a place of power.

By the time they reached the Isle, the sun was high. The mists had burned away, and with them, some of the visible mystery. The round church and beehive huts of the monks nestled at the base of the hill, with the community of nuns beside the sacred well beyond them. The lower meadows had sprouted a new crop of tents of hide and canvas, and men and horses were everywhere. The pressure of so many minds buzzed in Merlin's brain.

"Speak with Cataur," he told the king, "and when you are done, however it goes, come to me on the top of the Tor. You will not wish to take the time, but you must do so. From the summit you will be able to see more than the road across the vale—you will see your way." He held

Artor's gaze until the angry light in the king's eyes faded and he knew that the younger man was sensing, at least a little, the ancient power that would outlast all of them and their fears.

"Look at that arrogant son of a swine, parading in here as if he had won a victory instead of plunging the land into war!" exclaimed Cai. "I know how I'd reward him if I were high king!" He frowned as Cataur approached the awning that had been set up to shade the meeting, escorted by Leodegranus, the prince of Lindinis who was in a sense their host here. His hand drifted toward the pommel of his sword.

"Just as well you are not—" answered Betiver. "Artor will have to handle him like a man carrying coals through a hayfield, or we'll have all the west and south aflame. This deed of Cataur's has united the Saxons, but it could break the British alliance."

"And Artor knows it—" Gualchmai shook his head. "He's got a frown on him that would curdle new milk. Still, 'tis not entirely a bad thing. With every year the Saxons have been getting stronger. Do we smash them now, we'll not risk being too weak to do it in a few years' time. . . ."

His younger brother Gwyhir bared his teeth in a grin. He was pale of hair and combative, like his brother only in his height. The third brother, Aggarban, was short and darker. Men said that after the first son, all of Morgause's children had been festival got, of fathers unknown. In the north, where they held to the old ways, no one thought the worse of her. In the south they remembered that she was the king's sister, and if they spoke of it, did so in whispers.

"I hope we will fight—" said Aggarban. "You have had your shares of glory, but I still have to make my name!"

"You sound as if we should thank Cataur for starting this war!" Betiver said bitterly.

Gualchmai shrugged. "I will not blame him. I do admit it has all been a bit unexpected, but ye must bring a boil to a head before ye can lance it. Cataur is only forcing the king to do what one way or another had to come."

Even as Betiver frowned he had to admit that there was a certain hard logic in his words. But he remembered Oesc's fair head next to Artor's brown as they bent over the tabula board or stood at the butts for archery. Oesc had begun as Artor's prisoner, but in the end it seemed to him that they had found a kind of peace in each other's company that Artor had with no one else. The breaking of that bond must surely be hurting both of them now.

There was a little murmur of anticipation as Artor pushed through the crowd. For a moment he hesitated, glaring at the canopy beneath which Cataur waited. Then, without looking to see if his escort followed, he marched towards him. The Dumnonian prince stood up as Artor neared. His sandy hair had grown thinner, noticed Betiver. But the flush on his fair skin was probably from the heat, not shame.

The king's warriors stepped back out of earshot, facing the men of Cataur's houseguard. They could not make out words, but the rise and fall of the two voices came clearly, Artor's deep and tightly controlled and Cataur's higher, with the hint of a whine. But perhaps that was only Betiver's interpretation. Certainly the Dumnonian's face was getting even redder as the discussion went on.

"Say what you will!" Cataur's voice rose. "Giving the woman back now won't stop the war!"

"The war you wanted!" came Artor's shout in reply. The escorts moved closer as he went on. "Send the woman to my stronghold at Dun Tagell. The chieftains of Demetia are still gathering their men. I must go north to join them. Take your own men east and hold Aelle's forces for as long as you can. If you fail me I promise that when I have dealt with the Saxons I will come after you myself!"

He stood, and Cataur got to his feet as well, grinning tightly.

"My lord, we will do all that men can."

The afternoon was far advanced when Merlin felt the energy that pulsed around the summit change and came back from the aery realms in which he had been wandering. Looking down, he saw the pattern of the encampment dislimning as the Dumnonians moved out. Then he became aware of a subtler alteration and knew that Artor was climbing the hill. No other would dare. Even the monks came here only on feast days to make prayers to the Archangel Michael, whom they hoped would bind the old powers that lived in the Tor.

The strengthening breeze set dust whirling in a spiral, and he smiled. Could one bind the waters that flowed through the earth, or the wind that stirred his hair? Perhaps the monks' prayers kept them from feeling the power of the Tor, but even with his eyes open, Merlin could see the lines of power radiating out from the holy hill.

He turned as the high king appeared at the edge of the flattened oval of the summit, his hair blown, a sheen of perspiration on his brow. But the haze of anger that had pulsed around him that morning was gone. Perhaps he had worked off his fury on the climb.

"Have you brought me here to show me all the kingdoms of the world and the glory thereof?" Artor asked wryly when he had his breath again.

To the north and south, hills edged the vale. To the west one could guess at the blue shimmer of the sea. Eastward the land fell away to dim distances veiled by the smoke of burning fields.

Merlin shook his head. "Glory you shall see, but not of this world. Take a deep breath—this air comes pure from the heights of heaven."

"Cataur and Oesc are in *this* world—" Artor said angrily.

"Breathe!" Merlin's voice compelled obedience. The air the king had drawn in to argue with was expelled without words. He breathed in again, more slowly, and his eyes widened.

"What is it? I feel a tingling, and there are little sparkles in the air!"

"Look at me . . ." said the druid.

"There is a haze of brightness around you," whispered Artor after a moment had passed.

"Now, look at the land. . . ."

This time, the silence was longer. The king stood still, trembling, his eyes wide and unfocused.

"What do you see?"

"Light—" came the answer. "With every breath, light flows through the grass and stone and trees. . . ."

"Life," corrected the druid. "It is the Spirit that you are perceiving, that moves like a wind through all that is."

"Even the Saxons?"

"Even through them, though they do not perceive it. He who understands this mystery is part of the land. This is the power that will carry you to victory."

Nearby, someone was groaning. Oesc roused, smelled horses and old blood and the smoke of a watch fire, and knew he was encamped with Aelle's army. The groaning man must be Guthlaf, one of his houseguard who had taken an arrow through the thigh. But he would live, and they had won the battle. He turned over, wincing as the movement jarred stiff muscles, and gazed upward, where stars winked through a high haze of cloud. The gods had favored them with good weather for campaigning, and barring a few scratches, he had come through the fighting unscathed.

But he was tired to the bone. He tried to remember what it was like to sleep in a real bed with the soft warmth of a woman beside him. He had had Rigana for little more than a year—it was not long enough to offset a lifetime of loneliness. *Is she even alive? Is the child?* By day he could assure himself that Cataur would have no reason to kill her. But in the dark hours he imagined a lifetime spent grieving for her loss.

Even if Cataur had offered to give her back tomorrow, Oesc could not break the oaths that bound him to the war. That was the doom that haunted his nightmares. Living or dying, how could Rigana forgive him for not rescuing her? He had meant their marriage to join their two peoples in harmony, and instead it had led to a new and more devastating war.

It was small consolation to reflect that Cataur must be regretting his action as well. One of Ceretic's warriors was boasting that he had struck the Dumnonian prince from his saddle. The Britons had got their leader safely away, but it would be long before Cataur could fight again. After several preliminary skirmishes, the main forces had met near Sorviodunum, and the Dumnonians, if not quite defeated, had been prevented from retreating westward. Now the larger Saxon army was pursuing them across the plain.

Burdened with wounded, the British would go slowly. Aelle hoped to cut them off before they could join with the forces Artor was raising in Demetia.

Oesc felt a new set of muscles complain as he turned onto his side and closed his eyes once more. But the deep slumber he so badly needed eluded him. Instead he fell into a state halfway between sleep and waking in which he wandered through a landscape of warring ghosts.

At first he thought of the old story of Hild, whose curse set her father and lover to repeat their final battle throughout eternity. But this was a battle of Saxon against Briton, and it was Rigana who walked among them, shrieking imprecations. It seemed to him then that he followed after, begging her to forgive so that peace might come. And then she turned, and her face was that of a wælcyrige, one of the battle hags who choose the slain for Woden's hall.

Oesc halted, shaking his fists at the heavens. *"What do you want? When will you bring this slaughter to an end?"*

And it seemed to him then that a great wind swept across the battlefield, swirling up the bodies of men like fallen leaves and flinging them across the sky. And like the roar of that wind, came the answer—

"When you choose wisdom over war. . . . When you learn how to use the Spear!"

The Britons were retreating. Cataur's appeal had brought Artor's forces down from Demetia to his aid, but the Saxon army was larger than anyone had expected. In the open field, the Britons could not stand against them. Several skirmishes and one pitched battle had proved that in numbers at least, the Saxons had superiority. Every villa in their path had been looted, and the ruins of Cunetio still smoked behind them. But if the defenders were being forced to fall back, at least they were doing so in good order. Their losses had been relatively light—to some, that made their retreat all the more ignominious. Only Artor seemed unconcerned.

When the murmurs became too bitter to ignore, he called his chieftains to council.

They had made camp just outside the hamlet of Verlucio, a staging post on the main road that led from Calleva and the Midlands toward Aquae Sulis. The inhabitants, recognizing that any supplies they did not share with their own side would soon be taken by the Saxons, had been generous with food and drink, and the men were in a more mellow mood than they had been when the day began.

Even Gualchmai, who had been growling like a chained hound, seemed to have been pacified by a skin of wine. But Betiver, gazing at the circle of flushed or frowning faces, still felt a hard knot of anxiety in his gut.

"What is the matter, old friend?" came a voice at his elbow. "You are looking around you like a sheep that has just heard the first wolf howl." It was the king.

Betiver sighed. "It is not the wolves I fear just now, but the sheepdogs. They do not like to be beaten, and they do not like to run."

"And you fear the shepherd will not be able to command them?" Artor's eyes were as bright as if he were going into battle.

Betiver flushed. *He understands what is at stake here, despite his soft words.*

"Have faith. No man can guarantee victory always, but I do have a plan."

"My lord," Betiver answered softly, "I have believed in you since I was thirteen years old."

It was Artor's turn to color then. He turned away rather quickly and took his place in the folding camp chair with the crimson leather seat and back that he used as a portable throne. Gualchmai moved into position behind his right shoulder and Betiver took the left. Gradually, the men gathered before him grew still.

"Let me tell you a story—" the high king said into the silence. "Once I hunted a stag. He was an old beast, and wily, but I was confident that my dogs could run him down. But he knew the ground better than I did, and the chase went on and on. By afternoon, I was far from my own hunting runs. I had no food, and the trail was leading into the hills. But my prey was so close, I could not give up. And then, the ground rose suddenly and I looked up and saw the stag above me on a rock that jutted out from the cliff. Three dogs were killed as they tried to leap up at him. I lifted my spear, but before I could throw, the stag charged. His horns took out two more dogs as he crashed through the circle, and my horse reared and threw me. By the time I sorted myself out, he was long gone, and the dogs that remained to me were quite happy to head home. . . ."

For a long moment there was silence, then Agricola of Demetia let out a guffaw. "Is that why we've been bolting for the hills for the past ten-day?"

"You are trying to draw the Saxons into hostile territory?" asked Cunorix, whose Irish had, in the face of this new threat, been transformed into allies once more.

Artor let the babble of speculation run its course before raising his hand. "Aelle's army is too great for him to carry sufficient supplies. He must live off the land, but if he splits his forces to forage they risk coming upon a larger body of our own men. The farther he gets from his own lands the worse his problem becomes."

"And where do you propose to stand at bay?" a new voice put in.

"Aquae Sulis nestles among hills. In such broken country, the Saxons will find it hard to bring their numbers to bear. There is a hill that over-looks the Abona across the river from the town, above the place where the Calleva road joins the road to Corinium. It stands alone, and its summit is flat, big enough for our mounts and but not too big to defend. That is where I propose we make our stand. We have enough in our saddlebags to hold out for some days, and we can bring river water in barrels from the town. I have sent orders already to the people of Aquae Sulis to flee, to leave what food they cannot carry on the hill, and to take with them every scrap of food they can."

For a moment longer the issue was in doubt. Then Cunorix grinned. " 'Tis a trap, then, that we'll be setting for our foes."

"It is, and we the bait and the jaws of it both!"

Cunorix half drew his sword. "Then I'd best get busy sharpening mine—" More laughter followed, and Betiver relaxed. He should never have doubted, he thought then, that Artor could handle his men.

The hill bristled against the pale blue of the sky.

At first Oesc thought the uneven line was brush or treetops, but as they drew closer he could see the stubble of cut tree trunks and bushes on the slopes above. The sides of the hill had once been covered with foliage that might have hidden ascending enemies, but now they were denuded, trunks and branches woven into a spiky rampart around the sum-mit.

He swore softly. "Ceretic was so sure we had them on the run! But if Artor was running, this was his goal—he *meant* to lead us here."

Haesta, who was marching beside him, grunted agreement. "You may know less about leading armies, but you know Artor. Aelle should have listened to you. On the other hand, Artor may not have expected quite so many of us—" He squinted up at the hill. "They're safe for the moment, but where can they go?"

By nightfall, the hill was surrounded, and the Saxon warsongs drifted upward on the wind. On the next morning the first assault was mounted on the southern, and least precipitous, side of the hill. It was also the best defended, and the picked force that had ascended was soon retreating once more.

That afternoon they tried again with a general assault from all sides at once. In the process they discovered the hard way that the Britons had a good supply of arrows and retired with significant, though not crippling, losses. That night they tended their wounds, and in the chill hour just before dawn, sent warriors creeping silently up the western side of the hill. Just as the burning rim of the sun edged the eastern hills a second force charged the eastern side, screaming war cries, and the defenders, springing to the breastworks, were dazzled by the first light of day.

The western force made good use of their distraction, swarming over the piled logs and taking out the sentries, then pulling as much of the breastwork down as they could manage to give those who followed easier entry.

It should have worked. The Britons, waking dazed from sleep, thronged toward the eastern side of the hill, and the Saxons who were infiltrating from the west fell upon them from the rear with silent ferocity. Oesc, who was leading them, was the first to see the figure that reared up before them, glowing with pale light and crying out words of power in a voice that paralyzed the soul.

His warriors, not knowing what had come against them, froze in terror. Oesc recognized Merlin, but for the few crucial moments it took for the Britons to realize where the real threat lay, his knowledge of the druid's powers incapacitated him as completely as it had his men. Then the brightness faded, to be replaced by yelling shapes silhouetted against the rising sun. Now it was the Saxons who were blinded. They turned and ran.

For a moment Oesc glimpsed Artor, clad only in breeches, the dawn-light flaming from his sword. He cried out in challenge, but caught in the midst of his fleeing warriors, he was carried back to the gap in the breast-work and down the hill.

By the end of that day, the disadvantages of maintaining a seige with a large army in hostile territory were becoming clear. Artor and his warriors were surrounded by Saxons, but the Saxons were surrounded by trackless hills from which all sources of food seemed to have disappeared.

"If we are getting hungry, then they must be too," said Ceretic grimly. "And even if they have food, they must run out of water soon. They have horses up there, lads—tomorrow morning we'll attack again, and keep coming until we overrun the hill. Then we'll feast on horseflesh and offer the king's stallion to the gods."

They were fine words, thought Oesc, binding up a gash on his thigh, but if the Saxons did not succeed in bringing the Britons to battle, they would be eating each other soon. His gaze moved to the long, shrouded shape that lay with the rest of his gear. Until now he had not unwrapped it, for Artor had left his Sword in Londinium, safely sheathed in stone. But Merlin had used magic against them that morning. The next time the Saxons attacked, Oesc would use the Spear.

At sunset it was the high king's custom to make the rounds of the breastworks unescorted, stopping at each guard post to hearten the men on duty there. On the evening of the second day of the seige, Merlin fell into step beside him. He had been waiting for the right moment, when the king, driven to the limit of his resources, would be willing to hear his words.

"Have you come to point out my foolishness, as you used to do when I was a boy? I gambled that if I took refuge here, Aelle would be forced to raise the seige, and my pride may have lost not only the war, but Britannia," Artor said bitterly as they moved along the breastwork. "Tomorrow we must try to break free."

"You did not choose so badly. This hilltop has been a fortress before—" Merlin replied.

"What do you mean?" asked Artor. He paused to greet the men who were leaning against the tangle of logs at the post on the eastern side. Torches on tall poles cast an uncertain light down the slope, a garland of fire that was matched by the larger necklace of watchfires below. Between them, dark shapes lay among the stumps; bodies that neither side had dared to retrieve for fear of arrows from above or below.

"Did you think the gods had leveled this summit in foreknowledge that one day you would need a refuge?" Merlin said as they moved on. "Men lived here before the Romans came. That is why the top is flat and the edges so sheer. Your breastworks are built on the remains of the ramparts they raised to protect their village."

"I wish they were here! I speak words of cheer, but this morning we lost men we could not spare."

"What makes you think that they are not?" said the druid. "Now, in the hour between dark and daylight, all times are one. Open your ears and listen—open your eyes and see. . . ."

As Artor turned, frowning, Merlin touched his forefinger to the spot on his brow just between his eyes. The king staggered, blinking, and the druid held him, his own sight shifting. Overlaid upon the shapes of hide campaign tents he saw round houses of daub and wattle with conical roofs of thatch. The ghostly images of earthen ramparts crowned by a palisade veiled the breastwork of piled logs. And among the warriors of Artor's army moved the figures of men and women and children dressed in the striped and checkered garments of ancient days.

"I see . . ." whispered the king, his voice shaking. "But these are only memories."

"By my arts I can give such substance to these wraiths as will send the Saxons shrieking. But you must call them—"

"In whose name? To what power that they would recognize can I appeal?"

Merlin drew from his pouch a bronze disc with a woman's face in bas-relief. "This is an image of the Goddess—one of those they used to sell to folk who came to bathe in the waters of Sulis. The ancient ones will know it. Fix it to your shield and summon them in the name of the Lady of this land."

The time for tricks and surprises was over. Today must see an end-ing—both sides knew it, thought Oesc, tightening his grip on the Spear. Before the sun rose the Saxons had taken up their arms; the first rays glittered on ranks of helmets and spearpoints and shields. The toll was likely to be terrible, but by the end of it the Britons would be broken. He would be avenged.

He wondered why that knowledge brought no triumph. *I will weep for you, my king, but I will not hold my hand. . . .*

Saxon cowhorns blared in challenge, and from behind the ramparts, British trumpets shrilled a reply. On the southern side, where once had stood the gateway to the fortress, he glimpsed a shiver of movement. The tree trunks and brush were being pulled away. Of course, he thought then, this was the only slope on which the horses could hope to keep their footing. The momentum of the hill would aid that of the British charge.

Aelle had given Oesc the right flank. His thanes had formed the shieldwall in front of him, but all around him men edged back as they saw him fumbling with the wrappings that covered the Spear. The dawn wind was rising, tugging at the bindings, whipping back the hair that flowed from beneath his helm.

Are you so eager, lord of the slain? Soon, you shall have your prey!

The last knot came free and the transclucent stone of the spearhead glowed in the light of the rising sun. A tremor ran through the rune-carved shaft. Oesc tried to convince himself it was the wind.

Wood cracked above and a horse whinnied shrilly. Wind gusted, flattening the grass, and suddenly the whole world was in movement, logs bouncing and clattering downward, bowling over the first rank of Aelle's houseguard. The first of the horses followed.

Oesc tensed, balancing the Spear. In a single moment he glimpsed Artor's big black horse with the white blaze among them, and felt his arm swinging back of its own accord.

"To Woden I give you!" he cried. The god-power rushed through him as light flared from the boss of Artor's shield. That same power brought his arm forward, plucked the Spear from his hand and sent it arcing through the air, higher and higher. Surely the wind was lifting it, carrying it where the god required it to go.

Oesc followed it with his eyes, over the horsemen who were cascading down the hill through the opening in the breastwork and straight for the man who had sprung onto the logs beside it, his grey beard flying in the wind. He stared, ignoring the tumult around him, as that white-robed figure seemed to expand, reaching, and impossibly, caught the Spear.

To Merlin, it was a streak of incandescent power. He reached out with body and spirit, knowing only that he must keep it from plunging into the mass of men behind him. And then, like a striking eagle, it came to his hand, and agony flared through every nerve and limb. He wheezed as the air was squeezed from his lungs, breathed again in a great gasp and felt the pain replaced by ecstasy.

Consciousness whirled upward as through the gateway thundered wave after wave of men and horses. With awareness at once precisely focused and impossibly extended, Merlin heard each battle cry and knew the name of the man who uttered it. He heard the silent yelling of the wraiths who rose from the earth as Artor called them, felt them flow down the hill, and heard the terrified babble of the men who fell before them. He heard, as once before at Verulamium, the battle-shriek of Cathubodva's raven that weakened the sinews and fettered the will, as Artor swept back and forth across the field, scything down men as a reaper cuts grain.

He knew all words in all languages, and the language of the earth itself, the song of every blade of grass and leaf on tree.

And he heard, with a clarity beyond mortal hearing, a Voice that whispered, *"All those who battle on this field I claim—my speech will fill the mouths of their children's children; my law will rule this land. But today, to your king I give the victory. . . . "*

Oesc fought an army of shadows, with shadow-warriors at his side. Some of them had faces he knew—men he had led to battle, and men he had known as a child. It was when he saw Octha his father among them that he understood that this battlefield was not the British hill he had left, but the plain before Wælhall. He stopped then, and put down his sword. His father saw, and turned to him, gesturing towards the foe.

"Is this all," Oesc cried, *"Is there no other way but war?"* As he spoke the shadows faded, and he fell down a long tunnel and back into his body once more.

At least he assumed it was so, for he was very cold. With an effort he drew a breath, and felt the first tinglings of pain. With sensation came hearing—the cries of wounded men, and someone speaking nearby.

"Oesc, can you hear me?"

With another effort of will, Oesc made his eyes open. Artor was bending over him, his hair matted by the pressure of his helmet and the smudges of fatigue shadowing his eyes.

"My lord. . . ." It was barely a whisper. "He took Rigana. Why didn't you answer me?"

"I didn't know!" Artor's face contorted. "By our Lady I swear that you were on the march before I knew." He reached out to take Oesc's hand.

Oesc tried to return the grip, but nothing seemed to be happening. "I can't . . . feel . . ."

He sensed movement and saw that Artor was cradling his hand against his breast, but he felt nothing at all.

"A horse fell on him," said another voice. He could not turn his head to see. "I think his back is broken."

There was a moment of shock, and a rush of bitterness as Oesc understood that he would never hold Rigana in his arms, never see his son grow to be a man, never again watch the rich grasslands of Cantuware rippling in the wind from the sea. All his hopes, his ambitions . . . whirled away like dust on the breeze. . . . He fought for control.

This, then, was the Wyrd that the runes had foretold for him, the outcome of all the choices he had made. It was the gift of a hero to know when the time had come to cease fighting. To choose whether his spirit should dwell with the gods or stay to guard his people was the gift of a king.

"I don't remember that . . . only the fighting. . . ." With difficulty, he drew breath once more. The cold had increased; he didn't have much time. "My lord . . . find Rigana and my son. . . ."

"They are safe—" Artor said quickly. "I will bring them back to Cantium. And you—" His words failed.

Oesc remembered the shrine at Ægele's ford and the promise he had given there. "Make my mound next to Hengest's, and I will guard the land. I am . . . its king. But you . . . are different. You belong to all . . . Britannia."

A sudden flush of color came into Artor's face, as if only now was he realizing that with the Anglians tamed and the southern Saxons broken, for the first time in his reign he was truly the high king. He cleared his throat.

"Eormenric shall have your high seat, and while I live no one will dare to challenge him!"

Oesc managed a smile, and after another moment, the breath to speak again. "Only one last gift . . . to ask. . . ." Sudden anguish filled Artor's eyes, but Oesc held his gaze until he nodded acceptance. "Now. . . ."

Light glinted from the king's dagger. Still smiling, Oesc closed his eyes. There was a swift pressure, but no pain, only the sweetness of release as his heart's blood flowed out to feed the earth and he gave his breath back to the god.

THE BOOK OF THE CAULDRON

Contents

Prologue

Life came first from the sea.

Cradle of creation and sheltering womb, it contained all elements. Dissolved and coalescing, joining, growing, the elements combined to become beings of ascending complexity.

Water is transformation.

Rising and falling, dying and rebirthing, it nourishes the world. Perpetually moving, it obeys the laws of moon and tide. Constrained, it grows stagnant and dies; free flowing, it renews the world.

Water is the blood of the Goddess, flowing through the streams and rivers that vein the land. In the lakes and pools, fed from the depths by bubbling springs, She pours out her blessings.

Water is woman's magic.

As the sea floods in answer to the moon so does her womb; each month she bleeds and is renewed. In blood she creates a child and bloody, she bears it; from her breasts springs sweet milk to be its food. Women seek the sacred spring and make offerings to the Goddess whose name means the power that wells up from the depths to the heights, knowing that her magic and theirs is the same. . . .

On an island in the ocean, nine priestesses serve a sacred shrine. As each moon waxes and wanes they praise the Goddess in Her times and seasons. But often, when the moon is full, the priestess who is their leader walks by the shore of the sea. Moonlight glitters silver on the waters. She stretches out her arms to embrace that splendor, but it flows through her fingers. She aches with yearning to hold the power by which she herself is held, and slowly, within the womb of her head a vision grows.

When the chieftains of her people come to make their offerings she requires of them silver. Piece by piece, she melts it together, beats it out into flat sheets, molded with images of the Goddess. Ready for love or armed for war, healing the sick or giving songs to the bard, milking a cow or hunting a deer or bringing a ship safe to land, nursing her child or bearing the soul of a dead man across the sea, the Goddess appears in all Her guises, blessing humankind.

Section by section the pieces are shaped, riveted and soldered until they are one. From hand and heart a great cauldron is born, silver as the moon. River pearls are set into its rim, gleaming softly. Then, singing, the priestesses bear it to the sacred spring. One by one, each priestess fills her chalice. She lifts it high to catch the radiance of the moon. Then she pours it into the cauldron, shimmering with silver light.

The song grows deeper, becomes a wordless humming, a vibration that shivers the surface of the water. From beyond this world come overtones and harmonies. A mist of radiance glows above the water, twines upward, shapes itself into the form of a woman. Turning, She opens her arms, Her voice joins in the singing, and shapes it into words. She dips liquid from the cauldron; into each chalice She pours Her blessings, and all are filled.

And when at last, the priestesses return to awareness of who and where they are, the Cauldron is empty. But every full moon when they fill it with water from the sacred spring, that water glows, and all who drink of it are renewed.

Birth Pangs

A.D. 487

Just before sunset, a wind came down from the heights to ruffle the water. The Lady of the Lake breathed it in gratefully, for the day had been warm, a promise of the summer season that Beltain would usher in. In the lands of men, the young folk would be going out into the woods to gather greenery for the festival, and if they took rather longer than was strictly necessary to cut the branches, and came back with their clothing awry, even the Christians would hardly dare chastise them on this eve. But on the Isle of Maidens there was no need to bring in the wilderness, for it was all around them. And while man and maid performed the old earth magic, she and her priestesses would invoke the magic of the waters whose power enabled all these green and growing things to survive.

Beyond the screen of willow and the silver sheen of the water, the mountain crouched like an old woman, cloaked and hooded in misty blue, hunched against the dimming sky. Igierne had seen it so when, as a girl, she first claimed this spot as her private bathing place. Now she was an old woman herself. But the mountain remained the same.

She hung the rough towel across a branch and slid the cloak from around her shoulders, shivering a little at the touch of the air. For a moment she hesitated to remove her shift as well, but it was not going to get any warmer. Lips twisting wryly, she dragged it over her head and made her way down to the waterside.

White and wavering as a birch trunk, she saw her body reflected there. *I am a waning moon* . . . she thought wryly. Even her hair, once golden, was faded now to silver-fair. As a girl, she had spied on the older priestesses at their bathing and been astonished to find their bodies still so smooth. It surprised her still, looking down, to see her own shape so much younger than the face in her mirror. True, her breasts lay pendant upon her ribcage, and her belly had been stretched by the weight of two children, but her buttocks were round with muscle from walking, and her arms were firm.

If Uthir had been living, she would have rejoiced in his delight in her body, but he slept now beside his brother in the mound before the Giant's Dance. No longer was she high queen and his lady. Now it was her son Artor who ruled. When the princes of Britannia chose him, Igierne had offered to stay and manage his household, but the lords of Britannia, having accepted her son's right to rule them, wanted no motherly meddling in the process of turning him into a king. Even Merlin had been tolerated only grudgingly as his tutor, perhaps because they feared him.

And so she had returned to the Isle of Maidens to reclaim the role for which she had been born. She wrote to Artor with some regularity, seeking to supply the guidance she had not been allowed to give before, but increasingly her counsel came from her meditations as a priestess, rather than her memories of life as Uthir's queen. On the rare occasions when she visited her son, his court seemed like another world. These days, the health of her body mattered only because it served her soul. And that—she smiled down at the woman who looked back at her from the water—was still that of the maiden who had first bathed in these waters so long ago.

Still smiling, she stepped down the shelving strand into the water.

"Blessed be my feet, that I may walk in Thy ways . . . blessed be my legs, that I may stand before Thee . . . blessed be my womb, that I may be Thy shrine . . ." She scooped up water, purifying each part of her body, murmuring the words that would make her a fit vessel for the power of the Goddess to fill.

The Isle of Maidens lay hidden within the double enclosure of the Lake and its encircling hills. The Romans had massacred the Druid priesthood on the isle of Mona, and driven them from Afallon that men now called the Isle of Glass, but this sanctuary they had never found. In time its huts of daubed withies had been replaced by stone, but in some things the priestesses still held by the old Druid ways, and the most sacred of their rituals took place beneath the open sky.

If the island was doubly warded, the hazelwood formed the innermost barrier around its center, where a fissure in the island's rocky core had created a cave. The Sword-God's shrine had been a temple built by men, tolerated, but never truly belonging to the isle. The cave was its most ancient and original sanctuary. Three fires burned now before it, but the entrance remained in shadow.

Igierne lay back against the carved wood of her chair, willing her breathing to remain steady, waiting for her heartbeat to slow. Her pale hair lay loose upon her shoulders. For this ceremony her maidens were robed in white. Only she wore the black of the midnight sky, though her ornaments were of silver, set with moonstone and river pearls.

Overhead, a scattering of stars glimmered in the river of night. Long practice had taught her to sense the slow turning of the skies. The moon was in its third quarter, and would not rise till the night was half gone. Imperceptibly her breathing began to deepen. She straightened, hearing her own heartbeat echoed by the soft beat of a drum. Anticipation tightened her skin as the women began to sing—

"Thou art the source and the stream . . .
Thou art the desire and the dream . . .
that which is empty and that which fills,
that which receives and that which wills;
Thou art the part and Thou art the whole,
Thou art the body and Thou, the soul. . . ."

The mingled voices converged in a single note, sustained in a long vibration that thrummed in the still air. Elsewhere they called on the gods in other guises, and by other names, especially on this night, when the young God came forth from his leafy glades to couple with the Goddess in the fields. But here, at the heart of the isle, it was the Lady alone who ruled.

"Great Mother, be near us—" intoned Igierne.

"Hear us, be near us . . ." came the reply.

"Gateway to birth and doorway to death—" Ceincair's sweet voice rose above the rest.

"Hear us. . . ."

"Lady of hope and healing—" the litany went on, and with each salutation, the air seemed to thicken until it was difficult to breathe.

"Thou art the Cauldron of Changes, the Womb of Wisdom—" said Igierne, and at her words, Morut and Nest moved to the dark opening of the cave and began to pull the stones away. Beneath them was a wooden chest carved with triple spirals, and within the chest, something swathed in white silk which they set in the hollow of the stone before Igierne's chair.

As the cloth fell away, she felt her awareness shifting so that she saw with doubled vision the ancient cauldron of riveted silver plates on which goddess-faces and the images of strange beasts stood out in low relief, and a vessel of pure Light, outshining the fires.

A white-clad shape moved forward. From a silver pitcher, water poured into the cauldron in a glistening stream. The light grew brighter.

"I bring water from the ocean, the womb of the world. Receive the offering!" the voice was that of Nest.

Another moved into the radiance. "I bring water from the Tamesis, lifeblood of the land—" More water glittered through the air.

One by one the priestesses emptied their pitchers. The water they offered came from each of the great rivers that drained Britannia, and from the sacred springs.

"I bring water from the Isle of Mona . . ." chanted Morut.

"I bring water from the blood spring of Afallon . . ." sang Ceincair.

The light grew; glowing figures moved within a bright haze. Igierne stared into the glimmering depths of the Cauldron.

"Speak to us, Lady, " she whispered. "In this moment when the doors open between the worlds, show us what is to be. . . ."

With that prayer, all other awareness became peripheral. The light welled up around her and she was free.

She saw Britannia laid out below her, picked out in lines of light as one Beltain fire signaled another across the land. Disciplines practiced for so long they had become instinct turned her mind toward those whose future she must see.

Beltain fires blazed on the hills above Isca. Igierne's gaze followed the flicker of light and shadow as men and women danced around them. Her son Artor was there, with Betiver and Cai, and that odd Saxon boy who they said was Hengest's grandson. Girls came to the king, laughing, and he kissed them and drank the mead they offered, but though many of his men allowed themselves to be led off into the leafy shadows, and Gualchmai was no doubt there already, Artor remained by the fires.

Is this how you honor the Goddess, my child? Igierne thought ruefully, and heard, as if in agreement, a ripple of silvery laughter. But Artor had grown up suspecting himself a bastard, she remembered with sudden pain. No wonder if he took care where he sowed his own seed.

He must have a queen to act as your priestess, Lady! she told the bright darkness. *Show me the woman who will share his bed and his throne!*

The image shattered. Colors ran in swirls of liquid light, painting a land of folded hills and peaceful woodlands, altogether a gentler country than the Demetian shore. In a sheltered valley the villa of a British prince lay dark while his tribesmen revelled in the meadow below. But at the edge of the firelight something stirred. Igierne's vision focused; she saw a slim girl-child with amber eyes and a cloud of red-gold hair clutching an old blanket around her as she watched the dancing. Even standing, she seemed to sway like a young tree in the wind. She would be beautiful in motion.

As the image dimmed, the Voice of the Goddess sounded in Igierne's awareness once more—*"She is Leodagranus' daughter. Her name is Guendivar . . ."*

She is young, yet, thought Igierne, *too young to understand what this means, I must find her and prepare her for her destiny.*

Images flickered before her: Guendivar grown, her bright hair crowned with flowers . . . laughing, dancing, racing through the woods on a grey dappled mare . . . and older still, her face racked by grief and looking for the first time like that of a mortal woman and not a maiden of faerie. Igierne strove to see more, but the vision became a blur that left her dazed and dizzy, floating in the void.

With an effort she regained her focus. To foresee fate did not necessarily show one how to change it, for the ancients held that it was always changing, and in seeking to avoid the end foretold many a man had instead been its cause. Better to seek knowledge of events nearer to hand, so that one might, if not prevent, at least prepare to meet them.

Morgause . . . With a regretful recognition that her concern sprang more from duty than desire, Igierne sought to see the outcome of her daughter's pregnancy.

On the height of Dun Eidyn the Votadini warriors drank to their king. She saw Morgause bearing the horn among them, too heavily pregnant for dancing. From time to time she would pause, biting her lip for a moment before continuing her round.

The child will come very soon, thought Igierne, *does she know it?* But this was Morgause's fifth pregnancy. She must know her own body's signals by now. It was stubbornness, not ignorance, that kept her on her feet this Beltain Eve. Igierne suppressed the irritation that thoughts of her daughter too often inspired.

Will the birthing go well? What will this child bring to Britannia?

Vision was dazzled by the blaze of morning light on water. But in the next moment a tide of red replaced it. A child's angry wail deepened into the battlefield roar of an army. Fear for her daughter gave way to a deeper terror as she saw Morgause, her features sagging with middle age and twisted by hatred, and beside her, a boy whose features were a younger, fairer, reflection of her own, with a hint of someone else in the line of the jaw that Igierne could not quite recognize. Was it that which set something deep within to shivering, or was it the spark of malice in his eyes? Red darkness swirled across her vision: a raven banner tossed against a fiery sky. And then it was a flight of ravens, and a Voice that cried—

"He shall bring blood and fire and the end of an age . . . All things pass, else lack of balance would destroy the world."

Igierne writhed in soundless repudiation, knowing, even as she hated it, that this Voice also was divine. And then, like cool water, the Goddess as she had always known Her spoke in her soul.

"Fear not. While the ravens ward the White Mount, the Guardian of Britannia will remain. . . ."

She felt herself falling back into her body, starlight and firelight and the light of her visions shattering around her like a mosaic of Roman glass. Desperately she tried to fix the pieces in some pattern that would retain its meaning, but they were moving too fast.

"Merlin!" her soul cried, *"Merlin, hear me! Beware the child that is born the first of May!"*

Then it was over, though she ached in every limb. Igierne felt soft hands helping her to sit upright, heard a murmur of shock and concern.

"My lady, are you all right?"

"I will be . . ." she muttered. *Artor—* she thought, *I must speak with him soon.* Then she took a deep breath and opened her eyes to see the gibbous quarter-moon staring down at her from a sky that was already paling before the first light of Beltain's dawn.

At dawn on Beltain, Morgause went out with her women to bring water from the sacred spring. Before sunrise the air was brisk and Morgause was glad of the fleecy cloak she wore. Unbalanced by the great bulge of her belly, she moved carefully, picking her way down the rocky path in the uncertain torchlight and the light of the waning moon that was more deceptive still. From the group of maidens who walked with her came laughter, swiftly hushed. The child in her belly stirred, then stilled. Perhaps, she thought hopefully, the unaccustomed motion would lull him to sleep. He had kept her wakeful half the night with his kicking, as if he could not wait for the womb to open and set him free.

To walk from the fortress down to the base of the cleft below it and back could take half the morning, and the return climb required considerable stamina. The women, eyeing the queen's distended belly, had begged her to let one of the chieftains' daughters who attended her represent her in the ceremony, but Morgause refused. For a girl to take her place in Leudonus' bed during her pregnancies did not threaten her position, but her condition had not permitted her to dance at the Beltain fires. Morgause would allow no one to usurp any of the other sacred duties of the queen.

"It will be safe enough," she told them. "The babe is not due for another half moon." This was not quite true—she knew very well that this child had been conceived in the rites at the feast of Lugus, and so her pregnancy was now full term. But her other children had come behind time, so she told the lie without compunction.

Men might speculate, when the queen's sons were born some nine moons after a festival, but those who did not follow the old ways could never be certain they were not of Leudonus' begetting. The majority of the Votadini tribesmen believed, like Morgause, that her children were a gift from the gods.

For a moment vision blurred; the torchlit darkness of the road became the festival ground, and the chill of dawn the warm summer night of Lughnasaid. The people were shouting, a hero came to her in the darkness of the sacred enclosure, filled with the god, and then the dark fire of the goddess reft her own awareness away . . .

Morgause trembled again, remembering. It was only afterwards, listening to folk speak of the bull-fight and how the young king from the south had saved the fallen priest of Lugus and completed the ceremony, that she understood that it was Artor who had lain in her arms.

She had considered, in that moment of realization, seeking out the herbs that would cast the child from her womb. But the gods had willed that her brother's seed take root there. She did not dare deny them. Morgause was built for bearing, but a woman offered her life in childbed as a man marched into battle. Soon, now, the gods would judge both mother and child. And if such a child lived . . . surely he was meant for a mighty destiny.

A stone turned under her foot and she grasped at the arm of Dugech, who walked beside her.

"Lady, please, let me send for a litter to take you back to the dun!"

Morgause shook her head. To give up now would be an admission of weakness. She straightened defiantly.

"Then let us carry you down—"

Morgause started forward again without answering. The sky was growing lighter. The far side of the cleft stood in stark outline against that pallor; a gulf of darkness gaped below. *I am descending into the Underworld,* she thought, suppressing panic. For a moment she considered letting Dugech have her way, but now that the exercise had got her blood running, she felt better than she had before.

"The rite requires that I walk to the spring, and it will do me good. I have sat too long indoors. Only stay close so that I do not fall."

They moved on. The pallor above brightened to a pearly grey, and then, as the torch flames grew pale and the shapeless masses of shadow that edged the path became shrubs and trees lightened, with a hint of rose. They had reached the crossroads where the way that ran down the vale crossed the path that descended from the dun. Morgause turned. Behind the jagged peak of the Watch Hill the sky was beginning to flame with gold.

She tried to hurry then, ignoring the slow ache across her lower back. She wished now that she had called for the litter, but she had almost reached the spring. With relief she felt the pathway level out and took a deep breath of moist air. Beneath their mantles the white linen garments of her maidens glowed. Morgause paused to undo the pins that held her own cloak and straightened gratefully as its weight slithered to the ground. The flesh on her arms pebbled at the touch of the brisk air, but her blood was still heated from the walk and she did not mind the cold.

She beckoned to red-haired Leuku, who was carrying the bronze vessel, and strode toward the spring. To the east the sky was bright gold. Overhead the heavens glowed pale rose, but the scattered clouds, catching the sunlight, had hung out banners of flame.

The women stood in silence, watching that radiance intensify until the rock above was edged with a sliver of flame. As the sunwheel rolled up the sky, light blazed between the birches and sparkled on the waters of the well as if a fire had been kindled within. Pent breath was released in a shout—

"Water of life from the depths upwelling—" sang the queen.

"Bring us thy blessing!" her maidens chorused in reply.

"Fire of power from the heavens descending—"

"Bring us thy blessing!"

"Fire in the water kindling cool flame—" she sang then, and waited for the others to reply.

"Power we drink and protection we claim."

Carefully, she bent and tipped the rim of the kettle so that the glittering water trickled in. As she began to stand up, the ache across her loins became a sudden pang. For a moment Morgause could not move. When she could breathe again, she straightened, telling herself it had only been another preliminary pain. She had been having them for weeks, and knew them for the distant thunder that heralds the storm.

But with her next step, Morgause felt a trickle of warm fluid between her thighs, and understood that the time of waiting was done.

"My lady!" cried Dugech as the gush soaked the back of the queen's gown.

Morgause managed a smile. "The waters of my womb flow like those of the holy well. Let them be my offering. . . ." She held out the cauldron, and Leuku, her eyes wide, took it from her hands.

Without waiting for orders, Dugech whispered to one of the younger girls and sent her sprinting back up the trail.

"Let us spread our mantles to make a bed for you, lady, and you can lie down until the litter arrives."

Morgause shook her head. "I walked half the night to bear my first child. This labor will go easier if I get as far as I can under my own power." She knew that she was challenging the gods, but so long as she was moving, she could maintain the illusion that this process was under her control. Ignoring the shocked protest of the maidens, she started back along the trail.

From time to time a pain overwhelmed her and she would pause, gripping Dugech's shoulder until it passed. But it soon became apparent that this child was in a hurry to come into the world. By the time they reached the crossroads, the pains were coming swiftly. Morgause swayed, dragging in breath in hoarse gasps. The women were piling their cloaks on the grass beside the road. Dugech took one arm and Leuku the other, and Morgause could no longer resist them. Biting her lip against the pain, she let them help her down to lie with her back braced against the bank where the pale primroses grew.

Her fingers clenched in the new grass as the muscles of her belly contracted and released again. She was aware that the litter had arrived, but by then things had gone too far for her to be moved.

She fixed her gaze on the hollow moon, sliding down the western sky like a rind of pearl. She could hear the girls whispering. It was not right that the queen of the Votadini should give birth like a beggar woman beside the road. And at a crossroads too! At Beltain, when the folk of faerie moved from their winter quarters to their summer homes, more might be passing along that road than men. Morgause shook her head, denying her own fear. This pregnancy itself had been a challenge to the gods—it should be no surprise that the birth was the same.

"Draw the circle of safety around me if you are afraid—" she grunted between pangs, "and then get ready to catch the babe."

The muscles of her belly writhed again, and she was unable to suppress a groan. Between birthings one always forgot the pain, but it seemed to her that the violence of the pangs that tore her now was greater than any she had known, as if the womb were trying to turn itself inside out in its haste to expel the weight it bore.

"Mother . . ." she whimpered, and then bit back the word. Blood trickled from between her thighs to stain the crimson gown. Igierne was not there—had never been there, really, when Morgause needed her, even when they were living in the same hall. Why should she call for her now?

Morgause had always taken such pride in her ability to bear sons. But women died in childbirth, and she was no longer in her first youth. *Am I dying?* Her thoughts circled in confusion. *Is the Goddess claiming my offering?* Shadows danced before her eyes like dark wings.

I am in Your hands, Lady . . . I offer my life if it will serve you, and that of my child. She let out her breath in a long sigh, feeling a dim sorrow, but no fear.

Then another convulsion took her and she cried out once more. The rolling ache became a wrenching agony.

"Warrior, and mother of warriors—now you shall fight for your life!" came a voice from within. *"Cast the babe from your body, now!"*

Morgause drew up her legs and dug her heels into the soft earth and pushed with all the strength she had. The pressure increased, as if she were being split in two. Again her muscles clenched and she bore down. She felt the gush of birthblood and a burning pain in her sex as the child's head crowned. Against her closed eyelids the sunlight was a whirl of red brightness. She sucked in air, and then with the last of her strength, pushed once more.

There was a moment of pulsing relief as the babe slid, warm and slippery, between her thighs. She gasped for breath, and in echo, heard his furious challenge to the world. The babe was still yelling when Dugech tied off and cut the cord and laid him on her breast.

Morgause lay in drowsy stupor, the contractions of the birth fading from her wracked body like the last tremors of love. She felt the warm seep of blood from her womb sinking into the thirsty soil and found it hard to care. Anxious voices twittered around her, but she ignored them. Only when hard fingers began to knead her belly did she open her eyes with a weak cry.

"My lady, the afterbirth must be driven forth—" said Leuku as the queen protested. The baby was still squalling.

"Set the child to the teat," someone said then.

There were a few moments of confusion as they undid her gown. Morgause felt the babe rootling at her breast, and then a sudden sharp pang that shocked through her entire body as he fastened onto the nipple and her milk let down. Through the convulsions that followed as she was delivered of the placenta he hung on. It was only when he let go at last that she saw blood flowing from her nipple along with the milk and realized that her son had been born toothed and ready to take on the world.

From nearby came the deep rumble of male voices. Morgause looked up and saw Leudonus' grizzled head above the others.

"You have a fine son, my lord, for all that he came early into the world—" said Dugech, leading the king into the circle of women. Morgause's lips twitched as the other woman bent to take the swaddled child from her arms.

Dugech knew perfectly well that this boy, like the others, was full-term. Even Leudonus, who had sired his share of bastards, must know the difference by now, but if so, he had his own reasons to uphold the fiction. He frowned down at the squirming bundle Dugech had handed him, and silence fell while men waited for him to acknowledge paternity.

"A fine boy indeed. He has your hair," he said finally. And then, holding him up, "Let him be called Medraut, of the royal kindred. Let the Votadini welcome a future warrior!"

This, if not explicit, was close enough to an avowal. The walls of the cleft echoed to their shout of welcome. Morgause smiled. *A warrior,* she thought, *and more than a warrior. I welcome a king!* She could sleep now, knowing others would guard her child. The moon had finally disappeared, but through her closing eyelids, she still saw the red glow of the Beltain Sun.

If she slitted her eyes just so, thought Guendivar, the reflections from the warriors' spearpoints merged into a single dazzle of light. That was almost more fun than watching them throw the spears, and certainly better than listening to them argue about the casts. She had promised Telent that she would watch him compete today. He was in Prince Leodagranus' guard, and carried her around on his shoulders, though the last time she asked he had said that at almost seven, she was too old.

Guendivar chewed on her lower lip, watching as he prepared to cast anew. She knew that she was growing, but he was *very* tall. Perhaps she would go away now, to punish him.

At the thought, she was already in motion, flitting past the line of men like a white blossom before the wind. Her mother, who had been dozing in the shade of the figured cloth, sat up suddenly, calling, but by then Guendivar was halfway down the field and could pretend she had not heard. Petronilla was always trying to make her be polite and tidy; Guendivar had learned the advantages of evasion early on.

She wanted to see the rest of the festival. At the edge of the field, peddlers had set up their wares in bothies made of woven branches and strips of striped cloth. There were only a few, and their goods would have been considered paltry stuff when the Romans ruled, but only the older people remembered those days. In the old days they would probably have celebrated the festival in Lindinis, her father's town, instead of spending most of their time at the old villa in the hills. To the folk of the country-side, the red pottery oil lamps and the beads of Roman glass seemed very fine. Guendivar wandered among them, admiring, and one of the traders gave her a green ribbon to tie back her hair.

The afternoon was waning when she saw one of her mother's women advancing toward her with a decidedly repressive look in her eye. Rather suddenly Guendivar remembered that Petronilla had been quite explicit about the behavior that was expected of a chieftain's daughter at this festival. She knew that she had disobeyed, and she did not mind being punished once it was over, but the sun was still well above the trees!

Before the woman could grab her, Guendivar was off again, slipping behind a cart and then around the horse-lines and toward the protection of the trees. Perhaps her father's huntsmen knew these woods better than she did, but Guendivar did not think anyone else could find her once she was among the trees. And even a woodsman might think twice about entering the tunnels that a small girl could negotiate with ease.

One of them brought her out into a small glade surrounded by hazels. The grass in the center was flattened, as if someone had been sleeping there, and hanging on one of the hazel twigs was a flower crown. Guendivar began to smile.

To watch the dancing last night had been exciting, with the drumming and the naked bodies shining in the light of the fires. She had not quite understood what those men and girls were seeking when they leaped over the flames or ran, half-embraced and laughing, for the forest, but she knew it must be something wonderful, part of the magic she felt pulsing from the land itself on Beltain eve.

Guendivar could still sense it, a little, here in the glade. She sat still, senses extended, feeling the warmth of the afternoon radiating from the grass. The sounds of the festival seemed distant, and as she continued to sit and her eyelids grew heavy, more distant still. She had not gotten much sleep the night before, and the day had been busy. The warm air caressed her and she curled drowsily down into the tangled grass.

It was the change in the light that roused her, a ray of the sinking sun that found its way through the tangle of branches to her closed eyelids. Still half-asleep, she scrunched them shut more tightly and turned her head, but the sun's angle let the last of its radiance pour through the trees. Sighing, Guendivar rubbed her eyes and slitted them open.

Within the glade, every stock and stone was glowing, and each leaf and blade of grass was edged with flame. *Pretty . . .* she thought, watching with half-focused gaze, and stretched out her arm. *Everything has light inside, even me. . . .* Beneath the scratches and the smears of soil and the scattering of golden freckles, her pale flesh shone.

A flicker at the edge of vision caught her attention. Her vision refocused; something was moving there. Bemused by beauty, she did not stir, even when her vision transmuted the spiraling sparkles into attenuated figures that danced and darted about the glade. At first they seemed tiny, but they seemed able to change their size at will, and they moved as if weightless, or winged. And presently she realized that susurrus of sound was neither the wind nor music, but the chatter of high, sweet voices.

Fragments of old tales configured themselves into sudden certainty. Slowly Guendivar sat up, refusing to blink, lest the vision flicker away.

"I know you now . . ." she said softly. "You are faerie-folk. Have you just moved house into these woods today?"

For a moment even the motes of light seemed to stop moving. Then the air shimmered with faerie laughter.

"She sees us! She can see!" The faeries clustered around her in a glowing swirl. One of the figures floated upward to face her, expanding until it was as large as a child of three.

"Of course I can see you," answered Guendivar. "I have seen faeries before, I think," she added, remembering, "but they never talked to me."

"It is the moment between day and darkness, and in this child, the old blood runs true," said one of the others. *"But she will lose the vision when she is grown."*

Guendivar glared, but a new question was already on her lips. "Will you show me your country?"

"This is *our country—it is all around you, if you have the eyes to*

see—" came the answer, and indeed, when Guendivar lifted her eyes, the familiar shapes of tree and rock seemed doorways to unguessed dimensions. But she dared not look too long, for fear that her new friends would flit away.

"Then will you give me a wish?" she asked.

"Our gifts can be dangerous . . ." the faerie responded, but Guendivar only laughed.

"Am I in danger here?" She grinned. "My wish is that my heart shall stay as it is now, and I shall always be able to see faerie."

"Are you certain? Folk so sighted may find it difficult to live in the mortal world. . . ."

Guendivar shrugged. "I think it is boring already. It will not matter to me."

"It will matter . . ." said the faerie, with momentary sadness. Then it, too, laughed. *"But we cannot refuse you on this day."*

Guendivar clapped her hands, and as if on cue, the sun slid behind the hilltop and the light was gone. Her new friends were gone, too. For a moment she felt like crying, but it was getting cold, and she was hungry. She looked for the tunnel through the hazels, and found that to her altered vision, the world around her still shone from within.

The faerie had not lied to her. Laughing once more, Guendivar ran back to the world of humankind.

A Shadow on The Moon

Just at dusk, on an evening when the first sliver of the first new moon of summer hung above the brow of the hill, Merlin arrived at the Lake. As always, he came alone and unheralded, appearing like a spirit at the edge of the forest. Igierne, on her way to the rock at the highest point of the island for her evening meditation, felt his presence like a breath of scent, which at first teases, and then releases a flood of memories. She stopped short on the path, so that Morut nearly ran into her.

"Go down to the landing and send the boat across to the shore. We have a visitor."

Morut's eyes widened, but she did not question Igierne's knowledge. Smiling, Igierne watched her go.

When she had first returned to the Lake to reclaim her role as its Lady, after Artor was made king, Igierne had felt herself half an impostor. The skills required of a bean-drui needed focus, application, constant honing. She was like a warrior taking down the sword he has allowed to rust on the wall. And yet her mental muscles, though stiff and clumsy, still remembered their early training, and in time she found that the passing years had given her a depth of understanding that had not been there when she was a girl. There might be others on the island to whom these skills came more easily, but none with her judgment regarding how and when they should be used. And after a dozen years as Tigernissa of Britain, Igierne found it easy to rule a gaggle of women and girls.

But Merlin, she thought as she watched him coming towards her, had wisdom of a different and higher order still. When she was a young woman, he had seemed much older than she, but from the vantage of fifty-two, a man in his early sixties was a contemporary. It was not age that set him so apart from other men, but an inherent wildness, despite all his years in the courts of kings.

He wore his accustomed wolfskin over a druid's white gown. Both were well-worn, as if they had grown to his gaunt frame. But he looked strong. Later, as she poured mint tea into his bowl from the kettle that steamed over her fire, she realized that Merlin was assessing her as well.

"I am no longer the girl you knew in Luguvalium . . ." she said softly.

"You are still beautiful—" he answered her thought rather than her words "—as the forest in autumn, when the nuts ripen on the trees."

Igierne felt herself flushing, and shook her head. "My moon has passed the full, but it is the sun we should be speaking of. When did you last see Artor?"

Merlin raised one bushy eyebrow in gentle mockery, but allowed her self-deprecation to pass. "Two, or nearly three moons past. He is rebuilding the fort at Isca. Castra Legionis, they call it. It will serve as a staging area for campaigns against raiders from Eriu. It was very crowded and full of soldiers. I did not stay long."

"That is the main threat, then? Not the Saxons?"

The druid shrugged. "At present. Artor has tamed Hengest's cub and set him to guard the sheep in Cantium, but the rest of the Saxon pack are still hungry. Ceretic sits in Venta, licking his chops and eyeing the lands around him, and the Anglians roam the fens. Artor will have to deal with them eventually. But why do you ask me? Does not he write to you?"

"From time to time—" She tapped the carved wooden casket where she kept Artor's letters. "But a druid's sight is different from that of a king."

"I cannot rule for him, Igierne," Merlin answered her, "nor can you."

She frowned, thinking of the advice she had been sending. Someone must speak for the Goddess, until Artor had a queen. "Is that why you spend so much time roaming the wilds?" she countered. "What if something happens? What if he needs you?"

"I will know." His voice was a subterranean rumble, as if he spoke thorough stone. "The stars have shown me that a crisis is coming. For good or for ill, it will settle things with the Saxons for a generation. When that time comes, it is ordained that I be there."

Igierne felt the truth of that in her bones. For a few moments there was no sound but the hiss of the fire.

"I too have searched the future," she said finally. "Two years ago, at Beltain. This year I dared not—I was afraid. I remember the terror, but of what I saw I know only that the Lady of Ravens was there, and red war coming, and a child."

"I know Her . . ." Merlin's face twisted with ancient sorrow. "Only the White Raven can stand against her when the war horns blow."

"But what of the child?"

"You called out to me in that vision, and I heard—" Merlin threw up his hands in exasperation. "But what would you have me do? Should I have counselled Artor to order every child born on the first of May exposed? Even Caesar would have been unable to enforce such a decree! Foreknowledge is a deceptive gift, Igierne, for our hopes and fears distort the shapes of what we see. When I was young I searched the heavens constantly, but the older I get, the less I seek to know."

"But if you foresee a danger, you can avoid it—" she exclaimed.

"Can you? The Greeks tell of a man called Oedipus, whose efforts to flee his fate instead fulfilled it."

Igierne glared at him. She knew that as women got older they often became stronger, more resolute, while many men grew gentler in old age. Certainly it was so with Merlin. He, who in their young days had been hard as the hills, seemed now as elusive as wind or water.

"If I see danger coming to my country or my child I will confront it," she told him, leaning forward with her hands on her knees. "And I will not cease to fight that fate while life shall last."

"Perhaps that is *your* fate, Igierne," Merlin said gently, and smiled.

"Mother, Aggarban is wearing my red belt!"

"Why can't I have it? You said you weren't taking it with you—"

Gwyhir's reply was muffled, as if he had decided to take matters into his own hands. Morgause sighed. She had been regretting Leudonus' decision to send her second son to join his brother at the court of Artor, but just at this moment she did not care whether he went to Castra Legionis or the Devil, if she could have peace in her house once more.

"Let him have it, Gwyhir," she snapped, thrusting aside the curtain between her closet-bed and the central common area around the fire. "You were telling me only yesterday that the belt is too small."

"But he should *ask*, mother," said Gwyhir, straightening to his full height. He had got man-high in the past moons, but was still growing into his bones. His hair, lighter than Gualchmai's, stuck out at odd angles, giving him the look of a young bird.

Aggarban still wore the belt, though he was flushed and rumpled where his brother had grabbed him. He was dark and stocky, not much taller than the fourth brother, Goriat, even though he was almost four years older. Morgause looked at them and shook her head. She was too young to be the mother of such a brood of big, boisterous boys. At the moment, she wanted to send them *all* to Artor; all, that is, except for her sweet Medraut.

Her youngest son was turned two this spring. She had danced at the Beltain fires this year and gone into the woods afterwards with one of Leudonus' warriors. But she had not kindled. She told herself it meant nothing—there were three years between Gwyhir and Aggarban, after all, and four between Goriat and Medraut—but in her heart the fear was growing that Medraut would be her last child. Was he her punishment, or her key to greatness? She still did not know.

"Will you write and tell us all about Artor's fortress?" asked Goriat.

"I will be far too busy to write letters," answered his brother loftily, "riding, and training with the sword and spear. When I win my first fight I will let you know."

"And what if you lose?" Aggarban stuck out his tongue and darted out of the way of his brother's blow.

"Our brother Gualchmai is the greatest warrior the High King has," said Gwyhir. "He may beat me, but by the gods, nobody else will, once my training is done."

At least, thought his mother, he recognized that he still had a few things to learn. But in the long run, she shared his confidence. No son of hers could be anything but a champion.

"A fine lad," said Bliesbituth as they watched Gwyhir ride out with Leudonus and his men. He was a chieftain who often served as a courier between Fodreu and Dun Eidyn. "But why do you send him to the Romans? If you let him come to Pictland, we would marry him to one of our princesses and he might father kings." He smiled at his wife, a plump, pretty woman called Tulach, who was herself of the royal lineage.

"I have several sons," Morgause said diplomatically. "Perhaps one of the others—"

"You think I am flattering," said Bliesbituth, "but it is not so. Britannia was strong in the time of the emperors, but their time is ended. The

Votadini should look northward. We were never conquered; our warriors never gave up their swords. If all the peoples who live north of the Wall were to unite, we would be a power to reckon with. The Romans call us the Picts, the painted people, but we are the Pretani, the true Britons of this isle. The south is exhausted—our time is coming now."

Morgause felt the blood of generations who had fought to defend that Wall burning in her cheeks, but she held her tongue. From all accounts, Artor was keeping the Saxons and the men of Eriu in check; she was too tactful to remind Bliesbituth how her brother had dealt with the Picts three years before. The Romans, even at the height of their power, had been able to do little more.

Another thought chilled her suddenly. If all the might of Rome had been able to do no better, what did that say about the power of Alba? While Artor was young and strong, perhaps he could hold the north in check, but what about his successor? The lords of Britannia had refused to make her husband their king because his power was too far from the center of things, but in the time that was coming, it might be that only a king whose strength lay on the borders could hope to rule. *A king like my son* . . . she thought, smiling grimly, *my Medraut.* . . .

"And there is this to think on," said Tulach. "They say that the people of the south have abandoned their gods. The new religion teaches love, and peace. Is it any wonder that the empire has fallen? You think you keep the old ways here, my queen, but among the Pretani we have preserved the ancient traditions in all their purity. It is not only our menfolk who have power!" The silver ornaments clasped in the tight curls of her bronze brown hair chimed softly as she nodded.

Morgause smiled thinly. "It is true that there are many in Britannia who follow the Christos, but I am the daughter of the Lady of the Lake and the heir to its mysteries."

"No doubt, but there are things we could teach you, Morgause."

Morgause did not answer her. The dust of Leudonus' cavalcade was fading, and it was time to go in. She could not deny that for a moment Tulach's offer had tempted her. But the power that waited on the Isle of Maidens was bred in her, blood and bone. It had been too long since she had tasted its waters and breathed its air.

She should pay her mother a visit, she thought then, and take Medraut. It was time Igierne met her youngest grandchild.

"Well, Morgause, motherhood certainly agrees with you. You are blooming like a rose!" Ebrdila grinned toothlessly and patted the bench beside her. Behind her, the roses in Igierne's garden had been trained over an arbor. In this sheltered spot, the red blooms clustered in profusion, scattering bright petals upon the path.

True, thought Igierne, surveying her daughter with a more critical eye, *but this rose is beginning to look just a bit blown.*

Morgause still had a fine, full figure, but after five children, her breasts no longer rode high, and the muscles of her belly had not yet recovered their tone. But it was her face that had prompted the observation, as Igierne noted the permanent high color in the cheeks, and around the mouth, the first faint lines of discontent. Ebrdila's old eyes might not be able to see it—but then Morgause had been her special pet since the days when Igierne, newly married to Uthir, had left the girl in her care.

"Oh, I am very well!" Morgause gave the old woman a swift hug as she sat down beside her, "and so is my baby. Is he not a fine boy?" She smiled complacently at the child who was playing with the rose petals in the path.

"He is indeed," answered Ebrdila, "just like his mother!"

Igierne had to admit the boy was handsome, though most children, however ugly as babies or gawky as they grew, were plump and rosy at this age. Had Artor been so sweetly rounded when he was two, so seriously intent upon the wonders of the world? Regret for the lost years ached like an old wound in her breast. This boy's hair shone like burnished bronze in the sunlight—Morgause had been the same—but when he looked up, Igierne found herself disconcerted by his considering stare. Then he grabbed for another rose petal and laughed, and the odd moment was gone.

Igierne cleared her throat. "And how is Leudonus?" For a moment Morgause simply stared at her. *Your husband,* thought Igierne, *surely you remember him, even if he is not the father of this child.*

"He is in Isca with Artor," Morgause answered, a little defiantly. "He took Gwyhir into his household with Gualchmai. But surely you knew that—do not you and your son correspond? I thought he asked your advice every time he wiped—"

"Morgause!" Ebrdila chided gently, "There is no need to be coarse."

She had not criticized the content of the remark, only its expression. But at least Igierne now knew that the jealousy Morgause had felt for her brother when she was a girl was still there.

"And did Leudonus suggest that you spend his absence here?" she asked, trying to keep her tone from becoming sarcastic. "It has been a long time—"

Morgause frowned. "I found myself missing the Lake, and all those I love here," her daughter said then. "I did grow up here, after all."

"Indeed you did!" Ebrdila smiled happily and patted her hand.

I feel ill, thought Igierne, but she managed a smile as well. Whether she liked it or not, Morgause was born of the old blood. The Isle of Maidens was her heritage.

"Tonight the moon shines full, and we will honor her. It will be good to see you in the circle once more."

"Not the ritual on the hilltop, I hope—" said Morgause.

"But of course. The night will be clear," her mother replied.

Morgause grimaced. "I had hoped to see the Cauldron again. Artor bears the Sword, but the Hallow that remains on this isle is its equal in power. I am surprised you do not make more use of it!"

Igierne lifted one eyebrow. Was *that* why Morgause had come? "Would you take a war-axe to slice cheese? Neither Sword nor Cauldron are to be used unless need compels."

"True, but unless you practice with a weapon, you won't know how to use it when the need does arrive. Your son bears the Sword, but the Cauldron is my inheritance. Is it not time I began to learn its mysteries?"

From the look on her daughter's face, Igierne feared she had not been able to conceal her instinctive alarm.

"Not while you are still a mother and a ruling queen," she kept her voice even with an effort, wondering why she felt so reluctant to let her daughter anywhere near the Cauldron, since what Morgause had said was quite true. "I myself did not even begin to understand it until I was done with all that and retired to the Lake to give my whole heart to its Mysteries."

"No doubt you are right." Morgause shrugged dismissively. "And I am sure the ceremony on the heights will be very beautiful. It has been some time since I did much climbing, but if you can get up the mountain at your age, I should be able to manage as well."

"No doubt—" Igierne echoed with an edged smile. She had better walk by the lake this afternoon and meditate, she told herself, to clear her mind of anger before the ritual.

*　　*　　*

"Lady of the Silver Wheel,
Lady of the Three-fold Way,
Dreams and Destiny you deal,
Hear us, Goddess, as we pray . . ."

Women's voices echoed, soft and sweet across the water as the procession followed the path by the shore.

"Lady of the shining road,
Lady of the sacred round,
Holiness is your abode,
Help and healing there abound."

Breath shortened as the trail turned from the lake and began to wind up the hillside, but still the priestesses sang. Cupped by its encircling mountains, the island on the lake contained powerful magic, but by the time the full moon breasted those heights, it was high in the sky. The priestesses used the meadow where lay the circle of stones, where they could observe the moment she lifted above the horizon, to honor her.

Igierne felt the blood sing in her veins as the exercise warmed her, and smiled. Ebrdila no longer made this journey, but she herself could still keep up with the youngest of her priestesses. It was Morgause whose face was growing red with exertion as they climbed.

"Lady of the starry sky,
Lady of the sparkling sea,
Queen of all the hosts on high,
And the deeps of memory—"

They reached the summit at last, their shadows stretching black across the grass as the sun sank behind them. Northward, a cloudbank still hung in the heavens, but in the east the sky, tinted a pearly pink by sunset, was clear. Igierne could hear her daughter's harsh breathing ease as they spiraled around the slab of stone that lay on the grass. Cup and ring marks had been carved into its surface by some people long forgotten. Several still held a little water from the morning's rain.

"Lady of the moon's red tide,
Lady of the flowing breast,
Ever-changing, you abide,
Grant us motion, give us rest."

As each woman passed the stone, she bent, touched fingertip to the water and blessed herself, belly and breast and brow. Igierne felt her knee joints complain as she took her turn, and her sight darkened for a moment as she straightened again, but she kept her balance and moved on. She shook her head in self-mockery, knowing that if Morgause had not been there she would have stopped a moment to catch her breath at the top of the hill.

Eastward, the hills fell away in long folds to a dim haze that hid the more settled lands. And there, at the limit of vision, a luminous pallor was beginning to suffuse the sky. The priestesses waited, humming softly. The air brightened suddenly as the sun hung for an instant on the rim of the hills behind them. Then it was gone, and the world was lit by a gentle afterglow. Silently Igierne began to count, knowing that beyond the mountain the sun was still sinking towards the distant sea. The colors of the sky above deepened, the clouds catching the light in bands of gold and rose. She heard her own indrawn breath repeated around the semicircle, and they began to sing once more.

"Radiant Lady, bless the night,
Bless the waters and the skies,
Bless the world with silver light,
We summon you—arise, arise!"

Every month they honored the full moon, on the Isle when the weather was cloudy, and on the heights when the sky was clear, yet the hair lifted on Igierne's neck as a growing glow silhouetted the shape of a distant hill. And then, as if in answer to the compulsion of the song's final line, they saw the hill edged by a rim of blinding silver, and the huge, wonderful disc of the moon rose suddenly into the eastern sky.

Without thought she found her own arms rising with those of the others, as if to lift that bright orb into the sky. Swiftly the moon mounted the heavens, until the women stood with arms stretched high in adoration, hailing the Goddess with a wordless ululation of pure sound.

Gradually the human song faded until only the jubilant chirring of crickets could be heard. Some of the priestesses remained standing with uplifted arms to pray silently while others sank to the earth, sitting cross-legged with their hands open upon their knees. Igierne stayed where she was, staring at the moon's brightness until vision was overwhelmed by light.

Lady, hear and help me! her heart cried. *Here stands the child of my body—why do I find it so hard to love her? She is my daughter, not my enemy!* She heard the harsh rasp of her breath and stopped, willing the inner babble to still, remembering the many times she had told young priestesses that it did no good to ask the gods questions if you were not willing to listen for the answer.

She could hear Morgause breathing beside her. After a time, she realized they had found the same rhythm. She felt ashamed that she should be so surprised.

Is that Your answer? She stopped the thought, concentrating on her breathing, waiting. The moon was halfway up the sky, its color changing from the warm pearl glow of the horizon to a pure silver light. Listening, she heard Morgause's steady breathing grow ragged, as if she were trying to hold back tears.

What does she *have to cry about?* was Igierne's first, swiftly suppressed response. If this woman whose arrogance had irritated her so this afternoon was weeping, her sorrow must be all the greater for being hidden. There were those who must have thought the same of Igierne herself, in the days when she mourned secretly for her lost son while all men hailed her as Uthir's queen.

Ah, child, there was a time you would have brought your trouble to me and wept in my arms. How have we become such strangers? She turned to her daughter, intending to offer comfort. As she met Morgause's eyes, the younger woman's gaze grew stony and she turned away, but not before Igierne had seen upon her cheeks the silver track of tears.

Igierne stared at her back, feeling the tears start in her own eyes. *Sweet Lady, help her! Help us all!* came her heart's silent cry.

In the next moment a breath of wind stirred the grass and gently touched her hair. As it dried her cheeks, she thought that with it came a whisper, "*I am with you, even in your pain. . . .*"

As the harvest moon waned the north lay at peace. The grain was ripening, and on both sides of the Bodotria estuary, men labored to reap the golden sheaves. Braced against the side of the boat that was carrying her over the water, Morgause turned her face to the sea wind and breathed in freedom.

Leudonus was still in the south with Artor, and when Morgause announced her intention to visit the lady Tulach in Fodreu, there was no one in Dun Eidyn with the power to say her nay. Medraut had screamed when she detached his little hands from her gown and handed him to his nurse, but even his cries had no power against the imperative that ever since her visit to the Lake had beat like a drum in her brain—

My mother still loves Artor more! She will never share her secrets. Whatever magic I wield must be my own!

The land on the Pictish shore of the estuary was much the same as the country around Dun Eidyn. Why, she wondered, did the air seem fresher, and the colors more intense, on the other side? It was not only the change of scene that excited her, thought Morgause, for the Lake Country that surrounded the Isle of Maidens was a different land entirely, and she had only felt more constricted there. Perhaps it was because among the Picts she was bound by no ties of love or duty, only by whatever mutual obligations she should agree to in her search for power.

Tulach was waiting for her on the shore, accompanied by a half dozen tribesmen wrapped in tattered plaids and two older women in dusty black robes. They had enough ponies for the Votadini as well.

"Are you taking me to Fodreu?" asked Morgause as she mounted the shaggy little mare they had brought for her. Her own escort eyed the Pictish warriors uneasily, but with or without the consent of kinfolk, there had been marriages enough across the border that half of them had relations on the other side. As they moved out, their suspicions began to submerge in a murmur of genealogical comparison.

Tulach shook her head. "The place for the ritual I have in mind for you lies farther up the coast. We should reach it before nightfall."

"What is it?"

"A place of the old ones, who were here before Roman or Briton. The Picts are partly of that blood. You have such circles in the south as well, but you have forgotten how to use their magic. The old powers are still there, if you know how to call them. You will see."

Merlin knows how to call them, thought Morgause, remembering stories she had heard. Did she truly want to wield that magic, so ancient it seemed alien to her kind? But she had come too far to turn back now.

Her mother would never dream of challenging Merlin. Her mother, she reflected bitterly, was content to follow a woman's traditional path, supporting, encouraging, waiting in the shadows. Did Artor even bother to read the advice she sent him?

She took a deep breath of the damp sea-wind. Her older boys were already moving into Leudonus' world, but Medraut was still hers alone. *It is not advice I will give him, but commands,* she thought grimly, *when I come into my power. The princes of Britannia dream of bringing back the old days before they went under the yoke of Rome. I will bring back a time that is older still, the time of the queens!*

The rough-coated ponies made surprisingly swift progress on the uneven ground. By the afternoon they had travelled a fair distance north and eastward along the shore. They passed a village of fishermen, their overturned coracles sprouting like mushrooms from the stony strand, and paused for a meal of barley cakes baked on the hearthstone and washed down with heather beer. When they mounted once more, they took a new trail that wound upward through the shelving cliffs to a band of woodland below the moor. One of the warriors was now carrying a bag before him, with something inside it that jerked and struggled as they began to climb.

Just as dusk was falling they passed through a tangle of ash and alder

where a small burn trickled towards the sea. Beyond it, an area roughly
the size of Leudonus' hall had been roughly cleared. In the last of the
light she could see that it was bordered by a circle of stones, the largest
no more than waist-high. They were too choked by undergrowth to count,
but the grass around the three in the center, one upright and the others
tumbled, had been cut so that they stood clear.

As the priestesses dismounted, some of the warriors bound torches to
the poles that had been set into the ground, and the bag was laid beside
a tree. Then the men saluted Tulach and led the ponies back down the
hill.

"They know better than to be near when women work magic!" the
Pictish woman laughed. From her bag she took two black mantles, one of
which she handed to Morgause. "Take off your clothes and put this on.
Then wait here until we call."

True, the wind was growing cold, but Morgause suspected it was the
touch of the garment itself that had set her to shivering. To change one's
semblance was to change the soul; as the black wool replaced the garments
of the queen of the Votadini, she became someone else, someone she did
not know.

The other women had already lit the torches and suspended a bronze
kettle above a fire. The water inside it was beginning to steam. Morgause
felt her lips twist in bitter amusement—it appeared that she was going to
learn the mysteries of the cauldron after all.

Tulach moved sunwise around the inside of the circle, scattering herbs
and chanting something in the old tongue. Morgause blinked, wondering
if it were the gathering dusk that suddenly made it so hard to see.

Through the gloom she glimpsed Tulach coming towards her.

"Who are you, and why have you come here?"

"I am Morgause daughter of Igierne," she heard herself answering,
"and I come to offer my service to the old powers."

"That is well. Take up the offering—" she indicated the bag "—and
enter."

What happened after that was hard to remember. There was more
chanting in the strange language as the three old women cast herbs and
mushrooms and other nameless things into the cauldron. The aromatic
steam made Morgause dizzy, so that sometimes she thought she saw a
host of shapes around them and at others it was only the three.

"We stand upon the graves of old ones," Tulach told her. "Do not be
surprised if they are drawn to the ceremony."

Shortly thereafter the singing reached a climax. It was full dark now;
in the circle the flickering torches chased shadows around the fire.

"Take up the bag," said Tulach, "and carefully bring out what you find there."

Morgause had already concluded it must be an animal, and was not surprised to find she had hold of a large hare. Everyone knew that the hare was a creature of great magic. A fisherman who saw one on his way to the boats would turn back and stay home that day. It was never hunted, never eaten except when it was offered to the Goddess. At first the beast struggled, but when she made it breathe the steam, it abruptly went still. Tulach grasped it by the ears and handed her a flint knife.

"Kill it—" she said, "and give the blood to the stones."

The stone knife was sharper than she had expected, but it was still a messy business. Then Morgause got the big vein open, and held the body so that blood spurted over the rock, pooling in the hollows and running down the sides. One of the other women took the victim and began to skin it, and in a few minutes the disjointed body was simmering in the cauldron with the herbs.

The head sat dripping on the largest stone, and Morgause blinked, for the rock was surrounded by a pale glow. She looked around her and saw that the other stones were glowing as well with a light that owed nothing to the fire. With every movement, Tulach and the three priestesses trailed a glimmering radiance. Morgause felt her head swim and knew that she was already deep in trance. The tiny spark within that could still think yammered frantically. Why should they stop with the hare, when they could sacrifice a Votadini queen?

The other women had stripped off their black robes. For a moment she thought that beneath they were wearing blue-embroidered garments. Then she realized that she was seeing skin, tattooed in intricate patterns with woad. She was too dazed to prevent them from removing her black mantle as well, but within the circle the air was warm.

Tulach began to speak, her voice blurred as if it came through water. "We will make no permanent mark upon your skin, but the sacred signs we paint upon your body will mark your spirit shape so that the powers can see . . ."

She dipped a small brush into a bowl in which hare's blood had been mixed with something else and began to draw upon Morgause's breast and belly the same spirals that marked her own. The brush tickled as it passed, and left a tingling behind it. By the time the priestesses had finished painting her front and back, upper arms and thighs, her entire body was throbbing with a pleasant, almost sexual pain.

The soft heartbeat of a drum brought Morgause to her feet again.

"Now you are ready . . . now we call *Her*. . . ."

The drum beat faster, and Morgause found herself dancing as she had not danced since before her first child. Sweat sheened her body, adding its own meanders to the painted designs; she could smell her own female musk mingling with the scent of the herbs. It was very late; the distorted husk of the waning moon hung in the eastern sky.

The priestesses were singing. Presently Morgause recognized goddess-names within the murmur of incantation. She began to listen more carefully, understanding without knowing whether she was hearing with the ears or the heart.

The goddesses they were calling were older and wilder than any face of the Lady she had heard of on the Isle, names that resonated in earth and fire, in the stone of the circle and the whisper of the distant sea.

"Call Her!" sang Tulach as she whirled by. "Call Her by the name of your deepest desire!"

For a moment Morgause faltered. Then the drumming drew from her belly a moan, a shout, a cry of rage she had not known she held within.

She spun in place, light and shadow whirling around her. And then it was not shadow, but ravens, a cloud of black birds whose hoarse cries echoed her own.

"Cathubodva! Cathubodva! Come!"

Was she still moving, or was it the birds who swept her up to the heart of the maelstrom, where it was suddenly, shockingly, still?

"You have called Me, and I have come . . . what do you need?"

"I want what my mother had, what my brother has! I have as much right as he does to rule—I want to be Tigernissa—I want to be queen!"

"The power of the Black Raven, not the White, is Mine. I am the Dark Face of the Moon . . ." came the answer. *"I madden the complacent and destroy that which is outworn. I drink red blood and feast upon the slain. . . ."*

"My mother clings to a power she can no longer wield! My brother fights for a dream that died with Rome! Let me be your priestess, Lady, and do your will!"

"What will you sacrifice?"

"I have a young son, who is also the son of the king! Help me, and I will raise him to be your champion!"

Abruptly sound returned in a cacophony that whirled her with it into a chaos of fire and shadow until she knew no more.

III

First Blood

Bushes blurred by in a haze of green as Guendivar beat her heels against the white pony's sides. Then they burst out onto the sunny ridge, and the mare, seeing a clear trail before her, stretched out her neck and responded with a new burst of speed. Guendivar tightened her long legs around the blanket and whooped in delight. She was flying, lifting like a bird into the blue.

Then the road dipped, and the pony began to slow. Guendivar dug in her heels, but the mare snorted, shaking her head, and her canter became a jarring trot that compelled the girl to rein her in.

"Oh, very well—" she said crossly. "I suppose you deserve a rest. But you liked it too, didn't you, my swan? I wish you could really fly!"

Guendivar had gotten the pony for her seventh birthday. Now she was thirteen; too old, said her mother, to spend her days careering about the countryside. The dark shadow of adulthood was creeping towards her. Only on Cygnet's back could she be free.

A gull's cry brought her head up; she followed its flight, shading her eyes against the sunlight, as it wheeled above the ridge and away over the

Vale. It had been a beautiful summer, especially after last year, when there was so much rain. Through the mist she glimpsed the distant glitter of the Sabrina estuary. Closer, golden haze lay across the lowlands, reminding her of the waters that in the winter turned it into an inland sea. A few hillocks poked through like islands, dominated by a pointed cone in the middle of the Vale. In this light, even the Tor seemed luminous; she wondered if that was why some folk called it the Isle of Glass.

The pony had halted and was tugging at the rein as she tried to reach the grass. Guendivar hauled the beast's head up and got her going again, frowning as she became aware of a dull ache across her lower back. In a canter, Cygnet was as graceful as the bird from which she took her name, but her trot was torture.

Suddenly the bag of apples and bread and cheese tied to her belt seemed very attractive. Guendivar gave the pony a kick and reined her down the hill towards the spring.

It was little more than a seep in the side of the hill, but the constant trickle of water had hollowed out a small pool, fringed with fern and stone-crop and shaded by a willow tree. On the sunny slopes, the grass was ripening, but near the spring the spreading moisture had kept it a vivid green. Cygnet tugged at the rein, eager to be at it, and laughing, Guendivar swung her right foot over the pony's neck and slid down.

"You are a goose, not a swan," she exclaimed, "and just as greedy. But while we eat we may as well be comfortable." She turned to uncinch the blanket and stilled, staring at the blood that had soaked into the cloth.

Frantically she unbuckled the cinch and pulled off the blanket, searching for the injury. But the pony's sweat-darkened hide was whole.

Guendivar's racing pulse thundered in her ears. She tethered the mare so that she could graze, and then, very reluctantly, she loosened her breeches, a pair that had been her older brother's when he was a boy, and pulling them down, saw on the inseam the betraying red stain.

Swearing softly, she pulled the breeches off. She could wash them, and no one would know. But even as she bent over the pool she felt warmth, and saw a new trickle of red snake down her inner thigh.

That was when panic changed to despair, and she curled up on the grass and let the hot tears flow.

Guendivar was still sniffling when she became aware that she was not alone. In that first moment, she could not have told what had changed. It was like hearing music, though there was no sound, or a scent, though there was no change in the air. As she sat up, her senses settled on vision as a mode of perception, and she saw a shimmer that she recognized as the spirit of the pool. Words formed in her awareness.

"*You are different today . . .*"

"I've got my moonblood," Guendivar said bitterly, "and now everything is going to change!"

"*Everything is always changing. . . .*"

"Some changes are worse than others. Now my mother will make me stay home and spin while she talks to me about ruling a house and a husband! After this, she'll never let me ride alone again! I don't want this blood! I don't want to change!"

"*It was the blood that called me,*" came the reply.

"What?" She opened her eyes again. "I thought growing up would mean I couldn't see you."

"*Not so. When you are in your blood it will be easier. . . .*"

Guendivar felt the hairs lift on her arms. Around her the air was thickening with glimmering forms: the slender shape of the Willow girl bending over her; spirits of reed and flower; airy forms that drifted on the wind; squat shapes that emerged from the stones.

"Why are you here?" she whispered. "What does my woman blood mean to you?"

"*It means life. It means you are part of the magic.*"

"I thought it just meant having babies. I don't want to be worn out like my mother, bearing child after child that dies." Petronilla had borne eight infants, but only the oldest boys and Guendivar survived.

"*When man and maid lie down together in the fields they make magic. Before, you were only a bud on the branch. Now you are the flower.*"

Guendivar sat back, thinking about that. Abruptly she found herself hungry. She reached for the bag, and then, remembering, started to offer a portion to the pool.

"*You have something better to give us—*" came the voices around her. "*There is a special power in the first spurting of a boy's seed, and a girl's first flow. Wash yourself in the spring. . . .*"

Guendivar flushed with embarrassment, even though she knew that human conventions meant less than nothing to the faerie kind. But gradually her shame shifted to something else, a dawning awareness of power. She bent, and scooping up the cool water in her palm, poured it over her thighs until her blood swirled dark in the clear water. When she was clean, she washed out her breeches and the saddle cloth and laid them out in the sun to dry.

The faerie folk flitted around her in swirls of light.

"*Sleep a little . . .*" said the spirit of the pool, "*and we will send you dreams of power.*"

Guendivar lay back and closed her eyes. Almost immediately images began to come: the running of the deer, mare and stallion, sow and boar, men and women circling the Beltain fire. All the great dance of life whirled before her, faster and faster, shaping itself at last into the figure of a laughing maiden formed out of flowers.

When she woke at last, the setting sun had turned all the vale into a blaze of gold. But the spirits had disappeared. Her clothing was dry, and for the moment, her flow of blood seemed to have ceased. Swiftly she dressed and cinched the saddle cloth back onto the mare. She was still not looking forward to telling her mother what had happened. But one thing had changed—the thought of growing up no longer made her afraid.

For all the years of Guendivar's childhood, the Tor had been a constant presence, felt, even when clouds kept it from being seen. But except for one visit made when she was too little to remember, she had never been there. As soon as she told her mother what had happened to her, Petronilla had decided to take her to the nuns who lived on the Isle of Glass for a blessing. The prospect filled her with mingled excitement and fear.

It is like growing up— she thought as they reached the base of the isle and the curve of the lower hill hid the Tor from view. *For so long it loomed on the horizon, and now I cannot see it because I am almost there. I will only be able to see my own womanhood reflected in others' eyes.*

The top of the round church that the holy Joseph had built showed above the trees. Around it clustered the smaller huts that were the monks' cells, and a little farther, a second group of buildings for the nuns. Nearby was the guesthouse where the visitors would stay. As they climbed the road, the deep sound of men's voices throbbed in the air. The monks were chanting the noon prayers, her mother said. Guendivar felt the hair lift on her arms with delight as the sweet sounds drifted through the trees. Then the shadowed orifice of the church door came into view and she shivered. The music was beautiful, but cooped up in the darkness like that, how could men sing?

She sighed with relief as they continued along the hillside toward the houses of the nuns. To one side she saw apple trees, ripening fruit already weighting their branches, and to the other, neat gardens. Beyond was a tall hedge, hiding the base of the hill that nestled next to the Tor. She wondered what was behind it. There was something in the air of this place that made her skin tingle as it did when the faerie folk were near. If she could escape her mother's watchful eye, this would be a good place to explore.

A tall woman came out of one of the houses, robed in a shapeless gown of natural wool with a wooden cross hanging from a thong around her neck, her hair hidden by a linen veil. But when she looked up, Guendivar saw a broad smile and twinkling eyes. For a moment that gaze rested on her in frank appraisal. Then she turned to Guendivar's mother.

"So, Petronilla, this is your maid-child—she has grown like a flower in good soil, tall and fair!"

"Nothing so rooted," answered her mother ruefully. "She is a bird, or perhaps a wild pony, always off running about the hills. Guendivar, this is Mother Maruret. Show that you know how to give her a proper greeting!"

Still blushing, Guendivar slid down from her pony, took the woman's hand and bent to kiss it.

"You are welcome indeed, my child. My daughters will show you to your quarters. No doubt you will wish to wash before your meal."

Guendivar's belly growled in anicipation. Along with other changes, she was growing, and these days she was always hungry.

"You are not our only guests," said Mother Maruret as she led them towards the largest building. "The queen is here."

"Igierne?" asked Petronilla.

"Herself, with two of her women."

Petronilla lifted one eyebrow. "And you allow them to stay on the Isle?"

The nun smiled. "We have been in this place long enough to understand that the ways of the Creator of the World are many and mysterious. If the queen is deluded, how shall that trouble my own faith? But indeed, she has never been other than quiet and respectful when she was here . . ."

Guendivar listened, wide-eyed. She had heard many tales of Artor's mother, the most beautiful woman of her time. They said that King Uthir had fought a war to win her and killed her husband before her eyes, though others whispered that Merlin had murdered him with his magic. She lived now in the north, ran the tales, on a magic island. Of course by now Igierne must be quite old, but it would be exciting to meet her all the same.

But when they entered the guest-house, though the queen's two women were there, talking softly by the fire, Igierne was nowhere to be seen.

Just before dawn, Guendivar's mother awakened her. The girl rose quickly and dressed in the white gown they gave her—she had been fasting since noon the day before before, and the sooner this was over the sooner she could get some food. Stumbling with sleepiness, she followed her mother and the two nuns, one of them young and one an old woman, who led the way with lanterns out of the guesthouse and up the hill.

Her interest quickened when she saw they were approaching the hazel hedge. There was a gate set amid the branches. The young woman lifted the iron latch and motioned for them to go in.

On the other side was a garden. Already a few birds were singing, though the sky was still dim and grey. She could hear the tinkle of falling water, and as the light grew, she saw that it was flowing down through a stone channel into a large pool.

"The spring is farther up the hill," the young nun said in a low voice. Her name, she remembered, was Julia. "Winter and summer the pure water flows from the holy well. Even in years of drought it has never failed."

Petronilla glanced at the sky, then turned to her daughter. "It is almost time. Take off the gown and step into the pool."

"I was baptized when I was a babe," muttered Guendivar as she obeyed, "Was not that not purification enough?"

"This is to cleanse you from childhood's sins. You will emerge, a woman, transformed by the blood of your body and the water of the spirit." Her mother took the gown and folded it across her arm.

Of the spirit, or the spirits? wondered Guendivar, remembering the spring on the hillside. It gave her the courage to set her foot on the steps that entered the dark water.

In that first shocked moment, she could not tell if the water was holy, only that it was freezingly cold. She stifled a yelp and stood shaking, the water lapping the joining of her thighs.

"In the name of the Blessed Virgin, may you be cleansed and purified of all sin and stain . . ." murmured Sister Julia, dipping up water in a wooden bowl and pouring it over Guendivar's shoulders.

"In the name of Maria Theotokos, may you be cleansed and puri-fied—" Now it was her mother's turn.

"In the name of the Lady of Sorrows . . ." The old nun poured water over her head and stepped away.

In the name of all the gods, let me out of here before I freeze! thought Guendivar, edging back towards the steps. But her mother stopped her with a word. When Guendivar could escape her mother's eye, she ran free, but she had never yet dared to defy her directly. Shivering, the girl stood where she was.

The sky brightened to a luminous pink like the inside of a shell. Light lay like a mist above the water. Guendivar took a quick breath, and re-alized that her shivering had ceased and her skin was tingling.

"Spirit of the holy spring," her lips moved silently, "give me your blessing . . ." She scooped up water in her hand and drank, surprised at its iron tang. Then, before she could lose courage, she took a quick breath and submerged herself in the pool.

For a long moment she stayed there, her amber hair raying out across the surface, and each hair on her body lifted by its own bubble of air. The water she had swallowed sent a shock through every vein. The tingling of her skin intensified, as if the water were penetrating all the way to her bones. Then, just as it reached the edge of pain, it became light. The force of it brought Guendivar upright, arms uplifted, turning to face the rising sun.

She heard a sharp gasp of indrawn breath from one of the women. The sun was rising red above the slope of the hill. Rosy light glistened on her wet skin, glittered from the surface of the pool. For a moment she gazed, then the light brightened to gold and she could look no more.

"Receive the blessing of the Son of God—" her mother cried. But it was another voice that Guendivar heard.

"Be blessed by the shining sun, for while you walk in its light, no other power shall separate you from this bright and living world. . . . "

To that dawn ritual there was one other witness, who watched from the hillside as the women helped Guendivar from the pool and hid the radiance of her body in the shapeless robe of a penitent. When Igierne had first heard of the planned ritual, she had feared they meant to make the girl a nun; the actual intention was almost as hard to understand. What sins could a child of thirteen have committed? Before her marriage, Petronilla had spent some time as part of Igierne's court. She came from an old Roman family that had long been Christian. Igierne knew that it was not the stains of childhood that Guendivar's mother wanted to wash away, but her daughter's incipient sexuality.

If so, she had chosen the wrong place to do so. Igierne knew how to interpret the blaze of light she had seen in the pool, and she knew also that the colony of monks established here by Joseph of Arimathea had learned how to use the magic of the Tor, but had not changed it. The powers that dwelt here were ancient when the Druids first saw this hill. She should not be surprised that this girl, whose face she had first seen in vision, should be recognized by the spirits of the Tor.

But it did make it all the more imperative that she speak with Guendivar. It would be difficult, for Petronilla kept her daughter well guarded. When the women had left the pool Igierne made her own way down to it, and found tangled in the branches above the gateway a wisp of red-gold hair. She smiled, and pulling a few pale hairs from her own head, began to twine them together, whispering a spell.

The little community on the Tor retired early, the guests to sleep through the night, and the nuns to rest until they should be called to midnight prayer. At night, said the Christians, the Devil roamed the world, and only the incantations of the faithful kept him at bay. But to Igierne, the night was a friend.

When the sound of quiet breathing told her that the other women in the guesthouse were asleep, she rose, slipped her feet into sandals and took up a cloak, and went outside. If anyone had questioned her, she would have said she sought the privy, but in fact her goal was the orchard, where she found a seat, put on the ring of twined hair she had made that morning, and began to sing.

And presently, just as the moon was lifting above the trees, the door to the guest-house opened and a pale figure came through. Igierne told herself that it was only the effect of moonlight on a white gown that made Guendivar's figure seem luminous, but she could not help remembering the radiance of the morning and wondering.

Still, this opportunity must not be wasted. As Guendivar started down the path, Igierne gathered up her cloak and came out to meet her.

The girl started, eyes widening, but she stood her ground.

"Couldn't you sleep either?" Igierne asked softly. "Let us walk. The gardens are beautiful in the light of the moon."

"You're human—" It was not quite a question.

"As human as you are," Igierne answered, although when she remembered what she had seen that morning, she wondered.

"You are the queen—" Guendivar said then.

"The queen that was," Igierne replied, *as you are the queen that will be*. . . . But it was not yet time to say so aloud.

They came out from beneath the moon-dappled shadows of the orchard and continued along the path. The moon shone full in a luminous sky, so bright that one could distinguish the red of the roses that lined the path from the dim green of the hill.

"Where are we going?" Guendivar asked at last.

"To the White Spring. You bathed in the Red Spring this morning, did you not? The Blood Well? Perhaps you did not know there is another on the Tor."

"The Blood Well?" the girl echoed. "Then that is why . . . I thought—" Her voice became a whisper. "I thought that my flow had started again, that my blood had turned the water red."

"They should have explained," Igierne said tartly. "There is iron in the water, just as there is in our blood. Did they tell you the water would wash away your sins? In the old days, maidens bathed here to establish their female cycle. Barren women came also, that their wombs might become as bountiful as the well."

"I felt a tingling . . . all through my body . . ." Guendivar said then. "I suppose that now my mother will be trying to marry me off. She is very ambitious. But I'm not ready."

"Indeed—" Igierne knew too well what it was to be married young to an older man. But for the daughters of princes, a long maidenhood was a luxury. And how long could Artor wait before his ministers compelled him to take a bride? "Do you think you will be ready when you are fifteen?"

The girl shrugged. "That is the age at which my brother was allowed to ride to battle."

"It is the age at which my son became king . . ."

"That was a long time ago," said Guendivar.

Igierne's heart sank. What were the gods about, to make Artor wait so many years for his destined bride? Silent, she led the way down the path to the second gate, and the smaller enclosure where the White Spring welled up from the ground.

"What is this one for?" the girl asked.

"They say it brings hope and healing. You are in health, but sometimes the spirit needs healing as well. Let the water flow into this bowl, and then hold it up to catch the light of the moon."

Guendivar nodded. "There was sun-power in the Blood Well, but this feels different—" She lifted the bowl.

"I wish—" Igierne began, then paused. The girl looked at her expectantly. "Not many would have noticed that. If I thought there were any chance your mother would agree, I would take you for training on the Holy Isle . . ." *If only I could give Artor a queen who was an initiate of the ancient mysteries!*

"An island?" Guendivar shook her head. "I would feel prisoned if I could not gallop my pony beneath the sky. Why do you you live there?"

"Long ago the Romans sought to destroy all Druids because they were the ones who preserved the soul of our people and reminded them of what it was to be free. Those who survived their attacks fled to Alba or Eriu, or secret places in Britannia where they could survive. The Lake is one such, hidden among high hills, and also it is very beautiful."

"I suppose—" the girl said dubiously. "But what do you find to do there all day?"

Igierne laughed. "Our life on the Isle of Maidens is not so different from the way the nuns live here, although we call ourselves maiden not because we are virgin but because we are bound to no man. We spin and weave and grow herbs as other women do, and beyond that, we pray. Do you think that sounds boring?" she answered Guendivar's grimace. "Our prayers are no abject plea to a distant god, but an act of magic. We seek to put ourselves in harmony with the flow of energy through the world, and by understanding, to bend it—"

"To change things?" Guendivar asked.

"To help them to become what they should be, that all shall prosper."

For a few moments Guendivar considered this, her hair glistening in the light of the moon. Then, very softly, came another question. "Do you talk to the spirits, the faerie-folk?"

"Sometimes . . ." answered Igierne.

"I see them . . . they are my best friends. . . ."

The touch of faerie! That is the source of the strangeness I have seen in her, thought Igierne.

The girl shrugged ruefully. "Now you know more than I have ever told my mother. Do not tell her that we have spoken. She already looks at you as if she feared you might summon a chariot drawn by dragons to carry me away!" She stopped abruptly, and even in the gloom Igierne could tell that she was blushing.

"Does she think the Tigernissa of Britannia without honor? You are still a child, and in her ward. I will say only this, Guendivar—if in time to come you need help or counsel, write to me."

She could love this girl, she thought then, as her own daughter—more, she feared, than she had ever been able to love Morgause. But when the child was married to Artor she *would* be her daughter. Surely the goddess who had sent her that vision would not lie!

Guendivar nodded, set the bowl to her lips, and drank. After a moment she lifted her head, her eyes wide with wonder.

"The moon is in it—" With a ceremonial grace, she offered the bowl.

Moonlight flashed silver from trembling water as Igierne grasped the rim. The water was very cold, so pure it tasted sweet on the tongue. She closed her eyes, and let that sweetness spread through her. *Grant hope and healing . . .* she prayed, *to me and to Britannia. . . .*

Igierne held onto the wooden seat as her cart bumped up the street towards the Governor's Palace. She had forgotten how hot Londinium could get in the days between Midsummer and Harvest. Heat radiated from the stone walls of those buildings that remained, and the trees that had grown up among the ruins of others drooped with dusty leaves. Ceincair and Morut swayed in stoic silence beside her.

She ached in every joint from the jolting of the cart, her tunic was stuck to her back with perspiration, and her hair was full of dust despite the veil. For a moment of piercing regret, she wished she had never left the Lake. But there were baths at the palace—perhaps she would feel better when she was clean.

And then the cart pulled up at the gates. Guards straightened to attention, calling out her name. One or two were men she remembered from her days with Uthir. She smiled, giving orders, and for a little while, forgot that she was not still the queen.

By the time the three priestesses were settled it was evening, and Artor had returned to the palace. That was a relief. When Igierne had stopped in Isca on the way south she had heard he was in Londinium, but at any moment that could change. These days he seemed to conduct the business of Britannia from the back of a horse. She had sent a message to warn him of her coming, but she would not have been surprised to find him gone.

He was obviously not intending to stay long. The palace was understaffed, and the meal to which they sat down, though well-cooked, was little better than camp fare.

"I don't know why I should be surprised," said Igierne, taking another spoonful of lentil stew. "When I married him, your father was living on the same thing."

Artor gave her a wry smile. "A telling argument for any who still doubt my parentage. But in truth, I eat this way for the same reason he did. We are still at war. Icel is holding to the treaty I forced on him last summer, but the Irish in Demetia are making trouble again. I must ask you and your ladies to continue your prayers for us, for I will have to take my army westward soon."

Igierne sighed. Artor was taller, with a look that reminded her of her mother about the eyes, but his hair was the same nut brown, and his shoulders as broad as Uthir's had been. As Artor grew older, the resemblance sometimes took her breath away. Like Uthir, he was, in public, a Christian. But he knew very well that the priestesses of the Isle of Maidens did more than simply pray. That was not the issue now.

"No one who knew him would doubt that you are Uthir's son. Nor do I dispute that Britannia is still at war. But during all the years of our marriage it was the same. Nonetheless, your father and I managed to live like civilized people. There is no reason you cannot do so as well!"

"But I am not married . . ." he said softly, reaching for the wine.

Igierne stared unseeing at the faded frescoes on the wall behind him, thinking furiously. Every other time she had brought up the subject, he had turned the conversation. Why was he mentioning it now?

"Are you thinking of changing that?" she asked carefully.

Artor looked up, saw her face, and laughed. "Are you afraid I've fallen in love with someone unsuitable? When would I find the time?" He shook his head. "But even old Oesc has managed to find a woman—Prince Gorangonus' granddaughter, of all people. I've just returned from their wedding, where I gave the bride away. I always meant to marry once the country was secure, but at this rate, Oesc will have grandchildren by then." He took a deep breath. "I'm ready to consider it, mother, though I warn you, I have no time to go looking for a bride."

Igierne sipped wine, for a moment too astounded by this capitulation for words. "Perhaps you won't have to," she said slowly. "If my visions have not lied. There is a maiden, Prince Leodegranus' daughter, whom I believe the Goddess has chosen. But you will have to wait for her—she is only thirteen."

"She is a child!" he exclaimed.

"Any girl who is still unspoken for is going be young—" said Igierne. "Unless you choose a widow, but that is likely to cause complications." They both heard the unspoken, *As it did for me* . . .

"I won't force a maid into marriage with a man twice her age," Artor said grimly. "We must meet before things are settled."

"I will write to Leodegranus, and ask him not to betroth his daughter until you have seen her."

"She must be willing."

"Of course . . ." said Igierne, sighing. She herself had been willing to marry Gorlosius, and that had been a disaster. "Your sister had doubts about marrying Leudonus," she said aloud, "but she agreed to do it, and that pairing seems to have worked out well, even though he is much older than she."

She tried to interpret the play of expression on Artor's face at the mention of Morgause. She knew her daughter resented *him*, but Artor had hardly met his sister often enough to form an opinion.

"I have not seen her since we defeated Naiton Morbet and the Picts," he said finally. "She was . . . magnificent. Three of her boys are with me now, and they tell me that she is well."

Igierne nodded. "I last saw her five years ago, when she visited the Lake with her youngest child. She seemed troubled, but Leudonus was not the cause."

"What, then?" Artor straightened, and she knew he was thinking like a king once more.

"Since Medraut, there have been no more children, and Morgause is a woman who cherished her fertility. She wanted me to make her priestess of the Cauldron—I suspect she was looking for a new source of power."

"I knew you had kept the Sword of the Defender on the Isle of Maidens, but what is the Cauldron?" Artor asked.

"Perhaps, if there is ever a season of peace, you can visit the Lake and I will show you. It is a woman's mystery, but you are the High King, and there are some things you have a right to know." She paused, marshalling her memories. "It is silver . . . very ancient." She shook her head. "That is only what it looks like, not what it *is*. . . . The Cauldron . . . is the womb of the Goddess, the vessel from which comes the power to renew the world."

For a long moment, Artor simply stared. Then she saw a new light come into his eyes. ". . . To renew the world," he echoed. "Do you know how I have dreamed of it? I have been High King of Britannia since I was fifteen years old, and spent most of that time defending her. Do you understand what that means, Mother? All I have been able to do is react, to try and maintain the status quo. How I have longed to move forward, to make things better, to heal this land! If there is ever, as you say, a season of peace, I will beg you to invoke the Cauldron's power!"

Igierne reached out, and Artor took her hand. Her heartbeat was shaking her chest. For so long she had loved her son, yearned for him, and never known him at all. And now it seemed to her that she touched his soul through their clasped hands.

"I will be ready, my beloved. Together we will do it. This is what I too have been waiting for, all my life long!"

But even as her heart soared in triumph, Igierne wondered how Morgause was likely to react when she learned that Artor had been given yet one more thing that she herself had been denied.

Medraut was telling a story. Morgause heard his voice as she came around the side of the women's sun house, clear as a bard's, rising and falling as he spun out the tale.

"It was old Nessa's spirit I saw . . . hunched beside the fire just as when she lived. And anyone who takes that seat is her prey—first you'll feel a cold touch on your neck, and then—"

From the corner of his eye he saw his mother coming and fell silent. The younger children to whom he had been talking got to their feet, wide-eyed at the sight of the queen.

"Medraut, you will follow me—"

"As you wish, Mama," he answered politely. She had taught him not to talk back to her before he was three years old.

But as they neared the door she heard a stifled giggle from one of the children, and turning, surprised her son completing a swish of his hips that was obviously an imitation of her own walk. Her hand shot out and she gripped his ear and hauled him after her through the door.

"And what was *that?*" she asked, releasing him.

"Nothing—it was just to make them laugh," he added as she reached for him again, "so they'll like me."

Her fingers clenched in his hair, jerking it for emphasis. "You are a *prince,* Medraut. It is they who should be courting *you!* But if you *must* ridicule, attack those who are lower than yourself. It does not contribute to *your* standing to make them laugh at *me!* Do you understand?"

"I understand, Mama . . ." he whispered, and she let him go. His eyes glittered with tears, but weeping was another thing she had trained him out of long ago.

"You are a prince, my beloved," Morgause added, more gently. She set down the bag she was carrying, and bent, turning him to face her and gently stroking his hair. "Your blood is the highest in the land. And you are the brightest and best of my children. Remember that, Medraut. I will teach you things that none of the others could understand. You must not disappoint me, my little one. . . ." She took his face between her hands and kissed him on the brow.

As she straightened, she saw his gaze shift to the bag, which was twitching and bulging of its own accord.

"Is it alive?" he whispered.

"That is a surprise for you," she answered gaily, picking up the bag with one hand and offering the other to her son. As always, her heart lifted as his small fingers tightened on hers. *You are mine!* she thought, looking down at him, *the child of my heart and the son of my soul!*

"Are we going to do a ritual?" he asked as the turned down the path to the spring. "Is it something that you have been learning from Tulach and her friends?"

"Hush, child, we must not speak of that here," said Morgause. "What we will do is not one of their rites, though they have helped me to better understand it. You are seven years old. What I will show you today will set you on the road to power."

Medraut began to walk faster, and she smiled.

By the time they reached the spring, the sun was setting at the end of the gorge, and as it disappeared, the shadow of the cliff loomed dark across the grass. Sounds from the dun above them came to them faintly, as though from another world.

Morgause dropped the bag and hunkered down beside it, motioning to Medraut to do the same.

"This is the hour that lies between day and night. Now, we are between times, between the worlds. It is a good time to speak with spirits, and those that dwell in the sacred springs and holy wells are among the most powerful."

He nodded, gazing into the dark pool with wondering eyes. What did he see? When Morgause was a child she had sometimes glimpsed the faerie-folk. These days, she was learning to do so again, with the aid of certain herbs and spells.

Carefully, she showed him how to cleanse head and hands, and made him drink a little from the spring.

"Make your prayer to the spirit that lives here . . ."

Obediently he shut his eyes, lips moving silently. She would rather have heard what he was saying, but that did not matter now. Presently he looked up at her once more.

In the distance Morgause could hear the lowing of cattle, but by the spring it was very still. But there was a weight to that silence, as if something was listening. She picked up the bag and smiled.

"The spirit of the spring is waiting. Now you must make your offering. Open the bag—"

With nimble fingers, Medraut untied the strings and pulled at the opening, dropping it with a squawk as something white and feathered burst free. It was a cockerel, and it was not happy at having been confined in the bag. But its feet had been tied, so for all its flapping, it could not go far.

"Blood is life," said Morgause. "Wring the bird's neck, and let its blood flow into the pool."

Medraut looked from the cockerel to his mother and shook his head, eyes dark with revulsion.

"What, are you afraid of a little blood? When you are a warrior, you will have to kill men! Do it, Medraut—do it now!"

The child shook his head again and started to edge away. Morgause fought to control her anger.

"I teach you secrets that grown men would pay to learn. You will not deny me. See—" she gentled her voice, "it is easy—"

With a swift pounce, she captured his hands and pressed them around the neck of the fowl. The boy fought to free himself, still shaking his head and weeping. Morgause could not afford pity. Tightening her grip, she twisted, ripped the cockerel's head off and tossed it aside. Medraut cried out as blood spurted, but still she held his hands on the body of the bird, and did not know if the tremors that pulsed through their clasped fingers were those of the dying cockerel or of her son.

IV

Lady of The Eastern Gate

In the hour before dawn, the priestesses gathered in the largest of the roundhouses on the Isle of Maidens. Mist lay like a veil across the lake; glittered in golden haloes around the lamps. Silent and anxious, some still rubbing sleep from their eyes, they filed in and took their places around the hearth.

Igierne was waiting for them. From sunset of the night before, when her spirit, open in the evening meditation, had received Merlin's message to this moment, she had not been able to sleep at all. Since the beginning of this last and greatest Saxon rebellion, the priestesses had met three times daily to support with the strength of their spirits the Britons' campaign.

But this was the last battle, the final confrontation with the ancient enemy. Through Merlin's eyes she had seen the hill called Mons Badonicus where Artor's army stood at bay, the scattering of campfires on its summit surrounded by a multitude below. The men were tired, food was low, and their water was almost gone. With the dawning, they would stake all on one last throw and ride against the enemy.

The priestesses, huddled in their pale mantles against the chill, sat like a circle of stones, and like the stones, their strength was rooted in the earth of Britannia. With Igierne, they were nineteen—all the senior priestesses, and the most talented of the girls. She signaled to the drummer to begin her steady beat. Then she took a deep breath and let her own awareness sink down through the fluid layers around the island and deeper still into the bedrock that supported them. Slowly her pulsebeat steadied and her breathing slowed. Here, at the foundation of all things, there was neither hope nor fear. There was only pure Being, changeless and secure.

She could have remained in that safe and secret place forever, but though her anxiety had faded, the discipline of years brought her back to awareness of her need, fueled by her determination and deeper even than her fear for her country, to protect her child. Slowly she allowed her awareness to move upward, trailing a cord of connection to the earth below, until she reached the level where her body sat once more.

Igierne lifted her arms, and the drumming quickened. With the precision of long practice, the other priestesses stretched out their arms. One by one they connected, and as the circle was completed, a pulse of power flared from hand to hand. Now, with each breath, power was drawn up from the depths and through the body, out through the left palm to the hand it clasped and onward.

Around and around, with each circuit it grew, a vortex that spiraled above the hearth. Igierne kept it steady, resisting the temptation to release it all in one climactic explosion of energy. In her mind she held the image of Merlin, offering him the cone of power to support his own wizardry. As the link grew stronger, she sensed men and horses, confusion and blood-lust, exaltation and fear.

She held the circle even as she felt something flare towards him like a spear of light. But the shock as Merlin caught it shattered the link. For one terrified moment the spirits of the priestesses were tossed like leaves in a high wind. And then another power blossomed in the midst of them, rising from the hearth like a flame into which all other powers were subsumed.

Bright as fire, serene as pure water, strong as the earth below, Brigantia Herself arose from the midst of Her priestesses and directed their joined powers towards the goddess image on the boss of Artor's shield. Through Her eyes, Igierne saw the image blaze, saw an answering radiance in the faces of Britannia's warriors, and saw, as the Saxons felt the land itself turning against them, the enemy break and flee.

To Igierne, Aquae Sulis had always seemed an outpost of civility and culture in the midst of the wild hills. The warm stone of the temple of

Sulis and the enclosure surrounding the baths in the center of the city glowed in the afternoon sunshine, and the tiled roofs of the Roman buildings around them had the mellow beauty of an earlier age. Even the Saxon war had not really touched it, though the land to the north had been trampled and torn by the two armies. Igierne had wept, passing the twin mounds where they had burned the bodies of the slain Britons and those of their foes. In life, she reflected, they had been enemies, but in death they all fed the same soil.

The Saxons had kicked down a few doors when they searched Aquae Sulis for foodstuffs, but by Artor's order, the town had been stripped of booty and abandoned before the armies arrived. If the place had not been full of wounded soldiers, she might never have guessed there had been a war.

Those fighters who were still fit to travel were already off to their homes, or harrying the retreating Saxons. Most of the warriors who had been badly wounded were dead. Those who remained in Aquae Sulis had wounds which were not severe enough to kill them outright but required a longer convalescence. The minerals in the water healed torn flesh as its warmth eased aching muscles, and each morning the altar of Sulis bore new offerings.

At dawn, before the day's complement of wounded came to seek the goddess, Igierne and her women visited the baths. Some of the hot and cold pools that had been added to the facilities in the previous century were no longer usable, but the rectangular great bath was still protected by its vaulted ceiling. Seen through the steam that rose from the surface, the marble gods stationed around the pool seemed to nod and sway. Cradled in the warmth of the water, Igierne saluted them: Venus and Mercurius, Jupiter and Juno and Minerva, Ceres and Bacchus, Apollo and his sister Diana with her leaping deer.

Only Mars was missing from this place of healing. But on Mons Badonicus the Britons had made offerings enough to the god of war. Not only Oesc, but Ceretic, the leader of the West Saxons, had fallen there. Aelle, who had led the rebellion, was an old man. It would be a generation or more before the Saxons could hope to field such an army again.

Afterwards, relaxed and glowing, she joined Artor for breakfast in the house of the chief magistrate.

"You look well," he said as they sat down.

"I wish I could say the same for you," she answered. In the pitiless illumination of morning the lines that pain had drawn around his mouth and responsibility had graven on his brow showed even more clearly than they had by torchlight the night before. "You look as if you had lost the war."

"I lost a lot of good men," he said tonelessly. He had filled his bowl with porridge, but he was not eating it. "I lost Oesc."

"He was your enemy!"

Artor shook his head. "Never that. If I had not failed him, there would have been no war. I killed him," he said flatly.

"Not in hatred or anger . . ." she objected softly.

Her son sighed. "I was spared that, at least. It was by his request. His back was broken in the battle, and he wished the mercy stroke to come from my hand."

Igierne considered him, frowning. *You are wounded too, my son, as sorely as any of those men I saw outside the baths.*

"When Uthir died," she said slowly, "I saw no reason to go on. Morgause did not need me, and I did not know where you were. I was no longer a queen. It took time for me to understand that there was still a role for me to play, and things I was needed to do."

"Indeed . . ." Artor breathed, "I felt your presence on the battlefield. And then—" a memory of wonder flared briefly in his eyes "—the goddess came, Sulis Minerva, or Brigantia Herself, filling our hearts with fire. Britannia owes a great debt to the women of the Holy Isle."

"And now you need me again—" she said, not quite questioning. He did not answer. His face was grim, and she realized that he was not seeing her at all. "Artor," she said sharply, "why did you summon me here?"

"I do need you." His face brightened with a rueful smile. "There remains one task that is too much for my courage. Only a woman—a priestess—can help me now."

Igierne set down her tea and looked at him expectantly.

"I swore to Oesc that I would bury his ashes beside Hengest's mound . . . and I promised to see his wife and infant son back to Cantium."

"Cataur will give her up to you?"

"Has already given—" Artor said grimly, "which is the only reason his head is still connected to his shoulders. Enough Saxon blood has been spilled to satisfy even the Dumnonians. Rigana and her child are safe now at Dun Tagell. I want you to go there and escort her home."

Igierne sat back in her chair, staring, her mind awhirl with memory. "I have not seen Dun Tagell since your father took me away to be married, after Gorlosius died. . . ."

After a moment she realized how much of that ancient grief and anger must have shown in her face by its reflection in Artor's eyes.

"Does it get any easier, Mother? Do the rage and the sorrow fade in time?" he asked then.

"They do . . ." she said slowly, "if you seek healing; if from the destruction you build something new."

He nodded, still holding her gaze. "Healing is what we all need now. After so many years of warfare, Britannia, bruised and battered as she is, knows peace at last. The Sword and the Spear must be put to rest. It is time to bring forth the Cauldron and use its power."

"And for that you need the Lady of the Lake," answered Igierne, "I understand. But you also need a queen."

"Still trying to marry me off, Mother?" The pain lines vanished in a brief grin. "Well, perhaps you are right. I will arrange to visit Leodegranus—after I have confirmed Oesc's son as lord of Cantium."

"So—did Artor send you because he was afraid to face me?" Rigana turned, skirts flaring as the sea breeze caught them, but then there was always wind at Dun Tagell.

"There are a great many demands on the High King's time," Igierne answered neutrally.

"Oh, indeed!" Rigana took a quick step away from the cliff's edge, brown curls blowing across her face and head cocked like an angry bird. "Too many for him to pay attention when that bastard Cataur abducted me, and far too many for him to take the time to rescue me! I would still have a husband, and you would not have had this war, if there had not been so many demands on your son's time!"

Igierne took a firm hold on her own temper. "The women of Demetia whom he saved from slavery in Eriu might not agree with you, but hindsight is a wonderful counselor." She had met Oesc a time or two when he was Artor's hostage, and thought him a pleasant, if rather dour, young man. How had he ended up married to this virago? "He sent me because I know what it is to lose a husband," she continued. "Artor will be waiting for us in Cantium."

"With Oesc's ashes." Rigana's narrow shoulders slumped. "At night I lie awake, remembering all our bitter words. And yet I loved the man, even though he was Saxon and the heir of my family's ancient enemy."

"Artor loved him too," said Igierne quietly.

Together, the two women started along the path that wound about the edge of the rock. The stone wall was low here, a protection for those inside rather than a defense, for no boat could live among the rocks at the base of the sheer cliff that faced the dancing glitter of the sea. They picked their way thorugh the tumbled remains of beehive-shaped huts where monks had lived until Gorlosius turned Dun Tagell into a guardpost, following the curve of the rock back towards the hall.

"Oesc trusted him—" Rigana said bitterly. "He would not have turned against his own folk for my sake, but I think he might have done so, if Artor had called."

"He went to war with Artor for your sake," Igierne reminded her.

"Do you think I haven't blamed myself for that, too?"

"Blame Cataur—"

"Who goes unpunished!" Rigana exclaimed.

"Not entirely. I am told he will never sit a horse again."

"Artor should have killed him! He taunted me—called me a whore who had sold out to my country's enemy for the sake of a warm bed and a crimson gown!"

They had stopped once more. Below them the sea shone luminous as emerald in the slack water by the shore.

"He wanted to," answered Igierne, "but he needed Cataur's men. The greater good outweighed the desire for revenge—a lesson you will have to learn if you are to hold Cantium until your son is grown."

"Is *that* what Artor intends?" Rigana's eyes widened.

"Cantium is the Eastern Gate of Britannia. Artor trusted Oesc to hold it for him, and promised it to Oesc's son. You are of the old blood of the land. Until Eormenric comes of age, you will be Cantium's queen. You will have to choose a good man to lead the house-guard—" She stopped, for Rigana was not listening.

Overhead gulls darted and soared, squabbling. Rigana had turned towards the hall, and Igierne heard a fainter cry above the mewing of the birds.

"Eormenric—" Rigana crossed her arms above her breasts, where a dark stain was already spreading as her milk let down in response to the baby's cry, and hurried down the path.

Igierne followed more slowly, bracing herself against memories that surged like the waves of the sea. In her mind's eye, the bright afternoon gave way to moonlight, and once more she saw Uthir coming towards her. When a cloaked figure rose up before her, she was not surprised, and reached out eagerly.

"Lady . . . I greet you. . . ."

A woman's voice—Igierne recoiled, blinded by the light of day. Someone seized her hand and pulled her back to the path, and she stood shaking with reaction.

The woman who was holding her was a little bent, with grey in her hair, wrapped in a grey shawl. It took a moment for Igierne to realize that the glimmer of light around the stranger was no failure of vision, but the aura of power. She took a deep breath, centered herself, and looked again.

"You are Hæthwæge, Oesc's wisewoman," she said then. "Merlin has told me about you."

Hæthwæge smiled, and suddenly she did not seem so old. "And all Britannia knows the Lady of the Lake." Her nod was the salutation of one priestess to another. "I am glad that you have come."

To Igierne's relief, she used the British speech, accented but clear. "Do *you* understand why Artor kept Rigana here?"

The wisewoman's gaze grew bleak. "To keep her safe until Oesc's Wyrd was accomplished. The runes told me what had to be. I loved him dearly, but I knew his life would not be long. Now he goes back to the land."

Igierne looked at her with sudden calculation. That the Saxon woman had power was clear—but what, besides the runes, did she know?

"A time of peace is coming in which our peoples must learn to live together," she said slowly. "And it seems to me that as the years pass, those of us who follow the old ways, both Saxon and Briton, will find we have more in common with each other than we do with the priests of the Christians. You would be welcome at the Lake, to teach our young priestesses, and learn our mysteries."

Hæthwæge stopped short, her gaze gone inward as if she were listening. Then she laughed. "I would like that well, but you must know that where I go, there also goes the god I serve. He has always been very willing to learn from women, and I may teach what I have learned from him. But my duty lies now with Oesc's young son. Until Eormenric is taken from the care of women, I must stay by him. If you are still willing, when that day arrives I will come to you."

"I understand," said Igierne, "and Rigana is fortunate to have you at her side. But we have a journey to make. While we bear each other company, let us share what wisdom we may. . . ."

The harvest was in and the first storm of autumn had swept the west country, cleansing the land and setting the first touch of vivid color in the leaves. But when it was past, the gods seemed to have regretted their threat of winter, for the skies cleared and the air grew warm once more. The Vale of Afallon lay in dreaming peace, and the hills that sheltered it basked beneath the sun.

Even at the villa, where the family of Prince Leodagranus had gone to escape the heat of Lindinis, the air was hot and still. Guendivar, clad in the sheerest linen tunica her mother would permit her, untied the waist cord to let the garment flow freely from the brooches that held it at the shoulders and still felt rivulets of perspiration twining across her skin. Even the wool she was spinning felt slick beneath her fingers. She detached them distastefully and tossed the spindle onto the bench that ran along the covered porch.

Sister Julia started at the clatter, then returned her attention to the even strand that was feeding from the cloud of wool wrapped around her distaff onto her own. She had been Guendivar's constant companion for almost a year, when Petronilla, dazzled by the prospects implied by Queen Igierne's letter, had sent to the Isle of Glass for a nun to guard her daughter's chastity. Mother Maruret had offered them Julia, an orphan of good family who had not yet taken her final vows. She was plain enough to convince Guendivar's mother of her virtue, and at eighteen, young enough so that Guendivar would tolerate her company.

"How can you bear to spin in this weather?" Guendivar exclaimed, resting her hands on the railing and gazing out across the stubble of the hay-meadow. "If they could, I daresay even the sheep would be shedding their fleeces now. But then—" she turned back to Julia "—you always look so cool."

Julia flushed a little, and Guendivar laughed. She had discovered very early that the young woman's fair skin showed every shift in emotion. She was clad, as always, in a gown of heavy undyed linen, and when Guendivar looked more closely, she saw a sheen of perspiration on Julia's brow.

"You *are* hot! Well, that settles it. We are going down to the stream to bathe!"

"But your mother—" Julia stopped her spinning.

"My mother will not be back from Lindinis until tonight, but why should she object? The war is over, and all the lust-crazed soldiers are on their way home!"

It was too bad, really—for all their fears, not one warrior, lusty or not, had come near. It would have brought a little excitement into what had been an anxious but boring summer. Guendivar sighed, knowing her mother would have told her to use the bathhouse attached to the villa, but she saw no reason to make more work for the slaves when what she really wanted was to get out into the woods once more.

Before Julia could protest further, Guendivar had dashed inside for her sandals and some towel cloths and a blanket, and was running down the path. In the next moment, she smiled as she heard the young nun hurrying after her. By now, she had found that within the limitations of her mother's rules, Julia was quite persuadable. Guendivar would even have been glad of her companionship if she could just, once in a while, have spent some time alone.

It had been months since she had had a glimpse of faerie radiance. Did growing up mean that one could no longer see them? But they had *promised* that she would stay the same! Guendivar clung to that knowledge in the lonely nights when she lay awake watching the moon pass her window and listening to Julia's quiet breathing from the other side of the room. Sometimes she thought about simply climbing out the window, but Julia was a light sleeper and would rouse the household to follow her.

But I will do it! she promised herself as she reached the woods and slowed. *No one, not even the High King himself, will keep me locked in for long!*

Julia gave her a reproachful glance as she caught up with her. She was breathing hard and sweating visibly. Guendivar suppressed an impulse of pity. It was Julia's own fault—she knew where Guendivar was going, after all.

But now she could hear the cheerful gurgle of the stream as it purled among the stones of the ford. Below the ford the ground had been cleared so the sheep and the cattle could come down to drink there, but above it, where a screen of alders shaded the water, her father had hollowed out a bathing pool.

Guendivar dropped her towel and stripped off her tunica in a single motion, and made a dash for the pool.

"Oh, it's delicious!" she cried as the coolness closed around her. She ducked beneath the surface and came up laughing, splashed Julia, who had folded her gown and was testing the water with one toe, and laughed again to see it sparkle in the sun. She leaned backward to let the water embrace her and floated, her bright hair raying out around her, her breasts bobbing like pale apples.

Carefully, Julia waded in. Standing, the water lapped her breasts, larger than Guendivar's, though the younger girl was taller, with rosy nipples, erect now in response to the water. Julia's face might be plain, reflected Guendivar, but her body was rounded and beautiful. It was a shame to hide that curving waist beneath a nun's shapeless robe.

She allowed herself to sink beneath the surface once more, turning, opening her legs so the cool water rushed between her thighs. She felt the pressure of the current against her side—or was it the spirit of the pool? Her spirit reached out in wordless longing, and she felt the current curl around her in an insubstantial embrace.

Too soon she had to come up for air, and the moment was gone. She could only be grateful that she was wet already, so Julia could not see her tears. She gathered up her hair and twisted it to wring out the water, then started for the shore.

"Do you want to go back now?" asked Julia. She was washing her hair, black now with moisture, like the delta of shadow between her thighs.

"I will rest awhile and let the air dry me." Guendivar spread out the blanket where the old leaves lay thick beneath the trees and lay down.

Presently Julia joined her, sighing with content as she stretched out at Guendivar's side.

"What is it?" the other girl asked presently. "You look so sad. Is it something I have said or done?"

Damn— thought Guendivar, wiping her eyes. "I used to range the hills like a wild pony! I hate being penned in the house like a mare being kept until the stallion comes. It's not your fault, Julia. You make it almost bearable!"

"Oh, my dear—" Julia reached out to touch her shoulder. "Don't you want to marry the king?"

"He doesn't even know me! Maybe it will come to nothing. Maybe this is all no more than my mother's dream. But if the High King doesn't want me, she will find someone else, and I will be in prison forevermore!"

"Guendivar, it's all right!" murmured Julia, drawing her close as she began to weep once more, holding her pillowed against her soft breast until she had cried herself out and was still.

It had been a long time, thought Guendivar in the peace that followed, since her mother had held her so. Julia's skin was as cool and smooth as her mother's silken gown. Dreamily, as if she were stroking her cat, she slid her fingers down that soft side. Again, and again, she stroked, exploring the contours of muscle and bone beneath the smooth skin, until her hand cupped the curve of the other woman's breast.

Julia gasped, and Guendivar, opening her eyes, saw the betraying flush, rosy as sunrise, beneath the fair skin. "Please—you should not—"

"Touch you? But why not?" asked Guendivar. "Your skin is lovely." She squeezed gently, fingers circling until they found the pink nipple and felt it harden.

"I think . . . it is a sin. . . ." Julia took a quick breath and started to pull away, but Guendivar held her.

"My mother says it is a sin if I let a man touch my body, but you are not a man." Guendivar smiled. "Look, our breasts are nestling together like doves. . . ." She moved closer, feeling a sweet fire begin to burn warm within her own body at the contact of skin on skin. She licked her lips, wondering if that skin would be as sweet to the taste as it was to touch. Julia made a small desperate sound and turned her head away.

"You like me, don't you?" Guendivar asked in sudden doubt. "It's not just because my mother makes you stay—"

"Oh Guendivar, my sweet child, I love you," Julia whispered brokenly, "Didn't you know?" The stiffness went out of her body and she reached up to stroke Guendivar's hair.

"I don't know about love, but I know that you like holding me—" She smiled again and kissed Julia's lips. There was a last moment of resistance, and then the other girl's arms tightened around her.

Together they sank back down on the blanket, and she learned just how much Julia liked her as, clumsy as colts and sensuous as kittens, they discovered the pleasure touch could bring. And presently, lost in sensation, Guendivar forgot the future that prisoned her, and was free.

At Midwinter, the High King came to Lindinis. He was travelling from Londinium to visit Cataur in Isca Dumnoniorum, his message told them, and Lindinis would be a good place to break his journey. He would be there, he said, in time for the festival.

"He has not said he is coming to see *me*," said Guendivar. Scrubbed and scented and swathed in Roman silks, she sat on the chest in her mother's bedchamber, kicking her heels against its carven side.

"He wrote to ask your father if you were spoken for," answered Petronilla, peering into her mirror of polished bronze as she hung discs of gold filigree and garnets in her ears. "God knows how he knew that Leodagranus even *has* a daughter, but if he is coming here, it is you he wants to see. Perhaps he fears that if he marries into Demetia or Dumnonia, the others will be jealous, whereas an alliance with Lindinis will not upset the balance of power. But you come of the blood of the Durotrige princes, and your ancestry is as royal as any in Britannia. So you will be on your best behavior, my girl—" she turned to fix her daughter with a repressive glare "—and show yourself worthy to be Artor's bride."

And why should I want to be a queen? Guendivar wondered mutinously. *From all I have heard, they have even less freedom than other wives*—but she did not say so aloud. Her mother had explained quite clearly the advantages to her family, and threatened to send her back to the Isle of Glass with Julia if she refused.

"At least," Petronilla continued as she settled the veil over her hair, "you are in blooming looks."

Guendivar felt a betraying flush heat her cheeks and hoped her mother would put it down to maidenly modesty. It was Julia's care for her and the joy they had together that had made these past months bearable.

Sounds from the street below brought both of them to their feet, listening. Petronilla moved swiftly to the porch that overlooked the atrium and glanced down.

"They've come—quickly now, we must be ready to greet them—" She reached for her daughter's hand and towed her out of the room.

Guendivar's first thought was that Artor was old. After a second glance, she decided that perhaps he was merely very tired. He was tall and well-muscled, though rather thin, and his brown hair showed only a few threads of grey. He might even be rather good looking, if he ever relaxed. She wondered if she were judging him so harshly because he had hardly looked at her? Once they were all seated in the triclinium and the slaves began to bring in the food, the king had directed all his remarks to her father and brother.

Artor's nephew Gualchmai, an enormous young man who reminded her of a mastiff puppy her brother had once brought home, was doing his best to compensate.

"Those two louts who are swilling at the end of yon table are my brothers Gwyhir and Aggarban—" he said, gesturing broadly, the goblet of pale green glass seeming impossibly fragile in his big hand. "And there's two more at Dun Eidyn still to come."

Guendivar lifted one eyebrow. Gwyhir, sitting beneath the garland of winter greenery that had been draped across the frescoed wall, was almost as tall as his brother, Aggarban shorter and more solid, but still a big man.

"And you go everywhere with the king?" she asked.

"We do, along with Betiver, that narrow dark lad yonder who is nephew to Riothamus in Gallia, and Cai, who was Artor's foster-brother."

"He has formidable protectors." She saw him blink as she smiled.

"Aye, well—we lost some good men at Mons Badonicus, but seemingly we'll have less need of them from now on." Gualchmai looked as if he were trying to convince himself this was a good thing.

The slaves came in to clear the platters of venison and roast pork away and replace them with honeycakes and pies made from the apples of the vale. Soon the feast would be over. Would the men sit down to their drinking and send the women away? Guendivar no longer wished to avoid Artor; indeed, she had begun to think that if she did not arrange an encounter, she would have no chance to speak with him at all.

"I think my father is about to end the feasting—" she told Gualchmai. "You might tell your lord that even at midwinter I often walk in the atrium at night to breathe the fresh air. . . ."

"A good commander is always glad of information—" He grinned at her approvingly. "I will make certain that he knows."

Well, at least *he* seemed to like her, she thought as she followed her mother out of the room. If Artor did not want her, perhaps she could marry Gualchmai.

It was late, and even the hooded cloak was no longer quite sufficient to keep off the chill, when Guendivar heard a man's step upon the stones. Shivering, she stood up, and saw him stop short, then move slowly forward until he stood before her. She thought for a moment that it might be Gualchmai, come to tell her that Artor would not be there. But those senses with which she had learned to see the folk of faerie identified not the king's appearance but his unique aura of power.

"I am sorry—" he said finally. "I have kept you waiting, and you are cold." He shrugged off his crimson mantle and draped it around her shoulders. It still held the heat of his body and warmed her like a fire.

"But you will be cold—" she protested.

"I've campaigned in worse weather than this, in armor. *That* is cold!"

"I have never been cold without a way to get warm, never marched without food or panted from thirst, never done labor that I could not stop when I willed. Except for spinning, of course—" she added ruefully. He was surprisingly easy to talk to—perhaps it was because she could not see him. They were two spirits, speaking together in the dark.

"What *has* Gualchmai been telling you?" Artor said, on a breath of laughter. "I do not expect my queen to march with the army. I hope that in the next few years even *I* won't have to march with the army, at least not all the time."

"Would you then keep your wife like a jewel in a golden setting?" Guendivar's voice was very soft.

There was another charged silence, then Artor sighed. "Your brother tells me that you are a great rider, and can stay out all day, ranging the hills. I would not cage you, Guendivar, even in gold. If you wish it, I would be glad to have you riding at my side."

She straightened, trying to see his face. She was a tall girl, but still she had to look up at him. "From what Gualchmai says, you are never more than a moon in the same place. I think I will have to—"

"It is a bargain, then?" Relief made his voice unsteady as he set his hands on her shoulders.

"It is—" She had feared this marriage as a prison, but now she was beginning to think it might be an adventure. The pressure of his hands felt warm and secure.

"In the spring, then—" He stopped suddenly. "How old are you?"

"At the beginning of April I will be fifteen." She strove for dignity.

His hands dropped suddenly and he shook his head. "Sweet Goddess! And yet, if I was old enough to be king at that age, I suppose that you can be a queen."

Her assurance left her suddenly. "I will try—"

Artor eased back her hood. He took her face between his hands, gentle as if he were touching a butterfly, and kissed her on the brow.

V

The Flower Bride

A.D. 496

That year spring came early to Britannia, as if the land were adorning itself to celebrate the wedding of the High King. Every dell was scattered with creamy primroses; the woodland rides were flooded with bluebells, and in the hedges the starry white of hawthorn veiled each bough.

As the bridal procession left the Summer Country and made its slow way towards Londinium, folk thronged from tiled villas and thatched Celtic roundhouses, from shepherds' lonely huts and half-ruined towns to hail the bride whose marriage would set a seal of peace upon the land. Surely, they sang, the wars were truly ended, if the High King was at last giving them a queen. Where Guendivar passed, the road was strewn with flowers.

To Merlin, making his way southward from the Caledonian forest, the rumor of her progress was like a warm breath of wind from some fruitful southern land. He found himself hastening, moved by a hope he had not dared to feel for far too long. He had been born to serve the Defender of Britannia and set him on his throne, and he had succeeded in that task. None of them had dared to think about what might come afterward.

But now the land itself was providing the answer. After winter came the spring, after sorrow, this joy, after the death of the Britannia that had been ruled by Rome, a new nation in which all the gathered greatness of the peoples who had settled here could flower.

Igierne, riding south with Ceincair and Morut, could not help but contrast this wedding with her marriage to Uthir, that hurried, makeshift ceremony held in the dead of winter and the aftermath of a civil war to legitimize the child she was already carrying. Guendivar would come to her marriage a virgin, with neither memories of the past nor fears for the future to shadow the day. If the queen mother had not been so profoundly relieved at the prospect of passing on a part of the burden she had carried for so long, she would have envied her son's bride.

For Artor's sister, riding swiftly southward with her escort of Votadini tribesmen, each milestone on the old Roman road was a reminder of her own dilemma. For so long she had told herself that the freedom of a queen in Alba suited her far better than any title dying Britannia had to offer. Now she was about to find out if she really believed it. If Artor had never been born, her own descent from the House of Maximus might have given her husband a claim to torque and diadem. Yet the closer she got to Londinium, the more clearly Morgause understood that it was not Guendivar whom she envied, but Artor himself. She did not desire to be a consort, but the ruling queen.

Even in decline, the Romanized Britons for whom Boudicca was still a name with which to frighten children would never have accepted her. Artor's son would inherit his imperium. The only question was whether that son would be the child of her womb, or Guendivar's.

Artor himself, struggling with questions of personality and precedence, remembered the bright face of the girl he had met at midwinter and wondered if he had the right to plunge any woman into the political morass this wedding had become. Even the choice of a place to hold the ceremony had provoked a battle. Bishop Dubricius had offered his own church in Isca, but to marry there would have insulted the Dumnonians, already on the defensive because they were blamed for provoking the last Saxon war.

Artor could have been married in the bride's home, but Lindinis was only a secondary tribal civitas, and had no edifice large enough to hold all those who would want to come. Calleva or Sorviodunum were central, but too closely associated with the wars. At least Londinium had once been the country's undisputed capital, and in the basilica and the Palace of the Governors there would be room for all.

But as the first of May drew closer Artor would have been glad of an excuse to send some of them home again. Planning battles was much easier. He was beginning to think that the ancient custom of marriage by capture had a lot to recommend it. Guendivar had said she liked to ride— perhaps she would prefer being carried off. But when the king tried this theory out on his companions, they only laughed. Gualchmai, who had more experience with women than any three of the rest of them, assured him that women *liked* ceremonies with flowers and candles and uncomfortable new clothes.

As for Guendivar herself, she rode through the blossoming landscape in a haze of delight, accepting the gifts men brought her and the homage they paid her beauty; exulting in the movement of the horse beneath her, the brightness of the sunlight and the sweetness of the flowers. Focused on the excitement of each moment, she scarcely thought about the wedding towards which this journey was leading her.

"Old Oesc used to say these walls were like the work of etins— titans . . ." said Betiver, gesturing at the ruins of the gatehouse that had once guarded the Calleva Road. The rubble had been cleared away, but the gate had never been repaired.

Guendivar gazed around her with interest as they passed. "It looks old, and sad. Will Artor rebuild it?"

"Why should he trouble himself," asked Gualchmai, laughing, "when the walls are as full of holes as a cloak when the moths have been making free? Walls!" He made a rude gesture. "No good are they without brave men and sharp spears behind them!"

"Oh, indeed," said his brother Gwyhir, who rode just behind him, "and you yourself are as good as an army!"

Guendivar laughed. After three weeks on the road, she had taken their measure. Artor had sent the youngest and liveliest of his Companions to be her escort, and they had preened and pranced for her from Lindinis to Londinium. They reminded her of puppies showing off, even Betiver, who was said to have a permanent mistress in the town and a nine-year-old son.

"The high roof you see belongs to the basilica," he told her. "That is where the wedding feast will be—I think it is the only building in Britannia large enough to hold all the people Cai has invited. The church is nearer the river."

"And the palace?"

"Beyond the basilica, on the other side of the square. Of course only the main wing is still usable, but with luck, we'll be able to find enough sound roofs in Londinium to keep everyone dry!" He sent a suspicious glance skyward, but the overcast did not look as if it were going to deepen into rain.

Guendivar sighed. She had looked forward to staying in a palace, but this vast city, its old buildings leprous with decay, held little of the splendour of her dreams. Ghosts might dwell here, but not the folk of faerie. She thought wistfully of the fields through which they had passed to come here, adorned more richly than any work of the Romans with spring flowers.

But she must not let her escort sense her unease. "Is Artor here already?" she asked brightly. "Will he come to greet me?"

The Votadini brothers turned to Betiver, who replied with a wry smile, "I am sure that so soon as he knows you have arrived he will come to you—but as for where he is now—well, you will learn soon enough that Artor is not one for sitting still."

But the High King was not working. Igierne had arrived the previous day and, finding her son in the old office of the procurator, surrounded by scraps of paper, had carried him off to the river. As a boy he had learned the difficult art of paddling a coracle; she pressed him into service now as her boatman and ordered him to take her upstream.

High clouds had spread a silver veil partway across the heavens. Each stroke of the paddle set reflections rippling like pearl. From time to time some other craft, coming downstream, would pass them. Igierne lifted a hand to answer their hails, but Artor had not the breath to reply.

She watched him with a critical eye, noting the flex and stretch of muscle in his arms and back as he drove the round skin-covered craft against the current. Sometimes an eddy would spin them, and Artor needed all of his strength as well as skill to get them back on course. He was sweating freely by the time she told him to stop.

The coracle spun round once more, then began to drift gently back towards the city whose smoke hazed the river below them like a shadow of the clouds. Artor rested the paddle on his knees, still breathing hard.

"Do you feel better?" she asked.

For a moment he stared; then his exasperation gave way to wonder. "In fact, I do . . ."

"There is nothing like vigorous action to relieve strain, and you have been under a great deal, my child." He spent much time outdoors and his color was good, but she noticed more than one thread of silver in the brown hair, and there were new shadows around his eyes.

"I have never been required to plan a campaign of peace before," he said apologetically. "In war it is easy. If a man has a sword at your throat, he is an enemy. Here, I have only allies, who think they know what is needed better than I. I might believe them—if they could only all agree!"

Igierne laughed. "It is not so different among my priestesses on the Isle of Maidens." For a few moments they were silent, watching the ducks dive into the reedbeds as they passed. Then she spoke once more. "Tell me, is it easier to move the boat upstream or down?"

"Down, of course," he answered, one brow lifting in enquiry.

"Just so. Think—is not everything easier when you move with the current instead of fighting it?"

He nodded. "Like charging downhill."

"Like this wedding—" she said then. "Guendivar is the woman whom the fates have ordained for you. To make her your wife you don't have to fight the world. Let it be. Relax and allow her to come to you." She stopped suddenly. "Or are you afraid?"

He knew how to govern his face, but she saw his knuckles whiten as he gripped the oar.

"She is so young, Mother. She has never heard the ravens singing on a battlefield, or seen the life ebb from the face of a man you love. She has never known how fury can seize you and make you do terrible things, conscious of nothing until you come to yourself and see the blood on your hands. What can I say to her? What kind of a life can we have?"

"A life of peace," answered his mother, "though you will not have done with battles entirely while the Picts still ride southward and Eriu sends warriors across the sea. It is because she is innocent that you need this girl. You need say nothing—let her talk to you. . . . She will be Tigernissa, High Queen. Men fight for land, but the life of the land is in the waters that flow through it. The power of the waters belongs to the queen. It is for her to initiate you into its mysteries."

A gull swooped low, yammering, and when it saw they had no food, soared away. They could smell woodsmoke now, and on the shore the wharves of Londinium were beginning to come into view.

"The river has great power. See how swiftly we have returned? Beneath all the eddies, all the flotsam that rides its surface and the ruffling of the wind, the deep current of the river rolls. It is the same with the squabbles of humankind. Worship as you must for Britannia's peace, but never forget how strong these waters are as they move so steadily toward the sea. . . ."

*   *   *

The night before the wedding it rained. At dawn, clouds still covered the sky, but as they thinned, they admitted a little watery sunshine. When Guendivar came out of the palace, the wet stones of the pavement were shining. She gazed around her, blinking at the brightness. At that moment, even this place of wood and stone was beautiful. Her escort was already formed up and waiting. When they saw her, they began to cheer, drowning out the clamor that marked the progress of the groom's procession, already two streets away.

Her mother twitched at the hawthorn wreath that held the bridal veil. Its fiery silk had been embroidered with golden flowers. More flowers were woven into the crimson damask of her dalmatic and worked into its golden borders in pearls. Jewels weighted the wide neckband and the strip of gold that ran from throat to hem. It was a magnificent garment, fit for an empress of the eastern lands from which it had come—everyone said so. But it was so heavy Guendivar could hardly move.

Her mother gripped her elbow, pulling her forward. For a moment Guendivar resisted, filled with a wild desire to strip down to her linen undergown and make a dash for the open fields. How could they praise her beauty when her body was encased in jewels like a relic and her face curtained by this veil? It was an image they shouted for, like the icon of the Virgin that was carried in procession at festivals.

But she had given her word to Artor.

"She comes! She comes—" cried the crowd "—the Flower Bride!"

Stiff as a jointed puppet, Guendivar mounted the cart, its railings wound with primroses and violets and its sides garlanded with eglantine. As it passed through the streets, people strewed the road with all the blooms of May. They brightened the way, but could not soften the rough stones. Guendivar gripped the rail, swaying as the cart jolted forward.

They turned a corner and came into the square before the church, a modest whitewashed structure dwarfed by what remained of the imperial buildings that still surrounded it. The hills of the Summer Country seemed very far away.

The groom's escort was already drawn up beside it, and the bishop waited before the church door, his white vestments as heavily ornamented as her gown. Even Artor was cased in cloth of gold that glittered in the pale sunlight. *We are all images,* she told herself, *existing only to play our roles in this ceremony.* But what force could manipulate kings for its pleasure? The people, perhaps? Or their gods?

The cart halted. Guendivar allowed them to help her descend, and her father, grinning as if she were his sole invention, led her to the church door. Marriages were blessed by the Church, but they were not part of its liturgy. Still, the porch of the church seemed a strange place for a ceremony. Through the haze of silk she could see Artor, looking as stiff and uncomfortable as she. Bishop Dubricius cleared his throat, gathering the attention of the crowd.

"*In nomine Patris, et Filii, et Espiritu Sancti—*"

Guendivar felt her heart beat like that of a trapped hare as the sonorous Latin rolled on, a river of words that was sweeping her and Artor both away.

Only when the sound ceased did she rouse. Everyone was looking at her, waiting for her answer. Could she, even now, refuse? But as she gazed frantically around her the sun broke through the clouds, and suddenly all the world was a glitter of light. She shut her eyes against that brilliance, but behind her eyelids it still blazed.

"*Volo—*" she heard her own voice say.

There were more words, and then the deep murmur of Artor's reply. The priest bound their hands, turned them to show themselves to the people, whose joyous response smote the sky.

Then Artor led her into the darkness of the church for the nuptial mass.

The scent of flowers hung heavy in the hall, mingling unpleasantly with the odors of human sweat and spilled wine. From the high table on the dais at the end of the basilica, tables had been set end to end in front of the walls. Upon the benches of the king's side, all the princelings of Britannia, and on the queen's side, their wives and daughters, sat packed like pickles in a crock.

Morgause took another drink from her own cup, breathing deep to let the sharp fumes drive the other scents away. When the last of the Roman governors abandoned his post, the items he had left behind included some amphoras of good wine. It was a little past its prime—Artor had been right to use it now. She sighed, aware that the wine was making her melancholy. When she was a girl they had drunk wine like this in her father's hall, but in times to come they would have to swill like barbarians on mead and heather beer.

A clatter of steel on shield leather brought everyone upright as the sword dancers marched in. Some of the male guests leaped from their benches, reaching as if they expected to find their own weapons hanging behind them on the wall. Morgause grinned sourly. These were the champion dancers among her husband's tribesmen; it pleased her to see these fat southern lords, if only for a moment, feel afraid.

The dancers' tunics, though clean, were of rough wool, and the earthy hues woven into their mantles dull against the bright colors of the princes, but their swords flashed in the torchlight. Singing, they formed two squares. Shields lifted into position, and they began their deadly play.

The singers who had been performing earlier had almost been drowned out by the hum of conversation, but the sword dancers riveted everyone's attention. Even the little bride, who had been picking at the slice of roast boar with which Artor had served her, put down her knife to stare.

"They are Votadini?" asked the woman beside Morgause. She was called Flavia, invited because she had been foster-mother to Artor.

She nodded. "They come from a clan on our border with Alta Cluta."

"They are most . . . energetic . . ." Flavia replied. "Your husband must be proud. But I do not see him. Is he well?"

"Well enough," answered Morgause tightly, "but his joints pain him too much to make such a journey."

"Ah, I understand—" Flavia grimaced in sympathy. "I came in a horselitter, and still it was two days before I could walk without wincing! It is the price of growing old. Of course *you* are still young—" she said after an uncomfortable moment had passed.

Morgause thought of her own aches and kept silence. On her other side the mothers of the bride and groom were deep in conversation. Morgause had stopped resenting having to sit below Guendivar's mother, when she realized that Petronilla, puffed with pride though she might be, would save her from having to talk to Igierne.

"And what do you think of our new queen?" asked Flavia.

Morgause bared her teeth in a smile. "She is pretty enough, but very young—"

Young enough to be Artor's daughter, if he had been married off at the age I was. Young enough to be a sister to Artor's son. . . . Medraut had begged to come with her to the wedding. He was quite self-possessed for a nine-year-old—she had trained him well, but instinct counselled her to wait. Medraut's time was yet to come.

"But you yourself were married at much the same age, were you not, and to a much older man?" Flavia commented, far too acutely.

And now I am tied to an ancient who is good for nothing but to sit by the fire, while I am still in my prime! Morgause thought then. It would serve Guendivar right if she found herself in the same situation with Artor. It could happen—Leudonus was proof that some warriors lived to be old.

"It is not her age but her intelligence that will make the difference,"

Morgause answered tartly. "A pretty face alone will not hold a man's interest for long."

"Then we must hope that she can do so, for my Arktos was always a conscientious lad, and I suspect he will remain faithful, whether she loves him or no."

Morgause regarded her thoughtfully. Igierne, for all her lofty sentiments, knew less of her son than this woman who had raised him. She leaned forward until she could see the middle of the table. The bride had given up all pretense of eating and was looking distinctly uncomfortable. Her face was flushed as if she had drunk more than she was used to. Morgause suppressed a smile.

Carefully she swung her legs over the bench and stood. "It is time I visited the privies," she said loudly. "Would anyone like to keep me company?"

Guendivar's eyes focused suddenly. "I would! If I drink any more I will burst!"

Petronilla looked pained, but she assisted the bride to disentangle her robes and rise. There was anxiety in Igierne's eyes as as well, but what could be more natural than for a sister-in-law to escort the new queen?

Artor looked up, smiling with friendly concern. His companions had been seated at a lower table, but Gualchmai had left his place and was leaning with his arm draped across the top of the king's chair. He nodded politely to his mother, but his eyes were watchful. Morgause smiled blandly and took Guendivar's arm.

The old Roman lavatory facilities were still in use. Beyond them, a corridor opened out onto the colonnade. When they had finished and washed, Morgause paused.

"The air in the hall was so hot and warm; I still feel a little faint. Will you bear me company for a few moments in the fresh air?"

"Gladly—" answered Guendivar. "I had been hoping for a chance to speak with you," she added shyly. "You are still a reigning queen. I suspect there are things you can tell me that I will need to know."

Morgause peered at her through the darkness Shouts of laughter echoed faint from the hall. Could the child possibly be as ingenuous as she sounded?

"Do you love Artor?" she asked suddenly.

There was a constricted silence. "I agreed to marry him. I will do my best to make him happy."

Morgause considered. In these garments the girl looked like an overdressed doll, but she had good bones, and her hair, a reddish gold that curled to her waist, was beautiful. Did Artor want an ally or an adorer?

If he had chosen Guendivar for her pretty face, she would not hold his interest for long.

Duty was an unexciting bedfellow, but a good companion. What would this girl find it hardest to give? It occurred to her that it would serve Medraut better if Artor did not find too much comfort in his queen.

"My brother is not a bad man," she said thoughtfully, "but he has been a king as long as you have been alive. He is accustomed to obedience. And he has been at war for many years. He will want diversion. Amuse him—be playful—feign passion, even if you do not feel it. And if he seems cold, well, you will be surrounded by virile young men. If you are discreet, you can use them for your pleasure. It has worked well for me."

And that was true enough. But Artor was not Leudonus, who had known very well that his marriage was a political alliance, and never expected more. In Alba, the lustiness of the queen was as important as that of the king. And Alba was not a Christian land.

"You are young," said Morgause, "and know little of the body's demands. But as you mature you will find that a woman has needs too, and kings are very busy men. . . ."

A door opened and light and shadow barred the colonnade.

"They have missed us," Guendivar said quickly. "We had better go in—"

"But of course," answered Morgause. "You are the queen, and you command." But as she followed Guendivar back into the hall, she was smiling.

A murmur of appreciation greeted Guendivar's entrance. Morgause hung back a little, noting the gleam in men's eyes as they watched her come. This one would not have to entice men to her bed if she decided she wanted them—they would be lining up at her door. The remains of the feast lay about them like a looted battlefield. Men had drunk enough now to want something else, and tonight, all their lust was projected upon the king.

"Don't you think it time the little bride was bedded?" she said to Gualchmai as she passed. "She is ready, and he should not make her wait too long."

Some of the other men heard and began to bang their mugs against the planks of the table. "To bed, to bed—let Artor prove that he is king!"

Guendivar's face was nearly as scarlet as her gown, but even the women were laughing.

"Very well," said Petronilla with what dignity she could muster.

"Come, ladies, let us escort the queen to the bridal chamber and make her ready for her husband."

Shouting and singing, the women crowded around the new queen and bore her away. But Morgause remained, waiting in the shadow of a pillar as the masculine banter became ever more explicit, until the king was blushing almost as hotly as his bride.

Presently she saw the little nun who had been Guendivar's chaperone returning to tell them she was ready.

The men, for a moment abashed by her grave gaze, grew quieter. Morgause stepped forward.

"And will you also, sister, wish me joy?" Artor asked. "I thought you would be with the women who are helping Guendivar—"

"Oh, I have given her my advice already—" answered Morgause.

"And have you any counsel for me? Your sons have been as frank as farmers with suggestions on how I should practice a husband's craft."

If he had not mentioned her sons, perhaps, even then, Morgause would have kept silent. But she smiled and slid her hand gently along his upper arm.

"But you already know how to deal with a woman, dear brother, *don't you remember?*" she said very softly. "And you have a son to prove it, begotten ten years since at the feast of Lugus. His name is Medraut." Still smiling, she took his face between her hands and kissed him.

His lips were cold, and as she released him, she saw, bleak as the morning after battle, the dawn of desolation in his eyes.

The bed linen smelled of lavender. Guendivar ran her hands across the cloth, smooth with many launderings, and sighed. The linen was old, like this chamber, whose stones seemed to whisper tales of those who had lain here in the years since the mud huts of the Trinovantes were replaced by the stone and plaster of Rome.

She sat up, wrapping her arms around her knees. *What am I doing here?* She belonged in the open land of wood and field, not in this box of stone. Even the silk nightrobe in which they had wrapped her seemed alien. Weather permitting, she preferred to sleep bare. She considered pulling the garment off, but her mother had impressed upon her the need to behave modestly—it would never do to shock her new husband, after all.

Guendivar found it hard to believe that a man who had been living in military camps for half his life would be disturbed by bare skin. Did Artor really believe that she was the simpering maiden her mother had counselled her to be? She tried to remember their single conversation—it had seemed to her then that it was because she had red blood in her veins that he had liked her.

As she started to untie the neckstrings she heard shouting from the corridor and her fingers stilled. They were coming. Suddenly the garment seemed not a constriction, but protection. She pulled up the bedclothes and sat staring as the door swung open and torchlight, dimming the flicker of the lamps, streamed into the room.

The doorway filled with faces, their laughter faltering as they saw her sitting there. For a moment she saw herself with their vision: eyes huge in her white face, mantled in shining hair.

The crowd heaved as the men who were behind pushed forward, then moved aside to admit a figure that moved in a haze of gold, from the band around his brows to the embroidery on his mantle. But his face was in shadow, and though he was surrounded by a leaping, laughing crowd, his stillness matched her own.

"The way is clear!" came Gualchmai's shout. "Get in with you, man—I'll cover you!"

"Nay, it is Artor who will be covering his bride!" someone replied, and the hall rang with masculine laughter. They sounded like her brother and his friends when they had been drinking.

"For shame, lads—give the man some privacy!" That came from Betiver.

Morgause would have known how to command those boors to leave them. Guendivar recalled the Votadini queen's words to her and felt her skin grow hot with remembered embarrassment—perhaps Artor's sister would not have cared.

Then Artor turned to face his tormentors. Their laughter faded, and she wondered what they were seeing in his eyes. He swung round, and a long stride carried him over the threshold. His arm swept out and the heavy door slammed behind him.

The noise outside fell suddenly to a murmur; she thought they were singing and was glad she could not distinguish the words. Inside, the dark shape by the door seemed to gather silence around him until it was a palpable weight in the air. Guendivar drew the bedclothes closer, shivering. She had not expected her new husband to leap upon her, but why was he still standing there? Could he possibly be afraid?

When the silence had become more disturbing than anything she could imagine him doing, she cleared her throat.

"I do not know the etiquette of these things, but the priests assure me that you have a right to be here. Are you waiting for an invitation to lie down with me?"

Some of the tension went out of him and he laughed. "Perhaps I am. I will confess to you, Guendivar, that I have more experience in 'these things' than you do, but not . . . much—" His voice cracked. "I have a son."

She lifted an eyebrow. "Before he was married my father got three, and for all I know, more afterward. Did you think I would be scandalized?"

And yet it was strange that the High King could have a child that no one had heard of. Bastards begotten before marriage were not unusual, and for a man, no shame. If Morgause was to be believed, in Alba they were not shameful for a woman either, but this was hardly the moment to say so. For a moment she longed for the comfort of Julia's warm arms, even though she knew that for every hour they had lain together the other girl had spent three on her knees. It had always seemed strange to Guendivar to do penance for something that gave the same simple pleasure as a cat arching to the stroke of a caress, but at least she understood what Julia wanted when she was in her arms.

This male creature that radiated tension from the doorway was totally strange, but clearly, if she did not do something, he might well stand there until dawn.

"I am told that you begin by taking off your clothes," she said wryly. "Do you need help? It took three women to get me out of mine."

Artor laughed again, as if she had surprised him, and shook his head. But he did unbuckle his belt and then the brooch that held his mantle at the shoulder. The rustle of heavy silk seemed loud in the quiet of the room.

"And what do you suggest I do next?" he asked when he was down to the twist of linen about his loins.

Surely, she thought with an unexpected lift of the heart, that had been amusement she heard in his tone. But why should he need to ask? Did he really believe that one bastard had made him unfit to approach her?

"Next, you get into the bed . . ."

He drew a quick breath, and she had a sudden insight into how he must look before battle. She hoped he did not see her as an enemy. She twitched the covers aside and the leather straps of the bedstead creaked as he lay down. In the flicker of lamplight she could see the curves and planes of his body quite clearly. Except for his face and forearms, his skin was almost as fair as her own, scrolled here and there by the subtle pink or silvery tracery of old battle scars. She stared curiously. She had seen men's bodies before, stripped for labor in the fields or exposed to piss against a tree, but never at such close quarters.

After a moment she realized that Artor's breathing was too controlled. What was wrong? He hadn't been so tense when they talked at midwinter. Even this morning there had been open friendliness in his smile. This was not how she had imagined her wedding night would be.

"You did not marry me for love but because you needed an heir," Guendivar said finally. "So far as I know, there is only one way to get one. You may have a son, but he cannot inherit from you, so let us be about it. It would be a pity to disappoint all those people I hear making noise to encourage us out there!"

Artor turned, raising himself on one elbow to look at her. "I have been misled—men always speak of women as if they were creatures of flight and fancy, but I see it is not so—" He took her hand, callused fingers tracing spirals across her palm.

Guendivar drew a quick breath, all her senses focusing on his touch, from which warmth had begun to radiate in little bursts of sparks across her skin. *The female animal desires the male . . .* she told herself, *so why should I be surprised?* If they did not have love, lust was no bad foundation for a marriage, so long as it came linked with laughter. For surely there was nothing here to match the ecstasy she had found in the company of the faerie-folk, but she had not expected it.

"If it were, how could you trust us to manage your homes and raise your children?" she asked tartly, and then, while she still had the courage, lifted his hand and pressed it to her breast.

As his fingers tightened, the sparks became a flame that leaped from nipple to nipple and focused in a throbbing ache between her thighs. Her play with Julia had awakened her body, and since they began this wedding journey there had been no way for them to be alone. If Artor was surprised, his changed breathing told her that the fire had kindled him as well.

She slid her hands from his shoulders down the hard muscle of his sides. Were men's and women's bodies so different? Heart pounding, she brushed upward across his nipples and heard him gasp. Guendivar smiled then, and reached down to tug at his clout. Artor tensed, but at least he did not pull away, and when she eased back down on the bed he came with her, his movement pushing her gown above her thighs.

She could feel his male member hard against her and wished she could see it, but at last he was kissing her. Guendivar held him tightly, a part of her mind cataloguing the differences between his hard strength and Julia's yielding softness, while the remainder was being consumed by an expanding flame.

Artor pushed against her and she opened her thighs, trembling with mingled excitement and fear. This, certainly, was something she had not experienced with Julia! His hands tightened painfully on her shoulders and he thrust again. She felt a tearing pain, them the pressure abruptly eased. He continued to batter against her for a few moments longer, but it was with his body only—the part that had taken her maidenhead slid free, and she had not the art to arouse it again.

Presently he stilled and collapsed onto the bed beside her, breathing hard.

"Was it like this," she said softly when he was still, "when you begot your son?"

"I do not know . . . I do not remember . . ." he groaned, "but it cannot have been," he added bitterly, "or there would have been no child . . ."

Only then did she understand that the act had been incomplete for him as well.

"Dear God!" He turned onto his back and she saw that he was weeping. "What have I done? What did she do to me?"

Guendivar let out her breath in a long sigh. She would not, she gathered, come from this night with child. She sensed the pain in the man beside her without understanding it.

"It will be all right," she said presently, "we have time."

Gradually the rasp of his breathing slowed. "Time . . ." he groaned. "Ten years . . ."

Guendivar touched his shoulder, but he did not respond. After that, they were silent. Even the noise outside their door had ceased. The place between her thighs throbbed with a mingling of pleasure and pain. Presently she pulled the covers over her, and used her hand to release the tension Artor's touch had aroused.

Her husband lay very still beside her, and if he realized what she was doing, he made no sign.

That night, while Artor's Companions were finishing off the last of the Procurator's wine, the mother of his son lay in the arms of a lusty guardsman in a union which, however unblessed, was considerably more rewarding. Igierne slept alone in the room she had once shared with Uthir, plagued by troubled dreams. But Merlin watched out the night at the top of the ancient guard tower, striving to understand the portents he glimpsed in the stars, and in the church where Guendivar had been married, Julia lay stretched upon the cold stones, wrestling with her soul in prayer.

VI

The Sacred Round

Camalot smelled of raw wood and rang with the sound of hammers. It seemed to have grown every time the king's household returned to it, the timber and stone ramparts raised higher, the framing of the great henge hall and the other buildings more solid against the spring sky. The hill had been part of Guendivar's dowry, and if the past year had seen little progress in the intimate side of their marriage, externally, Artor had accomplished a great deal.

From the timber guard tower above the southwest gate the queen saw small figures of men and horses climbing the road. That would be Matauc of Durnovaria—she recognized the standard. He was an old man now, and Artor had not been sure he would come. No doubt curiosity had brought him, as it had so many others—Britannia was full of tales about the new stronghold Artor was building in Leodagranus' land.

Most of the other princes were here already—the place was full of men and horses, and the clusters of hide tents and brushwood bothies that sheltered their escorts nestled close to the wall. According to Leodagranus, it had been a Durotrige fortress when the Romans came, destroyed in the years after Boudicca's war, and then it had been the site of a pagan shrine. But Merlin said the Durotriges were only the latest of the peoples who had sheltered on the hill, tribes now so long gone that no one even remembered their names.

Cai had laughed at him, for on first sight its tree-choked slopes seemed no different from any of the surrounding hills. But when they reached the summit, they found a roughly flattened oblong with a swell of earth around it, and three additional ramparts carved into the side of the hill. The trees they cut to clear the site had provided timber to brace the rubble wall and planks for the breastwork that topped it.

Guendivar climbed the ladder from the sentry walk to the gatehouse often. Here, she could lean on the wickerwork railing and watch the bustle without being overwhelmed by it, and there was usually a breeze. Gazing out across the tree-clad hills she could almost imagine herself free.

Below her, men were setting more stones into the rough facing of the rampart. Just because Artor had called a consilium did not mean work could cease. From here Camalot was a place of circles within circles: the ramparts that ringed the hill, and the huts within the wall, and in the space to the east of the more conventional rectangular building where Artor had his quarters, the great henge hall.

In truth, it was not so much a hall as a shelter, for sections of its wickerwork walling could be removed to let in light and air. Its design had also been one of Merlin's suggestion, neither a Roman basilica nor even a Celtic roundhouse, although it most resembled the latter. Merlin said it was another inspiration from ancient days. The thatched roof was supported on a triple henge of stout wooden pillars, its diameter so great that a hundred and fifty warriors could sit in a circle around the central fire. The old sorcerer still made Guendivar uneasy, but there was no denying his ideas were sometimes useful.

She turned and saw the gate guard lifting an earthenware jug to his lips.

"Is that wine?" she asked, feeling suddenly dry.

The man blushed—surely he should have been accustomed to her by now. "Oh no, lady—'tis water only. My lord king would have my ears did I drink while on guard. But you're welcome to share it—" he added, flushing again. He wiped the rim of the jug with the hem of his tunic and offered it to her.

She eyed it a little dubiously, for his tunic was not over-clean, but she could not insult him by refusing it now. And the water was good, kept cold by the clay. She savored it, rolling it on her tongue, before swallowing. When she had drunk, she handed back the jug and smiled, a thirst that no water could ease fed by the admiration with which he gazed back at her. Tomorrow at the council she would see her beauty reflected in the gleam of other men's eyes.

A hail from below brought her around. She leaned over the railing and waved at Betiver, who had been sent to escort Matauc to the hill. The first gate had opened, and Betiver, preceding the horselitter in which the old man had travelled, was passing beneath the tower. Matauc would need some time to recover and refresh himself, but then Artor would no doubt be wanting her to extend an official welcome. It was time for her to go do so.

Dark and light, shadowed and bright, the oblong of the doorway flickered as the princes of Britannia came into the new henge hall. The flare and glint of gold, abruptly extinguished, dazzled the eye, and Betiver, standing at his accustomed place at Artor's shoulder, had to look away. After a moment his vision adjusted, and he began counting once more.

Light coming in beneath the low eaves where the wicker screens had been removed lent the lower parts of the interior a diffuse illumination, and the fire in the center cast a warm glow; beneath the peak of the roof, all was shadow. Betiver suppressed a smile as he watched the princes and their followers attempting to figure out which were the most honorable benches when the seating was circular. That was exactly why Merlin had suggested that Artor build this round hall. In the end, the choice of seats became roughly geographical, as the little groups found places near their allies and neighbors.

Matauc of Durnovaria had taken a seat beside Leodagranus, just down from Cataur of Dumnonia, who had brought his son Constantine. The Demetian contingent was dominated by Agricola, a war-leader from an old Roman family who made up in effectiveness for what he lacked in bloodlines. Being Roman, he did not call himself a prince, but Protector, though his powers were the same. He had also brought a son, called Vortipor. His northern neighbor was Catwallaun Longhand, still bearing the scars of his last campaign against the Irishmen of Laigin who had settled there under king Illan.

There were other, more familiar faces: old Eleutherius from Eboracum and his son Peretur, Eldaul who ruled the area around Glevum, and Catraut, who kept a wary eye on the Saxons of the east from Verulamium. As his gaze moved around the circle it was the younger men who drew Betiver's attention. They were the ones upon whose strength Artor would build Britannia, whose focus was on the future.

But the silver hairs of age and experience were still much in evidence.

Ridarchus had come down from Dun Breatann. He was as old as Leudonus, though he looked stronger. Men said he was married to a sister of Merlin. Betiver found it hard to imagine. Next to him was his half-brother Dumnoval, a grandson of the great Germanianus, who now held the Votadini lands south of the Tava under Leudonus, who had been too ill to come.

Instead, young Cunobelinus was there to speak for the Votadini of Dun Eidyn. There had some discussion about that earlier, for Gualchmai was Leudonus' named heir. But Gualchmai was sitting on Artor's right hand, as Cai held the place on his left, and no one had dared to ask whether that meant the northerner had renounced his birthright to serve the High King, or was claiming a greater one, as Artor's heir.

It seemed unlikely, for although in a year of marriage the queen had not kindled, she was young and healthy, and surely one day she would bear a child. As if the thought had been a summons, Betiver noted a change in the faces of the men across the circle and turned to see Guendivar herself, standing in a nimbus of light in the doorway.

Old or young, men fell silent as the High Queen made her way around the circle, carrying the great silver krater by the handles at each side. This, thought Betiver, was not the laughing girl who had become his friend, but the High Queen, remote and perfect as an icon in a dalmatic of creamy damask set with pearls, the finest of linen veiling her hair beneath the diadem. As she came to each man, she offered the krater. As the wine flowed over the bright silver, it caught the light with a garnet-colored glow.

"The blood of the grape is the blood of the land," she said softly. "And you are its strong arms. Drink in peace, drink in unity, and be welcome in this hall . . ."

"Lady, you lend us grace—" murmured Vortipor, and then flushed as he realized he had spoken aloud. But no one else seemed to notice—he was saying no more than what they all felt, after all.

Guendivar completed the circle and brought the krater to Artor. "The blood of the grape is the blood of the land, and you, Pendragon, are its head—"

Artor's hands closed over hers on the krater, drawing her closer as he lifted it to his lips. His face bore an expression Betiver had never seen there before—he could not tell if it were joy or pain. Then he let go, looking up at her.

"As you are its heart, my queen . . ." he murmured. For a moment his eyes closed. When he opened them again his features had regained their usual calm. Now it was Guendivar in whose eyes Betiver saw pain. For a moment the queen bowed her head, then she lifted the krater once more and with the same gliding gait bore it out of the hall.

Slowly the murmur of conversation resumed, but the mood had changed. It reminded Betiver of something—abruptly he remembered rapt faces in the church of his boyhood when the icon of the Virgin had been carried around. His breath caught—was the thought sacrilege? A churchman might say so, but his heart told him that a power that was in its way as holy as anything blessed by the church had rested upon the queen as she moved through the hall.

But Artor was speaking—

"In my own name, also, I bid you welcome. We have much to discuss, and more to think on. The Saxons are beaten and for a time their oaths will hold them. We must plan how to use that time to keep them divided in heart and in territory, so that they do not combine against us again. We must plan also a new campaign against the men of Eriu who have seized land in Demetia, and bring it once more under British rule. But these tasks, however pressing, are only a beginning. For too long, force has been our only governor—if we wish to restore the security we knew under the Romans, we must return to the rule of law."

Betiver shifted his weight as Artor's opening speech continued. If he had stayed at home in Gallia, he thought, he might have been addressing such a meeting in his own father's hall. But like Gualchmai, he had chosen to remain in Britannia and serve Artor.

In the afternoon Artor released the members of the council to rest, to think on the matters he had set before them, and to seek exercise. Betiver offered to guide some of the younger men around the countryside, and when he met them at the horse pens, he found that Guendivar, dressed for riding, was waiting too. Her presence might inhibit some of their speech, but she would not impede their exercise. He knew already that she could ride as well as any man. And if the princes were dubious—he smiled quietly—they were in for a surprise.

Certainly the girl who leaped unassisted to the back of the white mare Artor had given her was a very different creature from the image of sovereignty who had brought them wine in the hall. For riding, Guendivar wore breeches and a short tunic. Only the linen cloth that bound her hair showed her to be a woman, and the embroidered blue mantle pinned at the shoulder, a queen.

When they were mounted, it was she who led the way. Indeed, thought Betiver as he brought up the rear, she could have guided the visitors with no help from him. But as he watched her laugh at some word of Peretur's, or smile at young Vortipor, he realized that it was not her safety, but her reputation, he would be guarding today.

At the bottom of the steep hill, Guendivar reined in. They had departed through the gate on the northeast side of the hill, past the well. From its base, the road ran straight towards the little village that had grown up in the days when the only structure on the hill was the shrine. The queen's mare snorted and shook its head and she laughed.

"Swanwhite wants to stretch her legs!" She gestured towards the village. "Do you think you can catch her if we run?"

By the time they arrived at the village, both horses and riders were quite willing to keep to a more leisurely pace. Guendivar's head wrap had come off and her hair tumbled down her back in a tangle of spilled gold. Her cheeks were flushed, her eyes bright. She looked, thought Betiver, twice as alive as the woman who had stood beside Artor in the council hall, and he felt an odd pang in the region of his heart.

They ambled through the spring green of the countryside, talking. In the warmth of her presence, Vortipor and the other princes lost all their shyness. The air rumbled with their deep laughter. *She is charming them,* thought Betiver. *Artor should be pleased.*

Vortipor told them a long story about hunting stag in the mountains of Demetia, and Peretur countered with a tale of a bear hunt in the dales west of Eboracum. Everyone, it seemed, had some tale of manly prowess—vying with words, the young men strutted and pranced like stallions before a mare. It was Ebicatos, the Irishman who commanded the garrison at Calleva, who protested that the queen must be becoming bored by all these stories of blood and battle, though Betiver had seen no sign of it in her face. But when the Irishman praised her white mare for winning the race to the village, and began the tale of the Children of Lir, who had been transformed by a jealous stepmother into swans, Guendivar listened with parted lips and shining eyes.

Their ride brought them around in a wide half-circle to the southwest. When the hill loomed before them once more, they slowed. The young men gazed at it in amazement. It did not seem possible they had come all this way so quickly, but the sun, which had reached its zenith when they set out, was well along in its downward slide.

The evening session of the council would be beginning. Merlin had returned from his most recent wanderings, and tonight he would report on what he had seen. That should be more interesting than the endless debates they had been listening to, though it would no doubt lead to more.

"Ah, lady," cried Vortipor, "I wish we did not have to return. I wish we could ride westward without stopping until we reached the sea, and then our horses would all become swans, to carry us to the Isles of the Hesperides!"

"The Isles of the Blessed, the Isle of Fair Women, and the Isle of Birds—" murmured Ebicatos.

"There is no need, surely, when the fairest of all women is here with us on this hallowed isle," said Peretur. He caught her outstretched hand and kissed it fervently.

Betiver's breath caught as Guendivar's beauty took on an intensity that was almost painful. Then she shook her head and bitterness muted her radiance like a cloud hiding the sun.

"And here I must stay—" A sudden dig of the heels sent her mare curvetting forward. Startled to silence, the others followed.

What is this that I am feeling? Betiver asked himself as they began to climb the hill. *My sweet Roud is a good woman, and I love her and my son . . .*

The red-headed Alban girl whom he had tumbled in the inebriation of the Feast of Lugus eleven years before had been an unexpected mate, but a good one. It was a soldier's marriage, unblessed by the Church, but recorded by the clerks of Artor's army. But the contentment Roud brought him had nothing in common with the painful way his heart leaped when he looked at Guendivar. A glance at the other men told him that they felt the same. They would serve her—they would die for her—with no hope of any reward beyond a word or a smile.

She is Venus—the remnants of a Classical education prompted him, *and we are her worshippers. And that is only fitting, for she is the queen.* But as they clattered beneath the gatehouse he wondered why, with such a woman in his bed, did the king seem to have so little joy?

Artor is not happy. . . . Merlin glanced at the king from beneath his bushy brows and frowned. Seated on the king's right hand, he could not look at him directly, but the evidence of his eyes only confirmed what other senses had been telling him. Artor was paler than he had been, and thickening around the middle—those changes were a natural result of sitting so much in council chambers and eating well. But there was something haunted about his eyes.

It was not the council, which was going as well as such things ever did. It had become clear that Roman order would never return to Britannia until Roman law ruled once more. The princes must learn to think of themselves as *rectors,* and their war-leaders as *duces,* the generals of the country. Those who had ruled as chieftains had to become judges and magistrates, deriving their power from rector and emperor once more.

Thus, and in this way only, could they separate their civilization from the ways of the barbarians.

To Merlin, longing for his northern wilderness, they were both equally constricting, but he had been born to serve the Defender of Britannia, and with him, its Law. Artor's attempts to restore the old ways even looked as if they might be successful. He should have been, if not triumphant, at least well pleased. Something was wrong, and Merlin supposed it was his duty to try and set it right. The thought made him tired, and he yearned to be back in the forest and the undemanding society of the wild folk who lived there. One day, he thought then, he would seek those green mysteries and not return.

The tone of the voices around him changed and he brought his awareness back to the present. The discussion of titles and duties was coming to a close.

"That is well, then, and we can move to the next topic," said Artor. "The Saxons. Merlin has been going among them—they seem to respect him as a holy man—and I believe we can benefit from his observations."

Merlin's lips twitched. He had wandered through the territory of the enemy in times past in safety, protected by their respect for those they thought old or mad. Their response to him now was different, and he knew why.

As if the thought had awakened it, he felt a throb of force from the rune-carved Spear that leaned against his chair, and the familiar pressure in his mind, as if Someone were listening. The head of the Spear was shrouded in silk, and a wrapping of leather thongs hid the runes carved into the shaft, but it still carried the power of the god Woden, and when Merlin came to a Saxon farmstead, holding that staff and with his long beard flying and an old hat drawn down over his eyes, he knew whom they believed him to be.

Merlin got to his feet and moved to the central hearth, leaning on the Spear. Artor straightened, eyes narrowing, as if something within him scented its power. Or perhaps it was the Sword at his side that had recognized another Hallow. Once, the god of the Spear had fought the one that lived in the Sword, but now they seemed to be in alliance. He must explain to Artor what had happened, one day.

But for now, he had to tell these British leaders what he had seen in the Saxon lands.

"In Cantium, the lady Rigana has gathered a council of thanes to advise her. The child, Oesc's son, is healthy, and the men seem very willing to support an extended regency. Many of their young warriors died at Mons Badonicus. They have sufficient men to defend the coasts against small groups of raiders, but I do not believe they will be a danger to us until at least another generation is grown."

"That is all very well," said Catraut, "but what about the Saxons of the south and west?"

"Aelle is an old man—" said Merlin. *My age, but Mons Badonicus broke him. . . .* "He will not ride to war again. And Ceretic's son is little more than a boy. Even if he should seek vengeance, it is clear that his father's thanes will not support him."

"And the Anglians?" asked Peretur.

"There also, for different reasons, I see no danger," said Merlin, and began to lay out his analysis of Icel's position as sacred king, and the reasons why the oath he had given Artor would continue to bind him.

"Separate, these tribes do not present a danger. It is my counsel that you choose brave men to settle the lands that lie between their holdings. So long as the Saxons perceive their portions as tribal territories, they will find it hard to combine. They may hold half Britannia, but they will not see it that way, and so long as you, my lords, remain united, you will be the stronger."

Even Cataur of Dumnonia could see that this was good counsel. Merlin resumed his seat as the princes of Britannia began to debate which borderlands should be resettled, and where they would find the men.

That night, after everyone had eaten, Merlin walked along the sentryway built into the wall, troubled in his mind. While they feasted, he had watched Artor, seated at the central table with his lady beside him. The king should have been smiling, for the council had gone well that day. With a wife like Guendivar, he should have been eager to retire. But though Artor's body showed his awareness of her every movement, they did not touch, and his smiles did not reach his eyes. And when the queen made her farewells and departed into the royal chamber that was partitioned off from the main part of the hall, the king remained talking with Eldaul and Agricola by the fire.

A full moon was rising, its cool light glittering from the open water of pond and stream, and glowing softly in the mist that rose off the fields. The distant hills seemed ghostly; in that glimmering illumination, he could not tell if it was with the eyes of the flesh or of the spirit that he saw, away to the northwest, the pointed shape of the Tor.

Merlin had been standing there for some time, drinking in peace as a thirsty man gulps water, when he sensed that he was no longer alone. A pale shape moved along the walkway, too graceful to be any of the men. The White Phantom that was one meaning of her name . . . Guendivar. . . .

He drew his spirit entirely into his body once more and took a step towards her. She whirled, the indrawn gasp of her breath loud in the stillness, and pressed her back against the wall.

"It is true, you *can* make yourself invisible!"

"Not invisible, only very still. . . . I came to enjoy the peace of the night," he answered, extending his awareness to encompass her, smiling a little as the tension left her body and she took a step towards him.

"So did I . . ." she said in a low voice.

"I thought you would have been in bed by now, with your husband—"

She jerked, staring. "What do you mean? What do you know?"

"I know that all is not well between you. I know that you have no child . . ." he said softly.

She straightened, drawing dignity around her, and he felt her barriers strengthening.

"You have no right—" Her voice shook.

"I am one of the guardians of Britannia, and you are the High Queen. What is wrong, Guendivar?"

"Why do you assume the fault is mine? Ask Artor!"

He shook his head. "The power passes from male to female, and from female to male. You are the Lady of Britannia. If the difficulty is his, still, the healing must come from you."

"And I suppose the knowledge of how to do that will come from *you*? You flatter yourself, old man!" She turned, watching him over her shoulder.

Her hair was silver-gilt in the light of the moon. Even he, who had admitted desire for only one mortal woman in his lifetime, felt a stirring of the senses. But he shook his head.

"The body serves the spirit," he said steadily. "It is in the spirit that I would teach you."

"Tell the woman who wounded Artor to help him! Let him seek healing from the mother of his son! Then, perhaps, he can come to me!"

In the instant that shock held him still she flowed into motion. For a few moments he heard the patter of her retreating footsteps, and then she was gone. Even then, a word of power could have held her, but to such work as he would bid her, the spirit could not be constrained.

Igierne had foreseen this. But she had not seen the mother, only the child. The child would bring war to Britannia, but its mother had already struck a heavy blow. Who was she? In one thing, Guendivar had the right of it, he thought then. He must speak to Artor.

* * *

The fortress had been closed up for the night, but the guard on duty at the north gate was a very young man, and half in love with his queen, so he let her through. *They are all in love with me!* Guendivar thought bitterly. *All except the only one I am allowed to love.*

Stumbling in her haste, she made her way down the trail to the well. A pale shape swooped across the path and she started and nearly fell. For a moment she stared, heart pounding, then relaxed as she saw that it was only a white owl. On such a night, when the sky was clear and the full moon sailed in triumph through the skies, she felt stifled indoors. Even Julia's warm arms were a prison, where she stifled beneath the weight of the other woman's need.

Guendivar had thought a walk on the walls would allow her spirit to soar as freely as the bird, but Merlin was before her. What had she said to him? Surely he, who knew everything, must have known about Artor. The old sorcerer had offered her help—for a moment she wondered if she had been a fool to flee.

But how could a change in *her* do any good? The sin was Artor's, if sin it was—certainly he seemed to think so. He had attempted to be a husband to her two times after that first disastrous encounter, with even less success than on their wedding night. After that, they had not tried again. He was kind to her, and in public gave her all honor, but in the bed that should have been the heart and wellspring of their marriage, they slept without touching, proximity only making them more alone.

Guendivar knew this path well, but she had never been here in the night. In the uncertain light, the familiar shapes of the lower ramparts swelled like serpent coils. Beneath the melancholy calling of the owl she could hear the sweet music of running water. Everywhere else, the trees had been cut to clear a field of fire from the the walls of the fortress, but halfway down the hill, birch trees still clustered protectively around the spring.

Guendivar had never visited the hill until Artor began to build his fortress there, but the people of her father's lands had many tales of the days when it had been a place of pilgrimage. When the lords of Lindinis became Christian they had ceased to support the shrine, and after its last priestess died, the square building with its deep porch had fallen into decay. Now its tumbled stones were part of Artor's walls.

But the sacred spring from which the priestesses had drawn water to use in their spells of healing remained, bubbling up from the depths beneath the hill to form a quiet pool. The stone coping that edged it was worn, but the spout that channeled the overflow had remained clear. From there, it fell in a musical trickle down the hillside in a little stream. Moonlight, filtering through the birch trees, shrouded pool and stone alike in dappled shade.

Guendivar blinked, uncertain, in that glamoured illumination, of her way. The old powers had been banished from the hilltop, but here she could still feel them. She stretched out her arms, calling as she had called when she ranged the hills at home. Gown and mantle weighted her limbs; she stripped them off and unpinned the heavy coils of her hair. She stretched, exulting in the free play of muscle and limb. A little breeze lifted the fine strands and caressed her naked body, set the birch leaves shivering until the shifting dappling of moonlight glittered on the troubled waters of the pool.

Light swirled above it like a mist off the waters, shaping the form of a woman, clad, like Guendivar, only in her shining hair.

"Who are you?" Guendivar whispered. She was accustomed to the folk of faerie, but this was a being of nobler kind than any she had met before.

"*I am Cama, the curve of the hill and the winding water, I am the sacred round. It has been long . . . very long . . . since any mortal called to Me. . . . What is your need?*"

Guendivar felt her skin pebble with holy fear. The new faith had not yet succeeded in banishing the old wisdom so completely that she could not recognize the ancient goddess of this part of the land. But her cry had been wordless. She struggled for an answer.

"The water flows—the wind blows—but I am bound! I want to be free!"

"*Free . . .* " The goddess tested the sound as if she did not quite understand. "*The waters flow downhill to the sea . . . heat and cold drive the currents of the wind. They are free to follow their natures. Is that what you desire?*"

"And what is my nature? I am wed, but no wife!"

"*You are the Queen . . .* "

"I am a gilded image. I have no power—"

"*You* are *the power . . .* "

Guendivar, her mouth still opening in protest, halted, almost understanding. Then the owl called, and the insight was gone. She saw the figure of the Lady dislimning into a column of glimmering light.

"Help me!" she cried. She heard no answer, but the figure opened its arms.

Shivering, Guendivar climbed over the coping and stepped into the pool. Soft mud gave beneath her feet and she slid into the cold depths too swiftly for a scream. Water closed over her head, darkness enclosed her.

This is death, she thought, but there was no time for fear. And then she was rushing upwards into the light. Power swirled around her, but she was the center of the circle—*being* and *doing,* the motion and her stillness, one and the same.

In this place there was no time, but time must have passed, for presently, with no sense of transition, Guendivar found herself experiencing the world with her normal senses once more. The moon had moved a quarter of the way across the sky, and its light no longer fell full on the pool. She was standing, streaming with water, but the bottom of the pool was solid beneath her feet.

She felt empty, and realized that what had departed from her was her despair. Perhaps this serenity would not last, but she did not think she would ever entirely forget what she had seen.

VII

The Wounded King

Guendivar huddled next to the hearth of the house the king's household had commandeered, listening to the hiss of the fire and the dull thud of rain on the thatching. If she sat any closer, she thought unhappily, she would catch fire herself, but her back still felt damp even when her front was steaming.

None of the other dwellings in this village were any better. She pitied the men of Artor's army, shivering in the dubious shelter of tents made of oiled hide as they cursed the Irish. The euphoria of their great victory at Urbs Legionis—the city of legions that was also called Deva—had worn away. Illan, king of the men of Laigin who had settled in northern Guenet a generation ago, was on the run, but he was going to make the British fight for every measure of ground between Deva and the Irish Sea.

She laid another stick on the fire, wondering why she had been so eager to accompany Artor on this campaign. For most of the past week it had been raining, grey veils of cloud dissolving into the silver sea. With each day's march, the stony hills that edged the green pasturelands had grown nearer. Now they rose in a grim wall on the left, broken by an occasional steep glen from which shrieking bands of Irishmen might at any moment emerge to harry the army that was pushing steadily westward along the narrowing band of flat land between the mountains and the sea.

Artor was up ahead somewhere with the scouts. It had been foolish to think that their relationship might improve if she accompanied him. The king spent his days in the saddle, returning tired, wet, and hungry when night fell, usually escorting wounded men. Artor had not wanted to bring her, but during their brief courtship he had said she could ride with the army, and she had sworn she would neither complain nor slow them down.

There was no risk of the latter, Guendivar thought bitterly, since she travelled with the rearguard. As for complaining, so far she had held her tongue, but she knew that if she had to stay cooped up in this hut for much longer she was going to scream.

With that thought, she found that she was on her feet and turning towards the door. She pushed past the cowhide that covered it and stood beneath the overhang of the roof, breathing deeply of the clean air. It was damp, heavy with mingled scents of wet grass and seaweed. Mist still clung to the hilltops, but a fresh wind was blowing, and here and there a stray gleam of sunlight spangled the sea.

It might only be temporary, but the skies were clearing. Guendivar gazed longingly at the slopes whose green grew brighter with every moment. Surely, she told herself, they could not be entirely different from the gentle hills of her home. Some of the same herbs would grow there, plants that her old nurse had taught her to use in healing. . . .

The young soldier who had been assigned to her personal escort straightened as she came out into the open. His name was Cau, one of the men who had come down from the Votadini lands with Marianus. There was some tension between the followers of Marianus and Catwallaun, both grandsons of the great Cuneta, though Catwallaun's branch of the family had been settled in Guenet a generation before. Many of the newcomers resented being set to guard the rear of the army, but Cau had attached himself to Guendivar's service with a dedication reminiscent of those monks who served the Virgin Mary. He had left a wife back in Deva with their infant son, Gildas, but he still flushed crimson whenever Guendivar smiled.

"Look—it has stopped raining." She stretched out a hand, palm upward, and laughed. "We should take advantage of the change in weather. I would ride a little way into those hills to gather herbs for healing."

Cau was already shaking his head. "My lord king ordered me to keep you safe here—"

"The king has also ordered that his wounded be cared for. Surely he would not object if I go out in search of medicines to help them. Please, Cau—" she gave him a tremulous smile "—I think I will go mad if I do not get some exercise. Surely all the enemy are far ahead of us by now!"

Cau still looked uncertain, but he and his men were as frustrated by their inaction as she was. She suppressed a smile, knowing even before he spoke that he was going to agree.

After the stink and smoke of the hut, to be out in the fresh air was heaven. When the grasslands began to slope upward, they dismounted, and Guendivar wandered over the meadow searching for useful herbs while Cau followed with a basket and the other men sat their horses, grinning in their beards.

Guendivar made sure she found enough herbs among the grasses to justify the expedition. She picked the five-lobed leaves of Lady's Mantle and Self-heal with its clustered purple trumpets, both good for cleansing wounds. As they wandered farther, she glimpsed the creamy flowers and tooth-shaped leaves of Traveller's Joy, whose bark made an effective infusion for reducing fever, and Centaury, also good for fever, and for soothing the stomach and toning the system as well. Purging Flax went into the basket, and wild Marjoram to bathe sore muscles and reduce bruises.

It was a hard land, whipped by the sea winds, and nowhere did the useful plants grow in abundance, but by midafternoon they had nearly filled the basket. Her men had earned a rest, and Guendivar led them towards the musical trickle of water that came from a small ravine. The stream itself was hidden by a fringe of hazel and thorn, with a few straggling birch trees, but after all the running about she had been doing, its moist breath was welcome.

She had opened her mouth to tell Cau to bring the bread and cheese from her saddlebags when a wild shriek and a crashing in the bushes brought her whirling around. From out of the brush men came leaping, brandishing spears. There must have been fifty of them, against the dozen men of the queen's guard. Her escort spurred their mounts forward to meet them, but the ground was steep and broken; two horses went down and the others plunged as men ran towards them.

"Selenn! Run! Get help—" cried Cau. The last of the riders pulled up as the attackers surrounded the others, stabbing with their spears. In another moment he had hauled his mount's head around and was galloping down the slope.

Cau grabbed Guendivar's arm and thrust her down, standing over her with drawn sword. One enemy got too close and a sweeping swordstroke felled him, but a word from the leader directed the others towards the rest of her escort, and in minutes they were dead or captive, and the queen and her protector surrounded by leveled spears. Guendivar got to her feet, chin held up defiantly.

"You will be putting down your blade now, and none will harm you—" said the leader. An Irish accent, of course—but she had guessed that from the jackets and breeches of padded leather they wore.

"Artor will kill me . . ." muttered Cau, lowering his sword.

Guendivar shook her head. "It was my will, my responsibility—"

The enemy leader made a swift step forward, took the weapon and handed it to one of his men. He drew two lengths of thong from his belt and tied first Cau's and then Guendivar's hands.

"Come now, for we have far to go."

"You are mad," said the queen. "Release us, and perhaps Artor will not hunt you down."

"Lady, would you be refusing our hospitality?" He eyed her appreciatively. "I'm thinking that your king will pay well to have you back again."

One of the spears swung purposefully towards Cau's back. The warrior's grin told her he would not hesitate to spear his captive, and Guendivar started forward, knowing that Cau must follow her.

"It is myself, Melguas son of Ciaran, that has the honor to be your captor," he said over his shoulder, teeth flashing in his russet beard. His hair was more blond than red, confined in many small braids bound and ornamented with bits of silver and gold. He led the way at a swift trot and it took all Guendivar's breath to keep up with him.

"It is Guendivar daughter of Leodagranus who has the misfortune to be your captive, and lord Cau, who commands my guards," she said when they paused for a moment at the top of the slope. The ravine deepened here, and in the shelter of the trees ponies were waiting, surefooted native beasts that could go swiftly on the rough terrain.

"And do you think we did not know it? For many and many a day we have been watching you." Melguas tipped back his head, laughing, and she saw the torque of silver that gleamed beneath the beard.

"A damned cheerful villain," murmured Cau, but Guendivar closed her eyes in pain. This had been no evil chance, but the enemy's careful plan, waiting only on her foolishness. She thought of the three men of her escort whom the Irish had left dead on the field and knew their blood was on her hands.

Darkness had fallen by the time they stopped at last, and they had covered many miles. Sick at heart and aching from the pony's jolting,

Guendivar allowed Melguas to pull her off the horse and thrust her into a brush hut without protest. They left Cau to lie beside the fire, still bound, with a blanket thrown over him. It did no good to tell herself that Artor would be as wounded by the loss of any of his companions as by her capture—none of *them* could have been taken so easily.

That night she huddled in the odorous blankets in silent misery. How long, she wondered, before Selenn reached the rearguard and told his tale? How long for another messenger to get to Artor? By the time he could send men to her rescue, the rain she heard pattering on the brush would have wiped out their trail. *Perhaps he will think himself well rid of me. . . .* She contemplated the prospect of an endless captivity with sour satisfaction. She was glad now that Julia had been left behind in Camalot, so that she was not weighted by the burden of the sister's grief as well.

In the morning she was given a bowl of gruel and made to mount the pony once more. For most of the day they moved steadily, following the hidden paths through the hills. Here in the high country, the wind blew cold and pure, as if it had never passed through mortal lungs; an eagle, hanging in the air halfway between the earth and the sun, was the only living thing they saw. When Guendivar expressed surprise that the Irish should know these paths, Melguas laughed.

"My father is a prince in the land of Laigin, but 'tis here I was born and I am on speaking terms with every peak and valley."

As I am in the Summer Country, Guendivar thought then, wishing she were there now. "Are you taking me to King Illan?" she asked aloud.

"Surely—better than a wall of stone to protect us is the lovely body of Artor's queen."

"Do not be so certain," Guendivar said grimly.

"How not?" Melguas looked at her in surprise. "Are you not the White Lady, with the fertility of the land between your round thighs and its sovereignty shining from your brow?"

Not for Artor, thought Guendivar, but she would not betray him by saying so. These Irish seemed so confident of her value—what magic did queens have, there in Eriu, that these exiled sons should hold them in such reverence? Melguas had forced her obedience, but neither he nor his men had dared to offer her either insult or familiarity. *This is what Merlin was trying to tell me,* she thought then, *but I must be a fraud as well as a failure, for there is something missing within me that prevents me from becoming truly Artor's queen!*

That night they slept wrapped in cloaks beneath rude brush shelters. In the middle of the night, Guendivar felt the need to relieve herself and crawled out from the shelter, shivering as the chill touched her skin. The privy trench had been dug a little down the slope. When she was finished, she stood, gazing at the black shapes of the mountains humped against the stars. If this had been her own country, she would have tried to slip away in the darkness, but she did not know this land, and besides, Melguas was a careful commander, and though she could not see them, there would be guards.

She turned, and as if the thought had summoned him, saw a dark man-shape rising out of the rocks.

"Ah, lady, you are cold—let me make you warm—"

It was Melguas, but something within her had already known it. With a sense of inevitability, she felt his hands close on her shoulders, the scent of male sweat as he pulled her against him and kissed her mouth.

"I am a queen—" she whispered when he released her at last. "Is this how you respect me?" But her heart was thumping in her breast, and she had not wanted him to let her go.

"It is—as I would serve the land herself, had she a body I could worship . . ." The soft Irish voice was trembling, but his grip was firm.

I must stop this, Guendivar told herself as he pulled her close once more, his hands reverent on her skin. But if she cried out, no one would help her—there would only be more witnesses to her shame. His hand moved to her breast, and she swayed, all her frustrated sensuality asserting its claim. He laughed then, sensing her body yielding, and bore her to the shelter of a stony outcrop and on the soft grass laid her down.

Pressed against the earth by the weight of Melguas' body, the queen had no power of resistance. And at the moment of fulfillment, it seemed to her as if she *was* the earth, opening ecstatically to receive his love.

Guendivar woke, shamed and aching, to a soft drizzle that continued throughout the day. She drew her shawl over her head, peering at the faces of the warriors. But there were no sly looks or secret smiles, and if Melguas looked triumphant, her capture was excuse enough. Perhaps her secret was secure. She wondered if Cau suspected. Their captors had left him bound all night, and he must be feeling even worse than she was. He sat his pony without complaining, but he no longer smiled.

The cloud cover was beginning to darken when Melguas drew rein.

"Illan's camp lies yonder—" He gestured towards the next fold in the hills, and it seemed to Guendivar, accustomed after two days to the cold silences of the heights, that she could hear a distant murmur like a river in flood. "If you wish it, we will be stopping for a moment so that you may dress your hair and brush your garments and appear before my lord as a queen." There was a familiar warmth in his gaze.

Guendivar stared at him. Riding with Artor's men, she had packed away her royal ornaments so that they would think of her as a sister and comrade. After two days in the saddle, she must look like one of the women who followed the army, her face grimed and bits of brush tangled in her hair. *If all my jewels cannot make me a real queen, how will it serve if I tidy my hair?*

Melguas was waiting. Guendivar's mother had been constantly carping at her to at least *pretend* she was a lady. Why should this be any different? For three years now she had been pretending to be a queen. What had happened to her last night should have destroyed even the pretense of legitimacy, but her captor's belief compelled her. She took the comb the Irishman held out to her and began to untangle her braids.

Through the veil of her hair she could see the light in Melguas' eyes become a flame of adoration. As the red-gold strands blew out upon the wind the other men stared, even Cau had straightened in the saddle, watching with some of his old worship in his eyes. Their faces were mirrors in which she saw the reflection of a queen. She slowed, drawing out each stroke of the comb with intention, drawing from the men who watched her the power to become what they needed her to be.

And in that moment, when the attention of her captors was focused on her beauty, riders burst suddenly over the rim of the hill and the warcry of the Pendragon echoed against the sky.

Gualchmai was in the lead, as big and barbaric as any of the Irishmen. Melguas made a grab for Guendivar's rein, but she recovered from the first shock of recognition in time to boot her pony into motion. She dropped the comb and grabbed for its mane as the beast leaped into a jolting canter, managing to collect the reins herself in time to stop the animal before it ran away with her.

By this time Melguas and Gualchmai were trading blows, the clangor of steel assaulting the trembling air. She glimpsed Betiver and Cai and Gualchmai's brothers—Christ! Artor had sent all his Companions! And then she realized that he had not sent but led them, that the big man in silver mail and the spangenhelm that hid his features was Artor himself, charging into battle like the Great Bear.

She had never before seen Artor in combat. Gualchmai fought with more gleeful ferocity, Betiver with more precision, but Artor faced his foes with a grim intensity she had not observed in any other man, the Chalybe blade falling like the stroke of doom on any fighter who dared to face him.

Is this for me, wondered Guendivar, *or for his honor? Or for the sake of that imaginary being, the High Queen?*

Just as the Irishmen had overmatched her escort, they were overwhelmed by Artor's Companions, even though they outnumbered them. In a few moments, it seemed, her captors were dead or fleeing, except for Melguas himself, who was still holding off Betiver and Aggarban, laughing. But they fell back when Artor finished off his last opponent and strode towards them, his bloody sword poised.

"Not worthy of her—" Melguas said breathlessly, "but I see . . . you are an honorable man!"

Silently, Artor settled into a fighter's crouch, every line in his body expressing deadly purpose. Melguas' eyes narrowed, as if he had only now begun to appreciate the caliber of his enemy, and he braced his feet, lifting his sword. For a long moment, neither man stirred. Then, as if at some unspoken signal, both fighters blurred into action. The swords moved too swiftly for her eye to follow, but when the two figures separated, Artor was still upright, and Melguas was falling, a red gash opening like a flower across his belly and breast.

Guendivar let out a breath she had not known she was holding in a long sigh. Melguas lay where he had fallen, chest heaving in loud gasps as blood spread over his leather armor and began to drip onto the ground. She took a step forward, and then another, staring in appalled fascination at the wreck of the man who had made her captive.

"End it—" whispered Melguas. "You . . . have the best of me. . . ."

"My lord," Betiver started forward, dagger already drawn, "there is no need for you to soil your hands—"

Artor shook his head. "A good hunter always finishes off his kill." He took the dagger from Betiver and knelt beside his foe, laying his sword beside him on the ground.

Melguas twisted, his body contorting as if momentarily overcome by pain. Only Guendivar, coming closer, saw his fingers close on the hilt of the dagger strapped to his thigh. In the moment it took her mind to comprehend what her eyes had seen, Melguas jerked the weapon free and slashed upward beneath the hanging skirt of Artor's mail.

The king jerked away with a muffled oath.

"No good to her—" Melguas began, but Artor, his face suffused with fury, reeled forward, supporting himself on his left hand, and with his right plunged the dagger into his enemy's throat above the silver torque and tore sideways so that the Irishman's head flopped suddenly to the side, his eyes still widening in surprise.

Artor stared down at him, grimacing, then slowly collapsed to his side, blood spreading down the cloth of his breeches.

"Artor!" "My lord!" Gualchmai and Betiver cried out together as they reached his side. Carefully they stretched him out, dragging the mail aside. The dagger had torn the flesh of Artor's inner thigh and all the way up into the groin. The king made no sound, but his skin was paling, and his body quivered with the pain.

"He didn't get the artery—" murmured Betiver, peeling the cloth back from the wound. Blood was flowing steadily, but not in the red tide that no surgery could stop.

"Nor yet your manhood!" added Gualchmai, gripping Artor's shoulder. "Let it bleed for the moment—it will clean the wound. Do you lie now on your right side, and we'll get you out of this mail."

Guendivar's fists were clenched in her skirts, but these men knew more of wounds and armor than she. There was nothing she could do until they had got off sword belt and mail shirt and cut away his breeches and were looking for cloth with which to stanch the wound.

After three days in the saddle, her own clothes were none too clean, but she had more, and softer, fabric about her than anything the Companions had to offer. She hauled up her skirts and cut half the front of her shift away, folding it into a pad which she bound across the wound with her veil.

"You will have to make a litter," she told the men. "He cannot ride this way."

"Aye, and swiftly," agreed Gualchmai, "before the bastards that got away are bringing Illan down on us to finish the job."

"Betiver . . . you will lead the army—" whispered Artor as the men began to hack at a young oak tree that clung to the side of the hill. "Take most of the men and head straight for the coast. Pursuit should . . . follow you."

"And what of you, my lord?" Betiver kept his voice steady, but his face was nearly as pale as Artor's own.

"Gualchmai will take . . . me to the Lake . . . to Igierne."

"I will go with you," Guendivar said firmly. Artor, who had not met her gaze since she bandaged his wound, said nothing, and as she stared down the others, she realized that at least for this moment, she was queen in truth as well as name.

When her women came to tell her that a messenger had arrived, Morgause was not surprised—galloping hooves had haunted her dreams. The rider was the man she had sent to be her eyes and ears in Artor's army.

As she recognized him, she felt something twist painfully in her belly, and that did surprise her.

"What is it?" she asked, controlling her voice. "Has something happened to the king?"

"He is not dead, my lady," the man said quickly. "But he is wounded, too badly to continue the campaign. He has left Betiver in command."

"Not Gualchmai?" Morgause frowned.

"Your son is with Artor. They are progressing by slow stages northward—no one would say where or why."

"To the Lake—" Morgause said thoughtfully, "that has to be their destination. His wound must be serious indeed, if he goes to my mother for healing."

To Igierne, and to the Cauldron, she added silently, fists clenching in the skirts of her gown. Was the injury so severe, or had Artor seized the excuse to gain access to the Cauldron's mysteries?

"What is the nature of the wound?" she asked then.

"I do not know for certain," said the spy. "He is not able to ride. They say—" he added in some embarrassment "—that the king is wounded in the thighs . . ."

Morgause stifled a triumphant smile. The queen had borne Artor no child. Whether that was because the words she gave to each of them at their wedding had cursed their bed, or it was the will of the gods, she did not know. But if the king was injured in his manhood, it might be long before he could try again to beget an heir. Gualchmai was known to everyone as Artor's sister-son, the bravest of his Companions. Britannia would find it easy to accept him as the king's heir. And if he refused the honor, she still had Medraut. . . .

"You did well to bring me this news." Morgause paused, considering the messenger. He was called Doli, a man of the ancient race of the hills. In feature he was fine-boned and dark, devoted to her service by rites of the old magic. Some years earlier she had arranged for his sister to enter the community of priestesses on the Isle of Maidens.

"Now I have another task for you," she said then. "I wish you to ride to the Lake and pay a visit to your sister. If, as you say, the king's party is moving slowly, you may be there and gone before ever he arrives."

"And when I am come?" Doli lifted one dark eyebrow inquiringly.

"You will give her the flask I shall send with you, and a message. But this, I dare not commit to writing. I shall record it in your memory, and only when your sister Ia speaks the words, 'by star and stone' shall the message be set free.

"It is well—" Doli bowed his head in submission, then settled himself cross-legged on the floor, eyes closed and chest rising and falling in the ancient rhythm of trance.

When she sensed that his energy had sunk and steadied, Morgause called his spirit to attention by uttering his secret name. Then she began to chant the message that he must carry.

"Thus, the words of the Lady of Dun Eidyn who is called the Vor-Tigerna, the Great Queen, to Ia daughter of Malcuin. The priestesses will work the rite of healing for King Artor. Add the contents of the flask your brother shall give you to the water in the pool. When you do this, these are the words you must say: 'Thou art a stagnant pool in a poisoned land, a barren field and a fruitless tree. Thy seed shall fail, and thy sovereignty pass away. By the will of the Great Queen, so shall it be!' "

Morgause waited a moment, then spoke the ritual words to rouse Doli from his trance. Then she sent him off to be fed, and went herself to the hut where she prepared her herbs and brewed her medicines to distill a potion strong enough to counter the power of the Cauldron and all her mother's magic as well.

Asleep, Artor was so like Uthir that Igierne felt the pain of it in her breast each time she looked at him. Perhaps it was because he was ill, and the image of how her husband had appeared in his last years was still vivid in Igierne's memory. But Artor was only thirty-four, and she would not let him die. Even asleep his face showed the lines that responsibility had graven around his mouth and between his brows, and there were more strands of silver in the brown hair.

They had put the king to bed in the guest chamber of the Isle of Maidens, where a fresh breeze off the lake could blow through the window, bearing with it the scent the sun released from the pines. From time to time Artor twitched, as if even in sleep his wound pained him. The Irishman's blade had sliced through the muscles of the inner thigh and up into the groin, but it had not, quite, penetrated the belly. Nor had it cut into his scrotum, although the slash came perilously close. The great danger now was wound fever, for the rough field dressing had done little more than stop the bleeding, and during the jolting journey north the wound had become inflamed.

She leaned forward to stroke the damp hair off of his brow and felt the heat of fever, though it seemed to her that the strong infusion of willow-bark tea she had given Artor when he arrived had begun to bring the burning down. When he was a little rested, they would have to cleanse the wound and pack it with a poultice of spear-leek to combat the infection. As if in anticipation of the pain, Artor twisted restlessly, muttering, and she bent closer to hear.

"Guendivar . . . so beautiful. . . ." That he should call his wife's name was to be expected, but why was there such anguish in his tone? "Did he touch her? Did he . . . I have no right! It was my sin. . . ."

Frowning, Igierne dipped the cloth into the basin of cool water and laid it once more on his brow. She knew that Artor had been wounded by the Irishman who abducted the queen, but Guendivar swore she had not been harmed. Why was he babbling about sin?

"Be easy, my child . . ." she murmured. "It is all over now and you are safe here. . . ."

He shook his head, groaning, as if even in his delirium his mother's words had reached him. "She told me . . . I have a son. . . ."

Igierne sat back, eyes widening. "Who, Artor?" her voice hardened. "Whose son?"

"Morgause . . ." came the answer. "Why should she hate me? I didn't know. . . ."

"It is all right . . . the sin was not yours . . ." Igierne replied, but her mind was racing, remembering a sullen, red-headed boy sorting pebbles on a garden path. She had assumed the family resemblance came all from Morgause—but what if Medraut had a double heritage?

It was no wonder that Artor was fevered, if this knowledge was festering in his memory. It would not be enough to deal with the wound to his body—somehow, she would have to heal his soul.

The Lake was very beautiful, thought Guendivar, especially now, when the first turning leaves of autumn set glimmering reflections of gold and russet dancing in the water, and the tawny hills lifted bare shoulders against a sky that shone pure clear blue after the past days of rain. But after a week cooped up on the island with the priestesses, she felt as confined as she had with the army, and Gualchmai, who was camped with the other men in the meadow by the landing across from the island, had said he would be happy to escort her on a walk along the shore.

"If we are attacked," she said bitterly, "let them take me. I am not worth the lives of any more good men." Throughout that long ride northward, no one had accused her, no one suspected that she had lain in Melguas' arms. In the stress of the journey she had almost been able to forget it herself. But now, with nothing to do, the memory tormented her.

"Lady! You must not say it. You are the queen!" Gualchmai's voice held real pain.

She shook her head. "Igierne is the queen. On the way north Artor needed me, but I have neither the knowledge nor the magic to help him now."

"Nor do I, Guendivar—I would give my heart's blood if it would heal him, but I have no skill to fight the enemy he battles." Gualchmai's broad shoulders slumped.

Hearing the anguish in his voice, the queen found her own a little eased. She breathed in the spicy scent of fallen leaves and exhaled again in a long sigh, feeling tension go out of her. Leaves rustled with each footstep, and squirrels chittered to each other from the trees.

"But you fight his other foes," she said presently. "You are the bulwark of his throne."

"That is all I desire. I am happier on the field of battle than in the council hall. To deal with the bickering of the princes would drive me to blows within a year and plunge the land into civil war."

His tone had brightened, and Guendivar laughed.

"Surely the Lady of the Lake will make the king well again, and I will be spared the temptation," he said then. "She is a wise woman. And she has agreed to take my daughter as one of her maidens here."

"Your daughter! I did not know you had a child," exclaimed Guendivar.

"Until last year, I did not know it either," Gualchmai answered ruefully. "I got her on a woman of the little dark folk of the hills, one time I was out hunting and my pony went lame when I was yet far from home. She is as wild as a doe, but her hair is the same color as my own, and her mother died this past winter, so I must find her a home."

"What is she called?" asked the queen, finding it as hard to imagine Gualchmai a father as he did himself.

"Ninive—"

So Morgause is a grandmother! Does she know? wondered Guendivar, but she did not voice that thought aloud.

"Igierne will understand how to tame her," said Gualchmai. He stooped to pick up a spray of chestnuts brought down by the wind, and stripped off the prickly rind and the leathery shell before offering one to the queen. The nut inside was moist and sweet. "And she will make Artor well."

"She will," Guendivar echoed his affirmation. "His fever has been down for two days now, and they tell me that the wound is beginning to heal."

No man had ever entered the cave of the Cauldron, but in the dell below it, a basin had been hollowed out of the stone foundations of the island which could be filled with water for baths of purification or healing, and here, when there was great need, a man could come. It was large enough for several women to sit together or for a grown man to lie. Here, at dusk when the new moon was first visible in the evening sky, they brought Artor to complete his healing.

The Lady of the Lake sat on a bench at the head of the pool. It was set into the niche where the image of the Goddess had stood since the first priestesses came to the island. Or perhaps before—the image was fashioned from lead, bare-breasted above a bell-shaped skirt, in a style that had been ancient when the Romans came. A terra-cotta lamp cast a wavering light on the image. To Igierne, it seemed that She was smiling.

It would take many weeks before the king was entirely whole, but the wound had closed. For health to return, the balance of his body must be restored, and his bruised spirit persuaded to add its blessing. More lamps flickered around the pool, and the breeze from the lake brought with it the scent of woodsmoke from the fire where they were heating the water. Sometimes she longed for the natural hot springs of Aquae Sulis, and yet there was a more focused magic in the building of a fire and the brewing of the herbs that infused the water.

As the season turned towards autumn the nights were growing cold, but now, while the memory of the sun still glowed in the western sky, the air held the warmth of the afternoon. In the purple dusk the maiden moon hung like a rind of pearl. The air had the hush that comes with the end of day, but as Igierne listened, she began to perceive another sound. Her priestesses were singing as they escorted Artor along the path.

"Water of life, water of love—
We come from the Mother and to Her we return . . ."

Igierne got to her feet. As she raised her arms in welcome, the black folds of her sleeves fell back from her white arms. The silver-and-moonstone diadem of the high priestess was a familiar weight upon her brow.

"Water of healing flows from above,
We come from the Mother. . . ."

Two by two, the white-clad priestesses passed between the twin oak trees that guarded the pool, each carrying a vessel of water that steamed gently in the cooling air. The pairs separated to either side, kneeling to

pour the contents of the basins into the bath, then rising and turning away
to either side to return for more.

"*Water of passage, water of birth . . .*" the priestesses sang.

As the level of liquid grew, the scents of the herbs that had been
steeped in it grew heavy in the air—various mints and camomile, rosemary
and lavender, salvia and sweet woodruff and substances such as sea salt
and powdered white willow that had little fragrance but great power.

Some of them they grew on the island, and some they gathered in the
wild lands, and some were brought from afar. The fragrance was almost
dizzying in its intensity. And yet, as Igierne breathed in, something seemed
different from before, a hint of something spoiled. She took another breath,
testing the air, but it was no scent she recognized. She wondered if it were
physical at all, or if she was sensing some spiritual corruption. At the
thought, her hands moved instinctively in the gesture used to ward and
banish, and her awareness of the wrongness began to pass away.

"*Water of blessing flows from the earth . . .*"

She shook her head—perhaps it had been her imagination. She knew
that with age her senses had become less dependable.

Now the bath was three-quarters full. Nest and Ceincair were coming
through the gateway with Artor, wrapped in a green robe between them.
He moved slowly, depending on the priestesses for support, but he was
on his feet, though the beads of sweat stood out on his brow.

"*We come from the Mother and to Her we return . . .*" the women
sang, and then were still.

The king and his escorts stopped at the edge of the pool.

"Child of the Goddess, why have you come here?" asked Igierne.

"I seek to be healed in body and in soul—" came Artor's answer.
She held his gaze, hoping that it was true, for she had not been able to
get from him, waking, an explanation of the words he had muttered in his
fevered dream.

"Return, then, to the womb of the Mother, and be made whole."

The priestesses untied the cord and eased the robe from his shoulders.
Face and arms were sallow where illness had faded his tan, but the rest
of Artor's body was pale, growing rosy now as he realized he stood naked
before nine women. But their gaze was impersonal, half tranced already
by the ritual, and after a moment he regained his composure and allowed
Nest and Ceincair to steady him as he descended the steps into the pool.

He halted again at the first level, as if surprised by the heat, then,
biting his lip, continued downward until he stood in water halfway up his
thighs, the mark of his injury livid against the pale skin. At the end of
the bath there was a stone headrest. When the priestesses had helped him

all the way down, the headrest enabled him to lie half-floating, his body completely submerged.

The priestesses had settled themselves cross-legged around the pool, singing softly to invoke the healing powers of the herbs. From time to time one of them would fetch more water to maintain the heat of the bath. Gradually the tension faded from Artor's body. He lay with eyes closed, perspiration streaming from his face.

The singing continued as the night grew darker, gradually increasing in intensity. Igierne, who had been watching the gateway, saw first the pale figure appear within it, and then, as if some change in the air had aroused him, a sudden tension in the slack body of the king. He opened his eyes, and they widened as a light that transcended the blaze of the torches glowed around the shining robes of the priestess and the silver Cauldron in her arms.

The wonder remained as the maiden came fully into the light and he saw her dark hair, but the hope that had been there also was gone. Igierne understood. She had tried to persuade Guendivar to bear the Cauldron, and could not understand why the queen would not agree. Neither her son nor her daughter-in-law would share their secrets, but she understood now that Artor loved his queen. For a moment sorrow shook Igierne's concentration. Then the momentum of the ritual swept all other awareness away.

"Be reborn from the water of life!" her voice rang against the stones. "Be healed by the water of love!"

The priestess lifted the cauldron, and the hallowed water it held poured in a stream of light into the pool.

VIII

The Great Queen

The skirling of bagpipes throbbed like an old wound in the chill spring air, so constant that one forgot it until a touch, or a memory, brought the pain of loss to consciousness once more. King Leudonus was dead, and the Votadini were gathering to mourn him. The great dun on the rock of Eidyn was filled with chieftains, and the gorge below crammed with the skin tents and brushwood bothies of their followers. Morgause, marshalling provisions and cooks for the funeral feast, settling quarrels over precedence and ordering the rituals, was too busy to question whether what she felt was grief, or relief that he was gone.

These past ten years she had been a nurse to him, not a wife, watching his strength fade until he lay like a ruined fortress, never leaving his bed. And as the rule of the Votadini had passed into her hands, Morgause had become not only the symbol of sovereignty, but its reality. In his day, Leudonus had been a mighty warrior, but in the end death had taken him from ambush, with no struggle at all. She had drawn aside the curtain that screened his bed place one morning and found him stiff and cold.

It was just as well, thought Morgause as Dumnoval and the southern

Votadini chieftains came marching in, that grief did not overwhelm her, for upon the strength she showed now, her future here would depend. She had sent word to her sons who were with Artor, but she had little hope they would come. The spring campaign against those Irish who still clung to the coasts of Guenet and Demetia had just begun, and the king's nephews were among his most valued commanders.

Perhaps it was as well, for the fighting provided a credible excuse for Gualchmai's absence. As it was, she could pretend that only a greater duty kept him away, though it had long been clear to her just how little he cared for the lordship of his father's land. Nonetheless, just as her marriage to Leudonus had legitimated her authority, her status as mother to the heir might continue to do so, even when everyone knew his rule to be a fiction.

It was not, she thought as she offered the meadhorn to Dumnoval in welcome, as if she had not prepared for this day. There was scarcely a family in the land that had not cause to be grateful for food in a hard year, the loan of a bride-price to win a family alliance, gifts of weapons or cattle or honors. And so, as Dumnoval slid down off his pony, she greeted him as the Great Queen of Alba, receiving one of her men.

That evening she dressed in silk, its crimson folds glowing blood-red in the torchlight. Ornaments of amber and jet gleamed from her neck and wrists, amber drops swung from her ears. For some years now she had used henna to hide the silver in her hair, and kohl to emphasize her eyes. In the firelight, the marks that time and power had graven in her face were hidden. She was forever young, and beautiful. She passed among the benches, smiling, flattering, reminding them of her ties with the Picts and the benefits that a united Alba could bring, persuading them that they still needed her to be their queen.

The next morning, veiled, she walked behind Leudonus' bier, her son Goriat, who at seventeen towered like a young tree, on one side, and the thirteen-year-old Medraut, with his shining bronze hair and secret smile, on the other. Up from the Rock of Eidyn to the Watch Hill above it wound the procession, and then around the slope to the little lake on whose shores they had prepared the pyre. The ashes would be buried by the tribal kingstone below the ancient Votadini fortress, a day's journey to the southeast. It was here where the king had ruled that the Druids chanted their prayers and spells; and here, while the pipes wailed and the drums pounded heavy as heartbeats, that the holy fire released Leudonus' spirit to the winds.

That night the men drank to their dead king's memory while the bards chanted his deeds. The queen remained in the women's quarters, as was fitting. Morgause was grateful for the custom, for her woman's courses, which for several moons had been absent, had returned in a flood. She was lying in her bed, listening to the distant sounds of revelry and wondering whether she could sleep if she drank more mead, when she heard from the direction of the gate the sounds of a new arrival.

"My lady—" Dugech spoke from the door. "Are you still awake, Morgause?"

"Someone has come. I heard. Tell him to join the other drunkards in the hall—" she answered, lying back on her pillows again.

"But lady, it is your mother who is here!"

Morgause sat up, calculating swiftly the time it would have taken for a messenger to reach the Lake, and for Igierne to make the journey to Dun Eidyn. Did her mother have a spy here, as she herself did on the Isle of Maidens, or was it Ia, receiving the word from her brother, who had willingly or unwillingly let the high priestess know?

She swung her feet over the edge of the bed and reached for a shawl. Whatever the truth might be, she must suppress any reaction until she could find out why her mother was here.

Even the warmth of the firelight could not disguise the pallor of Igierne's skin, and Morgause was aware of an unexpected and surprisingly painful pang of fear. At times she had longed for the day when her mother would be gone and she should inherit her place on the Isle of Maidens. But not now, when she was battling to retain her hold on the Votadini. The idea that she might still long for her mother's love was a thought she could not allow.

"Bring us some chamomile tea, and show my mother's women where they will be sleeping," she told Dugech. Igierne had brought two priestesses whom Morgause did not know, an older woman and a dark-eyed girl with corn-colored hair, who were bringing in baskets and bundles.

"The burning was this morning. You missed it—" she said then. "Did you think I needed a shoulder to weep on? I am doing well. You did not have to make such a journey for my sake."

"Gracious as ever . . ." murmured Igierne, drinking from the cup of tea Dugech set before her. A little color began to return to her cheeks. "Perhaps I came to honor Leudonus."

"Since your son could not be bothered," said Morgause. "Or was Artor unable to come? I hear he has never quite recovered from his wounding two years ago, despite your attempts to heal him."

"He can ride—" Igierne answered, frowning. "Yet even if he could leave his army, the king would not have been here in time for the funeral. But I remember Leudonus in his youth, and even if you do not, I will mourn him. It was long since I had seen him, but he was one of the last men of Uthir's generation. The world is poorer for having lost him."

Morgause snorted and lifted a hand as men do to acknowledge a hit when they practice with swords. "Very well. But you cannot wonder that I am surprised to see you. We have not been close these past years."

"I will not quarrel with you regarding whose fault that is. I am too tired." Igierne set down her tea. "I had hoped that now you are a grandmother yourself, you might be able to put aside your resentment of me. . . ."

Morgause felt the color flood up into her face and then recede again. "What do you mean?"

"Gualchmai has a girl-child, did not you know? She is the daughter of some woman he met in the hills. She is twelve now. He sent her to me last year." At the words, the younger of her companions looked up, her eyes wide and dark as those of a startled doe. "Come, Ninive, and greet your grandmother—"

Seen close to, Ninive was obviously a child, gazing around her as if any sudden sound would send her bounding away. *A wild one, but I could tame her,* thought Morgause as the girl bent to kiss her hand. *Why did Gualchmai not give her to me?*

But at a deeper level, she knew. Her brother had stolen her two elder sons already, and now her mother was claiming the girl, the granddaughter that she could have trained as a priestess in a tradition older than anything in Igierne's mysteries. Igierne had been foolish to bring her here, or foolishly sure of her own power.

"You are very certain of her—" she said when Ninive had been sent off for more tea. "It is not an easy life, there on the island. What if the child wants a man in her bed and children at her knee? She ought to have the chance to choose—"

"Why do you think I brought her here?" Igierne replied, with that lift of the eyebrow that had always exasperated her daughter, so eloquent in its assumption of authority.

For a moment, Morgause could only stare. "How generous! Well, I will speak with Ninive after the assembly, and then we will see if she takes after you, or me. . . . But I can see why Gualchmai did not wish to bring a girl-child to Artor's court," she added reflectively.

"What do you mean?"

"My brother does not write to me, but others do," Morgause replied, "and there are many who say that the queen's bed is not empty, though Artor does not lie there."

"It is not so—" said Igierne, but Morgause suppressed a smile, seeing the uncertainty in her mother's eyes.

"Is it not? Well, I have no objection if Guendivar follows northern ways. If the king is not potent, it is up to the queen to empower the land."

"By taking lovers, as you have? Who fathered your sons, Morgause?"

Morgause laughed, having goaded her mother to a direct attack at last. "What man would dare to boast of having fathered a child on the queen, especially when it was not she with whom he lay, but the Goddess, wearing her form, and he himself possessed by the God? My children are more than royal, Mother, they are gifts of the gods!"

In the next moment she realized that this stroke had missed its mark. Igierne sat back and took another sip of tea.

"Ah—so that is how it came to pass. Beware, daughter, lest the gods call you to account for what you have made of their gifts to you."

Morgause frowned, aware of having revealed more than she meant to. But even if Igierne knew Medraut's parentage, what could she do? This child, at least, was her own, body and soul.

"You have had a long journey, Mother, and you must be weary," she said then. "And I must be fresh for tomorrow's assembly of the clans. Dugech will show you where you are to sleep." Morgause rose, summoning the woman who waited by the door. But despite her words, she herself tossed restlessly until the dawn.

Still, the gods had not abandoned her, for by the end of the council, the clans, while recognizing the claim of Dumnoval to lead the southern Votadini, and choosing Cunobelinus as warleader for the northern clans, had agreed that Morgause should continue to rule in Dun Eidyn as regent for Gualchmai. But Ninive chose to return to the Isle of Maidens with Igierne.

"They tell me that you are shaping well as a warrior." Morgause looked up at her fourth son as they stood on the guard path built into the rampart of Dun Eidyn. Goriat over-topped her by more than a head, and she was a big woman. Indeed, he towered over most men. She was not entirely certain who had fathered him, but as he grew it seemed likely that it was a man of Lochlann, who had come bringing furs and timber from the Northlands that lay eastward across the sea. She remembered the beauty of the trader's long-fingered hands.

"Men say that Gualchmai is the greatest warrior in Britannia. If I cannot surpass him, I have sworn to be the second." Goriat grinned.

"But are you the best fighter in Alba?" she asked then.

"I can take any man of the tribes—"

"South of the Bodotria," she corrected, "but you have not yet measured yourself against the men of the Pretani." Morgause gestured northward, where the lands of the Picts were blossoming in tender green beneath the sun.

Goriat shrugged. "If Artor fights them, I suppose I shall find out."

She looked up, startled by his tone. It was natural that he should think of following his brothers into his uncle's service, but she had not realized he considered it a certainty.

"Perhaps Artor will not have to fight them," she said carefully. "If one of his kindred is their warleader. . . . The Pretani have a princess of the highest lineage who is ripe for marriage. You know they seek outlanders to husband their royal women to avoid competition within the clans. They have sent a messenger, asking me for one of my sons. Marry the girl, and you will lead their armies and father kings."

"The Pretani!" Goriat exclaimed in revulsion.

"Alba!" Morgause replied. "If the Votadini and the Pretani make alliance, the north will be united at last!"

"And then may the gods pity Britannia!" He turned to face her, his long fingers curling into fists. "But it will not happen. If you think I will lend myself to this plot, Mother, you have gone mad. Play your games with Medraut, if you will, but I will stand on the other side of the board."

"You are an idiot without understanding," she hissed. "With one of my sons on the high seat of Britannia and my grandson on the sacred stone of the Pretani, we will rule this entire Hallowed Isle! You will go north, Goriat, or you will go nowhere! You think yourself a man and a warrior, but I am the Great Queen!"

Morgause turned and stalked away along the parapet, leaving him there. He was young and rebellious, but she held the purse-strings. His brothers had gone outfitted with arms and horses and servants as befitted their station, but her fourth son should have nothing until he agreed to do her will.

But the next morning, when she called for him, Goriat had disappeared.

For three days, Morgause raged. Then she began to think once more. For a time she considered sending Medraut to the Picts instead, but he was not yet a warrior, although in other areas he was precocious enough to give her concern. Yet even if he had been of an age to marry, Medraut had a different destiny. At heart, Morgause, like Goriat, held Britannia to be the greater prize, and of all her sons, Medraut was the one with the greatest right to it.

At Midsummer, the tribes of the north celebrated the sun's triumph by clan and district, making the offerings and feasting and blessing their cattle and their fields. Each year, it had been the custom of the queen to keep the festival with a different clan, but the summer after the death of Leudonus, she gave out that this year she would observe the holiday in seclusion, and her youngest son with her, in honor of her lord.

A few days before the solstice they set out east along the shore of the firth, towards a headland with a house to which Morgause had often retired when she needed to recuperate from the demands made on a queen. Her folk were accustomed to this, and there was no surprise when she dismissed all attendants except Dugech and Leuku. But none knew that the following evening a boat was beached on the shore below, whose crew spoke with Pretani tongues, or that it pushed off once more before the sun was in the sky, bearing the queen of the Votadini, her maid Dugech, and her son.

"Why does Leuku not come with us?" asked Medraut as the land grew dim behind them.

"She will keep a fire going in the house so that any who pass will believe we are all still there."

For a few moments he was silent. "Does that mean we will be gone for some time?"

"For a space of several days. It is time you saw how folk who have not abandoned the most ancient ways of our people keep the festival."

Medraut's eyes brightened as he realized that she was at last going to share with him the secret of her mysterious journeys.

At thirteen, he had reached an uneasy balance between boy and man. He would never, she thought, have the height and sheer muscular power of his brothers. But the size of his hands and feet promised growth, and even now, at a boy's most awkward age, he had an agility that should develop into uncommon speed and grace. Gualchmai and Gwyhir and Goriat possessed physical splendor, while Aggarban, when last she saw him, had been cultivating a dark truculence that was impressive in its own way. Her youngest son would have an elegance that verged on beauty. Already, when he chose to do so, Medraut knew how to charm.

And sexual maturity was coming early as well. She had seen him bathing with the other boys, and though the fuzz on his cheeks was not yet worth shaving, his man's parts were full sized, surrounded by a bush of red hair. Medraut had an eye for women already, and only the most dire of threats to her maidservants had preserved his virginity thus far. Morgause would have preferred that he hold on to that power, but since chastity was probably unattainable, she meant to channel the magic of Medraut's sexual initiation through ritual.

"And in what way, Mother, are the rites of the Pretani different from Votadini ways?"

From his expression, Morgause could tell that there was something strange about her answering smile. "There is more blood in them," she said softly, "and more power."

The current had been with them, and the northern shore was already near. On the beach, horsemen were waiting. Morgause felt her pulse begin to beat more strongly. She took a deep breath, scenting woodsmoke and roasted flesh on the wind.

They came to Fodreu in the evening when the sun, still clinging to his season of triumph, turned the smoke from a multitude of cookfires to a golden haze. Coming over the rim of the hill they could see the gleam of water where the Tava curved abruptly eastward. Just above the bend was a ferry, with rafts to take them across the swift-running stream, and then they were following the road along the far bank towards the royal dun. Drest Gurthinmoch had emerged victorious from the turmoil following the death of Nectain Morbet and married the queen. He reigned now over the Pretani of both north and south from a stout dun near the sacred grove that held the coronation stone.

But that was another mystery. Today, their way led to the wide meadow where a women's enclosure had been prepared for the honored guests of the Pretani queen. Here, Morgause parted from Medraut, with certain words of warning to the warrior assigned to escort him. Then she passed through the gateway where Tulach was waiting to escort her to the queen.

The inner enclosure had been hung with woolen cloths embroidered with sacred symbols. Behind the queen's high seat the hanging stirred in the draught, so that the red mare pictured upon it seemed to move. Above it were images of the comb and mirror, symbols of the Goddess who ruled both in this world and the next. The queen herself wore red garments, also heavily embroidered, and was eating dried apples from a woven platter held by one of her maidens.

Uorepona—the Great Mare—was for her both a name and a title, always borne by the ruling queen. She was older than her husband, having been queen to Nectain Morbet before him, a little woman with grey hair, her body sagging with age.

Morgause made her obeisance, wondering nervously if Uorepona had loved her first husband, and if so, whether she might seek vengeance on the sister of the man who had killed him.

"The Great Mare of the Pretani bids you welcome," said Tulach in the British tongue.

"The Great Queen of the Votadini gives thanks, and offers her these gifts in token of her friendship," answered Dugech, motioning one of the slaves to bring forward the casket. Courtesy was all very well, but too much humility would be taken as weakness.

The atmosphere warmed perceptibly as Uorepona examined the ivory comb, the ornaments of golden filigree, and the vessels of Roman glass. A length of crimson silk was unfolded and immediately put to service as a mantle. The queen's woman offered Morgause apples from the platter, and she began to relax, understanding that as an accepted guest, she would be safe from now on.

"I have brought with me my son to be initiated into manhood—" she said later that evening as they sat around the women's fire. "He is the son of a king and comes of a line of warriors, and has never lain with a woman. I will give you the first offering of his seed if you have among your servants a clean maiden to receive it."

Uorepona spoke to her women in the Pictish dialect and laughed, by which Morgause concluded that though she did not speak British well, she understood it. When she had finished, one of the women replied.

"He is the bronze-haired lad that came with you, is it not so? My lady says that if she were younger she would take his seed herself, but as she is old, she will set her ornaments upon one of her servants to stand in her stead. The lady Tulach shall help you to choose . . ."

The Great Mare was served entirely by women. Even the slaves were of good blood, captives taken in war. Almost immediately, one of the girls caught Morgause's eye, a slim child scarcely older than Medraut, though her breasts were grown. But what had attracted the queen's attention was the bright red-gold of her hair and her amber eyes. She was very like Guendivar. . . .

"That one—" she gestured. "Where is she from?"

Tulach shrugged. "She is British, taken as a child in Nectain Morbet's war, but her lineage is not known."

Morgause nodded. "She will do very well."

The longest day continued endlessly beneath the northern sky. Earlier, the men had competed in contests of strength and skill, and the cattle had been driven through the smoke of the herb-laden fires. Now the sun was sinking, although it would be close to midnight before the last light was gone from the sky. The scent of cooking meat drifted through the encampment as the carcasses of sacrificed cattle roasted over many fires, but the smell of blood still hung in the air.

Tonight, the gods of the Pretani must be rejoicing, thought Morgause. Even the Votadini festivals were not so lavish, and as Christianity strengthened in the south, Artor's feasts had become bloodless travesties. A distant drum beat was taken up by others; her blood pulsed in time to the rhythm that throbbed in the air. Soon, the Goddess would receive another kind of offering.

Morgause had been given a place of honor with the women. On the other side of the circle she could see Medraut, sitting with the other boys. He had a gift for languages, and his agile tongue had clearly mastered the speech of the Pretani well enough to make them laugh. But from time to time his gaze would flicker towards her, questioning.

Trust me— She sent reassurance back with her smile. *This is for your good. You will see. . . .*

The slaves brought platters of meat still steaming from the spit, and skins of mead and heather beer. Some of the men were already becoming drunken, but what was given to the boys had been diluted. The ritual required that they be merry, but not incapable. Chieftains rose in place to boast of their achievements and praise the king. Young warriors marched into the center of the circle and danced with swords. And presently, after Drest's bard had completed a song in his honor, the drumbeat quickened, and the boys, with the awkward grace of colts just beginning their training, danced into the circle in a wavering line.

Morgause had spared no pains in her son's education. At this age, all boys were somewhat ungainly, but Medraut had not yet begun the growth spurt that would make his body for a time a stranger's, and in addition to her more private teaching, he had been rigorously schooled in running and leaping, in riding and in swordplay, and in the stylized movements of the warrior's dance.

It was a tradition the Votadini shared with their northern neighbors. Medraut's thin body took on grace as he recognized the quickening rhythm, spine straightening, shoulders braced, and the belted kilt that was all he wore swinging as his feet stamped in time. This was a tradition of unarmed combat. The beat shifted and the boys paired off, leaping and feinting with clenched fists or open hands, proud as young cocks of their energy and skill.

Skinny torsos shone with perspiration; differences in conditioning became apparent as some of the boys began to slow. Medraut, who had learned a few movements not included in the formal sequence, leaned close to his partner as they switched positions, feet flickering, and in the next moment the other boy fell. Face flaming with shame, he pulled himself upright and shambled off to the sidelines to join those whose endurance had given out.

Again a shift in the drumbeat signaled a change, and the pairs became a line once more. Faster and faster the rhythm drove them, and the dancers circled and spun. Another boy fell, with no help from Medraut, and rolled away. The drumming crescendoed and fell silent. The boys stopped dancing, one or two of them sinking to their knees, chests heaving, as the power of the music let go. Medraut stood with his head up, perspiration running in glittering rivulets down his chest and sides. The hair that clung damply to his neck was the color of old blood, but he had the air of a young stallion that has won his maiden race and vindicated his breeding.

Now a shimmer of tinkling metal brought heads up, eyes widening. A line of young women was filing in, their garments sewn with bits of silver and bronze. Singing and clapping hands, they circled the boys, and then drew back, leaving the girl Morgause had chosen standing alone.

She moved along the line of boys, as if considering them. Her movements were stiff and her smile anxious, as if she were not quite certain she would be able to follow her instructions. Her bright hair, combed in a shining cape across her shoulders, stirred gently as she moved. The boys twitched and licked their lips as she passed them, and halted at last before Medraut, as she had been told to do.

Medraut's eyes widened, and his mother smiled. The ornaments the girl was wearing belonged to the Great Mare, but the gown was one he would recognize as her own, with her perfume still clinging to every fold. *When you take her in your arms you will see Guendivar's face, but it is my scent you will smell, and my magic that will bind you. . . .*

She had borne five strong sons in pain and suffering, and except for the last, she might as well have been a barren tree. One by one, Artor had seduced them away. Her granddaughter had been taken by Igierne. Medraut was all that remained to her, and she meant to use all her magic to make sure that the link between them stayed as strong as if the cord still connected him to her womb.

The maiden twirled before her chosen champion. From around the circle came a soft murmur of appreciation as she unpinned the brooch that held her garment at the shoulder and let it fall. The girls sang louder and she swayed, cupping her naked breasts in her two hands. They were small, but perfect, pale nipples uptilted beneath the necklet of amber and gold. Medraut's kilt stood out in a little tent before his thighs, and Morgause knew that the girl was arousing him.

The boy had been told what the reward would be if he did well in the dancing, just as the maiden had been told what to do. Did he understand how the act was accomplished? Surely no lad brought up in the dun could be ignorant—he had seen animals coupling, and humans as well, when the revelry became too drunken in the hall.

Seeing the admiration in Medraut's eyes, the girl smiled and held out her hand. He sent a quick glance of appeal towards his mother, who nodded. Then he allowed the maiden to lead him away to the bower that had been prepared for them. The other girls followed, singing, and the rest of the boys, relieved or resentful, went back to their place in the circle and began to tease the serving girls to give them more beer.

To the queens, they offered mead. Now that her son had met his challenge, Morgause could afford to relax. She accepted a beaker and drank deeply, tasting the fire beneath the sweetness and sighing as the familiar faint buzz began to detach her from the world.

The royal circle began to break up as they prepared to light the great bonfire that had been built in the center of the field where they had held the competitions earlier that day. The sun had set some time ago, and the half-light was fading, soft as memory, into a purple glow. In the east, the waning moon, late rising as an old woman, was just beginning to climb the sky.

Morgause got to her feet, taking a deep breath as the world spun dizzily around her. Her heartbeat pounded in her ears, or was it the Pictish drums she was hearing? Uorepona was retiring with her women, but Morgause felt desire rising within her. Since those few days during Leudonus' funeral, her courses had not come. Surely, if she worshipped the Goddess at the Midsummer fires, she would become fertile once more!

The drumming deepened. From the other end of the encampment a procession was coming, the light of torches danced and flickered across the grass. Morgause joined the throng that was forming a circle around the pyramid of logs. Tinder of all kinds had been stuffed within it, and the whole doused with oil. In times of danger, that frame of tinder would have held a man.

It will burn, she thought, taking her place in the circle, *and so will I. . . .*

Shouting, the torchbearers danced around the waiting pyre, rushing inward and then retreating once more. Again and again they surged, in and back and in again, while the first stars began to prick through the silken curtain of the sky. Each thrust was echoed by a cry from the crowd. The shouting got louder, the dance more frenzied, and Morgause swayed, feeling warmth kindle between her thighs. And then, as if the need of the gathered clans had driven them to climax, the dancers leaped forward and plunged their torches into the pyre.

The tinder caught, flame began to spark along the logs. Morgause felt a blast of warmth against her cheeks as fire billowed skyward. The drumming picked up and suddenly everyone was dancing. She laughed, whirling in place, and then began to move sunwise around the bonfire, hips swaying, arms outstretched.

One of the men caught her eye and began to dance with her, but she did not like his looks, and whirled away. Soon enough a bright-haired warrior found favor, mirroring her movements as they danced together, burning with the same flame. The dance brought them closer and closer, until her bobbing breasts brushed his chest. He seized her then, kissing her hungrily, and staggering like drunkards they wove among the other dancers until they reached the edge of the circle and collapsed together, bodies straining, on the grass.

Her warrior served her well, but when he had left her, Morgause still felt hunger. *Take me!* her heart cried as she began to dance once more, *fill me with your seed, and I will live forever!*

And soon another man came to her, and when she had exhausted him, a third. By this time, her clothing had gone, and she danced clad only in her own sweat and her necklaces of amber and jet. After that, she ceased counting. At one point she lay with two men together, and then, just as the early dawn was lightening the eastern sky, she enticed one of the drummers, for there were not many dancers left upright, though coupling figures still writhed upon the grass.

Morgause drew him down, pulling at his clothing with hasty caresses until he grunted and entered her. He was tired, and took his time at it, but a satiated exhaustion was finally overcoming her as well. She lay spread-eagled on the earth, quivering to his thrusts, until above his harsh breathing another sound caught her attention. She looked up, and gazing past the man's muscled shoulder saw Medraut, his hair glinting in the first light, disgust in his eyes.

"You are a man now—" Morgause said harshly. "This is what men do. Did you think you were so different?" Her partner groaned then and convulsed against her, and she laughed.

It was nearly noon when Morgause woke, her head throbbing from too much mead and her body aching from rutting in the grass. After she had bathed, she began to feel better and returned to the women's enclosure. Medraut was nowhere to be seen, but she recognized his maiden, working with the other slave girls to clear the detritus of the night's carousing away. She was wearing a bracelet that Morgause had last seen on her son's arm.

She ducked beneath the shade of the striped awning to pay her respects to the queen.

"Your son performed well last night," Uorepona said through her interpreter.

"He did. But now the girl may bear his child. Will you sell her to me?"

"If that is so, she would be all the more valuable," came the answer.

"I will be frank with you," said Morgause. "The children of princes must be begotten at the proper time and season. It is not my desire that there should be a child, nor that the vessel that received this holy sacrifice should be tainted by the use of one less worthy. But I cannot dispose of your property."

Uorepona bent to whisper into Tulach's ear.

"Ah—now I begin to understand you. But she is a pretty thing, and has been useful. If I had known your intention, I would have offered you a slave of less value."

"She was the best choice for my purpose," answered Morgause. "I will pay well."

Tulach nodded, and they began the delicate process of haggling.

For the two nights that remained of the festival, Medraut slept with the slave girl and hardly spoke to his mother at all. The girl herself had not been informed of the change of ownership, and when the time came for Medraut to depart, clung to him, weeping. The boy had already tried to persuade Morgause to bring the slave south with them and been refused. When at last they took the road towards the firth, there were tears in his eyes as well.

"Will we come back here? Will they be kind to her?" he asked as the grey waters of the Bodotria came into view.

"She will be well taken care of," answered Morgause, knowing that by now the slave collar would have been replaced by the mark of the strangler's cord. In time, she would tell Medraut that the girl was dead, and he would forget her.

"Why did you bring me here?" muttered the boy. "Every time something good happens to me, you take the joy away. . . ."

"You are a prince. You must learn to master your desires."

"As you did at the festival?" he snapped back, then flushed and looked away.

Morgause took a deep breath, striving to control her temper. This was the child of her heart, and she must not drive him off. "I had a reason," she said finally. "What is important is not *what* you do so much as why."

"And you won't tell me. . . . Will you answer any of my questions? You have taught me things you never showed my brothers, and they are princes too!"

Morgause took a deep breath. Was now the moment she had been awaiting? Now, when he was beginning to understand what it meant to be a man?

"Your brothers are only princes of the Votadini. You are by birth the heir to all Britannia."

Medraut reined in sharply, all color draining from his face, staring at her.

"Your father and I lay together unknowing, god with goddess, in the sacred rite of the feast of Lugus. But the seed that was planted in my belly was that of Artor," Morgause said calmly. "In the old days, you would have been proclaimed before all the people, but Britannia is ruled now by Christians, who would count what we did a sin. Nonetheless, you are Artor's only child."

From pale, Medraut's face had flushed red. Slowly his complexion returned to normal, but his eyes were shining.

Oh my brother, thought Morgause, *you fathered this child, but I possess his soul. . . .*

IX

A Vessel of Light

A.D. 502

In the second year of the new century, sickness stalked the land. It came with vomiting and fever, and when it killed, took by preference the young and strong. The first cases appeared in Londinium, where a few trading vessels still put in at the wharves, and the illness spread along the roads to such other centers of population as remained. Then it began to strike in the countryside. If not so deadly as the great plague that had devastated the empire some forty years before, it was fearful enough to make people flee the towns that were beginning to rise from the ashes of the Saxon wars.

That year, the rains of winter persisted into the summer months, blighting the grain. Those who were still healthy shivered along with the sick and cursed whichever gods commanded their loyalty. And some, especially those who held to the old ways, began to speak against the king.

Artor had never entirely recovered from the wound he got in the Irish wars. He could walk and fight and ride, but not for long. He had moved to Deva to direct the conclusion of the campaigning, but he had delegated its execution to Agricola in Demetia, and Catwallaun Longhand in the north of Guenet. And the British efforts had been rewarded with victory. Even the holy isle of Mona was now free. The only Irishmen remaining in Britannia were those who had given oath to defend it for Artor— Brocagnus in Cicutio, and others farther inland. To Cunorix, who had once been his hostage, he gave the defense of Viroconium, and the Irish mercenary Ebicatos was installed in Calleva.

But to the common folk of Britannia, coughing beneath their leaky thatching and watching the rain batter down the young grain, these great victories were distant and irrelevant. Any warrior could kill enemies, but the power that kept health in man and beast and brought good harvests came from the king.

And the king, or so ran the rumor, was not a whole man. For six years he had been married, and yet his young queen bore no child. Merchants who braved the dangers of the road to come to Camalot bore tales as well as cloth and knife blades and spices. By his life or by his death, it was the duty of the High King to heal the land.

Guendivar took a handful of coins from her pouch and pushed them past the packets of herbs and spices to the peddler. There were more than the pepper and nutmeg, the hyssop and saffron and sandalwood warranted, but she would not haggle. From the smile with which the old man took them, he understood that she was paying for the information as well.

If only, she thought as she gathered up her purchases in the corner of her mantle and set off for the kitchen, she could have acquired so easily some specific for the problems he had described to her. She had gone to Cama's sacred spring to pray, and learned only that she herself would be protected. And last Beltain, she had gone, veiled, to the sacred fires where the country folk still lit them in the hills, and allowed a fair young man to draw her into the woods during the dancing, but she had not kindled from his lovemaking. This year, it was likely to be too wet to even light the fire.

There was some lack in her, she thought sadly, as well as in the king. For her to bear a child would have stilled wagging tongues, no matter who the father might be. But she was a barren field. Since Melguas had seduced her when she was his captive, Guendivar had lain with several men, but despite their caresses, she, whose body throbbed with pleasure at the warmth of the sun on her back or the feel of a cat's soft fur, had responded to none of them. Only with the folk of faerie did she feel fully alive, and her responsibilities often prevented her from seeking them. If Merlin had been with them, she would have begged him to teach her the mysteries she had once refused. But his absences had grown longer in recent years.

She regretted now that shame had kept her from touching the Cauldron. If she had had the courage, it might have healed her, and through her, the king. Artor had spoken sometimes of the Cauldron's power to renew the land. But in the condition he was now he could never spare the time it would take to travel back to the Lake.

She stopped short, still standing on the muddy path between the royal hall and the cookhouse, heedless of the fine rain that was scattering beads of crystal across her mantle and her hair. Artor could not go to the Cauldron, but could the Cauldron come here?

She did not believe that the king could be brought to appeal to his mother, even—or perhaps especially—if it concerned his own safety. But perhaps the Lady of the Lake would respond to a message from the High Queen.

A change in the wind brought her the scent of cooking, and Guendivar began to walk once more. If she wished to appeal to Igierne, she must find a messenger—not one of Artor's warriors, who would insist on getting confirmation from his commander, but someone with the strength and wit to make the journey swiftly, who would carry the message simply because it was the queen's desire.

Folk looked up, smiling, as she pulled open the door. Guendivar had never thought to be glad of her mother's training, but she did understand how to talk to the men and women who served her, and the cooks were always glad to see her, knowing she would make no demands without reason, and do her best to see that they had the resources they needed to do their job. As for the queen, she had noticed that males were more likely to be reasonable when they were well fed, and in this, Artor's champions were no different from any other men.

"A peddler has come, and I have bought out his store of spices—" She spilled the contents of her mantle out onto the scrubbed wooden table.

The chief of the cooks, a big, red-faced man called Lollius, set down his cleaver to look at them. The others clustered around him, chattering as the packets were identified, except for one lad, a strongly built fellow who was so tall he had to stoop to get through the door. He had looked up briefly when she came in, coloring to the roots of his fair hair, and then returned his attention to the bulbs of spear-leek that he was peeling. The sharp scent hung in the air.

That one—thought Guendivar. *He is in love with me.*

That, of course, was not unusual—half of Artor's men dreamed of her, or some fantasy that they gave her name. But this lad, who despite his northern burr spoke better than fit his station, seemed to look at *her*. She moved around the tables as the cook held forth upon the virtues and uses of the spices, examining a vegetable, or sniffing the contents of a bowl, until she stood beside him.

"Will the spear-leek go into the stew?" she asked softly.

"Lollius says it will fight sickness," he answered. "Surely it is strong enough!" He ventured a shy smile.

"You are very deft. What do they call you?"

"Manus—" He flushed again. "*Manus Formosus*," he added, "because of my hands."

"Indeed, they are very well-shaped and beautiful," Guendivar agreed. "But that is not the name your mother gave you, and you did not gain those shoulder muscles using a paring knife, but swinging a sword. Who are you, lad?"

At that, his clever fingers, which had continued to strip the papery rind from the bulbs, fell still.

"I have sworn not to say . . ." Manus answered finally, "until I have been in the king's service for a year and a day."

"That time is almost over," said the queen. She remembered his arrival now, though he had been much thinner then, as if he had been long on the road and lived hard. "When it is done, you will ask my lord for the boon he promised. But until then, your service belongs to me."

"Always . . ." he muttered, though he would not meet her eyes.

"I wish you to carry a message to the Lady of the Lake. But none must know where you go or why. Will you do that for me?" There was a short silence. One of the other servants began to hack vigorously at a peeled turnip, and she drew Manus after her to the end of the table, wondering if the young man had heard.

"My lady, I will go," Manus answered at last.

"I am too old to go racketing about the countryside this way . . ." said Igierne, twisting uncomfortably. The other priestesses she had brought with her from the Isle of Maidens moved around the room, unpacking clothing and hanging cloaks and mantles up to dry, for they had reached Camalot on the wings of an oncoming storm. But the chest at the foot of her bed they left strictly alone.

"Is the bed too hard?" Guendivar patted the pillows into shape as Igierne lay back again. The queen's bright hair was hidden by a veil, and there were smudges of fatigue beneath her eyes. What business did *she* have looking so tired, wondered Igierne? She had not travelled for two weeks in the rain.

"The bed is well enough, but every heartbeat jolts me as if I were still in that damned horse-litter," she snapped in reply. "I thought to find Artor on his deathbed at the very least, but aside from an indoor pallor and some weight around his middle that's due to lack of exercise, he seems well enough. So why did you summon me?"

"You know in what state he was when he left the Isle of Maidens." Guendivar frowned. "He may be no worse, but he is certainly no better. But that is not why I wrote to you. It is the land that is sick, and the people who are dying, and if you do not understand that, then why did you come?"

Igierne sighed, letting go of her anger. "Not entirely because of your message, so you need feel neither guilt nor pride. For the past moon I have had evil dreams. . . ."

"Dreams of water rushing in a great wave, overwhelming the land?" asked Guendivar in a shaking voice.

Igierne raised herself on one elbow, remembering the potential she had once seen in this child—but no, Guendivar was twenty-one, a woman now. Was she at last beginning to grow into her power?

"Just so," she said softly. "I think it is one of the gifts of the queens to have such dreams. But the last of those dreams was different. With the water came a great light, and a voice that sang."

"I heard it too," whispered Guendivar, "though I could not understand the words. But the light came from the Cauldron."

Igierne nodded, her gaze moving involuntarily to the chest. In externals, it seemed no different than any of the others, though it was heavier because of the sheets of lead with which it was lined. Even so, she could feel the presence of the cauldron it held like a buzz along her nerves—perhaps it was that, and not the travel, that had made her so tired. Now she understood why it had always been kept within the shielding earth and stone of the shrine.

"What will you do with it?" the queen asked then.

"I do not know. The Goddess has not told me. We can only wait for her to show us Her will. . . ."

Throughout that night it rained steadily, and yet this was only the harbinger of a storm such as the West Country had rarely known, driven straight from the Hibernian Sea. In the levels below the Isle of Glass the sea-swell would be backing up the rivers and making islands of the high ground. Guendivar could imagine how the marsh-folk must be taking refuge on the Tor while the monks and the nuns chanted desperate prayers to their god.

In the sheltered lowlands, the waters were rising, but on the heights, one felt the full force of the wind. Artor's walls were small protection. The storm swept over the ramparts of Camalot to pluck at the thatching of the buildings within. Of them all, only the great round henge hall that Merlin had designed was entirely undamaged, though drafts swept through its wicker partitions and it flexed and shuddered with each onslaught of the storm. Father Kebi, the Christian priest who had spoken darkly of sorcery when the hall was being built, came meekly enough to take refuge with the others, though he crossed himself when he passed through the door. It was not council season, and many of Artor's chieftains were home on their own lands. With his Companions and his servants and the priestesses from the Isle of Maidens inside, there was just room for them all.

All that afternoon, Guendivar worked with her maidservants to bring food and drink and bedding, and then there was nothing she could do but take her place beside Artor, and force herself to keep smiling as she watched the torch flames flicker in the draught, and wait for the dawn.

Igierne shivered, wondering if the touch she had felt on her cheek had really been a drop of water. With her mind, she knew the hall would not fail them—she could sense Merlin's magic, binding post to pillar and thatching to beam—but her gut was not so certain. Ceincair helped her to settle her mantle more securely around her shoulders, and she thanked her, searching the crowd for her other priestesses as she turned.

"Where is Ninive?"

"She went to the side door, to relieve herself, she said, though I think she really wanted to see the storm," said Ceincair.

Igierne shook her head with a sigh. Bringing the child here had been a risk—in three years Ninive had learned a great deal, but she was still a woodscolt at heart, and if at times she found the serene society of the Isle of Maidens too confining, she must be suffering in this crowded hall. She was young and would take no harm from a wetting, but her absence was not the true cause of the priestess' unease.

It was the Cauldron.

Igierne had believed that the Goddess wanted her to bring it south, but what if her own concern for Artor had deceived her? In Eriu they had a tale of a woman who insulted a sacred spring and caused a flood that drowned the land. Was this a natural storm, or by taking the Cauldron from its spell-shielded sanctuary had she so unbalanced the elements that they would destroy Britannia? If it were required, she would take up the Cauldron with her own two hands and carry it to the sea, but she did not know what she ought to do. If the stakes had not been so high, Igierne would have accepted her panic as a necessary lesson in humility, but as it was, all she could do was close her eyes and pray.

"Lord have mercy upon us, Christ have mercy upon us," muttered the little priest as the storm raged. Betiver, who had hardly said a prayer since his childhood, found himself murmuring an echo, and so did many another of those who had been raised in Roman ways. A flare of lightning outlined the great door, and in another moment thunder clapped and rattled above them. Behind him, he heard men calling on Jupiter and Taranis and even Thunor of the Saxons.

He stiffened, veins singing with the same mingled fear and fury he felt before battle, and instinctively his gaze sought the royal high seat and his king. Artor, every nerve strained at attention as he waited for the next bolt to fall, nonetheless looked far better than the lethargic figure of yesterday. This was the valiant commander Betiver remembered from a hundred campaigns. Guendivar said something, and Artor leaned close to answer her, smiling and reaching out to grasp her hand.

It was almost the first time Betiver could remember seeing the king touch her, but before he could wonder, the lightning and thunder crashed around them once again.

Guendivar felt the warm strength of Artor's grip and squeezed back convulsively as the thunder shook the hall.

Lady, help us! For the sake of the king, for all this land! I will do whatever you ask, but I pray you, shelter us now!

She had never been afraid of thunderstorms, but this one had an unexpected and elemental power. Each flare of lightning showed clearly the unimportance of her own fears and frustrations. There was a life in the storm that had nothing to do with the problems of the queen of Britannia. Oddly enough, that relieved her. She sat, a still point in the midst of fury, rooted to the earth by the steady grip of her husband's hand, and waited for the next convulsion of the skies.

This time, the lightning's flare and the thunder were almost simultaneous. The hall trembled, the great doors sprang wide. Wind howled and every torch was extinguished, but in the same moment a blue iridescence burst through the opening and whirled about, edging post and beam and benches alike with livid light.

"It is Pentecost!" cried Father Kebi, "and the Holy Spirit has come to us in wind and fire!"

But the lightning passed, and the raging of the heavens was replaced by a sudden singing silence. They were in the eye of the storm. They sat, staring, while the blood beat in their ears, and the lightning focused to a single sphere of radiance that floated slowly around the interior of the hall. So bright it was that no man could say who bore it, or if indeed it moved by any human agency at all.

Guendivar stared at that brightness and knew that she was weeping, though she made no sound. From one person to another it passed, pausing for a few moments and then moving on, awarding as much time to a chieftain as to a serving lad, and to the woman who fed the pigs as to the priestesses who had come with Igierne. She saw it surrounding Julia, who crossed herself and then reached out, her cheeks shining with tears.

What are you? Who are you? the queen's heart cried as the light drew closer. Now it seemed to her that forms moved within that radiance; a procession of bright beings was passing through the hall. *What do you want from me?*

And then it was before her, swallowing up all other sensation except the pressure of her husband's hand.

An answer came. *"I am as full of wonders as Faerie, and as common as day. I am what you most desire. Now I stand before you, but only when I stand behind you will you understand Me truly, and be fulfilled."*

And then it seemed to her that the light shimmered, and she glimpsed within it a woman's form. The radiance surrounded her, and she tasted sweetness beyond the capacity of mortal food, though she never afterward was able to say if it had been truly taste instead of sight or sound.

Betiver heard singing, as he had heard it in the great church of Saint Martin as a child. With it came the sweetness of frankincense, filling the hall in great smoking clouds of light. The brightness drew closer, surrounded by a shifting glimmer like the movement of mighty wings. For a moment then he glimpsed a Chalice, through whose pure curve a rose-red radiance glowed.

"I am thy true Lord and thy Commander. Follow Me!" came a soundless Voice, and Betiver's spirit responded in an ecstasy of self-offering—

"I am Thy man until my life's end. How shall I serve Thee?"

"Serve Britannia ... serve the King. ... " came the answer, and he bowed his head in homage.

"Always ..." he murmured, "always, wherever the road may lead. ..."

To Igierne, alone among all that company, the visitation had a tangible form. She saw the glowing silver and knew it for the Cauldron, but as it approached, the image of the Goddess grew out of the low relief of its central panel to a full figure that expanded until it filled the hall.

"Brigantia, Exalted One, power upwelling—" she whispered, "watch over Your children."

"When have I failed to do so? It is you who turn away from Me . . ."

"Did I do wrong to bring the Cauldron to the king?"

"You did well, though a time will come soon when you will question that choosing. But for now, be comforted, for in the flesh your son has his healing, though he will not be whole in spirit until he sees Me in another guise."

The radiance intensified, growing until she could no longer bear its brilliance, carrying her to a realm where the spirit and the senses were one, and she knew no more.

To each soul in that circle the Cauldron came, after the fashion in which he or she could see it most clearly, and each one received the nourishment, in body and in spirit, that was most desired.

And presently folk began to blink and stir, gazing around them as if the painted pillars and the woven hangings, their own hands and each other's faces were equally strange and wonderful. It was no supernal radiance that showed them these things—that Light had disappeared. But the great door to the hall still stood open, and beyond it glowed a clear, rose-tinted sky, and the first golden rays of the rising sun.

Betiver looked exalted, as a warrior who has seen his victory. It was an expression that illuminated the faces of many of Artor's Companions, though they gazed around them now in confusion and loss.

"I had it—" whispered someone, "I almost understood—where has it gone?"

Igierne lay still, with her priestesses around her, but her breast rose and fell, and Guendivar knew that in time she would wake, restored. Father Kebi was murmuring prayers, on his face an unaccustomed peace. The cooks and the kitchen slaves gazed about them in amazement. But Manus' eyes shone like two stars.

Guendivar turned to her husband, understanding that she had seen the thing that was behind the faerie-folk who had once so enchanted her, and the source of their magic, though the images were fading so swiftly that she could no longer say just what it had been.

"What did you see, Artor?" she whispered. "What did you see?"

But he only shook his head, his eyes still wide, half-blinded by looking on too much light. She reached out, and he drew her to him and held her close against his heart, and for that moment, both of them were free.

Morgause gazed at the glory of the new day and cursed the gods. A night of elemental fury, followed by a dawning that might have belonged to the morning of the world, could only mean that Igierne had unveiled the Cauldron. The mysteries Morgause had studied during these past years had taught her how to sense the cycles of the land as once she had charted her own moontides, and she knew that this had been no natural storm. Such lore as she had been able to glean in the years she spent on the Isle of Maidens suggested that the precautions with which the Cauldron had always been surrounded were not only intended to control access to it— they were needed to control its power.

On the night just past they had surely seen the result of letting that power flow free. The ground was littered with leaves, and the woodlands were striped with pale slashes where entire branches had been torn from the trees. As the horses picked their way along the muddy trackway to- wards Camalot, she saw that the homes of men had fared even worse. Huts stood like half-plucked chickens, the bracing of their roofs bared where the thatching had been torn away. At that, the Celtic roundhouses, whose frames flexed with the storm, had fared better than the square-built Roman dwellings, which tended to crumble when the wind ripped off their terra-cotta tiles.

For anyone caught in the open, as she and her escort had been, the hours of darkness had been a nightmare. The cloak Morgause wore still steamed with moisture. Only the yew wood in which they had found shelter had saved them from an even worse battering by the storm.

And then, in the most secret hours before the dawning, the wind had dropped. For a few moments Morgause had wondered if the fury of the storm had transcended her powers of hearing. Then the air grew warmer, and she knew that the stillness betokened a Presence and no mere lack of sound.

Until then, she had hoped her suspicions might be mistaken. Her spy in Artor's kitchens knew only that Guendivar had summoned the Lady of the Lake. But in her dreams Morgause had seen the Cauldron rising like a great moon above the land. And so she had come south—but not swiftly enough to prevent her mother from bringing the Cauldron—the Hallow that was Morgause's birthright—to Artor.

This smiling morning only confirmed her in her conclusion. She felt orphaned; she felt furious. She had learned much from the witches of the Pretani, and yet she was a foreigner among them, always conscious that

they kept secrets she could never learn. With the Cauldron, she could face
them as an equal. During the past few years her desire for it had grown
from an irritation to an obsession. It had to be hers!

There was no point in following her mother to Camalot and confronting her—the damage was done. Still, Igierne must leave eventually. Better,
Morgause thought now, to keep her presence in the area a secret. Just
ahead, the road had been washed out by the storm. Any party attempting
to return to the Lake from the south must detour through the woodland.
The damaged forest could hardly have been better arranged for setting an
ambush. Limbs of alder and oak littered the ground, while sallow and
willow had bowed to the blast. The marsh grasses were half submerged
and the higher ground muddy. At her feet a marigold nodded in the light
breeze. Morgause wondered how it had escaped the fury of the storm.

"We will stop here," she told her men. "Uinist, set a watch and send
scouts around the woods to watch the southern road. Doli, it will be your
task to position the men where they can attack successfully. And when
we have finished, we will flee westward. If there is suspicion, they will
be searching the main road that leads north from Lindinis. No one will
expect us to skirt the higher ground and push towards the sea."

They had three days to wait before her men reported a large party
coming up the road from the direction of Camalot. The horselitter, Morgause knew, must be carrying her mother. But even without the scouts
she would have known who, and what, was coming—she could *feel* the
presence of the Cauldron, as if its recent exercise had increased its power.
She could feel it, and she wanted it, as a thirsty man desires the well.

Morgause ordered her men to do no harm to the Lady of the Lake.
Far better, she thought vengefully, to let her mother live with the knowledge of what she had lost, as she herself had had to live without her
birthright. The others they might kill, so long as they carried off all of the
baggage and gear.

And so she waited while her men disappeared into the woodland, and
just past the hour of noon, she heard women screaming and northern
warcries, and smiled.

"Mother, it was not your fault!" Artor grasped Igierne's hands, chafing
them. "Were it not for my weakness, the Cauldron would never have left
the Isle of Maidens."

"It was my message that brought you—" echoed Guendivar.

"—but my decision to respond . . ." Igierne forced out the words.

She was still shivering, as she had ever since the attack. The men of her escort had been killed, but Ninive had caught one of the horses and galloped back to Camalot for help. That had been at midmorning, and now it was nearly eventide. The Cauldron was gone, and since Uthir's death, she had known no greater disaster. Ceincair wrapped blankets around her and spoke of shock, but Igierne knew it was fear.

"But who *were* they?" asked Aggarban.

"Men, with spears and bucklers and shirts of hardened leather," answered Nest. "The only words I heard were in British as we speak it in the north, but not the Pictish tongue. They could have been reivers, or masterless men."

"I thought all such had been hunted down by the king's soldiers," said Guendivar.

Artor's eyes flickered dangerously. "So did I . . ."

"It does not matter who they are—we must be after them!" exclaimed Gualchmai. "If that was indeed the Cauldron that by the power of the gods came shining through the hall, I would give my heart's blood to see it again!"

"And I!" said Vortipor. Other voices echoed his vow.

When the priestesses returned to the House of Women after that night of storm and glory, they had found the Cauldron safe in its chest, and no one could be brought to admit having touched or moved it. But what else could it have been? Now it was gone, and Igierne shuddered to think of the disaster it might bring in hostile hands.

She coughed and tugged at Ceincair's sleeve. "Did you note, among the riders, any women?"

"I did not," answered the priestess. "Do you think that Morgause—" She fell silent, seeing Gualchmai's stricken gaze.

"Do you think it is not as hard for me to say it, grandson, as for you to hear?" asked Igierne. "But your mother has always desired the Cauldron. In your searching do not forget the northern roads." *And if she has taken it, the fault is mine—* her thought continued. *Morgause begged me to teach her its mysteries, and I refused.*

"We will search *all* the roads, Mother," said Artor. She heard him giving orders as she sank back into the shelter of her blankets.

"And we will take care of you here," added Guendivar, "where you can hear the reports as the searchers come in."

Igierne shook her head. "The quest must take place in the mortal realm, and it is the High Queen, the Tigernissa, who is for your warriors the image of the Goddess in the world. I will go back to the Lake . . . I should never have left it, for I am Branuen, the Hidden Queen, and the quest of the spirit must be directed from there. Perhaps the Cauldron will hear our prayers and make its own way home."

X

The Quest

A.D. 502

Of those who had ridden out from Camalot in search of the Cauldron, the first to return was Betiver. When he came in, Guendivar was in the herb hut, stripping the tender leaves from mints she had gathered in the woods. The sharp, sweet fragrance filled the air.

"Where is the king?" he asked when he had saluted her.

"He rode over to Lindinis. He should be back for the evening meal."

"The king is riding?" he asked, astonishment sharpening his tone.

"He is much better," Guendivar said softly, "and the weather has been fine as well. If anyone doubts that what we saw was holy, surely its works speak for it."

"*I* do not doubt it, though I believe that vision is all that I shall ever see—" He sank down upon a bench, the glow which his eyes always held when he looked at her intensifying. "Perhaps that is why I do not feel compelled to continue trying to see it again."

"What do you mean?" she asked, watching him closely.

"When the Light came to me, what I saw within it was the Chalice of our Lord, and I was fed, and made whole. We have no assurance that

the wonder that moved through the hall was the Cauldron. Igierne's priestesses say they did not take it from its chest, so how could it account for
such a miracle?"

Guendivar frowned thoughtfully. Igierne had told her that she saw the
figure of a goddess emerge from the Cauldron, while Julia's vision, like
that of Betiver, had been of the chalice of the Christian mass. She herself
had seen only luminous forms in a haze of light, and no vessel at all.

"The others who have gone said that the vision left them with an
aching desire to see it again . . ." she said then.

"That is so, but when I had gone away, I found that all I truly longed
for was here."

For a moment Betiver's gaze held hers, and she flinched, seeing his
unvoiced love for her naked in his eyes. She had become accustomed to
recognizing lust or longing when men looked at her. One or two had
threatened to seek death in battle when she would not return their passion.
Only Betiver seemed able to love her without being unfaithful either to
his concubine in Londinium or to his king. She had not realized what a
comfort that steady, undemanding devotion was until she noted her own
happiness at seeing him back again.

His tone flattened as he went on, "But the theft of the Cauldron must
not go unpunished, whatever its nature may be. I have sent word to all
our garrisons, and set a watch upon the ports, and having done so, see no
purpose in continuing to wander the countryside when I could better serve
Britannia by helping Artor."

"The king will be grateful," Guendivar said carefully, "and so will I.
It has been very quiet here, and lonely, with all of you gone."

The power of the Cauldron grew with the waxing of the moon. As
Morgause and her men worked their way cross-country along the edges
of the sodden lowlands, travelling by night and lying up during the day,
she found herself constantly aware of its presence, as even with eyes
closed, one can sense the direction of a fire. But this was a white flame,
cool as water, seductive as the hidden current in a stream. She could feel
her moods change as they had done before her moon cycles came to an
end. At some times the smallest frustration could drive her to fury or tears,
and at others, and these were ever more frequent as the moon grew from
a silver sickle towards its first quarter, she was uplififted on a tide of joy.

Slowly, for the paths were rough and they often had to backtrack and
find a new path, they travelled westward. Presently the folded hills with
their meadows and patches of woodland gave way to a high heathland
where a constant wind carried the sharp breath of the sea. In the days of

the empire, these hills had been well populated, for Rome needed the lead from Britannia's mines. But most of the shafts had been worked out or abandoned when the trade routes were interrupted, and grass grew on the piled earth and rock where they had been.

Morgause and her party moved more openly now, taking the old road to the mouth of the Uxela where the lead ships used to come in. Only once did they pass a huddle of huts beside a working mine shaft, and no one greeted them. At the rivermouth they saw the remains of the port, which now was home only to a few fishermen whose boats were drawn up on shore. Saltmarsh and mudflat stretched along the coast to either side of the narrow channel; at low tide the atmosphere was redolent with their rank perfume. But when it changed, the waters surged up the estuary of the Sabrina, bringing with them fresh sea air and seabirds crying on the wind.

And there, as if the gods themselves had conspired to help her, a boat was waiting.

"Go to the captain and ask where he comes from and what he carries," she told Uinist. "If he is loading lead to take to Gallia say no more, but if he is sailing northward, ask if he will accept a few passengers."

Morgause had meant to follow the estuary and strike across country from there, but as her awareness of the Cauldron grew, it had come to her that perhaps Igierne would be able to trace the movement of power. If the Cauldron were at sea, surely its identity would be masked by that of the element to which it belonged.

And so it was that Morgause took ship with three of her men while the others turned back with the horses, travelling in groups of two and three to divert any pursuers who might have traced them.

Aggarban returned to Camalot on a stretcher. Hearing the commotion, Guendivar came running from the hall. For a moment she thought they had brought her a corpse to bury, then she saw his chest rise and fall.

"We heard there were strange riders in the hills to the west," said Edrit, the half-Saxon lad whom Aggarban had taken into his service. "We caught up with them just as night was falling, and when they would not stop, we fought. In the confusion, my lord and I were separated. It took me too long to kill my man, and by the time I found my way back it was full dark. There was a dead man in the clearing, but I had to wait until morning to track my master. He was lying in his blood with the body of his opponent beside him. I bound up his wounds as best I could, and then I had to find a farm with a cart to bear him. I am sorry, my lady—" He gazed at her with sorrowful eyes. "I did the best I could. . . ."

"I am sure you did," she said reassuringly, one eye on the old woman, of all their folk the most skilled in treating injuries, who was examining Aggarban.

"He was unconscious when I found him," Edrit babbled on, "and by the time I came back with the cart, he was burning with fever. But now that we are here he will better. You will heal him, lady, I know!"

"If God wills it—" she answered cautiously, but he was looking at her as if she were the Goddess, or perhaps only the Tigernissa. Only now was Guendivar beginning to understand that for some, that was almost the same thing.

The healer had finished her examination

"Will he recover?" she asked.

"I believe so, with time and careful nursing," the woman answered her. "He can make back the blood he has lost, and his wounds are not too severe. But I don't like that fever."

No more did Guendivar, but she had promised Edrit that she would try to save his master. For three nights she took turns with the other women to sit by the wounded man, sponging his brow and listening to his mutterings, until the crisis came.

It was past midnight, and the queen herself was half asleep in her chair, when a groan woke her.

"Hold!" Aggarban spoke quite clearly but his eyes were closed. "Don't trouble to deny it—I know ye for a northern man. Is my mother tangled in this business?" There was a silence, as if someone invisible were answering, and then, once more, that terrible groan. When he spoke again, his voice was softer, edged by pain.

"Ah, my mother, you were in the Light that came through the hall— and then you abandoned us. Do you not care for your sons? But you never did, save for that red-haired brat. Festival-bastard, king's-get—oh, I have heard the tales. Can you name *any* of our fathers?" The accusations faded into anguished mutterings.

"Aggarban—" The queen wrung water from the cloth and laid it on his brow. "It's all right now, it's over . . . you must sleep and get well."

His eyes opened suddenly, and it seemed that he knew her. "Queen Guendivar . . . you shine like the moon . . . and are you faithless too?"

She recoiled as if he had struck her, but his eyes had closed. He stopped speaking, and after a few moments she took a deep breath and laying her hand on his brow, found it cool. Guendivar rose then and called the healer to examine him; and after, she went to her own bed, and wept until sleep came.

*   *   *

It was sunset, and the moon, now in its first quarter, hovered halfway up the sky. To Morgause, sitting on a coil of rope beside the stern rail, it looked like a cauldron into which all the light was trickling as the sky dimmed from rose to mauve and then a soft violet blue. When her gaze returned to the sea, she saw the undulating landscape before her, opalescent with color, its billows refracting blue and purple as they caught the light and subsiding into dusk grey when they fell.

The ship flexed and dipped, angling across the waves towards her evening anchorage. She was called the *Siren*, and in a week of travel Morgause had come to know her routine. Unless the weather was exceptionally fine and the wind steady, they put in each night at some sheltered cove, trading for fresh food and water and exchanging news. In these remote places there had been no rumor of the search for the Cauldron, but even here folk had felt the storm and rejoiced in the peace that came after. Those who had not died of the great sickness were on the mend, and hope had returned to the land.

At first, such interrupted progress had frustrated Morgause to the edge of rage. If the first few villages had been able to sell them horses, she would have left the ship and gone overland—to struggle with the hazards of the mountains would have matched her mood. But as day succeeded day, ever changing and always the same, she found her anger dissolving away. Even the presence of the Cauldron did not disturb her, for at sea, she was in its element and there was no separation between them.

Moving across the surface of the waters, suspended between earth and heaven, she found herself suspended also between the time before she took the Cauldron and whatever the future might hold. Her desire for the Cauldron was unchanging, but she wondered now why she had fought so hard to rule the north? Beside its reality, even her ambitions for Medraut paled. She was beginning to understand that whatever happened now, the woman who returned to the north would not be the same as the one who had ridden away a moon ago.

Vortipor rode in to Camalot with ravens wheeling around him. When those who came out to welcome him realized that the round objects dangling from his saddlebow were severed heads, they understood why.

The man who had taken them was brown and healthy and grinning triumphantly. The heads were rather less so, and even Vortipor did not protest too much when Artor tactfully suggested that Father Kebi might be willing to give them Christian burial.

"Though I doubt very much that they deserve it. I was outnumbered, and could not afford them time to confess their sins." He did not sound sorry.

"I trust that they deserved the death you gave them—" Artor observed, but the steel in his tone did little to dim the young man's smile.

"Oh, yes. The cave where they held me was littered with the remains of *their* victims. We'll have to send a party to give them a grave as least as good as that of their murderers."

"They were robbers, then," said Guendivar.

"Most certainly, but they bit off more than they could chew when they captured me! I am sorry, my lady, that I have no news of the Cauldron, but when the Light passed through the hall, what I saw was a Warrior Angel, and I can only serve the truth I see. . . ."

"None of us can say more than that," answered the king, and led him into the hall.

Even on dry land the ground seemed to be heaving. Morgause stumbled and halted, laughing. The *Siren* had put them ashore on the north bank of the Belisama, for her master would sail no farther. A half-day's journey would set them on the Bremetennacum road. It was far enough— no one would think to look for the fugitives here. Indeed, the fear of pursuit had ceased to trouble her, as had any ambivalence regarding her theft of the Cauldron.

It was *hers*, as the gods had always intended, and the time to claim her inheritance had arrived. When Doli began to ask her about the next stage of their journey, she waved him away.

"We can take thought for that tomorrow. Tonight is the full of the moon. Carry the chest up the beach—there, beyond the trees—and let no one disturb me." He was a Pict, and she knew he would not question his queen.

The sun was already sinking into the western sea, and as they reached the spot Morgause had chosen, a rim of silver edged the distant hill.

Swiftly she stripped off her clothes and stood, arms lifted in adoration, as the silver wheel of the moon rolled up the eastern sky. It had been long since she had saluted the moon with the priestesses, but she still remembered the beginning of their hymn.

"*Lady of the Silver Wheel, Lady of the Three-fold Way* . . . ." For a moment she hummed, trying to recall how the next lines ran, then words came to her—"*Thy deepest mysteries reveal, hear me, Goddess, as I pray!*" She repeated the phrase, sinking deeper into the chant, finding new verses to continue the song.

Words of power she sang, to confirm her mastery, but gradually it seemed to her that she was hearing other voices and singing the old words after all, and she did not know if they came from memory, or whether the familiar melody had somehow linked her in spirit to the priestesses who even now would be drawing down the moon on the Holy Isle.

"*Holiness is your abode . . . Help and healing there abound. . . .*" But Morgause had not wanted healing, only power.

"*Ever-changing, you abide . . . Grant us motion, give us rest. . . .*" As she sang the words, her strength left her and she sank down onto her scattered clothing, her breath coming in stifled sobs. It took a long time before she could find a stillness to match that of the night around her.

And all that while, the moon had continued to rise. Morgause sat watching it, and draped her mantle over her naked shoulders against the night chill. She realized gradually that the quiet was a breathing stillness, compounded of the chirring of frogs, the gentle lap of the waves against the sand, and the whisper of wind in the grass. And now, as she watched, she saw the first spark of light on the water, and the moon, lifting ever higher, began to lay down a path of light across the sea.

Ripple by ripple the moonpath lengthened. Moving with dreamlike slowness, Morgause rose, undid the hasps that had secured the chest, and raised the lid. White silk swathed the Cauldron. Gently she folded it back, and drew in her breath at the glimmer of silver inside. It was as bright as if newly polished. The priestesses on the Isle of Maidens used to whisper that it never grew tarnished or needed to be cleaned.

For a moment longer awe kept her from moving, then she lifted the Cauldron and carried it to the water's edge. The tide was fully in, and she had not far to go. The moon was high, serene in a sky of indigo, so bright that the sea showed deep blue as well, but moving across the river came a dancing glitter of light. Still holding the Cauldron, Morgause waded into the water, and when it lapped the tops of her thighs, she lowered the vessel and let it fill.

Here, where the outflow of the river met the tide, the water was both sweet and salt. *It is all the waters of the world,* thought Morgause, bearing the Cauldron back to the shore.

She set it down at the water's edge and knelt behind it. A last wave ran up the sand and splashed her, and then the tide began to turn, but the moonpath continued to lengthen, glistening on the wet sand, until the light struck first the rim of the Cauldron and then the water within, and began to glow.

It was the power she had glimpsed in her mother's ritual, increased a thousandfold. It was all she had ever hoped for, or desired. Heart pounding, Morgause gripped the rim of the Cauldron and looked in.

In the first moment, she saw only the moon reflected in the surface of the water. In the next, light flared around her. She did not know if the water had fountained or she were falling in. Glowing shapes moved around her; she blinked, and recognized the goddesses whose outer images had been embossed upon the Cauldron's skin. The Lady of the Silver Wheel and the Lady of Ravens, the Flower Bride and the Great Mother, the Lady of Healing and the Death Crone, all of them passed before her—but now she perceived them without the veils of form that human minds had imposed to shield eyes unready to gaze on glory.

Morgause floated in the center of their circle, trembling as one by one they turned to look at her. She tried to hide her face, but she had no hands, and no feet with which to run even if there had been anywhere to go. A naked soul, she cowered beneath that pitiless contemplation that beheld and judged every angry thought and selfish deed and bitter word. In that brilliance all her justifications and excuses dissolved and disappeared.

And with them, the separate images dislimned and flowed together until there was only one Goddess, who wore her mother's face, and gazed at her with all the love that Morgause had ever longed for in Her eyes, and then that image also gave way to a radiance beyond all forms and gender, and she knew no more.

Half a hundred of Artor's Companions had ridden out to search for the Cauldron. As the infant moon grew to maturity and then began to dwindle, more and more of them returned. Some, like Aggarban, came back wounded. Sullen and taciturn once his fever left him, Aggarban was recovering well, but there were others who reached Camalot only to die, or who never returned at all, and Guendivar could not help but wonder whether Morgause had managed to curse the Cauldron.

And yet there were others who came back with a new light in their eyes, having found, if not the Cauldron, the thing that gave it meaning. It had taken her some days to realize that Manus, who had accompanied Igierne back down from the north, had gone out to search with the other men. He had not returned either, but she could not explain why she was worried about a kitchen lad.

The days passed, and Cai came in. He seemed more peaceful than he had been, though he refused to say much of his journey.

"I never even found a trace of the theives," he told them. "But I do feel better—perhaps I just needed to get away. . . ."

Peretur had a strange tale of a girl he met by a sacred spring that made Guendivar wonder if he too had encountered the folk of faerie. Gwyhir returned triumphant, having surpassed Vortipor's tally of slain outlaws. Young Amminius did not come back, but sent word that he was leaving the world to join a hermit he had found in the forest.

By the dark of the moon, of the most notable warriors all had been accounted for save Gualchmai. At first, Artor refused to worry. His nephew was widely recognized as the best fighter in an army that was the best in Britannia. Surely he could deal with any foe who might challenge him. But as time went on with no word, men began to remember that even the greatest fighter could be taken down from ambush or overwhelmed by numbers. And yet, even outnumbered, Gualchmai must have given an account of himself that would make the heavens ring.

And then, as the first sliver of new moon glimmered in the afternoon sky, the gate guard sent word that a single rider was coming up the road, a big man with a shock of wheat-colored hair. That hair, and the red-and-white shield, were famous all over Britannia. By the time Gualchmai rode through the gate, the entire population of Camalot was turned out to meet him.

"What is it?" he asked, looking around him. "Is there a festival?"

Whatever he had been doing, it was not fighting, for there was not a mark upon him. In fact he looked younger. The tunic he was wearing was new, made from green linen with embroidery around the neck and hems.

"To look at you, there must be!" exclaimed Gwyhir. "Where have you been, man? We've been worried about you!"

"Oh . . ." A becoming flush reddened Gualchmai's skin. "I didn't realize." There was another pause. "I got married . . ." he said then.

He could hardly have caused a greater uproar, thought Guendivar, if he had announced a new invasion of Saxons. In time of war, Gualchmai was a great fighter. In peace he had gained an equal reputation as a lover of women. One could believe almost any feat in the bedchamber or the battlefield. But not marriage.

He told them about it later, when they were all gathered in the hall. He had taken the northern road, and after a day found the tracks of a large party of men. Gualchmai followed them onto a path that led through a patch of woodland, catching up just in time to break up an attack on an ancient Roman two-wheeled carriage with two women and an old man inside.

"Her name is Gracilia, and she was a widow, living in an old villa and struggling to keep the farm going with three slaves."

"She must be very beautiful . . ." said Vortipor, but Guendivar wondered. It had always seemed to her that Gualchmai was so successful with women just because he found *all* of them beautiful.

"She . . ." Gualchmai gestured helplessly, seeking for words. "She is what I need."

She is his Vessel of Light— thought Guendivar as the conversation continued.

"I thought I had made Britannia safe because there were no more enemies attacking from outside her borders," said Artor at last, "but you are not the only one to have encountered worse evil within. My own injuries kept me confined to Camalot for too long. In the future it will be different, I swear."

For three days, after the full of the moon, Morgause lay half conscious and drained of energy. When Doli, concerned because she had not called him in the morning, had gone to her, he had found the Cauldron back in its chest and his mistress lying unconscious beside it. Morgause had no memory of having put it there, but for some time, her memories of the entire night remained fragmented, like something remembered from a dream.

But certain facts remained with her, and as the days passed, they became clearer.

The Cauldron's power was far greater than she had imagined, and far less amenable to human control, and the Isle of Maidens was the only place where it might be safely kept in this world.

The Goddess for whom it was the physical gateway was also greater than Morgause had allowed herself to believe, and the aspects that she had for the past ten years worshipped were no more adequate to represent the whole than the pallid version she had scorned the priestesses of the Isle of Maidens for honoring.

Her mother loved her, and the hostility between them was as much her own fault as it was Igierne's.

When a week had passed and Morgause could stand up without her legs turning to water, she ordered her men to break camp and took the road north towards Luguvalium. They traveled slowly while her strength was returning, and so the moon had grown dark and was beginning to wax once more when they came to the fortress of Voreda.

That night they sheltered in the barracks, abandoned for nearly a century. In the morning, Morgause led the way to the track that wound westward through the hills.

Once, she had known this way well. Now, she took in the prospect revealed by each turn of the road with new eyes. Never before had she been so conscious that this was a place outside ordinary reality, a realm of mountains sculptured by giants, rising like guardians behind the familiar hills. They hid a secret country that she, always so preoccupied by her own concerns, had never really known.

In body Morgause grew steadily stronger. Her past was forgotten, the future unknown. She greeted each dawn with increasing eagerness, wondering what the new day would bring, until they crested the last rise and saw through the black fringe of pine trees a glint of blue.

Where the trail curved round towards the trees stood an ancient boulder. When she had lived here as a child, the maidens used to call it the throne.

Someone was sitting there.

Even before Morgause could see the figure clearly, she sensed who it must be. *Just as my mother knew that I would be coming,* she thought then. *I always believed that we fought because we were too different, but perhaps it was because we are too much the same. . . .*

With a few words she halted Uinuist and Doli. She dismounted, then and took the rein of the pony to whose back the chest had been bound, and started towards the stone.

As she drew closer, Morgause realized that she was not the only one who had changed. She had never believed that her mother could look so fragile. The sunlight that dappled the ground beneath the pine needles seemed to shine through her.

There was another thing. Igierne was a trained priestess, and Morgause had seen her often in the willed and disciplined stillness of ritual. But there had always been a tension, a sense of leashed power in reserve, like a warhorse on a tight rein. Now, her mother simply sat still.

"I have brought the gift of the Goddess back to its place . . ." said Morgause, letting the lead rope fall.

"You do not say that you have brought it back to *me,*" observed Igierne.

"It is not yours," said Morgause. "Nor is it mine . . . that is what I have learned."

"If you know that, you have learned a great deal."

"I have indeed . . ." Morgause gave a rather shaky sigh and dropped down to sit cross-legged in the dust at her mother's feet. Through the trees she could see sunlight dancing on the blue water, and knew the Lake for another vessel of power.

Manus was nearly the last of the seekers to come back to Camalot, and when he returned, he rode clad as a warrior, escorting a young priestess who had been sent by Igierne.

"I am glad to see you!" said Guendivar when the babble of welcome had died down. "But what is all this?" she indicated his armor. "You have changed!"

He blushed as everyone turned to look at him once more, but all could see that he wore the gear as one accustomed, not like a kitchen boy who had stripped some armor from a body he found by the road.

"Why did the Lady send *you* to guard her messenger?" wondered someone.

Aggarban pointed the stick upon which he had been leaning at the kitchen boy.

"And why are ye wearing a Votadini plaid?"

"Because it is mine!" snapped Manus, reddening once more. "And you are a blind oaf, brother, that never stooped to *look* at the folk who serve ye, or ye would have recognized me before!"

There was a moment of stunned silence, and then Gualchmai guffawed with laughter. "Oh indeed, he has ye there, Aggarban. And in truth he does have the look of Goriat, does he not, Gwyhir?"

"Oh, he does, he does—" agreed the second brother, his gaze travelling upward, "but much, much larger. . . ." And then everyone, even Artor, who had finished his conversation with the priestess, began to laugh.

"And he has outdone you all," said the king, "for Goriat has found the Cauldron, or at least brought word of it. That is the message my mother has sent to me. The sacred vessel is safe in its shrine, and the Lady of the Votadini is there as well."

"*Mother?*" exclaimed the three older brothers, amazement stamping their faces with a momentary identity.

"Was it Morgause who stole it, then?" exclaimed Cai amidst a rising babble of speculation.

"The message does not say, and whatever lies between my sister and my mother is their own affair," Artor said repressively.

"If the Cauldron has been found, then all our wandering warriors can come home," Guendivar said then.

"It will not matter," observed Betiver. "Pagan though it was, I think the Cauldron was what the priests mean by a sacrament—an earthly symbol that points the way to something beyond. That was what we saw that night, and that is what they are looking for."

"Perhaps we have been too successful," Cai said ruefully. "When we were constantly in danger from the Saxons or the Irish, men had no time to worry about much beyond their own skins."

"And now they worry about their sins. . . ." Artor sighed.

"Take comfort, my lord. So long as human beings must live in the world, they will need good government, and heaven does not hold the only beauty of which men dream."

For a moment, Betiver's glance touched Guendivar. Then he looked away. But others had followed the motion, and now she stood at the center of all men's gaze. She heard their thought clearly, though it was not with her physical ears.

"For some, the Vessel of Light is here . . ."

Igierne made her way along the edge of the Lake. Beyond the farther shore, the humped shapes of the mountains rose up against the luminous blue of the night sky like a black wall, shutting out the world. Beyond the lapping of the water and the crunch of her footsteps on stone and gravel, the night was still. The surface was uneven and she moved carefully, using her staff for support, for her stiff joints would not be able to save her if she should fall. It was one of the disadvantages of growing older, and at this moment, she felt both old and tired.

But for the first time in many moons, she was at peace. Her daughter had come home as Igierne's own mother had foretold. Morgause had much to unlearn as well as to learn before the rage and hatred in which she had lived for so many years were entirely replaced by wisdom and love. Igierne did not suppose that their relationship would always be peaceful, but at least they now *had* one, instead of a state of war. And the Lady of the Lake had no desire to break her daughter's will—to rule the Isle of Maidens, Morgause would need to be strong, as she had been strong. But Igierne could foresee, now, a time when she herself would be able to let go.

The Lake slept beneath the stars, reflecting only an occasional flicker of light, and on the island, the priestesses slept likewise. Only the Lady of the Lake was still wakeful. On the eastern point a bench had been set for those who wished to salute the sun or watch the moonrise. With a sigh Igierne settled herself upon it and laid down the staff. Her priestesses came here often when the moon was new or full. But the waning moon was an old woman who rose late and ruled the silent hours between midnight and dawn, and she had few worshippers.

She is like me . . . Igierne smiled to herself. Let Morgause learn to wield the full moon's power. Her coming had freed her mother to study the secrets of the waning moon and the dark, to truly become the raven whose wings shine white in the Otherworld—Branuen, the Hidden Queen.

As if the thought had been a summons, Igierne glimpsed behind the mountain a pallid glow. In another moment, the Crone's silver sickle appeared in the sky.

"Lady of Wisdom, be welcome," whispered Igierne. "Cut away that which I need no longer, and purify my spirit, until it is time for me to return to your dark Cauldron and be reborn. . . ."

THE BOOK OF THE STONE

Contents

ALBA

FODREU
DUN BARA
DUN EIDYN
TRIMONTIUM

DUN BREATANN

CALEDONIAN
FOREST

CAMBOGLANNA
LUGUVALIUM

THE LAKE

BRITANNIA

VOREDA

EBURACUM

MONA

LINDUM

ANGLIA

DEVA

DEMETIA

CAMULODUNUM

GUENET

LONDIMIUM

CASTRA LEGIONIS

AQUAESULIS

CANTUWAREBURH

ISLE OF GLASS

CANTUWARE

CAMALOT

VENTA BELGARUM

DUMNONIA

CALLEVA

GIANTS DANCE

///// = SAXON LANDS

ISCA
DUMNONIDRUM

Prologue

Earth is the mother of us all, and the bones of the earth are made of stone. Stone is the foundation of the world.

Born from fire, stone heaves skyward, taking a thousand forms. Cooling and coalescing, it endures the wearing of water, the rasp of the wind, becomes soil from which living things can grow. The earth convulses, burying the soil, and pressure compresses it into rock once more. As age follows age, the cycle repeats, preserving the bones of plant and animal in eternal stone. The lives of her creatures are but instants in the ages of the earth, but the stone preserves their memories.

Stone is the historian of humanity. The first primates to know themselves as men make from stone the tools that carry their identity. Time passes and the ice comes and goes again. Humans cut wood with tools of stone and build houses, till the soil and form communities. Laboring together, they drag great stones across the land, raise menhirs and barrows, great henges to chart the movements of the stars, and grave them with the spiral patterns of power.

With boundary stones the tribes mark off their territories, but in the center of each land lies the *omphalos,* the navel stone, the sacred center of their world. When the destined king sets foot upon it, the stone sings in triumphant vindication for those who have ears to hear.

But kings die, and one tribe gives way to another on the land. The makers of the henges pass away, and only their stones remember them. Wise Druids incorporate them into their own mysteries. The men of the Eagles net the land with straight tracks of stone, and around the king stones the grass grows high. But the earth turns, and in time the Romans, too, are gone.

But stone endures.

The bones of the earth uphold the world. In the stones of the earth, all that has been lives still in memory.

The Seed Once Sown

The bones of the earth were close to the surface here.

Artor let the horse he was leading halt and gazed around him at grey stone scoured bare by the storms, furred here and there by a thin pelt of grass where seeds had rooted themselves in pockets of soil. Harsh though they were, the mountains where once the Silure tribesmen had roamed had their own uncompromising beauty, but they had little mercy for those footed creatures that dared to search out their mysteries. Sheepherds followed their sheep across these hills, but even they rarely climbed so high.

The black horse, finding the grass too short and thin to be worth grazing, butted Artor gently and the high king took a step forward. In the clear light Raven's coat gleamed like the wing of the bird that had given him his name. The stallion had gone lame a little past mid-morning. The stag they were trailing was long gone, and the rest of the hunters after it. The track that Artor was following now, though it crested the ridge before descending into the valley, was the shortest way home.

A stone turned beneath his foot and he tensed against remembered pain. But his muscles, warmed by the exercise, flexed and held without a twinge. Indeed, at forty-two, he was as hale and strong as he had ever been. And Britannia was at peace after untold years of war.

It still seemed strange to him to contemplate a year without a campaign. He would have to think of something—public works, perhaps—on which his chieftains could spend their energy so they did not begin fighting one another. He had even begun to hope that he might find it in him to be a true husband to Guendivar.

Artor was still not quite accustomed to being able to move freely—for three years the wound that Melwas' spear had torn through his groin had pained him. The night when the Cauldron, borne through the hall of Camalot by invisible hands, had healed them all was scarcely three months ago.

And a good thing, too—half lamed, he could never have made this climb under his own power. But, now, gazing out across a landscape of blue distances ribbed by ridge and valley, the king blessed the mischance that had brought him here. On the Sunday past, Father Paternus had preached about the temptation of Christ, whom the Devil had carried off to a high place to show him all the kingdoms of the world and their glory. Looking around him, Artor thought that the writer of the gospel must have gotten it wrong somehow, for he himself was high king of all he could see, and the sight of it did not fill him with pride and power, but with wonder.

And, he thought as the next moment brought new awareness, with humility. How could any man look upon this mighty expanse of plain and mountain and say he ruled it all?

Below him the land fell away in long green slopes towards the estuary of the Sabrina, touched here and there with the gold of turning leaves. A smudge of smoke dimmed the tiled roofs of Castra Legionis; beyond them he could just make out the blue gleam of the Sabrina itself. Closer still he glimpsed the villa from which the hunting party had set out that morning. To the south across the water stretched the dim blur of the Dumnonian lands. Eastward lay the midlands, and beyond them Londinium and the Saxon territories. Looking north he could imagine the whole length of the island, all the way to the Alban tribes beyond the Wall. The sky to the north was curdled with clouds. A storm was coming, but he had a little time before it was here.

From this mountaintop, the works of humankind were no more than smudges upon the hallowed isle of Britannia, set like a jewel in the shining silver of the sea.

But it does not belong to me— Artor thought then. *Better to say that I belong to the land.*

A nudge from Raven brought him back from his reverie and he grinned, turning to rub the horse behind his swiveling ears, where the black hide sweated beneath the bridle. Men were not made to live on such heights, and at this time of year darkness would be gathering before he reached shelter. He patted the black's neck, took up the reins, and started down the hill.

For years, thought Medraut, these hills had haunted his dreams. But he had not visited the Isle of Maidens since his childhood, and he had convinced himself that the dark and looming shapes he remembered were no more than a child's imaginings. He was accustomed to mountains— the high, wild hills of the Pictish country, and the tangled hills of the Votadini lands. Why should these be so different? But with every hour he rode, the humped shapes grew closer, and more terrible.

They are my mother's hills . . . he thought grimly. *They are like her.* As he dreaded these hills, he dreaded the thought of confronting her. But he was fifteen, and a man. Neither fear could stop him now.

At Voreda he found a shepherd who agreed to guide him in exchange for a few pieces of gold. For three days they followed the narrow trail that led through the high meadows and down among the trees. Like many men who have lived much alone, the shepherd was inclined to chatter when in company, and gabbled cheerfully until a glare from Medraut stopped him. After that, they rode in a gloomy silence that preyed upon the young man's nerves until he was almost ready to order the shepherd to start talking again.

But by then they had reached the pass below the circle of stones, and Medraut could see the Lake, and the round island, and the thatched roofs of buildings gleaming through its trees. He paid the shepherd then and sent him away, saying that from here he could follow the trail to the coast without a guide. He did not particularly care if the old man believed him, as long as he went away. The remainder of this journey must be accomplished alone.

To be alone was frightening, but it carried with it the heady taste of freedom. Throughout the years of his growing, his mother had always been present even when she was not physically there, as if the belly cord still connected them. And then, three months ago, when the full moon hung in the sky, the link had disappeared.

For weeks he had been half paralyzed with terror, expecting every messenger to tell them that Morgause was dead. It was Cunobelinus, riding through the great gates with his men behind him, who informed Medraut that his mother was at the Lake with the priestesses of the Isle of Maidens, and that from now on Cunobelinus himself would serve as regent as well as warleader for the northern Votadini, and rule from Dun Eidyn.

The new regent was civil, and his people treated Medraut as a royal prince when they had time to notice him at all. It was not loss of status that had sent him southward. It was the thing he had learned while he still feared Morgause dead that burned in his belly and had driven him here to confront her. It was hard to admit anger when one was torn by the grief of loss. But his mother was still alive.

Medraut was free to hate her now.

"What are you doing here?"

Medraut spun around, for a moment too astonished not to have sensed that his mother had entered the small, whitewashed chamber where the priestesses had placed him to answer her. Tuned since birth to her presence, he should have vibrated like a harpstring when its octave is plucked. But the link between them was broken; if he had doubted, he felt the truth of that now.

"Without a word, you abandoned me. Is it so surprising I should come to see how you fared?"

Morgause eyed him uncertainly. Clearly she too felt the difference in the energy between them, all the more, he reflected angrily, because she had not been expecting it. Obviously she had not known their bond was broken. Since she went away she had not thought about him at all.

"As you see," she said finally, "I am well."

His eyes narrowed. "You are changed." And indeed it was so, though at first glance it was hard to describe what had altered. Where before she had always worn black and crimson, now she was dressed in the dark blue of a senior priestess on the Isle. But that was only external. Perhaps it was the fact that her high color had faded that made her seem different, or the new silver in her hair. Or perhaps it was the aura of power, almost of violence, that had always surrounded her, that was gone.

Medraut probed with his inner senses, as she had taught him, and recoiled, blinking. The power was still there, but leashed and contained. It occurred to him that her inner stillness might, if anything, make her stronger. A frightening thought, but it would make no difference, he reminded himself. After today nothing she did could hurt him anymore.

His mother's shoulders twitched in a shrug—a subtle, complex movement that simultaneously suggested apology, pride, and oddly, laughter. She looked at him directly then, and he shivered.

"So are you." Her voice was without expression. She asked again, "Why did you come?"

"To accuse you—" The words came out in a whisper, and Medraut cleared his throat angrily. "You killed her. Without a word to me. You had Kea murdered! Why?!"

He had expected disdain or anger, but not the flat incomprehension with which Morgause gazed back at him.

"The slave girl!" he said desperately. "The one I slept with at Fodreu!" How inadequate those words were for what Kea had done for him, making of her forced choice a gift that transformed him, as if by receiving his first seed, she had given birth to him as a man.

For a moment her eyes flashed in the way he remembered, then she sighed. "Did you love her? I am sorry."

He cleared his throat. "Sorry that I loved her, or that you had her put down like a sick dog?"

"At the time . . . it seemed best to ensure that there should be no child," Morgause answered at last.

"Do you truly believe that? Surely you wisewomen could have made sure any child she might conceive was not born!" He shook his head, temples beginning to pound with the sick headache that came from suppressing rage. "If death was a fit remedy for inappropriate conception, you should have hanged yourself on the nearest tree when you found yourself pregnant with me!

"You did not kill her because of my child, *Mother* . . . " all the bitterness Medraut had carried so long poured out at last, "but because of *yours*. I think you ordered Kea's death because you feared I might love her more than you!"

Morgause's hands fluttered outward in a little helpless gesture that snapped the last of his control.

"Well, you failed! I hate you, Queen-bitch, royal whore!" He flew at her and discovered that even without stirring she still had the power to stop him, shaking, where he stood.

"You are a prince! Show some control!"

"I am an abomination! I am what you have made me!"

"You will be free of me . . ." Morgause said tiredly. "I will not be returning to Dun Eidyn."

"Do you think that will make a difference, when every room holds your scent, and every stone the impress of your power. I am going south. Perhaps my *father* will teach me what it means to be a man. He could hardly do a worse job of it than you!"

The long hours in the saddle had given him the time to think it through. His mother had raised him to believe himself meant for a special destiny, and for two years now, he had thought himself true heir to Britannia. But in discovering her treachery, he had begun to question every-thing, and it had come to him that Artor's high seat was not hers to bestow. Neither would the inheritance come to him through Christian law. It was Artor himself he must persuade if he wanted his heritage.

"You will do nothing of the kind!" For the first time, Morgause looked alarmed. "You will stay in Alba and inherit the Votadini lands. Artor has all of your brothers. He does not need you."

"Do you still hate him, Mother?" Medraut asked maliciously. "Or has this conversion to holiness taken even that away?"

"Artor . . ." she said stiffly, "is no longer my concern."

"Nor am I, mother dear, nor am I . . ." Medraut's fury was fading, to be replaced by a cold detachment, as if the rage had burned all his hu-manity away. He liked the feeling—it took away the pain. "I am the age Artor was when he became king, no longer subject to a woman's rule. Will you lock me up to keep me from going where I choose?"

"If I have to—" Morgause said shortly.

Medraut laughed as she left him. But when he opened the door to follow, he found it guarded by two sturdy young women who looked as if they knew how to use the short spears gripped in their hands. In some things his mother's lessons still served him well. His first outraged re-sponse was suppressed so swiftly they scarcely noted it.

"Have you come to protect me? I am afraid my mother still considers me a child." He eyed them appreciatively and his smile became a complicit grin. They were young and, living among women, must be curious about beings of a gender they saw only at festivals. In another moment one of the girls began to smile back, and he knew that she, at least, was not seeing him as a child at all.

"Do not say that it serves me right, after all the trouble I gave you, to find an enemy in my son!" exclaimed Morgause, whirling to glare at Igierne, who sat still in her great carven chair. So still—even in the throes of her confusion, Morgause felt a pang. With each day Igierne seemed to grow more fragile, as if her substance was evaporating like the morning dew.

But her voice, when she replied, was strong. "Have I said so? But if he is rebelling, surely you, of all mothers, ought to understand."

"That is not what has upset me. Medraut has grown as I shaped him, and now that I no longer desire to do so, I am afraid to loose him upon the world."

"You shaped him," observed the third woman, who had been sitting with Igierne when Morgause slammed through the door into the room.

"But the wisefolk of my land teach that the Norns are three. You bear responsibility for what has been, maybe, but now your son is becoming a new person, and he must choose what shall be."

"What do you know of it, outlander?" Morgause spat back. Igierne lifted a hand in protest, and Morgause bit back her next words. She had grown unaccustomed to self-control.

Hæthwæge gazed back at her, unfazed, and Morgause glared. She had been raised to think of the Saxon kind as enemy, and found Hæthwæge's name and race alike disturbing, but Igierne had welcomed her, and in truth, the old woman who had helped to raise the child-king of Cantuware had knowledge they could use.

"I was not happy when the time came for me to give up Eormenric to the care of men—it still seems to me that seven is too young," Hæthwæge said then. "But it is true that a child needs the teaching of both male and female to grow. Let Medraut's father take him if he needs a stronger hand."

There was a short, charged silence.

"His father is the high king. . . ." Through clenched teeth Morgause got out the words.

"Ah—and he is your brother. . . ." Hæthwæge nodded. "I know that the Christians are not understanding about such things."

For a moment longer Morgause stared at her. Then she began, rather helplessly, to laugh. Weathered and bent like an old elder tree, Hæthwæge played the role of a simple village wisewoman very well, but Morgause could see past the mask. If the *wicce* had made light of the danger, it was on purpose, to comfort her.

She was trying to think of a polite rejoinder when there was a knock at the door. In the next moment it swung open and they saw Verica, one of the young priestesses who had been set to guard Medraut.

"He's gone!"

Morgause felt suddenly cold.

"Did he harm Cunovinda?" asked Igierne.

"Oh Vinda is just fine—unless you call a broken heart a wound," Verica said bitterly. "I left her guarding a locked door, and when I returned it was open and she was crying her eyes out because he had persuaded her to open it and then left her!"

It could have been worse, thought Morgause numbly. He could have taken the girl with him, and then killed or abandoned her. Who knew what Medraut might do?

"He is beyond your reach, daughter," Igierne said then, and Hæthwæge added, "He will make his own wyrd now. . . ."

"That is so, but this child's wyrd could shake a kingdom," said Igierne.

Morgause nodded. What that fate might be she dared not imagine, but she knew where he was going, and for the first time in her life, felt pity for Artor.

The high king of Britannia sat in his chair of state to receive the ambassadors. The basilica at Calleva would have been more impressive, or the one in Londinium, but the long chamber that had once been the pride of the commander of the fort at Isca had been restored when he rebuilt the town's defenses. The walls bore no frescoes, but they had been newly whitewashed, with a bright band of geometric designs painted along the top and bottom, and there were touches of gilding on the columns that ran down the nave. The cloaks of the chieftains and princes who had crowded inside, chequered and banded or bright with embroidery, made a vivid spectacle. Artor had been in Castra Legionis for a little over a month, long enough for everyone in the area who had a petition or a grievance to travel here.

But for this audience Artor had chosen to wear the full panoply of an emperor, and the length of time it had been since the previous occasion was marked by the difficulty they had in finding a jewel-sewn mantle in a shade that would match the deep green tunic, with its orphreys and apparels of gold woven brocade. That had been when they made peace with King Icel, said Betiver when Artor tried to remember. Then, thought the king as he tried to shift position without dislodging the stiff folds of the mantle, he had wanted to impress barbarians. Today his purpose was to appear as an heir of Rome's imperium before other heirs of Rome.

Artor felt Betiver stir nervously in his place behind the chair and turned his head to smile reassuringly.

"I should have been the one to welcome him," muttered the younger man. "But I didn't know what to say. Christ! It's been more than twenty years!"

Twenty years ago, Betiver had been an awestruck boy and Artor himself just learning to wield the power of a king, and now the child who had been left with him to seal an alliance was one of the supports of his kingdom.

"He is your father," Artor said aloud. "He will forgive. It is I who should earn his wrath for keeping you here—"

Then the great double doors at the end of the hall swung open, and men moved aside to clear an aisle as the embassy from Gallia marched in.

Johannes Rutilius seemed smaller than Artor remembered, worn by the years. For the men of Gallia, as for Britannia, those years had been filled by fighting. Rutilius walked with a limp now, and there was abundant silver in his hair. But he still stood erect, and the only change in his expression came when he realized who the warrior standing behind Artor must be.

But the formal Latin greetings did not falter, nor did Artor's welcome.

"Is your lord in good health?" he asked. "He must be ripe in years."

Rutilius sighed as he sank into the chair they brought for him. "He is old indeed, and not much time is left to him. Hence this embassy. When I came before, we offered you alliance. Now I come to ask for the help you swore to give. Riothamus is dying, my lord, but Chlodovechus of the Franks is in the flower of his age, seeking to extend the Frankish lands in the north, while Alaric II leads the Visigoths of Tolosa against us in the south.

"The only son of Riothamus, Daniel Dremrud, was killed some years ago, fighting in the German lands. My lord's grandsons intrigue against each other—" He cast a tired glance at a dark young man who stood glowering among the warriors who had escorted him into the hall.

"Budic, there, is one of them. Five years ago, he and his brother Maxentius attacked Civitas Aquilonia in the south of Armorica, to which they had a claim from their mother's father. Now Budic's brother has expelled him in turn. He hopes you will give him an army with which to take it back again."

"Then Riothamus is not asking my support for Budic as his heir?" asked Artor.

"We are Romans," Rutilius said simply: "And the Empire has always prospered when we sought heirs not of the body but of the spirit. Well, I know that it is so—does not my own son cleave to you before his own kin?"

He looked past Artor to Betiver, who flushed painfully, but he was smiling. He gestured towards Artor's mantle. "And I see that you, my lord, also hold to the spirit of Rome—so you will understand."

"What?" Artor said into the silence. "What does he wish of me?"

"You will make up your own mind whether to give aid to Budic in Aquilonia—but Riothamus judges neither of his grandsons of the stature to defend Gallia. The Emperor of the East is far away, and an Ostrogoth rules in Rome. The last strength of the West lies here, lord, in Britannia, where you have driven out the wild Irish and set the Saxon beneath your heel. What will your soldiers do now?"

There was a little stir among the watching warriors as Rutilius looked around.

"Bring them to Gallia, *princeps*, and Riothamus will make you his heir. Your fame is great in Armorica, and the grandsons of the men who followed Maximian will flock to your standard. Come to our aid, my lord Artor, and we will make you Emperor!"

The old dream reborn! Struggling to keep his face impassive, Artor sat back in his chair, the ghosts of Magnentius and Maximian, who had led the legions of Britannia to fight for the Empire, whispering in his ear. Constantine himself had been acclaimed in Eboracum before marching south to his destiny. Aegidius and his son Syagrius had tried to restore the Western Empire in Gallia, but without the resources of Britannia they could not endure. His foster-father Caius Turpilius had brought him up on these tales.

But with the power of Britannia and the blessing of Riothamus behind him, Artor might well succeed where no other man could. He had already succeeded in uniting Britannia, which neither Vitalinus nor Ambrosius nor Uthir had been able to do. Was it for this that he had been healed of his injury? He blinked, dazzled at the prospect. Oh, what a noble dream!

"My lord?" said a voice close by, and Artor forced his attention to the present once more.

"This is . . . an unexpected . . . offer," he managed to say. "It will require careful thought and discussion."

"Of course," answered Rutilius.

"You are my guest, and have scarcely tasted our hospitality," the king said in a more normal tone. "Let Betiver be my deputy, and do his duty to both of us in arranging for your lodging. Budic shall be our guest as well. Whatever the future may hold, I am still king in Britannia, and there are men waiting whose petitions I must hear."

Medraut ran his hand up the kitchen girl's leg beneath her skirts and pulled her back to the bed. "One more kiss—don't waste it. Once we reach the court you may never see me again."

"Let me go, you silly boy—I'll be late—" she protested, but she was laughing, and when he held her down and kissed her, she sighed and melted against him.

It was his turn to laugh, then, as a single smooth movement brought him off the bed and upright. He crossed to the basin he had made her bring to the room, and began to wash. It was little more than a cubbyhole, with a single pallet that would hold two people only if they were very friendly. But if Medraut had not had a knack for gaining what the Irish liked to call the "friendship of the thighs," he would not have been here.

He remembered, with momentary regret, the young priestess who had helped him to escape from the Isle of Maidens. Her kisses had been shy but sweet; it was too bad he had not had the time to take her maidenhead. To seduce one of the girls whose virginity his mother—the hypocrite— was guarding would have been a satisfactory first step to his revenge.

"You are mad," said the kitchen girl, who still lay on the bed with her skirts rucked up about her thighs. "The high king does not hand out places at his court to every nameless wanderer. Even the lord Goriat served for two seasons in the kitchen."

"Oh, I have a name," answered Medraut, "though I have not shared it with you." In truth, he had already forgotten hers. "But Goriat will no doubt remember you. Bring me to him, and you will have done all I require."

"Oh, you *are* a proud one!" she exclaimed, lifting her chin with a mocking sniff. "I will bring you to my lord, and see how far you fly when he throws you out the door!"

Ignoring her, Medraut went to his pack and pulled out the garments he had carried all the way from Dun Eidyn. At the flare of crimson silk, the girl fell silent, her eyes widening as he pulled on breeches of finely woven brown wool and shoes of tooled calfskin whose laces criss-crossed up his calves. The silk unrolled into a tunic, ornamented at shoulders and hem with bands embroidered with silver thread. From the folds of his chequered mantle he pulled a silver torc, and twisting, slid it around his neck, pulled a comb through his dark auburn hair and picked up the mantle.

"Who *are* you?" breathed the girl.

"Take me to Goriat, and you may learn—" Medraut gave her a sardonic smile. "If you remember what I told you to say. . . ."

During the time it took for her to lead him from the cubbyhole in the old barracks through the narrow lanes of the fortress to the wide porch before the audience hall he refused to say another word.

He had learned that Gualchmai was newly wedded, and away on his wife's lands in the south, and Aggarban still on sick leave. That did not matter. It was Goriat who would be most likely to recognize him, and who must stand, however reluctantly, his ally. He had no difficulty recognizing him, standing with Gwyhir in the midst of laughing warriors, for his brothers overtopped most of the other men by a head.

Only the court and its servants could enter. He had to depend on the girl to make her way through the men to Goriat. He saw his brother turn, frowning. Medraut grinned. He had told the girl to say a message had come for "Dandelion," Goriat's baby-name, but he gave it in the dialect of the north. In another moment both of his brothers were pushing through the crowd.

"It's the brat!" exclaimed Goriat, staring at Medraut. Then he looked anxiously around him. "Where's Mother?"

"With the holy bitches at the Lake, rump aimed at the moon and nose in the dust, muttering sorceries. . . ."

"Oh . . . my . . . mother's baby boy has fled the nest indeed!" breathed Gwyhir. "I thought that you at least would stay with her in Dun Eidyn!"

"I thought she would have married you off to a Pictish princess by now," said Goriat. "That's what she tried to do to me!"

He blinked at the venom in Medraut's answering glare, but it was quickly quenched. There was no way, he thought, that Goriat could know about Kea.

"I do hope that Gualchmai was not expecting to stand on the Votadini coronation stone—" he said aloud. "Cunobelinus rules there now, and even for Leudonus' son I do not think he will give it up again."

"And Mother did not fight it? She simply walked away?" repeated Gwyhir in amazement. "Has she gone mad?"

Medraut shrugged. When, he wondered, had Morgause ever been sane?

"I have come south to seek my fortune with the rest of you," he said then. "They say that our mother's brother is throned on high in yonder hall. Will not one of you escort me there and make the introductions?"

The messenger from Dun Breatann had been speaking for some time. Artor focused his attention with an effort as a change in the man's voice heralded a conclusion. "And so, it is the request of my master Ridarchus that the high king journey to confer with him on this matter—"

What matter? Artor had been thinking of Gallia and had scarcely heard. The Irish—that was it—the king of the Dal Riadans had offered alliance. He cleared his throat and straightened.

"I will consider Ridarchus' request, but it is my judgment that the men of Eriu will lie quiet at least until next spring. I will come, but I must consider the needs of the rest of Britannia before I decide on when."

That was a tactful answer that would not bind him, but it was true. Even if he decided to accept Riothamus' offer, he must spend some time settling things here before he could leave. Perhaps Betiver could lead a token force to Gallia. . . .

The man from Dun Breatann bowed and backed away. The crowd

stirred, and he saw the fair heads of Goriat and Gwyhir moving above the others like swans on a stream.

"My lord uncle!" called Gwyhir. "We have brought a new recruit to your service!"

Another man was with them—no, a boy just beginning his growth spurt, with dark red hair. Artor caught the gleam of a silver torc, but the features were a blur. His heart pounded suddenly, as if he had come upon an enemy unaware.

"The last of my mother's sons has come south to join us," added Goriat heartily. "Here is Medraut, lord king. Will you welcome him?"

Artor stared down at the boy's bent head. He had recognized him already, without yet understanding. But how had the time passed so quickly? This boy was almost grown! Medraut did not resemble his brothers, though there was the promise of height in those long bones. But as he began to get up, the king suppressed an instinctive recoil, for in that fine-boned face he saw Morgause. He wondered if his sister had told her son the truth about his parentage.

"Is it your wish to serve me, boy?" His voice sounded harsh in his own ears.

"You shall be as a father to me . . ." answered Medraut, and smiled.

A Circle of Kings

The plain stretched away to a grey line of hills, a new layer of green grass poking through last year's trampled straw. Medraut's mare jerked at the rein, reaching for a bite, and he hauled up her head. Since joining Artor's court the previous autumn he had gotten a lot more practice in riding. Even in winter the high king moved often, and his household went with him. Medraut found these southern lands fair and fat, with their thick woods and fertile fields, but to one accustomed to the harsh vistas of the north, their very luxuriance felt confining.

From Castra Legionis they had travelled south to Dumnonia, and then to Camalot for the Midwinter holy days. He wished they could have stayed there, for Artor's queen had been kind to him. Guendivar's golden beauty reminded him of his lost Kea. But perhaps it was just as well they did not stay long, he thought then. She might not have been so friendly if someone had told her he was Artor's son.

If so, he had only himself to blame, he thought ruefully. Or perhaps his brothers—when they persisted in treating him as if he were still a child there had been a stupid argument, and he had retorted that of them all, only he and Gualchmai could truly say who their fathers had been. They had only agreed to keep silent on the matter after tempers had cooled, but someone must have overheard. He could tell by the way people looked at him, afterward.

He would not make that mistake again, he told himself, shifting in the saddle. And yet perhaps it was just as well, if Artor was going to acknowledge him, that the news did not come as a complete surprise.

They had finished the winter in Londinium, and now they were on their way north once more. But the straightest way to Alba would have been to follow the old Roman road to Lindum, through the Anglian lands. Instead, the royal party had turned west through Calleva to Sorviodunum before taking the track that led north to this plain, the largest expanse of open land in Britannia.

Medraut shivered. It was cold here, with nothing to break the wind. Even at high summer, he suspected, that wind would blow. Now, a week after the Feast of the Resurrection, the wind probed the weave of his cloak with chill fingers and whispered like a restless soul.

Ahead he could see the first of the barrows that marched across the plain. Perhaps that was why the thought had come to him. He grimaced. His mother would have welcomed the ghosts, avid and smiling. His . . . father . . . riding near the head of the line, sat his big black horse easily, his watchful gaze revealing no emotion at all.

Medraut squeezed the red mare's sides and moved forward. There was plenty of room to go abreast, and the warrior who had been riding nearest reined aside to let him bring his mare up next to the king. Artor's grey gaze flickered towards him and away.

Do I make you uneasy, my father-uncle? The king had made him welcome with the greatest courtesy, but there was always a tension between them. Was it guilt that made Artor so wary, wondered Medraut, or had his mother warped him into something that no one could love?

"This is not the way to Glevum—" he said aloud.

"Not the most direct, it is true," Artor replied.

"Then why have we come here? No doubt it is very interesting, but is your kingdom so peaceful that you can waste time sightseeing? I thought you were eager to see the land settled so that you could go to Gallia—"

"When Maximian set out to claim the Imperium, the wild tribes of the north attacked like wolves when the shepherd has left the fold. Until I am satisfied regarding our defenses, I will not leave these shores. Betiver and the men he has taken yonder will bolster Riothamus until I come."

"Betiver is the old man's sister-son—" Medraut observed with a side-long smile. "Are you not afraid that Riothamus will make him his heir?"

"It would be very natural," Artor said softly, his gaze still on the land ahead. "If that should come to pass I would rejoice for Betiver and swear alliance gladly, though I would miss his presence at my side."

Medraut's heart raced in his breast. *He means to make me his heir! I am sure of it, or why would he be talking to me this way?*

"There—" said Artor as they reached the top of the rise. "That is why we have come here."

Medraut straightened, shading his eyes with his hand. To their right, the line of barrows stretched away across the plain. The nearest was larger than the others, its sides still rough beneath the furring of grass, as if it had not yet had time to settle completely into the land.

"These are the graves of ancient kings, gone back to the earth of the land they loved."

Medraut shivered as he heard the echo of his thoughts in Artor's words.

"The mound at the end holds the bones of the British princes whom Hengest killed by treachery on the Night of the Long Knives. My uncle Ambrosius is buried there, and Uthir, my father, as well."

My grandfather . . . thought Medraut. This was a heritage his mother did not share, and he looked at the mound curiously, trying to remember what he had heard about those long ago days when the Saxons had overrun the land in blood and fire.

"Well, you have avenged them," he said then. "The Saxon wolf is tamed."

"For now," Artor agreed. "While we stay strong. But in Gallia, the Franks and Burgunds and Visigoths that were settled on the land to defend it rule the Romans now. They may pretend to adopt our ways, but even Oesc—" He broke off, shaking his head. Then he gestured towards the mounds. "It will take time to make us all one people. When the bones of Saxon and Briton are mingled together with the dust of this land perhaps we may trust them. But it will take time."

Medraut looked at him skeptically. Old men, he had heard, tended to live in the past. The high king looked strong, but there was silver in his beard. Was he getting old?

The wind blew more strongly. From overhead he heard the harsh cry of a raven and looked upward. The bird circled the riders once and then flapped away to the westward. Medraut, turning to track its flight, stilled, staring at the circle of stones that seemed to have risen out of the ground. He had seen Roman buildings that were larger, but never such mighty pieces of stone. Standing proud as kings come to council, their stark simplicity chilled his soul.

Something in his silence must have alerted the king, for Artor followed his gaze and smiled.

"It is the Giant's Dance. Merlin brought me here when I was a boy."

Medraut twitched involuntarily at the sound of that name. The Druid had arrived at Castra Legionis not long after he himself had come there. There was no reason to think it had anything to do with him. Men said that Merlin had always come and gone at his own will—not even the high king could command him. But there was something in the dark stare beneath those bushy brows that made Medraut feel naked. He had been surprised at the depth of his own relief when the old man went away once more.

"Why?" he asked baldly.

Artor looked at him, one eyebrow lifting. "Come and see—" With a word to Cai, he reined his horse towards the stone circle, and after a moment's astonished hesitation, Medraut followed.

As he neared the circle, he looked over his shoulder. The rest of the column was continuing its march across the plain. The boy looked around him nervously. Had the king decided he posed too great a danger and found this opportunity to get rid of him? Reason told him it was unlikely. Artor could have gotten away with such a deed far more easily in Londinium than this empty land where everyone would know.

"Don't be afraid," said Artor, interpreting his hesitation correctly even if, one hoped, he did not divine its cause. He pulled up before a stone that stood in front of the others like a sentinel, slid off of his mount and motioned to Medraut to do the same. "At this time of day and at this season, the circle is not dangerous."

Medraut started forward. As he passed through the outer circle of uprights he flinched. A buzz, more felt than heard, vibrated through his bones.

"Don't you feel it?" he asked as Artor turned inquiringly. "This place is warded."

"Not precisely—Merlin says that a current of power flows between the stones. I have learned to sense such things, but when I was your age I could not feel it. Is this a natural talent, Medraut, or *her* teaching?"

The boy felt himself flushing. No need to ask whom he meant. What had his mother done to Artor to make *him* fear her? He took another step towards the middle trilithon. Everything beyond the circle appeared to waver, as if he were looking at it through glass.

"Wait—" Artor set his hand on Medraut's shoulder. He twitched, but the touch steadied him, and he did not pull away. Together, they moved between the huge capped uprights of the inner circle into the level space within. As they neared the altar stone Medraut sensed a subliminal hum, as if he were standing next to a hive of bees.

Artor's gaze had gone inward. "Power flows beneath the soil as water flows through riverbeds, from circle to circle, and from stone to stone. Here, two great currents cross. It is a place of mighty magic."

"Have you brought my brothers here?" Medraut asked softly after a time, still anchored by the king's hand.

Artor shook his head.

"You know, don't you . . ." Medraut said then, "about me. . . ."

For the first time, he allowed himself to stare at the man who had fathered him. The high king, if not quite so tall as Medraut's older brothers, was still bigger than most men, his torso heavy with muscle. His features were too rugged for beauty, weathered by years of responsibility into a mask of power. But there were laughter lines around the grey eyes that watched him from beneath level brows. Except, perhaps, in those eyes, he could see nothing of himself in this man at all.

The king let go of his shoulder, looking away. "She did not tell me you existed until you were ten years old."

"Why didn't you take me away from her?"

"I had no proof . . ." Artor whispered.

At ten, Medraut had still believed that his mother was good, and that he himself would grow up to be a hero one day. If the king had taken him then, his son might have been able to love him.

"You were newly married and expected to get a legitimate child," he said flatly. "But you have none. Will you make me your heir?"

"You have a son's claim on me, Medraut. But I am more a Roman than a Briton when it comes to the Imperium. They did not make me king because I was my father's son, or not wholly, but because of the Sword."

Artor's hand settled over the pommel of the blade at his side, and Medraut shivered as a new note pierced the circle's hum, so high and clear that it hurt to hear. He knew about the Sword, of course, but it was always the Cauldron that his mother had coveted. This was man's magic, and this too, he thought with a tremor of excitement, was his heritage.

The sound faded as the high king's hand moved once more to his side, and he sighed. "When the time comes, if there is a man fit to hold it, he will become the Defender of Britannia. I will do what I can for you, but I can make no promises."

Medraut frowned. *If you had raised me, Father, I might believe that. But in the North we know that bloodright binds the king to his land. Britannia belongs to me. . . .* But he did not voice those thoughts aloud.

*   *   *

The road from Mamucium to Bremetennacum led through low hills. The king and his escort had spent the night in the abandoned fort above the river. The timber barracks buildings had long ago collapsed, but the gatehouse and parts of the praetorium, where once the commander of the garrison had ruled, still provided some shelter. But it was a cheerless camp, for the town outside the walls had fallen into ruin a generation before.

It was fear that had killed the town, thought Artor, not the Saxons, for there was no sign of burning. The people who had once inhabited those mute, overgrown heaps of rubble had simply moved away. *But they will return . . .* he told himself. *The site on the river is a good one. From these ruins some day a mighty city will rise.*

Something moved in the tangle of hazels that flanked the road. By the time he identified the whistle of arrows Artor was already turning, flattening himself against the stallion's neck as he grabbed for his shield. A horse squealed, rearing. Behind him a man slid from his mount, a black-feathered arrow jutting from his chest. Artor straightened, peering back down the line from the shelter of his shield. He sighed with unexpected relief as he saw that Medraut, who had been riding with Goriat, had his shield up as well.

An arrow thunked into his own, and he realized that the enemy were concentrating their fire on the forward part of the line. Masterless men who lived by banditry, he thought. This time they had chosen the wrong prey.

"Vanguard, dismount!" he cried. "Goriat, take your riders and hit them from the rear!"

He slid from the saddle. A swat sent Raven trotting down the road. Afoot, Artor and his men were smaller targets. Though he had no recollection of drawing it, his sword was in his hand. It flared in the sunlight as he ran towards the trees.

Branches thrashed, scratching his shield. Artor crashed through them, glimpsed a man's shape and thrust. The blade bit and someone yelled. The king jerked the sword free and pushed onward. From ahead came more yelling. He cut down two more enemies before he reached the clearing where the horsemen had caught the fleeing men.

Several bodies lay crumpled on the grass. The fifteen or so outlaws who remained glared at the horsemen whose circle held them, lances pointing at their breasts. The king straightened, shield still up, waiting for his pulse to slow. It was more than a year since he had drawn his sword in anger; the fading rush of battle fury warred with the ache of stressed muscles and the smart where a branch had whipped across his brow.

That felt too good— he thought wryly, *like the first beaker of beer at the end of a long, hot day.* Automatically, he was making a headcount of friend and foe. He noted Medraut's auburn head and once more, tension he had not been aware of suddenly eased. Why? There were others— Betiver or Gualchmai—whom he loved better than he did this sullen boy, but he had never sagged with relief after a fight to find them still alive.

Medraut's face was pale with excitement, his eyes burning like coals. A bloodstained scarf was tied around his arm. Artor swallowed as he saw it. He would have to get the boy some armor. The others were his friends, but this boy was his future. *I have a hostage to fortune now.*

He shook himself and strode forward. "Cai, get rope to bind them."

The prisoners were a sorry lot, stinking and unshaven, clad in tattered wool and badly cured leather. One man was missing an ear. But the weapons they had thrown down looked well-used.

"We're poor men, lord—" whined one of the prisoners, "refugees from the Saxon wars."

"Indeed? It seems to me that you speak like a man of Glevum—"

"My father was from Camulodunum," the complainer said quickly. "He was a sandalmaker there. But the towns are dying, and where shall I practice the trade he taught me now? Surely you'll not be too harsh with folk who are only trying to survive!"

"Work then!" Artor said harshly. "Britannia is full of abandoned farms. Learn to get food by the sweat of your own brows, rather than taking it from better men! You complain that there are no towns!" He shook his head in disgust. "When you make the roads unsafe for honest travelers, how in the Lady's name do you expect towns to survive?"

"Shall we hang them here, lord?" called one of the horsemen, and the robber's face showed his fear.

Artor shook his head. "There is still a magistrate at Bremetennacum. These wretches shall be judged by the people on whom they have preyed."

There was blood on his blade, but it seemed to him he could feel a hum of satisfaction from the sword. Carefully he wiped it and slid it into the sheath once more. When he looked up, he met Medraut's considering gaze.

He says he will not make me his heir, thought Medraut, watching the high king as he took his place on the bench the monks had set out for him, *but why has he brought me along on this journey if not to show me what it is to be a king?*

Gaining Artor's throne was not going to be easy. The gash where the arrow had nicked his arm throbbed dully and he adjusted the sling to support it, remembering the first shock of pain, and the next even more disturbing awareness that the arrow had come from behind. He had said nothing to Artor, for he could prove nothing. But the psychic defenses honed by years with Morgause had snapped back into place like a king's houseguard. It was only when he felt that familiar wary tension return that he realized that traveling with his father, he had begun to let them down.

The fort at Bremetennacum had fallen into ruin, but the townsfolk here had managed to maintain their ditch and palisade. Perhaps the reason was the rich bottomlands of the valley and the river with its easy access to the sea. The land was good here, and so was the trade, but that only made the place a more attractive target for raids. The magistrates who had been seated on their own benches beside him gazed sourly around them, torn between gratitude to the king for capturing the robbers and resentment of the pace at which they were required to deal with them.

They had sentenced the leaders to hang, but the remainder they enslaved, arguing that it was justice that those who had stolen the fruit of others' labors should be denied the use of their own. As the last of the prisoners was marched off to death or servitude, the townsmen straightened, anticipating the feast that had been prepared to honor their visitor.

But Artor was not yet done with them.

"We've cleared out one nest of vermin, and you and your goods will have safe passage to Mamucium and Deva—for a time. But what happens when some other ruffian decides to settle in? I cannot be everywhere, and who will protect you then?"

"We are merchants and farmers, lord, not fighting men—" one of the magistrates said sullenly. He gestured in the direction in which the prisoners had gone. "If we were, do you think we would have suffered that lot for so long?"

"If you cannot defend yourselves, then I will have to appoint you a protector . . ." the king said slowly. "Is that what you desire?"

"Oh, my lord—" Another man looked up eagerly. "Indeed it is! He and his men can stay at the old fort, and—"

Artor's features creased in a sardonic smile, as if he had heard this before. "And who will rebuild it? And what will they eat? An ill-fed man cannot swing a sword—"

"But you—We supposed—" The magistrates wilted beneath his glare.

"I will give you Paulinus Clutorix, a veteran of the Saxon wars, and three experienced men."

"But that's not enough—"

"Very true," Artor continued briskly. "He will take on more, enough to mount a regular patrol, and he will drill every man of fighting age in this valley in the use of arms so that when the time comes to go after a band of outlaws, or you see yon river bobbing with Irish coracles, you'll have a force sufficient to deal with them."

The town fathers were frowning. Their reluctance seemed strange to Medraut, who had grown up among a warrior people who had never been forbidden by the Romans to bear arms. But he could see that some of the younger men were grinning. He had seen his father fight the day before. Now, he was seeing how Artor ruled.

"And there will be a levy, in goods or coin, upon each household for their keep." The townsmen began to protest while Artor's warriors tried to hide their grins. The king held up one hand. "Did you assume I would send gold? How do you think I feed my men if not by taking tithes and levying taxes? At least this way you will know where your tax money goes. And the burden must be shared by everyone—" He gazed sternly around him. "Even the monks who own these rich fields. . . ."

Now it was the churchmen who were protesting. The defending force would have their prayers, of course, but their produce belonged to God. In Artor's face there was no yielding. Medraut suppressed an anticipatory grin.

"Good father, if prayer had protected you from outlaw spears or Irish swords I might agree," said the king. "But I have seen too many burnt monasteries. Pay your share, holy brethren, if you expect my men to come to your call!" He sat back, eyes glinting, a grim smile twitching the brown beard.

Morgause had always said that Artor let the priests rule him, but Medraut saw now that it was not so. He sat hunched on his bench, resting his chin on his fist as he watched. In how many other ways had she been wrong? The priests would call his birth ungodly, but he was *glad* now to be Artor's son. And if he worked hard, he thought, perhaps the wary courtesy with which the high king treated him would change to true affection, and Medraut could prove himself a worthy heir. . . .

"It looks . . . defensible . . ." said Gwyhir, whose turn it was to ride beside the king.

Artor laughed. The firth of the Clutha lay before them, its waters a shifting sheet of silver beneath the high clouds. Low hills ran along the peninsula behind it, featureless as if carved from shadow. The great rock of Altaclutha rose from those opalescent waters like an island, its sheer sides carved by the gods into a fortress that needed little help from man to be secure. From this distance, he could scarcely distinguish the stone walls and slate roofs from the native stone, and the causeway that connected it to the land was hidden from view.

"Dun Breatann is the fortress of the Britons indeed. Since my father's time the Rock has guarded the west of Alba. But Ridarchus is old now, and I do not know his heir."

"It is Morcant Bulc, is it not?" Gwyhir answered him. "Ridarchus' grandson. They came once to Dun Eidyn when I was a child."

Artor nodded. He did not want to think about inheritance, but he supposed it was his duty. Unbidden, the face of Medraut came to mind. He had hoped to learn more of the boy on this long journey up from the south, and to some extent he had done so. But Medraut's smooth surface repelled intimacy. How he could have come from the same nest as his brothers was cause for amazement. Gualchmai could not conceal a thought if he tried. Aggarban's sullen silences were easily read, and the eyes of Gwyhir and Goriat were deep pools into which one had only to gaze to see their souls.

Medraut was clearly doing his best to please, thought the king. He was observant, and did not make the same mistake twice, but he reminded the king of a man struggling to learn a new language, learning by rote the turns of phrase for which he had no natural ear. It was not because he had been brought up in Alba—his brothers had been accepted by Artor's household immediately. But their actions, even their mistakes, came from the heart. One sensed that Medraut's were the result of calculation.

In the next moment Artor shook his head, blaming his distrust on his own fears. Most likely the boy was simply shy.

The high king glanced back along the line. Men who had been slumped in the saddle reined in straying mounts and straightened to military alertness when they felt his eye upon them. Artor turned back, gesturing to Gwyhir to blow his horn. The sound echoed across the pewter waters, and in a few moments he heard an answer from the dun, faint and sweet with distance, like an echo of faerie horns.

The night after their arrival a storm rolled in from the sea, dense clouds wrapping close about the Rock, blanketing the ever-changing tides. For five days they huddled beneath the slate roofs of the fortress, the only thing solid in a dissolving world. But the ale-vats of Dun Breatann were deep, and if it was wet outside, the drink flowed just as freely within.

"I gather that your journey here was not altogether peaceful—" said Ridarchus, indicating the bits of bandage that still adorned some of Artor's men.

Unlike his brother-in-law, Merlin, who still towered like a tree, Ridarchus had shrunk with the years, flesh and bone fined down to a twisted, sinewy frame. Only his nose still jutted fiercely. Sitting there with his black mantle and glinting dark eyes he reminded Artor of a raven. And like the bird, Ridarchus had grown wise with years.

"It's true, and makes your hospitality all the more welcome. But you will find the roads to the south safer, for awhile."

"You should have found them safe already, once you entered my lands," rasped Ridarchus. "I must thank you for ridding me of young Cuil and his band. But his death has won you few friends here, I warn you. He was popular with the common folk, with whom he used to share his booty."

"Do they not understand that without safe roads there will be no trade, and no long-term prosperity?"

"In their children's time, perhaps," said the prince, "but Cuil gave them gifts they could hold in their hands."

"I suppose so, and I am sorry he was killed in the fighting," said Artor, "for he was the brother of a man who captained the queen's guard when we campaigned in Demetia, and after I had drawn his teeth I would have spared him." He blinked as a change in the wind outside rippled through the hangings that were supposed to keep out draughts and sent smoke billowing sideways from the central fire.

"Maybe now news will reach us as well," said Ridarchus. "We hear little of what is happening in the world outside this isle."

Artor shook his head. "The Empire of the West is beseiged on every side. Theoderic rules in Italia, and has just married his daughter Amalafrida to Thraseric of the Vandals in the north of Africa. In Gallia, Chlodovechus is expanding his borders in all directions. Three years ago he captured Burdigala. They say that the Romans in the Gothic lands fought for Alaric, their Gothic ruler, but the Franks were still too strong for them. Alaric made peace and paid Chlodovechus tribute last year."

"Will the Visigoths become a subject kingdom then?"

Artor shrugged. "They have a foothold in Iberia already—they have moved so many times, perhaps they will all pass over the Pyrenaei montes and abandon the south of Gallia to the Franks entirely."

The men who sat around the fire were singing, first the warriors from the dun, and then, as they caught the chorus, Artor's men as well. The king did not see Medraut among them and wondered where he had gone.

"I perceive that this matters to you," Ridarchus said after a moment had passed. "But we have our own troubles here in Britannia. Why do you care what happens across the sea?"

"No doubt Cassivellaunus might have said the same, before Caesar came," Artor observed dryly. "The Franks have proved themselves a war-like people. If they are not controlled now, your son's sons may see them at your gates. And there are men of our blood in Gallia who will certainly be overrun."

"I have heard a rumor that you mean to cross the sea yourself." Ridarchus cocked his head, bright eyes fixing the king.

"Riothamus has appealed to me. But before I go I must make Britannia secure."

"Hence this journey—" Ridarchus said slowly.

The high king nodded. "Until the Saxons came, the wild tribes of the North were always the greatest danger, and after them, the men of Eriu. When I have done what I can for you, I will move on to Dun Eidyn and seek a treaty with the Pictish king."

Ridarchus signaled to one of the serving girls to bring them more ale. He drank, then set his beaker down with an appreciative sigh.

"You can make a treaty for me, too, if you will—" he said then. "You know that for many years there have been men of Eriu on the peninsula of Cendtire, the old Epidii lands. Far from increasing the danger from their kinfolk across the water, I think they have protected us. They have been good neighbors, and we have fought side by side when the Picts got too strong. But perhaps too many of them have left Dal Riada, for in Eriu, Feragussos their king can no longer hold against the Ui Niall.

"Do you see those two men in the saffron tunics, there by the door?" He paused to drink once more and Artor followed the direction of his gaze. "They arrived a little before you did. They are men of Cendtire, ambassadors. Feragussos wishes to move himself and his court and the rest of his clan here from Dal Riada, and offers friendship. I could tolerate their presence unofficially, but I would not enter into such an alliance without your good will."

Particularly, thought Artor, *when I am sitting in your hall.* But he smiled. "I agree. I shall prepare a letter of invitation to Feragussos and welcome him as an ally."

Medraut moved away from the shelter of the inner wall, leaning against the wind. For the moment it had ceased to rain, but there was still enough moisture in the air to sting. He picked his way across the uneven rock to the breast-high wall that edged the clifftop and clung to it, gulping deep breaths of the brisk wind.

To the south and west stretched the silver dimpled waters of the Clutha. Beneath banks of low cloud he could just make out the darker masses of the far shore. He looked up as a gull screamed overhead, flung across the sky by the wind.

Free— he thought, *what would it feel like to be that free?* Even through the thick folds of his woolen mantle he was beginning to feel the chill, but after the odorous warmth of the hall it was welcome. He turned, his gaze moving from the watchtower on the highest point of the Rock to the great hall set into the niche halfway down one side.

He wondered why he felt so constricted—he could find no fault with Ridarchus' hospitality . . . and then, as the gull called again, he remembered the seabirds wheeling above the Bodotria, and realized it was the scent of northern fires, and the sound of northern voices, that had disturbed him. They reminded him of Dun Eidyn.

I can't go back there, he thought, and still less did he desire to revisit Pictland, where he would remember Kea every time he turned around. But where could he run to? Certainly not to his mother. He had proved that he could manage on his own, but then he had been traveling with a goal, a place at the court of the high king. It was no part of his life-plan to become a nameless wanderer upon the roads. He wondered if Gualchmai and his new wife would take him in.

The sky was darkening. He felt one cold drop strike his hand and then a spattering of others as the heavens began to open once more. He sucked in a last breath of the cold, salt-tanged air and started back towards the inner wall. The squall was coming quickly now; he pulled his mantle over his head and hunched against the rain.

After the wall, one gained the next level by a steep flight of steps cut into the rock. Fighting the buffeting of the wind, Medraut had nearly gained the top when he sensed something dark rise up before him, recoiled, and slipped on the rain-slick stone. He flailed wildly, but there was nothing to hold onto. His falling body hit one outcrop and then another, and slid to the base of the wall.

When he came to himself, it was full dark. He hurt all over, and he was *cold*. Head throbbing, he tried to remember what had happened. If someone had pushed him, why had they not taken advantage of his unconsciousness to toss him into the sea? And if not, why was he still lying here? But if no one had seen him fall, surely someone should be wondering where he had gone. . . .

At least he could feel all his limbs. Very carefully, he tried to move. Everything ached, but it was only in his right leg that he felt real pain. Still, it was only going to get colder. He had to get up somehow.

Medraut had made it to the steps when he heard voices from above.

Torches flared wildly as the wind caught them. Someone was calling his name.

"Look, there at the foot of the stair," someone cried.

"Here—" He let his dark mantle fall back so that the paler tunic could be seen. "I'm here. . . ."

He tensed as someone hurried towards him, torch held too high for features to be seen. Then the man was kneeling, and Medraut looked up into the anxious eyes of Artor the king.

The storm had passed, but the high king of Britannia remained at Dun Breatann. The boy, Medraut, had broken his leg, and was not yet fit to ride. That Artor should stay for the sake of a nephew was a matter of wonder, but presently men began to speak of a greater wonder, that the nephew was also a son. Artor knew they said it, though he did not know from whom the rumor first had come. It was inevitable, he thought, that the truth would eventually be known. That did not disturb him so much as the whisper he had heard as he lifted his son in his arms.

"Still living? A pity—if the bastard broke his neck it would be better for the king and for us all!"

Artor had not recognized the voice, and the situation could only be made worse by questioning, but in the dark hours of the night he lay wakeful, remembering the moment of thought, instantly suppressed, in which he had hoped it might be true.

He was still there a week later, when horns proclaimed the arrival of another party and the Saxon lords rode in. When Artor had spoken with them he went to the terrace where Medraut, his leg splinted and bound, sat looking out at the sea.

"Who has come?" asked the boy, looking up at him.

Artor continued to gaze at the bright glitter of sun on water. "The brother of Cynric, who rules the south Saxons now," he said without turning. "I had sent to them before we left Londinium, requesting his son as hostage, to guarantee the peace while I am in Gallia."

"And he has refused?"

Artor shook his head, turning to face his son. "They have brought me the boy. Ceawlin is his name."

"Then why are you troubled? And why are you telling this to me?" Medraut swung his splinted leg down from the bench and sat up, the sunlight sparking on his hair in glints of fire.

Artor stared at him, striving to see past the coloring and the fine bones that reminded him so painfully of Morgause. *Who are you really, boy? What is going on behind those eyes?*

"He desires me to send a man of my own kindred in exchange—'*to increase understanding between our peoples. . . .*'"

"And Goriat doesn't want to go, so you are thinking of sending me?" Medraut asked mockingly, and Artor felt his face grow red.

"Were you pushed down those stairs?" He held the boy's gaze and saw a glimmer of some emotion, swiftly shut away.

Artor had been king since he was the same age as this boy and he thought he knew how to judge men, but Medraut's personality offered no point of attachment on which to build a relationship.

Is that really true? he asked himself suddenly. *Or is it that you have been afraid to try?* He had kept the boy with him for almost a year, but how much time together had they really had?

After a moment, Medraut looked down.

"It was dark and raining . . . I thought there was someone, but I could not really see. I will tell you this, though. The arrow that wounded me in the south came from behind."

"You did not tell me!" Artor took a step forward, frowning, but Medraut's eyes were limpid as the sea.

"I had no proof, my lord, nor do I now. . . ."

Artor stood over him, fists clenching. *What are you hiding?* he thought, and then, *What am I?* He felt a vast weariness as his anger drained away.

"I will send you to the Saxons. Here, I cannot guarantee your safety, but Cynric will guard you like a she-wolf her last cub." *Against his own people, and mine,* his thought went on, *and perhaps against me. . . .*

"If you wish it, I will obey," answered Medraut, looking away.

Artor eyed at him narrowly, hearing in the boy's voice something almost like satisfaction, and wondered why.

III

In The Place of Stones

To travel across the neck of Alba in high summer, neither pursued nor pursuing, was pure pleasure. The Roman forts that had once defended the Antonine Wall were now no more than dimpled mounds, but the road that connected them was still passable. To the north rose the outriders of the highlands, blue with distance, the nearer slopes cloaked like an emperor in heather. Alba was all purple and gold beneath a pale northern sky, and the air had the same sweet tang as the peat-brown waters that rippled down from the hills.

Artor breathed deeply and sat straighter, as cares he had not known he carried fell away. Even the weather held fair, as if to welcome him.

"It won't last," said Goriat. "A week, or two, and we'll see fog and rain so thick you'd think it was winter in the southern lands."

"All the more reason to enjoy it now!" Artor grinned back at him, and Raven, sensing his rider's mood, pranced and pulled at the rein. "By the time the weather changes, we'll be safe at Fodreu."

Cai, who was riding on his other side, made a sound halfway between a grunt and a growl. "If we can trust them—I still say you're a fool to put yourself in their power!"

Goriat opened his eyes at the language, but Artor only smiled. There were times when Cai forgot the king was not still the little foster-brother who had followed him about when they were young. But the blood Cai had shed in his service since then, thought Artor, entitled him to a few blunt words. He was only four years older than the king, but he looked ten, the dark hair grizzled, and his face weathered and lined.

"Maybe so," Artor answered mildly, "but if they can't be trusted, better to find out now than have them break the border while I'm in Gallia!"

"Hmph!" Cai replied. "Or else you just enjoy the risk. I remember how it was when we were boys . . ."

Goriat kicked his horse in the ribs and drew level, brows quirked enquiringly.

"Whenever things got too quiet, Artor would find some fool thing to do. . . ." Cai exchanged rueful smiles with the king.

"Was I that bad?" asked Artor.

"Remember the miller's donkey?"

Artor's grin grew broader.

"What did he do?" asked Goriat in an awed voice.

"Tied the donkey to a threshing flail—"

"It could have worked," protested the king. "We use oxen to grind the corn, after all."

"What happened?" Goriat persisted, obviously delighted to be let in on this secret history.

"The donkey ate the grain and both Artor and I got a beating. They said I should have stopped him, but I knew even then the futility of trying to change Artor's mind when he gets that look in his eye," Cai answered resignedly.

"I learned something, though . . ." Artor continued after a moment had passed. "Beasts, or men, must be led in the direction their nature compels them. It is my judgment that the Picts are ready for peace. I would hate to think that I have grown so accustomed to fighting that I crave it as a drunkard his wine! Still, just in case, Cai has the right of it: there is one whom I have no right to lead into danger—" He glanced back down the line, seeking the gleam of Ceawlin's ruddy hair.

"Goriat, go back down the line and bring Cynric's cub up here to ride with me."

"And that's another risk . . ." mumured Cai as the younger man rode off.

"The child is nine years old! Do you fear he will attack me?" exclaimed Artor.

"He is a fox kit. I am afraid you will love him, and be hurt when he goes back to his wild kin. . . ."

Artor shut his lips, remembering the incident Cai referred to. He was grateful that his foster-brother had not mentioned Oesc, whom he had also made his hostage, and loved, and at Mons Badonicus been forced to kill. *His* little son must be almost eight by now.

He shook off the memory as Goriat returned, the frowning child kicking his pony to keep up with him. Despite his Saxon name, Ceawlin had the look of the Belgic royal house from whom his grandfather Ceretic had come.

Our blood is already mingling, thought Artor. *How long before we will be one in spirit?* He thought once more of the other little boy, Oesc's son, whose mother was Britannic and royal as well.

"Are you enjoying the journey?"

The grey glance flickered swiftly upward, then Ceawlin fixed his gaze on the road once more.

"You will have seen more of Britannia by now than any of the boys at home." Artor saw the frown began to ease and hid a smile. "But perhaps you miss the southern lands. It is in my mind to send you to stay at Camalot, under the care of my queen."

"Does she have a little boy?"

Artor twitched, momentarily astonished that the question should bring such pain. But Ceawlin could have no idea he had even struck a blow, much less how near to the bone. Would Guendivar learn to love this fox kit he was sending her? Or would she weep in secret because her husband had not been able to give her a child?

Goriat was telling the boy about Camalot, where the children of the folk who cooked and kept the livestock and stood guard ran laughing along the walls. The princes and chieftains brought their sons when they came visiting, but they were all British. At least Oesc had had Cunorix and Betiver as companions.

"Perhaps we will send for Eormenric of Cantuware to keep you company—" he said then. "Would you like that?"

Ceawlin nodded. "His father was my grandfather's ally."

Cai raised an eyebrow. This kit was not going to be easy to tame.

Eormenric had been raised by his mother to be Artor's friend. Still, he would need friends among the Saxons as well, and perhaps Ceawlin would be more willing to listen to another boy. They could guard each other's backs against the British child-pack, and Guendivar would win them over as she did everyone.

Artor closed his eyes for a moment, seeing against his eyelids the gleam of her amber hair. When he was at home, the knowledge of how he had failed her was sometimes so painful he longed to be away. But when he was far from her, Guendivar haunted his dreams.

"That is settled, then," he said briskly. "Goriat, I will give you an escort to take the boy south, and letters to the queen." Then, as the young man looked mutinous, "Do not fear for my safety—Cai here will be suspicious enough for two. Besides, was there not some story that the Picts wanted you to husband one of their princesses? I fear to let them set eyes on you!"

At the blush that suffused Goriat's cheeks everyone began to laugh, and Artor knew that his nephew would not dare to protest again.

Two more days of travel brought them a glimpse of bright water to the east, where the estuary of the Bodotria cut deeply into the land. Here their ways parted, Goriat and his men to continue on to Dun Eidyn and then south with the boy, and Artor and his party north to seek the headwaters of the Tava and the Pictish clanholds of Fodreu.

"Goriat was right! The fair weather didn't last," grumbled Cai. "Damn this Devil's murk—how are we to see our road?"

Artor wiped rain from his eyes and peered ahead. The weather had closed in as predicted, and all day they had travelled through a drizzling rain. If they had not come so far already, he might have been tempted to turn around, but at this point he judged them close to Fodreu. If they could find it, he thought gloomily. But they were as likely to get lost going back as keeping on. He could only hope that the Picts kept a good watch on their hunting runs, and would guide them in.

The track they followed wound between rolling hills. From time to time he glimpsed above them the shadows of higher mountains, as if they had been conjured from the mists for a moment, only to vanish away. *Merlin could conjure them back again*, he thought wistfully. *I wish Merlin were here*.

The black horse stumbled on the rocky path and instinctively he tightened the rein, sending reassurance with knees and hands. Raven collected himself and began, more carefully, to move once more. Artor shifted position on the saddle, whose hard frame was beginning to chafe through the damp leather breeches. The superb steel of his sword, kept oiled and clean, would be all right, but it seemed to him that the lesser metal of his mail shirt, inherited from some barbarian auxiliary, was beginning to rust already.

Another few steps and the black horse checked again, head up and nostrils flaring.

"It's all right, old boy—" The king leaned forward to pat the damp neck, and stilled as the humped shapes of shrub and boulder on the hillside ahead of them began to move. Dim figures of men on shaggy ponies seemed to emerge from the hill.

Someone shouted a warning, and Cai kicked his mount forward to cover the king, sword hissing from its sheath. He was swearing softly. Artor himself straightened, reaching for the hilt of his own blade. Then he paused. Why weren't they yelling? And why had there been no preliminary flight of arrows to cut the Britons down?

Behind him his own men were frantically struggling to string their bows. Artor lifted one hand. "Wait!"

Quivering with tension, the Britons stared as the Pictish riders emerged from the mist. They rode swathed in lengths of heavy cloth striped and chequered in the natural colors of the wool, to which the moisture beaded and clung. As they came closer, Artor noted that they smelled like sheep too.

The first riders were small men, wild haired and heavily bearded, but they drew aside for another, tall as a Briton, with the gold torque of a chieftain glinting from beneath his plaid. He halted his pony without appearing to signal and surveyed the strangers from beneath bent brows.

"Who is leader of the southern men?" His accent was odd, but his speech clear enough.

The king moved out from behind Cai, hand still lifted in the sign of peace. "It is I, Artor of Britannia. We seek the dun of Drest Gurthinmoch, King of all the Picts. Can you take us there?"

The Pictish chieftain nodded. "He sent us to find you. Fire and food are waiting, and"—his lips twitched beneath the russet mustache—"dry clothes."

That night, as he sat drinking heather ale at the Pict-king's fire, Artor reflected that Drest Gurthinmoch's hospitality was certainly preferable to his hostility. Artor's stiffening muscles made movement painful, but a good fire and a full belly more than compensated. And above all, he was glad, as the Pictish chieftain had promised, to be dry.

Overhead the peak of the thatched roof rose to unknown distances behind the smoke that veiled it, but at the level of the fire the air was clear. Artor had seen roundhouses in the western parts of Britannia, but never one of such size. In Roman lands, princes preferred the elegant villas, plastered and painted, of the conqueror. The roundhouse that formed the center of King Drest's dun was nearly as wide as the basilica in Calleva, its concentric uprights carved and painted with zig-zags, crescents and circles and the abstract renderings of boar and salmon, bull and horse and bird that he took to be the totems of the Pictish clans.

My ancestors lived like this before the Romans came . . . Artor thought then. He felt as if he had gone into a faerie hill where time ran backwards, returning him to the past.

King Drest was speaking. Artor turned, cupping one ear as if it was the noise, and not his own abstraction, that had made him miss the Pict-king's words.

"It is good my men found you," said Drest in his gutteral accent. The speech of the Pict-lords was as old-fashioned as their hall, a Brythonic dialect mixed with other words from a language he did not know.

"Truly—" Artor replied. "It was ill weather to be out on the moors."

"Ach—'tis of another danger I'd be warning you," the Pict replied. "There are worse things than weather, or even the wild beasts that haunt the hills."

His voice had lowered to a conspiratorial whisper and Artor leaned back, brows lifting, sensing a story.

"You'd not be likely to meet Bloody Comb, now, riding in a large and well-armed company. But he's a fearsome sight to a lone traveler, with his red eyes and his talon nails."

"And a bloody head?"

Drest grimaced. "It is the head of the traveler that grows bloody, when the creature has pelted him with heavy stones, and carries off the blood in his cap to feed."

"Bloody Comb is fearsome," said one of his chieftains, grinning, "but the Hidden People are more dangerous, they that live under the hills."

"It is because they look like men," a big man with fair hair put in. "But old age does not touch them. They steal our women, and change their sickly babes for our own."

"Do they have treasure?" asked Artor, remembering some of the tales he had heard. These stories were known everywhere, though the fair folk seemed to dwindle in the Roman lands.

"Surely, for they have been here since the first mothers of our folk came into this land. They are creatures of night and shadow, but they grow weak and ugly if you catch them in the full light of day. You can kill them then with ease."

"And they would liefer die than reveal where their treasure is hid," said the chieftain. "Like the female we caught two moons past. She screamed, but would say nothing until she died."

Artor looked away, trying not to imagine the treatment that had made the woman, whatever she was, scream. Suddenly the barbaric splendor of Drest Gurthinmoch's dun seemed less attractive. And yet he had to admit that many Romans, if they had believed in the treasure at all, might have done the same.

"I see that I have had a narrow escape," he said in a neutral tone, "and bless the fate that led me to Drest Gurthinmoch's dun. If I had known your hospitality was so generous, I would have come before. . . ."

Without a sword in your hand? The echo of his words showed clearly in the sardonic gleam of the Pict-king's eyes.

"If there has been less than friendship between your people and mine, it was not by my will—" Artor said quietly.

"Nor by mine—" his host agreed. "But we will speak more of that in the morning. For now, let you drink with me, and we shall see if the Britons can match the Pretani as well at the ale-vats as they do on the battlefield!" He began to laugh.

Artor awoke with a throbbing head. When he staggered out to the horse trough he saw that it was well past dawn. His memories of the preceding evening were chaotic, culminating in a tide of boozy good fellowship that had borne him to his bed. *I hope I may not have sworn away half Britannia . . . what* do *they put in their beer?*

By the time he had doused his head in the chill water, he was feeling less like a victim of Bloody Comb, and could greet Drest Gurthinmoch, stout, ruddy, and apparently unaffected by the night's carouse, without wincing as his own words echoed against his skull.

"Come," said the Pict, "we will walk, and complete your cure in the sweet air."

Artor grimaced. His condition must be more obvious than he had thought. Still it was a good suggestion, and as movement worked the stiffness out of his muscles, he began to feel more like a man, if not yet entirely like a king.

The royal dun lay on the shore of the Tava, which here ran deep and smoothly between two lines of hills. Beyond the great feasting hall lay the house of the queen, its thatching dyed in patterns of dull red and green and blue. The gate to the palisade was open, and in the meadow horses and cattle were grazing. At first Artor thought he had been brought out here to admire them, but the Pict-king led him along a path that led towards the trees. Seeing the noble stand of oaks that rose before him, Artor understood that he was being taken to the *nemeton* of the tribe.

The meadow had been full of sounds—the whicker of a pony and the stamp of hooves, bee song, and the twitter of birds—but the *nemeton* was very still. The whisper of wind in the upper leaves seemed to intensify the silence below. As they came to the edge of the clearing, Artor felt a change in pressure and stopped short.

Drest Gurthinmoch turned back, smiling. "Ah, you feel it? That is well, but the guardians will allow you to enter, since you are with me." He reached out, and after a moment Artor grasped his hand.

For a moment the shift dizzied him; then he was in, surrounded by trees that seemed to watch him like the standing stones at the Giant's Dance. And in the center of this circle there also lay a stone.

"The king stone . . ." said the Pict. "When I stood upon it at my king-making, it cried out, for those who know how to hear. Do you not have the custom in your land?"

Artor considered the chunk of sandstone, a rough rectangle of a height for a man to sit on, with an indentation that might have been a footprint on its upper side. In the north, he knew, every tribe had its navel stone, the focus of gatherings. There were sacred stones in Britannia as well, but where the Romans ruled, their use had been forgotten.

"No longer—" he whispered.

"I come here when I need to think like a king. . . ." Drest motioned him to sit beside him on the fallen log that lay at the edge of the clearing. "Why do you want to cross the narrow sea?"

The sudden question took Artor by surprise. No point in asking the old wolf how he knew it—no doubt he had an informant in Artor's household just as there were men in Pictland who carried news to the British king.

"To fight the Franks," he said at last.

"Why? They do not raid your shores."

"Not yet. But they are hungry. One day, like the Romans, they will cross the sea. Better to stop them now than wait until they are in our hunting runs—or yours."

Drest looked thoughtful. "So this war that you go to will defend us as well?"

"That is what I believe." Artor was thinking, he realized, like a Roman, who had protected their borders by conquering what lay beyond them. But the Romans had not known when to stop. He would be wiser.

The Pict-king grunted. "Then I will guard your back."

Artor sat up, skin flushing with the release from tension he had not known he carried until now.

"Blood seals an alliance better than breath," Drest said then. "It is a pity that you have no child."

I have a son. . . . Medraut's face sprang suddenly to mind, but Artor kept silent.

"One of your sister's sons will be your heir, as is right, but she bore several. It would be well if one of them could be sent here to wed one of our royal women." He looked at Artor slyly. "One day your blood might rule the Pretani after all . . ."

Artor licked dry lips. "They are grown men. I . . . cannot choose for them. But I will ask."

"Or a man of your Companions, though my people will not see that as so binding. Still, they would value for his own sake any man trained in your war-band."

Artor's lips twitched at the compliment. "I will ask."

The Britons took care to delay their departure until the sun returned, but Artor was fast learning that the weather this far north could never be relied on. By the time they reached the firth, a chill wind was gusting in from the sea, driving dark clouds that trailed veils of rain. He only hoped that the Picts were more trustworthy than the sky.

Across the firth he could see in silhouette the Rock of Dun Eidyn, stark against the clouds. But the water between frothed with foam. Clearly no boat would ply those seas until the wind died down. The king halted his black horse at the edge of the sand, gazing across the heaving waves with a longing that surprised him. He wanted to be back in his own country!

Cai was saying something about a wood in whose shelter they could wait out the storm, but Artor shook his head.

"I've never liked boats anyway," he said crossly. "We'll ride east, go around."

Cai shook his head gloomily, but he turned away and began to give the necessary orders all the same. The king felt a moment's compunction—he knew that the knee his foster-brother had injured at Mons Badonicus gave him trouble in wet weather, but no doubt it would ache as much sitting still in a damp forest as on the trail.

Yet for a time it seemed that Artor's decision had been a good one. Away from the sea the storm's strength lessened, and the rain diminished to a drizzle as night drew near. Their campsite was damp, but even when wet, the lengths of tightly woven natural wool that King Drest had given them to use as riding cloaks stayed warm.

In the morning the air seemed warmer, and the rain had almost ceased, but before they had been an hour on the trail they wished it back again, for the rain-soaked earth was giving up its moisture in the form of fog. Heavy and clinging, it weighted the lungs and penetrated to the bone. A trackway seemed to lead away to the right; they turned their mounts uphill, hoping to get above the fog and find shelter. The Picts who had escorted them knew the lay of the land, but none had the intimate local knowledge of each rock and tree that could have guided them now.

The mist deadened sound. They had dismounted, and Artor could hear the clop and scrape behind him as Raven picked his way over mud and stone. The sounds of the other horses came faintly, and as darkness fell, their shapes faded to shadows more sensed than seen. Something loomed ahead and the black horse threw up his head, snorting in alarm. Artor pulled him down, stroking the sweated neck to soothe him. It was only a big boulder, though in the half-dark it humped like a crouching beast. He led Raven around it, and pulled him gently after the receding shape of the horse ahead of him.

Or at least that was what he thought he was doing. He had walked for perhaps as long as it takes to boil an egg before he realized that the figure he thought he was following was another boulder. He paused, listening. The heavy whuff of Raven's breathing was the only sound.

For a moment the king stood and swore. Then he fumbled for the strap that held his horn. He set it to his lips and blew, the sound dull in the heavy air. From somewhere above him came an answer. Artor loosened the rein and the horse started forward.

Three more times after that he blew the horn, and each time the reply came more faintly, until he could hear nothing at all. It was full dark now, and if he wandered further, he risked damaging the horse's legs in some unseen hole. The ground was rising. He stubbed his toe on a large stone and stepped aside, finding more even ground beyond it. His mount stopped short, trembling, and Artor yanked on the rein. Even in the thick air he noticed the shift in pressure that told him the rock he had just passed had been no ordinary boulder, but by now he scarcely cared. If the place made the horse nervous, perhaps wild creatures would avoid it. In any case, he could go no further now.

He hobbled the horse by feel and removed the bridle, ungirthed the saddle pad and laid it on the ground next to an upended slab of stone. Another slab lay half over it, and he pulled the pad beneath it, grateful for whatever protection it might afford. Then, wrapping the Pictish plaid around him, he lay down.

It was warmer than he had expected in the shelter of the stones. He felt pieces of something like broken pottery beneath the blanket and swept them aside. Fragments of warning tugged at his memory, but exhaustion was already overwhelming him. He was asleep before he could decide whether he ought to be afraid.

"Artor . . . Defender of Britannia . . . arise. . . ."

Blinking, the king sat up. He was glad to wake from the old nightmare about Mons Badonicus, but as he stared around him he wondered if he had passed into another dream. It was still night, but there was no mist within the circle, and the stones glowed. In their eerie light he saw that his shelter consisted of a slab of rock balanced on two others like a small table, but instead of the bare earth he expected beneath it, he saw a lighted tunnel that led down into the hill.

"Artor, come to Me. . . ."

The king glanced swiftly around him. His horse stood hipslung, head low in sleep. The call was coming from the depths. A whisper from his waking mind warned him not to answer, but the voice was sweet as his mother's croon, golden as Guendivar's laughter. No mortal could have resisted that call.

He knelt, peering into the opening. And it seemed to him that the space grew larger, or perhaps it was he who was becoming small, for what he saw now was a tunnel through which he could walk easily.

The light flared before him. When he could see once more, he found himself in a round chamber carved out of the rock. He could not see the passage through which he had entered, and there were people all around him. With a start of of pure terror, he understood that the Hidden People had him in their power.

Artor took a deep breath and looked around him. They did not seem hostile. Men and women stared back at him. They had the look of some of the men he had seen among the Picts, sturdy of body with grey eyes and thick-springing earth-brown hair, but they were not dressed like any-one he had ever seen. Warriors went bare-chested, their loins wrapped in woolen kilts held by belts ornamented with plaques of gold. Their skin was blue with tattooed designs, and at their sides hung leaf-shaped bronze swords. Other men wore the skins of beasts, clasped on one shoulder. There were women in gathered skirts and shawls, their hair coiled in netted caps, while others wore a single garment held at the shoulders with brooches of bronze or gold.

They had wealth enough, whoever they were—gold at wrist and ear, and crescent necklets of beaten gold. As he wondered, the crowd parted and a man robed in white wool appeared. He had a look of Merlin, but he was smaller, his breast and shoulders sheathed in gold. An imperious gesture summoned Artor, and the people drew back, pointing at his mail shirt and his sword.

At the back of the cave a woman sat throned on an outcropping of stone. There were carvings on it; he realized that the entire cavern was carved in spirals so that its contours blurred. But he had no attention to spare for them now. Those same spirals twined across the ivory flesh of the woman's bare torso—no, not merely a woman, he thought as he noted the diadem of gold that gleamed from the cloud of dark hair—a queen. She was very like Drest Gurthinmoch's woman whom the Picts called the Great Mare. A skirt of painted linen fell in stiff folds beneath her belly; for mantle she had the thick furs of forest cats, the wicked heads drawn over her shoulders. Cairngorms glinted from their slanted eyes.

"Defender. . . ."

Unbidden, Artor fell to his knees. Her eyes, too, were like those of the Pictish queen.

"What do you want of me?" His voice was harsh in his own ears.

"Defend this land—"

"I have done so since I was fifteen winters old."

"Defend your people," the queen said then. "All of them—the children of the earth-folk as well as the children of the sun."

Artor set his hand on the pommel of his sword. "I am pledged to deal justly with all those who dwell in this hallowed isle."

"Men need not justice only, but hope, and a dream." Her voice was harsh honey.

Artor shook his head. "How can I give them that, Lady? I am only a man. . . ."

"You are the child of the Bear, you are the Raven of Britannia," she continued implacably. "Are you willing to become her eternal king?"

Artor remembered the oaths he had sworn at his anointing. But this was something different, a bright shadow on the soul. As he hesitated, she spoke again.

"There is a price to be paid."

"What do you want?"

"Touch the Stone, and you will understand."

For a long moment he stared at her. "Where shall I find it?" he whispered at last.

Her eyes held his, and his head began to swim. "It is here . . ." The stone on which she was sitting began to glow. As Artor reached towards it her words were echoed from all around him: "Here . . . *here* . . . *HERE*!"

The blaze became blinding and he fell into light.

Artor awakened to a sharp and localized pain just above his breastbone. His eyes opened, and he became very still. Beneath his nose he glimpsed the dull gleam of a flint spearhead. His gaze followed the shaft to the man who held it. For a moment he thought he was still dreaming, for the spearman was stocky, with a brown bush of hair like the warriors he had seen in the cavern. Then he realized that this man was weathered, his hide cape tattered with wear. He was not alone.

"Who are you?" one of the other men asked in guttural Brythonic. He was a little better dressed than the others, but Artor recognized his captors as the people of the hills against whom the Pict-lords had warned him. But he knew them now for the first inhabitants of this land. One of the strangers held Raven by the bridle. The black horse stamped and shook his head, but did not try to get away.

Moving very slowly, the king edged away from under the spear and sat up, brushing more potsherds away as he set down his hand. Someone gasped and made a sign of warding.

"I am the Defender of Britannia . . ." he answered, his mind still filled with echoes of his dream.

"You are here all night?"

Artor nodded. The sky was still grey, but the mist no longer hugged the hills. A light wind gave hope that it might clear later in the day.

"I was lost in the mist." He looked around him, only now appreciating the strangeness of his refuge. "This place seemed . . . warm."

"You sleep with the Old Ones. . . ." The speaker showed broken teeth in a grim smile. "This is their tomb."

Artor looked around him at the kerb of stones and the megaliths in whose shelter he had lain, understanding now the nervousness with which they eyed him.

"I am a living man."

The speaker reached out and gripped his shoulder. "He is solid," he confirmed.

"I feel hollow—" Artor added with a smile. "I have not eaten since yestermorn."

"We kill strangers who come into our hunting runs—do the children of the Great Mare not tell you so?" the first man said bitterly.

Artor drew up his knees and rested his arms upon them, knowing it would be fatal to show himself afraid. "If your ancestors did not take my soul, it is not for you to do so."

The speaker muttered to the others then turned back again. "I know you. You are the one they call the Bear, the lord of the sun-people beyond the Wall."

"I am he." Artor nodded, wondering if admitting it was wise. But he found himself compelled to speak truth here.

"Come—it is not well to stay in a place of the old ones, even by day. We give you food and lead you to your men. We watch them since sunset past, but they do not see us there." The grim smile flickered again. "But there is a price."

"There is always a price—" said Artor, remembering his vision of the night. "Name it."

"Speak for us to the children of the Great Mare. They drive us from the best lands already. Let them leave us alone, not hunt us like deer."

Artor looked at them, noting bad teeth and thinning hair, legs bowed with malnutrition. Saxon and Roman, Briton and Pict alike were newcomers next to these, the original inhabitants of Britannia. Slowly he got to his feet and set his hand on the pommel of the Chalybe sword.

"Will you take me as your king?"

The speaker looked him up and down, then grinned. "By star and stone we swear it."

"Then by star and stone I will swear also to protect you."

IV

The Orchard

Artor walked with his mother by the Lake, where the apple orchard came down to the shore. Igierne used a cane now, and paused often to catch her breath. It was clear that movement was painful, but she had refused to stop, nor did she complain. When they came to the long rock that had been shaped roughly into a seat she eased down with a sigh.

He stood behind her, one hand resting lightly on her thin shoulder. Trees circled the lake and clung to the lower slopes of the hills, dark masses of evergreen mingled with bare branches just showing the first haze of spring green. On the apple trees, buds were swelling, their branches framing the shining silver water and the shaded masses of surrounding hills that held the lake like a cup in their strong hands.

Here the bones of the earth showed strong and clear. In the mountains Artor found an enduring beauty for which the changing displays of leaf and flower were only an adornment—like his mother, he thought, whose fine bone structure retained its beauty despite the softly wrinkled skin.

"It is beautiful," Igierne said softly. "It is worth the labor of getting here for the refreshment of spirit it brings."

"I might say the same," answered the king. He had spent much of the winter with Cunobelinus at Trimontium, and seen him sworn king over the Votadini on the stone at the base of its hill, and at the moment the chieftain's foot touched the stone, Artor had heard the earth's exultant cry.

From there he had travelled down the eastern coast. He was glad now that he had decided to follow the old Roman Wall west again to the Isle of Maidens. Since the last time he had seen her, his mother had grown visibly more frail.

"Look—" She pointed towards the eastern hills. "There is the path that leads up to the circle of stones."

"I stopped there on my way," said Artor, remembering the ring of stones. Some had fallen, and the tallest were no more than breast high, as if the earth were slowly reclaiming a broken crown. "How many are there? I counted three times and the answer was never the same."

"Ah, that secret belongs to our Mysteries—"

Artor shook his head, laughing. "Is that why those stones are so— *alive*? Most of the circles I have seen are somnolent as an old dog in the sun. But the ones on the hill hummed with energy."

"And how would you know that?" Igierne turned to look up at him.

Artor kept his gaze on the hills. "Because I have met the folk who built them. Or their spirits. I wish I had thought to ask them *why*!"

"Tell me—" Igierne's voice changed, and Artor knew that she was speaking as Lady of the Lake. Easing down beside her, he began to describe the night he had spent beneath the ancient stones.

"And now," he ended, "it is as if I were growing new senses. I can tell, before I even touch it, if a stone has weathered naturally or was shaped by the Old Ones of this land. Who was the Lady I saw, and what did her question mean?"

"I would guess . . . she was a great queen of the elder days, so bound to the land that after her death she would not pass onward to the Blessed Isles, but became one with the spirits of the earth. To some . . ." she spoke ever more slowly, "that choice is given. They become part of the Otherworld that lies like a veil above our own. In some places the fabric is folded, and there, the two worlds touch."

"That grave was one of them . . ." he said slowly. "As are all the places where the old ones worked the stones. . . ."

"In their proper times and seasons, it is so."

Artor realized that he was gripping the rock on which he sat. Beneath his palm its chill surface was warming; he felt a vibration as if some great beast purred beneath his hand, and let go quickly.

"What is the price? And where is the Stone? The Votadini king stone belongs to that land and that people only. Where is the Stone that will hail me as king and emperor?"

Igierne shook her head. "That is *your* mystery." She looked at him again. "Why do you want to be emperor? Is it the old dream of glory that draws you—the need to avenge Maximian?"

"Perhaps it was . . . at first," he replied. "I admit that Riothamus' offer was flattering. But I have been thinking about it as I travelled around this land. The Lady commanded me to defend all the races who dwell in Britannia, from the earth-folk to the Saxons. At its best, the justice of Rome did that, but the Pax Romana has failed."

"Will you impose a Pax Britannica upon the world?"

"Perhaps, to keep this Island safe, that is what I will have to do. . . ."

Igierne sighed. "You have seen the tumbled stones of the second wall that the Romans built to defend the first one that Hadrianus made. Each conquest only gave them a new land that had to be protected. But in the end they could not hold all they had taken. To be accepted by all of Britannia is more than any other prince of our people has achieved—do you truly believe that you can be a king for Gallia as well?"

"Mother, I do not know. But to bring peace to the world and justice to its peoples, we need a dream. I think I have to try. . . ."

Morgause was in the weaving shed, supervising the younger priestesses as they checked the bags of raw fleece, when she realized that someone was standing in the doorway. She looked up, eyes narrowed against the glare. For a moment he was only a shape outlined in light; then she recognized the broad shoulders and height of the king. Slowly she straightened. For the three days of Artor's visit she had managed to avoid him, but there was no evading a confrontation now.

"Verica, I must go—make sure that any bags that have gotten moths in them over the winter are taken to the other shed. If we wash the fleeces thoroughly, we may be able to save some of the wool."

The younger priestess nodded, and Morgause made her way past the women to the door.

"Ah—" Artor essayed a smile. "I am glad you came out to me. I would rather charge a Saxon army than intrude on all those chattering girls."

"Truly? I thought there was nothing you would not dare—" Morgause fought to keep her tone even.

Artor shook his head. "Will you walk with me? We need to speak about Medraut." Together, they moved down the path.

"What has he done?"

"Why should you ask that? Was he so difficult a child to raise?" Artor asked quickly.

Not at all. Not until the last. . . . Morgause pulled her shawl more tightly around her, for clouds were gathering, pushed by a chilly wind. "Your tone suggested he was in trouble . . ." she said aloud.

"On the way north there were . . . accidents. I sent Medraut to the Saxons—to Cynric at Venta Belgarum, who for the sake of his own cub's life will guard him as the apple of his eye. It would seem that the secret of Medraut's parentage has become known, and perhaps there are some who think they would be doing me a favor to get rid of him."

"Perhaps they are right," Morgause answered bitterly. "Why should you trust him, when he is what I made him? You have good reason to distrust *me.*"

"For the Lady's sake, Morgause! It may be that he should never have been born, but he is here, and he deserves a chance. I have not come here to blame you, but you know him better than anyone else. Like it or not, he is my son. I need to understand. . . ."

Morgause stared up at the brother she had hated so long and so intimately betrayed. He was still strong, but there was silver in the brown hair, and his face was carved by lines of responsibility and power. He seemed so sure of himself, as if he had never doubted his own integrity, that she almost began to hate him once more.

Should I tell him that Medraut is brilliant and seductive and dangerous? How much am I willing to admit? How much do I dare? Looking back, the woman who had manipulated and schemed seemed like a stranger, but the reverberations of that woman's past actions still troubled the present, like the ripples from a cast stone.

"Medraut is very intelligent," she said slowly, shame moderating her words. "But his brothers were too much older—he has been very much alone. He does not have much experience of friendship." She paused. "I raised him to think he had a right to your throne."

"That is the one thing I cannot give him," Artor replied, his gaze troubled. "Even if his birth were acceptable, what I have to leave will go to the man best fitted to hold it. To the man, if there is one, who is chosen by the spirit of this Sword. I told him that. I do not know if he believed me—" he said then, gripping the hilt of the weapon that hung at his side.

"Then you must somehow teach him to be worthy of it," said Morgause, "for that is what he will desire."

Perhaps, she thought, *in rejecting me, Medraut will reject what I taught him.* But she found that hard to believe.

Artor was staring out across the lake, his gaze as grey as the troubled surface of the water.

"One thing I would ask of you—" she said aloud. "To take Gualchmai's daughter with you when you go. She is a wild creature of the moors, not suited by nature for the quiet life we have here. Perhaps Guendivar will be able to tame her."

"Very well. What is her name?"

"She is called Ninive."

At the feast of Christ's Resurrection, the queen and her household journeyed from Camalot to the Isle of Afallon to hear mass at the round church there. Sister Julia was here, having finally taken full vows as a nun, but to Guendivar, it was as if she walked with the ghost of the girl she had once been. Here, Queen Igierne had set her on the path to her destiny. And now she was woman and queen, but not a mother.

Men were beginning to whisper that that strange boy, Medraut, was Artor's son. It seemed to Guendivar that they looked on her less kindly now, holding her a barren stock and no true queen. *But even the most fertile field will not bear without sowing*, she thought bitterly. If she was at fault, it was not because she could not conceive, but because she had not been able to awaken the manhood of the king.

When the service was over, Guendivar walked out of its scented darkness and stood blinking in the sunshine. On this day, the Church forgot its mysteries of blood and sorrow and rejoiced in life reborn, and the world seemed to echo that joy. Above the smooth peak of the Tor, the clouds from last night's storm hung white and fluffy in a blue sky.

The wind was chilly enough for her cloak to be welcome, but there was a promise of warming weather in the heat of the sun. She could not waste such a day cooped up with a flock of chattering women—but she glimpsed two small heads, one red, one fair, by the horse trough, and began to smile.

"Ceawlin! Eormenric! Come walk with me!" she called.

"Oh my lady, wait—" Netta, the woman who tended the boys, came bustling over. "The wretched children have soaked each other with their splashing and must have dry things!"

Eormenric shook himself like a puppy and Ceawlin looked mutinous as Guendivar bent to touch the cloth.

"They are a little damp, truly, but the day is growing warmer. They will dry off soon enough if they run about in the sun!" She turned to the boys. "Will you escort me, my warriors? I would walk in the orchard for awhile."

Yipping gleefully, they dashed ahead, then circled back around her. Fox-red Ceawlin had the features of his Belgic forebears, but in thought and speech he was all Saxon. It was Eormenric, in appearance a lanky, blond reincarnation of Oesc, his father, who was most fluent in the British tongue and easy with their ways. That was the doing of Rigana, who had been born a princess of Cantium and now was Cantuware's queen. Artor had been wise to ask her to send her son to Camalot. The boys had become fast friends.

The apple trees were leafing out, with only a few flowered branches remaining to bear witness to their former snowy glory. Guendivar had pulled one down to smell the scent when she heard a cry behind her.

Ceawlin lay sprawled on the grass, like a doll dropped by some child in play. Eormenric bent over him, then straightened, gazing at Guendivar in mute appeal.

"He fell out of the tree—"

Guendivar knelt. She could feel her own heart thumping alarm as she felt at his throat for the pulse that beat in answer to her own.

"Did he fall on his head?" she asked, sitting back on her heels.

"I think so—" answered Eormenric. "Is he going to die?"

"Not today," she said, hoping it was true. "But he will have a sore head when he wakes up." Carefully she felt his limbs.

Ceawlin stirred, whimpering. "*Modor. . . .*"

It needed no knowledge of Saxon to interpret that. Guendivar settled herself with her back to the tree trunk and gathered the boy against her breast. For a moment she remembered how the priest had wept over the image of Christ's mother with her dead son in her arms. But this boy would not die—she would not allow it! She tightened her grip on Ceawlin, and as naturally as a puppy, Eormenric snuggled beneath her other arm.

"It will be all right," she murmured. "All will be well. . . ."

The tree at her back was a steady support, the scent of crushed grass intoxicating. Guendivar leaned into its strength, and suddenly it seemed to her as if she had become the tree, rooting herself in the awakening earth and drawing up strength through her spine. Power welled through her from the depths of the earth to the child in her arms.

Ceawlin stirred again, and this time when his eyes opened there was recognition in his gaze. She waited for him to tense and pull away, but he only sighed and burrowed more comfortably against her.

She steadied her breathing, willing the shift in vision that would show her the spirits of the apple trees. The world began to change around her, but the shift was going too fast. Held in this moment, she went deeper than ever before. She *was* the solid earth and the warmth of the sunlight, the wind that stirred her hair and the pliant strength of the tree, a woman's body and the children in her arms, all part of a single whole. Life was reborn from the womb of earth with the springtime as the Christian god came forth from his earthen tomb. And in that moment, Guendivar understood that she was not barren at all.

She did not count the passing of time, but surely the sun had not moved far across the sky when she became aware that someone was speaking. For a time she simply listened to the musical rise and fall of the language, for it was a tongue she did not know. The sound seemed to come from all around her, as if the wind were speaking in the leaves.

"Come to the holy temple of the virgins
Where the pleasant grove of apple trees
Circles an altar smoking with frankincense."

The words became more distinct, and she realized that now she was hearing the British tongue.

"The roses leave shadow on the ground
And cool springs murmur through apple branches
Where shuddering leaves pour down profound sleep."

It must be true, thought Guendivar, for Ceawlin, eyes closed and breathing even, had passed into a healing slumber, and even Eormenric lay quiet against her breast. But her expanded soul was returning to the confines of her body. She heard with her mortal senses, therefore the words she was hearing must have some tangible source.

"In that meadow where horses have grown glossy,
And all spring flowers grow wild,
The anise shoots fill the air with aroma."

She straightened a little, turning her head, and saw a man, his limbs as gnarled and brown as the branches, sitting in one of the apple trees. In that first moment, the sight seemed quite normal, as if he had grown there. And so she was not startled when returning awareness resolved the abstract pattern of bearded face and skin-clad body into the figure of Merlin.

Seeing her gaze upon him, the Druid slid down from the tree and took up the staff that had been leaning against it.

"And there our queen Aphrodite pours
Celestial nectar in the gold cups,
Which she fills gracefully with sudden joy."

"Heathen words . . ." Guendivar said softly, "for such a holy day."

"Holy words, first sung for the Goddess by a lovely lady in the Grecian isles. In those days it was the death of Her lover Attis that the women mourned in the spring. The gods die and are reborn, but the Goddess, like the earth, is eternal. You know this to be true—I see the understanding in your eyes." Merlin came closer and squatted on his haunches, the staff leaning against his shoulder.

"Perhaps . . . but I am no goddess, to be hailed with such words."

"Are you not?" He laughed softly. "At least you are Her image, sitting there with your sons in your arms."

Guendivar looked at him in alarm, remembering the sense of union she had experienced only a few moments ago. How could the old man know what she was feeling? The last time he had tried to talk to her she had run from him, but she could not disturb the sleeping boys.

"And you are Her image to your husband's warriors, their Lady and Queen."

"But not to my husband," Guendivar said bitterly.

"All things change, even he, even you. Is it not so?"

"Even you?" she asked then.

He laughed softly, long fingers stroking lightly over the staff that lay against his arm. Its head was swathed in yellowed linen, but she could see now that strange symbols were carved up and down the shaft.

"I have been a salmon in the stream and a stag upon the hill. I have been an acorn in the forest, and the falcon floating in the wind. I was an old man once, but now I am as young as the cub just born this spring. . . ."

It was true, she thought. He had not moved like an old man, though the hair that covered his body was grizzled as a wolf's pelt, and streaks of pure silver glinted in his hair and beard.

"I think sometimes that I will be old without ever having seen my prime, passing directly from virginity to senility . . ." Guendivar said then.

"Do you believe that to bear in the body is the only fertility? I was a father to Artor, though another man begot him. It is not what you receive, but what you give, that will grant you fulfillment. You must become a conduit for power."

Ceawlin stirred, and she soothed him with a gentle touch. "How?" she asked when the boy had settled once more.

"You have done it already, when you brought the earth power through the tree. Build up an image of the Lady of Life standing behind you, and you will become a doorway through which Her force can flow."

Did she dare to believe it might be so? She would have questioned him further, but Eormenric opened his eyes and seeing Merlin, sat up, staring. Ceawlin, disturbed by his motion, began to wake as well.

"What's *he* doing here?" whispered Eormenric.

"He is wise in all the ancient magics," Guendivar answered. "He will make sure that your friend is well. . . ."

And Merlin, taking his cue, rose in a single smooth motion and came to her, passing his hands above the boy's body and resting them on his brow. Ceawlin, who lay with eyes rolling like those of a frightened horse, whispered something in the Saxon tongue.

"What did he say?" Guendivar asked Eormenric.

"He called the old man by the name of Woden and asked if he had come to take him to his hall . . ."

Merlin grunted and got to his feet. "Nay, child, I am a prophet sometimes, but no god." He stood looking down at the boy, his face growing grim. "I foresee for you a long life, and many victories."

His dark gaze lifted to meet hers, and Guendivar recoiled, wondering what it was he had seen. But without another word he turned and strode off and in a few moments had disappeared among the trees.

Guendivar stared after him. If he was not a god, she thought then, still, Merlin was something more than a man.

On a day of mingled sunlight and shadow towards the end of May, the high king of Britannia returned to Camalot. Another year's storms had weathered the timbers, and the thatching had been bleached by another year's suns to a paler gold. Artor remembered it half finished, all raw wood and pale stone, but now buildings and fortifications alike seemed to have grown out of the hill.

As always, he approached Camalot with mixed emotions. This was his home, the heart of his power, and here, in perpetual reminder of his greatest failure, was Guendivar. If he had been able to give her children, would she by now have grown fat and frowsy? But he had not, and so she remained in essence virgin, forever young, beautiful, and not to be possessed by any man.

Then they were passing beneath the gate, and the entire population of the fortress surged around him, obliterating thought in an ecstasy of welcome.

It was late that night before Artor and his queen were alone. He found himself grateful that the day had left him physically exhausted. Without the distracting demands of the body, it would be easier to remember the things he had to say.

Guendivar sat in her sleeping shift on the chest at the foot of their bed, combing out her hair. Long habit had taught him not to think of her with desire, but there were times when her beauty broke through his defenses.

She is a woman, he thought, his gaze lingering on the firm curves of breast and thigh, *no longer the green girl I took from her father's hall. A woman,* the thought went on, *who deserves better than I have been able to give. . . .*

He paused in his pacing and turned. "My lady, we need to talk—"

She picked up the comb again, features still half-veiled by the golden fall of her hair, but he sensed her attention. Her movement made the lamp flame flicker, sending a flurry of shadows across the woven hangings on the wall.

He cleared his throat. "I told you once that I had a son, but not by whom. I begot him on my sister, when I lay with her, all unknowing, at the rites of Lughnasa."

There was a charged silence, then the comb began to move once more.

"If you did not know, there was no sin—" Guendivar said slowly, then paused, thinking. "It is that boy Medraut, isn't it? The youngest son of Morgause who came to you last winter."

Artor nodded. "I hoped to keep his birth hidden, but the word has gotten around. It may be that he himself told someone the secret. Medraut can be. . . . strange."

"Do you wish to make him your heir?" she asked, frowning.

"Were he as good a man as Gualchmai, still the priests would never stand for it. Medraut cannot inherit, but men are saying . . . that his existence proves my fertility. Some of the chieftains came to me, suggesting that I should take another queen."

"Do you wish to divorce me?" Guendivar set down the comb and faced him, her eyes huge in a face drained of color.

"Guendivar—" Despite his will he could hear his voice shaking. "You know better than anyone that the fault lies in me. But it has come to me that by holding you to a barren bed I have wronged you. I thought things might have changed—in the North, I tried to take a girl, but I could do nothing. Morgause has repented, but she cannot alter the past. If you wish it, I will release you from the marriage, free you to find a man who can be a husband to you in fact as well as name."

She turned away and began once more, very slowly, to pull the ivory comb through her hair. "And if I do, and my new husband gets me with child, and men begin to say that the king has lost his manhood?"

"Be damned to them, so long as you are happy!" What was she thinking? He wished he could see her eyes!

"Then be damned to those who say that I am sterile. I wish no other husband than you."

Artor had not known he was holding his breath until it rushed out of him in a long sigh. Guendivar set down the comb and began to braid the golden silk of her hair. Her gaze was on the long strands, but he could see the smooth curve of cheek and brow, and her beauty smote him like a sword. The leather straps that supported the mattress creaked as he sat down.

"And I . . . no other queen. . . ." He forced the words past a thickened throat.

Guendivar tied off her braid, blew out the lamp on her side of the bed, and climbed in.

"You have guarded my honor," he said then. "Now I ask you to guard Britannia. Except for Cataur, I have spoken with all of the princes. I will go to Dumnonia to gather ships, and my army will make the journey to Gallia. When I cross the sea, I want you to rule. I think my treaties will hold, but if they do not, I will leave you Gualchmai to lead the warriors, and Cai to handle the administration. Someone must make our proud princes work together. You have power over men, my queen. The authority will be yours."

Guendivar raised herself on one elbow. The light of the remaining lamp seemed to dance in her eyes. "You have given me those two Saxon cubs to raise already, and now you will give me a kingdom to rule?"

"I know of none other to whom I would entrust it," he said slowly, shrugging off his chamber robe and tossing it to the foot of the bed.

"Then I will be the mother of many," she said softly, "and watch over the land until you return. But while you are still here, come to bed." She paused, and for a moment he thought she would say something more, but her gaze slid away from his, and she lay back down.

At the beginning of summer the Isca flowed calmly past the old capital of the Dumnonii. In the riverside meadow where the feasting tables had been arranged, a fresh wind was blowing up off the water, and though Artor could not see it, he thought he could smell the sea. He leaned back in the carved chair that once had graced the home of a Roman magistrate and took a deep breath, seeking the current of fresh air above the heavy scents of roasting meat and ale.

This campaign had been too long in the planning, but this summer, surely, he would see Gallia. On the plain above Portus Adurni his army was gathering even now. He had made all secure behind him. Only Dumnonia remained to settle, and the king was beginning to think that Cataur's country would be more trouble than the rest of Britannia combined.

"Do not be telling me that this campaign has nothing to do with you!" exclaimed Betiver, who had come back from Gallia to help with the final preparations. "In the North they provided men and horses, as I have heard, and they have far less reason to fear the Frankish power. I have been in Armorica, my friends, and I know well that half the country is ruled by princes from Dumnonia and Kernow. It is your own lands and kin we will be fighting for! The king expects you be to generous with ships and men."

Artor eyed Cataur, who sat at the other end of the long table, with a grim smile. The northerners might well think it worth the price to be out from under the king's eye for awhile, whereas the Dumnonians were unwilling to give up the independence they enjoyed across the sea. But that freedom from royal control was a luxury that they could no longer afford.

Cataur was shaking his head, complaining about bad harvests and hard times.

"The seasons have been no worse here than elsewhere," Artor put in suddenly, "and you never suffered from the Saxons. Even here in Isca you have found folk from Demetia to repopulate the town. You have the ships, and men who sail to Armorica every moon to steer them. And you shall have them back again once they have made a few voyages for me."

"Very well, that is fair enough." Abruptly Cataur capitulated, grinning through teeth gone bad with age. He had never really recovered from the wound he took in the last Saxon revolt, and his sons led his armies now.

"I will not ask you for more than a company of men," the king went on, "and your son Constantine to lead them. Together, we will raise more troops among your cousins in Armorica."

Cataur scowled at that, but Constantine was smiling. Not quite old enough to fight at Mons Badonicus, he had grown up on tales of the heroes of the Saxon wars. Artor suspected he regretted never having had a chance to win his own glory. Long ago Cataur had been a contender for the kingship, and Constantine, who came of the same blood as Uthir, was a potential heir. Let him come and show what he was made of in this war.

"And from the Church," Artor went on, "I will ask only a tithe of grain—"

The abbot of Saint Germanus, who was also bishop for Dumnonia, sat up suddenly.

"It is for men to tithe to the Church, not the Church to men!"

Cups and platters jumped as Artor's fist struck the table, impatience getting the better of him at last, and everyone sat up and paid attention.

"Do you wish your brethren in Gallia to pay in blood instead? The Frankish king may call himself a Christian, but his warriors have little respect for churchmen. The murdered monks win a martyr's crown, but that does little good to the souls for whom they cared!"

In the silence that followed he sensed movement under the table. He had drawn back his foot to kick, thinking it a dog, when he heard a giggle. Frowning, he pushed back his chair, reached down, and hauled up by the neck of his tunic the small, dark-haired boy who had been hiding there.

"And whose pup are you?" Artor tried to gentle his tone as he set the boy on his knee.

The color that had left the child's face flooded back again. "Marc'h . . . son of Constantine. . . ."

The king shook his head, smiling. "I think you are Cunomorus, a great hunting dog who is waiting to steal the bones! Here's one for you, with the meat still on—" He took a pork rib from his platter, put it in the boy's grubby hand, and set him down. "Run off now and gnaw it!"

Flushing again at the men's laughter, the child scampered away.

"My lord, I am sorry—" Constantine's face was nearly as red as his son's.

"He's a fine lad, and does you credit," answered Artor, with a momentary twinge of regret because he had not known his own son's childhood. "Enjoy him while you can." Perhaps, when his army was assembling at Portus Adurni, he would have the time to visit Medraut in Venta and say farewell.

He looked down the table, his expression sobering, and the Dumnonians sighed and prepared to take up the argument once more. If they fought in battle as hard as they were fighting in council, Artor thought ruefully, this campaign was certain to go well.

Medraut walked with his father along the bank of the Icene, where some forgotten Roman had planted apple trees. Long untended, they had grown tall and twisted; the ground between them littered with branches brought down by storms. But the trees had survived, and on their branches the green apples were beginning to swell.

I am like those apples, thought Medraut. *Wild and untended, still I grow, and no power can keep me from fulfilling my destiny.*

Just over the hill, three thousand men were camped in tents of hide; the meadows behind them were full of horses, but here in the old orchard they might have been in a land deserted since the last legion sailed over the sea. To Medraut, Britannia still held a world of wonders. Why did the king want to go away?

Artor was gazing across the marshes, his eyes clouded by memory.

"I fought a battle here, when I was a little younger than you . . ." said the king. "The man I loved best in the world was killed, and I took Oesc, who became my friend, as a hostage."

"And now I am hostage to Ceretic's son—" observed Medraut. "How history repeats itself!"

Artor gave him a quick look, and Medraut realized he had not entirely kept the bitterness out of his tone. Since they had last met he had gotten taller, and he no longer had to look up to meet his father's eyes.

"They are not treating you well?" There was an edge to the king's reply that made Medraut smile.

For a moment he considered telling Artor that Cynric had been harsh to him just to see what his father would do. But whether or not Artor believed him, the consequences would not serve his purpose. He shook his head, scooped up a little green apple that had fallen untimely, and began to toss it from hand to hand.

"Oh they have been kind enough. Indeed, they remind me of my own tribesmen in the North. No doubt I fit better here than I would among the cultured magnates of Demetia. That, if anything, is my complaint. I left my mother's dun because I wanted to learn about my father's world."

"Would you rather I sent you to Londinium?" Artor asked, frowning. "I suppose I could arrange for you to be tutored there. Or perhaps one of the monasteries . . ."

"*Father!*" Medraut did not try to keep the mockery from his laugh. "You cannot imagine that the good monks would welcome *me*! Nor do I wish a tutor! If you want me to learn the ways of the Romans, take me with you to Gallia! You have just told me—at my age, you were fighting battles. Do you want the Saxons to be your son's instructors in the arts of war?"

He watched as anger flushed and faded in the king's face, or was it shame? *He grows uncomfortable when I remind him,* Medraut noted, *but he is too honest to deny it.* It had occurred to him, some months into his exile, that Artor could easily deny their relationship and brand him a deluded child. He realized now that it would be against the king's nature to do that—it was a useful thing to know.

"I wish they did not teach their own!" came the muttered reply. "But you must learn from them what you can. You are getting your growth, but if you were with me there would still be danger. In Gallia the priests

have great influence. I will have a hard enough time getting them to accept
me. . . ."

*And your incestuous bastard would be a burden you do not want to
bear!* It would have been different if his father had loved him. But why
should he? Medraut knew well that his begetting had been an accident,
and his birth a revenge. He should count himself lucky that the king felt
any responsibility towards him at all.

It did not occur to him to wonder why he should want Artor's love.
There was only the pain of realization, and an anger he did not even try
to understand.

"So you will not take me with you?"

"I cannot—" Artor spread his hands, then let them fall to his side.
He turned and began to walk once more. "I am leaving the government
of Britannia in the hands of my queen. If there is trouble here, you must
go to Guendivar."

Medraut nodded, then, realizing his father could not see him, mumbled something the king could take as agreement. His eyes were stinging,
and he told himself it was the wind. But as anguish welled up within him,
he threw the apple in his hand with all his strength. It arched up and out,
then fell into the river with a splash. Together he and Artor watched as
the current caught and carried it towards the sea.

V

The High Queen

A.D. 507–512

At Camalot someone was always coming or going, and one got used to the noise, especially now, when a series of hot days in early June had opened every window and door. But the voices outside the small building where the queen did her accounts were getting louder. Guendivar set down the tallies of taxes paid in beef or grain as Ninive came in, her fair hair curling wildly in the damp heat.

"My lady—there's a rider, with messages from Gallia—"

The queen's heart drummed in her breast, but she had learned to show no sign. Suddenly she could feel the fine linen of her tunica clinging to back and breast, and perspiration beading on her brow. But she waited with tightly folded hands as the messenger, his tunic still stained with salt from the journey oversea, came in.

"The king is well—" he said quickly, and she realized that her face had betrayed her after all, but that did not matter now. She recognized Artor's seal on the rawhide case in which he sent his dispatches, and held out her hand. The swift, angular writing that she had come to know so well blurred, then resolved into words.

" . . . *and so I am settled once more at Civitas Aquilonia. The rains have been heavy here, and there is some sickness among the men, but we hope for better weather soon.*"

She would have been happy to share the sunshine they were having here. But if the weather on both sides of the narrow sea was the same, Armorica would be drying out by now. Artor had not been used to write to her when he travelled in Britannia. But now the queen seemed to be his link to home. Deciphering his handwriting was only one of the many skills she had acquired since the king left her to rule in his name.

"*The news from the south of Gallia continues bad, at least for the kingdom of Tolosa. Chlodovechus is moving against the Goths at last, and this time I do not think Alaric will be able to hold. For us, it means peace for as long as it takes for the Franks to digest their new conquest. But in another year or two, they will look about them and notice that this last Roman stronghold is still defying them.*

"*I judge that I have that long to forge alliances among the British chieftains of Armorica that will withstand the storm. Dare I hope to restore the Empire of the West? I no longer know—but where once I saw Gallia as territory to be regained, now I see men who have put their trust in me, and whom I must not betray. . . .*"

There was a break in the writing. The remainder of the letter was written in a different shade of ink, the writing more angular still.

"*Tolosa has fallen. The Visigoths are in full retreat, and the Franks boast that they will keep them on the run all the way to the Pyrenaei montes and beyond. They are probably correct. Alaric must want very much to put a range of mountains between him and his foes. He will be safe in Iberia, for a time. But I predict that one day a Frankish king will follow, dreaming of Empire. Unless, that is, we can break their pride. Already we are seeing refugees from Tolosa, both Romans and Goths. If they wish to join the fight here they will be welcome. Some, I may send to you in Britannia.*

"*Watch well over my own kingdom, my queen. You hold my heart in your hands. . . .*"

How, she wondered, was she to take that? Surely, Artor was referring to the land, but for a moment she wondered what it would be like to claim not only his duty, but his love. She had almost understood it, listening to Merlin's poetry. But even unclothed, Artor kept his spirit armored, and the moment of possibility had passed. It would require some power even greater than Merlin's, she thought sadly, to bring him to her arms. . . .

She tried to tell herself that her husband's absence had at last made her a queen. Was she still fair? She did not know—men had learned that she was better pleased by praises for her wisdom. She had grown into the authority Artor had laid upon her, and discovered that she had a talent for rule. She might have failed him as a wife, but not as Britannia's queen.

But each letter revealed more of the man hidden within the king, the human soul who had guarded himself so carefully when they were alone. Artor had been back to Britannia only three times since beginning the Gallian campaign, brief visits spent settling disputes between the princes or persuading them to send him more men. Guendivar had scarcely seen him.

And she missed him, this husband whom she was only now coming to know. If it was her beauty that had unmanned him, she hoped that she had lost it. She reached for a piece of vellum, and after a moment began to set down words.

"To my lord and husband, greetings. The weather here has turned hot and fair and we have hope for a good harvest. I can send you some of last year's grain store now, and the taxes from Dumnonia. Gualchmai has brought his wife to Camalot. She is an intelligent woman, well read in the Latin poets, not at all the sort one would have expected Gualchmai to choose. But he is happy with her—the wild boy grown up at last. The news from the North is not so good. Morgause writes that your lady mother is ailing. If we hear more, I will send you word. . . ."

Guendivar paused, remembering the lake that lay like a jewel in the lap of the mountains, and the hush that one feared to break with any but sacred sounds. She had been there only once, but the memory was vivid. And yet she had no desire to return. She was a child of the southern lands, and her heart's home was the Vale of Afallon.

Merlin moved through the forest as a stag moves, scarcely stirring a leaf as he passed. But when he reached the river he was an otter, breasting the surface with undulant ease. When night came, the senses of a wolf carried him onward. But when he noticed at last that he was weary, he sank down between the roots of an ancient oak and became a tree.

Waking with the first light of morning, he thought for a moment that he was a bird. The pain of limbs that had stiffened with inaction brought him back to awareness of his body. He stretched out one forelimb, blinking at the sinewy length of a human arm, furred though it was with wiry, silver-brindled hair. Splayed twigs became fingers that reached out to the smooth, rune-carved wood of the Spear, which he had continued to carry through all his transformations.

With that touch, full consciousness returned to him, and he remembered his humanity. To stay a bird would have been easier, he thought grimly. A bird had no thought beyond the next insect, the next song. The long thoughts of trees, slowly stretching towards the skies, would be better still. A man could remember the message that had started him on this journey; a man could weep, trying to imagine a world without Igierne.

He gazed at the wooded heights above him and knew that the instinct that guided him had led him deep into the Lakeland hills, where once the Brigantes had ruled. A few hours more would bring him to the Isle of Maidens. Animal senses tugged at his awareness—he scented wild onion on the hillside, and grubs beneath a fallen log. Food he must have, and water, but it was necessary that he complete this journey as a man.

When Merlin came to the Lake it was nearing noon. The water lay flat and silver beneath the blue bowl of the sky; even the trees stood sentinel with no leaf stirring. Human reason told him that such calms often preceded storms, but a deeper instinct gibbered that the world was holding its breath, waiting for the Lady of the Lake to give up her own. When he climbed into the coracle drawn up on the shore, he pushed off carefully, as if even the ripples of his passage might be enough to upset that fragile equilibrium.

The priestesses had set Igierne's bed in the garden, beneath a wick-erwork shade. Merlin would have thought her dead already if he had not seen the linen cloth that covered her stir. Nine priestesses stood around her, chanting softly. As he approached, the woman who sat at the head of the bed straightened, and he saw that it was Morgause. The clear light that filtered through the wicker showed clearly the lines that had been carved into her face by passion and by pride, but it revealed also the enduring strength of bone. Distracted by the surface differences in coloring and the deeper differences in spirit, he had never realized how much she looked like her mother.

Igierne's eyes were closed; her breathing labored and slow. Her silver hair rayed out upon the pillow, combed by loving hands, but he could see the skull beneath the skin.

"How long—"

"Has she lain thus?" asked Morgause. "She weakened suddenly two days since."

"Have you called on the power of the Cauldron?"

Morgause shook her head, frowning. "She forbade it."

Merlin sighed. He should have expected that, for the power of the Cauldron was to fulfill the way of nature, not to deny it. Morgause spoke again.

"Yesterday she would still take broth, but since last night she has not stirred. She is going away from us, and there is nothing I can do."

"Have *you* slept?" When she shook her head, he touched her hand. "Go, rest, and let me watch awhile. I will call you if there is any change."

It was good advice, though Merlin did not know if he had given it for her sake, or his own. Her anger and her need battered against his hard-won composure.

When she had gone he leaned the Spear against the post, sat down in her place, and took Igierne's hand. It was cool and dry; only when he pressed could he feel the pulse within. He closed his eyes, letting his own breathing deepen, matching his life-force to hers.

"*Igierne . . . my lady . . . Igierne. . . .*" Awareness extended; he felt himself moving out of the body, reaching for that place where her spirit hovered, tethered to her body by a silver cord that thinned with every beat of her heart.

"*Merlin, my old friend—*" He sensed Igierne as a bright presence, turning towards him. "*Do not tell me I must come back with you, for I will not go!*" The radiance that surrounded them quivered with her laughter.

"*Then let me come with you!*"

"*Your flesh is still bound to the earth. It is not your time. . . .*"

"*The years pass, yet my body only grows stronger. The only thing that held my spirit to the human world was my love for you!*"

"*When you wandered, I watched over you from the Lake . . .*" came her reply. "*Now I will love you from the Hidden Realm. It is not so far away—*"

He could sense that this was true, for beyond the flicker of her spirit, a bright doorway was growing. He was aware that Morgause had returned, but her grief could not touch him now. From a great distance, it seemed, his mortal senses told him that Igierne's breath came harshly, rattling in her chest. The chanting of the priestesses faltered as someone began to weep, then resumed.

"*Your children still need you—*" he thought hopelessly.

"*My children are grown! Surely they know I love them. Merlin, you would not condemn me to live on in a body that is outworn! Help me, my dear one. Let me go!*"

He was not so sure of that, but it was his own need, not that of Morgause, that reached out and drew the spirit of the younger woman into the link as well.

"*There you are, my daughter—you see—*" Igierne moved closer to the light. "*This is what I tried to tell you. There is only this last bit, that is a little . . . difficult, and then all will be well. This, too, is part of your training. Help me. . . ."*

He could sense when the turmoil in Morgause's spirit began to give way to wonder.

"You see the doorway opening before you—" The words that the younger woman whispered came from ritual, but they carried conviction now, and resonated in both worlds. "The bright spirits of those you love await you, ready to welcome you home. . . ."

And as she spoke, Merlin realized that it was so. He glimpsed those radiant beings drawing nearer, and recognized, with a certainty beyond the senses, Uthir, and behind him Igierne's parents, Amlodius and Argantel.

"Go through the gate. Let our love support you through your own self-judgment. Over you the dark shall have no power. Farewell—we release you into the Lady's waiting arms. . . ."

Somewhere far away, the failing body struggled for breath, sighed, and was still. But that hardly mattered. For a moment, Merlin's inner vision embraced the brightness and he saw Igierne clearly, growing ever younger as she moved away from them until she was the gold-crowned maiden whom he had loved. And then she passed through the portal. The Light intensified beyond mortal comprehension, and Merlin was blown back into the pallid illumination of an earthly day.

The surface of the lake wrinkled as wind brushed the water. A vanguard of cloud was just rising beyond the western hills. Morgause shivered, though the temperature had barely begun to drop; the cold she felt came from the soul. Merlin, beside her, moved as she had seen men move coming half-stunned from the battlefield.

"It was a good death—" she said aloud. "Why am I so angry?" Behind them the ritual wailing of the priestesses swelled and faded like the rising wind, but Morgause felt her throat hard, the muscles tight, and her eyes were dry.

"Because your mother has abandoned you," came the deep rumble of his reply. "Even a death less triumphant than this one is a release for the one who passes. We grieve for ourselves, because she has left us alone."

Morgause stared. For most of her life she had hated this man, the architect of her father's death and her mother's first treachery. Of all people in the world, she had not expected him to understand.

"I remember when my grandmother was dying," she said then. "My mother wept, while I played, uncomprehending, on the shore. Argantel foretold that I would be the Lady of the Lake one day. For so many years

I fought my mother, fearing she would deny me my destiny. And now that fate is come upon me, and I am afraid."

"So was she . . ." answered Merlin. "Like you, she had been long away from the Lake. But you have had your mother's teaching. Much of the old wisdom has been lost—it is for you to preserve what you can. I do not know your mysteries . . ." he said with some difficulty, "but you have the Cauldron. Call upon your Goddess—surely She will comfort you."

"And you—" she answered him.

Merlin shook his head. "My goddess has gone out of the world. . . ."

Morgause looked at him in amazement, understanding only now that this man, like her father, had been denied Igierne's love. The wind blew again, more strongly, hissing in the trees. Merlin had turned to gaze across the lake to the heights where, even in those few moments, the clouds had doubled their size.

"I must go—" he said then. "Your mother is High Queen now in the Otherworld, and in this world, the Tiernissa is Guendivar. But you are Lady of the Lake, Morgause—the Hidden Queen, the White Raven of Britannia. Guard it well!"

He held her gaze, and she saw a woman crowned with splendor reflected in his eyes.

"I am the Lady of the Lake . . ." she affirmed, accepting his vision of her at last. "And who are you?"

The certainty in Merlin's eyes flickered out, to be replaced by desolation. "I am a leaf blown by the wind . . . I am a sea-smoothed rock . . . I am a sun-bleached bone . . . I do not know what I am, save that my body lives still in a world that my spirit finds strange. Up there"—he gestured towards the hills—"perhaps I may learn. . . ."

Above the trees, one entered the kingdom of the wind. Merlin struggled upward, reeling as a new gust swept across the slope and the purple bells of the heather rang with soundless urgency. A wren was tossed skyward, crying, caught by the blast. Clouds boiled above him, flinging splatters of rain. Merlin stumbled, jabbed the Spear into the earth to keep his balance, and pulled himself upright once more.

"Blow! Blow! Cry out in rage!" he shouted, shaking his fist at the sky. This violence of nature might be harsh to the body, but it matched the anguish in his soul. "World, weep, let my grief gust forth with every blast of wind!"

He took a step forward, realized he could climb no higher, and sank to his knees. "Why—" he gasped, "am I still alive?"

There were words in the blast that whipped at hair and beard. Merlin grasped the shaft of the Spear, feeling it thrum beneath his hands like a tree in the wind, and abruptly their meaning became clear.

"Unless you will it, you shall not leave this world. . . . "

"Am I less than human, then?"

"Perhaps you are more. . . ."

Merlin shivered. The Voice was all around him, in the wail of the wind, the vibration of the spearshaft, the rasp of air in his throat. He shook his head.

"Who are you?"

The air rippled with laughter. *"I am every breath you take, every thought you think; I am ecstasy."* The laughter rolled once more. *"You carry My Spear. . . ."*

Merlin recoiled. "The god of the Saxons!"

"You may call me that, or Lugos, if it makes you feel easier, or Mercurius. I have walked in many lands, and been called by many names. When men use wit and will and words, I am there. And you have borne my Spear for a dozen winters. Why are you so surprised?"

"Why did you allow it? What do you want with me?"

"O, man of Wisdom! Even now, do you not understand?"

Abruptly the wind failed. The storm was passing. Merlin stared as the light of sunset, blazing suddenly beneath the clouds, filled the world with gold. His grief for Igierne might never leave him, but now his mind buzzed with phrases, riddles, insights and imaginings, and a great curiosity. Holding onto the Spear, he levered himself upright once more. Then he plucked it from the earth and started down the mountain.

Dust rose in golden clouds, stirred by the feet of the harvesters. The cart they drew was piled with sheaves of corn and garlanded with summer flowers. Singing rose in descant to the rhythmic creak of wheels as they pushed it towards the meadow below the villa where the harvest feast had been laid. Guendivar, sitting with Cai and Gualchmai in the place of honor, drew her veil half over her face. But the precaution was needless, for as evening drew nearer, a light breeze had come up to blow the dust away.

She had been glad of Cai's invitation to keep the festival in the place where Artor had been a boy. It was Cai's home now, though the king's service had allowed him to spend little time here. His health had not been good, and she had come partly in hopes of getting him to take some rest. He did seem to be better here. She had smiled at his stories, trying to imagine the great king of Britannia as an eager boy. Her only regret was that Artor was not here with them. Five years he had spent campaigning in Gallia, with little result that she could see. He had not even returned when his mother died the year before.

The procession rounded the last curve, and she heard the chorus more clearly:

"Oh where is he hidden, and where has he gone?
The corn is all cut, and the harvest is done!"

The workers who had cut and bound the last sheaf, that they called "the neck," or sometimes, "the old man," held it high. They had already been soaked with water from the river to bring luck, but in this weather they did not seem to mind. Guendivar remembered with longing the secret pool where she used to bathe when she was a girl, and how she and Julia had discovered the pleasure their bodies could bring. These days, most of the time she felt as virgin as the Mother of God, but as she watched the reapers pursuing the women who had followed to bind the sheaves, she had to suppress a spurt of envy for the fulfillment she had been denied.

"In the first flush of springtime, the young king is born
The ploughed fields rejoice in the growth of the corn—
Oh where is he hidden, and where—"

Guendivar felt unexpected tears prick in her eyes. Men called her the Flower Bride and swore that her beauty was unchanged. But it was not the way of nature for spring to last forever. . . .

The cart was drawn up before the tables and the men who had hitched themselves to it threw off the traces. The woman who had been carrying the last sheaf handed it over to laughing girls, who bore it to the central upright of the drying shed and tied it there, wreathed with flowers. The light of the setting sun, slanting through the trees, turned stalk and seed to gold.

"The sun rises high and the fields they grow green.
Our king now is bearded, so fair to be seen—"

Cai held out his beaker to be refilled as the serving girl came by and sat back with a sigh. "It seems strange to sit here drinking cider, after so many years of war."

"And Artor not here to enjoy it," Gualchmai replied. "It is not right for the king to be so long from his own land. If he had the army with which we won at Mons Badonicus, by now he would be emperor!"

Still singing, men and women joined hands and began to dance around the post.

"The sun rises high and the fields turn to gold,
The king hangs his head, now that he has grown old—"

"Too many died on the quest for the Cauldron, and some of us are getting older . . ." He eyed Gualchmai wryly, rubbing his left arm as if it pained him. "Except, of course, for you."

Gualchmai frowned, uncomprehending. Years of war had battered his face like bronze, the sandy hair was receding from his high brow, but his arms were still oak-hard.

"It is too peaceful," he said truculently, and Guendivar laughed. "My lord set me here to guard you, but all our enemies are still frightened of his name." He sighed, and then turned to look at her, his eyes pleading. "Let me go to him, lady. Those Frankish lords would not dare to laugh if I were with him. Artor needs me. I am of use to no one here!"

"The reaper swings high and the binder bends low,
The king is cut down and to earth he must go."

Guendivar shivered, touched by a fear she thought she had forgotten. For so long, Artor had been a bodiless intelligence that spoke to her through the written word, she had nearly forgotten he wore mortal flesh that was vulnerable to cold, hunger, and enemy swords.

"Ninive, bring me my shawl—" she said, but the girl was not there. It should not have surprised her; the child made no secret of her discomfort in large gatherings. No doubt she was wandering in the woods on the hill, and would return when darkness fell. And in truth, the chill the queen felt was an internal one, that neither shawl nor mantle could ease.

"Very well—" Both men turned to look at her. "It comforts me to have you here, and your wife will not thank me for letting you go, but I agree that Artor needs you more."

The harvesters rushed inward towards the last sheaf, arms upraised.

"And we shall make merry with bread and with beer,
Until he returns with the spring of the year. . . ."

Then the circle dissolved into laughter as they descended on the vats of harvest ale.

Grinning, Gualchmai downed his own in a single swallow and held out his cup for more.

"But be sure that you make good on your boast, my champion," Guendivar said then. "Beat the breeches off the Franks and bring my lord swiftly home."

"Oh where is he hidden, and where has he gone?
The corn is all cut, and the harvest is done!"

Merlin walked in the oakwood above the villa in the golden light of a harvest moon. He had to remind himself that Turpilius and Flavia were both dead these twenty years and the farm belonged to Cai, for seen from the hillside, nothing seemed to have changed. Even from here the sound of celebration came clearly. Around the threshing sheds torches glittered; the revellers moving among them in a flickering dance of light and shadow. Stubbled fields gleamed faintly beyond them, waiting to rest through the fallow moons of wintertide.

He had intended to join the celebration, but the rites of the seeded earth were not his mysteries. Long experience had taught him that his presence would cast a chill on the festival, like a breath of wind from the wilderness beyond their fenced fields. It was far too beautiful a night to sleep, and these days he needed little rest, and had no need for the shelter of walls.

And so he walked, hair stirred lightly by the breathing darkness, feeding on the rich, organic scents of leaf mold and drying hay. On such a night it was easy to forget the dutiful impulse that had sent him south to offer his counsel to Artor's queen. He belonged in the wilderness, with only his daimon for companion and the god of the Spear for guide.

These days, the god was always with him. But the bright spirit that he called his daimon, the companion of his childhood, he had not seen for many years. Now that he was ancient he found himself remembering her bright eyes and shining hair ever more vividly. It was the fate of the old, he had heard, to become childlike.

Thinking so, he laughed softly, and out of the night, like a shiver of bells, came an answer.

Merlin stood still, senses questing outward. It was beyond belief that a man could have been present without his knowledge on this hill. What he found at last was a glimmering whiteness perched in an oak tree, the human mind so tuned to the rhythms of the night he had thought it a perturbation of the wind.

"The hour grows late—" came a silvery voice from the branches. "Why does the greatest Druid in Britannia wander the hills?"

Merlin shaped his sight to an owl's vision and saw a fine-boned face haloed by fair hair. For a moment he could not breathe. It was the face of his daimon, and yet she was no part of his imagining—even as a child, he had always understood the difference between the images that came from outside and those that lived within. And now he could sense the warmth of a human body and hear the faint whisper of breath. She stirred, and he glimpsed the glint of embroidery on her gown.

"Why is a maiden of the court sitting in a tree?"

"You do not know me, and yet we are kin." She laughed again. "I am Gualchmai's daughter by a woman of the hills, and if I cannot be roaming there, in this oak I can at least pretend to be free."

"That is so. I have myself lived for a time in a tree. Would it displease you to have an old man's company?" To his sight, a radiance seemed to flow from her slim form, more lovely than the light of the moon.

She cocked her head like a bird. "I have never before met anyone who felt like a part of the forest. You know all its secrets, is it not so? Stay then, and talk to me. . . ."

Merlin swayed, as if something were melting within him that had been frozen since Igierne died. He put out his hand to the oak tree, and carefully eased himself to the solid ground.

"Gladly . . ." he said softly. "Gladly will I stay with you."

Merlin's return was a wonder that had men buzzing for a season. When they saw how often he walked with the girl Ninive, they laughed, thinking they knew the reason. But Guendivar, having promised Gualchmai that she would watch over his child, understood that there was nothing sexual in the attraction between the old man and the maiden. And she had other, more pressing, concerns.

Gualchmai's departure had not loosed all Britannia's old enemies upon them, as some had feared. The Picts were holding to Artor's treaty, and there was only an occasional raider from Eriu. It was the princes of Britannia who were beginning to grow restive, like horses kept too long in pasture who forget the governance of bit and rein. Merlin told her that after Uthir died it had been the same. The counsel of the Druid was valuable; with his guidance Guendivar grew into her queenship like a tree in fertile soil. But he could not show an iron fist to the princes. She wrote to Artor, but another year passed, and he did not return.

Gualchmai had been gone for two years when new trouble between the men of Dumnonia and the West Saxons impelled her to appeal to Artor again. She had summoned Constantine and Cynric to meet with her at Durnovaria. The spring had been a fine one, and they had no excuse for not traveling. But if she could not reconcile them with her wisdom, she and they both knew that she had no teeth with which to compel obedience.

Through her window came the rich, organic scent of the river that Durnovaria guarded, mixed with the sharper tang of the sea. Few men lived permanently in the town—even the prince preferred to spend most of his time at his villa in the hills. But folk still gathered here for the weekly market, and the clamor of mixed tongues made a deeper background to the crying of gulls. Guendivar set down the vellum on which she had been working and took up the most recent letter that Artor had sent to her.

"Pompeius Regalis paid me a visit last month; he is building a strong-hold near Brioc's monastery in the west of the coastal plain and has realized he needs allies. There are so many Dumnonians there now the place is called by their name. His son Fracanus was with him. He has invented a new sport that he persuaded some of my men to try. Instead of racing their horses with chariots, they measure out a course and put up the lightest boys into the saddle. Of course it is dangerous if the lad is thrown, but the horses do go faster. . . ."

Guendivar shook her head. In conversation, Artor had never been one for humor, but in these letters he seemed anxious to amuse as well as to inform her. Indeed, she had learned more of his mind since he went over the sea than when they lived together.

"Summer is almost upon us. I believe that I can get Regalis and Conan of Venetorum to agree to an alliance, and with them, Guenomarcus of Plebs Legionorum. With them behind me, I will count Armorica as secured. The sons of Chlodovechus, having settled matters in Tolosa, are gazing northward, and the Britons who took up land in Lugdunensis have asked our aid."

That meant that Artor would be fighting soon, might be in battle even now. Guendivar realized that her grip had creased the vellum, and gently let it fall. The king had spent his life in warfare and rarely taken any harm. And now he had Gualchmai. Why should the prospect concern her now? Was it because he was not fighting for Britannia?

From the direction of the city gate came a blare of cowhorns; the babble in the marketplace crested to a roar. Cynric had arrived at last. Guendivar closed her eyes, massaging the skin above her brows. Then she rolled and tied Artor's letter, stood and called for her maidens to attire her in the stiff ceremonial garments of the high queen.

Robed in a Druid's snowy white and leaning on Woden's Spear, Merlin waited behind the high queen's throne. In almost three years, he had become accustomed to wearing civilized garments once more. Ninive accepted the weight of woven cloth and metal pins when she wanted to run like a wild pony across the moors. For her sake, he could do the same.

Men wondered what deep purpose lay behind his return, but he had no plan, no intentions. In his heart he knew that Ninive was not his daimon incarnate in a maiden's flesh. But she held him to the human world. He looked at her now, standing with the other girls who served the queen. For a moment their eyes met, and he heard the cry of a falcon soaring above the headlands, and the hushed roar of the sea.

The long chamber where once the magistrates of Durnovaria had held their meetings was beginning to fill. Constantine sat on the south side with the chieftain whose lands lay on the Saxon border beside him. A half dozen of his houseguard muttered behind him, fists straying to their hips and then away when they remembered that they had been required to leave their swords outside.

A side door opened and he saw Guendivar, framed like an icon against the darkness of the passageway. She was mantled in gold, her pointed face framed by the pearl lappets of a Byzantine diadem. But the splendor in which she walked was only a visible focus for the penumbra of power, and men rose to greet her with a reverence that was more than formal. The queen ascended the dais and took her seat, and the two youths who had escorted her, one red as a fox, the other fair, took their places to either side of the carved chair. Eormenric looked about him smiling, but red Ceawlin gazed at the door with a face like carved bone.

The double doors at the end of the hall swung open. Tall men came through it. The flaming hair of their leader was dusted now with ash, but it was bright enough to set an answering flame ablaze in Ceawlin's eyes.

"*Waes hael, drighten. Wilcume!*" said the queen, who had learned a little Saxon from her hostages.

Cynric blinked, then brought up his arm in acknowledgment. He and his men wheeled and took their places on the northern wall.

Merlin let his mind drift, the point and counterpoint of complaint and accusation like the mutter of distant thunder. Behind Cynric he could just make out a darker head amongst the fair and brown. The Saxon leader stepped forward, gesturing, and a ray of light from the upper window touched the head of the man behind him with a gleam of bronze. That was no Saxon! Merlin stepped out from behind the queen's chair, extending other, secret, senses towards the stranger.

As if he had felt the touch, the bronze-haired man straightened and turned, and Merlin recoiled, recognizing, in a face that was a masculine reflection of Morgause, the grey gaze of Artor the king. Any other identity of form or feature might have been put down to their common inheritance from Igierne, but not those eyes, which had come to Artor from Uthir, who was father to him alone.

"Lady, as you have deemed, so shall it be. Eadwulf will bring his kinsmen back from the western bank of the river. We give up our claim to the land—" Cynric's voice grew louder, and the Dumnonian lords began to grin. "I call your *Witan*, your council, to witness that we of the West Seax have kept faith with you. In your hall my son has grown to manhood. You have taught him much. Now it is time for him to come back to his own land and learn the ways of the folk that he will one day rule. In exchange, I return to you the son of your king!"

As Medraut stepped forward, a whisper of amazement, of question, of commentary swept the hall like the wind that heralds the storm. Those who remembered the Pendragon were marking the resemblance that identified Medraut not only as Artor's nephew but as his son. The tablet-woven banding on his dark tunic was all Saxon, like the seax-knife that hung at his side. But the brooch that held his mantle was of Pictish work, and the pride of the House of Maximian shone in his eyes. He halted, and half a hundred glances flickered from his face to that of the queen.

Surely, thought Merlin, Artor must have told her—but for nine years Medraut had been hidden among the Saxons like a hound among wolves. It had been too easy for all of them to forget that one day he would return to hunt with his own pack once more.

If she was surprised, Guendivar gave no sign. Speaking softly, she turned to Ceawlin, and the eagerness burning in his eyes for a moment dimmed as he bent to kiss her hand.

"I will not forget you, lady," he said hoarsely. Then, as if she had slipped his leash, he bounded to his father's side.

"And Eormenric"—she turned to the other youth—"you have spent as many years among us as your father did when he was young. I will not keep you here when your companion has gone."

For a moment the fair lad's face flamed. "My father loved King Artor," he said in a low mice. "But my loyalty is given to *you*. If ever you have need of me, you have only to call." He bent his head, turned, and went out of the hall.

Cynric and his son had moved a little aside, so that Medraut stood alone. Would the queen welcome him? Would she spurn him? Would she hail him as nephew or son? His face had gone very white, and as he looked at Guendivar, something anguished flickered in his eyes.

Fragmented images fluttered behind Merlin's vision. He grasped for them, and for a moment glimpsed dark shapes battling beneath the hard light of noon. His spirit reached out for comprehension to the daimon who from childhood had guided him, and in the next moment he found he was staring at Ninive, standing solid and alive beside the queen. For so long he had fled the power of foreknowledge that had haunted his childhood. Now, when he needed it, the only meaning he understood lay in the fair face of one young girl.

Guendivar leaned forward, stretching out her hand. "Come, Medraut— I bid you welcome home. . . ."

VI

A Wind from The North

A.D. 513

"My lady, a man has come—from Gallia. . . ."

Medraut's voice was quiet, the northern burr worn smooth by his years among the Saxons. Guendivar dropped the ball of embroidery wool she had been winding. As it rolled across the floor, Medraut bent smoothly and scooped it up, handing it back to her with a bow. Since he had been so unexpectedly returned to them, he had become an accepted presence in her court.

The thin lad who had appeared so briefly at Camalot nine years before had never met her eyes. Now she understood why, knowing him for Artor's son. She was glad that the king had told her himself, and not left her to learn it from gossip, or worse still, from Cynric. If Medraut's birth troubled him, he no longer let it show. His mother had trained him well, the queen thought wryly—he certainly knew how to make himself useful among the women. But his silent appearances still startled her, and she was no closer to understanding him.

"With news?" It was three months since she had heard from Artor, and a wet winter was turning into a chilly spring.

"He bears letters, but he is no messenger—"

At the sardonic tone, Guendivar lifted one eyebrow, but to comment would be to admit weakness, and instinct and experience both told her that with this one she must always seem strong.

"Shall I receive him here, or make him wait for a formal audience?" she asked, waiting curiously for his reply.

Since Medraut's arrival, she had searched her soul, grateful that she had suppressed her first furious impulse to send the boy back to Morgause. He had not asked to be born. Certainly, she thought with some resentment, she could not conceive when the king was in Gallia, even if Artor had been potent in her bed. Medraut was Artor's only son; even with his ambiguous heritage, he could be Artor's heir.

"Not here—" Medraut gazed around at the domestic clutter of the Women's Sunhouse. "And yet, I think this man is one you will wish to bind to your service. His name is Theodoric, a Goth of the kingdom of Tolosa and a man of the sea. Dress richly, but meet him in the garden."

Guendivar nodded slowly. Whether or not Medraut had the instinct for kingship, he certainly understood how to manipulate men. She glanced at the angle of the sun.

"That is good advice. Just after noon, bring him to me there."

Guendivar was already waiting on the stone bench beside the lavender bush when Theodoric entered the garden. One forgot that for a hundred years the Goths had been part of the Empire, not always peacefully, to be sure, but living side by side with Romans, learning their ways and their laws. They were even some kind of heretical Christians, she had heard. Certainly this man, tall and weathered by sun and wind though he might be, was no barbarian.

"I am Theodoric son of Theudebald—" The Goth stopped before her, bowing.

The queen rose to meet him, extending her hand. "Praefectus Classis," she continued in Latin, "be welcome to Britannia. Has my husband given you letters to bring to me?"

"He has, and said that to deliver them safely should be my best recommendation to you. I parted from the lord Artor on the last day of February." From the case at his side he drew a tubular letter case and held it out to her.

"Truly?" she said, calculating, "then you have made a swift passage. In a moment I will read what he has to say of you, but for now you must tell me about yourself, and why you have come."

"Lady, I need a home." A flush stained the bronzed cheeks, but he met her eyes steadily. "The Franks have driven my people over the mountains and into Iberia. The Goths are carving out a new kingdom, but it is all inland, whereas I am a man of the sea. I know how to sail it, how to fight upon it, how to build ships and defend harbors."

"And Britannia has many miles of coastline, and enemies who attack her from the sea—" finished Guendivar. "Now I understand why Artor sent you."

He straightened, relieved, but not surprised at her understanding. *What,* she wondered, *did Artor tell him about me?*

"What remains of the Gothic navy waits at Aquilonia—five vessels with their crews and captains who will sail at my command. I offer it to you."

"Our most present danger is the Irish, who attack the coasts of Demetia at will. Make your base at Glevum—I will send to the lord Agricola, who rules Demetia, to provide you with supplies. With your skills and his resources, we may hope to dislodge the Irish who have settled there and discourage them from trying again. Does that sound well to you?"

"It does indeed," he breathed. "I will write to my men immediately, and my ship can carry any messages you may have for the lord Artor." He started to turn, then paused, staring at her. "But perhaps you will want to read the king's letter first. To take me at my own word like this—you are very trusting."

"Perhaps." She smiled. "Although, if I have second thoughts, I can always send riders after you. But I hope that my lord would not have left his land in my charge if he did not trust my ability to read men."

For a moment longer Theodoric looked at her. Then, once again he bowed, not the courteous inclination with which he had greeted her, but the full reverence he might have made at the court of an emperor.

"Domina, I came here hoping to find safe harbor. But I have also found a queen. . . ."

Guendivar felt her own cheeks growing warm, but managed a gracious nod. "Medraut—" she called. She had not seen him, but she suspected he would not be out of earshot, and indeed it was only a moment before he appeared. "Escort our new admiral and help him to whatever he needs."

When he had gone, she sat down on the bench once more, and with fingers that trembled a little, opened the leather tube and pulled out the vellum roll inside.

"My lady, I must write swiftly, for Theodoric wishes to catch the morning tide. He has a good reputation among the Goths, and seems a

sensible man, but we here have no need for a navy. I give him to you for the defense of Demetia. Use him well.

"The Franks have marched more swiftly than I expected, despite the rain, and our supplies are getting low. Whatever you can send will be very welcome. The sons of Chlodovechus quarrel among themselves, but they can combine efficiently enough when they recognize an enemy. So far Theuderich, the eldest and most experienced among them, is still holding onto the leadership, even though he is not the son of Queen Chlotild, but of a concubine.

"Yesterday they brought us to battle, a hard-fought, muddy encounter that left no clear victor. We did not retreat—perhaps that may be counted as a victory. But it was costly. My nephew Aggarban was killed in the fighting, and there are many wounded.

"Riothamus still lives, but he is failing. Soon, I fear he will leave us, and I will have to decide whether or not to claim his sovereignty. I care for these people, and I believe that many of them have come to look to me with love and loyalty. But this is not my land. Last summer my journeys took me deep into Gallia, and there I found a town called Aballo, which in our tongue is the same as Afallon, the place of apples. And I closed my eyes, and saw the vale and the Tor so clearly I nearly wept with longing to be there. And you were there, standing beneath the apple trees."

There was a break in the writing there, as if he had been distracted, or perhaps too overcome to continue. Guendivar found her own eyes prickling with unshed tears, and shook her head. *How can you write such things,* she wondered angrily, *and not come home to me?* Wiping her eyes, she picked up the scroll once more.

"You will have to tell Medraut about his brother's death. About the boy himself, I do not know what to say. I did not understand him that season he was with me, and I cannot imagine what nine years among the Saxons have made of him. I can only trust that the powers that protect Britannia had some purpose in bringing him to birth."

Once more there was a space. The writing that followed was smaller, and precise, as if he had been exerting all his control.

"You, my queen, are the one most wronged by his existence. If you, of your charity, will keep him by you I will be grateful, but if it seems better, send him away. I leave him in your hands."

There was a blot on the page, as if he had started to write *"I wish . . ."* and then crossed it out. Beyond that she saw only the scrawled letters of his name.

"I wish!" Guendivar repeated aloud, glaring at the page and wondering whether this was trust or desperation. Should she be honored or angry? Either way, Medraut was her problem now. She would have to make another attempt to talk to him.

Artor, Artor, you have been too long away. What will it take to bring you home again? She rolled up the vellum and slid it into its case once more.

Guendivar had intended to talk with Medraut that evening, but just as they sat down to their meal a messenger arrived. He was from King Icel, his news an attack on Anglia by raiders from the northern land that is called Lochlann in Eriu, and by the Romans Skandza. They had picked their way through the shoals of the Metaris estuary and struck southward through the fens, burning farmsteads and carrying off livestock, goods, and men. Icel did not precisely ask for aid—he had, after all, been given those lands on the understanding that he would defend them—but the implication that he would welcome some support was clear.

"Otherwise, he would have simply reported his victory," said Cai. "We must send a troop—enough men so they will know we have not abandoned them. I can raise some from my own country, and perhaps the Dumnonians—"

"Will send no men to aid Saxons, as you know very well!" Guendivar interrupted him. "And you are not going to lead them, whoever they are. I need you here!"

That was not entirely true, but Cai must know as well as she did that he was in no condition for campaigning. He did not protest her decision, and that worried her. In the past year he had grown short of breath, and his high color was not a mark of health. Cai refused to discuss his condition with her or with Merlin. To keep him from exhausting himself further was the most she could manage.

"The messenger will need a day or two to recover. I will think on what we may do."

The queen was still worrying over the problem that evening when Medraut knocked at the door of the accounting house.

For the first time, she regretted allowing Gualchmai to go to Gallia. Or Theodoric to depart for Demetia—but the Anglians would not have been impressed by a Goth newly come to Britannia, no matter how good his navy. And she dared not send a Dumnonian prince, who was as likely to encourage the Northmen to attack Icel as to defend him. She needed someone of unquestioned British background who could deal with the Saxons.

"They are saying," said Medraut as he entered, "that my brother Aggarban is dead."

Guendivar set down the tax rolls she had been pretending to examine. "It is so. He died from wounds taken in battle. I am sorry."

Medraut shrugged. "He was some years older, and left home when I was only five years old. I did not know him well."

There was an uncomfortable silence.

"Will you sit?" she asked finally, setting the scroll she had been pretending to read aside. "The nights are still chilly. I will ask Fulvia to bring us some chamomile tea."

"Let me call her—" There was a hint of indulgence in Medraut's smile. He indicated the table covered with scrolls and wax tablets. "You have labored enough this evening already." He rose and went to the door.

Guendivar kept her face still. In the past six years she had learned to recognize the subtle tension of manipulation. It was unusual to find such skill in a man so young, but she thought that constant practice had made her even more skillful at it than he.

"The Goth, Theodoric, brought letters from the king," she said when Medraut had taken his seat once more.

"—my father," he completed her sentence.

Guendivar lifted an eyebrow. Was that the way he wanted it? "The king your father has left it to me to decide whether to keep you here or to send you elsewhere." She watched Medraut carefully, uncertain whether the tightening she thought she saw in his face came from the flicker of the lampflame or from unease.

But if she had worried him, he covered it quickly—when he lifted his head she saw the skin stretched across the strong, graceful bones of his face as smoothly as a mask.

"Since he has abandoned both kith and kingdom, it is fitting that his son, like Britannia, should be in the keeping of his queen. . . ."

"Say, rather, that he has left both in a mother's care . . ." she corrected blandly.

"Oh, pray do not!" Medraut's tone was sardonic, but she could see that she had shaken him. "You forget—my mother is Morgause!"

Guendivar blinked. She was only too aware how Morgause had damaged Artor—for the first time it occurred to her to wonder how she might have warped her son. She thought, *I will be the good mother Medraut never had,* and suppressed the anguished resentment that Artor had never allowed her to be the wife she should have been.

Medraut was still watching her, and Guendivar gave him a gentle smile. "Has your mother turned you against all women, then?"

He shook his head, lamplight sending ripples of flame along the smooth waves of auburn hair. The grey gaze that was so like Artor's held her own. But as she met his eyes, she realized that the expression there was nothing like Artor's at all.

"And has my father turned you against all men, leaving you to lie in an empty bed for so many years?"

Guendivar stiffened. Medraut's voice was very soft, his eyes hidden now by the sweep of downturned lashes so that she could not tell whether sympathy or irony glimmered there.

"That is not a question you may ask of me!"

"Then who can?" He straightened, and now it was she who could not look away. "Who has a better right to question what happens in King Artor's bed than you and I? We have a unique relationship," he said bitterly. "It was you, my lady, who chose to begin this conversation—you cannot take refuge in the ordinary courtesies now!"

Guendivar struggled to keep her composure. "It is clear," she said tightly, "that you do not want another mother."

"A mother?" He shuddered. "For that, you would have had to take me when I was born. But you were only six years old. Did you realize, my lady, how nearly of an age we are?" He reached out to her.

"What do you want, Medraut? What am I to do with you?" she said desperately, trying to forget that for a moment she had wanted to take his hand.

"Use me! Let me show what I can do, not as Artor's mistake or the tool of Morgause, but as myself, a prince of the line of Maximian!" he exclaimed. "Send me to the Anglians! Who else do you have who can understand them? They will not care about my birth, except to recognize that it is royal. There are stories of such matings in their own lore. With thirty men, or sixty, well-mounted, I could show them that the arm of Britannia is still long, even when her king is away!"

Guendivar could not fault his reasoning. But even as she agreed, she realized that it was not for his sake that she wanted him away, but for her own.

Medraut coughed as a shift in the wind brought the acrid reek of burning thatch. The black horse tossed its head uneasily and he jerked on the rein. The British had joined forces with Icel's men at Camulodunum and followed the trail of burnt farmsteads northward. And now, it would appear they had found the enemy. That same wind carried a singsong gabble of northern voices. He lifted his hand, a swift glance catching the attention of the British who rode behind him and the Anglian spearmen who marched with Creoda, a broad-built young man with ashy brown hair who was Icel's youngest son.

Creoda was the only one of Icel's children born in Britannia. He had been a boy during Artor's Anglian wars, brought up on his elder brother's tales of vanished glories. Medraut had not found it difficult to get him talking—he was much like the sons of the chieftains in Cynric's hall, enjoying the benefits of peace, but chafing because they had been born too late to be heroes. It was only when fending off marauders like these Northmen that they got the chance to fight at all.

Carefully they moved forward, the British on the road, the Anglians spreading out through the tangle of second-growth woodland where the old Roman fields were going back to the wild. Then the road curved, and suddenly the trees were gone. Beyond the young barley that the Anglian settler had planted in his home field they could see the burning farmstead.

Medraut yelled and bent forward, digging his heels into the black's sides. As the horse lurched into a gallop, he dropped the knotted reins on its neck, shrugged his shield onto his arm and plucked his spear from its rest at his side. He noted the bodies of the farmfolk without emotion, attention fixed on the foe. The raiders were dropping their booty and snatching up the weapons they had laid aside, but he had caught them by surprise. They were still scattered when the British hit them, stabbing and slashing with spear and sword.

The buildings were still smouldering when the fighting ended. Medraut drew a deep breath, grinning, exulting in the rush of blood through his veins. It had been like this when he had ridden with Cynric to break up a fight between two feuding clans of Saxons—the tension before the conflict and the exaltation after, as if he were drunk on a dark mead of war. Growing up in the hulking shadows of his brothers, he had sometimes despaired of ever becoming a warrior—but Cynric had trained him well. Though he did not have Goriat's height or Aggarban's heavy muscles, he had learned to make full use of the swift flexibility of his lean frame.

A dozen northern bodies sprawled in the farmyard, blood and mud darkening their fair hair. The rest, near forty in number, stood together by the well, their weapons heaped before them, glaring at the circle of Anglian spearmen who had caught those who tried to flee. Two of Creoda's men had been killed and several wounded; one of the British had broken a leg when he was pulled from his horse. But Medraut himself had not a mark on him, while three of the fallen had died at his hand. He was *good* at fighting—a gift he owed neither to father nor mother, but to Cynric's teaching and his own hard-won skill.

He grinned savagely, surveying his prisoners.

"Does one of you have the Roman tongue?" he asked.

A young man with hair so pale it seemed white in the spring sunlight straightened. Medraut had already guessed him to be the leader from the gold armring he wore.

"*Appeto Galliam*—" he said in rough Latin, using a verb which could mean either traveling to a place or attacking it, to indicate that he had been to Gallia.

"That I can believe!" murmured one of the British.

"*Mercator*—" the Northman continued. *As a merchant*—

"And that, I do not believe at all!"

"*Gippus, filius Gauthagastus regulus.*" The prisoner touched his chest. *Gipp son of Gauthagast.* . . .

"*Medrautus filius Artorius.*" He tapped his own breast, ignoring the little murmur of reaction from his men. "So, we have a king's son to ransom," he added in the Saxon tongue.

"A second son only," said Gipp in the same language. "You will not get much for me."

"Oh, I will get something—" Medraut smiled sweetly. "Where are the others?"

"The rest of you swine!" snarled Creoda when the prisoner did not answer.

"Gone by now, full-laden—" The Northman grinned. "They left us six days ago, but we were still hungry."

"This time, you have bit off more than you can chew," said Creoda, but the news had clearly relieved him.

Medraut nodded. "Who are your best seamen? They shall take your ship back to the North with word to your people. The rest of you will come with us to Camulodunum. Creoda, will you set up a rotation of guards?"

"Gladly! And send a messenger to my father." He favored Medraut with an approving smile. "You fight like one of our own, son of the Bear. We have done good work today!"

The Britons and their Anglian allies moved slowly southward, for some of the Northmen were wounded and could not go fast. But the weather had cleared and the roads were beginning to dry. With all their enemies accounted for, they could afford to relax.

On the third evening, knowing that the next day's march would bring them to Camulodunum, Medraut took a skin of ale and sat down beside his prisoner.

"Tomorrow we will come to Camulodunum," he said, offering the ale.

"A Roman town—who now lives there?" Gipp answered in the same tone. If he harbored fears for his future, he was doing well at hiding them.

"Anglians. The town was falling into ruin. Icel sent one of his chieftains to hold the place by the terms of his treaty with King Artor."

Gipp lifted an eyebrow. "I thought the Anglians conquered this land." He drank, and passed the skin of ale back again.

"Then why do I ride with them?" asked Medraut. "Artor defeated Icel's army twenty years ago. But by then, all the Britons had fled and there was no one to till the land. So Artor took the Anglians into his kingdom, to protect it from raiders."

"Like me. . . ." Gipp grinned. "They do not do so well, eh?"

"They have mostly settled the richer lands inland, not the coasts. Is this land much like your own?"

Gipp laughed. "It would be hard for a place to be more different. Halogaland is all mountains, with little pockets of pasture clinging above the narrow fjords. This land—so flat—" He gestured at the mixed marsh and woodland around them. "Seems very strange. But there are no rocks. A man could grow anything in this soil."

"Have you seen many lands?" Medraut wiped his mouth and passed the ale-skin back again.

"Oh, there are always kings who look for good fighting men. I marched with Ela when he attacked the Geats, after they took in the banished sons of his brother. He killed Heardred, the Geatish king, but Adgils and Admund escaped him. They say Beowulf rules there now, and he is a hero of whom there are already many tales. I think there would be little profit in following Ela now."

"It is profit you look for, not glory?" Medraut rested his forearms on his knees, considering the other man.

Gipp's high-boned face creased in a smile. "They say in my country that cattle and kinsmen will die, and only a man's fame live after. But I have won my name in battle, and it seems to me that so long as I live in this world I will need the cattle and the kin. I would not be sorry to settle down with a plump wife and a good farm. But at home there is little land."

"And that is why you think your father will not ransom you?"

Gipp shrugged. "A man cannot escape his wyrd."

"Well—" Medraut got to his feet, motioning to the Northman to keep the ale-skin. "Perhaps we will find some other use for you."

*   *   *

The bright, hot weather of June was smiling on the land when Medraut came back to Camalot. The fortress was full of men and horses—Guendivar had called the princes of Britannia to council, and their retinues sat drinking and dicing in stable and ramparts and hall.

He had stayed with the Anglians long enough to get Icel's agreement to settle Gipp at the mouth of the Arwe, north of Camulodunum, to hold the place for the Anglians as they held the whole of Anglia for Artor. But the Northman knew whom he had to thank for his good fortune. Medraut had not decided what use he might make of the warrior, but it never hurt to have the gratitude of a good fighting man.

Medraut was twenty-six years old. At his age, his father had already been king for ten years. He himself had spent the equivalent years with Cynric, and what had they gotten him?

The sons of the Saxons are not the only ones who dream of glory, he thought ruefully as he gazed at the grizzled locks of the princes who sat at council in the great roundhouse with their sons behind them. *Where, in this empire Artor is building, is there a place for me?*

The queen had summoned the assembly to set the levies for this year's taxes. It was not going well.

"Ten years! Next year it will be ten years since the king was sailing oversea!" exclaimed Cunobelinus, his northern accent striking with a painful familiarity in Medraut's ear. " 'Tis as long, surely, as it took the Greeks to take the city of Troy!"

"And will that be the end of it? Or will Artor, like Ulysses, be another ten years returning home?" Peretur echoed him.

"The seas that separate our shores from Gallia are neither so great nor so treacherous as the Mare Internum," the queen said tartly, "but even if it were so, when Artor returns he will find me as faithful as Penelope."

"My lady—no one doubts your fidelity," Eldaul of Glevum said gently, "only the need for it. The king of Britannia belongs at home."

"Oh, he may bide abroad for another ten years with my good will and conquer all the way to the gates of Roma," put in Paulinus of Viroconium, "so long as he does not require my taxes! Let the men of Gallia support his army if they desire his presence so greatly."

There was a murmur of agreement from many of the others.

"We have done well enough without him, these past years!" said someone at the other end of the hall. Medraut peered through the shadows and recognized the prince of Guenet.

Cunobelinus turned towards him, glaring. "But without the king, how long will the Pax Artoria be lasting? Drest Gurthinmoch has honored his treaty, but a new generation of warriors is growing up on tales of the riches of Britannia. How long will he be able to hold them? If he thinks that Artor has abandoned us, how long will he try?"

"The king has not abandoned us!" exclaimed Guendivar, two spots of color burning in her cheeks.

Perhaps not, my lady, thought Medraut, *but he certainly appears to have abandoned* you! She was very beautiful in her anger. He thought with distaste of his mother, who had also had to rule alone when Leodonus began to fail. But Morgause had lusted after power.

What do you lust for, Guendivar, he wondered, gazing at her, *or do you even know?* Last night he had dreamed of Kea, the Pictish slave who had been his first woman. Like the queen, she had been sweetly rounded, with hair like amber in the sun. At the time, he had thought her beautiful, but compared to Guendivar's radiance, her light was only an oil-lamp's flame.

"Artor asks for our taxes—for gold and for grain—" Peretur of Eburacum was speaking now. "And for the defense of Britannia we have never denied him—" His grim gaze swept the assembly, as if tallying those who *had* sometimes refused their support, even during the Saxon wars. "But I am loathe to give up resources which, if the Picts break the Border, we will need ourselves!"

The babble of response was like the roar of a distant sea. Guendivar surveyed the assembly, cheeks flaming with anger, and rose to her feet, staring them down until silence fell once more. But when she spoke, her voice was calm.

"Clearly, there are many factors here to be considered, and we have sat long at our debate. Hunger is not the best counselor. Let us go out to the meal that my cooks have been preparing, and meet again when the sun begins its descent once more."

As he followed the others from the roundhouse, Medraut continued to watch the queen. Though her women had come out to escort her, she seemed very much alone, her brow furrowed with the anxiety she had been too proud to show in the hall.

Britannia may be able to endure without Artor, he thought then, *but if he does not return, what will happen to the queen?* His gaze followed her as she entered her own quarters, and he blinked, his vision for a moment overlaid with memory of the dream in which little Kea had lain in his arms.

"Medraut!"

At the shout, he turned, and saw the heir to Viroconium hurrying towards him. Martinus was a puppy, with an open face and eager eyes, but he might have his uses. Medraut paused, arranging his features in a pleasant expression.

"I hear that you fought wild savages from Lochlann last spring. What were they like? How many did you kill?"

With some effort, Medraut maintained his smile. Martinus' voice was both penetrating and loud; others were turning, younger men for the most part, second sons and chieftains' heirs. He saw Caninus of Glevum, who was a good fighter already, and the two cousins from Guenet, Cunoglassus and Maglocun. In another moment, a group was gathering, and Medraut grinned.

"They are fierce fighters indeed, but no monsters. If you like, I will tell you the tale. . . ."

Whatever he might say was bound to be more interesting than the political debates of their elders, thought Medraut as he led his audience to the shade below the palisade.

"You all know that we defeated the Anglians twenty years ago, and gave them lands in the east that our own people had abandoned; on condition that they should defend them."

"My grandfather says the king betrayed his own people, making that treaty—" said Marc'h, a lanky thirteen-year-old who was the son of Constantine. "He should have killed them all."

"Huh—*your* grandfather started the last Saxon war!" someone else replied.

"Perhaps—" Medraut cut in once more, "but then the land would have been empty, and these same Northmen you call savages might have come instead, and been much harder to deal with. The Saxons, and the Anglians, are not bad people—I have lived among them, and I know. They become more like us the longer they live in our land."

"They hold a quarter of Britannia," muttered Marc'h. "My grandfather says they will try to gobble down the rest of it one day."

Medraut shook his head. "Not if we are strong and stand together. Not if their kings see an advantage in being our allies. I fought shoulder to shoulder with Icel's son, Creoda, and now he calls me friend."

"The campaign—tell us—" came a babble of voices, and Medraut began his tale. He did not exaggerate, or at least, only a little. The men of Demetia who had ridden with him could disprove any claims that were too extravagant, after all. But he had learned among the Saxons that a man owed it to himself to claim his victories.

"And so I have the gratitude of both the Anglians and the Northmen!" Medraut allowed himself a small smile. "There is still glory to be won without ever leaving Britannia."

"The lord Peretur says that the Picts are sure to start a new war soon," said a young guardsman from Eburacum. "He says if the king does not come back soon, Britannia will be as it was in the time of the Vor-Tigernus, when the princes fought each other and left the land at the mercy of its enemies."

"It is true," Medraut said thoughtfully. "We need a strong king, who will put Britannia first. . . ." He stopped, seeing a sudden doubt in some of their faces, while others nodded agreement. Had he meant to hint at rebellion? He hardly knew himself, but the seed was planted now.

"And what if Artor does not come back? What if he and your brothers and all the experienced fighting men are killed by the Franks?" Martinus cried.

"We still have the queen—" answered Medraut. "During these past years, will any deny that she has governed well?"

"But she cannot lead an army—"

"Perhaps not, though I seem to remember that the queens of our people did just that, when the Romans were conquering this land. But she does not need to. I come from the North, where they still understand that the queen is the source of sovereignty. If the high king falls, or fails, it is for Guendivar to choose a lord to lead this land."

VII

Bitter Harvest

A.D. 514

The yearly levies of gold and grain were due at the end of summer, when the corn harvest was in. Each year since the king had departed, it seemed to Guendivar, the totals had diminished. Were the princes lying in their reports, or had Artor's absence really drained the fertility from the land? In the North, folk held that the soil's productivity depended on the queen. That was no help, she thought, staring at the smoke-stained plaster of the wall. How could the land be fecund when the queen was barren?

"Do you have the tally from Dumnonia?" asked Medraut from the other side of the room.

"Such as it is—" she answered. "According to this, there is scarcely a stalk of grain in Kernow, and hardly a fish in the sea." She leaned from her chair to hand him the scroll.

Putting another table in the room for him to use had made for cramped quarters, but Guendivar did not grudge it. Medraut had a sharp brain, and his mother, whatever his feelings about her might be, had trained him well. In the past year he had turned into an able assistant.

And now he was more necessary than ever. The queen felt her eyes filling with remembered sorrow. For the past year Cai had insisted on continuing to work even when it was clear he was in pain, and just after midsummer his noble heart had given way at last. She still missed his dour, steady support, but at least Medraut was taking on some of his labor.

"You cannot blame the Dumnonians for wishing to keep their harvest for their own use when they know that what they give us will go to support a war across the sea," he said then.

"Can't they see the need?" Guendivar exclaimed.

"To a farmer in Kernow or a sheepherd in the Lake Country, Gallia seems very far away—"

"I'm sure the Armoricans thought the Franks were distant too," Guendivar replied tartly, "but now they are at their gates. It does not need a Merlin to prophesy that if the Franks are not stopped in Gallia, one day the cliffs of Dubris may see their sails."

"But not today—" repeated Medraut, "and this day, this harvest, is what the people see. They do not understand why their king has abandoned them. They cannot share his dreams."

"What can I do?" She shook her head despairingly. The changes had been slow, and small, but each day the king was away from his kingdom, the web of obligation and loyalty that had held Britannia together frayed a little more. "How can I make them understand?"

"It is Artor's dream!" he exclaimed, rising. "Let *him* persuade them. It is not fair to lay this burden on you!"

"At least this is something I *can* do for him," Guendivar said sadly.

"And this is something I can do for you . . ." Medraut replied.

Guendivar felt a gentle touch on her shoulder, and then his strong fingers kneading, banishing the tension that knotted the muscles there. She gave an involuntary sigh, leaning into the pressure of his hands. She had not realized how tightly she had been braced against the demands of each day.

"Is that better?" he said softly.

"Wonderful . . . where did you learn to do this?"

There was a silence, while he pressed the points that would release the tensions at the base of her neck.

"My mother also was a ruling queen, although, unlike you, she lusted after power. But after a day among the accounts she too grew stiff and sore. She taught me how to massage the pain away. In the evenings I would stand behind her, as now I stand behind you, while her harper played."

"She taught you well. . . ."

"Oh indeed." His voice grew bitter. "She taught me many things . . ."

For a moment his grip was almost painful. She made a stifled sound of protest and he grew gentle again.

"What did Morgause do, to hurt you so?" Guendivar asked at last.

"Sometimes I think her first sin was to give birth to me. But no child hates its life. She was my whole world, then." He sighed. "And I believed that I was hers. I knew she favored me more than my brothers. She kept me always by her, directing my every step, and thought, and word. I loved her—I had no one else to love."

"Was that so bad? Or did she change?"

"Change? Not until it was too late for me," Medraut replied. "When I began to feel a man's urges, she took me to the Picts. There were a number of boys of my age there—they showed us a beautiful girl and said she should choose as her lover the lad who did best in the games. She had amber hair like yours," he added softly, "but she was wearing one of my mother's gowns. I know now that it was all arranged beforehand, but at the time I thought her a princess, whom I had won in fair competition with the other boys.

"And perhaps I would have!" he burst out then. "I was skillful and strong. I did well! But after that night, in which I discovered the joy that men find in women's arms, she confessed that she was only a slavegirl, and that she had been told which boy to choose. She wept in my arms, my little Kea, for by then she loved me, and I believed that I loved her, too.

"I begged my mother to buy her for me, but she said the girl was bestowed elsewhere. It was more than a year before I found out that my mother had already purchased Kea herself and ordered her strangled before we had even arrived back at Dun Eidyn."

"But why?" exclaimed Guendivar.

"The reason given was that she must never open to another the womb that had received my first seed! I think that my mother saw how I loved Kea, and feared a rival. . . . But by the time I found out what had happened, Morgause no longer cared whether I loved her. She had left me and whatever plot she had meant to use me in, and run back to her own mother at the Isle of Maidens. I came south, hoping to find better treatment at the hands of my father. But he has abandoned me too, just as he abandoned you!"

"Oh, Medraut!" she exclaimed, half turning. "I am so sorry!"

For a moment the knowing fingers stilled. "Poor little queen . . . so beautiful and wise. She cares for everyone else, but who will care for her?" He began to work again, stroking down along her arms, massaging the muscles of forearm and hand, especially the right, cramped from long hours with stylus and quill.

"Such a fair white hand—it doesn't deserve such labor—" He turned it over and began very gently to explore the countours of the palm.

Guendivar shivered. He stood very close, his arms curved around her. It seemed natural to lean against him, savoring the warm strength of the male body that supported her own.

"It deserves . . . to be kissed—" Medraut lifted her hand and gently pressed his lips to the sensitive center of her palm.

"Oh!" She pulled her hand away, still quivering from the jolt of energy that had passed through her body at his touch. "It tickles—" she stammered, stiffening.

Medraut said nothing, but the strong hands drifted back up to her shoulders, gentling her like a nervous mare, and then to her neck and scalp. She relaxed once more, the dangerous moment past.

"You spoke of a plot. What did Morgause plan? I know she did not intend your conception," she said then.

Again, for a moment, the clever fingers stilled. "Not my conception, but from the hour of my birth she raised me to be her puppet on Artor's throne, because he had stolen Igierne's love, and because she knew the princes of Britannia would never accept her as queen. Now, of course, she is the holy Lady of the Lake herself, and would never dream of disloyalty—"

He drawled out the words with bitter irony.

"And you?" Guendivar said softly.

"I was brought up to serve a queen. You are my lady now. . . ." Gently he stroked her hair. She sat, half-tranced as his hands moved down to caress her cheek, turning her head as he came around to kneel beside her, and reached to kiss her lips.

His mouth was sweet and warm. She trembled, feeling her blood leap in answer, and his hand tightened, drawing her closer. Now his lips claimed what they had only requested before. Guendivar stiffened, and he let her go.

"I am your father's wife . . ." she whispered.

"But not my mother—" he said thickly. "This, at least, is not incest."

She straightened, taking a deep breath to slow her pulse. "Soon, Artor will return. I will keep faith with him."

"But what if he breaks faith with you? What if he never returns?" Medraut's gaze held hers.

"He will come back!" she said desperately. "Help me, Medraut, I need you. But between us there can be nothing more."

Medraut sat back on his heels, his expression relaxing to its usual look of irony. "Lady, I will remember. . . ."

The queen turned back to her papers, though she did not see them, knowing that she would remember as well.

When the first chill winds of fall plucked leaves from the trees and gleaned the stubbled fields, the princes of Britannia went hunting. It had become Guendivar's custom, in the years of Artor's absence, to progress through the kingdom during the time between harvest and midwinter, allowing her household to enjoy the sport, renewing acquaintance with the chieftains, and collecting any taxes that were still in arrears. This year it was Dumnonia whose contribution was still lacking, and so it was that at the Turning of Autumn the royal household found itself at Caellwic, an old hillfort south of Din Tagell that Constantine used as a hunting lodge.

The stags were in rut already. The woodland rang with their bellowing. Men stopped when they heard that harsh music, listening, and Medraut recognized the excitement that pulsed in his own veins in the glitter of other men's eyes.

"Go—" said Constantine, who was prevented by a twisted knee from riding. "It is clear that until you have had your sport no one will have any patience for sitting in council. I only wish I could go with you!"

They set out early the next morning, guided by a little dark fellow called Cuby who reminded Medraut of the hidden people of the northern hills. Several of the riders had brought dogs with them, lean grey sighthounds that strained at their tethers and curly-haired brachets that could follow a blood trail all the way to Annuen.

"A stag—you get now, while still has flesh—" The little man laughed softly. "Wears self to bone, rutting and fighting. This time o'year, thinks with his balls!"

"Like you, Ebi—" said Martinus of Viroconium to one of his friends.

The young man in question flushed. He had acquired a reputation second only to Gualchmai's for affairs with women, and since the latter's marriage, might even have surpassed him.

"And why not?" said someone else in a lower tone. "We must prove our manhood in bed if we are not allowed to do so in war!"

Medraut smiled without speaking, paying more attention to the tone than the words. The men who had come out with him were mostly of his own generation, sons of chieftains, or of men who had gone with Artor over the sea. He watched how they rode and handled their weapons, considering which of them he might want to add to the guard with which he had garrisoned Camalot.

They came down off the high moorland into a wooded valley and their guide held up a hand for silence. Medraut leaned back, gripping hard with his knees as his mount slid down the bank. Somewhere ahead he could hear the gurgle of a stream. His pony threw up its head, snorting, and he reined in hard as half a dozen dark heads popped up from among the hazels. They spoke to Cuby in a soft gabble, and the guide turned back to the riders with a grin.

"They say there is fine deer in meadow downstream. You go carefully, bows ready, and they drive him."

One of the dogs whined and was hushed. The hounds pulled at their leashes, quivering, knowing that soon they would be freed to run.

"Very well," said Medraut. He turned to the other riders. "Mark your targets as you will, but the king stag belongs to me!"

He kicked his mount into the lead. They moved off through the autumn woods, dappled with the golden shadows of the turning leaves. The riders, wrapped in hunting mantles chequered in the earth tones of natural wool, seemed to blend into the branches. Fallen foliage deadened the horses' footfalls; only a soft rustle accompanied their progress, with the squeak of saddle leather and the occasional chink of steel.

There was a tense moment when Martinus reined his mount in hard and it squealed. Medraut rounded on him, frowning, and Martinus pointed to the black-and-white ripple of an adder winding away among the leaves. Martinus was notorious for his fear of serpents; hopefully they would not encounter another. Medraut sighed, and motioned him to move on.

Presently the trees began to thin. Beyond them he glimpsed the meadow, and the red-brown shapes of deer. He reined back and lifted a hand to alert the others, then loosened his rein. His mount took a few steps forward, paused to snatch a mouthful of greenery, then moved on. Through the veil of leaves he saw one of the deer lift its head, ears swiveling, and then, sensing only the random movements of grazing quadrupeds, return to its own meal.

Slowly the hunting party moved through the wood, men peeling off at Medraut's signal to tie their mounts to trees and ready their bows. They could see the deer clearly now, grazing at the other end of the meadow— seven soft-eyed does and the stag who was courting them, his flanks a little ragged, but his head upheld proudly beneath its antler crown. The old king of the forest he was, a stag of twelve tines who had survived many battles and begotten many fawns.

Ho, old man, thought Medraut, *you are looking for the young stag who will try to steal your does. But the creature that comes against you now will take not only your females but land and life itself! Beware!*

The does were grazing, but the stag stood with head up, nostrils flaring as he tested the wind. He was clearly uneasy, but the random movements of the horses had deceived him, and the scent he was seeking was that of his own kind. Medraut saw the edge of the wood before him and reined his own mount in. Moving slowly, he slid from the saddle, using the body of the horse to hide his own from view. With equal care he unslung his bow and nocked an arrow.

A two-legged shape flickered in and out of view at the other end of the meadow. Among the deer, heads jerked up. They began to move, alerted, but not yet alarmed.

Come here, my king . . . thought Medraut, *this way. Your life belongs to me!*

Again the half-seen movement. Now the wind must be bringing scent as well, for a doe jumped to one side. The others stiffened and the stag's heavy head swung round. In another moment they would flee. Medraut lifted the bow, his own muscles quivering with strain.

Off to his left someone sneezed. The deer exploded into motion. Medraut, his gaze fixed on the stag, turned as it leaped forward, awareness narrowing to the gleam of red hide. He felt the arrow thrum from between his fingers, saw it sink into the shining flank, then the stag flashed past him and crashed off through the trees.

He jerked the rein free and flung himself onto his horse's back. A grey shape hurtled past him, barking excitedly. From behind him, hunting horns sounded the chase in bitter harmony. Medraut dug his heels into the pony's sides and sent it after, lips peeled back in a feral grin.

The minutes that followed were a confusion of thrashing leaves and whipping branches. His shot had been a good one, but the stag was strong, and by the time blood loss began to slow him he was halfway down the valley.

Medraut heard a furious yammering of dogs and slapped his pony's neck with the reins. Through the trees he saw a plunging shape, red and brown as it passed through sunlight and shade. Five hounds had brought the stag to bay against an outcropping of stone. As Medraut pulled up, he heard hoofbeats behind him and saw Martinus on a lathered mount.

"Over there—" he shouted. "Keep the dogs to their work!"

Martinus nodded and urged his horse forward, sounding the death on his horn and encouraging the hounds with yips and cries. Medraut had dismounted and tied his own mount, and was working his way around the side, pulling the short hunting sword from its sheath. He heard other riders arriving, but none would dispute his claim. He eased around the tumbled rocks, calculating his approach.

The hart, wheeling to face the darting dogs, was oblivious to its danger. One dog was bleeding from a gashed flank already, and as Medraut crept closer, the stag's head dipped and it hooked another, yelping, into the air. Medraut darted forward, slashing at the tendon that ran down the hind leg, leaping back as the beast lurched, three-legged, towards him.

For a moment he met the white-rimmed gaze, furious and disdainful even now. Then the antlers scythed downward in a wicked slash.

Medraut leaped sideways, aiming for the spot behind the shoulder where a swift stab could pierce upward to the heart. But the stag was faster. Twelve blades blurred towards him. He dropped his sword and threw himself forward, under the tines, then jumped, grabbing the beast's neck and jerking up his legs to avoid the striking hooves.

Overbalanced, the stag fell. Medraut, pinned beneath it, twisted an arm free to draw his dagger, stabbing. His body strained against that of the deer in a desperate embrace, his face jammed against the rank hide, until with a last spasm the stag gave up the battle and lay still.

"My lord! Lord Medraut!"

Dimly, he heard the cries. He struggled to sit up as men pulled the carcass off of him. He got to his feet, amazed to find nothing broken, though battered limbs were already beginning to complain. The neck of the hart was a bloody mess, its eyes already dull. He kicked the body and raised his arms, red to the elbow.

"The old king is dead!" he cried, his voice shrill with release. "The victory is mine!"

In the eyes of the men around him he saw relief, and wonder, and a feral excitement that matched his own. They began to cry out his name as horns belled victory. In that moment, the forest, and the dead deer, and the shouting hunters were one. He looked at them and felt a visceral jolt of connection, as if the spirit of the stag had entered him. *They are mine!* he thought. *This land is mine! I claim it as a conqueror!*

Bitter as memory, the music of the horns was carried by the wind from the tree-choked valley to the bare high moorland that looked over the sea. Merlin paused to listen, the sprig of thyme forgotten in his hand.

"Medraut has made his kill," said Ninive. "Tonight there will be venison for the table."

"I would that were all that Medraut brought with him—" The words came from somewhere below Merlin's conscious awareness.

"What do you mean?" asked the girl, her fair hair lifting in the breeze.

Merlin shrugged, knowing neither what he feared nor from whence the knowledge came.

Eyes narrowing, she gestured towards the plant in his hand. "You said you would teach me. This lore of herbs and healing I could learn at the Isle of Maidens. But you are the prophet of Britannia—teach me how to *know*. . . ."

He spread his hands helplessly, letting the thyme fall to the ground. Standing with her face uplifted to the sky, Ninive seemed made of light, her pointed features one with the face of the daimon that lived within his soul.

"How can I teach you? You *are* knowledge."

"When you look at me, what do you see? And what do I see when I look at you?" She gave him a long, enigmatic look. "What you cannot say, perhaps you can show—" she said softly. Then her voice sharpened. "Speak, O man of wisdom. In the name of your daimon I conjure you. How goes it with the high king in Gallia?"

Merlin felt the first wave of vertigo and gripped the shaft of the Spear with both hands, thrusting the point into the earth as if to root it there. Vision came and went in waves, so he closed his eyes, feeling the ashwood shaft in his hands become the trunk of a great tree mighty enough to uphold worlds. Supported by its strength, he relinquished his attempt to hold onto normal consciousness and let his spirit soar.

In the first moments, awareness extended, borne on the wings of the wind. Below him tossed the grey waves of the sea. Then vision began to focus; he saw hacked woodlands and broad fields trampled to mud where armies had passed. In the dim distance where he had left his body, a voice called his name. He knew that he answered, but not what he said to her.

There was the smoke of a burned village; the air trembled with the echo of battle. Awareness focused further; he saw the standard of the Pendragon and men in battered Roman armor locked in a struggle against big, fairhaired men in high-peaked spangenhelms with gilded figures of eagles glittering from their shields.

He saw Artor bestriding the body of Gwyhir, hewing Franks with mighty strokes until Gualchmai clove a way through the tangle to stand with him. Horns blared, and a wedge of cavalry bore down upon the fray, Betiver in the lead. The Franks fell back then, running towards the mounts they had left at the edge of the field. Betiver pursued. The long Roman lances stabbed and more blood fed the ground.

The scene changed then. It was sunset, and within a circle of torches he could see the body of an old man, wrapped in a purple mantle and laid upon a pyre. Artor took a torch from one of the soldiers and plunged it between the logs, then stood back, the flicker of light gilding the hard planes of his face, as the fire caught the oil-soaked wood and blazed high.

Men crowded around him. One held a cloak like the one that had wrapped the corpse. Artor was shaking his head, but they cast the purple across his shoulders. Others surged forward, shields on their arms, and knelt as the king, still protesting, was lifted. Cheering, they raised him on their shields. Merlin could see mouths opening in unison, heard the echo of their shouting in his soul—*"Imperator! Imperator!"*

Awareness recoiled in a whirl of purple and flame, and he opened his eyes, gasping in the red light of the dying day.

"The king—" he croaked, and coughed, trying to sort through the maelstrom of fading images. "What did I say?"

"Riothamus is dead," said Ninive in a shaken voice, "and they have acclaimed Artor as emperor. . . ."

The Isle of Afallon lay wrapped in the dreaming peace of autumn. Guendivar sat beside the Blood Spring, watching yellow leaves swirl slowly across the pool.

"He will never return, Julia," she said sadly. "I feel it in my heart. If they have made Artor emperor, he has his desire. Why should he return to me, or to Britannia?"

"If you can trust the sorcerer's vision," observed the other woman a trifle grimly. The years had changed Julia little, save for the white veil of a sworn nun that covered her cropped hair. "Every day, it seems, we hear a new tale. Some say that it was Artor, not Riothamus, who died."

Guendivar shook her head. "He is not dead. I would know. . . ."

"Because you are his wife?" Julia lifted one eyebrow. "He has never truly been a husband to you."

"Because I am Artor's queen," corrected Guendivar, "and the land itself would break into lamentation if he departed this world."

Julia snorted disbelievingly. "After ten years does the land even remember him? It is you, my dear one, who are the source of sovereignty. What will you do?" After the death of Mother Madured, the nuns had chosen Julia to lead them, and she spoke with authority.

"Theodoric has sent a ship to Aquilonia for news. I will decide when we know for sure—"

"If you have time!" Julia rose to her feet, shaking her head. "Artor has been too long away, and Britannia is humming like a hive. If he does not come back himself along with the messenger, he may find that the land has given herself elsewhere! But whatever happens, my queen, remember that there will always be a place for you at Afallon."

Guendivar tried to smile. Once she had thought this isle a prison, but now she could appreciate the power that lay beneath its peace. All the disciplines of the nuns barely allowed them to endure the energies that pulsed in the chill waters of the spring. She leaned over the water, seeing her own face as a design in flowing planes amid the spiral flow of the current. She dipped up water and the image dislimned, forming anew in the shining drops that fell from her hands.

Both women turned at the sound of a step on the stones. It was one of the novices, still nervous before the queen of Britannia.

"Lady, the lord Medraut would speak with you. . . ."

"He cannot come here," Julia began, but Guendivar was already rising.

"Tell him to join me in the orchard," she said, pulling the veil up over her hair.

The apples had been harvested, and the leaves were falling. Only a few wizened fruits, too small to be worth the effort to reach them, still clung to the highest boughs. But though the trees were bare, they were not barren, for with the new year they would flower and fruit once more.

Unlike me . . . the queen thought bitterly. She paced between the trees and turned, frowning, as Medraut shut the gate and came towards her. Lean and well-knit, with the sunlight burnishing his auburn hair, at least he did not remind her of Artor.

"The horses are ready. If we would reach Camalot before dark, we must go now."

"Why should I go back? If Artor does not return, I am no longer queen." Guendivar could feel the kingdom crumbling around her, or perhaps it was she herself who was drying up and flakng away. Medraut caught her by the shoulder as she started to turn.

"Guendivar!" His grip tightened. "You are the source of sovereignty! Britannia needs you—*I* need you! My lady, my beloved, don't you understand?"

She retreated, shaking her head, and he followed, still holding her, until her back was against a tree.

"Guendivar. . . . Guendivar. . . ." He pulled the veil from her head and, very gently, touched her hair. "You are source and the center, the wellspring and the sacred grove."

She stood, scarcely breathing, as his hand moved from her hair to her cheek. This was not the disguised seduction he had tried before. Gentle he might be, but there was an authority in his grip that she could not deny. She turned her head, but he forced it back again, and then he was kissing her, hard and deep, and she felt the power begin to leave her limbs.

"Artor is gone . . ." he murmured into her hair. "He has abandoned us, and without a king, the princes will tear this poor land apart like wolves. I can lead them, I know it, but only you can legitimate my rule!"

His hand slid down her neck, pushing the tunica from her shoulder to cup her breast, and she began to tremble, long-suppressed responses flaming into awareness once more.

"Guendivar . . . Guendivar. . . . Marry me, and I will love you as he never could. I know how to serve a queen!" He bowed before her, hands sliding down her sides until he knelt, holding her against him, head pressed against the joining of her thighs.

"I am your father's wife . . ." she whispered, fighting to stay upright. If once he got her on her back upon the grass, she would have no power to stop whatever he might do.

And why am I resisting? she wondered. When had Artor ever come to her with such passion, such need?

"He has renounced the marriage, and you are no kin to me—" he said thickly. "Come to me, Guendivar, give me the right to rule. . . ."

"Not here . . ." she whispered. "This is holy ground. . . ."

Medraut leaned back a little, gazing up at her with darkened gaze. "But you will lie with me, won't you, my dearest? You will marry me?"

Guendivar shuddered, her body aching with need. It was too late, she thought. She had no choice, now—she had already given too much away. Without volition, the words came to her. "When you are king. . . ."

The queen sat in her place in the round Council Hall, an image of sovereignty draped in cloth of gold. Medraut had taken his seat on the other side of the king's empty chair.

Soon, he thought, *it will be* my *chair!* As soon as the men he had summoned to his Midwinter Feasting agreed. . . . The blazing fire in the center of the circle flickered on faces sharpened by interest, glinted on the softness of fur lined mantles and the glint of gold. The houseposts were wreathed with evergreen, set with holly and ivy and mistletoe.

To call them together had been a risk, he knew. It might have been safer to simply proclaim himself king. If Artor had left the Sword behind, Medraut could have proved his right by pulling it from the stone. His mother had explained the trick of it, and he was of the blood—twice over, he thought with a sardonic grin.

But he could call himself Basileus of Byzantium, or lord of the Blessed Isles, and it would mean nothing if no one followed him. He must be acclaimed by the princes of Britannia, or by enough of them to impress the remainder. Camalot was garrisoned with men he had chosen. He had sent word already to Aelle and Cynric and Icel, and knew that they would send him warriors when he called. But to rule Britannia, he needed the support of these men.

He gazed around the chamber, counting those of whom he was certain, and those he judged weak enough to be swayed. There were some, like Theodoric in Demetia and Eldaul of Glevum, whom he knew would accept no heir until they saw Artor in his grave. The invitations sent to them had all—so sorry—gone astray. Of the older men, he had only Cataur of Dumnonia, who had never been Artor's friend, with his son Constantine by his side.

But Martinus of Viroconium, newly succeeded to his father's seat, would stand behind him, and so would Caninus of Glevum, whatever his father might say. The boys from Guenet, Maglouen and Cunoglassus, though young, came of noble kin. Where the sons were seduced by dreams of glory, the fathers might be persuaded by lower taxes and a more accommodating authority.

Medraut waited, poised as the hawk that hovers over the field, until all had taken their places, waited until the silence was becoming uncomfortable, before he got to his feet in an easy movement that focused their attention. He had dressed with care in a long tunic of Byzantine brocade dyed a crimson so deep it was almost purple. His black cloak was lined with wolfskin. Around his neck glinted a king's torque of twisted gold.

"Lords of Britannia, I bid you welcome. It is the queen who has called you here to council, as is her right. I speak in her name—" He bowed to Guendivar, who inclined her head, her features as expressionless as those of a Roman statue beneath the veil.

"And why does she—or you—summon us here?" Cataur called out in reply.

"To take counsel for the future of this island, for ten long years bereft of her king." He waited for the murmur to subside.

"Have you had word of Artor's death?" asked Paulinus of Viroconium.

"We have had rumors only. There was a great battle with the Franks, and many were killed. My informants saw a funeral pyre and were told that the Britons were burning their king."

The outbreak of response to this was sharper. Many here had resented Artor's rule, but he had also been much loved. Guendivar looked up abruptly at his words, for she believed the confused tale of Merlin's prophecy, that it was Riothamus who had died.

"Perhaps he is not dead"—he shrugged—"although I do not understand why, if Artor lives, he has not sent word. Perhaps they have made him emperor, and he no longer cares for Britannia." Medraut spread his hands. "My lords—does it really matter? He is not here! Is that the act of a lord who cares for his people?" he exclaimed.

"The season of storms is on us, bad for sailing," said someone, but the rest of the men were shouting agreement.

"Is that the way of a Defender of the land? The way of a king?" Medraut continued, drawing more shouts with each repetition.

He moved away from his seat and began to pace around the circle. "Last year men from the North attacked the coast of Anglia. I led a troop of British warriors, and rode with Icel's son Creoda to defeat them. We parted in friendship, but do you think the Anglians did not notice that Britannia has no king to defend her? They accepted me only because I am King Artor's . . . kin."

Medraut saw eyes flickering towards his face and away again. They had become accustomed to him—time to remind them who he really was.

"I spent nearly nine years among the Saxons, and learned their tongue. After a time they forgot to watch their words around me. They are quiet now, but they have not given up their dreams of conquering the rest of this isle. For a decade the fear of Artor's name has held them, but a new generation of warriors is growing up who have not learned to respect British arms. Whether by fear or friendship, they must be fettered anew, and this can only be done by a king."

The fire wavered as the pressure inside the hall was changed by a gust of wind outside, as if to echo his words.

"And do you claim the kingship?" cried one of the Dumnonian lords.

Medraut took a deep breath. For this he had been born; he had been trained up by his mother to be her weapon against the king. Now that Morgause had renounced vengeance, to take Artor's place would be his revenge on her. And he wanted it, more than he had ever wanted anything, except perhaps for his mother's love, or Kea, or Guendivar.

"I do. I have the right, whether you count me as son or sister-son, and I have the will." His voice rang through the hall. "Artor wasted your sons and your wealth in a senseless foreign war. I will keep both safe in Britannia. He kept a tight rein on the princes of this land; but the Saxon wars are long past, and we can afford to rule with less central authority. There must be one man with the power, and the prestige, to deal with them. All these things I will do as your king!"

"What says the lady Guendivar?" asked Constantine.

Medraut turned to the queen and held out his hand. She rose to her feet, paler, if possible, than she had been before.

"Artor has abandoned us," she said in a low voice. "Let Medraut take the rule. . . ."

He bent before her, then straightened, standing of a purpose where firelight would veil him in gold.

"Medraut!" called Martinus and Cunoglassus, and after them a dozen others took up the cry. They shouted his name till the rafters rang, and when the acclamation died away at last, Medraut sat down in the great carved chair of the king.

VIII

Beltain Fires

A.D. 515

Artor splashed through the icy waves, struggling to keep his feet against the surge, until the tide retreated behind him. A few more steps and the stony shore was solid beneath his feet. He sank to his knees, plunging his fingers deep into the swirled ridges of pebble and sand.

Britannia! For so long, as winter storms lashed the narrow sea, he had thought he would never get here. But this holy earth was truly his homeland—it spoke to him as the soil of Gallia could never do. He bent and kissed the stones.

The ground trembled to the tread of the men and horses that were struggling ashore all around him. As he straightened again, the mists thinned and he saw the pale glimmer of the chalk cliffs that flanked the harbor. For two months they had haunted him, seen first in the dream that had brought him home. Even now the images made him writhe: Medraut in the king's high seat, Medraut with his arms around Guendivar. At first, he had thought the vision some bastard offspring of his own fears. But the dream had the flavor of Merlin's power, and as Artor got his men into winter quarters after that last, triumphant battle, he had begun to believe it, even before Theodoric's storm-battered galley brought the news.

Medraut had proclaimed himself high king. He held Camalot and Londinium, and Dumnonia stood his ally. He had made his own treaties with the Saxons, and the rest of the Island was on the verge of civil war. And Guendivar had pledged herself to be his queen.

That was the blade that pierced Artor's heart. Until she betrayed him, he had not realized how much of his soul he had given to his queen. He lifted his head, trying to see through the mists. He had half expected to find Merlin waiting for him to come ashore. If the Druid knew enough to warn him, why had he not put a stop to Medraut's treachery?

"My lord! Did you fall?" Goriat's tall form bent beside him.

Artor shook his head, but the damp of the voyage had stiffened his joints, and he accepted a hand to help himself get up again. There was not much left in Goriat of the youth who had once served in the kitchens of Camalot, he thought grimly, except for the innocence in his eyes. He looked much like Gualchmai, both of them hard muscled and fair and taller than the other men, though Gualchmai's sandy hair was laced with silver now. Aggarban and Gwyhir lay in the earth of Gallia. Since hearing the news from Britannia, the two brothers who survived no longer counted Medraut as kin.

"Well, at least there's no enemy here to meet us—" Goriat squinted past the remains of the old fortress of Dubris towards the downs.

Artor nodded. No doubt that was why Merlin had shown him these cliffs in his dream. In the season of storms he dared no longer crossing, and Dumnonia and the lands the south Saxons ruled would be held against him. Only in Cantium could he hope to land unopposed, if Rigana and Eormenric stayed true.

He looked around him, shading his eyes as the pale February sunlight broke through the fog. Shadow shapes of boats darkened the shoreline. The strand was a confusion of horses and men. It was the warriors of Britannia he had with him—the others had been left with Betiver in Gallia. Men fought best for their own land. The sorrow here was that the same might be said of both sides.

"Get the gear unloaded and form up the baggage train. I'll want to meet with troop commanders as soon as possible. We'll march on Cantuwareburh in the morning."

A day later, Artor was sitting in Hengest's hall. The beams were darker, the walls covered by embroidered cloths, but otherwise it was much as he remembered from Oesc's wedding to Rigana, some twenty-one years before. The year before Mons Badonicus, that had been, when Oesc was killed. Rigana's slenderness had become a whipcord strength, her features sharpened by maturity; in appearance, she seemed little changed. He did not think that she had mellowed, though she seemed to have her temper under better control. But Eormenric was grown to manhood, and Artor winced to see his father look out of his eyes.

Oesc, wherever he is now, has more reason to be proud of his son than I do of mine, he thought bitterly.

"Oh yes, Medraut has sent messengers," observed Rigana, as if she had read his thought. "Gifts as well. We smiled, and took them. Why not?" she went on. "There was no point in defiance until we knew your plans—" She untied a soft leather bag from her belt and plopped it in front of Artor with a musical clink of gold.

"What, did you think I still held Oesc's death against you?" Rigana added wryly. "It was Cataur and Ceretic who destroyed him. And the West Seax and the Dumnonians are Medraut's allies." She turned to her son, whose face had changed at the mention of Ceretic's name. "I know you fear to face your friend Ceawlin in battle, but this is the way of the world. When he thought it needful to avenge me, your father went even against Artor, whom he loved. . . ."

The king watched his own fingers clench on his drinking horn until the knuckles whitened, and forced them to release again. "If you will raise the men of your *fyrd* to follow me, under a good commander, I will be grateful," he said harshly. "But you, boy, stay home to guard Cantuware. This conflict has set brother against brother and father against son already. I will not ask you to fight against your friend."

Rigana's gaze softened. "I see you are still capable of mercy. Remember it, when you have the victory."

"Do you think I will win?"

"When the people see that you have come back to them, they will turn to you," she answered him, "save for those who have been driven so far they think no forgiveness is possible."

"You are talking about Medraut, and . . . the queen?" Odd, how he could not say her name.

"Consider this—Guendivar supports his cause, but she has not married him. Leave a way open for her to come to you. . . ."

Artor stared at her, thinking on the things she did not say. Rigana was the Lady of Cantium; she knew the queen could bestow the sovereignty of the land on the man who served her well. Perhaps Guendivar had not yet given herself to Medraut, but he himself had been no use to her either. He recognized now that it was one reason he had stayed away.

"She must hate me—" he whispered, knowing that until he was able to forgive himself, he could not forgive his queen. And until then, he had no choice but to press on with the bloody business of war.

The king's forces marched swiftly through the chill spring rains, taking the old Roman road westward towards Londinium. At Durobrivae their camp was attacked in the hour before dawn by tall, fair men whose sleek ships had crossed the estuary of the Tamesis. By the time they were beaten off, several wagonloads of supplies had been burned and a number of men killed. The one prisoner they took told them he was a Northman from the settlement Gipp had made on the coast of the Anglian lands, and then, laughing, tore off the bandage with which they had stopped his bleeding and died.

The art of making friends with barbarians, thought Artor grimly, was a gift his son seemed to have inherited. But he said nothing, and ordered his army to continue on.

There were several skirmishes before they reached Londinium, but the city was not held against them. There was no need. Medraut had already stripped it of all supplies. Even in Artor's youth the city had been decaying. There was little left of it now. Still, it was good to take shelter beneath such roofs as remained intact while the king's scouts tried to find out which way the enemy had gone. There he found Betiver's son by the Votadini girl who for nearly twenty years had been his concubine. To have the young man at his side was some small consolation for having had to leave Betiver with the rest of his troops in Gallia.

Thus, it was the middle of the month of Mars before word came that the rebel forces were gathering near Ambrosiacum on the great western plain.

Medraut stood before the Mound of the Princes, watching his father's army form up across the plain. They were armed, as were his own forces, but had not put on their helmets. Artor had called for a parley. Medraut wondered if it could possibly succeed. A chill wind rustled the husks of last year's grass and ruffled the new blades of green, its force scarcely checked by the ancient stones of the Giant's Dance, and he refastened his wolfskin cloak above his mail.

He had not done so badly, he thought, looking over his men. The South and much of the West had declared for him, and those few who resisted, like Eldaul of Glevum, had been overcome. But except for a few skirmishes, the rebels had not yet faced Artor's army, and the old king's reputation was worth a legion. It was Constantine who had insisted that they try negotiation now.

Medraut wondered whether he was confused by old loyalties or simply afraid. Artor's men might be veterans, thought Medraut as he watched uneasily, but they were *old;* experienced they might be, but their strength had been worn away in the Gallian campaigns. He told himself there was no need to fear.

The wind died, and Medraut looked over his shoulder, seized by the odd sense that the spirits in the mound were watching him. He smiled sardonically. They must be very confused. A war of Briton against Briton would be familiar enough, but behind Artor marched Jutes from Cantuware, while Saxons led by Cynric and Cymen and Anglians under Creoda rode in his own train.

The movement before him shivered to stillness. From Artor's army a horn blew shrill, to be answered after a moment from his own side. Constantine of Dumnonia stepped forward, his thinning hair blowing in the breeze. From Artor's side, the spokesman was Gualchmai, grim-faced and frowning, limping a little from some wound got in the Gallian wars. There was a murmur of disbelief from the Dumnonians when they saw him come forward. If the king had sent Gualchmai, it was not to negotiate, but to deliver terms.

Gualchmai halted, his thumbs hooked through his belt, surveying the enemy. Medraut flinched at the chill in his brother's blue gaze.

"So, we are standing together. If I had my will, I'd answer the boasts of your little prince with a good hiding, but I am bound to hear ye out, so say on—"

"My lord Medraut . . ." Constantine coughed to stop his voice from wavering, "requires that the high king give him the North to govern and recognize him as heir to Britannia."

"Fine words for a rebel!" growled Gualchmai. "My lord king requires first that Medraut return his lady and queen. After that, he may find the patience to receive your surrender!"

"Surrender?" Constantine tried to laugh. "When our army outnumbers yours?"

"We've beaten the Franks, who smashed every other army that faced them. D'ye think we'd have any trouble with yours?"

"It is a hard thing, when brother fights brother . . ." Constantine said piously. "And in any case, it is not for us to dispose of the Lady Guendivar—the choice of where she should go is hers."

The queen had been left in the care of a household of holy women who had settled at Ambrosiacum, and even Medraut did not know what she would do. Sometimes the aching tenderness with which he courted her gave way to visions in which he held that smooth white body splayed beneath him, victim of his desire. But he was too much his mother's son to dare to force her. He had felt her need for him—surely he was the one she would choose!

"Promise the prince a territory to govern and his place as heir, and we will disband," Constantine went on.

Let me have the North, thought Medraut, *and Artor will have to face Cynric and Cymen here*. . . . It would be good to get back to his own country. Once across the Wall he would be dealing with folk who had never really accepted the rule of Britannia. And beyond them waited the Picts, allies even more powerful than the Saxon tribes.

Artor nodded, and Gualchmai turned to Constantine with a sigh. "Let it be so."

But not for long, thought Medraut. Artor had not met his gaze, but in the grey light he could see the lines in the older man's face and the silver in his hair. He remembered how the stag had gasped out its life beneath his blade. *You are old, my father—and soon my time will come.*

"We'll drink together to seal the bargain," the Dumnonian replied, "and our lords shall swear to keep faith on the holy cross." Young Maglocun brought out a silver-banded horn filled with ale, and Father Kebi was pushed forward across the grass with crucifix in hand, eyeing the warriors around him like a wether among wolves.

On both sides, the men moved forward, the better to see. And at that moment, someone yelled and steel flashed in the sun. Every head turned. Medraut saw Martinus' face contort in disgust, and a flicker of black-and-white in the grass. The bare blade in his hand lifted, stained with red.

But a greater light was already flaring from the wheeling arc of Gualchmai's sword. "Treachery!" he cried, and then he clove Martinus through the shoulder and struck him down.

For an instant longer Medraut stared. The scene had shattered like a broken mosaic, horns blaring, men running everywhere. Then Cunoglassus pulled him back, shoving helm and shield into his hands. He fumbled to fix the straps, saw Cymen with his houseguard forming a shieldwall, and ran towards its protection.

In the years that came after, few could tell the true story of that deadly, confused conflict before the ancient circle of stones; a battle begun without plan and ending in darkness, with no clear victor. Folk knew only that more blood dyed the plain that day than had ever moistened the pagan altar stone. When it was over, the remnants of Medraut's army marched northward. From that time, news of the war came to the Britons of the South only as rumors that blended to create an imagined reality.

But to Artor, searching the battlefield with flickering torch in hand, it was all too real. Though most of the fallen came from the ranks of his foes, the toll among the men he had brought back from Gallia was heavy as well. He moved among the heaped bodies, recognizing here a man who had saved his life in Armorica, and there a fellow who had always been able to make his comrades laugh.

And near the hour of midnight, when the flesh grows cold on the bones, he found Gualchmai.

The king saw first the corpses, heaped in a distorted circle as if some dark elf had tried to construct a hillfort from the bodies of the slain. He had seen such ramparts before, where some brave soldier had stood at bay, but never so high. He was still staring at it when Goriat came up to him.

"Have you found your brother?" Artor asked, and Goriat shook his head. "Well, perhaps we should look there—" the king said then, indicating the heap of slain.

Wordless, Goriat handed Artor his torch and began to drag the bodies aside. They had fallen in layers—Icel's Anglians atop men from Dumnonia, and beneath them warriors from Cynric's band, all slain by the strokes of a sword. When Goriat had cleared a narrow pathway, Artor followed him to the center. Gualchmai lay there in a pool of red, the great sword still clenched in his hand. No single warrior could have killed him—it was loss of blood from too many wounds that had felled him at last.

"I used to dream of surpassing him," whispered Goriat. "But no warrior will ever enter Annuen with such a noble escort as these."

Artor nodded agreement, then stiffened as Gualchmai stirred. In the next moment he was kneeling beside him, feeling for a pulse beneath the blood-stiffened beard.

"Gualchmai, lad, can you hear me?" He cradled his nephew's head on his lap, stroking his brow. "Goriat, go for a wagon, bring blankets and water, run!" Gualchmai's flesh was cold, but his chest still rose and fell.

"Artor. . . ."

He could barely hear the whisper of sound. "Hush, lad, I am here."

"My fault . . . it was an adder . . . I saw . . . as my sword fell. . . . I have paid."

"Gualchmai, you must live," Artor said desperately. "I loved you and Betiver best of all in the world. Without you, how can I survive?"

Perhaps it was a trick of the torchlight, but he thought Gualchmai's lips curved in a smile. "The king . . . will never die. . . ."

When Goriat and the others arrived, Artor was still sitting with Gualchmai's head pillowed on his thigh, but on the king's cheek they could see the glistening track of tears, and they knew that the champion of Britannia was gone.

"My lord, what shall we do now?"

"Bury Gualchmai in the Mound of the Princes, and dig a grave for the rest of our folk who have fallen here," said Artor. From his eyes the tears still flowed, but his voice was like stone. "Where is the enemy?"

"The Dumnonians are scuttling westward like rats to their holes, but Medraut has gone north," answered Goriat. "They say he has taken the queen and the lady Ninive."

"Then north we shall go as well. Whether he flees to Alba or to Ultima Thule, there is no place on this earth so distant that I will not follow him."

By the day, the air rang with the sound of adze and hammer as Medraut's soldiers rebuilt the palisade of Dun Bara, the fort on the hill. Escorted, Guendivar paced the old earthworks, Ninive beside her. Battered and bruised by the pace of their journey northward, she had prayed only for its ending, but as her body recovered, she began to realize how small was the difference between prize and prisoner.

Beyond the half-built walls she could see a long sweep of hill and moorland and a bright glitter of water beyond them. It was the estuary of the Tava, they had told her. On the other side lay the dark masses of Fodreu. Even the Votadini lands, thought Guendivar as she refastened her cloak, would have seemed strange to her, but Medraut had carried her deep into the country of the Pretani, the Painted People, who had always been the enemies of Britannia. Wind and water tasted different here, and the soil was strange. Here, she was no longer a queen.

Ninive, on the other hand, had grown stronger with every step northward. "My mother was a Royal Woman of the Hidden People, the first folk to inhabit this land," she said, laughing, her fair hair flying in the wind. "I ran wild as a moorland pony until I was eleven years old. Then Gualchmai rode that way out hunting, as he had done when he met my mother and begot me. She was dead by then, and he took me to the Isle of Maidens, to Igierne. Only in this land have I ever been truly free!"

Guendivar shook her head, understanding only that when Medraut ordered her to choose one woman to come with her she had been wise to take Ninive. Had Merlin come north as well? Some of Medraut's men claimed to have seen a Wild Man beyond the flicker of their fires, but if it was the Druid, he had made no attempt to speak with her.

And why should he? she thought bitterly. *I have given him no reason to think I need rescuing. He waits for Ninive, not for me. . . .*

She shivered, and turned towards the roughly thatched hut they had built for the women while they worked on Medraut's hall. It was dark and had few comforts, but at least there was a fire.

That night, Medraut returned, with a band of laughing Pictish warriors, a herd of hairy black cattle, and a line of laden horses. Soon fires were burning and two of the cows were cooking, the large joints roasting over the coals while the rest boiled in crude bags made from their own hides.

For Guendivar he brought a straw-filled mattress and warm woolen blankets, and a mantle of chequered wool in shades of earthy green that he said was a gift from the Pictish queen.

"I am grateful," she said dully when Bleitisbluth, the smooth-tongued Pict who had become Medraut's shadow, had left them, "particularly since I am sure she has no wish to share her land with another queen. This is not my country, Medraut. How long will you keep me here?"

"Is it not?" He grinned whitely, and she realized that he had already had his share of the heather beer. "Pretani is just another word for Briton, and though this land never bowed to Rome, Alba and the south are all part of the same hallowed isle!"

"But these are Picts!" she said in a low voice. "They have always been our enemies!"

"The enemies of the soft southern tribes," he answered, "and the foes of Rome, not mine."

Guendivar could see that was true. Medraut stood now in kilt and mantle chequered in soft ochre and crimson. Of his southern gear he retained only the golden torque. His bare breast was shaded blue with the sinuous spirals of Pictish tatooing, his brow banded with Pictish gold.

"I have endured the rites by which they make a man a warrior. At the feast of Beltain we will swear formal alliance, and I will make for you a wedding feast in the old way that our people followed before ever Christian priest came into this land."

As Medraut's hands closed on her shoulders she stepped backward, but the doorpost was behind her, and there was nowhere to go. She trembled as his mouth claimed hers, feeling even now, as his hands moved over her body, the traitorous leap in the blood.

"Lie with me, Guendivar . . ." he said thickly, his touch growing more intimate. "Open your womb, white lady, and let me possess you utterly. Then I will truly be king!"

"When we are wedded—" she gasped. "I am no use to you if men think me your whore."

For a moment longer he gripped her, until she wondered if the conflict between lust and logic would break him—or her. Then, with an oath, he jerked away.

"*Wise* Guendivar . . ." he said furiously. "You deny me with such reasonable words. But in half a moon I will have you, spread-eagled on the feasting table if need be, so that all men may see that you are mine!" He thrust her away and pushed through the cowhide that hung across the door.

The fire flared as it flapped shut behind him, and Guendivar sank to her knees, her breath coming in shuddering sobs.

"Help me, Ninive!" she whispered as the younger woman put her arms around her. "What can I do?"

"You want him, don't you . . ." murmured Ninive, helping her to sit down by the fire.

"*Him?*" The queen shivered. "Not now, not anymore. But a man's strength to hold me, that I do—Medraut has lit the fire, damn him, and I burn! You don't understand, do you?" She lifted her head to look at Ninive. "Have you never felt your flesh quicken at the touch of a man?"

The other woman shook her head, her great eyes dark and quiet as forest pools.

"Not even Merlin?" Guendivar asked then.

"The love of the body is not what the Druid wants from me. . . ." Her lips curved in a secret smile.

The queen stared at her, but she had not the strength just now to try to understand. "It does not matter. But if Merlin were here, I would beg him to carry me away. . . ."

"Is that truly your will?" Ninive said slowly.

"Oh, my dear, I have known for moons that Medraut is no true king, but where could I go? Artor may have sworn to retrieve me, but he will not want me back again. Still, I will not weaken him further by joining myself to a man who would destroy Britannia! Better I should die in the wilderness, or live a hermit for the rest of my days, than become Medraut's queen!"

"Eat something, my lady, and rest while you may," said Ninive, her gaze gone inward. "And in the dark hours, when the men lie drunk or sleeping, we shall see. . . ."

Sure that sleep was impossible, Guendivar obeyed, but exhaustion claimed her, and when she roused at last to Ninive's whisper, it was from a dream of the Isle of Apples and the sacred spring.

The hearthfire was cold and the doorflap had been thrust aside. Mist curled through the opening, and when she emerged, wrapped in the Pictish cloak, she could see no more than the snoring shape of little Doli, the Pictish servant whom Medraut had set to guard her. Beyond him rose the bulk of the half-built hall. Then, as if he had precipitated from the mist, another figure was there, tall, swathed in a mantle, leaning on a spear.

He gestured, and Ninive took the queen's arm and drew her after, past men sprawled in sleep and drowsing horses, through the open gate of the fortress and down the hill into the waiting fog.

To Guendivar, it was as if they passed through the mists of the Otherworld. But by morning, her aching legs told her that they had covered many miles. They took refuge in a shallow cave, its entrance hidden by hawthornes whose buds were just on the edge of bloom. Guendivar had barely a moment to long for the Pict-queen's mattress before she fell asleep in Ninive's arms.

The next night also they travelled, though the queen's sore feet and aching muscles would not let her go fast or far. If Medraut had set the Picts to search for her she saw no sign of them, and trusted Merlin's woodcraft to keep their passage unknown. On the third day, he brought them horses—sturdy moorland ponies who could cross rough terrain without injury and would keep on going long after the endurance of a warhorse failed.

They moved south and east through the hills, Merlin pacing like a shadow ahead and beside them. His hair and beard were now entirely silver, but despite his age, he pushed on. Each morning there would be a handful of spring greens and some small creature, a hare or grouse or hedgehog, to cook over their little fire. Where Guendivar was sore and exhausted, Ninive grew lean and hardy, kirtling up her skirts and letting down her hair until she was no longer a royal lady but a woods-colt who could keep pace with Merlin.

On the fifth day of their journey, the pace eased, and they began to travel by day. They had crossed over into the lands of the Votadini, where the Picts would not yet follow. That night, Merlin asked her where she wished to go.

"Artor is on his way northward, though he goes slowly, trying to heal the destruction Medraut wrought as he passed. There is hardly a family that this rebellion has not divided, a thousand sparks that must be stamped out before he can fight the real fire."

"I cannot face him!" Guendivar drew back, trying to read the dark eyes beneath Merlin's bushy brows. He walked now in the skin garments of a Wild Man, the only touch of civilization about him the rune-carved Spear. It seemed to her that from time to time he leaned on it more heavily; that the pace he had set for them during the past days was slower, but she did not dare to ask if he were well.

"If I could choose, I would return to the South, to my own country. Perhaps I could take refuge with the holy women at the Isle of Afallon."

"Do you not understand?" He shook his head. "The choice is always yours—you are the queen."

Guendivar stared at him, tears burning down her cheeks, her throat aching so that she could not say a word.

"But the time for decision is not yet upon us," he went on as if he had not seen. "We will continue south towards the Wall, and perhaps on the journey you will find better counsel."

The days lengthened towards Beltain, and the land began to bloom. Now creamy primroses appeared in sunny patches, and the first bluebells nodded beneath the leafing trees. The moorlands were starred with white heather and budding bilberry. Just so, thought Guendivar, the land had arrayed itself when she rode to her wedding, and wondered if she would ever be done with tears.

They made their way eastward along the shore of the Bodotria, and then turned south to follow the old Roman road. Travel grew easier and she lost count of the days.

And then, one evening as the sun began to sink behind the hills, she heard the faint throb of drums. She kicked the pony into a trot and caught up with Merlin.

"What is it? Is there war?"

He shook his head, smiling oddly. "It is the eve of Beltain. . . ."

"Do you know some warded spot where we will be safe through the dark hours?"

"My child, why are you so frightened? Have you forgotten everything you knew?" He picked an early hawthorne blossom from the hedge and laid it in her hand. "Do not fear—where I lead you we will be welcome."

They rode onward through the long spring dusk. Across the valley she saw three peaks in silhouette against the sky. The drumming came now from one direction, now from another, soft with distance. Ninive had made wreaths for herself and Merlin, out of primrose and fragrant herbs. She held another up to Guendivar, and the queen had already set it on her brow before she realized it was a hawthorne crown.

For a moment Guendivar wanted to throw it down, remembering the wreath that had held her bridal veil. But the air was full of a rich, green smell, and she was no longer the child who had been Artor's bride. *Let them do as they will . . .* she thought with sweet melancholy, *it does not matter what happens to me.*

It was almost dark, but Merlin led them unflagging onto a track that wound across the moor. The western horizon still glowed, but above them, stars were blossoming in the sky. They had come around behind the tall northeastern peak where the remains of earthen ramparts rose, and were approaching the space between the other two hills.

The drumming was much louder. A prickle of fear chilled her.

"Ninive—what is it? Where are we going?"

For a moment the younger woman paused. "Oh my lady, those are the drums of my own people! I did not know that any still lived in these lands!" She ran ahead up the path.

But Merlin took Guendivar's bridle and led the horse up around the curve of the hill, stopping once or twice to catch his breath before pressing on. In the fold between the middle and southern peaks rose a rocky bump, where a bonfire sent sparks whirling up to dance with the stars. Dark figures cavorted around it, clad, like Ninive, who had cast off her tunic and run to join them, only in wreaths of flowers. The dancers clustered around her, chattering in a swift guttural language Guendivar did not know, but as Merlin led her into the circle of firelight they fell silent.

She stared into eyes dark as Ninive's, memory whirling with fragments of fearful tales of the people of the hills. After a long moment, she realized that they were as frightened as she. Merlin spoke then, his deep voice rumbling like an echo of the drums, and the fear changed to wonder. Women pulled heather and covered it with skins to make a seat, and when she slid down from the pony, escorted her there. As the drumming began once more, a small girl shyly offered her a wooden bowl filled with a dark liquid that tasted like honey mixed with fire.

"What did you tell them," she asked Merlin, "to make them welcome me this way?"

He smiled down at her, his hair bright as a snowy peak in the sun. "I told them the truth—I said that I had brought their queen."

She should have been angry, but the mead had lit a fire in her belly, and the drumming was beating in her blood. She looked at him and laughed. If eating this food bound her to the Hidden Realm, perhaps she could forget Artor.

The dancing continued. Guendivar ate roasted meat and dried berries, mixed with other things she did not try to identify. There was always more mead when her bowl emptied, the fire's reflection burning across the surface like liquid gold. She grew warm, and pulled off gown and tunica until she was as naked as the dancers. Men and women jumped together over the fire and wandered off into the darkness, laughing softly. The sighs of their passion whispered in time to the beat of the drums.

In the heavens, the stars were dancing, wheeling across the sky in patterns ancient when the world was new. She thought it must be near midnight when something in the music began to change.

People were still leaping around the fire, but they were not the same. They had put on the skins of animals, or perhaps they *were* animals, coupling in the compulsion of spring. She blinked, peering through the swirling smoke, and could not tell. Merlin would know, she thought then, but he too had disappeared, or changed. The drumming had a deeper note, as if the earth itself had become a single vibrating skin. That beat throbbed in her belly, bringing her swaying to her feet. From some depths she had never suspected, a sound rose in her throat and burst free in a wordless cry.

All around her, people were joined in the night's ecstasy, exulting in the passion that she had never been free to enjoy—she, whose fulfillment should have renewed them all! Guendivar took a step forward, stretching her arms to the skies.

"Come!" she cried to the night, to the fire, to the earth beneath her feet. "Oh my beloved, in the name of the Lady, come to me!"

And in the moment between one breath and another, from forest and flame and shadow, He came.

Furred like a beast, like a man He walked upright, and the antlers of the king of the wood crowned His brow. Erect, He came to her and bore her away in His strong arms. Filling and fulfilling He served her, pressing her down upon the moist earth, and the passion that until now had lain potential within her welled up in response, and flowed out from her into the land.

Guendivar was awakened in the dawning by the singing of many birds. Warm wool wrapped her, but the grass against her face was chill with dew. She stretched, muzzily aware of a pleasant soreness, and opened her eyes. The Pict-queen's cloak covered her, and her head was pillowed on her folded clothes. She blinked again; the world around her was a delicate dazzle of light. Through the branches of the hawthorne she could see a translucent sky whose banners of cloud were beginning to flush with gold. But each leaf was outlined in its own radiance, and moving among them she glimpsed vortices of whirling light.

She sat up, and clearing vision showed her luminous forms that expanded, as if in response to her attention, until they were the size of children, staring back at her with shining eyes.

"We hail the Queen!" sang the sweet voices. *"We hail the Hawthorne Bride! The Lady has come to the land!"*

"I know you . . ." whispered Guendivar, looking back in memory at the girl-child who had played with the faerie folk in the woods of the Summer Country long ago. For a moment, her vision blurred. Prisoned within walls, surrounded by humans with all their blind needs, she had forgotten how to see. . . .

"We live between the worlds. Between sunrise and sunset we can fly from one end to the other of this Isle. Will you stay with us, Lady, or will you ride?" Bird song and faerie song mingled in a cascade of harmonies.

"The queen has come to the land, but the king still wanders—" she answered.

Merlin had tried to tell her what was needed, but she had been unable to understand. She looked from the bright spirits to her own flesh—it felt solid, but her skin had a translucent glow, as if she could see the pulse of power.

"Between sunrise and sunset, my fair ones, take me to Britannia's true king. . . ."

IX

The Turning

It was the evening of Beltain, and the sun was withdrawing westward, trailing tattered standards of flame. From the Wall, Artor could see the flicker of bonfires here and there upon the land. *Like detachments that have been cut off from their main force and must stand alone against the dark*—A very military metaphor for the fires of spring, he thought grimly, but his heart was a battlefield, with no room for anything but war.

Some of the fires burned in the old fortress of Vercovicium, where his army had made camp. It was a central location, and until he knew whether Medraut meant to strike southward through Luguvalium or Dun Eidyn, as good a place as any to wait for news.

Here, the Wall took advantage of natural escarpments, with a view of the open country to either side. The water of the loughs reflected the sky's conflagration in fragments of flame. There were fires there as well, where the folk of scattered farmsteads had gathered to celebrate the festival.

On this night, no army would move. In the fort, his men could safely drink as much of the local beer as they had been able to collect on their march northward, but liquor would not drown Artor's sorrows. Instead he had set out to walk the Wall.

It curved away to the eastward, climbing the escarpments and swooping through the dales, even now, when parts of it were crumbling, a mighty testament to the empire it had defended. As he walked, the king fingered a fragment of bronze he had found among the stones, an old military badge with the image of an eagle, wishing it had the power to call to his aid the spirits of the men who had set these stones, as the image of the goddess had raised the ghosts at Mons Badonicus.

He had done what he could to pacify the land behind him, swearing new oaths with the sons of King Icel, and fighting a series of swift and bloody conflicts with the rebel lords of Demetia and Pagus and Guenet. They were a flock of fighting cocks, each crowing on his own dunghill. How quickly they had forgotten the host of enemies that waited beyond the farmyard wall!

This Wall, he thought, as his footfalls rang against the solid masonry. He peered into the shadow that was creeping across the northern lands. There lay the darkness that would extinguish the light of Britannia, where Medraut was gathering the wild tribes of the North. Their last defense was this slender line of stone.

Ahead, indeed, a section had fallen. Carefully, Artor clambered downward until he stood on the springy turf. The slope fell away before him, rising again to a pair of outcrops in stark silhouette against the fading sky. In the cleft between them he saw the sudden spark of a fire and started towards it.

Any one of his men who ventured thus into hostile territory, without orders and unsupported, would have been mucking out stables for a week, but Cai and Gualchmai were no longer here to scold him. Silent through the dusk, the king made his way forward, summoning all the woodcraft Merlin had taught him to move unseen. And in truth he did not think it was an enemy, but some sheepherd who would not grudge a stranger the warmth of his Beltain fire.

That flame, burning in the lee of a sandstone boulder, was the only light remaining in a darkening world. Artor closed his cloak to hide his mail and stepped towards it, wondering what they could be burning to make the air smell so sweet, as if the open moorland had somehow gathered all the rich scents of a woodland spring. He blinked at shadows laced with whirling sparkles of brightness that fled away at his approach until there was only one shape by the fire. As he drew nearer it straightened, light shining on a tangle of golden hair and glowing on the folds of a cloak striped and chequered in spring green.

Guendivar. . . .

Artor stopped short, staring. *A vision,* he thought numbly, *born of my need.* But no image in his memory matched this face that was both older than he remembered and as fresh as the hawthorne flowers that wreathed her brow. Would a vision have mud clinging to the hem of her tunica and leaves caught in her hair?

She is real! He could not even imagine how she came to be here. A flash of heat and chill together pebbled his skin.

"I bring a Beltain blessing from Britannia to her king. . . ." Her voice trembled as if the anxieties of humanity warred with the magic that still starred her eyes. He swallowed, remembering what reason she had to be afraid.

"What right have you to give such a blessing, who have betrayed both Britannia and me?"

Her cheeks grew first red, then pale, but her voice was steady as she replied. "The right of a priestess of Brigantia, whose land this is. I have not betrayed *her*, and what I give I have the right to take away."

"You have taken away my heart, and given another my bed and my throne!" Artor said bitterly, setting his hand on the hilt of his sword. "I should slay you where you stand!"

"Not your bed," she said in a low voice, "empty though it has been. The blade you bear is a Sword of Justice, which would refuse to touch me. You would do better to ask what gifts I bestow."

He let go of the pommel as if stung. His bed had been barren indeed, he thought in shame, but his soul was singing at the knowledge that Medraut had not lain with her there. "What are your gifts . . . Lady?" The words limped from his lips.

"Sovereignty. Potency. Power."

Artor believed her. She had never been so beautiful arrayed in silk and gold as she was now, standing by the fire in her smudged gown. And in that moment he knew himself an empty husk, unfit to serve her.

"Guendivar. . . ." The anger that had strengthened his voice drained away. Throughout this war that fury had sustained him. He had nothing, now. "I have tried to hate you," he said tiredly, "but whatever you have done, it was my sin and my failure that was the cause. Can you believe that little though I showed it, you have always had my love?"

"My dear—" she said with a tenderness that pierced his heart. "I have had your letters. Do you think I did not know? But you did not come, and I grew heartsick and confused, and did what I thought I must for the sake of the land. If there is blame, much of it must be mine."

He stood before her with bowed head and empty hands. "I have lived by the sword for forty years, Guendivar, and I am tired. My peace is broken, and my people tear at each other like wolves. I have nothing left to give. . . ."

"Did I not say it?" she said softly. "The gifts are mine. I am the Tiernissa, the Queen. Come to me. . . ."

Step by unsteady step, he made his way around the fire. She reached up to unclasp the penannular brooch that pinned his cloak and began to unbuckle the belt that held his sword. He stopped her, glancing around him, calculating the distance back to the Wall.

"We are warded by sentinels more vigilant than any of your soldiers," said Guendivar. "Take off your armor, Artor, and perhaps you will be able to see. . . ."

Piece by piece the king laid his garments aside, until he stood defenseless in that place where faith is the companion of despair. It did not matter whether he believed her. Love or death would be equally welcome, if they came in her arms. The queen had also thrown down her green mantle and unpinned the fibulae that held her gown, so that she stood dressed only in her hawthorne crown.

"Thus do I salute you, for you are the head of the people—" She stretched to kiss his brow.

Behind his closed eyes light flared, illuminating past and present so that he saw and understood the meanings and connections between all things.

Her hands moved down his shoulders and the blossoms of her crown brushed soft against his breast as her lips pressed the skin above his heart. "I salute you, for you are the protector of the nation—"

At the words, fire filled his breast, and a purifying protective tenderness that would dare all dangers, not from hatred, but for love.

Then Guendivar bent to his thighs, her fingers sliding softly along the track left by Melwas' spear. He drew in a sharp breath as her lips touched his phallus and he felt it rise.

"I salute you, for you are the Lord of the Land—"

Artor clutched at her shoulders, shaken by the raw pulse of power that leaped from the earth to flare through every limb, his stiffened member straining against her hand.

She tipped her head back, gazing up at him. "Oh my beloved, come to me!"

No man living could have resisted that command. The queen drew him down beside the stone, her white thighs opening to enfold him, and in her arms the power that filled him found its rightful outlet at last.

Conquered and conqueror, giving and receiving, very swiftly Artor ceased to distinguish between Guendivar's ecstasy and his own. And in the ultimate moment, when the entire essence of being was focused to a single point, even that blossomed in an expansion of awareness that included himself and Guendivar and the earth beneath them and all the hallowed isle.

Afterward, he and Guendivar lay beside the fire, wrapped in their cloaks against the chill they had not felt before. When her head rested thus, upon his shoulder, Artor knew there could be no wrong anywhere. If he had not been filled with joy, he could have wept for all the nights when they had lain separate in the royal bed.

"If we had a ship we could sail away to the Blessed Isles," he murmured against her hair.

She shook her head a little, nestling closer. "I think we have run far enough, you and I. It is we who must bring a blessing to *this* Isle."

"As you have given it to me. . . ." Artor smiled. "But what power brought you to me here?"

"Merlin took me from Medraut's fort. God knows what tales they will be telling—they must think that Ninive and I vanished into the air!" Her laughter faded as she told the tale. "But it was the fair folk who brought me to this place, though I hardly expected the High King of Britannia to be wandering alone on the moor."

"Not quite alone. There are something over four thousand men camped in the old fort—" He gestured towards the irregular line of the Wall, dark against the stars. "I had meant to pursue Medraut all the way to Fodreu, but now I do not know what I should do."

"Stay here," answered Guendivar, "where you have a source of supply and some protection. Medraut is raising the North against you—better to meet him on your own home ground." She began to speak of what she had learned during her captivity concerning the strength of the enemy and Medraut's plans.

"I suppose we should get up," he said finally. "My men will be wondering what has become of *me*."

"Need we go back quite yet?" Guendivar laughed a little, reaching up to kiss his ear.

To his delight, Artor's body responded—he had wondered if their loving would be a reproduceable miracle. He kissed her, and matters proceeded from there, and this time, if their joining did not quite reach the earlier excesses of ecstasy, he was better able to appreciate the solid reality of the woman in his arms.

Merlin sat with eyes half-closed and his back against an oak tree, listening to his heart drum in his breast. Nearby, Ninive was building up the fire and preparing a framework of willow twigs to cook the string of trout she had caught in the stream. From time to time she would glance at him, frowning, but she had said no word.

She's afraid to ask... he thought grimly. *Well, that's no wonder.* What had begun as a shortness of breath on the journey through Pictland had become a general weakness, as if with every step the life within him was bleeding back into the soil. Three weeks had passed since Beltain, and they had scarcely gone the distance he used to run in a day.

He himself did not feel fear so much as amazement that the body which had endured so many years past the normal span of men was failing at last. *It could have chosen a better moment to go,* he thought then. But most men, he had heard, found themselves unready when their time came at last.

He had rescued Guendivar, and the faerie folk told him she was reunited with the king. Indeed, he had hardly needed telling, for the joy of their reunion had reverberated through the land. But the spirits spoke also of a mighty hosting in the land of the Pretani. He had dreamed of a fort above a river, where men fought and died. Soon, Artor would face his greatest battle, and Merlin would not be there.

When he closed his eyes, he saw the face of the daimon of his prophecies, wide-eyed with wisdom and ethereally fair. When he opened them, he saw Ninive, as bright of hair, but with fine skin browned by sun and wind, and anxiety clouding her dark eyes. She had gone back entirely to the dress of her mother's people, a woolen skirt whose ragged fringe brushed her knees, and a skin cape pinned at the breast by a sharpened bone. Barefoot, she could fade into the woods like one of the folk of faerie. She knew the wildlands as he did, the perfect companion for his wanderings, but could she become something more?

"My lord, the fish is cooked—see how the flesh flakes off the bones." Ninive knelt beside him, offering the trout on a dock leaf.

"I will try." He smiled. He picked up fragments of the trout with a delicate touch.

"I am thinking," said Ninive when they were done, "that if I were to leave food here for you, I could fetch help and bring you to some farmstead where you could rest. . . ."

He shook his head. "We have to go on."

"Not all the way to the Wall!" she protested. "It would be harvest before we arrived, and you—" She broke off, looking away.

"Will likely not get there," he finished for her. "Do you think I do not know?" The face she turned to him was anguished, and he stretched out a hand already thinner than it had been a week ago. "My little one, do you care so much for me?"

Ninive gestured around her. "You have given me back my soul!" She took his hand and pressed her forehead against it. With his other hand, very gently, he touched her hair.

"I am ninety years old and had begun to fear myself immortal. In truth, I am relieved to find it is not so. In the forest, when a creature grows too weak to hunt food, death comes soon. I would tell you to leave me here—"

"I would not do it!" she interrupted.

"But I must ask something harder. Great forces are gathering against the king, and I cannot be there. I have dreamed of a future that fills me with fear. I must use the time that is left to me so that something will survive."

She stared at him, her eyes dark as forest pools. "What do you need me to do?"

"There is a place that I must find before Midsummer Day. It lies deep in the Forest of Caledon—" He gestured southward. "When we reach it, we will work a mighty magic."

Beltain, or perhaps the queen, had brought in the summer. Even along the Wall, flowers bloomed and grass grew tall, and on the moors the heather, weighted with an emperor's wealth of purple bloom, hummed with the song of bees. Now the days lengthened rapidly towards midsummer's epiphany.

Artor made good use of the time. New messages had gone out across Britannia, proclaiming that king and queen were once more united, and calling the warriors to a great hosting at Vercovicium. At this season the demands of the fields kept many on their farmsteads, but each day, it seemed, another group of riders would come jogging along the Military Way that ran below the Wall.

"You see, they are still loyal," said Guendivar, gazing down from the walkway of the fortress wall at the moving tapestry of men and horses below.

"It is your name that has brought them," Artor replied, putting his arms around her. "They know that the sovereignty of Britannia is returned to me."

She leaned against him, the warmth of his touch still filling her with wonder. It was now well into June, and the weather had turned bright and fair; the long northern dusk spread a veil of amethyst across the hills. In the evening peace, sounds carried clearly.

"What is that?" she asked, as a noise like distant thunder began to overwhelm the ordinary sounds of the camp below.

She felt Artor stiffen. He lifted his hand to shade his eyes from the westering sun, staring at the Military Way, where something was moving, dust boiling behind it in a plume. She turned to look up at him. Already the hard stare of the commander was replacing the tenderness in his eyes.

"A messenger," he said grimly, "who rides at too headlong a pace to bear good news."

Medraut had taken Luguvalium. The chieftains of the Selgovae, still resenting the taxes Artor had laid upon them a dozen years ago, had joined him in a swift drive southward, and Morcant Bulc of Dun Breatann, denying his father's treaties, had joined them. The main body of the Picts had not yet appeared, but their most likely route would be eastward through the Votadini lands. Artor had been aware of the danger, and ordered Cunobelinus to stay where he was and defend Dun Eidyn. But if Medraut held one end of the Wall and the Picts the other, the king's force would be caught in between.

The solution, obviously, was to attack Medraut first and destroy him. Artor got his men to Luguvalium in two days of hard marching and was preparing to attack the fort by the time Guendivar, following more slowly, caught up with him.

The wind carried a faint reek of something burning, and the air resounded with the yammering of crows. Guendivar gazed up at her husband, searching for words with which to say good-bye.

All her life, she had heard stories of Artor's battles, but she had never before seen him armed for war. The gilded scales of his hauberk gleamed in the sunlight and his mantle was of the purple of emperors. The big black horse stamped and snorted as he reined it in outside the little church at the edge of the town where he had taken her.

"Stay here, my heart—" he said, leaning down to touch her hair. "If we destroy them here, I will come for you, but if they flee, we will be pursuing, and you will be safer behind us." His shield was new, but the horse's harness and Artor's leather leg wrappings and the heavy wool tunic showed signs of hard wear.

"But how will I know—"

"If we win, I daresay someone will tell you." He laughed, his teeth flashing in the close-cropped beard. It was threaded with silver, but his hair still grew strongly. Her hands clenched as she fought the desire to bury her fingers in its thick waves once more.

"And if we lose—" His face sobered. "You must stay hidden and make your way south somehow. Do not fail me, my lady, for if I fall, only you can pass on the sovereignty."

"Do not say it!" she exclaimed. "I will not lose you now!"

"Guendivar . . . I will always be with you. . . ."

Behind him a horn blared and the king straightened, sliding the helmet he had carried in the crook of his arm onto his head. With nasal and side-flanges covering most of his face, he was suddenly a stranger. The stallion reared and Artor reined it around. The men of his escort fell in behind him, and then they were away.

The queen stared after them, and only when the echo of hoofbeats on cobblestones had faded did she allow the tears to come.

All through that endless day she prayed, kneeling on the worn planking of the church's floor, though she hardly knew which god it was to whom she addressed her prayers. About the middle of the afternoon, she heard a great clamor that gradually diminished until there were only a few dogs barking, and then, one by one, the voices of the people of the town.

Presently the old priest who served the church came back again.

"The king is safe, or at least he was an hour ago. But the Perjurer broke through his lines and fled with most of his men, and our army has gone after him, save for a detachment left under Prince Peretur to guard you and the town. Let us praise the Lord of Hosts, who gives victory!"

At night the Forest of Caledon was full of whispers; the wind continuing its conversation with the trees. Merlin felt the vibration through the trunk behind him, just as it thrummed through the shaft of the Spear at his side. Sitting so, his thoughts matched themselves to the long slow rhythms of the forest, and the rustle of leaf and twig became the words of a dialogue between the Goddess who lived in the earth and the God.

As the journey continued, the Druid understood them ever more clearly. By day he clung to the pony Ninive had brought for him, riding by balance. At night, when the girl lay breathing softly by the embers of their fire, Merlin became a tree, drawing from soil and sky the energy he needed to go on. But the earth drummed with distant hoofbeats and the wind rang with the crying of ravens, calling their kindred to a great killing, and he dared not succumb to the forest's peace.

And each day the hours of twilight lengthened as the season turned towards the solstice, all powers drawing together to resolve the conflict that had unbalanced the land.

At the Isle of Maidens, Morgause woke from evil dreams. It lacked a week to midsummer, and the priestesses were preparing for the festival, but her nightmares had been filled with blood and battle. She saw Artor and Medraut facing each other in battered armor, fury stamping their faces with its own likeness, and felt the perspiration break out on her brow. In that confrontation she sensed some great turning of fate, and it filled her with fear.

She left her chamber, calling to her maidens. "Pack journey food and blankets. Nest and Verica, you will come with me."

"But Lady," they protested, "what about the sacred rites, the festival?"

"This year the Lady of Ravens is celebrating her own ritual," she said heavily. "I must be at the Wall by Midsummer Day. . . ."

"Midsummer Eve . . ." said Goriat, surveying the winding river and the bluff above it, where lights twinkled from the old fortress. "At home, the clans will be gathering to light their solstice fires, throwing flaming brands high into the air to make the crops grow, and carrying the torches through the fields."

"In the South, also," answered Artor.

He felt as if he were thinking with two minds, one part evaluating the site's military potential while the other appreciated the beauty of the scene. The fort stood on a crag with a steep escarpment. Below stretched flats through which a small river wound. The higher ground was astir with men and horses as the Britons settled in.

"How strange that this stream should also have the name of Cam," the younger man said then.

The king shrugged. "Britannia is full of rivers that turn and wind in their courses, and I suppose many of them must bear that name." He walked along the riverbank, his officers following.

"You must wish it was the one that runs near Camalot."

"Only if I were inside its walls," Artor answered with grim humor. "If I must attack a fortress, I am glad it is not a place of my own building. Camboglanna was strong once, but now it is in disrepair, and Medraut is not provisioned for a seige."

"He has trapped himself, then—" Goriat grinned.

Vortipor shook his head. "Not if the Picts arrive to relieve him. That's our danger. He can't outrun us, so he hopes to outwait us—"

"—Until he outnumbers us. I see." Goriat squinted up at the fort.

"The old Romans built well. To see that ragtag of northerners occupying Camboglanna galls my soul! An attack uphill from this side would be difficult, and I don't suppose the far side is any better."

Peretur shrugged. "The Wall joins the edge of the fort on both sides and there is only one gate, still in good repair."

Goriat turned to Artor. "We'll have to winkle him out of there somehow, my lord."

Artor's gaze was still on the river—the gleam of late sunlight on the water shone like Guendivar's hair. *I have been fighting too long.* He sighed. *I want to take her with me somewhere they have never heard of warfare—perhaps the Blessed Isles.* But he had to fight one more battle. If he could win that one perhaps he would be done.

"I'll send a message. Medraut has run from me twice now. If force won't budge him, we'll see what shame will do."

They gazed up at the road that crossed the overgrown vallum ditch before the walls. Dark figures moved on the walkway above it, bows in their hands.

"I'll deliver it," said Goriat with a sigh. "We were brothers once. He might hesitate before ordering those archers to shoot me. . . ."

Above Camboglanna, two ravens circled, then swung out over the river and settled, calling, in the branches of a gnarled thorn tree.

Raven wings filled Merlin's vision with fragments of shadow. He clung to the saddle bow, drawing breath harshly, willing the wheeling world to slow. Over the tumult in his head he heard someone calling him—

"My lord, I have found the spring!"

He opened his eyes and found Ninive, a fixed point around which the world stilled to comprehensible shape and meaning. The ravens were at Camboglanna. Here, there were only the irregular flitterings of wren and tit, and the musical gurgle of a tiny stream.

Before him, the narrow leaves of young rowan trees moved gently in the breeze, their edges gilded by the westering sun. Below spread a hawthorne to whose twigs a few fading white blossoms still clung. Beyond them he saw a noble oak tree.

"The water flows from that outcrop of rock just beyond the trees—" Ninive danced back across the jumble of fallen leaves and mossy boulders. Through the tangle of branches loomed the side of the hill.

"It is the place. . . . The headwaters of the Cam," he muttered, nodding as he recognized each feature of the image that had haunted his dreams. "And the day—have we come too late? Tell me, what is the day?"

"By the calculations you gave me at the beginning of this journey, this will be the shortest night of the year," she replied.

He sat back with a long sigh. "Midsummer Eve. They will fight tomorrow by the river."

"Can you help?" asked the girl. "Will the water carry your power to Artor?"

"Can anyone turn fate?" he murmured. "Now, at least, I have a chance to try!"

He slid from the pony's back, and with Ninive and the Spear to prop him, made his way to the oak, whose knobbed root made a seat above the stream. There he sat, extending his senses to encompass every part of the wood around him, and waited, as at Camboglanna two armies were waiting, for the dawning of the longest day.

The first sunlight gleamed from the river and from the helmets of the men who stood beside it: Artor's army, in full battle array. Medraut could see them clearly. So could his men. They were talking about the damned letter. Did they think he could not hear?

He had burned the parchment, but the words were burned in his memory.

"You boast of your courage, but twice now you have run from my wrath. You boast of your right to rule, but the queen has fled you and returned to my bed. . . ."

Guendivar! Oh, Artor had known that would enrage him. In dreams he still held her rounded body in his arms.

The hateful words echoed in his inner ear—his mother's scolding voice, speaking his father's words.

"Like a greedy child, you have tried to seize your inheritance, and by doing so, forfeited all claim! You are coward and craven—tainted in blood and corrupt in mind."

And if I am, Mother, he thought in bitter reply, *I am what you and he have made me!* And still the accusations rolled on.

"And these things all men shall know for truth if you do not come out and face me, body to body and soul to soul!"

Ravens were circling in the air below, calling out to their goddess the tally of the slain. He had only to wait, Medraut thought furiously, and they would all be safe. But these bloodthirsty fools whom he commanded were chafing to avenge their defeat at Luguvalium.

"My lord," said Bleitisbluth, "the men are angry. The enemy have been shouting evil things. The Rome-king left a garrison in Luguvalium, and we outnumber them. Better to order our warriors to attack while you still can!"

The raven voices grew louder, blended to a single voice, calling to him. *Guendivar is lost to me,* he thought, *I must serve the Lady of Ravens now. . . .*

"Very well—if they are so eager for battle, fight they shall!" Certainty came to Medraut like a spark kindling tinder, and with it a fierce exultation. He reeled off a list of chieftains, their order and numbers. "The remainder will form a reserve force, hidden here, with me."

Medraut watched from the gatehouse as his army rolled down to meet the waiting force below. The men of the North rode their sturdy ponies to battle, but they fought on foot, with shield and spear. The narrow flats by the river favored them. He had expected that Artor would not be able to use his cavalry to full advantage, and indeed, he could see that the king himself was fighting dismounted.

As the morning passed, the purple cloak was everywhere on the field, the pendragon floating above it as Artor's standard bearer strove to keep up with him. As noon drew nearer, the sun's strength grew.

He is an old man, thought Medraut, *and it's getting hotter. Soon, he will fail!*

From below came clouds of dust, stopping the throat and stinging the eyes. The only color was the crimson of blood, bright as the cloak of the goddess of battles in the pitiless radiance of Midsummer Day.

What kept Merlin upright was the Spear. He had taken his stand in the space between the oak, the mountain ash trees, and the thorn, just where the waters of the Cam emerged from the stone. His heart galloped like Artor's warhorse, vision pulsing in time to its beat. Increasingly he relied on inner senses, extending them through air and soil until his body no longer contained his awareness. He risked losing focus entirely, but his control would last long enough, he thought, for what he had to do.

"Cast the circle, Ninive—"

The girl's voice rose and fell as she paced sunwise around him, sprinkling the sacred herbs, chanting in the old tongue of her mother's people. She was weeping, but her voice stayed strong, and he had time for a moment of pride. Nine times she made the circuit, and with each circumnambulation the Druid's consciousness drew inward, trading the diffuse awareness of his earlier state for a more powerful and precise connection with the space immediately around him, as if he stood within a pillar of crystal bounded by oak and ash and thorn.

Then she completed the spell, and he needed his control no longer, for the magic upheld him. Ninive was a spark of light before him, sensed rather than seen.

"The hour moves towards the triumph of the sun, the longest day! I summon you, O Prophet of Britannia, to say what shall come to this land."

For a moment Merlin knew nothing. Then the daimon within him awakened and his mind reeled beneath the flood of foreknowledge.

"The Red Dragon gives birth to a Boar and a litter of little Foxes that between them shall tear and worry at the land. Men and women shall cry out and flee their rulers, and give their name to Armorica, for it is the princes of their own people that oppress them. And then the White Dragon shall rise from his sleep and devour them, from Land's End to the Orcades."

Immensities of time and space rushed before him; he saw strange armies marching across Britannia, steel roads and devastated forests and cities covering the land. He saw a crossed banner that circled the world. The images he saw he could not comprehend, and presently he waited in silence once more.

"When these things come to pass, O Prophet, where will you be?" A new question came.

"I will be Lailoken in the court of Gwendoleu, and in the court of Urien I will be Taliessin. I shall not leave this land, but ever and again I will shape myself as her need compels me. Going in and out of the body, my voice will be heard in Britannia throughout the ages." In vision, all those lives were clear before him, and Merlin laughed.

"The sun nears her nooning, master, and there is one thing more to ask. Say now what fate is twined for Artor the king!"

The vision that had spanned centuries folded cataclysmically inward, arrowing like lightning towards its goal. Merlin saw the bloody field of Camboglanna, and Artor, catching his breath as he leaned upon a broken spear. Goriat lay dead beside him, but his enemies were fleeing up the hill. Above them the God of the Sword and the Lady of Ravens hovered, invisible to mortal eyes. And then the air rang with the bitter music of warpipes, and from the fortress a troop of mounted men came riding, and Medraut sped before them.

The bean-sidhe *is wailing-* thought Artor, *that doom-singing demon that Cunorix used to speak of so long ago.* He wiped sweat from his eyes with the back of his hand and peered up at the fort, knowing already that it was something worse. The army he had faced was gone, but Medraut, whom he had sought in vain all through the battle, was coming out at last.

Now, he thought despairingly, *when I am already tired.* But this was no time to stand swearing.

"Edrit, run—tell Vortipor to get ready!" he called to the warrior who bore his standard, and started to slog back to the high ground. Medraut had been clever to field a reserve force when the battle was almost done. But Artor had been clever too.

He heard a gleeful shout as the enemy sighted him, and struggled towards the line of willow trees.

On the other side, Vortipor waited with the best riders the British had. A boy was holding Artor's big black stallion, a descendent of the first Raven he had ridden to war. Edrit boosted him into the saddle and handed him a javelin and a horseman's round shield. Taking up the reins, he peered through the screen of branches. Medraut's troop had reached the bottom of the hill. They were losing speed as they spread out along the road.

He turned back to his men. "Has it been hot here, waiting? It was hot work down there too! But now it's your turn, my lads, and you are the veterans of Gallia. Keep your formation, and that rabble will scatter like bees from an overturned hive!"

Someone murmured, "But they can still sting!" And the others laughed.

They started forward, Vortipor taking the point and Artor riding among the men on the wing. As the rebels turned towards the river, the king's men burst through the willows, urging their mounts to full gallop as the slope lent them momentum.

"Artor!" cried the British riders. "Artor and Britannia!"

They were going to hit the enemy at an angle. The king wrapped his long legs around Raven's sides, dropped the knotted reins on the horse's neck, and cocked his arm, poising the javelin to throw.

He sighted on Medraut, then the point of the British wedge struck, and Artor was carried past him. Training ingrained to the point of instinct selected a new target; he cast, and a man fell. A spearpoint drove towards him; he lifted his shield and grunted as it took the weight of the weapon, shifted his weight and jerked as the horse moved, and felt the spear tear from the man's grip and clatter to the ground.

He thrust the shield outward to protect his body as he reached across his belly to grip the hilt of the Chalybe sword. *May the Defender be with me!* he prayed, and felt a tremor of eagerness shock through his hand. At the battle of Verulamium the god of the Sword had come himself to counter an alien magic, but this was a battle of men, and Artor dared ask only for the strength to endure to the end.

The black horse was fresh and knew its trade, wheeling to knock a smaller beast sideways so that Artor could finish the rider with a slash of his sword. Then another shape loomed up before him. He struck, and struck again. The sweat ran hot beneath his armor, for the sun stood high. After each blow his arm came back up more slowly, yet still he slew, seeing Medraut's mocking face on every foe.

The sun stood high, and all the wood trembled beneath the weight of its glory. The circle of power where Merlin stood was a dazzle of light. But his inner sight was filled with the image of Artor, fighting on while all around him men fled or fell.

An enemy sword cracked the king's shield; Merlin saw him lose his balance and tumble from the horse's back. In the next moment his opponent was downed by a thrown javelin. Artor struggled to his knees at the water's edge, shieldless, but still clinging to his sword. The king looked up. Medraut stood before him.

Merlin gripped the shaft of the Spear. "Is it time?" he whispered, and the rune-carved wood quivered like a live thing in his hand. In all the forest, there was no sound but the sweet music of the infant stream. "This is my will," he said aloud, "that my spirit shall neither sleep nor seek the Summerland, but continue to wander the world!

"I am the wind on the wave!" Merlin cried.

"I am the fire in the wood!

"I am the sun beneath the sea and the seed in the stone.

"Before time's beginning I was with the gods, and I will sing at its end.

"I am Wild Man and Witega, Druid and daimon—

"I invoke the land of Britannia to the aid of her king!"

The Spear whirled in his hand, and he plunged it, point downward, into the moist soil. Deep, deep it sank, to the roots of creation, but the wooden shaft was expanding, extending branches to embrace the sky. For an eternal moment, Merlin was the Tree, linking earth and heaven.

Then the world collapsed around him in a roar of falling stone. But the essence that had been Merlin was already shaping itself to root and branch, to soil and stone and the rising wind, but most powerfully to the winding waters at his feet. Swift as thought he sped southward towards Camboglanna.

X

Raven of The Sun

Medraut was a faceless shadow between Artor and the sun.

"So, my lord father, you kneel before me! Will you admit you are beaten at last?"

The king squinted up at him, licking blood from a lip that had split when he hit the ground. His helmet had come off; the air felt cool on his sweat-soaked hair. It was a little past noon.

"I kneel to the earth, whose power brought me down," he said evenly. "Are you going to let me get up, or do I have to fight you from my knees?" They were getting wet; he looked down and realized that he had fallen in the shallows at the edge of the stream.

Medraut slowly lifted his sword. *He's tired,* Artor observed, but he himself was exhausted. Perhaps it would be easier to fight from here. Or to let Medraut kill him. They were surrounded by the dead and dying. He had lost his army, he thought numbly, and Britannia.

The river ran purling past his foot, sweet and clear. When Medraut still did not answer, the king scooped up a handful of water.

His first thought was that he had not known he was so thirsty. He dipped up more, and felt his tissues expanding like parched earth in the rain. With the third mouthful, he sensed the triumphant surge of Merlin's spirit making him one with everything around him. The cool sweetness of water, the solid strength of earth, the dry heat of the air—he felt them all with an intensity that was almost pain.

A movement that would have been impossible a moment before brought the king to his feet. Medraut jumped back, staring.

"Thank you . . ." Artor whispered, but it was not his opponent to whom he was speaking. He swayed, and Medraut started forward, sword swinging high.

A smooth twist brought the king on guard, bringing up the Sword of the Defender two-handed to deflect Medraut's blow. The clangor as the two blades met echoed across the vale. Artor's knees bent slightly, the great sword drifting up to hover above his right shoulder.

"Why did you do this, Medraut? Why did you try to destroy Britannia?"

His son looked at him uncomprehending. "I wanted to rule—"

Artor shook his head. "The land cannot be ruled, only served."

Medraut's mouth twisted and he lunged. "You left her! You left *me*!"

For a moment the king hesitated, the truth of that accusation piercing more deeply than any enemy sword. Then strength surged up from the soil once more and he knew that he was still the Lady's Champion.

Artor leaped back, sword sweeping down and to the side, knocking his son's weapon away and spinning him so that for a moment they stood with shoulders touching, as if they met in the dance.

"I was promised everything, and then betrayed," hissed Medraut. "I came to you, since my mother had cast me aside like a tool she no longer wanted to use. And you banished me to the barbarians and *forgot* me! I've had to fight for my life, my name. . . ." He whirled away, the rest hanging unspoken between them—*for Guendivar. . . .*

"Surrender and you shall rule the North," said Artor, his breath coming fast.

"I could win it all yet, *Father*. . . ." Medraut advanced with a series of flashing blows that kept the king busy defending.

"Not while I live!" Artor knocked the younger man's last stroke aside with a force that sent him reeling.

"You will die, at my hand, or the hand of time—" answered Medraut, panting. "The heirs of Britannia are young foxes, eager to gnaw out their own little kingdoms, and that will be the end of your dream."

Instinctively Artor settled to guard, but his mind was whirling. He bore the Sword of the Defender, but what could a dead man defend? He looked up at the mocking face of his son. Men called Medraut the Perjurer, but surely Deceiver would be a better name, sent to tempt him to despair. And yet the power of that impossible moment of connection with the land still sang in his veins.

"Oh Medraut, is there room for nothing in your heart but hate?"

"You took the only thing I might have loved!" Medraut cried out in answer, and ran at him with wildly swinging sword.

Artor retreated, using all his skill to fend that blade away. The boy was a good swordsman, but he was battering with berserker fury as if he meant to obliterate, not merely kill. Forty years of experience kept the king's weapon between him and that deadly blade. It was those same battle-trained reflexes, not Artor's will, that halted Medraut's charge at last with a stop-thrust that pierced through hauberk and breastbone and out the other side.

For a moment they stared into each other's eyes. Then Medraut's features contorted. His weapon slipped from his hand, and Artor felt the weight of the boy's body begin to drag down the sword. He stepped back, and the blade slid free as Medraut fell, the bright blood—his son's blood—staining the steel.

The air rang with silence.

"Father. . . ." A little blood was running from Medraut's mouth. The king knelt beside him, laying down the Chalybe sword, reaching to ease off his son's helm and smooth back the hair from his brow as if he had been a little child. Medraut's eyes widened, meeting his father's gaze unbarriered at last, shock transmuting gradually into an appalled understanding.

Then he twisted, hand clutching at his side. "It is not *my* blood," he whispered, "that will consecrate the ground—"

He convulsed once more, thrusting the dagger that had been sheathed at his hip up beneath Artor's mail. It seared along the old scar where Melwas had wounded the king long ago and stabbed upward into his groin.

For a moment all other awareness disappeared in a red wave of agony. When it began to recede, Artor looked down and saw that Medraut lay still and sightless, his face upturned to the sun.

Oh, Lady— thought the king, *is this your sacrifice?*

He could feel the warm seep of blood across his thigh and the beginnings of a deeper agony. Slowly he lowered himself to the earth beside the body of his son, vision flashing dark and bright with each pulse, fixing on the pebble that lay beside him. A glowing spiral spun within the stone. Artor's fingers closed upon its solid certainty.

This is the king stone . . . the heart of Britannia. It was beneath my feet all along.

His hearing must be going too, he thought then, for his head rang with strange music . . . like Gaulish battle horns. . . .

Guendivar gasped and reached out to Peretur for support as pain stabbed upward through her womb.

"My lady, what is it? Are you ill?"

She tried to straighten, staring round at the men who had come with her to the marketplace. Blood and dust and sunlight filled her vision; she saw an old fortress on a hill.

"Camboglanna . . ." she whispered. "Artor has been wounded!"

As the words articulated her inner vision, she was aware of a great surge of mingled grief and exultation that seemed to rise from the very soil.

"Lady, the king told us to guard you here!" said Peretur in alarm.

She shook her head. "The battle is over. If you want to keep me safe, then follow, for go to him I will!" She started towards the stables, and after a moment the men came after her.

To Morgause, the moment was like a shadow on the sun, a shudder in the soil. She stood swaying in the road, suddenly finding it hard to breathe. Luguvalium lay a day and a half behind them. To left and right rose the outriders of the moors. Ahead, the Wall marched over the first of the crags, and brown dust stained the sky.

"What is it?" cried her priestesses. "What do you hear?"

"I hear a calling of ravens," whispered Morgause, "I hear the groans of dying men. The blood of kings soaks into the soil. We must go quickly, if we are to get there in time!"

"In time for what?" asked Nest, hurrying after her, but Morgause did not reply.

Ninive stood weeping before the tumble of earth and stone where once a cliff had been. Oak and ash and thorn had disappeared beneath the landslip, and with them all trace of the Druid who had used her aid to perform his last and greatest act of magic, but from beneath the rubble, the little stream still trickled, singing to the stones.

Merlin had accomplished what he intended, but had he saved the king? She knew only that there had been a great shift in the fabric of reality. What would he want her to do? Ninive dried her tears and stood listening, and it seemed to her that in the whisper of the wind and the gurgle of the stream she heard his voice once more.

She picked up the bag in which she had carried their food, and began to follow the course of the Cam south, toward the Wall.

Consciousness returned slowly. Artor drew a very careful breath, wondering how long he had lain wounded for his body to have already begun to learn ways to avoid the pain. He could feel the wound as a dull ache in his lower belly, but his flesh held the memory of a throbbing agony.

People were talking in low voices nearby—someone must have survived. He must have wakened before, already fevered, for he had thought that Morgause was there, and Betiver. The king opened his eyes and blinked, recognizing a Roman hauberk and curling dark hair threaded with grey.

"My lord! You are with us again!" Betiver turned and knelt beside him, his fine features bronzed with campaigning and drawn with strain.

"And so are you," answered Artor. "Old friend, what are you doing here?" He had been unconscious for some time, he thought, for his wound had been bandaged, and he was lying inside some roughly repaired building in the fortress.

"We could get no news—" Betiver said helplessly. "I thought you might need me. I came as swiftly as I could—dear God, if only I had come in time!"

"You did." The king's gaze moved around the room, seeing only Betiver's men. "We won. . . ."

"The field was already yours when I got here," said Betiver. "My men have scoured it, seeking survivors. A few of the rebels got away. Vortipor is alive, though wounded, and a few others—pitifully few."

Artor drew a long sigh and winced as his belly began to ache again. "I saw Goriat fall . . ." he said.

Betiver nodded. "Morgause has gone out to look for him. We were grateful to have someone so skilled in leechcraft join us," he added with reluctant appreciation. "It was she who dressed your wound."

"My poor sister. She has lost all her sons . . ." said Artor. *And so have I,* he thought then, and the tide of grief that followed bore him once more down into the dark.

Once, as a child, she had been told the tale of Niobe, who had boasted too loudly of her children, and seen them taken by the gods. Now, thought

Morgause as she searched the field of Camboglanna, she wept Niobe's tears.

The dead lay scattered like chaff in a newly reaped field; ravens stalked among them, gleaning their share of the grisly harvest. Selgovae and Saxons lay sprawled together, Dumnonians and Demetians, men from every corner of Britannia, in death there was no distinction between Medraut's rebels and those who had stayed loyal to Artor. This was not like the Saxon wars, when Britons had fought invaders from across the sea. There could be no winner in such a conflict as this had been, no matter which side claimed victory.

She had found Goriat early on. With him, she mourned Aggarban and Gwyhir and Gualchmai, but in a sense, she had lost them all a long time ago. The grief that kept her creeping from one body to another, turning them to peer at contorted faces, had been born when her youngest son left the Isle of Maidens, cursing her name.

That longest of days was beginning to draw to an end by the time she discovered Medraut. Betiver had said that his body had lain next to that of the king, but after Artor was taken up, the corpse must have been moved by the men who had served with the king in Gallia. It had not only been moved, she saw now, but hacked and slashed in posthumous vengeance so that without Betiver's description she would not have known which wound had been made by the Chalybe sword.

She carried water from the river and bathed the body as once she had bathed her child. They had stripped Medraut as well as mutilating him, but she could still see that her son had grown into a beautiful man—fair in body, at least, if not in soul. Cleansed of blood, his face bore a familiar sneering smile.

"And whose fault was that?" she muttered as she covered him with her veil. "Surely you were my most successful creation, a weapon aimed and sharpened which has finally struck home." He had pierced her to the heart as well.

"Is this all my doing?" Morgause gazed around her, shivering despite the warmth of the sun. "Ah, Medraut, even now I cannot hate you without hating myself as well!"

At the Isle of Maidens she had been kept too busy to think about the past; now it overwhelmed her. If she had had a blade, in that moment she might have executed her own self-judgment, but the fallen weapons had already been collected.

A raven fluttered to the ground nearby, its beak opening in a groan; in a moment two more followed it.

"You shall not have him!" Morgause exclaimed, and in their cries she heard an answer.

"I shall have all of them . . . from my bloody womb they are born, and in blood they return to me. Weep, my daughter, for all slain sons, and for all the mothers who will mourn them—weep with Me!"

The lamentations of the ravens rang around her, but the wail that rose from her belly to her breast to burst from her throat was far louder—a ullullation of mourning that echoed from the escarpment. Hearing it, men crossed themselves or flexed fingers in the sign of the Horns, looking over their shoulders.

But Morgause, when that cry had gone out of her, felt her own burden of grief a little lessened, knowing she did not mourn alone. Presently she heard the creak of wheels as men came with the cart to gather the corpses for the funeral pyre.

"Treat him with honor," Morgause said harshly, as they bent to take up Medraut's body, "for he came of the blood of kings."

"Lady, will you return to the fortress?" asked the troop leader. "They said that the king has awakened and is in pain."

The king . . . she thought numbly. Artor still needed her. She would have to live, at least for awhile.

"He is still alive?" Guendivar slid down from the horse and staggered as her muscles cramped from the long ride. Torchlight chased distorted shadows across the yard of the fortress. It was after midnight, but she had insisted they continue without stopping, desperate to reach Artor.

"The king lives," said Betiver, "but—"

She stumbled past him up the steps of the praetorium, where the roof had been repaired with rough thatching. An oil-lamp cast a fitful light on the sleeping man and the woman who sat by him. At Guendivar's step, she rose, and the queen stiffened, recognizing in the drawn features a reflection of Medraut.

Morgause stepped back abruptly, as if she had seen that moment of recoil. "You will wish to be with him. There is no more I can do for now." With a rustle of draperies she left the room.

The queen sank down upon the bench and took Artor's hand. It was warm, as if within, the solstice fires still burned. She laid her own fingers, chilled by her ride, upon his brow, and saw the flickers of pain that moved beneath his dreaming fade, and the firm lips within the curling beard curve in a little smile.

Presently his eyes opened. "I dreamed I was in Demetia . . . the Irish campaign. But you are here. . . ."

Guendivar nodded. She had been with him in Demetia too, but not like this, her soul seeking his like a homing bird.

"And I am here"—Artor grimaced —"for awhile. . . ." She started to protest, but he shook his head. "I always expected to die in battle, but I had hoped for a clean kill."

"It is only the wound fever," she said desperately. "We healed you before!"

"Well, we shall see. . . ." His voice trailed off. "God knows, now that we are together at last, I want. . . ." His eyes closed. She bent over him in panic, but it was only sleep.

She set her arms about him, calling on the goddess who had filled her at Beltain, and presently there came to her, not the exultant sexual power that had awakened the king's manhood, but a brooding, maternal tenderness—Brigantia, comforting her fallen champion, her most beloved child.

Through the remaining hours of darkness, a little longer than the night before, Guendivar dozed, cradling her king in her arms. When the light of morning began to filter through the thatching, she heard voices outside and, looking up, saw Ninive. As the young woman entered the room, Artor stirred.

"You were with Merlin—" said the king. In the strengthening day-light, Guendivar could see all too clearly how the fever had already begun to burn his flesh away.

Ninive nodded and came to the foot of the bed, looking like a wood spirit in her tattered cape, with leaves still caught in her hair.

"We were in the Forest of Caledon. He wanted to come to you—"

"But something happened. He touched me during the battle. What did he do?" the king asked harshly.

"Age came on him suddenly, as it does, in the wild . . ." Ninive said with difficulty. "He used the last of his strength to make a great magic. And when it was over I felt him all around me, as if he had not gone away, but become present everywhere in the world."

"Perhaps it must be so," Artor murmured then. "It was ever the way for the prophet to go before the king. . . ."

Later that morning, when the king had slipped once more into uneasy sleep, Guendivar consented to walk out into the sunlight and take a little food. They had set up a rude table and there was some thin ale and barley bread and hard cheese. Presently, she was joined by Ninive and Morgause.

"How bad is the king's wound?" asked the girl.

Guendivar fixed her eyes on the broken gate, through which she could see the edge of the bluff and the gleam of river beyond, as if she could bear to hear the answer but not to read it in the older woman's eyes.

"Bad enough, if the blade has only penetrated the layers of muscle that sheathe the belly. But if it opened the gut . . ." Morgause shook her head. "There is nothing I can do."

Guendivar turned. "You are the Lady of the Lake! We must take him there," she said desperately. "The Cauldron healed him before!"

Morgause stared at her as if, sunk in her own sorrow, she had forgotten who she was.

"Could he endure the jolting of a horselitter for so long?" asked Ninive, looking from one to the other.

"He will die if he stays here," Morgause said slowly. "Perhaps, if a coracle would float this far upstream, we could take him by water part of the way."

"We will do it!" Guendivar stood up suddenly. "I am the Tiernissa, and even Betiver will obey!"

"You are the Tiernissa, queen in the realm of men," said Morgause, something kindling in her face that had not been there before, "as I am the Hidden Queen, the White Raven who reigns in the country of the soul."

"Among my mother's people I might be counted a queen as well," said Ninive, "though the forest is where I rule."

"With three queens to care for him, surely Artor will be healed!" exclaimed Guendivar, and in that moment, when the sun shone so brightly on the hills, she could even believe it true.

As the coracle began its journey downriver, Morgause saw two ravens lift from the old thorn tree and fly away before them. On the next day, there were a dozen, and after that, always at least that many, circling the boat and flying ahead or behind it.

Guendivar would stiffen when she saw them, as if to defend the king, though the birds showed no signs of hunger. The warriors who paced them along the bank had another interpretation, and said that Lugos and the Lady of Battles had sent their birds to guard their champion. Ninive said it was Woden, who had given Merlin his Spear.

But Morgause remembered how Artor had found the head of Brannos in the White Mount at Londinium, and claimed the old king's place as Guardian of Britannia. It was said that the ravens had come to him that day, recognizing their chieftain. Perhaps it was the ravens of Brannos that followed Artor now, but whether they escorted him to death or to greater glory she could not tell.

At first some of the men waded with the coracle as it floated down the river, easing it over the shallows and clearing obstructions. But presently the water became deeper, and needed only an occasional dip of the boatman's paddle to keep the king moving smoothly towards Luguvalium. Always, while the other two rode with the warriors, one of the queens sat with him, singing, and laying cloths cooled by the waters of the river upon his burning brow.

Morgause could sense Artor's pain even when she was not beside him. The infusions of white willow she gave him did little to dull it. She had fed him a stew of leeks and caught their scent from the wound. She was sure now that there was a perforation there, and putrefaction in the belly, and when delirium set him babbling of old battles she was almost glad.

Before the Cam reached the Salmaes firth, they turned aside into the river that flowed north from Voreda, and moved upstream, towing the coracle where necessary by ropes pulled by men on the shore. Each night was just a little longer, and it seemed that the king's strength ebbed with the lessening of the sun's power. He was still fighting—she thought sometimes that was why he so often dreamed of war—but more and more often, consciousness fled entirely to give his tortured body a few hours of uneasy rest.

When they came at last to Voreda, they paused to construct a horselitter, and began the final part of the journey into the hills.

Morgause took a deep breath. Always, in the great hills, there was a living silence, a mingling of wind in leaves and the voice of waterfalls, or perhaps it was the breathing of the mountains themselves that she heard. Overhead, a raven rested on the wind. They had halted in the shade of a stand of birches to breathe the horses just before the last rise, and in the quiet, that hush filled her awareness.

The heavy warmth of the lowlands had sapped strength of mind and body, but Morgause felt new vigor flowing into her with every step she took into the hills. As she walked back along the line to check on Artor, it seemed to her that surely he must be the better for it as well. And indeed, she found him awake, staring around him with fever-bright eyes.

"Where are we?" he whispered.

"We are just below the circle of stones on the brow of the hill."

The king nodded. "I remember."

"Beyond the next turning the trail runs downward. Soon we will see before us the Lake and the Island."

"I do not think I will ever come there—" said Artor with a sigh.

Morgause took his wrist, and felt the pulse flicker like a guttering candle flame. Guendivar and Ninive had dismounted as well, and seeing them talking, came to join her.

"What is it?" asked Guendiver, bending to smooth the sweat-soaked hair back from Artor's brow. "Is there more pain?" Morgause could hear the effort it took to keep her voice even.

"Oh, my beloved," he breathed, "it is beyond pain. The sinews of my being are withering, and each step frays them further. I cannot go on. . . ."

"My king," Betiver said desperately, "we are almost to the Lake!"

Ninive took Morgause's arm. "Lady, let him wait in the circle; perhaps he will draw some strength from its power. Cannot we run ahead and bring the Cauldron here?"

Ninive had been a priestess at the Lake, thought Morgause. She was her granddaughter, heir to her power—perhaps the Goddess spoke through her now.

"The circle of stones . . ." echoed Artor. "I can feel it calling. Sister, if you have forgiven me for the wrong I did you by my birth, let me rest there. . . ."

"My brother," she asked, "can you find it in your heart to forgive *me*?"

He shook his head a little. "Our son's blood cancelled all debts, Morgause."

"I will go," she said softly, though her voice shook. "Wait for me, Artor! Wait for me!"

As she started down the trail, she heard his whisper behind her—"I will . . . if I can. . . ."

Artor lay upon the breast of the mountain, embraced by the open sky. He could sense the strength of the stones like a royal guard, he himself at their center, and the hill on which they stood surrounded by mountains, and this land of lake and mountain itself the still center of the circles of the world.

They had wished to build a shade above him, but he would not have it. He needed the light. He breathed more easily here than he had in days, but he had no illusions about his condition. From time to time the dark shape of a raven moved across his field of vision. *Soon*, he thought, *I will come with you. Be patient for just a little while.*

In his lucid moments it had gradually come to him that his disintegration had progressed too far for even the Cauldron to heal. Its power was to restore the natural order, and Nature's way, for a body so wasted as his, was to let the spirit go.

The kingdom he had ruled from Camalot was ended, and who would guard Britannia now? He twitched restlessly, remembering the young foxes of Medraut's prophecy. What would come to the land if one of them should try to set himself above the others, brandishing the Chalybe sword? Even the priestesses of the Isle could not guard it against a determined attacker—

He must have moaned, because suddenly Betiver was leaning over him. "My lord, do you need water?"

Artor swallowed. "The Sword—bring it here. . . ." He closed his eyes for a moment, until he felt the familiar ridges of the hilt beneath his hand. He tried to grip it, amazed at how little strength remained in his fingers. But even that was enough for him to feel the current of power.

Defender . . . he prayed, *what is Your will for this blade?* and, in the next moment, trembled beneath a flood of images as he understood what he must do.

Guendivar's hands were cool upon his face, lifting him, and he felt a little water from the skin bag dribble across dry lips. He looked up at Betiver.

"Take the Sword down to the Lake's edge, and with all the power that is in you, throw it in."

"Artor! It is the strength of the kingdom!" exclaimed Betiver.

"It is—it will always be—so long as it does not fall into evil hands! Take it and go, and tell me what befalls!"

When Betiver had departed, Artor lay back again, waiting for his racing pulse to slow. His frame seemed hardly solid enough to keep the gallop of his heart from carrying him away. His body was an empty vessel being filled by the sunlight, or perhaps it was the fever that was burning away his mortality as the dross is burned when the Goddess puts on her smith's apron and purifies the ore in the fire.

Artor's skin is so transparent, thought Guendivar, *he is like a vessel filled with light.* . . . She had always known him as strong and, in his way, attractive; now, with flesh wasted to reveal the pure line of bone, he was beautiful. *And I am going to lose him.* Her stomach churned with the ripple of fear that had become all too familiar since the battle on the Cam.

He seemed to be sleeping, but she could not be sure. Through the link that had grown between them since Beltain, she sensed that for much of the time he lived in the dim borderland between sleep and waking— or perhaps it was the borders of the Otherworld. She had talked to him often on this journey, not knowing whether he could hear her, but there was still so much to say.

"I have missed so much," she said in a low voice. "Children, and the comfort of your arms through the long years. I weep because I could not give you a true son to carry that sword after you were gone. But to no other woman was this blessing given, to rule beside you as your queen. And if the kingdom we tried to build must fall, still, we tried, and for a little while at least we kept back the dark."

Gently she stroked his hair. "If you must leave me, I think I will go south again, to Afallon. Would you like to come with me, my love, so that one day we may lie together upon the holy isle?"

She heard a footstep, and looked up as Betiver came up the hill. He was empty-handed, and she frowned. Had so much time passed?

"And see, here is Betiver back again," she said then, and Artor opened his eyes, so perhaps he had been listening after all.

"Is it done?" asked the king. "What did you see?"

Betiver was staring at the grass. A muscle jumped in his jaw. "The wind on the water, and a splash. What more could there be?"

"The Sword going into the Lake!" said Artor with a strength that made everyone turn to see. "For you have not done what I asked! Go once more, Betiver, and obey my command, if I am still your king."

Ravens rose in a black cloud, carking with angry voices as Betiver started back down the hill. Several flapped after him, winged shadows of Artor's will.

Guendivar and the warriors sat in silence, waiting for his return. And yet the time seemed still too short for a man to have climbed down to the Lake and back when Betiver came again.

"Betiver, I trusted you!" The king's voice thinned with sorrow. "For five and twenty years you have been with me, closer than kin! Will even you betray me at the end?"

Betiver stretched out his hands, his cheeks glistening with tears. "My lord, wait for them to bring the Cauldron, and heal you, and take the Sword back again! Or if you must leave us, do not deprive us of the only hope we will have! You have named no successor! How shall we choose a true king, if not by the Sword?"

"You are all my heirs!" the king said strongly. "Everyone who hears my story! And it is not by arms that the heritage I leave you shall be defended. . . ." Artor's head moved weakly against the pillow. "You must find hope in your hearts, not in the Sword. . . ." He tried to speak again and coughed. Guendivar saw he did not have the strength for more.

"Betiver," she said with the steel she had learned in ten years as regent for the king, "I command you to do Artor's will, in the name of the love you bear for me. . . ." His eyes lifted to hers, and she saw the desperation go out of them, replaced by a grief as deep as her own.

"Lady," he answered in a breaking voice, "my son also lies among the dead on Camboglanna's field."

His steps were slow as he started down the hill towards the Lake once more.

Morgause sat in the bow of the boat, swaying as Nest poled them towards the shore. The Cauldron was cradled in her arms. Ninive crouched before her, holding the bag that held the medicines and other gear it had taken them all this while to find, for they might have to spend some time on the hill before Artor could be moved again.

We have the time . . . Morgause affirmed silently, turning on her seat to gaze up the hill. *He is safe in the circle. He will live till I return. . . .*

Beneath its wrappings the Cauldron quivered against her belly, as if she held something living. For so many years she had desired it and, seizing it, had herself been possessed and transformed by its power. But for more than a dozen years she had served as its priestess, handling it only with the prescribed and warded touch of ritual. This intimate contact dizzied her.

Brigantia be with me, she prayed. *Let me work Thy will!*

A movement on the shore caught her eye and she leaned forward, staring. "Nest, turn the boat," she commanded suddenly. "Toward the little beach by the boulder."

Betiver stood at the water's edge, holding the Sword. Even from here she could see that he was weeping.

"What are you doing?" she cried. "Is Artor—"

"Oh, Lady, he commanded me to throw it in!" Betiver called back, his face working.

The boat rocked as Morgause stood up. Before Artor, the women of her blood had been the Sword's keepers.

"Stop! You must not—" she began, but Betiver was already drawing back the blade, whirling it up and around behind him.

For a moment, at the height of his swing, the Sword seemed to hover, blazing in the light of the sun. Then it flew free, soaring above the water in an arc of flame. Morgause lurched forward, felt Ninive clutch at her legs at the same moment as the Cauldron leaped from fingers that no longer had the power to hold it.

The Cauldron spun across the water like a silver wheel, the Sword drove downward. Where they met, Light flared outward, blinding the senses. But as Morgause fell back, it was not the afterimage of Sword and

Cauldron that remained imprinted behind her eyelids, but that of a goddess, reaching up from the waters of the Lake to embrace the god. . . .

Artor jerked back to consciousness, gasping. *I am dying!* he thought, but his pain-wracked body still imprisoned him. It was the world that was whirling, to settle at last into a new configuration, and he understood that the perfect balance for which he had been striving since first he drew the Sword from the Stone was at last attained.

"Guendivar!" He reached out to her. "Do you feel it? It is done!"

She caught his hand against her breast, and he felt her heart beating almost as wildly as his own. He grinned as a warrior does at the end of a battle fought past the borders of desperation, and beyond hope, won. In her face he saw a reflected wonder.

"Help me to move—" he said with sudden authority. "Set me with my back against a stone."

The queen nodded, and men came to lift him, grim understanding in their eyes. They set him against one of the boulders that marked out a rectangle at the eastern edge of the circle, its face worn smooth by the centuries. It made a royal seat, he thought, for the death of a king.

Artor took a deep breath, and let it slowly out. The cold stone warmed against him; a vibration travelled down his spine and into the depths of the earth, then fountained upward. And now he could hear it—the stones were singing, crying out in recognition of his sovereignty. Could not the others hear? He coughed, and coughed again, feeling the bonds that held soul to body fray.

Guendivar knelt beside him, weeping.

"My love . . . my love . . ." he whispered, understanding now so many things. "We cannot lose each other. I will never be far away from you. When my body sleeps in the earth, my spirit will watch over Britannia. . . . Watch with me, my queen, until we are joined once more. . . ."

She took his hand, and Artor smiled. He was aware of voices—Betiver and Morgause and Ninive, panting from their swift climb, but he could not find the strength to speak to them. He let his eyes close.

Through his eyelids he could still see sunlight; his other senses seemed to sharpen. The borders of his body could no longer hold him; awareness expanded outward through earth and air and water. Beyond the surfaces he had always accepted as reality, he perceived the real Britannia, the true country of the heart that no matter what evils passed in the world of men would always endure. This was his kingdom. Why, he wondered, had it taken him so long to understand?

*   *   *

To Guendivar, the light that had filled Artor's face seemed slowly to fade. But the radiance all around her was growing. Blinking back tears, she looked up from the emptied body, wondering where he had gone.

From Morgause came an anguished cry, and as if that had been a signal, the ravens rushed upward in a glistening dark cloud. Three times above the still body the black birds circled, calling out in grief and triumph. Then from their midst Guendivar saw one Raven rise and wing southward, its feathers turning incandescent in the sun.

Rex Aeternus

A.D. 1189

"They say that you know all the Breton tales," says the king. "Can you sing of King Arthur as well?" He taps a leather-bound book on the table before him. "Here are the *Lais* of Marie, that she dedicated to me. I have read the *Brut* also, and Geoffrey's *Historia,* when I was a young man. And I have heard very many songs of the jongleurs of your country. You will be hard put, I warn you, to find anything that I have not heard!"

The bard inclines his head. He is old, but seems strong, with a pair of dark eyes beneath bushy brows. He is a very big man.

"Lord king, I know many tales that no one has heard, of Artor, and other things." In the light from the pointed window, his beard glints silver against the dusty white of his robe.

"Hah!" says King Henry. "Sit, then, for I've a fox that gnaws my vitals, and a good tale may help me to forget the pain." He has filled the castle of Chinon with beautiful things. The stool to which he gestures the bard has a seat of red leather and feet carved like griffons' claws.

"That was how King Arthur died," says the bard. "Stabbed in the belly by his son." He speaks the French tongue with the deep music of the Celtic lands.

The king gives him a sharp look. "My sons have done the same, both Richard, who fights me, and John, who intrigues with that viper Philippe Auguste while smiling and praising my name. But you surprise me," he goes on, sipping more wine. "Mostly the Bretons say that Arthur never died, but sleeps in the Western Isles, or in a cavern in the hills, or in the vale of Avalon. The Welshmen, too, especially when they are preaching rebellion."

"Those who speak of Avalon come closest to the truth," rumbles the bard. "He is buried there."

"Now how did that come to pass?" Henry pulls his robe more closely around him and leans back in his carved chair, one eyebrow raised.

"The battle of Camlann was fought in the north of Angleterre, near the Wall," says the bard, "not in Cornuailles, as so many say. And when Arthur was dead, his body was carried south by Queen Guenivere and buried in Inis Witrin, which is the Isle of Avalon."

"Indeed?" The king cocks his head, willing to be amused. "Say then, if you know so much, what manner of man was Arthur, and how old he was when he met his end?"

"A big man, like you, and fifty-five years of age when he died. He too quarreled with churchmen for the good of the land, and dreamed of an empire in Gaul."

Henry frowns. "I have passed him, then, for I am fifty-six. I wonder, do you mean to threaten or to flatter me?"

The bard shrugs. "Arthur walked the earth, and loved greatly, and strove greatly to make good laws and keep the peace and preserve the land from her enemies."

"So also have I," the king replies, more softly. "But you take the magic from the story, telling it so!"

"Is it not a greater wonder that this same history should still be recounted some six centuries after Arthur died, and in every country of Christendom?" the bard answers more softly still.

King Henry shakes his head, laughing. "You will never make your fortune telling such tales to mortal kings! We prefer to believe that Arthur lived in an age of marvels, and avoid comparisons!"

"But what if it were true?"

"If it could be proved, you mean?" Suddenly the king grasps his sinewy arm. "Who are you, to know such things?"

For a moment the bard considers him. Then, very gently, he smiles, and Henry finds his grip loosening. "I have been called by many names. I am a Wild Man in the wood, and a bard in the courts of kings. I am a wanderer upon the roads of the world, and the prophet of Arthur. And you yourself can prove the truth of my words—"

He leans forward. "The abbey at Glastonbury burned five years ago, and the monks are still rebuilding. Command them to dig deep between the two pyramids in the churchyard. They will find there a coffin hollowed from a log of oak, and in it the bones of Arthur, and at his feet, Guenivere, with a leaden cross that gives their names."

"That would settle the Welsh!" exclaims the king, then sobers. "They claim Arthur as their Defender, but so do the English, and we Normans likewise, for my grandson bears his name. These days, he belongs to everyone. Why is that, do you suppose?" Henry says then. "Why should he matter so?"

"Because he loved Britannia . . ." answers the bard. "Because for a little while he kept her safe against the dark." He sits back, considering the king.

"I tell you these things so that you may know that such deeds can be achieved by mortal men. And yet what the Welsh and the Bretons tell you is the truth as well. Arthur's spirit never departed—neither to Heaven nor to the Otherworld. He watches over the Hallowed Isle. . . ."

PEOPLE AND PLACES

A note on pronunciation:

British names are given in fifth-century spelling, which does not yet reflect pronunciation changes. Initial letters should be pronounced as they are in English. Medial letters are as follows:

SPELLED	PRONOUNCED
p	b
t	d
k/c	(soft) g
b	v (approximately)
d	soft "th" (modern Welsh "dd")
g	"yuh"
m	v
ue	w

PEOPLE

CAPITALS = major character
* = historical personnage
( ) = dead before story begins
[ ] = name as given in later literature
Italics = diety or mythological personnage

*Aelle—king of the South Saxons
Aggarban [Agravaine]—third son of Morgause
*Agricola—prince of Demetia
*Alaric II—king of the Visigoths
(*Ambrosius Aurelianus—emperor of Britannia and Vitalinus' rival)
(*Amlodius—Artor's grandfather)
Amminius—one of Artor's men
ARTOR [Arthur]—son of Uthir and Igierne, high king of Britannia

(Artoria Argantel—Artor's grandmother)
Beowulf—king of the Geats in Denmark
BETIVER [Bedivere]—nephew to Riothamus, one of Artor's Companions
Bleitisbluth—a Pictish chieftain
Brigantia/Brigid—British goddess of healing, inspiration, and the land
*Budic—a grandson of Riothamus, lord of Civitas Aquilonia
CAI—son of Caius Turpilius, Artor's foster-brother and Companion
*Caninus [Aurelius Caninus]—son of the prince of Glevum, ally of Medraut
CATAUR [Cador]—prince of Dumnonia
Cathubodva—Lady of Ravens, a British war goddess
*Ceawlin—son of Cynric and grandson of Ceretic
Ceincair—a priestess on the Isle of Maidens
(*Ceretic [Cerdic]—king of the West Saxons)
*Chlodovechus [Clovis]—king of the Franks in Gallia
*Chlotild—queen of the Franks
*Conan—lord of Venetorum
*Constantine—son of Cataur, prince of Dumnonia
*Creoda—son of Icel of Anglia
*Cuil—a brigand
*Cunobelinus—warleader of the northern Votadini
*Cunoglassus—a prince of Guenet, ally of Medraut
Cunovinda—a young priestess on the Isle of Maidens
*Cymen—Aelle's eldest son
*Cynric—son of Ceretic, king of the West Saxons
*Daniel Dremrud—son of Riothamus
Doli—a Pictish warrior in the service of Morgause
*Drest Gurthinmoch—high king of the Picts
(*Dubricius—bishop of Isca and head of the church in Britannia)
*Dumnoval [Dyfnwal]—lord of the Southern Votadini
Edrit—a young warrior in the service of Aggarban
Eldaul the younger [Eldol]—prince of Glevum
*Eormenric—son of Oesc, child-king of Cantuware
*Feragussos [Fergus]—king of the Scotti of Dal Riada
*Gipp—Norse founder of Gippewic in Essex, Medraut's ally
GORIAT [Gareth]—fourth son of Morgause
(Gorlosius [Gorlois]—first husband of Igierne, father of Morgause)
Gracilia—wife of Gualchmai
GUALCHMAI [Gawain]—first son of Morgause
GUENDIVAR [Gwenivere]—Artor's queen

*Guenomarcus—lord of Plebs Legionorum

Gwyhir [Gaheris]—second son of Morgause

Hæthwæge—a Saxon wisewoman

(*Hengest—king of Cantuware, leader of Saxon revolt)

*Henry II—king of England

*Icel—king of the Anglians in Britannia

IGIERNE [Igraine]—Artor's mother, Lady of the Lake

Johannes Rutilius—brother-in-law to Riothamus, Betiver's father

Julia—a nun from the Isle of Glass, Guendivar's companion

(Kea—a British slave girl among the Picts, Medraut's first woman)

Father Kedi—an Irish priest at the court of Artor

Leodegranus [Leodegrance]—prince of Lindinis, Guendivar's father

(Leudonus [Lot]—king of the Votadini)

Maglouen [Maelgwn]—a prince of Guenet, Medraut's ally

(*Magnus Maximus [Maxen Wledig]—general serving in Britain who was
     proclaimed emperor 383–388)

Marcus Conomorus [Mark of Cornwall]—son of Constantine

Martinus of Viroconium—an ally of Medraut

Maxentius—a grandson of Riothamus

MEDRAUT—fifth son of Morgause, by Artor

Melwas [Meleagrance]—an Irishman born in Guenet, abductor of Guen-
     divar

MERLIN—druid and wizard, Artor's advisor

Morcant Bulc—heir to Dun Breatann

MORGAUSE—daughter of Igierne and Gorlosius, queen of the Votadini

(*Naitan Morbet—king of all the provinces of the Picts)

Nest—a priestess on the Isle of Maidens

Ninive—daughter of Gualchmai by a woman of the hills

(*Oesc—grandson of Hengest and king of Cantuware, Eormenric's father)

*Othar, Ela, Adgils, Admund [Othere, Onela, Eadgils, Eadmund]—King
     Ottar of Sweden, his brother Ali, his sons Adils and Eadmund

Paulinus Clutorix—lord of Viroconium

*Peretur [Peredur]—son of Eleutherius, lord of Eboracum

*Pompeius Regalis [Riwal]—lord of Domnonia

*Ridarchus—king at Alta Cluta and protector of Luguvalium

Rigana—widow of Oesc, Eormenric's mother

*Riothamus—ruler of Armorica

*Theodoric—a Gothic admiral in the service of Britannia

*Theuderich—king of the Franks, son of Chlodovechus and a concubine
     and one of his successors, along with Chlodomer, Childebert, and Lo-
     thar (by Queen Clotild)

Uorepona—the "Great Mare," high queen of the Picts
(Uthir [Uther Pendragon]—Artor's father)
Verica—a young priestess on the Isle of Maidens
(*Vitalinus, the Vor-Tigernus—ruler of Britannia who brought in the Saxons)
*Vortipor—son of Agricola, prince of Demetia

PLACES

Afallon [Avalon]—Isle of Apples, Glastonbury
Alba—Scotland
Altaclutha—kingdom of the Clyde
Ambrosiacum—Amesbury
Anglia—Lindsey and Lincoln
Annuen [Annwyn]—the land of the dead
Aquae Sulis—Bath
Armorica—Britanny
Belisama fluvius—River Ribble, Lancashire
Bodotria aestuarius—Firth of Forth
Britannia—Great Britain
Caellwic—Kelliwic, Cornwall
Caledonian forest—southern Scotland
Calleva—Silchester
Camalot [Camelot]—Cadbury Castle, Somerset
Camboglanna [Camlann]—fortress of Birdoswald, the Wall
Camulodunum—Colchester
Cantium, Cantuware—Kent
Castra Legionis—Caerleon
Cendtire—Kintyre peninsula
Civitas Aquilonia—Quimper, Brittany
Clutha—River Clyde
Demetia—Pembroke and Carmarthen
Domnonia—Cotes du Nord, Brittany
Dumnonia—Cornwall and Devon
Dun Bara—Barry Hill, Perth
Dun Breatann—"fortress of the Britons," Dumbarton Rock
Dun Eidyn—Edinburgh Rock
Durnovaria—Dorchester, Dorset
Durobrivae—1. Rochester, Kent; 2. Water Newton, Cambridge
Fodreu—Fortriu, Fife

Forest of Caledon—Caledonian forest, southern Scotland
Gallia—France
Giants' Dance—Stonehenge
Gippewic—in Essex
Glevum—Gloucester
Guenet [Gwynedd]—Denbigh and Caernarvon
Isca (Silurum)—Caerwent
Isle of Glass (Inis Witrin)—Glastonbury
Isle of Maidens in the Lake—Derwentwater, Cumbria
Lindinis—Ilchester, Somerset
Lindum—Lincoln
Londinium—London
Metaris aestuarius—the Wash
Mona—Anglesey
Plebs Legionorum—St. Pol de Léon, Brittany
Pyrenaei montes—the Pyrenees
Sabrina fluvia—the Severn River and estuary
Segontium—Caernarvon, Wales
Sorviodunum—Salisbury
Summer Country—Somerset
Tava—River Tay
Tolosa—Toulouse
Urbs Legionis (Deva)—Chester
Uxela fluvius—River Axe, Severn estuary
Venetorum—Vannes, in Brittany
Venta Belgarum—Winchester
Venta Siluricum—Caerwent, Wales
Viroconium—Wroxeter
Voreda—Old Penrith, Cumberland